O9-BUD-446

THE EDITH WHARTON READER

The Edith Wharton Reader

EDITED BY
LOUIS AUCHINCLOSS

Charles Scribner's Sons
New York

A-1.65[H]

Printed in the United States of America
Library of Congress Catalog Card Number 65-14613

CONTENTS

INTRODUCTION
BY LOUIS AUCHINCLOSS

Introduction

AMY LOWELL said once that her greatest handicap was to have been born into the class which is commonly assumed to be incapable of artistic creativity. Edith Wharton might well have echoed this sentiment. She had to suffer in her apprenticeship to the trade of letters from the prejudice of friends and relations, not so much that a lady *should* not write, as that she *could* not, that her work was not basically a thing to be taken seriously. While this point of view, mysteriously enough, has never been applied retroactively to the upper classes of past eras—*vide* the recent movement to attribute Shakespeare's plays to an earl—it still controls our own. Gossip has even tried to confer illegitimacy on Mrs. Wharton to explain her literary achievement.

It is true, of course, that an upper class training may hamper an incipient artist by inhibiting his emotions, and in fields of direct personal exhibition, as the stage and the dance, it may well be fatal. But the novelist need expose no more of himself than he wishes, and the Manhattan society into which Edith Newbold Jones was born in 1862 provided her with subject material for a lifetime. It was a serene, ordered hierarchy, as honest as it was unadventurous, as loyal as it was unambitious, living on its rent rolls with only a mild ostentation and hardly dreaming of the advent of the "lords of Pittsburgh" who were to turn its brownstones into houses of mirth. If the Jones' had taught their daughter nothing but her reverence for the English language, they would have done enough. As she said in her memoirs:

"Usage, in my childhood, was as authoritative an element in speaking English as tradition was in social conduct. And it was because our little society still lived in the reflected light of a long established culture that my parents, who were far from intellectual, who read little and studied not at all, nevertheless spoke their mother tongue with scrupulous perfection, and insisted that their children should do the same."

Raw material and the language with which to fashion it—it was not such a bad inheritance, after all. But that was the sum of it; the rest had to be rejected, even if it took half a lifetime to do so. Edith Jones Wharton married within her family's world and lived for years the life of European travel and New York dinner parties that was expected of her and that she seems to have expected of herself. It was not until early middle age that she recognized her true vocation. She had always scribbled, but then, perhaps to relieve the tensions of an unhappy marriage, she began to write.

With an early success she abandoned New York and even America. Everything opened up at once. She wanted not only to be a writer but to live in a world of physical beauty where artists and writers were appreciated by the highest in the land. She wanted houses and gardens as well as books; she wanted to unite the pleasures of the eye and the ear with those of the mind; she wanted a society that was disciplined as well as charming, intellectual as well as lively. For her it could be found only in France.

She was too much a perfectionist in the art of living, too much of a lady, to admit what her great output of more than forty volumes signified to her. She devotes only a single chapter of her autobiography to her writing, her "secret garden" as she calls it, and Percy Lubbock notes that her books had to be written in "the bare margin of such a populous and ornamented existence." But one suspects in this her favorite pose of "priestess of the life of reason." What her work really meant to her is seen in a letter to her niece:

"It's a great satisfaction, isn't it, to find one's work recognized and know that the dedicated sense one had within one corresponds to an outward reality? I know that feeling and am sure you'll agree with me that it's about the best there is in this world of uncertainties."

Three collections of short stories, two novelettes and an historical novel preceded her first major work. The short stories are in the early Jamesian, or perhaps more properly, the Hawthorne tradition. They deal with the problems of artists and writers, frequently in

Europe, and the conflict between the soul's aspiration and the lure of popular success. They are finely wrought, exquisite pieces, and the crisp, clear, flowing style, the merciless vision, the apt, glittering metaphors, the sense conveyed of a pellucid, almost masculine intelligence, softened only by a quick sense of humor, make the prose of the author's first efforts equal to that of her best period. And there is compassion, too, behind that hard stare, pity for the addled old lecturer in "The Pelican" who pretends to be boring her audiences for the sake of her little boy when in fact he is fully grown and supporting her, pity for the vain sweet decayed old gentle lady in "The Rembrandt" who wants to sell her egregious fake to a museum.

The Valley of Decision (1902), in Edith Wharton's own words, was not really a novel at all, "but only a romantic chronicle, unrolling its episodes like the frescoed legends on the palace walls which formed its background." She was now at forty-two ready to tackle a big subject in a form more compact and centripetal; she was ready for the novel of manners. "Fashionable New York," in all its flatness and futility, cried to be dealt with as the theme most available to her hand.

> "The problem was how to extract from such a subject the typical human significance which is the story-teller's reason for telling one story rather than another. In what aspect could a society of irresponsible pleasure-seekers be said to have, on the 'old woe of the world,' any deeper bearing than the people composing such a society could guess? The answer was that a frivolous society can acquire dramatic significance only through what its frivolity destroys. Its tragic implication lies in its power of debasing people and ideals. The answer, in short, was my heroine, Lily Bart."

Lily Bart, the beautiful, luxury-loving, sentimental heroine of *The House of Mirth* belongs by birth to old New York but by preference to "the invaders," the holders of the great new fortunes who had turned Fifth Avenue into a bank of derivative Loire chateaux and established new criteria in the pursuit of pleasure which made the stately diversions of the past seem as innocent and quaint as a game of slap-jack on a rainy afternoon. Lily likes to think that she aspires to a better life, but she is never willing to sacrifice even a rubber of bridge to it. There is only one way she can save herself from the gulf of debts and loans with its fatal pit of being "talked about," and that is by a rich marriage, but her repugnance to such a step constitutes her sole integrity and brings about her destruction. For in those worlds, the old as well as the new, money is everything, and poverty is as obscene to Lily's aunt, Mrs. Peniston, as it is to her coarse admirer, Mr. Rosedale.

Lily's physical beauty, a motif sounded again and again in the novel, becomes in the end the symbol of everything society would like to be and is not, and hence of everything that it feels compelled to destroy. The pursuit and tearing to pieces of Lily Bart becomes a terrible obsession that unites the occupants of the brownstones with those of the marble chateaux in a joint frenzy of hate, but in the end, when Lily lies dead, her beauty is still unconquered:

> "He stood looking down on the sleeping face which seemed to lie like a delicate impalpable mask over the living lineaments he had known. He felt that the real Lily was still there, close to him, yet invisible and inaccessible; and the tenuity of the barrier between them mocked him with a sense of helplessness."

The House of Mirth, published in 1905, inaugurated Edith Wharton's major period which was to last until shortly after the first world war. She continued her studies of New York society in *The Fruit of the Tree* and *The Custom of the Country* and in such penetrating short stories as "Autre Temps." Dozens of her contemporaries attempted to describe the same world; none did it with her authenticity. But her human interest was not confined to the fashionable world. In *Ethan Frome* she caught with brilliant success the bleak Massachusetts winter landscape and its penetration into the souls of the poor farmers who lived in it. In *Bunner Sisters* she traced the desperate struggle for survival of two old maids with a notions shop who are victimized and ruined by a seedy jeweler. And in *Summer* she explored the dullness of life and the drabness of seduction in a hot, dead New England village. Mrs. Wharton had been raised on the Victorian novelists who regarded the whole social scene as their province. Like George Eliot and Elizabeth Gaskell, and like Ellen Glasgow, her nearer contemporary, she felt equipped to write about anything that crossed her line of vision. Later she was to make the mistake of writing about life in the

American Midwest which she knew only through the eyes of Sinclair Lewis, but that was still twenty years off.

She remained in France during the first world war and worked unremittingly for relief organizations. She was swept up in the war fever and suffered afterwards from a flattened sense that the victory had cost too much. What had been paid, it seemed to her, was nothing less than the whole shelf of *lares* and *penates* that she had been brought up to revere. They seemed to have more validity now that they were gone. Even the New York of her childhood, that "cramped horizontal gridiron of a town," began to have a new charm when viewed nostalgically across the devastation of the war years and over the shoulders of a new and heedless generation. She saw her parents and their friends in a different light:

> "When I was young it used to seem to me that the group in which I grew up was like an empty vessel into which no new wine would ever again be poured. Now I see that one of its uses lay in preserving a few drops of an old vintage too rare to be savoured by a youthful palate."

Ellen Olenska, the heroine of *The Age of Innocence* (1920), the great novel that Mrs. Wharton wrote to preserve those few vintage drops, echoes this feeling of nostalgia. She has come back from a stormy European marriage to the dull port of her hometown and is inclined to find New York society stodgy and futile. Newland Archer, however, teaches her otherwise. "It was you," she tells him afterwards, "who made me understand that under the dullness there are things so fine and sensitive and delicate that even those I most cared for in my other life look cheap in comparison."

Of course, Archer has the opposite experience: Ellen opens *his* eyes to the provincialism of a society that until then he has regarded as very splendid. It is Henry James' *The Ambassadors* on the opposite side of the Atlantic: Ellen seeks to liberate Archer, but she ends by persuading him to remain true to his New York inheritance and to his New York wife. Archer uses his fresh vision not to win a new existence but to preserve and give a needed richness to the old. Edith Wharton was a conservative in her heart as well as in her manners. Despite the fact that she came to it in her own case, she always found divorce vulgar, and she was inclined to feel that human beings rarely bettered and usually degraded themselves when they broke through the fences of tradition. It was not so much the breaking of the fences that she minded—she always admired boldness and resolution—it was what one found on the other side. Like so many of her contemporaries she always associated illicit love with second class watering places.

The Age of Innocence is not only a novel perfect in form; it is a glowing series of pictures of the times. New York is seen in the early 1870s, in Mrs. Wharton's own childhood, and is bathed in the bright but accurate colors of her vivid nostalgia. Society in *The House of Mirth* is shown as it existed when she was already an adult and hence is seen with a more jaundiced eye. The "age of innocence" is pre-robber baron, when society, although worldly, found tradition at least as important as money.

Edmund Wilson said that Mrs. Wharton was not only the pioneer but the poet of interior decoration. It took the author of *The Decoration of Houses* and *Italian Villas and Their Gardens* to paint New York as it looked:

> ". . . the house had been boldly planned with a ballroom, so that, instead of squeezing through a narrow passage to get to it (as at the Chiverses') one marched solemnly down a vista of enfiladed drawing-rooms (the sea-green, the crimson and the *bouton d'or*), seeing from afar the many-candled lustres reflected in the polished parquetry, and beyond that the depths of a conservatory where camellias and tree-ferns arched their costly foliage over seats of black and gold bamboo."

Except in the four charming novelettes that make up the series *Old New York* (1924) and in her unfinished novel, *The Buccaneers,* Edith Wharton did not use again the material of her childhood New York. It is most unfortunate that she did not. Willa Cather, who suffered from the same kind of post-war disillusionment, turned to the historical novel and did her finest work. Edith Wharton, by insisting on the role of censor of modern morals, allowed herself to become a crank.

She had disregarded Henry James' famous warning that she should be tethered in "native pastures" even if it reduced her to a "backyard in New York," but this would not have mattered had she transferred her attention to Europeans or kept it fixed on the Americans whom she remembered. James himself, after all, wrote his greatest fiction after more than two decades of expatriation. But Edith Wharton assumed that she could borrow her young Americans from the novels of Sinclair Lewis. For many long prosperous years, right up until her death in 1937, she ventilated her mind and filled her pocketbook, writing slick satires about her fellow countrymen whom she no longer understood. Yet one doubts if she would ever have admitted the taint of commercialism. As she grew older, it became easier to convince herself that she had never relaxed her standards.

Happily, a "reader" need contain only the best. I have chosen to open and close this selection with excerpts from Mrs. Wharton's lucid and instructive autobiography, *A Backward Glance,* which contains some of her finest writing. It is, as one might guess, a very restrained account of her life, but the story is all there for the careful reader. I have included the first halves of her two great novels, *The House of Mirth* and *The Age of Innocence*; two novelettes about poverty, both of purse and heart, *Ethan Frome* and *Bunner Sisters;* and two of the four novelettes making up the series *Old New York.* There are also two of her early stories, a poem and three ghost stories, a genre in which she achieved near perfection.

I know of no accepted definition of the novel of manners, but it has always struck me that it is most successful when dealing with a hierarchical society. Edith Wharton possessed, in addition to a sharp eye and a quick sense of the ludicrous, a profound knowledge of the New York upper class as it existed at her birth and for half a century preceding it. She had been an intent observer of the assault upon this society of the heirs to the great new fortunes made after the Civil War, and she comprehended that this assault was bound to end less in defeat than in merger—a merger that she always regarded as somehow dishonorable. When she employed her talent upon this subject she became America's first-ranking novelist of manners.

In her memoirs she repudiated the assumption that she regarded any of her work as likely to be of lasting interest. Yet at least two of her novels and many of her novelettes and short stories are bound to be. The picture of upper class New York in the 1860s, and again in the early 1900s, when it controlled the finances of the nation, is an important part of our social and economic history, and nowhere else can it be seen as vividly as in the pages of Edith Wharton. George Templeton Strong's magnificent diary describes the world of her childhood; he knew her parents and many of their friends and was himself a kind of Newland Archer. The diary is a vital historical document, but to read it after *The Age of Innocence* is like viewing a faded Brady daguerrotype after a brilliant conversation piece by Eastman Johnson.

Louis Auchincloss

New York
August 1, 1964

THE
EDITH WHARTON READER

FROM *A Backward Glance*

CHAPTER 3 LITTLE GIRL

§ 2

THE OLD New York to which I came back as a little girl meant to me chiefly my father's library. Now for the first time I had my fill of books. Out of doors, in the mean monotonous streets, without architecture, without great churches or palaces, or any visible memorials of an historic past, what could New York offer to a child whose eyes had been filled with shapes of immortal beauty and immemorial significance? One of the most depressing impressions of my childhood is my recollection of the intolerable ugliness of New York, of its untended streets and the narrow houses so lacking in external dignity, so crammed with smug and suffocating upholstery. How could I understand that people who had seen Rome and Seville, Paris and London, could come back to live contentedly between Washington Square and the Central Park? What I could not guess was that this little low-studded rectangular New York, cursed with its universal chocolate-coloured coating of the most hideous stone ever quarried, this cramped horizontal gridiron of a town without towers, porticoes, fountains or perspectives, hide-bound in its deadly uniformity of mean ugliness, would fifty years later be as much a vanished city as Atlantis or the lowest layer of Schliemann's Troy, or that the social organization which that prosaic setting had slowly secreted would have been swept to oblivion with the rest. Nothing but the Atlantis-fate of old New York, the New York which had slowly but continuously developed from the early seventeenth century to my own childhood, makes that childhood worth recalling now.

Looking back at that little world, and remembering the "hoard of petty maxims" with which its elders preached down every sort of initiative, I have often wondered at such lassitude in the descendants of the men who first cleared a place for themselves in a new world, and then fought for the right to be masters there. What had become of the spirit of the pioneers and the revolutionaries? Perhaps the very violence of their effort had caused it to exhaust itself in the next generation, or the too great prosperity succeeding on almost unexampled hardships had produced, if not inertia, at least indifference in all matters except business or family affairs.

Even the acquiring of wealth had ceased to interest the little society into which I was born. In the case of some of its members, such as the Astors and Goelets, great fortunes, originating in a fabulous increase of New York real estate values, had been fostered by judicious investments and prudent administration; but of feverish money-making, in Wall Street or in railway, shipping or industrial enterprises, I heard nothing in my youth. Some of my father's friends may have been bankers, others have followed one of the liberal professions, usually the law; in fact almost all the young men I knew read law for a while after leaving college, though comparatively few practised it in after years. But for the most part my father's contemporaries, and those of my brothers also, were men of leisure—a term now almost as obsolete as the state it describes. It will probably seem unbelievable to present-day readers that only one of my own near relations, and not one of my husband's, was "in business". The group to which we belonged was composed of families to whom a middling prosperity had come, usually by the rapid rise in value of inherited real estate, and none of whom, apparently, aspired to be more than moderately well-off. I never in my early life came in contact with the gold-fever in any form, and when I hear that nowadays business life in New York is so strenuous that men and women never meet socially before the dinner hour, I remember the delightful week-day luncheons of my early married years, where the men were as numerous as the women, and where one of the first rules of conversation was the one early instilled in me by my mother: "Never talk about money, and think about it as little as possible."

The child of the well-to-do, hedged in by nurses and governesses, seldom knows much of its parents' activities. I have only the vaguest recollection of the way in which my father and mother spent their days. I know that my father was a director on the principal charitable boards of New York—the Blind Asylum and the Bloomingdale Insane Asylum among others; and that during Lent a ladies' "sewing class" met at our house to work with my mother for the poor. I also recall frequent drives with my mother, when the usual afternoon round of card-leaving was followed by a walk in the Central Park, and a hunt for violets and hepaticas in the secluded dells of the Ramble. In the evenings my parents went occasionally to the theatre, but never, as far as I remember, to a concert, or any kind of musical performance, until the Opera, then only sporadic, became an established entertainment, to which one went (as in eighteenth century Italy) chiefly if not solely for the pleasure of conversing with one's friends. Their most frequent distraction was dining out or dinner giving. Sometimes the dinners were stately and ceremonious (with engraved invitations issued three weeks in advance, soups, "thick" and "clear", and a Roman punch half way through the *menu*), but more often they were intimate and sociable, though always the occasion of much excellent food and old wine being admirably served, and discussed with suitable gravity.

My father had inherited from his family a serious tradition of good cooking, with a cellar of vintage clarets, and of Madeira which had rounded the Cape. The "Jones" Madeira (my father's) and the "Newbold" (my uncle's) enjoyed a particular celebrity even in that day of noted cellars. The following generation, interested only in champagne and claret, foolishly dispersed these precious stores. My brothers sold my father's cellar soon after his death; and after my marriage, dining in a *nouveau riche* house of which the master was unfamiliar with old New York cousinships, I had pressed on me, as a treat not likely to have come the way of one of my modest condition, a glass of "the famous Newbold Madeira".

My mother, if left to herself, would probably not have been much interested in the pleasures of the table. My father's Dutch blood accounted for his gastronomic enthusiasm; his mother, who was a Schermerhorn, was reputed to have the best cook in New York. But to know about good cooking was a part of every young wife's equipment, and my mother's favourite cookery books (Francatelli's and

Mrs. Leslie's) are thickly interleaved with sheets of yellowing note paper, on which, in a script of ethereal elegance, she records the making of "Mrs. Joshua Jones's scalloped oysters with cream", "Aunt Fanny Gallatin's fried chicken", "William Edgar's punch", and the special recipes of our two famous negro cooks, Mary Johnson and Susan Minneman. These great artists stand out, brilliantly turbaned and ear-ringed, from a Snyders-like background of game, fish and vegetables transformed into a succession of succulent repasts by their indefatigable blue-nailed hands: Mary Johnson, a gaunt towering woman of a rich bronzy black, with huge golden hoops in her ears, and crisp African crinkles under vividly patterned kerchiefs; Susan Minneman, a small smiling mulatto, more quietly attired, but as great a cook as her predecessor.

Ah, what artists they were! How simple yet sure were their methods—the mere perfection of broiling, roasting and basting—and what an unexampled wealth of material, vegetable and animal, their genius had to draw upon! Who will ever again taste anything in the whole range of gastronomy to equal their corned beef, their boiled turkeys with stewed celery and oyster sauce, their fried chickens, broiled red-heads, corn fritters, stewed tomatoes, rice griddle cakes, strawberry short-cake and vanilla ices? I am now enumerating only our daily fare, that from which even my tender years did not exclude me; but when my parents "gave a dinner", and terrapin and canvas-back ducks, or (in their season) broiled Spanish mackerel, soft-shelled crabs with a mayonnaise of celery, and peach-fed Virginia hams cooked in champagne (I am no doubt confusing all the seasons in this allegoric evocation of their riches), lima-beans in cream, corn soufflés and salads of oyster crabs, poured in varied succulence from Mary Johnson's lifted cornucopia—ah, then, the *gourmet* of that long-lost day, when cream was cream and butter butter and coffee coffee, and meat fresh every day, and game hung just for the proper number of hours, might lean back in his chair and murmur "Fate cannot harm me" over his cup of Moka and his glass of authentic Chartreuse.

I have lingered over these details because they formed a part—a most important and honourable part—of that ancient curriculum of house-keeping which, at least in Anglo-Saxon countries, was so soon to be swept aside by the "monstrous regiment" of the emancipated: young women taught by their elders to despise the kitchen and the linen room, and to substitute the acquiring of University degrees for the more complex art of civilized living. The movement began when I was young, and now that I am old, and have watched it and noted its results, I mourn more than ever the extinction of the household arts. Cold storage, deplorable as it is, has done far less harm to the home than the Higher Education.

And what of the guests who gathered at my father's table to enjoy the achievements of the Dark Ladies? I remember a mild blur of rosy and white-whiskered gentlemen, of ladies with bare sloping shoulders rising flower-like from voluminous skirts, peeped at from the stair-top while wraps were removed in the hall below. A great sense of leisure emanated from their kindly faces and voices. No motors waited to rush them on to ball or opera; balls were few and widely spaced, the opera just beginning; and "Opera night" would not have been chosen for one of my mother's big dinners. There being no haste, and a prodigious amount of good food to be disposed of, the guests sat long at table; and when my mother bowed slightly to the lady facing her on my father's right, and flounces and trains floated up the red velvet stair-carpet to the white-and-gold drawing-room with tufted purple satin arm-chairs, and voluminous purple satin curtains festooned with buttercup yellow fringe, the gentlemen settled down again to claret and Madeira, sent duly westward, and followed by coffee and Havana cigars.

My parents' guests ate well, and drank good wine with discernment; but a more fastidious taste had shortened the enormous repasts and deep bumpers of colonial days, and in twenty minutes the whiskered gentlemen had joined the flounced ladies on the purple settees for another half hour of amiable chat, accompanied by the cup of tea which always rounded off the evening. How mild and leisurely it all seems in the glare of our new century! Small parochial concerns no doubt formed the staple of the talk. Art and music and literature were rather timorously avoided (unless Trollope's last novel were touched upon, or a discreet allusion made to Mr. William Astor's audacious acquisition of a Bouguereau Venus), and the topics chiefly dwelt on were personal: the thoughtful discussion of food, wine, horses ("high steppers" were beginning to be much sought after), the laying out and planting of countryseats, the selection of "specimen" copper beeches and fern-leaved maples for lawns just beginning to be shorn smooth by the new hand-mowers, and those plans of European travel which filled so large a space in the thought of old New Yorkers. From my earliest infancy I had always seen about me people who were either just arriving from "abroad" or just embarking on a European tour. The old New Yorker was in continual contact with the land of his fathers, and it was not until I went to Boston on my marriage that I found myself in a community of wealthy and sedentary people seemingly too lacking in intellectual curiosity to have any desire to see the world.

I have always been perplexed by the incuriosity of New England with regard to the rest of the world, for New Yorkers of my day were never so happy as when they were hurrying on board the ocean liner which was to carry them to new lands. Those whose society my parents frequented did not, perhaps, profit much by the artistic and intellectual advantages of European travel, and to social opportunities they were half-resentfully indifferent. It was thought vulgar and snobbish to try to make the acquaintance, in London, Paris or Rome, of people of the class corresponding to their own. The Americans who forced their way into good society in Europe were said to be those who were shut out from it at home; and the self-respecting American on his travels frequented only the little "colonies" of his compatriots already settled in the European capitals, and only their most irreproachable members! What these artless travellers chiefly enjoyed were scenery, ruins and historic sites; places about which some sentimental legend hung, and to which Scott, Byron, Hans Andersen, Bulwer, Washington Irving or Hawthorne gently led the timid sight-seer. Public ceremonials also, ecclesiastical or royal, were much appreciated, though of the latter only distant glimpses could be caught, since it would have been snobbish to ask, through one's Legation, for reserved seats or invitations. And as for the American women who had themselves presented at the English Court—well, one had only to see with whom they associated at home!

However, ruins, snow-mountains, lakes and water-falls—especially water-falls—were endlessly enjoyable; and in the great cities there were the shops! In them, as Henry James acutely noted in "The Pension Beaurepas", the American woman found inexhaustible consolation for the loneliness and inconveniences of life in foreign lands. But, lest I seem to lay undue stress on the limitations of my compatriots, it must be remembered that, even in more sophisticated societies, cultivated sight-seeing was hardly known in those days. One need only glance through the "Travels" of the early nineteenth century to see how little, before Ruskin, the average well-educated tourist of any country was prepared to observe and enjoy. The intellectual few, at the end of the eighteenth century, had been taught by Arthur Young to travel with an eye to agriculture and geology; and Goethe, in Sicily, struck Syracuse and Girgenti from his itinerary, and took the monotonous and exhausting route across the middle of the island, in order to see with his own eyes why it had been called the granary of Rome. Meanwhile the simpler majority collected scraps of marble from the Forum, pressed maidenhair fern from the temple of Vesta at Tivoli, or daisies from the grave of Shelley, and bought edelweiss gummed on card-board from the guides of Chamonix, and copies of Guido's "Aurora" and Caravaggio's "Gamesters" from the Roman picture-dealers.

At that very time a handsome blue-eyed young man with a scarred mouth was driving across the continent in his parents' travelling carriage, and looking with wondering eyes at the Giottos of the Arena Chapel and the Cimabues of Assisi; at that time a young architect, poor and unknown, was toiling through the by-ways of Castile, Galicia and Andalusia in jolting *diligences,* or over stony mule-tracks, and recording in a series of exquisite drawings the unknown wonders of Spanish architecture; and Browning was dreaming of "The Ring and the Book"—and Shelley had long since written "The Cenci". But to the average well-to-do traveller Hawthorne's "Marble Faun", Bulwer's "Last Days of Pompeii" and Washington Irving's "Alhambra" were still the last word on Spain and Italy.

PREFATORY NOTE TO "THE PELICAN" AND "THE REMBRANDT"

Edith Wharton's first volume of fiction, *The Greater Inclination,* containing "The Pelican," appeared in 1899 when she was thirty-seven. Travelling at the time, she went into a bookseller's in London to ask what was new and interesting and discovered that she was famous. As a stylist, she had started off at her best. The writing in "The Pelican" is as polished and lucid as that in *The Age of Innocence.* It inaugurated a lifetime series of satires of ladies (their descendants were to be drawn by Helen Hokinson) who, like Mrs. Ballinger in *Xingu,* "pursue Culture in bands, as though it were dangerous to meet alone."

Two years later a second volume of stories, *Crucial Instances,* enjoyed an equal success. It contained "The Rembrandt," the first of many tales about the visual arts, the most famous of which was to be *False Dawn.* More so than writers today, Mrs. Wharton and her contemporaries, Henry James, Paul Bourget, Henry Fuller, Oscar Wilde, Rudyard Kipling and Marcel Proust, were fascinated by paintings and painters. "The Rembrandt" may be a slight tale, but it is handled with the greatest skill and charm.

The Pelican

SHE WAS very pretty when I first knew her, with the sweet straight nose and short upper lip of the cameo-brooch divinity, humanized by a dimple that flowered in her cheek whenever anything was said possessing the outward attributes of humor without its intrinsic quality. For the dear lady was providentially deficient in humor: the least hint of the real thing clouded her lovely eye like the hovering shadow of an algebraic problem.

I don't think nature had meant her to be "intellectual"; but what can a poor thing do, whose husband has died of drink when her baby is hardly six months old, and who finds her coral necklace and her grandfather's edition of the British Dramatists inadequate to the demands of the creditors?

Her mother, the celebrated Irene Astarte Pratt, had written a poem in blank verse on "The Fall of Man;" one of her aunts was dean of a girls' college; another had translated Euripides—with such a family, the poor child's fate was sealed in advance. The only way of paying her husband's debts and keeping the baby clothed was to be intellectual; and, after some hesitation as to the form her mental activity was to take, it was unanimously decided that she was to give lectures.

They began by being drawing-room lectures. The first time I saw her she was standing by the piano, against a flippant background of Dresden china and photographs, telling a roomful of women preoccupied with their spring bonnets all she thought she knew about Greek art. The ladies assembled to hear her had given me to understand that she was "doing it for the baby," and this fact, together with the shortness of her upper lip and the bewildering co-operation of her dimple, disposed me to listen leniently to her dissertation. Happily, at that time Greek art was still, if I may use the phrase, easily handled: it was as simple as walking down a museum-gallery lined with pleasant familiar Venuses and Apollos. All the later complications—the archaic and archaistic conundrums; the influences of Assyria and Asia Minor; the conflicting attributions and the wrangles of the erudite—still slumbered in the bosom of the future "scientific critic." Greek art in those days began with Phidias and ended with the Apollo Belvedere; and a child could travel from one to the other without danger of losing his way.

Mrs. Amyot had two fatal gifts: a capacious but inaccurate memory, and an extraordinary fluency of speech. There was nothing she did not remember—wrongly; but her halting facts were swathed in so many layers of rhetoric that their infirmities were imperceptible to her friendly critics. Besides, she had been taught Greek by the aunt who had translated Euripides; and the mere sound of the aiç and oiç that she now and then not unskilfully let slip (correcting herself, of course, with a start, and indulgently mistranslating the phrase), struck awe to the hearts of ladies whose only "accomplishment" was French—if you didn't speak too quickly.

I had then but a momentary glimpse of Mrs. Amyot, but a few months later I came upon her again in the New England university town where the celebrated Irene Astarte Pratt lived on the summit of a local Parnassus, with lesser muses and college professors respectfully grouped on the lower ledges of the sacred declivity. Mrs. Amyot, who, after her husband's death, had returned to the maternal roof (even during her father's lifetime the roof had been distinctively maternal), Mrs. Amyot, thanks to her upper lip, her dimple and her Greek, was already esconced in a snug hollow of the Parnassian slope.

After the lecture was over it happened that I walked home with Mrs. Amyot. From the incensed glances of two or three learned gentlemen who were hovering on the door-step when we emerged, I inferred that Mrs. Amyot, at that period, did not often walk home alone; but I doubt whether any of my discomfited rivals, whatever his claims to favor, was ever treated to so ravishing a mixture of shyness and self-abandonment, of sham erudition and real teeth and hair, as it was my privilege to enjoy. Even at the opening of her public career Mrs. Amyot had a tender eye for strangers, as possible links with successive centres of culture to which in due course the torch of Greek art might be handed on.

She began by telling me that she had never been so frightened in her life. She knew, of course, how dreadfully learned I was, and when, just as she was going to begin, her hostess had whispered to her that I was in the room, she had felt ready to sink through the floor. Then (with a flying dimple) she had remembered Emerson's line—wasn't it Emerson's?—that beauty is its own excuse for *seeing,* and that had made her feel a little more confident, since she was sure that no one *saw* beauty more vividly than she—as a child she used to sit for hours gazing at an Etruscan vase on the bookcase in the library, while her sisters played with their dolls—and if *seeing* beauty was the only excuse one needed for talking about it, why, she was sure I would make allowances and not be *too* critical and sarcastic, especially if, as she thought probable, I had heard of her having lost her poor husband, and how she had to do it for the baby.

Being abundantly assured of my sympathy on these points, she went on to say that she had always wanted so much to consult me about her lectures. Of course, one subject wasn't enough (this view of the limitations of Greek art as a "subject" gave me a startling idea of the rate at which a successful lecturer might exhaust the universe); she must find others; she had not ventured on any as yet, but she had thought of Tennyson—didn't I *love* Tennyson? She *worshipped* him so that she was sure she could help others to understand him; or what did I think of a "course" on Raphael or Michelangelo—or on the heroines of Shakespeare? There were some fine steel-engravings of Raphael's Madonnas and of the Sistine ceiling in her mother's library, and she had seen Miss Cushman in several Shakespearian *rôles,* so that on these subjects also she felt qualified to speak with authority.

When we reached her mother's door she begged me to come in and talk the matter over; she wanted me to see the baby—she felt as though I should understand her better if I saw the baby—and the dimple flashed through a tear.

The fear of encountering the author of "The Fall of Man," combined with the opportune recollection of a dinner engagement, made me evade this appeal with the promise of returning on the morrow. On the morrow, I left too early to redeem my promise; and for several years afterwards I saw no more of Mrs. Amyot.

My calling at that time took me at irregular intervals from one to another of our larger cities, and as Mrs. Amyot was also peripatetic it was inevitable that sooner or later we should cross each other's path. It was therefore without surprise that, one snowy afternoon in Boston, I learned from the lady with whom I chanced to be lunching that, as soon as the meal was over, I was to be taken to hear Mrs. Amyot lecture.

"On Greek art?" I suggested.

"Oh, you've heard her then? No, this is one of the series called 'Homes and Haunts of the Poets.' Last week we had Wordsworth and the Lake Poets, to-day we are to have Goethe and Weimar. She is a wonderful creature—all the women of her family are geniuses. You know, of course, that her mother was Irene Astarte Pratt, who wrote a poem on 'The Fall of Man'; N. P. Willis called her the female Milton of America. One of Mrs. Amyot's aunts has translated Eurip—"

"And is she as pretty as ever?" I irrelevantly interposed.

My hostess looked shocked. "She is excessively modest and retiring. She says it is actual suffering for her to speak in public. You know she only does it for the baby."

Punctually at the hour appointed, we took our seats in a lecture-hall full of strenuous females in ulsters. Mrs. Amyot was evidently a favorite with these austere sisters, for every corner was crowded, and as we entered a pale usher with an educated mispronunciation was setting forth to several dejected applicants the impossibility of supplying them with seats.

Our own were happily so near the front that when the curtains at the back of the platform parted, and Mrs. Amyot appeared, I was at once able to establish a comparison between the lady placidly dimpling to the applause of her public and the shrinking drawing-room orator of my earlier recollections.

Mrs. Amyot was as pretty as ever, and there was the same curious discrepancy between the freshness of her aspect and the staleness of her theme, but something was gone of the blushing unsteadiness with which she had fired her first random shots at Greek art. It was not that the shots were less uncertain, but that she now had an air of assuming that, for her purpose, the bull's-eye was everywhere, so that there was no need to be flustered in taking aim. This assurance had so facilitated the flow of her eloquence that she seemed to be performing a trick analogous to that of the conjuror who pulls hundreds of yards of white paper out of his mouth. From a large assortment of stock adjectives she chose, with unerring deftness and rapidity, the one that taste and discrimination would most surely have rejected, fitting out her subject with a whole wardrobe of slop-shop epithets irrelevant in cut and size. To the invaluable knack of not disturbing the association of ideas in her audience, she added the gift of what may be called a confidential manner—so that her fluent generalizations about Goethe and his place in literature (the lecture was, of course, manufactured out of Lewes's book) had the flavor of personal experience, of views sympathetically exchanged with her audience on the best way of knitting children's socks, or of putting up preserves for the winter. It was, I am sure, to this personal accent—the moral equivalent of her dimple—that Mrs. Amyot owed her prodigious, her irrational success. It was her art of transposing second-hand ideas into first-hand emotions that so endeared her to her feminine listeners.

To any one not in search of "documents" Mrs. Amyot's success was hardly of a kind to make her more interesting, and my curiosity flagged with the growing conviction that the "suffering" entailed on her by public speaking was at most a retrospective pang. I was sure that she had reached the point of measuring and enjoying her effects, of deliberately manipulating her public; and there must indeed have been a certain exhilaration in attaining results so considerable by means involving so little conscious effort. Mrs. Amyot's art was simply an extension of coquetry: she flirted with her audience.

In this mood of enlightened skepticism I responded but languidly to my hostess's suggestion that I should go with her that evening to see Mrs. Amyot. The aunt who had translated Euripides was at home on Saturday evenings, and one met "thoughtful" people there, my hostess explained: it was one of the intellectual centres of Boston. My mood remained distinctly resentful of any connection between Mrs. Amyot and intellectuality, and I declined to go; but the next day I met Mrs. Amyot in the street.

She stopped me reproachfully. She had heard I was in Boston; why had I not come last night? She had been told that I was at her lecture, and it had frightened her—yes, really, almost as much as years ago in Hillbridge. She never *could* get over that stupid shyness, and the whole business was as distasteful to her as ever; but what could she do? There was the baby—he was a big boy now, and boys were *so* expensive! But did I really think she had improved the least little bit? And why would n't I come home with her now, and see the boy, and tell her frankly what I had thought of the lecture? She had plenty of flattery—people were *so* kind, and every one knew that she did it for the baby—but what she felt the need of was criticism, severe, discriminating criticism like mine—oh, she knew that I was dreadfully discriminating!

I went home with her and saw the boy. In the early heat of her Tennyson-worship Mrs. Amyot had christened him Lancelot, and he looked it. Perhaps, however, it was his black velvet dress and the exasperating length of his yellow curls, together with the fact of his having been taught to recite Browning to visitors, that raised to fever-heat the itching of my palms in his Infant-Samuel-like presence. I have since had reason to think that he would have preferred to be called Billy, and to hunt cats with the other boys in the block: his curls and his poetry were simply another outlet for Mrs. Amyot's irrepressible coquetry.

But if Lancelot was not genuine, his mother's love for him was. It justified everything—the lectures *were* for the baby, after all. I had not been ten minutes in the room before I was pledged to help Mrs. Amyot carry out her triumphant fraud. If she wanted to lecture on Plato she should—Plato must take his chance like the rest of us! There was no use, of course, in being "discriminating." I preserved sufficient reason to avoid that pitfall, but I suggested "subjects" and made lists of books for her with a fatuity that became more obvious as time attenuated the remembrance of her smile; I even remember thinking that some men might have cut the knot by marrying her, but I handed over Plato as a hostage and escaped by the afternoon train.

The next time I saw her was in New York, when she had become so fashionable that it was a part of the whole duty of woman to be seen at her lectures. The lady who suggested that of course I ought to go and hear Mrs. Amyot, was not very clear about anything except that she was perfectly lovely, and had had a horrid husband, and was doing it to support her boy. The subject of the discourse (I think it was on Ruskin) was clearly of minor importance, not only to my friend, but to the throng of well-dressed and absent-minded ladies who rustled in late, dropped their muffs and pocket-books, and undisguisedly lost themselves in the study of each other's apparel. They received Mrs. Amyot with warmth, but she evidently represented a social obligation like going to church, rather than any more personal interest; in fact, I suspect that every one of the ladies would have remained away, had they been sure that none of the others were coming.

Whether Mrs. Amyot was disheartened by the lack of sympathy between herself and her hearers, or whether the sport of arousing it had become a task, she certainly imparted her platitudes with less convincing warmth than of old. Her voice had the same confidential inflections, but it was like a voice reproduced by a gramophone: the real woman seemed far away. She had grown stouter without losing her dewy freshness, and her smart gown might have been taken to show either the potentialities of a settled income, or a politic concession to the taste of her hearers. As I listened I reproached myself for ever having suspected her of self-deception in saying that she took no pleasure in her work. I was sure now that she did it only for Lancelot, and judging from the size of her audience and the price of the tickets I concluded that Lancelot must be receiving a liberal education.

I was living in New York that winter, and in the rotation of dinners I found myself one evening at Mrs. Amyot's side. The dimple came out at my greeting as punctually as a cuckoo in a Swiss clock, and I detected the same automatic quality in the tone in which she made her usual pretty demand for advice. She was like a musical-box charged with popular airs. They succeeded one another with breathless rapidity, but there was a moment after each when the cylinders scraped and whizzed.

Mrs. Amyot, as I found when I called on her, was living in a sunny flat, with a sitting-room full of flowers and a tea-table that had the air of expecting visitors. She owned that she had been ridiculously successful. It was delightful, of course, on Lancelot's account. Lancelot had been sent to the best school in the country, and if things went well and people didn't tire of his silly mother he was to go to Harvard afterwards. During the next two or three years Mrs. Amyot kept her flat in New York, and radiated art and literature upon the suburbs. I saw her now and then, always stouter, better dressed, more successful and more automatic: she had become a lecturing-machine.

I went abroad for a year or two and when I came back she had disappeared. I asked several people about her, but life had closed over her. She had been last heard of as lecturing—still lecturing—but no one seemed to know when or where.

It was in Boston that I found her at last, forlornly swaying to the oscillations of an overhead strap in a crowded trolley-car. Her face had so changed that I lost myself in a startled reckoning of the time that had elapsed since our parting. She spoke to me shyly, as though aware of my hurried calculation, and conscious that in five years she ought not to have altered so much as to upset my notion of time. Then she seemed to set it down to her dress, for she nervously gathered her cloak over a gown that asked only to be concealed, and shrank into a seat behind the line of prehensile bipeds blocking the aisle of the car.

It was perhaps because she so obviously avoided me that I felt for the first time that I might be of use to her; and when she left the car I made no excuse for following her.

She said nothing of needing advice and did not ask me to walk home with her, concealing, as we talked, her transparent preoccupations under the guise of a sudden interest in all I had been doing since she had last seen me. Of what concerned her, I learned only that Lancelot was well and that for the present she was not lecturing—she was tired and her doctor had ordered her to rest. On the doorstep of a shabby house she paused and held out her hand. She had been so glad to see me and perhaps if I were in Boston again—the tired dimple, as it were, bowed me out and closed the door on the conclusion of the phrase.

Two or three weeks later, at my club in New York, I found a letter from her. In it she owned that she was troubled, that of late she had been unsuccessful, and that, if I chanced to be coming back to Boston, and could spare her a little of that invaluable advice which—. A few days later the advice was at her disposal. She told me frankly what had happened. Her public had grown tired of her. She had seen it coming on for some time, and was shrewd enough in detecting the causes. She had more rivals than formerly—younger women, she admitted, with a smile that could still afford to be generous—and then her audiences had grown more critical and consequently more exacting. Lecturing—as she understood it—used to be simple enough. You chose your topic—Raphael, Shakespeare, Gothic Architecture, or some such big familiar "subject"—and read up about it for a week or so at the Athenæum or the Astor Library, and then told your audience what you had read. Now, it appeared, that simple process was no longer adequate. People had tired of familiar "subjects"; it was the fashion to be interested in things that one hadn't always known about—natural selection, animal magnetism, sociology and comparative folk-lore; while, in literature, the demand had become equally difficult to meet, since Matthew Arnold had introduced the habit of studying the "influence" of one author on another. She had tried lecturing on influences, and had done very well as long as the public was satisfied with the tracing of such obvious influences as that of Turner on Ruskin, of Schiller on Goethe, of Shakespeare on English literature; but such investigations had soon lost all charm for her too-sophisticated audiences, who now demanded either that the influence or the influenced should be quite unknown, or that there should be no perceptible connection between the two. The zest of the performance lay in the measure of ingenuity with which the lecturer established a relation between two people who had probably never heard of each other, much less read each other's works. A pretty Miss Williams with red hair had, for instance, been lecturing with great success on the influence of the Rosicrucians upon the poetry of Keats, while somebody else had given a "course" on the influence of St. Thomas Aquinas upon Professor Huxley.

Mrs. Amyot, warmed by my participation in her distress, went on to say that the growing demand for evolution was what most troubled her. Her grandfather had been a pillar of the Presbyterian ministry, and the idea of her lecturing on Darwin or Herbert Spencer was deeply shocking to her mother and aunts. In one sense the family had staked its literary as well as its spiritual hopes on the literal inspiration of Genesis: what became of "The Fall of Man" in the light of modern exegesis?

The upshot of it was that she had ceased to lecture because she could no longer sell tickets enough to pay for the hire of a lecture-hall; and as for the managers, they wouldn't look at her. She had tried her luck all through the Eastern States and as far south as Washington; but it was of no use, and unless she could get hold of some new subjects—or, better still, of some new audiences—she must simply go out of the business. That would mean the failure of all she had worked for, since Lancelot would have to leave Harvard. She paused, and wept some of the unbecoming tears that spring from real grief. Lancelot, it appeared, was to be a genius. He had passed his opening examinations brilliantly; he had "literary gifts"; he had written beautiful poetry, much of which his mother had copied out, in reverentially slanting characters, in a velvet-bound volume which she drew from a locked drawer.

Lancelot's verse struck me as nothing more alarming than growing-pains; but it was not to learn this that she had summoned me. What she wanted was to be assured that he was worth working for, an assurance which I managed to convey by the simple stratagem of remarking that the poems reminded me of Swinburne—and so they did, as well as of Browning, Tennyson, Rossetti, and all the other poets who supply young authors with original inspirations.

This point being established, it remained to be decided by what means his mother was, in the French phrase, to pay herself the luxury of a poet. It was clear that this indulgence could be bought only with counterfeit coin, and that the one way of helping Mrs. Amyot was to become a party to the circulation of such currency. My fetish of intellectual integrity went down like a ninepin before the appeal of a woman no longer young and distinctly foolish, but full of those dear contradictions and irrelevancies that will always make flesh and blood prevail against a syllogism. When I took leave of Mrs. Amyot I had promised her a dozen letters to Western universities and had half pledged myself to sketch out a lecture on the reconciliation of science and religion.

In the West she achieved a success which for a year or more embittered my perusal of the morning papers. The fascination that lures the murderer back to the scene of his crime drew my eye to every paragraph celebrating Mrs. Amyot's last brilliant lecture on the influence of something upon somebody; and her own letters—she overwhelmed me with them—spared me no detail of the entertainment given in her honor by the Palimpsest Club of Omaha or of her reception at the University of Leadville. The college professors were especially kind: she assured me that she had never before met with such discriminating sympathy. I winced at the adjective, which cast a sudden light on the vast machinery of fraud that I had set in motion. All over my native land, men of hitherto unblemished integrity were conniving with me in urging their friends to go and hear Mrs. Amyot lecture on the reconciliation of science and religion! My only hope was that, somewhere among the number of my accomplices, Mrs. Amyot might find one who would marry her in the defense of his convictions.

None, apparently, resorted to such heroic measures; for about two years later I was startled by the announcement that Mrs. Amyot was lecturing in Trenton, New Jersey, on modern theosophy in the light of the Vedas. The following week she was at Newark, discussing Schopenhauer in the light of recent psychology. The week after that I was on the deck of an ocean steamer, reconsidering my share in Mrs. Amyot's triumphs with the impartiality with which one views an episode that is being left behind at the rate of twenty knots an hour. After all, I had been helping a mother to educate her son.

The next ten years of my life were spent in Europe, and when I came home the recollection of Mrs. Amyot had become as inoffensive as one of those pathetic ghosts who are said to strive in vain to make themselves visible to the living. I did not even notice the fact that I no longer heard her spoken of; she had dropped like a dead leaf from the bough of memory.

A year or two after my return I was condemned to one of the worst punishments a worker can undergo—an enforced holiday. The doctors who pronounced the inhuman sentence decreed that it should be worked out in the South, and for a whole winter I carried my cough, my thermometer and my idleness from one fashionable orange-grove to another. In the vast and melancholy sea of my disoccupation I clutched like a drowning man at any human driftwood within reach. I took a critical and depreciatory interest in the coughs, the thermometers and the idleness of my fellow-sufferers;

but to the healthy, the occupied, the transient I clung with undiscriminating enthusiasm.

In no other way can I explain, as I look back on it, the importance I attached to the leisurely confidences of a new arrival with a brown beard who, tilted back at my side on a hotel veranda hung with roses, imparted to me one afternoon the simple annals of his past. There was nothing in the tale to kindle the most inflammable imagination, and though the man had a pleasant frank face and a voice differing agreeably from the shrill inflections of our fellow-lodgers, it is probable that under different conditions his discursive history of successful business ventures in a Western city would have affected me somewhat in the manner of a lullaby.

Even at the time I was not sure I liked his agreeable voice: it had a self-importance out of keeping with the humdrum nature of his story, as though a breeze engaged in shaking out a table-cloth should have fancied itself inflating a banner. But this criticism may have been a mere mark of my own fastidiousness, for the man seemed a simple fellow, satisfied with his middling fortunes, and already (he was not much past thirty) deep-sunk in conjugal content.

He had just started on an anecdote connected with the cutting of his eldest boy's teeth, when a lady I knew, returning from her late drive, paused before us for a moment in the twilight, with the smile which is the feminine equivalent of beads to savages.

"Won't you take a ticket?" she said sweetly.

Of course I would take a ticket—but for what? I ventured to inquire.

"Oh, that's *so* good of you—for the lecture this evening. You needn't go, you know; we're none of us going; most of us have been through it already at Aiken and at Saint Augustine and at Palm Beach. I've given away my tickets to some new people who've just come from the North, and some of us are going to send our maids, just to fill up the room."

"And may I ask to whom you are going to pay this delicate attention?"

"Oh, I thought you knew—to poor Mrs. Amyot. She's been lecturing all over the South this winter; she's simply *haunted* me ever since I left New York—and we had six weeks of her at Bar Harbor last summer! One has to take tickets, you know, because she's a widow and does it for her son—to pay for his education. She's so plucky and nice about it, and talks about him in such a touching unaffected way, that everybody is sorry for her, and we all simply ruin ourselves in tickets. I do hope that boy's nearly educated!"

"Mrs. Amyot? Mrs. Amyot?" I repeated. "Is she *still* educating her son?"

"Oh, do you know about her? Has she been at it long? There's some comfort in that, for I suppose when the boy's provided for the poor thing will be able to take a rest—and give us one!"

She laughed and held out her hand.

"Here's your ticket. Did you say *tickets*—two? Oh, thanks. Of course you need n't go."

"But I mean to go. Mrs. Amyot is an old friend of mine."

"Do you really? That's awfully good of you. Perhaps I'll go too if I can persuade Charlie and the others to come. And I wonder"—in a well-directed aside—"if your friend—?"

I telegraphed her under cover of the dusk that my friend was of too recent standing to be drawn into her charitable toils, and she masked her mistake under a rattle of friendly adjurations not to be late, and to be sure to keep a seat for her, as she had quite made up her mind to go even if Charlie and the others wouldn't.

The flutter of her skirts subsided in the distance, and my neighbor, who had half turned away to light a cigar, made no effort to reopen the conversation. At length, fearing he might have overheard the allusion to himself, I ventured to ask if he were going to the lecture that evening.

"Much obliged—I have a ticket," he said abruptly.

This struck me as in such bad taste that I made no answer; and it was he who spoke next.

"Did I understand you to say that you were an old friend of Mrs. Amyot's?"

"I think I may claim to be, if it is the same Mrs. Amyot I had the pleasure of knowing many years ago. My Mrs. Amyot used to lecture too—"

"To pay for her son's education?"

"I believe so."

"Well—see you later."

He got up and walked into the house.

In the hotel drawing-room that evening there was but a meagre sprinkling of guests, among whom I saw my brown-bearded friend sitting alone on a sofa, with his head against the wall. It could not have been curiosity to see Mrs. Amyot that had impelled him to attend the performance, for it would have been impossible for him, without changing his place, to command the improvised platform at the end of the room. When I looked at him he seemed lost in contemplation of the chandelier.

The lady from whom I had bought my tickets fluttered in late, unattended by Charlie and the others, and assuring me that she would *scream* if we had the lecture on Ibsen—she had heard it three times already that winter. A glance at the programme reassured her: it informed us (in the lecturer's own slanting hand) that Mrs. Amyot was to lecture on the Cosmogony.

After a long pause, during which the small audience coughed and moved its chairs and showed signs of regretting that it had come, the door opened, and Mrs. Amyot stepped upon the platform. Ah, poor lady!

Some one said "Hush!", the coughing and chair-shifting subsided, and she began.

It was like looking at one's self early in the morning in a cracked mirror. I had no idea I had grown so old. As for Lancelot, he must have a beard. A beard? The word struck me, and without knowing why I glanced across the room at my bearded friend on the sofa. Oddly enough he was looking at me, with a half-defiant, half-sullen expression; and as our glances crossed, and his fell, the conviction came to me that *he was Lancelot.*

I don't remember a word of the lecture; and yet there were enough of them to have filled a good-sized dictionary. The stream of Mrs. Amyot's eloquence had become a flood: one had the despairing sense that she had sprung a leak, and that until the plumber came there was nothing to be done about it.

The plumber came at length, in the shape of a clock striking ten; my companion, with a sigh of relief, drifted away in search of Charlie and the others; the audience scattered with the precipitation of people who had discharged a duty; and, without surprise, I found the brown-bearded stranger at my elbow.

We stood alone in the bare-floored room, under the flaring chandelier.

"I think you told me this afternoon that you were an old friend of Mrs. Amyot's?" he began awkwardly.

I assented.

"Will you come in and see her?"

"Now? I shall be very glad to, if—"

"She's ready; she's expecting you," he interposed.

He offered no further explanation, and I followed him in silence. He led me down the long corridor, and pushed open the door of a sitting-room.

"Mother," he said, closing the door after we had entered, "here's the gentleman who says he used to know you."

Mrs. Amyot, who sat in an easy-chair stirring a cup of bouillon, looked up with a start. She had evidently not seen me in the audience and her son's description had failed to convey my identity. I saw a frightened look in her eyes; then, like a frost flower on a windowpane, the dimple expanded on her wrinkled cheek, and she held out her hand.

"I'm so glad," she said, "so glad!"

She turned to her son, who stood watching us. "You must have told Lancelot all about me—you've known me so long!"

"I haven't had time to talk to your son—since I knew he was your son," I explained.

Her brow cleared. "Then you haven't had time to say anything very dreadful?" she said with a laugh.

"It is he who has been saying dreadful things," I returned, trying to fall in with her tone.

I saw my mistake. "What things?" she faltered.

"Making me feel how old I am by telling me about his children."

"My grandchildren!" she exclaimed with a blush.

"Well, if you choose to put it so."

She laughed again, vaguely, and was silent. I hesitated a moment and then put out my hand.

"I see you are tired. I shouldn't have ventured to come in at this hour if your son—"

The son stepped between us. "Yes, I asked him to come," he said to his mother, in his clear self-assertive voice. "*I* haven't told him anything yet; but you've got to—now. That's what I brought him for."

His mother straightened herself, but I saw her eye waver.

"Lancelot—" she began.

"Mr. Amyot," I said, turning to the young man, "if your mother will let me come back to-morrow, I shall be very glad—"

He struck his hand hard against the table on which he was leaning.

"No, sir! It won't take long, but it's got to be said now."

He moved nearer to his mother, and I saw his lip twitch under his beard. After all, he was younger and less sure of himself than I had fancied.

"See here, mother," he went on, "there's something here that's got to be cleared up, and as you say this gentleman is an old friend of yours it had better be cleared up in his presence. Maybe he can help explain it—and if he can't, it's got to be explained to *him*."

Mrs. Amyot's lips moved, but she made no sound. She glanced at me helplessly and sat down. My early inclination to thrash Lancelot was beginning to reassert itself. I took up my hat and moved toward the door.

"Mrs. Amyot is under no obligation to explain anything whatever to me," I said curtly.

"Well! She's under an obligation to me, then—to explain something in your presence." He turned to her again. "Do you know what the people in this hotel are saying? Do you know what he thinks—what they all think? That you're doing this lecturing to support me—to pay for my education! They say you go round telling them so. That 's what they buy the tickets for—they do it out of charity. Ask him if it isn't what they say—ask him if they weren't joking about it on the piazza before dinner. The others think I'm a little boy, but he's known you for years, and he must have known how old I was. He must have known it wasn't to pay for my education!"

He stood before her with his hands clenched, the veins beating in his temples. She had grown very pale, and her cheeks looked hollow. When she spoke her voice had an odd click in it.

"If—if these ladies and gentlemen have been coming to my lectures out of charity, I see nothing to be ashamed of in that—" she faltered.

"If they've been coming out of charity to *me,*" he retorted, "don't you see you've been making me a party to a fraud? Isn't there any shame in that?" His forehead reddened. "Mother! Can't you see the shame of letting people think I was a d— beat, who sponged on you for my keep? Let alone making us both the laughing-stock of every place you go to!"

"I never did that, Lancelot!"

"Did what?"

"Made you a laughing-stock—"

He stepped close to her and caught her wrist.

"Will you look me in the face and swear you never told people you were doing this lecturing business to support me?"

There was a long silence. He dropped her wrist and she lifted a limp handkerchief to her frightened eyes. "I did do it—to support you—to educate you"—she sobbed.

"We're not talking about what you did when I was a boy. Everybody who knows me knows I've been a grateful son. Have I ever taken a penny from you since I left college ten years ago?"

"I never said you had! How can you accuse your mother of such wickedness, Lancelot?"

"Have you never told anybody in this hotel—or anywhere else in the last ten years—that you were lecturing to support me? Answer me that!"

"How can you," she wept, "before a stranger?"

"Haven't you said such things about *me* to strangers?" he retorted.

"Lancelot!"

"Well—answer me, then. Say you haven't, mother!" His voice broke unexpectedly and he took her hand with a gentler touch. "I'll believe anything you tell me," he said almost humbly.

She mistook his tone and raised her head with a rash clutch at dignity.

"I think you'd better ask this gentleman to excuse you first."

"No, by God, I won't!" he cried. "This gentleman says he knows all about you and I mean him to know all about me too. I don't mean that he or anybody else under this roof shall go on thinking for another twenty-four hours that a cent of their money has ever gone into my pockets since I was old enough to shift for myself. And he shan't leave this room till you've made that clear to him."

He stepped back as he spoke and put his shoulders against the door.

"My dear young gentleman," I said politely, "I shall leave this room exactly when I see fit to do so—and that is now. I have already told you that Mrs. Amyot owes me no explanation of her conduct."

"But I owe you an explanation of mine—you and every one who has bought a single one of her lecture tickets. Do you suppose a man who's been through what I went through while that woman was talking to you in the porch before dinner is going to hold his tongue, and not attempt to justify himself? No decent man is going to sit down under that sort of thing. It's enough to ruin his character. If you're my mother's friend, you owe it to me to hear what I've got to say."

He pulled out his handkerchief and wiped his forehead.

"Good God, mother!" he burst out suddenly, "what did you do it for? Haven't you had everything you wanted ever since I was able to pay for it? Haven't I paid you back every cent you spent on me when I was in college? Have I ever gone back on you since I was big enough to work?" He turned to me with a laugh. "I thought she did it to amuse herself—and because there was such a demand for her lectures. *Such a demand!* That's what she always told me. When we asked her to come out and spend this winter with us in Minneapolis, she wrote back that she couldn't because she had engagements all through the south, and her manager wouldn't let her off. That's the reason why I came all the way on here to see her. We thought she was the most popular lecturer in the United States, my wife and I did! We were awfully proud of it too, I can tell you." He dropped into a chair, still laughing.

"How can you, Lancelot, how can you!" His mother, forgetful of my presence, was clinging to him with tentative caresses. "When you didn't need the money any longer I spent it all on the children—you know I did."

"Yes, on lace christening dresses and life-size rocking-horses with real manes! The kind of thing children can't do without."

"Oh, Lancelot, Lancelot—I loved them so! How can you believe such falsehoods about me?"

"What falsehoods about you?"

"That I ever told anybody such dreadful things?"

He put her back gently, keeping his eyes on hers. "Did you never tell anybody in this house that you were lecturing to support your son?"

Her hands dropped from his shoulders and she flashed round on me in sudden anger.

"I know what I think of people who call themselves friends and who come between a mother and her son!"

"Oh, mother, mother!" he groaned.

I went up to him and laid my hand on his shoulder.

"My dear man," I said, "don't you see the uselessness of prolonging this?"

"Yes, I do," he answered abruptly; and before I could forestall his movement he rose and walked out of the room.

There was a long silence, measured by the lessening reverberations of his footsteps down the wooden floor of the corridor.

When they ceased I approached Mrs. Amyot, who had sunk into her chair. I held out my hand and she took it without a trace of resentment on her ravaged face.

"I sent his wife a seal-skin jacket at Christmas!" she said, with the tears running down her cheeks.

The Rembrandt

"YOU'RE *so* artistic," my cousin Eleanor Copt began.

Of all Eleanor's exordiums it is the one I most dread. When she tells me I'm so clever I know this is merely the preamble to inviting me to meet the last literary obscurity of the moment: a trial to be evaded or endured, as circumstances dictate; whereas her calling me artistic fatally connotes the request to visit, in her company, some distressed gentlewoman whose future hangs on my valuation of her old Saxe or of her grandfather's Marc Antonios. Time was when I attempted to resist these compulsions of Eleanor's; but I soon learned that, short of actual flight, there was no refuge from her beneficent despotism. It is not always easy for the curator of a museum to abandon his post on the plea of escaping a pretty cousin's importunities; and Eleanor, aware of my predicament, is none too magnanimous to take advantage of it. Magnanimity is, in fact, not in Eleanor's line. The virtues, she once explained to me, are like bonnets: the very ones that look best on other people may not happen to suit one's own particular style; and she added, with a slight deflection of metaphor, that none of the ready-made virtues ever *had* fitted her: they all pinched somewhere, and she'd given up trying to wear them.

Therefore when she said to me, "You're *so* artistic," emphasizing the conjunction with a tap of her dripping umbrella (Eleanor is out in all weathers: the elements are as powerless against her as man), I merely stipulated, "It's not old Saxe again?"

She shook her head reassuringly. "A picture—a Rembrandt!"

"Good Lord! Why not a Leonardo?"

"Well"—she smiled—"that, of course, depends on *you.*"

"On me?"

"On your attribution. I dare say Mrs. Fontage would consent to the change—though she's very conservative."

A gleam of hope came to me and I pronounced: "One can't judge of a picture in this weather."

"Of course not. I'm coming for you to-morrow."

"I've an engagement to-morrow."

"I'll come before or after your engagement."

The afternoon paper lay at my elbow and I contrived a furtive consultation of the weather-report. It said "Rain to-morrow," and I answered briskly: "All right, then; come at ten"—rapidly calculating that the clouds on which I counted might lift by noon.

My ingenuity failed of its due reward; for the heavens, as if in league with my cousin, emptied themselves before morning, and punctually at ten Eleanor and the sun appeared together in my office.

I hardly listened, as we descended the Museum steps and got into Eleanor's hansom, to her vivid summing-up of the case. I guessed beforehand that the lady we were about to visit had lapsed by the most distressful degrees from opulence to a "hall-bedroom"; that her grandfather, if he had not been Minister to France, had signed the Declaration of Independence; that the Rembrandt was an heirloom, sole remnant of disbanded treasures; that for years its possessor had been unwilling to part with it, and that even now the question of its disposal must be approached with the most diplomatic obliquity.

Previous experience had taught me that all Eleanor's "cases" presented a harrowing similarity of detail. No circumstance tending to excite the spectator's sympathy and involve his action was omitted from the history of her beneficiaries; the lights and shades were indeed so skilfully adjusted that any impartial expression of opinion took on the hue of cruelty. I could have produced closetfuls of "heirlooms" in attestation of this fact; for it is one more mark of Eleanor's competence that her friends usually pay the interest on her philanthropy. My one hope was that in this case the object, being a picture, might reasonably be rated beyond my means; and as our cab drew up before a blistered brown-stone door-step I formed the self-defensive resolve to place an extreme valuation on Mrs. Fontage's Rembrandt. It is Eleanor's fault if she is sometimes fought with her own weapons.

The house stood in one of those shabby provisional-looking New York streets that seem resignedly awaiting demolition. It was the kind of house that, in its high days, must have had a bow-window with a bronze in it. The bow-window had been replaced by a plumber's *devanture,* and one might conceive the bronze to have gravitated to the limbo where Mexican onyx tables and bric-a-brac in buffalo-horn await the first signs of our next æsthetic reaction.

Eleanor swept me through a hall that smelled of poverty, up unlit stairs to a bare slit of a room. "And she must leave this in a month!" she whispered across her knock.

I had prepared myself for the limp widow's weed of a woman that one figures in such a setting; and confronted abruptly with Mrs. Fontage's white-haired erectness I had the disconcerting sense that I was somehow in her presence at my own solicitation. I instinctively charged Eleanor with this reversal of the situation; but a moment later I saw it must be ascribed to a something about Mrs. Fontage that precluded the possibility of her asking any one a favor. It was not that she was of forbidding, or even majestic, demeanor; but that one guessed, under her aquiline prettiness, a dignity nervously on guard against the petty betrayal of her surroundings. The room was unconcealably poor: the little faded "relics," the high-stocked ancestral silhouettes, the steel-engravings after Raphael and Correggio, grouped in a vain attempt to hide the most obvious stains on the wall-paper, served only to accentuate the contrast of a past evidently diversified by foreign travel and the enjoyment of the arts. Even Mrs. Fontage's dress had the air of being a last expedient, the ultimate outcome of a much-taxed ingenuity in darning and turning. One felt that all the poor lady's barriers were falling save that of her impregnable manner.

To this manner I found myself conveying my appreciation of being admitted to a view of the Rembrandt.

Mrs. Fontage's smile took my homage for granted. "It is always," she conceded, "a privilege to be in the presence of the great masters." Her slim wrinkled hand waved me to a dusky canvas near the window.

"It's *so* interesting, dear Mrs. Fontage," I heard Eleanor exclaiming, "and my cousin will be able to tell you exactly—" Eleanor, in my presence, always admits that she knows nothing about art; but she gives the impression that this is merely because she hasn't had time to look into the matter—and has had me to do it for her.

Mrs. Fontage seated herself without speaking, as though fearful that a breath might disturb my communion with the masterpiece. I felt that she thought Eleanor's reassuring ejaculations ill-timed; and in this I was of one mind with her; for the impossibility of telling her exactly what I thought of her Rembrandt had become clear to me at a glance.

My cousin's vivacities began to languish and the silence seemed to shape itself into a receptacle for my verdict. I stepped back, affecting a more distant scrutiny; and as I did so my eye caught Mrs. Fontage's profile. Her lids trembled slightly. I took refuge in the familiar expedient of asking the history of the picture, and she waved me brightly to a seat.

This was indeed a topic on which she could dilate. The Rembrandt, it appeared, had come into Mr. Fontage's possession many years ago, while the young couple were on their wedding-tour, and under circumstances so romantic that she made no excuse for relating them in all their parenthetic fulness. The picture belonged to an old Belgian Countess of redundant quarterings, whom the extravagances of an ungovernable nephew had compelled to part with her possessions (in the most private manner) about the time of the Fontages' arrival. By a really remarkable coincidence, it happened that their courier (an exceptionally intelligent and superior man) was an old servant of the Countess's, and had thus been able to put them in the way of securing the Rembrandt under the very nose of an English Duke, whose agent had been sent to Brussels to negotiate for its purchase. Mrs. Fontage could not recall the Duke's name, but he was a great collector and had a famous Highland castle, where somebody had been murdered, and which she herself had visited (by moonlight) when she had travelled in Scotland as a girl. The episode had in short been one of the most interesting "experiences" of a tour almost chromo-lithographic in vivacity of impression; and they had always meant to go back to Brussels for the sake of reliving so picturesque a moment. Circumstances (of which the narrator's surroundings declared the nature) had persistently interfered with the projected return to Europe, and the picture had grown doubly valuable as representing the high-water mark of their artistic emotions. Mrs. Fontage's moist eye caressed the canvas. "There is only," she added with a perceptible effort, "one slight drawback: the picture is not signed. But for that the Countess, of course, would have sold it to a museum. All the connoisseurs who have seen it pronounce it an undoubted Rembrandt, in the artist's best manner; but the museums"—she arched her brows in smiling recognition of a well-known weakness—"give the preference to signed examples—"

Mrs. Fontage's words evoked so touching a vision of the young tourists of fifty years ago, entrusting to an accomplished and versatile courier the direction of their helpless zeal for art, that I lost sight for a moment of the point at issue. The old Belgian Countess, the wealthy Duke with a feudal castle in Scotland, Mrs. Fontage's own maiden pilgrimage to Arthur's Seat and Holyrood, all the accessories of the naïf transaction, seemed a part of that vanished Europe to which our young race carried its indiscriminate ardors, its tender romantic credulity: the legendary castellated Europe of keepsakes, brigands and old masters, that compensated, by one such "experience" as Mrs. Fontage's, for an after-life of æsthetic privation.

I was restored to the present by Eleanor's looking at her watch. The action mutely conveyed that something was expected of me. I risked the temporizing statement that the picture was very interesting; but Mrs. Fontage's polite assent revealed the poverty of the expedient. Eleanor's impatience overflowed.

"You would like my cousin to give you an idea of its value?" she suggested.

Mrs. Fontage grew more erect. "No one," she corrected with great gentleness, "can know its value quite as well as I, who live with it—"

We murmured our hasty concurrence.

"But it might be interesting to hear"—she addressed herself to me—"as a mere matter of curiosity—what estimate would be put on it from the purely commercial point of view—if such a term may be used in speaking of a work of art."

I sounded a note of deprecation.

"Oh, I understand, of course," she delicately anticipated me, "that that could never be *your* view, your personal view; but since occasions *may* arise—do arise—when it becomes necessary to—to put a price on the priceless, as it were—I have thought—Miss Copt has suggested—"

"Some day," Eleanor encouraged her, "you might feel that the picture ought to belong to some one who has more—more opportunity of showing it—letting it be seen by the public—for educational reasons—"

"I have tried," Mrs. Fontage admitted, "to see it in that light."

The crucial moment was upon me. To escape the challenge of Mrs. Fontage's brilliant composure I turned once more to the picture. If my courage needed reinforcement, the picture amply furnished it. Looking at that lamentable canvas seemed the surest way of gathering strength to denounce it; but behind me, all the while, I felt Mrs. Fontage's shuddering pride drawn up in a final effort of self-defense. I hated myself for my sentimental perversion of the situation. Reason argued that it was more cruel to deceive Mrs. Fontage than to tell her the truth; but that merely proved the inferiority of reason to instinct in situations involving any concession to the emotions. Along with her faith in the Rembrandt I must destroy not only the whole fabric of Mrs. Fontage's past, but even that lifelong habit of acquiescence in untested formulas that makes the best part of the average feminine strength. I guessed the episode of the picture to be inextricably interwoven with the traditions and convictions which served to veil Mrs. Fontage's destitution not only from others but from herself. Viewed in that light the Rembrandt had perhaps been worth its purchase-money; and I regretted that works of art do not commonly sell on the merit of the moral support they may have rendered.

From this unavailing flight I was recalled by the sense that something must be done. To place a fictitious value on the picture was at best a provisional measure; while the brutal alternative of advising Mrs. Fontage to sell it for a hundred dollars at least afforded an opening to the charitably disposed purchaser. I intended, if other resources failed, to put myself forward in that light; but delicacy of course forbade my coupling my unflattering estimate of the Rembrandt with an immediate offer to buy it. All I could do was to inflict the wound: the healing unguent must be withheld for later application.

I turned to Mrs. Fontage, who sat motionless, her finely-lined cheeks touched with an expectant color, her eyes averted from the picture which was so evidently the one object they beheld.

"My dear madam—" I began. Her vivid smile was like a light

held up to dazzle me. It shrouded every alternative in darkness and I had the flurried sense of having lost my way among the intricacies of my contention. Of a sudden I felt the hopelessness of finding a crack in her impenetrable conviction. My words slipped from me like broken weapons. "The picture," I faltered, "would of course be worth more if it were signed. As it is, I–I hardly think–on a conservative estimate–it can be valued at–at more–than–a thousand dollars, say–"

My deflected argument ran on somewhat aimlessly till it found itself plunging full tilt against the barrier of Mrs. Fontage's silence. She sat as impassive as though I had not spoken. Eleanor loosed a few fluttering words of congratulation and encouragement, but their flight was suddenly cut short. Mrs. Fontage had risen with a certain solemnity.

"I could never," she said gently–her gentleness was adamantine –"under any circumstances whatever, consider, for a moment even, the possibility of parting with the picture at such a price."

§ 2

Within three weeks a tremulous note from Mrs. Fontage requested the favor of another visit. If the writing was tremulous, however, the writer's tone was firm. She named her own day and hour, without the conventional reference to her visitor's convenience.

My first impulse was to turn the note over to Eleanor. I had acquitted myself of my share in the ungrateful business of coming to Mrs. Fontage's aid, and if, as her letter denoted, she had now yielded to the closer pressure of need, the business of finding a purchaser for the Rembrandt might well be left to my cousin's ingenuity. But here conscience put in the uncomfortable reminder that it was I who, in putting a price on the picture, had raised the real obstacle in the way of Mrs. Fontage's rescue. No one would give a thousand dollars for the Rembrandt; but to tell Mrs. Fontage so had become as unthinkable as murder. I had, in fact, on returning from my first inspection of the picture, refrained from imparting to Eleanor my opinion of its value. Eleanor is porous, and I knew that sooner or later the unnecessary truth would exude through the loose texture of her dissimulation. Not infrequently she thus creates the misery she alleviates; and I have sometimes suspected her of paining people in order that she might be sorry for them. I had, at all events, cut off retreat in Eleanor's direction; and the remaining alternative carried me straight to Mrs. Fontage.

She received me with the same commanding sweetness. The room was even barer than before—I believe the carpet was gone—but her manner built up about her a palace to which I was welcomed with high state; and it was as a mere incident of the ceremony that I was presently made aware of her decision to sell the Rembrandt. My previous unsuccess in planning how to deal with Mrs. Fontage had warned me to leave my farther course to chance; and I listened to her explanation with complete detachment. She had resolved to travel for her health; her doctor advised it, and as her absence might be indefinitely prolonged she had reluctantly decided to part with the picture in order to avoid the expense of storage and insurance. Her voice drooped at the admission, and she hurried on, detailing the vague itinerary of a journey that was to combine long-promised visits to impatient friends with various "interesting opportunities" less definitely specified. The poor lady's skill in rearing a screen of verbiage about her enforced avowal had distracted me from my own share in the situation, and it was with dismay that I suddenly caught the drift of her assumptions. She expected me to buy the Rembrandt for the Museum; she had taken my previous valuation as a tentative bid, and when I came to my senses she was in the act of accepting my offer.

Had I had a thousand dollars of my own to dispose of, the bargain would have been concluded on the spot; but I was in the impossible position of being materially unable to buy the picture and morally unable to tell her that it was not worth acquiring for the Museum.

I dashed into the first evasion in sight. I had no authority, I explained, to purchase pictures for the Museum without the consent of the committee.

Mrs. Fontage coped for a moment in silence with the incredible fact that I had rejected her offer; then she ventured, with a kind of pale precipitation: "But I understood—Miss Copt tells me that you practically decide such matters for the committee." I could guess what the effort had cost her.

"My cousin is given to generalizations. My opinion may have some weight with the committee—"

"Well, then—" she timidly prompted.

"For that very reason I can't buy the picture."

She said, with a drooping note, "I don't understand."

"Yet you told me," I reminded her, "that you knew museums didn't buy unsigned pictures."

"Not for what they are worth! Every one knows that. But I—I understood—the price you named—" Her pride shuddered back from the abasement. "It's a misunderstanding then," she faltered.

To avoid looking at her, I glanced desperately at the Rembrandt. Could I—? But reason rejected the possibility. Even if the committee had been blind—and they all *were* but Crozier—I simply shouldn't have dared to do it. I stood up, feeling that to cut the matter short was the only alleviation within reach.

Mrs. Fontage had summoned her indomitable smile; but its brilliancy dropped, as I opened the door, like a candle blown out by a draught.

"If there's any one else—if you knew any one who would care to see the picture, I should be most happy—" She kept her eyes on me, and I saw that, in her case, it hurt less than to look at the Rembrandt. "I shall have to leave here, you know," she panted, "if nobody cares to have it—"

§ 3

That evening at my club I had just succeeded in losing sight of Mrs. Fontage in the fumes of an excellent cigar, when a voice at my elbow evoked her harassing image.

"I want to talk to you," the speaker said, "about Mrs. Fontage's Rembrandt."

"There isn't any," I was about to growl; but looking up I recognized the confiding countenance of Mr. Jefferson Rose.

Mr. Rose was known to me chiefly as a young man suffused with a vague enthusiasm for Virtue and my cousin Eleanor.

One glance at his glossy exterior conveyed the assurance that his morals were as immaculate as his complexion and his linen. Goodness exuded from his moist eye, his liquid voice, the warm damp pressure of his trustful hand. He had always struck me as one of the most uncomplicated organisms I had ever met. His ideas were as simple and inconsecutive as the propositions in a primer, and he spoke slowly, with a kind of uniformity of emphasis that made his words stand out like the raised type for the blind. An obvious incapacity for abstract conceptions made him peculiarly susceptible to the magic of generalization, and one felt he would have been at the mercy of any Cause that spelled itself with a capital letter. It was hard to explain how, with such a superabundance of merit, he managed to be a good fellow: I can only say that he performed the astonishing feat as naturally as he supported an invalid mother and two sisters on the slender salary of a banker's clerk. He sat down beside me with an air of bright expectancy.

"It's a remarkable picture, isn't it?" he said.

"You've seen it?"

"I've been so fortunate. Miss Copt was kind enough to get Mrs. Fontage's permission; we went this afternoon."

I inwardly wished that Eleanor had selected another victim; unless indeed the visit were part of a plan whereby some third person, better equipped for the cultivation of delusions, was to be made to think the Rembrandt remarkable. Knowing the limitations of Mr. Rose's resources I began to wonder if he had any rich aunts.

"And her buying it in that way, too," he went on with his limpid smile, "from that old Countess in Brussels, makes it all the more interesting, does n't it? Miss Copt tells me it's very seldom old pictures can be traced back for more than a generation. I suppose the fact of Mrs. Fontage's knowing its history must add a good deal to its value?"

Uncertain as to his drift, I said: "In her eyes it certainly appears to."

Implications are lost on Mr. Rose, who glowingly continued: "That's the reason why I wanted to talk to you about it—to consult you. Miss Copt tells me you value it at a thousand dollars."

There was no denying this, and I grunted a reluctant assent.

"Of course," he went on earnestly, "your valuation is based on the fact that the picture isn't signed—Mrs. Fontage explained that;

and it *does* make a difference, certainly. But the thing is—if the picture's really good—ought one to take advantage—? I mean—one can see that Mrs. Fontage is in a tight place, and I wouldn't for the world—"

My astonished stare arrested him.

"*You* wouldn't—?"

"I mean—you see, it's just this way;" he coughed and blushed: "I can't give more than a thousand dollars myself—it's as big a sum as I can manage to scrape together—but before I make the offer I want to be sure I'm not standing in the way of her getting more money."

My astonishment lapsed to dismay. "You're going to buy the picture for a thousand dollars?"

His blush deepened. "Why, yes. It sounds rather absurd, I suppose. It isn't much in my line, of course. I can see the picture's very beautiful, but I'm no judge—it isn't the kind of thing, naturally, that I could afford to go in for; but in this case I'm very glad to do what I can; the circumstances are so distressing; and knowing what you think of the picture I feel it's a pretty safe investment—"

"I don't think!" I blurted out.

"You—?"

"I don't think the picture's worth a thousand dollars; I don't think it's worth ten cents; I simply lied about it, that's all."

Mr. Rose looked as frightened as though I had charged him with the offense.

"Hang it, man, can't you see how it happened? I saw the poor woman's pride and happiness hung on her faith in that picture. I tried to make her understand that it was worthless—but she wouldn't; I tried to tell her so—but I couldn't. I behaved like a maudlin ass, but you shan't pay for my infernal bungling—you mustn't buy the picture!"

Mr. Rose sat silent, tapping one glossy boot-tip with another. Suddenly he turned on me a glance of stored intelligence. "But you know," he said good-humoredly, "I rather think I must."

"You haven't—already?"

"Oh, no; the offer's not made."

"Well, then—"

His look gathered a brighter significance.

"But if the picture's worth nothing, nobody will buy it—"

I groaned.

"Except," he continued, "some fellow like me, who doesn't know anything. *I* think it's lovely, you know; I mean to hang it in my mother's sitting-room." He rose and clasped my hand in his adhesive pressure. "I'm awfully obliged to you for telling me this; but perhaps you won't mind my asking you not to mention our talk to Miss Copt? It might bother her, you know, to think the picture isn't exactly up to the mark; and it won't make a rap of difference to me."

§ 4

Mr. Rose left me to a sleepless night. The next morning my resolve was formed, and it carried me straight to Mrs. Fontage's. She answered my knock by stepping out on the landing, and as she shut the door behind her I caught a glimpse of her devastated interior. She mentioned, with a careful avoidance of the note of pathos on which our last conversation had closed, that she was preparing to leave that afternoon; and the trunks obstructing the threshold showed that her preparations were nearly complete. They were, I felt certain, the same trunks that, strapped behind a rattling vettura, had accompanied the bride and groom on that memorable voyage of discovery of which the booty had till recently adorned her walls; and there was a dim consolation in the thought that those early "finds" in coral and Swiss wood-carving, in lava and alabaster, still lay behind the worn locks, in the security of worthlessness.

Mrs. Fontage, on the landing, among her strapped and corded treasures, maintained the same air of stability that made it impossible, even under such conditions, to regard her flight as anything less dignified than a departure. It was the moral support of what she tacitly assumed that enabled me to set forth with proper deliberation the object of my visit; and she received my announcement with an absence of surprise that struck me as the very flower of tact. Under cover of these mutual assumptions the transaction was rapidly concluded; and it was not till the canvas passed into my hands that, as though the physical contact had unnerved her, Mrs. Fontage suddenly faltered. "It's the giving it up—" she stammered, disguising herself to the last; and I hastened away from the collapse of her splendid effrontery.

I need hardly point out that I had acted impulsively, and that reaction from the most honorable impulses is sometimes attended by moral perturbation. My motives had indeed been mixed enough to justify some uneasiness, but this was allayed by the instinctive feeling that it is more venial to defraud an institution than a man. Since Mrs. Fontage had to be kept from starving by means not wholly defensible, it was better that the obligation should be borne by a rich institution than an impecunious youth. I doubt, in fact, if my scruples would have survived a night's sleep, had they not been complicated by some uncertainty as to my own future. It was true that, subject to the purely formal assent of the committee, I had full power to buy for the Museum, and that the one member of the committee likely to dispute my decision was opportunely travelling in Europe; but the picture once in place I must face the risk of any expert criticism to which chance might expose it. I dismissed this contingency for future study, stored the Rembrandt in the cellar of the Museum, and thanked heaven that Crozier was abroad.

Six months later he strolled into my office. I had just concluded, under conditions of exceptional difficulty, and on terms unexpectedly benign, the purchase of the great Bartley Reynolds; and this circumstance, by relegating the matter of the Rembrandt to a lower stratum of consciousness, enabled me to welcome Crozier with unmixed pleasure. My security was enhanced by his appearance. His smile was charged with amiable reminiscences, and I inferred that his trip had put him in the humor to approve of everything, or at least to ignore what fell short of his approval. I had therefore no uneasiness in accepting his invitation to dine that evening. It is always pleasant to dine with Crozier and never more so than when he is just back from Europe. His conversation gives even the food a flavor of the Café Anglais.

The repast was delightful, and it was not till we had finished a Camembert which he must have brought over with him, that my host said, in a tone of after-dinner perfunctoriness: "I see you've picked up a picture or two since I left."

I assented. "The Bartley Reynolds seemed too good an opportunity to miss, especially as the French government was after it. I think we got it cheap—"

"Connu, connu," said Crozier pleasantly. "I know all about the Reynolds. It was the biggest kind of a haul and I congratulate you.

Best stroke of business we've done yet. But tell me about the other picture—the Rembrandt."

"I never said it was a Rembrandt." I could hardly have said why, but I felt distinctly annoyed with Crozier.

"Of course not. There's 'Rembrandt' on the frame, but I saw you'd modified it to 'Dutch School'; I apologize." He paused, but I offered no explanation. "What about it?" he went on. "Where did you pick it up?" As he leaned to the flame of the cigar-lighter his face seemed ruddy with enjoyment.

"I got it for a song," I said.

"A thousand, I think?"

"Have you seen it?" I asked abruptly.

"Went over the place this afternoon and found it in the cellar. Why hasn't it been hung, by the way?"

I paused a moment. "I'm waiting—"

"To—?"

"To have it varnished."

"Ah!" He leaned back and poured himself a second glass of Chartreuse. The smile he confided to its golden depths provoked me to challenge him with—

"What do you think of it?"

"The Rembrandt?" He lifted his eyes from the glass. "Just what you do."

"It isn't a Rembrandt."

"I apologize again. You call it, I believe, a picture of the same period?"

"I'm uncertain of the period."

"H'm." He glanced appreciatively along his cigar. "What are you certain of?"

"That it's a damned bad picture," I said savagely.

He nodded. "Just so. That's all we wanted to know."

"We?"

"We—I—the committee, in short. You see, my dear fellow, if you hadn't been certain it was a damned bad picture our position would have been a little awkward. As it is, my remaining duty—I ought to explain that in this matter I'm acting for the committee—is as simple as it's agreeable."

"I'll be hanged," I burst out, "if I understand one word you're saying!"

He fixed me with a kind of cruel joyousness. "You will—you will," he assured me; "at least you'll begin to, when you hear that I've seen Miss Copt."

"Miss Copt?"

"And that she has told me under what conditions the picture was bought."

"She doesn't know anything about the conditions! That is," I added, hastening to restrict the assertion, "she doesn't know my opinion of the picture." I thirsted for five minutes with Eleanor.

"Are you quite sure?" Crozier took me up. "Mr. Jefferson Rose does."

"Ah—I see."

"I thought you would," he reminded me. "As soon as I'd laid eyes on the Rembrandt—I beg your pardon!—I saw that it—well, required some explanation."

"You might have come to me."

"I meant to; but I happened to meet Miss Copt, whose encyclopædic information has often before been of service to me. I always go to Miss Copt when I want to look up anything; and I found she knew all about the Rembrandt."

"All?"

"Precisely. The knowledge was in fact causing her sleepless nights. Mr. Rose, who was suffering from the same form of insomnia, had taken her into his confidence, and she—ultimately—took me into hers."

"Of course!"

"I must ask you to do your cousin justice. She didn't speak till it became evident to her uncommonly quick perceptions that your buying the picture on its merits would have been infinitely worse for—for everybody—than your diverting a small portion of the Museum's funds to philanthropic uses. Then she told me the moving incident of Mr. Rose. Good fellow, Rose. And the old lady's case was desperate. Somebody had to buy that picture." I moved uneasily in my seat. "Wait a moment, will you? I haven't finished my cigar. There's a little head of Il Fiammingo's that you haven't seen, by the way; I picked it up the other day in Parma. We'll go in and have a look at it presently. But meanwhile what I want to say is that I've been charged—in the most informal way—to express to you the committee's appreciation of your admirable promptness and energy in capturing the Bartley Reynolds. We shouldn't have got it at all if you hadn't been uncommonly wide-awake, and to get it at such a price is a double triumph. We'd have thought nothing of a few more thousands—"

"I don't see," I impatiently interposed, "that, as far as I'm concerned, that alters the case."

"The case—?"

"Of Mrs. Fontage's Rembrandt. I bought the picture because, as you say, the situation was desperate, and I couldn't raise a thousand myself. What I did was of course indefensible; but the money shall be refunded to-morrow—"

Crozier raised a protesting hand. "Don't interrupt me when I'm talking ex cathedra. The money's been refunded already. The fact is, the Museum has sold the Rembrandt."

I stared at him wildly. "Sold it? To whom?"

"Why—to the committee.—Hold on a bit, please.—Won't you take another cigar? Then perhaps I can finish what I've got to say.—Why, my dear fellow, the committee's under an obligation to you—that's the way we look at it. I've investigated Mrs. Fontage's case, and—well, the picture had to be bought. She's eating meat now, I believe, for the first time in a year. And they'd have turned her out into the street that very day, your cousin tells me. Something had to be done at once, and you've simply given a number of well-to-do and self-indulgent gentlemen the opportunity of performing, at very small individual expense, a meritorious action in the nick of time. That's the first thing I've got to thank you for. And then—you'll remember, please, that I have the floor—that I'm still speaking for the committee—and secondly, as a slight recognition of your services in securing the Bartley Reynolds at a very much lower figure than we were prepared to pay, we beg you—the committee begs you—to accept the gift of Mrs. Fontage's Rembrandt. Now we'll go in and look at that little head. . . ."

PREFATORY NOTE

TO "THE HOUSE OF MIRTH"

The House of Mirth was published in 1905 and deals with a New York society almost exactly contemporaneous. Fusion had already occurred between the old Knickerbocker society and the flamboyant millionaires of oil, steel and railroads. "Bellomont," the remodeled manor house of the Trenors on the Hudson, might be Staatsburg, rebuilt by a Livingston who had married a Mills, and the Van Osburghs, who are possessed of Manhattan's biggest fortune and related at the same time to all the old families, could be the Astors, by then intermarried with the Armstrongs and Schermerhorns. The men in *The House of Mirth* still go downtown to work, but it is more to increase their fortunes than to earn their bread. Morals are freer, though forms are still strictly observed. There is time, too much time, for cards, for balls, for yachting. It is a surfeited, bored society that has lost its taste for anything but the most trifling novelty.

Its diversion here will be to destroy Lily Bart, who has too much taste to fight it on its own terms and too little character to eschew it. Without money her beauty and charm are frail weapons against those whose jealousy they simply arouse. The novel traces the slow but inevitable fall of Lily from her precarious perch as the spoiled, dependent darling of the rich all the way down to the cheap boarding house and the overdose of sleeping pills. What follows is the first half of the novel. At its conclusion Lily has alienated the last friend who could save her, Lawrence Selden, and although she does not yet know it, she is doomed.

FROM *The House of Mirth,* BOOK I

§ 1

SELDEN paused in surprise. In the afternoon rush of the Grand Central Station his eyes had been refreshed by the sight of Miss Lily Bart.

It was a Monday in early September, and he was returning to his work from a hurried dip into the country; but what was Miss Bart doing in town at that season? If she had appeared to be catching a train, he might have inferred that he had come on her in the act of transition between one and another of the country-houses which disputed her presence after the close of the Newport season; but her desultory air perplexed him. She stood apart from the crowd, letting it drift by her to the platform or the street, and wearing an air of irresolution which might, as he surmised, be the mask of a very definite purpose. It struck him at once that she was waiting for some one, but he hardly knew why the idea arrested him. There was nothing new about Lily Bart, yet he could never see her without a faint movement of interest: it was characteristic of her that she always roused speculation, that her simplest acts seemed the result of far-reaching intentions.

An impulse of curiosity made him turn out of his direct line to the door, and stroll past her. He knew that if she did not wish to be seen she would contrive to elude him; and it amused him to think of putting her skill to the test.

"Mr. Selden—what good luck!"

She came forward smiling, eager almost, in her resolve to intercept him. One or two persons, in brushing past them, lingered to look; for Miss Bart was a figure to arrest even the suburban traveller rushing to his last train.

Selden had never seen her more radiant. Her vivid head, relieved against the dull tints of the crowd, made her more conspicuous than in a ball-room, and under her dark hat and veil she regained the girlish smoothness, the purity of tint, that she was beginning to lose after eleven years of late hours and indefatigable dancing. Was it really eleven years, Selden found himself wondering, and had she indeed reached the nine-and-twentieth birthday with which her rivals credited her?

"What luck!" she repeated. "How nice of you to come to my rescue!"

He responded joyfully that to do so was his mission in life, and asked what form the rescue was to take.

"Oh, almost any—even to sitting on a bench and talking to me. One sits out a cotillion—why not sit out a train? It isn't a bit hotter here than in Mrs. Van Osburgh's conservatory—and some of the women are not a bit uglier."

She broke off, laughing, to explain that she had come up to town from Tuxedo, on her way to the Gus Trenors' at Bellomont, and had missed the three-fifteen train to Rhinebeck.

"And there isn't another till half-past five." She consulted the little jewelled watch among her laces. "Just two hours to wait. And I don't know what to do with myself. My maid came up this morning to do some shopping for me, and was to go on to Bellomont at one o'clock, and my aunt's house is closed, and I don't know a soul in town." She glanced plaintively about the station. "It *is* hotter than Mrs. Van Osburgh's, after all. If you can spare the time, do take me somewhere for a breath of air."

He declared himself entirely at her disposal: the adventure struck him as diverting. As a spectator, he had always enjoyed Lily Bart; and his course lay so far out of her orbit that it amused him to be drawn for a moment into the sudden intimacy which her proposal implied.

"Shall we go over to Sherry's for a cup of tea?"

She smiled assentingly, and then made a slight grimace.

"So many people come up to town on a Monday—one is sure to meet a lot of bores. I'm as old as the hills, of course, and it ought not to make any difference; but if *I'm* old enough, you're not," she objected gaily. "I'm dying for tea—but isn't there a quieter place?"

He answered her smile, which rested on him vividly. Her discretions interested him almost as much as her imprudences: he was so sure that both were part of the same carefully-elaborated plan. In judging Miss Bart, he had always made use of the "argument from design."

"The resources of New York are rather meagre," he said; "but I'll find a hansom first, and then we'll invent something."

He led her through the throng of returning holiday-makers, past shallow-faced girls in preposterous hats, and flat-chested women struggling with paper bundles and palm-leaf fans. Was it possible that she belonged to the same race? The dinginess, the crudity of this average section of womanhood made him feel how highly specialized she was.

A rapid shower had cooled the air, and clouds still hung refreshingly over the moist street.

"How delicious! Let us walk a little," she said as they emerged from the station.

They turned into Madison Avenue and began to stroll northward. As she moved beside him, with her long light step, Selden was conscious of taking a luxurious pleasure in her nearness: in the modelling of her little ear, the crisp upward wave of her hair—was it ever so slightly brightened by art?—and the thick planting of her straight black lashes. Everything about her was at once vigorous and exquisite, at once strong and fine. He had a confused sense that she must have cost a great deal to make, that a great many dull and ugly people must, in some mysterious way, have been sacrificed to produce her. He was aware that the qualities distinguishing her from the herd of her sex were chiefly external: as though a fine glaze of beauty and fastidiousness had been applied to vulgar clay. Yet the analogy left him unsatisfied, for a coarse texture will not take a high finish; and was it not possible that the material was fine, but that circumstance had fashioned it into a futile shape?

As he reached this point in his speculations the sun came out, and her lifted parasol cut off his enjoyment. A moment or two later she paused with a sigh.

"Oh, dear, I'm so hot and thirsty—and what a hideous place New York is!" She looked despairingly up and down the dreary thoroughfare. "Other cities put on their best clothes in summer, but New York seems to sit in its shirt-sleeves." Her eyes wandered down one of the side-streets. "Some one has had the humanity to plant a few trees over there. Let us go into the shade."

"I am glad my street meets with your approval," said Selden as they turned the corner.

"Your street? Do you live here?"

She glanced with interest along the new brick and limestone house-fronts, fantastically varied in obedience to the American craving for novelty, but fresh and inviting with their awnings and flower-boxes.

"Ah, yes—to be sure: *The Benedick*. What a nice-looking building! I don't think I've ever seen it before." She looked across at the flat-house with its marble porch and pseudo-Georgian façade. "Which are your windows? Those with the awnings down?"

"On the top floor—yes."

"And that nice little balcony is yours? How cool it looks up there!"

He paused a moment. "Come up and see," he suggested. "I can give you a cup of tea in no time—and you won't meet any bores."

Her colour deepened—she still had the art of blushing at the right time—but she took the suggestion as lightly as it was made.

"Why not? It 's too tempting—I'll take the risk," she declared.

"Oh, I'm not dangerous," he said in the same key. In truth, he had never liked her as well as at that moment. He knew she had accepted without afterthought: he could never be a factor in her calculations, and there was a surprise, a refreshment almost, in the spontaneity of her consent.

On the threshold he paused a moment, feeling for his latchkey.

"There's no one here; but I have a servant who is supposed to come in the mornings, and it's just possible he may have put out the tea-things and provided some cake."

He ushered her into a slip of a hall hung with old prints. She noticed the letters and notes heaped on the table among his gloves and sticks; then she found herself in a small library, dark but cheerful, with its walls of books, a pleasantly faded Turkey rug, a littered desk, and, as he had foretold, a tea-tray on a low table near the window. A breeze had sprung up, swaying inward the muslin curtains, and bringing a fresh scent of mignonette and petunias from the flower-box on the balcony.

Lily sank with a sigh into one of the shabby leather chairs.

"How delicious to have a place like this all to one's self! What a miserable thing it is to be a woman." She leaned back in a luxury of discontent.

Selden was rummaging in a cupboard for the cake.

"Even women," he said, "have been known to enjoy the privileges of a flat."

"Oh, governesses—or widows. But not girls—not poor, miserable, marriageable girls!"

"I even know a girl who lives in a flat."

She sat up in surprise. "You do?"

"I do," he assured her emerging from the cupboard with the sought-for cake.

"Oh, I know—you mean Gerty Farish." She smiled a little unkindly. "But I said *marriageable*—and besides, she has a horrid little place, and no maid, and such queer things to eat. Her cook does the washing and the food tastes of soap. I should hate that, you know."

"You shouldn't dine with her on wash-days," said Selden, cutting the cake.

They both laughed, and he knelt by the table to light the lamp under the kettle, while she measured out the tea into a little tea-pot of green glaze. As he watched her hand, polished as a bit of old ivory, with its slender pink nails, and the sapphire bracelet slipping over her wrist, he was struck with the irony of suggesting to her such a life as his cousin Gertrude Farish had chosen. She was so evidently the victim of the civilization which had produced her, that the links of her bracelet seemed like manacles chaining her to her fate.

She seemed to read his thought. "It was horrid of me to say that of Gerty," she said with charming compunction. "I forgot she was your cousin. But we're so different, you know: she likes being good, and I like being happy. And besides, she is free and I am not. If I were, I daresay I could manage to be happy even in her flat. It must be pure bliss to arrange the furniture just as one likes, and give all the horrors to the ash-man. If I could only do over my aunt's drawing-room I know I should be a better woman."

"Is it so very bad?" he asked sympathetically.

She smiled at him across the tea-pot which she was holding up to be filled.

"That shows how seldom you come there. Why don't you come oftener?"

"When I do come, it's not to look at Mrs. Peniston's furniture."

"Nonsense," she said. "You don't come at all—and yet we get on so well when we meet."

"Perhaps that's the reason," he answered promptly. "I'm afraid I haven't any cream, you know—shall you mind a slice of lemon instead?"

"I shall like it better." She waited while he cut the lemon and dropped a thin disk into her cup. "But that is not the reason," she insisted.

"The reason for what?"

"For your never coming." She leaned forward with a shade of perplexity in her charming eyes. "I wish I knew—I wish I could make you out. Of course I know there are men who don't like me—one can tell that at a glance. And there are others who are afraid of me: they think I want to marry them." She smiled up at him frankly. "But I don't think you dislike me—and you can't possibly think I want to marry you."

"No—I absolve you of that," he agreed.

"Well, then——?"

He had carried his cup to the fireplace, and stood leaning against the chimney-piece and looking down on her with an air of indolent amusement. The provocation in her eyes increased his amusement—he had not supposed she would waste her powder on such small game; but perhaps she was only keeping her hand in; or perhaps a girl of her type had no conversation but of the personal kind. At any rate, she was amazingly pretty, and he had asked her to tea and must live up to his obligations.

"Well, then," he said with a plunge, "perhaps *that's* the reason."

"What?"

"The fact that you don't want to marry me. Perhaps I don't regard it as such a strong inducement to go and see you." He felt a slight shiver down his spine as he ventured this, but her laugh reassured him.

"Dear Mr. Selden, that wasn't worthy of you. It's stupid of you to make love to me, and it isn't like you to be stupid." She leaned back, sipping her tea with an air so enchantingly judicial that, if they had been in her aunt's drawing-room, he might almost have tried to disprove her deduction.

"Don't you see," she continued, "that there are men enough to say pleasant things to me, and that what I want is a friend who won't be afraid to say disagreeable ones when I need them? Sometimes I have fancied you might be that friend—I don't know why, except that you are neither a prig nor a bounder, and that I shouldn't have to pretend with you or be on my guard against you." Her voice had dropped to a note of seriousness, and she sat gazing up at him with the troubled gravity of a child.

"You don't know how much I need such a friend," she said. "My aunt is full of copy-book axioms, but they were all meant to apply to conduct in the early fifties. I always feel that to live up to them would include wearing book-muslin with gigot sleeves. And the other women—my best friends—well, they use me or abuse me; but they don't care a straw what happens to me. I've been about too long—people are getting tired of me; they are beginning to say I ought to marry."

There was a moment's pause, during which Selden meditated one or two replies calculated to add a momentary zest to the situation; but he rejected them in favour of the simple question: "Well, why don't you?"

She coloured and laughed. "Ah, I see you *are* a friend after all, and that is one of the disagreeable things I was asking for."

"It wasn't meant to be disagreeable," he returned amicably. "Isn't marriage your vocation? Isn't it what you're all brought up for?"

She sighed. "I suppose so. What else is there?"

"Exactly. And so why not take the plunge and have it over?"

She shrugged her shoulders. "You speak as if I ought to marry the first man who came along."

"I didn't mean to imply that you are as hard put to it as that. But there must be some one with the requisite qualifications."

She shook her head wearily. "I threw away one or two good chances when I first came out—I suppose every girl does; and you know I am horribly poor—and very expensive. I must have a great deal of money."

Selden had turned to reach for a cigarette-box on the mantelpiece.

"What's become of Dillworth?" he asked.

"Oh, his mother was frightened—she was afraid I should have all the family jewels reset. And she wanted me to promise that I wouldn't do over the drawing-room."

"The very thing you are marrying for!"

"Exactly. So she packed him off to India."

"Hard luck—but you can do better than Dillworth."

He offered the box, and she took out three or four cigarettes, putting one between her lips and slipping the others into a little gold case attached to her long pearl chain.

"Have I time? Just a whiff, then." She leaned forward, holding the tip of her cigarette to his. As she did so, he noted, with a purely impersonal enjoyment, how evenly the black lashes were set in her smooth white lids, and how the purplish shade beneath them melted into the pure pallor of the cheek.

She began to saunter about the room, examining the bookshelves between the puffs of her cigarette-smoke. Some of the volumes had the ripe tints of good tooling and old morocco, and her eyes lingered on them caressingly, not with the appreciation of the expert, but with the pleasure in agreeable tones and textures that was one of her inmost susceptibilities. Suddenly her expression changed from desultory enjoyment to active conjecture, and she turned to Selden with a question.

"You collect, don't you—you know about first editions and things?"

"As much as a man may who has no money to spend. Now and then I pick up something in the rubbish heap; and I go and look on at the big sales."

She had again addressed herself to the shelves, but her eyes now swept them inattentively, and he saw that she was preoccupied with a new idea.

"And Americana—do you collect Americana?"

Selden stared and laughed.

"No, that's rather out of my line. I'm not really a collector, you see; I simply like to have good editions of the books I am fond of."

She made a slight grimace. "And Americana are horribly dull, I suppose?"

"I should fancy so—except to the historian. But your real collector values a thing for its rarity. I don't suppose the buyers of Americana sit up reading them all night—old Jefferson Gryce certainly didn't."

She was listening with keen attention. "And yet they fetch fabulous prices, don't they? It seems so odd to want to pay a lot for an ugly badly-printed book that one is never going to read! And I suppose most of the owners of Americana are not historians either?"

"No; very few of the historians can afford to buy them. They have to use those in the public libraries or in private collections. It seems to be the mere rarity that attracts the average collector."

He had seated himself on an arm of the chair near which she was standing, and she continued to question him, asking which were the rarest volumes, whether the Jefferson Gryce collection was really considered the finest in the world, and what was the largest price ever fetched by a single volume.

It was so pleasant to sit there looking up at her, as she lifted now one book and then another from the shelves, fluttering the pages between her fingers, while her drooping profile was outlined against the warm background of old bindings, that he talked on without pausing to wonder at her sudden interest in so unsuggestive a subject. But he could never be long with her without trying to find a reason for what she was doing, and as she replaced his first edition of La Bruyère and turned away from the bookcases, he began to ask himself what she had been driving at. Her next question was not of a nature to enlighten him. She paused before him with a smile which seemed at once designed to admit him to her familiarity, and to remind him of the restrictions it imposed.

"Don't you ever mind," she asked suddenly, "not being rich enough to buy all the books you want?"

He followed her glance about the room, with its worn furniture and shabby walls.

"Don't I just? Do you take me for a saint on a pillar?"

"And having to work—do you mind that?"

"Oh, the work itself is not so bad—I'm rather fond of the law."

"No; but the being tied down: the routine—don't you ever want to get away, to see new places and people?"

"Horribly—especially when I see all my friends rushing to the steamer."

She drew a sympathetic breath. "But do you mind enough—to marry to get out of it?"

Selden broke into a laugh. "God forbid!" he declared.

She rose with a sigh, tossing her cigarette into the grate.

"Ah, there's the difference—a girl must, a man may if he chooses." She surveyed him critically. "Your coat's a little shabby—but who cares? It doesn't keep people from asking you to dine. If I were shabby no one would have me: a woman is asked out as much for her clothes as for herself. The clothes are the background, the frame, if you like: they don't make success, but they are a part of it. Who wants a dingy woman? We are expected to be pretty and well-dressed till we drop—and if we can't keep it up alone, we have to go into partnership."

Selden glanced at her with amusement: it was impossible, even with her lovely eyes imploring him, to take a sentimental view of her case.

"Ah, well, there must be plenty of capital on the lookout for such an investment. Perhaps you'll meet your fate to-night at the Trenors'."

She returned his look interrogatively.

"I thought you might be going there—oh, not in that capacity! But there are to be a lot of your set—Gwen Van Osburgh, the Wetheralls, Lady Cressida Raith—and the George Dorsets."

She paused a moment before the last name, and shot a query through her lashes; but he remained imperturbable.

"Mrs. Trenor asked me; but I can't get away till the end of the week; and those big parties bore me."

"Ah, so they do me," she exclaimed.

"Then why go?"

"It's part of the business—you forget! And besides, if I didn't, I should be playing bézique with my aunt at Richfield Springs."

"That's almost as bad as marrying Dillworth," he agreed, and they both laughed for pure pleasure in their sudden intimacy.

She glanced at the clock.

"Dear me! I must be off. It's after five."

She paused before the mantelpiece, studying herself in the mirror while she adjusted her veil. The attitude revealed the long slope of her slender sides, which gave a kind of wild-wood grace to her outline—as though she were a captured dryad subdued to the conventions of the drawing-room; and Selden reflected that it was the same streak of sylvan freedom in her nature that lent such savour to her artificiality.

He followed her across the room to the entrance-hall; but on the threshold she held out her hand with a gesture of leave-taking.

"It's been delightful; and now you will have to return my visit."

"But don't you want me to see you to the station?"

"No, good-bye here, please."

She let her hand lie in his a moment, smiling up at him adorably.

"Good-bye, then—and good luck at Bellomont!" he said, opening the door for her.

On the landing she paused to look about her. There were a thousand chances to one against her meeting anybody, but one could never tell, and she always paid for her rare indiscretions by a violent reaction of prudence. There was no one in sight, however, but a char-woman who was scrubbing the stairs. Her own stout person and its surrounding implements took up so much room that Lily, to pass her, had to gather up her skirts and brush against the wall. As she did so, the woman paused in her work and looked up curiously, resting her clenched red fists on the wet cloth she had just drawn from her pail. She had a broad sallow face, slightly pitted with small-pox, and thin straw-coloured hair through which her scalp shone unpleasantly.

"I beg your pardon," said Lily, intending by her politeness to convey a criticism of the other's manner.

The woman, without answering, pushed her pail aside, and continued to stare as Miss Bart swept by with a murmur of silken linings. Lily felt herself flushing under the look. What did the creature suppose? Could one never do the simplest, the most harmless thing, without subjecting one's self to some odious conjecture? Half way down the next flight, she smiled to think that a char-woman's stare should so perturb her. The poor thing was probably dazzled by such an unwonted apparition. But *were* such apparitions unwonted on Selden's stairs? Miss Bart was not familiar with the moral code of bachelors' flat-houses, and her colour rose again as it occurred to her that the woman's persistent gaze implied a groping among past associations. But she put aside the thought with a smile at her own fears, and hastened downward, wondering if she should find a cab short of Fifth Avenue.

Under the Georgian porch she paused again, scanning the street for a hansom. None was in sight, but as she reached the sidewalk she ran against a small glossy-looking man with a gardenia in his coat, who raised his hat with a surprised exclamation.

"Miss Bart? Well—of all people! This *is* luck," he declared; and she caught a twinkle of amused curiosity between his screwed-up lids.

"Oh, Mr. Rosedale—how are you?" she said, perceiving that the irrepressible annoyance on her face was reflected in the sudden intimacy of his smile.

Mr. Rosedale stood scanning her with interest and approval. He was a plump rosy man of the blond Jewish type, with smart London clothes fitting him like upholstery, and small sidelong eyes which gave him the air of appraising people as if they were bric-a-brac. He glanced up interrogatively at the porch of the Benedick.

"Been up to town for a little shopping, I suppose?" he said, in a tone which had the familiarity of a touch.

Miss Bart shrank from it slightly, and then flung herself into precipitate explanations.

"Yes—I came up to see my dress-maker. I am just on my way to catch the train to the Trenors'."

"Ah—your dress-maker; just so," he said blandly. "I didn't know there were any dress-makers in the Benedick."

"The Benedick?" She looked gently puzzled. "Is that the name of this building?"

"Yes, that's the name: I believe it's an old word for bachelor, isn't it? I happen to own the building—that's the way I know." His smile deepened as he added with increasing assurance: "But you must let me take you to the station. The Trenors are at Bellomont, of course? You've barely time to catch the five-forty. The dress-maker kept you waiting, I suppose."

Lily stiffened under the pleasantry.

"Oh, thanks," she stammered; and at that moment her eye caught a hansom drifting down Madison Avenue, and she hailed it with a desperate gesture.

"You're very kind; but I couldn't think of troubling you," she said, extending her hand to Mr. Rosedale; and heedless of his protestations, she sprang into the rescuing vehicle, and called out a breathless order to the driver.

§ 2

In the hansom she leaned back with a sigh.

Why must a girl pay so dearly for her least escape from routine? Why could one never do a natural thing without having to screen it behind a structure of artifice? She had yielded to a passing impulse in going to Lawrence Selden's rooms, and it was so seldom that she could allow herself the luxury of an impulse! This one, at any rate, was going to cost her rather more than she could afford. She was vexed to see that, in spite of so many years of vigilance, she had blundered twice within five minutes. That stupid story about her dress-maker was bad enough—it would have been so simple to tell Rosedale that she had been taking tea with Selden! The mere statement of the fact would have rendered it innocuous. But, after having let herself be surprised in a falsehood, it was doubly stupid to snub the witness of her discomfiture. If she had had the presence of mind to let Rosedale drive her to the station, the concession might have purchased his silence. He had his race's accuracy in the appraisal of values, and to be seen walking down the platform at the crowded afternoon hour in the company of Miss Lily Bart would have been money in his pocket, as he might himself have phrased it. He knew, of course, that there would be a large house-party at Bellomont, and the possibility of being taken for one of Mrs. Trenor's guests was doubtless included in his calculations. Mr. Rosedale was still at a stage in his social ascent when it was of importance to produce such impressions.

The provoking part was that Lily knew all this—knew how easy it would have been to silence him on the spot, and how difficult it might be to do so afterward. Mr. Simon Rosedale was a man who made it his business to know everything about every one, whose idea of showing himself to be at home in society was to display an inconvenient familiarity with the habits of those with whom he wished to be thought intimate. Lily was sure that within twenty-four hours the story of her visiting her dress-maker at the Benedick would be in active circulation among Mr. Rosedale's acquaintances. The worst of it was that she had always snubbed and ignored him. On his first appearance—when her improvident cousin, Jack Stepney, had obtained for him (in return for favours too easily guessed) a card to one of the vast impersonal Van Osburgh "crushes"—Rosedale, with that mixture of artistic sensibility and business astuteness which characterizes his race, had instantly gravitated toward Miss Bart. She understood his motives, for her own course was guided by as nice calculations. Training and experience had taught her to be hospitable to newcomers, since the most unpromising might be useful later on, and there were plenty of available *oubliettes* to swallow them if they were not. But some intuitive repugnance, getting the better of years of social discipline, had made her push Mr. Rosedale into his *oubliette* without a trial. He had left behind only the ripple of amusement which his speedy despatch had caused among her friends; and though later (to shift the metaphor) he reappeared lower down the stream, it was only in fleeting glimpses, with long submergences between.

Hitherto Lily had been undisturbed by scruples. In her little set Mr. Rosedale had been pronounced "impossible," and Jack Stepney roundly snubbed for his attempt to pay his debts in dinner invitations. Even Mrs. Trenor, whose taste for variety had led her into some hazardous experiments, resisted Jack's attempts to disguise Mr. Rosedale as a novelty, and declared that he was the same little Jew who had been served up and rejected at the social board a dozen times within her memory; and while Judy Trenor was obdurate there was small chance of Mr. Rosedale's penetrating beyond the outer limbo of the Van Osburgh crushes. Jack gave up the contest with a laughing "You'll see," and, sticking manfully to his guns, showed himself with Rosedale at the fashionable restaurants, in company with the personally vivid if socially obscure ladies who are available for such purposes. But the attempt had hitherto been vain, and as Rosedale undoubtedly paid for the dinners, the laugh remained with his debtor.

Mr. Rosedale, it will be seen, was thus far not a factor to be feared—unless one put one's self in his power. And this was precisely what Miss Bart had done. Her clumsy fib had let him see that she had something to conceal; and she was sure he had a score to settle with her. Something in his smile told her he had not forgotten. She turned from the thought with a little shiver, but it hung on her all the way to the station, and dogged her down the platform with the persistency of Mr. Rosedale himself.

She had just time to take her seat before the train started; but having arranged herself in her corner with the instinctive feeling for effect which never forsook her, she glanced about in the hope of seeing some other member of the Trenors' party. She wanted to get away from herself, and conversation was the only means of escape that she knew.

Her search was rewarded by the discovery of a very blond young man with a soft reddish beard, who, at the other end of the carriage, appeared to be dissembling himself behind an unfolded newspaper. Lily's eye brightened, and a faint smile relaxed the drawn lines of her mouth. She had known that Mr. Percy Gryce was to be at Bellomont, but she had not counted on the luck of having him to herself in the train; and the fact banished all perturbing thoughts of Mr. Rosedale. Perhaps, after all, the day was to end more favourably than it had begun.

She began to cut the pages of a novel, tranquilly studying her prey through downcast lashes while she organized a method of attack. Something in his attitude of conscious absorption told her that he was aware of her presence: no one had ever been quite so engrossed in an evening paper! She guessed that he was too shy to come up to her, and that she would have to devise some means of approach which should not appear to be an advance on her part. It amused her to think that any one as rich as Mr. Percy Gryce should be shy; but she was gifted with treasures of indulgence for such idiosyncrasies, and besides, his timidity might serve her purpose better than too much assurance. She had the art of giving self-confidence to the embarrassed, but she was not equally sure of being able to embarrass the self-confident.

She waited till the train had emerged from the tunnel and was racing between the ragged edges of the northern suburbs. Then, as it lowered its speed near Yonkers, she rose from her seat and drifted slowly down the carriage. As she passed Mr. Gryce, the train gave a lurch, and he was aware of a slender hand gripping the back of his chair. He rose with a start, his ingenuous face looking as though it had been dipped in crimson: even the reddish tint in his beard seemed to deepen.

The train swayed again, almost flinging Miss Bart into his arms. She steadied herself with a laugh and drew back; but he was enveloped in the scent of her dress, and his shoulder had felt her fugitive touch.

"Oh, Mr. Gryce, is it you? I'm so sorry—I was trying to find the porter and get some tea."

She held out her hand as the train resumed its level rush, and they stood exchanging a few words in the aisle. Yes—he was going to Bellomont. He had heard she was to be of the party—he blushed again as he admitted it. And was he to be there for a whole week? How delightful!

But at this point one or two belated passengers from the last station forced their way into the carriage, and Lily had to retreat to her seat.

"The chair next to mine is empty—do take it," she said over her shoulder; and Mr. Gryce, with considerable embarrassment, succeeded in effecting an exchange which enabled him to transport himself and his bags to her side.

"Ah—and here is the porter, and perhaps we can have some tea."

She signalled to that official, and in a moment, with the ease that seemed to attend the fulfilment of all her wishes, a little table had been set up between the seats, and she had helped Mr. Gryce to bestow his encumbering properties beneath it.

When the tea came he watched her in silent fascination while her hands flitted above the tray, looking miraculously fine and slender in contrast to the coarse china and lumpy bread. It seemed wonderful to him that any one should perform with such careless ease the difficult task of making tea in public in a lurching train. He would never have dared to order it for himself, lest he should attract the notice of his fellow-passengers; but, secure in the shelter of her conspicuousness, he sipped the inky draught with a delicious sense of exhilaration.

Lily, with the flavour of Selden's caravan tea on her lips, had no great fancy to drown it in the railway brew which seemed such nectar to her companion; but, rightly judging that one of the charms of tea is the fact of drinking it together, she proceeded to give the last touch to Mr. Gryce's enjoyment by smiling at him across her lifted cup.

"Is it quite right—I haven't made it too strong?" she asked solicitously; and he replied with conviction that he had never tasted better tea.

"I daresay it is true," she reflected; and her imagination was fired by the thought that Mr. Gryce, who might have sounded the depths of the most complex self-indulgence, was perhaps actually taking his first journey alone with a pretty woman.

It struck her as providential that she should be the instrument of his initiation. Some girls would not have known how to manage him. They would have over-emphasized the novelty of the adventure, trying to make him feel in it the zest of an escapade. But Lily's methods were more delicate. She remembered that her cousin Jack Stepney had once defined Mr. Gryce as the young man who had promised his mother never to go out in the rain without his overshoes; and acting on this hint, she resolved to impart a gently domestic air to the scene, in the hope that her companion, instead of feeling that he was doing something reckless or unusual, would merely be led to dwell on the advantage of always having a companion to make one's tea in the train.

But in spite of her efforts, conversation flagged after the tray had been removed, and she was driven to take a fresh measurement of Mr. Gryce's limitations. It was not, after all, opportunity but imagination that he lacked: he had a mental palate which would never learn to distinguish between railway tea and nectar. There was, however, one topic she could rely on: one spring that she had only to touch to set his simple machinery in motion. She had refrained from touching it because it was a last resource, and she had relied on other arts to stimulate other sensations; but as a settled look of dulness began to creep over his candid features, she saw that extreme measures were necessary.

"And how," she said, leaning forward, "are you getting on with your Americana?"

His eye became a degree less opaque: it was as though an incipient film had been removed from it, and she felt the pride of a skilful operator.

"I've got a few new things," he said, suffused with pleasure, but lowering his voice as though he feared his fellow-passengers might be in league to despoil him.

She returned a sympathetic enquiry, and gradually he was drawn on to talk of his latest purchases. It was the one subject which enabled him to forget himself, or allowed him, rather, to remember himself without constraint, because he was at home in it, and could assert a superiority that there were few to dispute. Hardly any of his acquaintances cared for Americana, or knew anything about them; and the consciousness of this ignorance threw Mr. Gryce's knowledge into agreeable relief. The only difficulty was to introduce the topic and to keep it to the front; most people showed no desire to have their ignorance dispelled, and Mr. Gryce was like a merchant whose warehouses are crammed with an unmarketable commodity.

But Miss Bart, it appeared, really did want to know about Americana; and moreover, she was already sufficiently informed to make the task of farther instruction as easy as it was agreeable. She questioned him intelligently, she heard him submissively; and, prepared for the look of lassitude which usually crept over his listeners' faces, he grew eloquent under her receptive gaze. The "points" she had had the presence of mind to glean from Selden, in anticipation of this very contingency, were serving her to such good purpose that she began to think her visit to him had been the luckiest incident of the day. She had once more shown her talent for profiting by the unexpected, and dangerous theories as to the advisability of yielding to impulse were germinating under the surface of smiling attention which she continued to present to her companion.

Mr. Gryce's sensations, if less definite, were equally agreeable. He felt his confused titillation with which the lower organisms welcome the gratification of their needs, and all his senses floundered in a vague well-being, through which Miss Bart's personality was dimly but pleasantly perceptible.

Mr. Gryce's interest in Americana had not originated with himself: it was impossible to think of him as evolving any taste of his own. An uncle had left him a collection already noted among bibliophiles; the existence of the collection was the only fact that had ever shed glory on the name of Gryce, and the nephew took as much pride in his inheritance as though it had been his own work. Indeed, he gradually came to regard it as such, and to feel a sense of personal complacency when he chanced on any reference to the Gryce Americana. Anxious as he was to avoid personal notice, he took, in the printed mention of his name, a pleasure so exquisite and excessive that it seemed a compensation for his shrinking from publicity.

To enjoy the sensation as often as possible, he subscribed to all the reviews dealing with book-collecting in general, and American history in particular, and as allusions to his library abounded in the pages of these journals, which formed his only reading, he came to regard himself as figuring prominently in the public eye, and to enjoy the thought of the interest which would be excited if the persons he met in the street, or sat among in travelling, were suddenly to be told that he was the possessor of the Gryce Americana.

Most timidities have such secret compensations, and Miss Bart was discerning enough to know that the inner vanity is generally in proportion to the outer self-deprecation. With a more confident person she would not have dared to dwell so long on one topic, or to show such exaggerated interest in it; but she had rightly guessed that Mr. Gryce's egoism was a thirsty soil, requiring constant nurture from without. Miss Bart had the gift of following an undercurrent of thought while she appeared to be sailing on the surface of conversation; and in this case her mental excursion took the form of a rapid survey of Mr. Percy Gryce's future as combined with her own. The Gryces were from Albany, and but lately introduced to the metropolis, where the mother and son had come, after old Jefferson Gryce's death, to take possession of his house in Madison Avenue—an appalling house, all brown stone without and black walnut within, with the Gryce library in a fire-proof annex that looked like a mausoleum. Lily, however, knew all about them: young Mr. Gryce's arrival had fluttered the maternal breasts of New York, and when a girl has no mother to palpitate for her she must needs be on the alert for herself. Lily, therefore, had not only contrived to put herself in the young man's way, but had made the acquaintance of Mrs. Gryce, a monumental woman with the voice of a pulpit orator and a mind preoccupied with the iniquities of her servants, who came sometimes to sit with Mrs. Peniston and learn from that lady how she managed to prevent the kitchen-maid's smuggling groceries out of the house. Mrs. Gryce had a kind of impersonal benevolence: cases of individual need she regarded with suspicion, but she subscribed to Institutions when their annual reports showed an impressive surplus. Her domestic duties were manifold, for they extended from furtive inspections of the servants' bedrooms to unannounced descents to the cellar; but she had never allowed herself many pleasures. Once, however, she had had a special edition of the Sarum Rule printed in rubric and presented to every clergyman in the diocese; and the gilt album in which their letters of thanks were pasted formed the chief ornament of her drawing-room table.

Percy had been brought up in the principles which so excellent a woman was sure to inculcate. Every form of prudence and suspicion had been grafted on a nature originally reluctant and cautious, with the result that it would have seemed hardly needful for Mrs. Gryce to extract his promise about the overshoes, so little likely was he to hazard himself abroad in the rain. After attaining his majority, and coming into the fortune which the late Mr. Gryce had made out of a patent device for excluding fresh air from hotels, the young man continued to live with his mother in Albany; but on Jefferson Gryce's death, when another large property passed into her son's hands, Mrs. Gryce thought that what she called his "interests" demanded his presence in New York. She accordingly installed herself in the Madison Avenue house, and Percy, whose sense of duty was not inferior to his mother's, spent all his week days in the handsome Broad Street office where a batch of pale men on small salaries had grown grey in the management of the Gryce estate, and where he was initiated with becoming reverence into every detail of the art of accumulation.

As far as Lily could learn, this had hitherto been Mr. Gryce's only occupation, and she might have been pardoned for thinking it not too hard a task to interest a young man who had been kept on such low diet. At any rate, she felt herself so completely in command of the situation that she yielded to a sense of security in which all fear of Mr. Rosedale, and of the difficulties on which that fear was contingent, vanished beyond the edge of thought.

The stopping of the train at Garrisons would not have distracted her from these thoughts, had she not caught a sudden look of distress in her companion's eye. His seat faced toward the door, and she guessed that he had been perturbed by the approach of an acquaintance; a fact confirmed by the turning of heads and general sense of commotion which her own entrance into a railway-carriage was apt to produce.

She knew the symptoms at once, and was not surprised to be hailed by the high notes of a pretty woman, who entered the train accompanied by a maid, a bull-terrier, and a footman staggering under a load of bags and dressing-cases.

"Oh, Lily—are you going to Bellomont? Then you can't let me have your seat, I suppose? But I *must* have a seat in this carriage—porter, you must find me a place at once. Can't some one be put somewhere else? I want to be with my friends. Oh, how do you do, Mr. Gryce? Do please make him understand that I must have a seat next to you and Lily."

Mrs. George Dorset, regardless of the mild efforts of a traveller with a carpet-bag, who was doing his best to make room for her by getting out of the train, stood in the middle of the aisle, diffusing about her that general sense of exasperation which a pretty woman on her travels not infrequently creates.

She was smaller and thinner than Lily Bart, with a restless pliability of pose, as if she could have been crumpled up and run through a ring, like the sinuous draperies she affected. Her small pale face seemed the mere setting of a pair of dark exaggerated eyes, of which the visionary gaze contrasted curiously with her self-assertive tone and gestures; so that, as one of her friends observed, she was like a disembodied spirit who took up a great deal of room.

Having finally discovered that the seat adjoining Miss Bart's was at her disposal, she possessed herself of it with a farther displacement of her surroundings, explaining meanwhile that she had come across from Mount Kisco in her motor-car that morning, and had been kicking her heels for an hour at Garrisons, without even the alleviation of a cigarette, her brute of a husband having neglected to replenish her case before they parted that morning.

"And at this hour of the day I don't suppose you've a single one left, have you, Lily?" she plaintively concluded.

Miss Bart caught the startled glance of Mr. Percy Gryce, whose own lips were never defiled by tobacco.

"What an absurd question, Bertha!" she exclaimed, blushing at the thought of the store she had laid in at Lawrence Selden's.

"Why, don't you smoke? Since when have you given it up? What —you never— And you don't either, Mr. Gryce? Ah, of course—how stupid of me—I understand."

And Mrs. Dorset leaned back against her travelling cushions with a smile which made Lily wish there had been no vacant seat beside her own.

§ 3

Bridge at Bellomont usually lasted till the small hours; and when Lily went to bed that night she had played too long for her own good.

Feeling no desire for the self-communion which awaited her in her room, she lingered on the broad stairway, looking down into the hall below, where the last card-players were grouped about the tray of tall glasses and silver-collared decanters which the butler had just placed on a low table near the fire.

The hall was arcaded, with a gallery supported on columns of pale yellow marble. Tall clumps of flowering plants were grouped against a background of dark foliage in the angles of the walls. On the crimson carpet a deer-hound and two or three spaniels dozed luxuriously before the fire, and the light from the great central lantern overhead shed a brightness on the women's hair and struck sparks from their jewels as they moved.

There were moments when such scenes delighted Lily, when they gratified her sense of beauty and her craving for the external finish of life; there were others when they gave a sharper edge to the meagreness of her own opportunities. This was one of the moments when the sense of contrast was uppermost, and she turned away impatiently as Mrs. George Dorset, glittering in serpentine spangles, drew Percy Gryce in her wake to a confidential nook beneath the gallery.

It was not that Miss Bart was afraid of losing her newly-acquired hold over Mr. Gryce. Mrs. Dorset might startle or dazzle him, but she had neither the skill nor the patience to effect his capture. She was too self-engrossed to penetrate the recesses of his shyness, and besides, why should she care to give herself the trouble? At most it might amuse her to make sport of his simplicity for an evening—after that he would be merely a burden to her, and knowing this, she was far too experienced to encourage him. But the mere thought of that other woman, who could take a man up and toss him aside as she willed, without having to regard him as a possible factor in her plans, filled Lily Bart with envy. She had been bored all the afternoon by Percy Gryce—the mere thought seemed to waken an echo of his droning voice—but she could not ignore him on the morrow, she must follow up her success, must submit to more boredom, must be ready with fresh compliances and adaptabilities, and all on the bare chance that he might ultimately decide to do her the honour of boring her for life.

It was a hateful fate—but how escape from it? What choice had she? To be herself, or a Gerty Farish. As she entered her bedroom, with its softly-shaded lights, her lace dressing-gown lying across the silken bedspread, her little embroidered slippers before the fire, a vase of carnations filling the air with perfume, and the last novels and magazines lying uncut on a table beside the reading-lamp, she had a vision of Miss Farish's cramped flat, with its cheap conveniences and hideous wall-papers. No; she was not made for mean and shabby surroundings, for the squalid compromises of poverty. Her whole being dilated in an atmosphere of luxury; it was the background she required, the only climate she could breathe in. But the luxury of others was not what she wanted. A few years ago it had sufficed her: she had taken her daily meed of pleasures without caring who provided it. Now she was beginning to chafe at the obligations it imposed, to feel herself a mere pensioner on the splendour which had once seemed to belong to her. There were even moments when she was conscious of having to pay her way.

For a long time she had refused to play bridge. She knew she could not afford it, and she was afraid of acquiring so expensive a taste. She had seen the danger exemplified in more than one of her associates—in young Ned Silverton, for instance, the charming fair boy now seated in abject rapture at the elbow of Mrs. Fisher, a striking divorcée with eyes and gowns as emphatic as the head-lines of her "case." Lily could remember when young Silverton had stumbled into their circle, with the air of a strayed Arcadian who has published charming sonnets in his college journal. Since then he had developed a taste for Mrs. Fisher and bridge, and the latter at least had involved him in expenses from which he had been more than once rescued by harassed maiden sisters, who treasured the sonnets, and went without sugar in their tea to keep their darling afloat. Ned's case was familiar to Lily: she had seen his charming eyes—which had a good deal more poetry in them than the sonnets—change from surprise to amusement, and from amusement to anxiety, as he passed under the spell of the terrible god of chance; and she was afraid of discovering the same symptoms in her own case.

For in the last year she had found that her hostesses expected her to take a place at the card-table. It was one of the taxes she had to pay for their prolonged hospitality, and for the dresses and trinkets which occasionally replenished her insufficient wardrobe. And since she had played regularly the passion had grown on her. Once or twice of late she had won a large sum, and instead of keeping it against future losses, had spent it in dress or jewelry; and the desire to atone for this imprudence, combined with the increasing exhilaration of the game, drove her to risk higher stakes at each fresh venture. She tried to excuse herself on the plea that, in the Trenor set, if one played at all one must either play high or be set down as priggish or stingy; but she knew that the gambling passion was upon her, and that in her present surroundings there was small hope of resisting it.

Tonight the luck had been persistently bad, and the little gold purse which hung among her trinkets was almost empty when she returned to her room. She unlocked the wardrobe, and taking out her jewel-case, looked under the tray for the roll of bills from which she had replenished the purse before going down to dinner. Only twenty dollars were left: the discovery was so startling that for a moment she fancied she must have been robbed. Then she took paper and pencil, and seating herself at the writing-table, tried to reckon up what she had spent during the day. Her head was throbbing with fatigue, and she had to go over the figures again and again; but at last it became clear to her that she had lost three hundred dollars at cards. She took out her cheque-book to see if her balance was larger than she remembered, but found she had erred in the other direction. Then she returned to her calculations; but figure as she would, she could not conjure back the vanished three hundred dollars. It was the sum she had set aside to pacify her dress-maker—unless she should decide to use it as a sop to the jeweller. At any rate, she had so many uses for it that its very insufficiency had caused her to play high in the hope of doubling it. But of course she had lost—she who needed every penny, while Bertha Dorset, whose husband showered money on her, must have pocketed at least five hundred, and Judy Trenor, who could have afforded to lose a thousand a night, had left the table clutching such a heap of bills that she had been unable to shake hands with her guests when they bade her good night.

A world in which such things could be seemed a miserable place to Lily Bart; but then she had never been able to understand the laws of a universe which was so ready to leave her out of its calculations.

She began to undress without ringing for her maid, whom she had sent to bed. She had been long enough in bondage to other people's pleasure to be considerate of those who depended on hers, and in her bitter moods it sometimes struck her that she and her maid were in the same position, except that the latter received her wages more regularly.

As she sat before the mirror brushing her hair, her face looked hollow and pale, and she was frightened by two little lines near her mouth, faint flaws in the smooth curve of the cheek.

"Oh, I must stop worrying!" she exclaimed. "Unless it's the electric light—" she reflected, springing up from her seat and lighting the candles on the dressing-table.

She turned out the wall-lights, and peered at herself between the candle-flames. The white oval of her face swam out waveringly from a background of shadows, the uncertain light blurring it like a haze; but the two lines about the mouth remained.

Lily rose and undressed in haste.

"It is only because I am tired and have such odious things to think about," she kept repeating; and it seemed an added injustice that petty cares should leave a trace on the beauty which was her only defence against them.

But the odious things were there, and remained with her. She returned wearily to the thought of Percy Gryce, as a wayfarer picks up a heavy load and toils on after a brief rest. She was almost sure she had "landed" him: a few days' work and she would win her reward. But the reward itself seemed unpalatable just then: she could get no zest from the thought of victory. It would be a rest from worry, no more—and how little that would have seemed to her a few years earlier! Her ambitions had shrunk gradually in the desiccating air of failure. But why had she failed? Was it her own fault or that of destiny?

She remembered how her mother, after they had lost their money, used to say to her with a kind of fierce vindictiveness: "But you'll get it all back—you'll get it all back, with your face." . . . The remembrance roused a whole train of association, and she lay in the darkness reconstructing the past out of which her present had grown.

A house in which no one ever dined at home unless there was "company"; a door-bell perpetually ringing; a hall-table showered with square envelopes which were opened in haste, and oblong envelopes which were allowed to gather dust in the depths of a bronze jar; a series of French and English maids giving warning amid a chaos of hurriedly-ransacked wardrobes and dress-closets; an equally changing dynasty of nurses and footmen; quarrels in the pantry, the kitchen and the drawing-room; precipitate trips to Europe, and returns with gorged trunks and days of interminable unpacking; semi-annual discussions as to where the summer should be spent, grey interludes of economy and brilliant reactions of expense—such was the setting of Lily Bart's first memories.

Ruling the turbulent element called home was the vigorous and determined figure of a mother still young enough to dance her ball-dresses to rags, while the hazy outline of a neutral-tinted father filled an intermediate space between the butler and the man who came to wind the clocks. Even to the eyes of infancy, Mrs. Hudson Bart had appeared young; but Lily could not recall the time when her father had not been bald and slightly stooping, with streaks of grey in his hair, and a tired walk. It was a shock to her to learn afterward that he was but two years older than her mother.

Lily seldom saw her father by daylight. All day he was "down town"; and in winter it was long after nightfall when she heard his fagged step on the stairs and his hand on the school-room door. He would kiss her in silence, and ask one or two questions of the nurse or the governess; then Mrs. Bart's maid would come to remind him that he was dining out, and he would hurry away with a nod to Lily. In summer, when he joined them for a Sunday at Newport or Southampton, he was even more effaced and silent than in winter. It seemed to tire him to rest, and he would sit for hours staring at the sea-line from a quiet corner of the verandah, while the clatter of his wife's existence went on unheeded a few feet off. Generally, however, Mrs. Bart and Lily went to Europe for the summer, and before the steamer was half way over Mr. Bart had dipped below the horizon. Sometimes his daughter heard him denounced for having neglected to forward Mrs. Bart's remittances; but for the most part he was never mentioned or thought of till his patient stooping figure presented itself on the New York dock as a buffer between the magnitude of his wife's luggage and the restrictions of the American custom-house.

In this desultory yet agitated fashion life went on through Lily's teens: a zig-zag broken course down which the family craft glided on a rapid current of amusement, tugged at by the underflow of a perpetual need—the need of more money. Lily could not recall the time when there had been money enough, and in some vague way her father seemed always to blame for the deficiency. It could certainly not be the fault of Mrs. Bart, who was spoken of by her friends as a "wonderful manager." Mrs. Bart was famous for the unlimited effect she produced on limited means; and to the lady and her acquaintances there was something heroic in living as though one were much richer than one's bankbook denoted.

Lily was naturally proud of her mother's aptitude in this line: she had been brought up in the faith that, whatever it cost, one must have a good cook, and be what Mrs. Bart called "decently dressed." Mrs. Bart's worst reproach to her husband was to ask him if he expected her to "live like a pig"; and his replying in the negative was always regarded as a justification for cabling to Paris for an extra dress or two, and telephoning to the jeweller that he might, after all, send home the turquoise bracelet which Mrs. Bart had looked at that morning.

Lily knew people who "lived like pigs," and their appearance and surroundings justified her mother's repugnance to that form of existence. They were mostly cousins, who inhabited dingy houses with engravings from Cole's Voyage of Life on the drawing-room walls, and slatternly parlour-maids who said "I'll go and see" to visitors calling at an hour when all right-minded persons were conventionally if not actually out. The disgusting part of it was that many of these cousins were rich, so that Lily imbibed the idea that if people lived like pigs it was from choice, and through the lack of any proper standard of conduct. This gave her a sense of reflected superiority, and she did not need Mrs. Bart's comments on the family frumps and misers to foster her naturally lively taste for splendour.

Lily was nineteen when circumstances caused her to revise her view of the universe.

The previous year she had made a dazzling début fringed by a heavy thunder-cloud of bills. The light of the début still lingered on the horizon, but the cloud had thickened; and suddenly it broke. The suddenness added to the horror; and there were still times when Lily relived with painful vividness every detail of the day on which the blow fell. She and her mother had been seated at the luncheon-table, over the *chaudfroid* and cold salmon of the previous night's dinner: it was one of Mrs. Bart's few economies to consume in private the expensive remnants of her hospitality. Lily was feeling the pleasant languor which is youth's penalty for dancing till dawn; but her mother, in spite of a few lines about the mouth, and under the yellow waves on her temples, was as alert, determined and high in colour as if she had risen from an untroubled sleep.

In the centre of the table, between the melting *marrons glacés* and candied cherries, a pyramid of American Beauties lifted their vigorous stems; they held their heads as high as Mrs. Bart, but their rose-colour had turned to a dissipated purple, and Lily's sense of fitness was disturbed by their reappearance on the luncheon-table.

"I really think, mother," she said reproachfully, "we might afford a few fresh flowers for luncheon. Just some jonquils or lilies-of-the-valley——"

Mrs. Bart stared. Her own fastidiousness had its eye fixed on the world, and she did not care how the luncheon-table looked when there was no one present at it but the family. But she smiled at her daughter's innocence.

"Lilies-of-the-valley," she said calmly, "cost two dollars a dozen at this season."

Lily was not impressed. She knew very little of the value of money.

"It would not take more than six dozen to fill that bowl," she argued.

"Six dozen what?" asked her father's voice in the doorway.

The two women looked up in surprise; though it was a Saturday, the sight of Mr. Bart at luncheon was an unwonted one. But neither his wife nor his daughter was sufficiently interested to ask an explanation.

Mr. Bart dropped into a chair, and sat gazing absently at the fragment of jellied salmon which the butler had placed before him.

"I was only saying," Lily began, "that I hate to see faded flowers at luncheon; and mother says a bunch of lilies-of-the-valley would not cost more than twelve dollars. Mayn't I tell the florist to send a few every day?"

She leaned confidently toward her father: he seldom refused her anything, and Mrs. Bart had taught her to plead with him when her own entreaties failed.

Mr. Bart sat motionless, his gaze still fixed on the salmon, and his lower jaw dropped; he looked even paler than usual, and his thin hair lay in untidy streaks on his forehead. Suddenly he looked at his daughter and laughed. The laugh was so strange that Lily coloured under it: she disliked being ridiculed, and her father seemed to see something ridiculous in the request. Perhaps he thought it foolish that she should trouble him about such a trifle.

"Twelve dollars—twelve dollars a day for flowers? Oh, certainly, my dear—give him an order for twelve hundred." He continued to laugh.

Mrs. Bart gave him a quick glance.

"You needn't wait, Poleworth—I will ring for you," she said to the butler.

The butler withdrew with an air of silent disapproval, leaving the remains of the *chaudfroid* on the sideboard.

"What is the matter, Hudson? Are you ill?" said Mrs. Bart severely.

She had no tolerance for scenes which were not of her own making, and it was odious to her that her husband should make a show of himself before the servants.

"Are you ill?" she repeated.

"Ill?—No, I'm ruined," he said.

Lily made a frightened sound, and Mrs. Bart rose to her feet.

"Ruined—?" she cried; but controlling herself instantly, she turned a calm face to Lily.

"Shut the pantry door," she said.

Lily obeyed, and when she turned back into the room her father was sitting with both elbows on the table, the plate of salmon between them, and his head bowed on his hands.

Mrs. Bart stood over him with a white face which made her hair unnaturally yellow. She looked at Lily as the latter approached: her look was terrible, but her voice was modulated to a ghastly cheerfulness.

"Your father is not well—he doesn't know what he is saying. It is nothing—but you had better go upstairs; and don't talk to the servants," she added.

Lily obeyed; she always obeyed when her mother spoke in that voice. She had not been deceived by Mrs. Bart's words: she knew at once that they were ruined. In the dark hours which followed, that awful fact overshadowed even her father's slow and difficult dying. To his wife he no longer counted: he had become extinct when he ceased to fulfil his purpose, and she sat at his side with the provisional air of a traveller who waits for a belated train to start. Lily's feelings were softer: she pitied him in a frightened ineffectual way. But the fact that he was for the most part unconscious, and that his attention, when she stole into the room, drifted away from her after a moment, made him even more of a stranger than in the nursery days when he had never come home till after dark. She seemed always to have seen him through a blur—first of sleepiness, then of distance and indifference—and now the fog had thickened till he was almost indistinguishable. If she could have performed any little services for him, or have exchanged with him a few of those affecting words which an extensive perusal of fiction had led her to connect with such occasions, the filial instinct might have stirred in her; but her pity, finding no active expression, remained in a state of spectatorship, overshadowed by her mother's grim unflagging resentment. Every look and act of Mrs. Bart's seemed to say: "You are sorry for him now—but you will feel differently when you see what he has done to us."

It was a relief to Lily when her father died.

Then a long winter set in. There was a little money left, but to Mrs. Bart it seemed worse than nothing—the mere mockery of what she was entitled to. What was the use of living if one had to live like a pig? She sank into a kind of furious apathy, a state of inert anger against fate. Her faculty for "managing" deserted her, or she no longer took sufficient pride in it to exert it. It was well enough to "manage" when by so doing one could keep one's own carriage; but when one's best contrivance did not conceal the fact that one had to go on foot, the effort was no longer worth making.

Lily and her mother wandered from place to place, now paying long visits to relations whose house-keeping Mrs. Bart criticized, and who deplored the fact that she let Lily breakfast in bed when the girl had no prospects before her, and now vegetating in cheap continental refuges, where Mrs. Bart held herself fiercely aloof from the frugal tea-tables of her companions in misfortune. She was especially careful to avoid her old friends and the scenes of her former successes. To be poor seemed to her such a confession of failure that it amounted to disgrace; and she detected a note of condescension in the friendliest advances.

Only one thought consoled her, and that was the contemplation of Lily's beauty. She studied it with a kind of passion, as though it were some weapon she had slowly fashioned for her vengeance. It was the last asset in their fortunes, the nucleus around which their life was to be rebuilt. She watched it jealously, as though it were her own property and Lily its mere custodian; and she tried to instil into the latter a sense of the responsibility that such a charge involved. She followed in imagination the career of other beauties, pointing out to her daughter what might be achieved through such a gift, and dwelling on the awful warning of those who, in spite of it, had failed to get what they wanted: to Mrs. Bart, only stupidity could explain the lamentable dénouement of some of her examples. She was not above the inconsistency of charging fate, rather than herself, with her own misfortunes; but she inveighed so acrimoniously against love-matches that Lily would have fancied her own marriage had been of that nature, had not Mrs. Bart frequently assured her that she had been "talked into it"—by whom, she never made clear.

Lily was duly impressed by the magnitude of her opportunities. The dinginess of her present life threw into enchanting relief the existence to which she felt herself entitled. To a less illuminated intelligence Mrs. Bart's counsels might have been dangerous, but Lily understood that beauty is only the raw material of conquest, and that to convert it into success other arts are required. She knew that to betray any sense of superiority was a subtler form of the stupidity her mother denounced, and it did not take her long to learn that a beauty needs more tact than the possessor of an average set of features.

Her ambitions were not as crude as Mrs. Bart's. It had been among that lady's grievances that her husband—in the early days, before he was too tired—had wasted his evenings in what she vaguely described as "reading poetry"; and among the effects packed off to auction after his death were a score or two of dingy volumes which had struggled for existence among the boots and medicine bottles of his dressing-room shelves. There was in Lily a vein of sentiment, perhaps transmitted from this source, which gave an idealizing touch to her most prosaic purposes. She liked to think of her beauty as a power for good, as giving her the opportunity to attain a position where she should make her influence felt in the vague diffusion of refinement and good taste. She was fond of pictures and flowers, and of sentimental fiction, and she could not help thinking that the possession of such tastes ennobled her desire for worldly advantages. She would not indeed have cared to marry a man who was merely rich: she was secretly ashamed of her mother's crude passion for money. Lily's preference would have been for an English nobleman with political ambitions and vast estates; or, for second choice, an Italian prince with a castle in the Apennines and an hereditary office in the Vatican. Lost causes had a romantic charm for her, and she liked to picture herself as standing aloof from the vulgar press of the Quirinal, and sacrificing her pleasure to the claims of an immemorial tradition. . . .

How long ago and how far off it all seemed! Those ambitions were hardly more futile and childish than the earlier ones which had centered about the possession of a French jointed doll with real hair. Was it only ten years since she had wavered in imagination between the English earl and the Italian prince? Relentlessly her mind travelled on over the dreary interval. . . .

After two years of hungry roaming Mrs. Bart had died—died of a deep disgust. She had hated dinginess, and it was her fate to be dingy. Her visions of a brilliant marriage for Lily had faded after the first year.

"People can't marry you if they don't see you—and how can they see you in these holes where we're stuck?" That was the burden of her lament; and her last adjuration to her daughter was to escape from dinginess if she could.

"Don't let it creep up on you and drag you down. Fight your way out of it somehow—you're young and can do it," she insisted.

She had died during one of their brief visits to New York, and there Lily at once became the centre of a family council composed of the wealthy relatives whom she had been taught to despise for living like pigs. It may be that they had an inkling of the sentiments in which she had been brought up, for none of them manifested a very lively desire for her company; indeed, the question threatened to remain unsolved till Mrs. Peniston with a sigh announced: "I'll try her for a year."

Every one was surprised, but one and all concealed their surprise, lest Mrs. Peniston should be alarmed by it into reconsidering her decision.

Mrs. Peniston was Mr. Bart's widowed sister, and if she was by no means the richest of the family group, its other members nevertheless abounded in reasons why she was clearly destined by Providence to assume the charge of Lily. In the first place she was alone, and it would be charming for her to have a young companion. Then she sometimes travelled, and Lily's familiarity with foreign customs—deplored as a misfortune by her more conservative relatives—would at least enable her to act as a kind of courier. But as a matter of fact Mrs. Peniston had not been affected by these considerations. She had taken the girl simply because no one else would have her, and because she had the kind of moral *mauvaise honte* which makes the public display of selfishness difficult, though it does not interfere with its private indulgence. It would have been impossible for Mrs. Peniston to be heroic on a desert island, but with the eyes of her little world upon her she took a certain pleasure in her act.

She reaped the reward to which disinterestedness is entitled, and found an agreeable companion in her niece. She had expected to find Lily headstrong, critical and "foreign"—for even Mrs. Peniston, though she occasionally went abroad, had the family dread of foreignness—but the girl showed a pliancy, which to a more penetrating mind than her aunt's, might have been less reassuring than the open selfishness of youth. Misfortune had made Lily supple instead of hardening her, and a pliable substance is less easy to break than a stiff one.

Mrs. Peniston, however, did not suffer from her niece's adaptability. Lily had no intention of taking advantage of her aunt's good nature. She was in truth grateful for the refuge offered her: Mrs. Peniston's opulent interior was at least not externally dingy. But dinginess is a quality which assumes all manner of disguises; and Lily soon found that it was as latent in the expensive routine of her aunt's life as in the makeshift existence of a continental pension.

Mrs. Peniston was one of the episodical persons who form the padding of life. It was impossible to believe that she had herself ever been a focus of activities. The most vivid thing about her was the fact that her grandmother had been a Van Alstyne. This connection with the well-fed industrious stock of early New York revealed itself in the glacial neatness of Mrs. Peniston's drawing-room and in the excellence of her cuisine. She belonged to the class of old New Yorkers who have always lived well, dressed expensively, and done little else; and to these inherited obligations Mrs. Peniston faithfully conformed. She had always been a looker-on at life, and her mind resembled one of those little mirrors which her Dutch ancestors were accustomed to affix to their upper windows, so that from the depths of an impenetrable domesticity they might see what was happening in the street.

Mrs. Peniston was the owner of a country-place in New Jersey, but she had never lived there since her husband's death—a remote event, which appeared to dwell in her memory chiefly as a dividing point in the personal reminiscences that formed the staple of her conversation. She was a woman who remembered dates with intensity, and could tell at a moment's notice whether the drawing-room curtains had been renewed before or after Mr. Peniston's last illness.

Mrs. Peniston thought the country lonely and trees damp, and cherished a vague fear of meeting a bull. To guard against such contingencies she frequented the more populous watering-places, where she installed herself impersonally in a hired house and looked on at life through the matting screen of her verandah. In the care of such a guardian, it soon became clear to Lily that she was to enjoy only the material advantages of good food and expensive clothing; and, though far from underrating these, she would gladly have exchanged them for what Mrs. Bart had taught her to regard as opportunities. She sighed to think what her mother's fierce energies would have accomplished, had they been coupled with Mrs. Peniston's resources. Lily had abundant energy of her own, but it was restricted by the necessity of adapting herself to her aunt's habits. She saw that at all costs she must keep Mrs. Peniston's favour till, as Mrs. Bart would have phrased it, she could stand on her own legs. Lily had no mind for the vagabond life of the poor relation, and to adapt herself to Mrs. Peniston she had, to some degree, to assume that lady's passive attitude. She had fancied at first that it would be easy to draw her aunt into the whirl of her own activities, but there was a static force in Mrs. Peniston against which her niece's efforts spent themselves in vain. To attempt to bring her into active relation with life was like tugging at a piece of furniture which has been screwed to the floor. She did not, indeed, expect Lily to remain equally immovable: she had all the American guardian's indulgence for the volatility of youth. She had indulgence also for certain other habits of her niece's. It seemed to her natural that Lily should spend all her money on dress, and she supplemented the girl's scanty income by occasional "handsome presents" meant to be applied to the same purpose. Lily, who was intensely practical, would have preferred a fixed allowance; but Mrs. Peniston liked the periodical recurrence of gratitude evoked by unexpected cheques, and was perhaps shrewd enough to perceive that such a method of giving kept alive in her niece a salutary sense of dependence.

Beyond this, Mrs. Peniston had not felt called upon to do anything for her charge: she had simply stood aside and let her take the field. Lily had taken it, at first with the confidence of assured possessorship, then with gradually narrowing demands, till now she found herself actually struggling for a foothold on the broad space which had once seemed her own for the asking. How it happened she did not yet know. Sometimes she thought it was because Mrs. Peniston had been too passive, and again she feared it was because she herself had not been passive enough. Had she shown an undue eagerness for victory? Had she lacked patience, pliancy and dissimulation? Whether she charged herself with these faults or absolved herself from them, made no difference in the sum-total of her failure. Younger and plainer girls had been married off by dozens, and she was nine-and-twenty, and still Miss Bart.

She was beginning to have fits of angry rebellion against fate, when she longed to drop out of the race and make an independent life for herself. But what manner of life would it be? She had barely enough money to pay her dress-makers' bills and her gambling debts; and none of the desultory interests which she dignified with the name of tastes was pronounced enough to enable her to live contentedly in obscurity. Ah, no—she was too intelligent not to be honest with herself. She knew that she hated dinginess as much as her mother had hated it, and to her last breath she meant to fight against it, dragging herself up again and again above its flood till she gained the bright pinnacles of success which presented such a slippery surface to her clutch.

§ 4

The next morning in her breakfast tray, Miss Bart found a note from her hostess.

"Dearest Lily," it ran, "if it is not too much of a bore to be down by ten, will you come to my sitting room to help me with some tiresome things?"

Lily tossed aside the note and subsided on her pillows with a sigh. It *was* a bore to be down by ten—an hour regarded at Bellomont as vaguely synchronous with sunrise—and she knew too well the nature of the tiresome things in question. Miss Pragg, the secretary, had been called away, and there would be notes and dinner-cards to write, lost addresses to hunt up, and other social drudgery to perform. It was understood that Miss Bart should fill the gap in such emergencies, and she usually recognized the obligation without a murmur.

Today, however, it renewed the sense of servitude which the previous night's review of her cheque-book had produced. Everything in her surroundings ministered to feelings of ease and amenity. The windows stood open to the sparkling freshness of the September morning, and between the yellow boughs she caught a perspective of hedges and parterres leading by degrees of lessening formality to the free undulations of the park. Her maid had kindled a little fire on the hearth, and it contended cheerfully with the sunlight which slanted across the moss-green carpet and caressed the curved sides of an old marquetry desk. Near the bed stood a table holding her breakfast tray, with its harmonious porcelain and silver, a handful of violets in a slender glass, and the morning paper folded beneath her letters. There was nothing new to Lily in these tokens of a studied luxury; but, though they formed a part of her atmosphere, she never lost her sensitiveness to their charm. Mere display left her with a sense of superior distinction; but she felt an affinity to all the subtler manifestations of wealth.

Mrs. Trenor's summons, however, suddenly recalled her state of dependence, and she rose and dressed in a mood of irritability that she was usually too prudent to indulge. She knew that such emotions leave lines on the face as well as in the character, and she had meant to take warning by the little creases which her midnight survey had revealed.

The matter-of-course tone of Mrs. Trenor's greeting deepened her irritation. If one did drag one's self out of bed at such an hour, and come down fresh and radiant to the monotony of note-writing, some special recognition of the sacrifice seemed fitting. But Mrs. Trenor's tone showed no consciousness of the fact.

"Oh, Lily, that's nice of you," she merely sighed across the chaos of letters, bills and other domestic documents which gave an incongruously commercial touch to the slender elegance of her writing-table.

"There are such lots of horrors his morning," she added, clearing a space in the centre of the confusion and rising to yield her seat to Miss Bart.

Mrs. Trenor was a tall fair woman, whose height just saved her from redundancy. Her rosy blondness had survived some forty years of futile activity without showing much trace of ill-usage except in a diminished play of feature. It was difficult to define her beyond saying that she seemed to exist only as a hostess, not so much from any exaggerated instinct of hospitality as because she could not sustain life except in a crowd. The collective nature of her interests exempted her from the ordinary rivalries of her sex, and she knew no more personal emotion than that of hatred for the woman who presumed to give bigger dinners or have more amusing house-parties than herself. As her social talents, backed by Mr. Trenor's bank-account, almost always assured her ultimate triumph in such competitions, success had developed in her an unscrupulous good nature toward the rest of her sex, and in Miss Bart's utilitarian classification of her friends, Mrs. Trenor ranked as the woman who was least likely to "go back" on her.

"It was simply inhuman of Pragg to go off now," Mrs. Trenor declared, as her friend seated herself at the desk. "She says her sister is going to have a baby—as if that were anything to having a house-party! I'm sure I shall get most horribly mixed up and there will be some awful rows. When I was down at Tuxedo I asked a lot of people for next week, and I've mislaid the list and can't remember who is coming. And this week is going to be a horrid failure too—and Gwen Van Osburgh will go back and tell her mother how bored people were. I didn't mean to ask the Wetheralls—that was a blunder of Gus's. They disapprove of Carry Fisher, you know. As if one could help having Carry Fisher! It *was* foolish of her to get that second divorce—Carry always overdoes things—but she said the only way to get a penny out of Fisher was to divorce him and make him pay alimony. And poor Carry has to consider every dollar. It's really absurd of Alice Wetherall to make such a fuss about meeting her, when one thinks of what society is coming to. Some one said the other day that there was a divorce and a case of appendicitis in every family one knows. Besides, Carry is the only person who can keep Gus in a good humour when we have bores in the house. Have you noticed that *all* the husbands like her? All, I mean, except her own. It's rather clever of her to have made a specialty of devoting herself to dull people—the field is such a large one, and she has it practically to herself. She finds compensations, no doubt—I know she borrows money of Gus—but then I'd *pay* her to keep him in a good humour, so I can't complain, after all."

Mrs. Trenor paused to enjoy the spectacle of Miss Bart's efforts to unravel her tangled correspondence.

"But it isn't only the Wetheralls and Carry," she resumed, with a fresh note of lament. "The truth is, I'm awfully disappointed in Lady Cressida Raith."

"Disappointed? Hadn't you known her before?"

"Mercy, no—never saw her till yesterday. Lady Skiddaw sent her over with letters to the Van Osburghs, and I heard that Maria Van Osburgh was asking a big party to meet her this week, so I thought it would be fun to get her away, and Jack Stepney, who knew her in India, managed it for me. Maria was furious, and actually had the impudence to make Gwen invite herself here, so that they shouldn't be *quite* out of it—if I'd known what Lady Cressida was like, they could have had her and welcome! But I thought any friend of the Skiddaws' was sure to be amusing. You remember what fun Lady Skiddaw was? There were times when I simply had to send the girls out of the room. Besides, Lady Cressida is the Duchess of Beltshire's sister, and I naturally supposed she was the same sort; but you never can tell in those English families. They are so big that there's room for all kinds, and it turns out that Lady Cressida is the moral one—married a clergyman and does missionary work in the East End. Think of my taking such a lot of trouble about a clergyman's wife, who wears Indian jewelry and botanizes! She made Gus take her all through the glass-houses yesterday, and bothered him to death by asking him the names of the plants. Fancy treating Gus as if he were the gardener!"

Mrs. Trenor brought this out in a *crescendo* of indignation.

"Oh, well, perhaps Lady Cressida will reconcile the Wetheralls to meeting Carry Fisher," said Miss Bart pacifically.

"I'm sure I hope so! But she is boring all the men horribly, and if she takes to distributing tracts, as I hear she does, it will be too depressing. The worst of it is that she would have been so useful at the right time. You know we have to have the Bishop once a year, and she would have given just the right tone to things. I always have horrid luck about the Bishop's visits," added Mrs. Trenor, whose present misery was being fed by a rapidly rising tide of reminiscence; "last year, when he came, Gus forgot all about his being here, and brought home the Ned Wintons and the Farleys—five divorces and six sets of children between them!"

"When is Lady Cressida going?" Lily enquired.

Mrs. Trenor cast up her eyes in despair. "My dear, if one only knew! I was in such a hurry to get her away from Maria that I actually forgot to name a date, and Gus says she told some one she meant to stop here all winter."

"To stop here? In this house?"

"Don't be silly—in America. But if no one else asks her—you know they *never* go to hotels."

"Perhaps Gus only said it to frighten you."

"No—I heard her tell Bertha Dorset that she had six months to put in while her husband was taking the cure in the Engadine. You should have seen Bertha look vacant! But it's no joke, you know—if she stays here all the autumn she'll spoil everything, and Maria Van Osburgh will simply exult."

At this affecting vision Mrs. Trenor's voice trembled with self-pity.

"Oh, Judy—as if any one were ever bored at Bellomont!" Miss Bart tactfully protested. "You know perfectly well that, if Mrs. Van Osburgh were to get all the right people and leave you with all the wrong ones, you'd manage to make things go off, and she wouldn't."

Such an assurance would usually have restored Mrs. Trenor's complacency; but on this occasion it did not chase the cloud from her brow.

"It isn't only Lady Cressida," she lamented. "Everything has gone wrong this week. I can see that Bertha Dorset is furious with me."

"Furious with you? Why?"

"Because I told her that Lawrence Selden was coming; but he wouldn't, after all, and she's quite unreasonable enough to think it's my fault."

Miss Bart put down her pen and sat absently gazing at the note she had begun.

"I thought that was all over," she said.

"So it is, on his side. And of course Bertha hasn't been idle since. But I fancy she's out of a job just at present—and some one gave me a hint that I had better ask Lawrence. Well, I *did* ask him—but I couldn't make him come; and now I suppose she'll take it out of me by being perfectly nasty to every one else."

"Oh, she may take it out of *him* by being perfectly charming—to some one else."

Mrs. Trenor shook her head dolefully. "She knows he wouldn't mind. And who else is there? Alice Wetherall won't let Lucius out of her sight. Ned Silverton can't take his eyes off Carry Fisher—poor boy! Gus is bored by Bertha, Jack Stepney knows her too well—and —well, to be sure, there's Percy Gryce!"

She sat up smiling at the thought.

Miss Bart's countenance did not reflect the smile.

"Oh, she and Mr. Gryce would not be likely to hit it off."

"You mean that she'd shock him and he'd bore her? Well, that's not such a bad beginning, you know. But I hope she won't take it into her head to be nice to him, for I asked him here on purpose for you."

Lily laughed. *"Merci du compliment!* I should certainly have no show against Bertha."

"Do you think I am uncomplimentary? I'm not really, you know. Every one knows you're a thousand times handsomer and cleverer than Bertha; but then you're not nasty. And for always getting what she wants in the long run, commend me to a nasty woman."

Miss Bart stared in affected reproval. "I thought you were so fond of Bertha."

"Oh, I am—it's much safer to be fond of dangerous people. But she *is* dangerous—and if I ever saw her up to mischief it's now. I can tell by poor George's manner. That man is a perfect barometer —he always knows when Bertha is going to——"

"To fall?" Miss Bart suggested.

"Don't be shocking! You know he believes in her still. And of course I don't say there's any real harm in Bertha. Only she delights in making people miserable, and especially poor George."

"Well, he seems cut out for the part—I don't wonder she likes more cheerful companionship."

"Oh, George is not as dismal as you think. If Bertha didn't worry him he would be quite different. Or if she'd leave him alone, and let him arrange his life as he pleases. But she doesn't dare lose her hold of him on account of the money, and so when *he* isn't jealous she pretends to be."

Miss Bart went on writing in silence, and her hostess sat following her train of thought with frowning intensity.

"Do you know," she exclaimed after a long pause, "I believe I'll call up Lawrence on the telephone and tell him he simply *must* come?"

"Oh, don't," said Lily, with a quick suffusion of colour. The blush surprised her almost as much as it did her hostess, who, though not commonly observant of facial changes, sat staring at her with puzzled eyes.

"Good gracious, Lily, how handsome you are!——Why? Do you dislike him so much?"

"Not at all; I like him. But if you are actuated by the benevolent intention of protecting me from Bertha—I don't think I need your protection."

Mrs. Trenor sat up with an exclamation. "Lily!—— *Percy!* Do you mean to say you've actually done it?"

Miss Bart smiled. "I only mean to say that Mr. Gryce and I are getting to be very good friends."

"H'm—I see." Mrs. Trenor fixed a rapt eye upon her. "You know they say he has eight hundred thousand a year—and spends nothing, except on some rubbishy old books. And his mother has heart-disease and will leave him a lot more. *Oh, Lily, do go slowly,*" her friend adjured her.

Miss Bart continued to smile without annoyance. "I shouldn't, for instance," she remarked, "be in any haste to tell him that he had a lot of rubbishy old books."

"No, of course not; I know you're wonderful about getting up people's subjects. But he's horribly shy, and easily shocked, and—and——"

"Why don't you say it, Judy? I have the reputation of being on the hunt for a rich husband?"

"Oh, I don't mean that; he wouldn't believe it of you—at first," said Mrs. Trenor, with candid shrewdness. "But you know things are rather lively here at times—I must give Jack and Gus a hint—and if he thought you were what his mother would call fast—oh, well, you know what I mean. Don't wear your scarlet *crêpe-de-chine* for dinner, and don't smoke if you can help it, Lily dear!"

Lily pushed aside her finished work with a dry smile. "You're very kind, Judy: I'll lock up my cigarettes and wear that last year's dress you sent me this morning. And if you are really interested in my career, perhaps you'll be kind enough not to ask me to play bridge again this evening."

"Bridge? Does he mind bridge, too? Oh, Lily, what an awful life you'll lead! But of course I won't—why didn't you give me a hint last night? There's nothing I wouldn't do, you poor duck, to see you happy!"

And Mrs. Trenor, glowing with her sex's eagerness to smooth the course of true love, enveloped Lily in a long embrace.

"You're quite sure," she added solicitously, as the latter extricated herself, "that you wouldn't like me to telephone for Lawrence Selden?"

"Quite sure," said Lily.

The next three days demonstrated to her own complete satisfaction Miss Bart's ability to manage her affairs without extraneous aid.

As she sat, on the Saturday afternoon, on the terrace at Bellomont, she smiled at Mrs. Trenor's fear that she might go too fast. If such a warning had ever been needful, the years had taught her a salutary lesson, and she flattered herself that she now knew how to adapt her pace to the object of pursuit. In the case of Mr. Gryce she had found it well to flutter ahead, losing herself elusively and luring him on from depth to depth of unconscious intimacy. The surrounding atmosphere was propitious to this scheme of courtship. Mrs. Trenor, true to her word, had shown no signs of expecting Lily at the bridge-table, and had even hinted to the other card-players that they were to betray no surprise at her unwonted defection. In consequence of this hint, Lily found herself the centre of that feminine solicitude which envelops a young woman in the mating season. A solitude was tacitly created for her in the crowded existence of Bellomont, and her friends could not have shown a greater readiness for self-effacement had her wooing been adorned with all the attributes of romance. In Lily's set this conduct implied a sympathetic comprehension of her motives, and Mr. Gryce rose in her esteem as she saw the consideration he inspired.

The terrace at Bellomont on a September afternoon was a spot propitious to sentimental musings, and as Miss Bart stood leaning against the balustrade above the sunken garden, at a little distance from the animated group about the tea-table, she might have been lost in the mazes of an inarticulate happiness. In reality, her thoughts were finding definite utterance in the tranquil recapitulation of the blessings in store for her. From where she stood she could see them embodied in the form of Mr. Gryce, who, in a light overcoat and muffler, sat somewhat nervously on the edge of his chair, while Carry Fisher, with all the energy of eye and gesture with which nature and art had combined to endow her, pressed on him the duty of taking part in the task of municipal reform.

Mrs. Fisher's latest hobby was municipal reform. It had been preceded by an equal zeal for socialism, which had in turn replaced an energetic advocacy of Christian Science. Mrs. Fisher was small, fiery and dramatic; and her hands and eyes were admirable instruments in the service of whatever cause she happened to espouse. She had, however, the fault common to enthusiasts of ignoring any slackness of response on the part of her hearers, and Lily was amused by her unconsciousness of the resistance displayed in every angle of Mr. Gryce's attitude. Lily herself knew that his mind was divided between the dread of catching cold if he remained out of doors too long at that hour, and the fear that, if he retreated to the house, Mrs. Fisher might follow him up with a paper to be signed. Mr. Gryce had a constitutional dislike to what he called "committing himself," and tenderly as he cherished his health, he evidently concluded that it was safer to stay out of reach of pen and ink till chance released him from Mrs. Fisher's toils. Meanwhile he cast agonized glances in the direction of Miss Bart, whose only response was to sink into an attitude of more graceful abstraction. She had learned the value of contrast in throwing her charms into relief, and was fully aware of the extent to which Mrs. Fisher's volubility was enhancing her own repose.

She was roused from her musings by the approach of her cousin Jack Stepney who, at Gwen Van Osburgh's side, was returning across the garden from the tennis court.

The couple in question were engaged in the same kind of romance in which Lily figured, and the latter felt a certain annoyance in comtemplating what seemed to her a caricature of her own situation. Miss Van Osburgh was a large girl with flat surfaces and no high lights. Jack Stepney had once said of her that she was as reliable as roast mutton. His own taste was in the line of less solid and more highly-seasoned diet; but hunger makes any fare palatable, and there had been times when Mr. Stepney had been reduced to a crust.

Lily considered with interest the expression of their faces: the girl's turned toward her companion's like an empty plate held up to be filled, while the man lounging at her side already betrayed the encroaching boredom which would presently crack the thin veneer of his smile.

"How impatient men are!" Lily reflected. "All Jack has to do to get everything he wants is to keep quiet and let that girl marry him; whereas I have to calculate and contrive, and retreat and advance, as if I were going through an intricate dance, when one misstep would throw me hopelessly out of time."

As they drew nearer she was whimsically struck by a kind of family likeness between Miss Van Osburgh and Percy Gryce. There was no resemblance of feature. Gryce was handsome in a didactic way—he looked like a clever pupil's drawing from a plaster-cast—while Gwen's countenance had no more modeling than a face painted on a toy balloon. But the deeper affinity was unmistakable: the two had the same prejudices and ideals, and the same quality of making other standards non-existent by ignoring them. This attribute was common to most of Lily's set: they had a force of negation which eliminated everything beyond their own range of perception. Gryce and Miss Van Osburgh were, in short, made for each other by every law of moral and physical correspondence— "Yet they wouldn't look at each other," Lily mused, "they never do. Each of them wants a creature of a different race, of Jack's race and mine, with all sorts of intuitions, sensations and perceptions that they don't even guess the existence of. And they always get what they want."

She stood talking with her cousin and Miss Van Osburgh, till a slight cloud on the latter's brow advised her that even cousinly amenities were subject to suspicion, and Miss Bart, mindful of the necessity of not exciting enmities at this crucial point of her career, dropped aside while the happy couple proceeded toward the tea-table.

Seating herself on the upper step of the terrace, Lily leaned her head against the honeysuckles wreathing the balustrade. The fragrance of the late blossoms seemed an emanation of the tranquil scene, a landscape tutored to the last degree of rural elegance. In the foreground glowed the warm tints of the gardens. Beyond the lawn, with its pyramidal pale-gold maples and velvety firs, sloped pastures dotted with cattle; and through a long glade the river widened like a lake under the silver light of September. Lily did not want to join the circle about the tea-table. They represented the future she had chosen, and she was content with it, but in no haste to anticipate its joys. The certainty that she could marry Percy Gryce when she pleased had lifted a heavy load from her mind, and her money troubles were too recent for their removal not to leave a sense of relief which a less discerning intelligence might have taken for happiness. Her vulgar cares were at an end. She would be able to arrange her life as she pleased, to soar into that empyrean of security where creditors cannot penetrate. She would have smarter gowns than Judy Trenor, and far, far more jewels than Bertha Dorset. She would be free forever from the shifts, the expedients, the humiliations of the relatively poor. Instead of having to flatter, she would be flattered; instead of being grateful, she would receive thanks. There were old scores she could pay off as well as old benefits she could return. And she had no doubts as to the extent of her power. She knew that Mr. Gryce was of the small chary type most inaccessible to impulses and emotions. He had the kind of character in which prudence is a vice, and good advice the most dangerous nourishment. But Lily had known the species before: she was aware that such a guarded nature must find one huge outlet of egoism, and she determined to be to him what his Americana had hitherto been: the one possession in which he took sufficient pride to spend money on it. She knew that this generosity to self is one of the forms of meanness, and she resolved so to identify herself with her husband's vanity that to gratify her wishes would be to him the most exquisite form of self-indulgence. The system might at first necessitate a resort to some of the very shifts and expedients from which she intended it should free her; but she felt sure that in a short time she would be able to play the game in her own way. How should she have distrusted her powers? Her beauty itself was not the mere ephemeral possession it might have been in the hands of inexperience: her skill in enhancing it, the care she took of it, the use she made of it, seemed to give it a kind of permanence. She felt she could trust it to carry her through to the end.

And the end, on the whole, was worth while. Life was not the mockery she had thought it three days ago. There was room for her, after all, in this crowded selfish world of pleasure whence, so short a time since, her poverty had seemed to exclude her. These people whom she had ridiculed and yet envied were glad to make a place for her in the charmed circle about which all her desires revolved. They were not as brutal and self-engrossed as she had fancied—or rather, since it would no longer be necessary to flatter and humour them, that side of their nature became less conspicuous. Society is a revolving body which is apt to be judged according to its place in each man's heaven; and at present it was turning its illuminated face to Lily.

In the rosy glow it diffused her companions seemed full of amiable qualites. She liked their elegance; their lightness, their lack of emphasis: even the self-assurance which at times was so like obtuseness now seemed the natural sign of social ascendency. They were lords of the only world she cared for, and they were ready to admit her to their ranks and let her lord it with them. Already she felt within her a stealing allegiance to their standards, an acceptance of their limitations, a disbelief in the things they did not believe in, a contemptuous pity for the people who were not able to live as they lived.

The early sunset was slanting across the park. Through the boughs of the long avenue beyond the gardens she caught the flash of wheels, and divined that more visitors were approaching. There was a movement behind her, a scattering of steps and voices: it was evident that the party about the tea-table was breaking up. Presently she heard a tread behind her on the terrace. She supposed that Mr. Gryce had at last found means to escape from his predicament, and she smiled at the significance of his coming to join her instead of beating an instant retreat to the fire-side.

She turned to give him the welcome which such gallantry deserved; but her greeting wavered into a blush of wonder, for the man who had approached her was Lawrence Selden.

"You see I came after all," he said; but, before she had time to answer, Mrs. Dorset, breaking away from a lifeless colloquy with her host, had stepped between them with a little gesture of appropriation.

§ 5

The observance of Sunday at Bellomont was chiefly marked by the punctual appearance of the smart omnibus destined to convey the household to the little church at the gates. Whether any one got into the omnibus or not was a matter of secondary importance, since by standing there it not only bore witness to the orthodox intentions of the family, but made Mrs. Trenor feel, when she finally heard it drive away, that she had somehow vicariously made use of it.

It was Mrs. Trenor's theory that her daughters actually did go to church every Sunday; but their French governess's convictions calling her to the rival fane, and the fatigues of the week keeping their mother in her room till luncheon, there was seldom any one present to verify the fact. Now and then, in a spasmodic burst of virtue—when the house had been too uproarious over night—Gus Trenor forced his genial bulk into a tight frock-coat and routed his daughters from their slumbers; but habitually, as Lily explained to Mr. Gryce, this parental duty was forgotten till the church bells were ringing across the park, and the omnibus had driven away empty.

Lily had hinted to Mr. Gryce that this neglect of religious observances was repugnant to her early traditions, and that during her visits to Bellomont she regularly accompanied Muriel and Hilda to church. This tallied with the assurance, also confidentially imparted, that, never having played bridge before, she had been "dragged into it" on the night of her arrival, and had lost an appalling amount of money in consequence of her ignorance of the game and of the rules of betting. Mr. Gryce was undoubtedly enjoying Bellomont. He liked the ease and glitter of the life, and the lustre conferred on him by being a member of this group of rich and conspicuous people. But he thought it a very materialistic society; there were times when he was frightened by the talk of the men and the looks of the ladies, and he was glad to find that Miss Bart, for all her ease and self-possession, was not at home in so ambiguous an atmosphere. For this reason he had been especially pleased to learn that she would, as usual, attend the young Trenors to church on Sunday morning; and as he paced the gravel sweep before the door, his light overcoat on his arm and his prayer-book in one carefully-gloved hand, he reflected agreeably on the strength of character which kept her true to her early training in surroundings so subversive to religious principles.

For a long time Mr. Gryce and the omnibus had the gravel sweep to themselves; but, far from regretting this deplorable indifference on the part of the other guests, he found himself nourishing the hope that Miss Bart might be unaccompanied. The precious minutes were flying, however; the big chestnuts pawed the ground and flecked their impatient sides with foam; the coachman seemed to be slowly petrifying on the box, and the groom on the doorstep; and still the lady did not come. Suddenly, however, there was a sound of voices and a rustle of skirts in the doorway, and Mr. Gryce, restoring his watch to his pocket, turned with a nervous start; but it was only to find himself handing Mrs. Wetherall into the carriage.

The Wetheralls always went to church. They belonged to the vast group of human automata who go through life without neglecting to perform a single one of the gestures executed by the surrounding puppets. It is true that the Bellomont puppets did not go to church; but others equally important did—and Mr. and Mrs. Wetherall's circle was so large that God was included in their visiting-list. They appeared, therefore, punctual and resigned, with the air of people bound for a dull "At Home," and after them Hilda and Muriel straggled, yawning and pinning each other's veils and ribbons as they came. They had promised Lily to go to church with her, they declared, and Lily was such a dear old duck that they didn't mind doing it to please her, though they couldn't fancy what had put the idea in her head, and though for their own part they would much rather have played lawn tennis with Jack and Gwen, if she hadn't told them she was coming. The Misses Trenor were followed by Lady Cressida Raith, a weather-beaten person in Liberty silk and ethnological trinkets, who, on seeing the omnibus, expressed her surprise that they were not to walk across the park; but at Mrs. Wetherall's horrified protest that the church was a mile away, her ladyship, after a glance at the height of the other's heels, acquiesced in the necessity of driving, and poor Mr. Gryce found himself rolling off between four ladies for whose spiritual welfare he felt not the least concern.

It might have afforded him some consolation could he have known that Miss Bart had really meant to go to church. She had even risen earlier than usual in the execution of her purpose. She had no idea that the sight of her in a grey gown of devotional cut, with her famous lashes drooped above a prayer-book, would put the finishing touch to Mr. Gryce's subjugation, and render inevitable a certain incident which she had resolved should form a part of the walk they were to take together after luncheon. Her intentions in short had never been more definite; but poor Lily, for all the hard glaze of her exterior, was inwardly as malleable as wax. Her faculty for adapting herself, for entering into other people's feelings, if it served her now and then in small contingencies, hampered her in the decisive moments of life. She was like a water-plant in the flux of the tides, and today the whole current of her mood was carrying her toward Lawrence Selden. Why had he come? Was it to see herself or Bertha Dorset? It was the last question which, at that moment, should have engaged her. She might better have contented herself with thinking that he had simply responded to the despairing summons of his hostess, anxious to interpose him between herself and the ill-humour of Mrs. Dorset. But Lily had not rested till she learned from Mrs. Trenor that Selden had come of his own accord.

"He didn't even wire me—he just happened to find the trap at the station. Perhaps it's not over with Bertha after all," Mrs. Trenor musingly concluded, and went away to arrange her dinner-cards accordingly.

Perhaps it was not, Lily reflected; but it should be seen, unless she had lost her cunning. If Selden had come at Mrs. Dorset's call, it was at her own that he would stay. So much the previous evening had told her. Mrs. Trenor, true to her simple principle of making her married friends happy, had placed Selden and Mrs. Dorset next to each other at dinner; but, in obedience to the time-honoured traditions of the match-maker, she had separated Lily and Mr. Gryce, sending in the former with George Dorset, while Mr. Gryce was coupled with Gwen Van Osburgh.

George Dorset's talk did not interfere with the range of his neighbour's thoughts. He was a mournful dyspeptic, intent on finding out the deleterious ingredients of every dish and diverted from this care only by the sound of his wife's voice. On this occasion, however, Mrs. Dorset took no part in the general conversation. She sat talking in low murmurs with Selden, and turning a contemptuous and denuded shoulder toward her host, who, far from resenting his exclusion, plunged into the excesses of the *menu* with the joyous irresponsibility of a free man. To Mr. Dorset, however, his wife's attitude was a subject of such evident concern that, when he was not scraping the sauce from his fish, or scooping the moist breadcrumbs from the interior of his roll, he sat straining his thin neck for a glimpse of her between the lights.

Mrs. Trenor, as it chanced, had placed the husband and wife on opposite sides of the table, and Lily was therefore able to observe Mrs. Dorset also, and by carrying her glance a few feet farther, to set up a rapid comparison between Lawrence Selden and Mr. Gryce. It was that comparison which was her undoing. Why else had she suddenly grown interested in Selden? She had known him for eight years or more: ever since her return to America he had formed a part of her background. She had always been glad to sit next to him at dinner, had found him more agreeable than most men, and had vaguely wished that he possessed the other qualities needful to fix her attention; but till now she had been too busy with her own affairs to regard him as more than one of the pleasant accessories of life. Miss Bart was a keen reader of her own heart, and she saw that her sudden preoccupation with Selden was due to the fact that his presence shed a new light on her surroundings. Not that he was notably brilliant or exceptional; in his own profession he was surpassed by more than one man who had bored Lily through many a weary dinner. It was rather that he had preserved a certain social detachment, a happy air of viewing the show objectively, of having points of contact outside the great gilt cage in which they were all huddled for the mob to gape at. How alluring the world outside the cage appeared to Lily, as she heard its door clang on her! In reality, as she knew, the door never clanged: it stood always open; but most of the captives were like flies in a bottle, and having once flown in, could never regain their freedom. It was Selden's distinction that he had never forgotten the way out.

That was the secret of his way of readjusting her vision. Lily, turning her eyes from him, found herself scanning her little world through his retina: it was as though the pink lamps had been shut off and the dusty daylight let in. She looked down the long table, studying its occupants one by one, from Gus Trenor, with his heavy carnivorous head sunk between his shoulders, as he preyed on a jellied plover, to his wife, at the opposite end of the long bank of orchids, suggestive, with her glaring good-looks, of a jeweller's window lit by electricity. And between the two, what a long stretch of vacuity! How dreary and trivial these people were! Lily reviewed them with a scornful impatience: Carry Fisher, with her shoulders, her eyes, her divorces, her general air of embodying a "spicy paragraph"; young Silverton, who had meant to live on proof-reading and write an epic, and who now lived on his friends and had become critical of truffles; Alice Wetherall, an animated visiting-list, whose most fervid convictions turned on the wording of invitations and the engraving of dinner-cards; Wetherall, with his perpetual nervous nod of acquiescence, his air of agreeing with people before he knew what they were saying; Jack Stepney, with his confident smile and anxious eyes, half way between the sheriff and an heiress; Gwen Van Osburgh, with all the guileless confidence of a young girl who has always been told that there is no one richer than her father.

Lily smiled at her classification of her friends. How different they had seemed to her a few hours ago! Then they had symbolized what she was gaining, now they stood for what she was giving up. That very afternoon they had seemed full of brilliant qualities; now she saw that they were merely dull in a loud way. Under the glitter of their opportunities she saw the poverty of their achievement. It was not that she wanted them to be more disinterested; but she would have liked them to be more picturesque. And she had a shamed recollection of the way in which, a few hours since, she had felt the centripetal force of their standards. She closed her eyes an instant, and the vacuous routine of the life she had chosen stretched before her like a long white road without dip or turning: it was true she was to roll over it in a carriage instead of trudging it on foot, but sometimes the pedestrian enjoys the diversion of a short cut which is denied to those on wheels.

She was roused by a chuckle which Mr. Dorset seemed to eject from the depths of his lean throat.

"I say, do look at her," he exclaimed, turning to Miss Bart with lugubrious merriment—"I beg your pardon, but do just look at my wife making a fool of that poor devil over there! One would really suppose she was gone on him—and it's all the other way round, I assure you."

Thus adjured, Lily turned her eyes on the spectacle which was affording Mr. Dorset such legitimate mirth. It certainly appeared, as he said, that Mrs. Dorset was the more active participant in the scene: her neighbour seemed to receive her advances with a temperate zest which did not distract him from his dinner. The sight restored Lily's good humour, and knowing the peculiar disguise which Mr. Dorset's marital fears assumed, she asked gaily: "Aren't you horribly jealous of her?"

Dorset greeted the sally with delight. "Oh, abominably—you've just hit it—keeps me awake at night. The doctors tell me that's what has knocked my digestion out—being so infernally jealous of her. —I can't eat a mouthful of this stuff, you know," he added suddenly, pushing back his plate with a clouded countenance; and Lily, unfailingly adaptable, accorded her radiant attention to his prolonged denunciation of other people's cooks, with a supplementary tirade on the toxic qualities of melted butter.

It was not often that he found so ready an ear; and, being a man as well as a dyspeptic, it may be that as he poured his grievances into it he was not insensible to its rosy symmetry. At any rate he engaged Lily so long that the sweets were being handed when she caught a phrase on her other side, where Miss Corby, the comic woman of the company, was bantering Jack Stepney on his approaching engagement. Miss Corby's rôle was jocularity: she always entered the conversation with a handspring.

"And of course you'll have Sim Rosedale as best man!" Lily heard her fling out as the climax of her prognostications; and

Stepney responded, as if struck: "Jove, that's an idea. What a thumping present I'd get out of him!"

Sim Rosedale! The name, made more odious by its diminutive, obtruded itself on Lily's thoughts like a leer. It stood for one of the many hated possibilities hovering on the edge of life. If she did not marry Percy Gryce, the day might come when she would have to be civil to such men as Rosedale. *If she did not marry him?* But she meant to marry him—she was sure of him and sure of herself. She drew back with a shiver from the pleasant paths in which her thoughts had been straying, and set her feet once more in the middle of the long white road. . . . When she went upstairs that night she found that the late post had brought her a fresh batch of bills. Mrs. Peniston, who was a conscientious woman, had forwarded them all to Bellomont.

Miss Bart, accordingly, rose the next morning with the most earnest conviction that it was her duty to go to church. She tore herself betimes from the lingering enjoyment of her breakfast-tray, rang to have her grey gown laid out, and despatched her maid to borrow a prayer-book from Mrs. Trenor.

But her course was too purely reasonable not to contain the germs of rebellion. No sooner were her preparations made than they roused a smothered sense of resistance. A small spark was enough to kindle Lily's imagination, and the sight of the grey dress and the borrowed prayer-book flashed a long light down the years. She would have to go to church with Percy Gryce every Sunday. They would have a front pew in the most expensive church in New York, and his name would figure handsomely in the list of parish charities. In a few years, when he grew stouter, he would be made a warden. Once in the winter the rector would come to dine, and her husband would beg her to go over the list and see that no *divorcées* were included, except those who had showed signs of penitence by being re-married to the very wealthy. There was nothing especially arduous in this round of religious obligations; but it stood for a fraction of that great bulk of boredom which loomed across her path. And who could consent to be bored on such a morning? Lily had slept well, and her bath had filled her with a pleasant glow, which was becomingly reflected in the clear curve of her cheek. No lines were visible this morning, or else the glass was at a happier angle.

And the day was the accomplice of her mood: it was a day for impulse and truancy. The light air seemed full of powdered gold; below the dewy bloom of the lawns the woodlands blushed and smouldered, and the hills across the river swam in molten blue. Every drop of blood in Lily's veins invited her to happiness.

The sound of wheels roused her from these musings, and leaning behind her shutters she saw the omnibus take up its freight. She was too late, then—but the fact did not alarm her. A glimpse of Mr. Gryce's crestfallen face even suggested that she had done wisely in absenting herself, since the disappointment he so candidly betrayed would surely whet his appetite for the afternoon walk. That walk she did not mean to miss; one glance at the bills on her writing-table was enough to recall its necessity. But meanwhile she had the morning to herself, and could muse pleasantly on the disposal of its hours. She was familiar enough with the habits of Bellomont to know that she was likely to have a free field till luncheon. She had seen the Wetheralls, the Trenor girls and Lady Cressida packed safely into the omnibus; Judy Trenor was sure to be having her hair shampooed; Carry Fisher had doubtless carried off her host for a drive, Ned Silverton was probably smoking the cigarette of young despair in his bedroom; and Kate Corby was certain to be playing tennis with Jack Stepney and Miss Van Osburgh. Of the ladies, this left only Mrs. Dorset unaccounted for, and Mrs. Dorset never came down till luncheon: her doctors, she averred, had forbidden her to expose herself to the crude air of the morning.

To the remaining members of the party Lily gave no special thought; wherever they were, they were not likely to interfere with her plans. These, for the moment, took the shape of assuming a dress somewhat more rustic and summerlike in style than the garment she had first selected, and rustling downstairs, sunshade in hand, with the disengaged air of a lady in quest of exercise. The great hall was empty but for the knot of dogs by the fire, who, taking in at a glance the out-door aspect of Miss Bart, were upon her at once with lavish offers of companionship. She put aside the ramping paws which conveyed these offers, and assuring the joyous volunteers that she might presently have a use for their company, sauntered on through the empty drawing-room to the library at the end of the house. The library was almost the only surviving portion of the old manor-house of Bellomont: a long spacious room, revealing the traditions of the mother-country in its classically-cased doors, the Dutch tiles of the chimney, and the elaborate hobgrate with its shining brass urns. A few family portraits of lantern-jawed gentlemen in tie-wigs, and ladies with large head-dresses and small bodies, hung between the shelves lined with pleasantly shabby books: books mostly contemporaneous with the ancestors in question, and to which the subsequent Trenors had made no perceptible additions. The library at Bellomont was in fact never used for reading, though it had a certain popularity as a smoking-room or a quiet retreat for flirtation. It had occurred to Lily, however, that it might on this occasion have been resorted to by the only member of the party in the least likely to put it to its original use. She advanced noiselessly over the dense old rug scattered with easy-chairs, and before she reached the middle of the room she saw that she had not been mistaken. Lawrence Selden was in fact seated at its farther end; but though a book lay on his knee, his attention was not engaged with it, but directed to a lady whose lace-clad figure, as she leaned back in an adjoining chair, detached itself with exaggerated slimness against the dusky leather of the upholstery.

Lily paused as she caught sight of the group; for a moment she seemed about to withdraw, but thinking better of this, she announced her approach by a slight shake of her skirts which made the couple raise their heads, Mrs. Dorset with a look of frank displeasure, and Selden with his usual quiet smile. The sight of his composure had a disturbing effect on Lily; but to be disturbed was in her case to make a more brilliant effort at self-possession.

"Dear me, am I late?" she asked, putting a hand in his as he advanced to greet her.

"Late for what?" enquired Mrs. Dorset tartly. "Not for luncheon, certainly—but perhaps you had an earlier engagement?"

"Yes, I had," said Lily confidingly.

"Really? Perhaps I am in the way, then? But Mr. Selden is entirely at your disposal." Mrs. Dorset was pale with temper, and her antagonist felt a certain pleasure in prolonging her distress.

"Oh, dear, no—do stay," she said good-humouredly. "I don't in the least want to drive you away."

"You're awfully good, dear, but I never interfere with Mr. Selden's engagements."

The remark was uttered with a little air of proprietorship not lost on its object, who concealed a faint blush of annoyance by stooping to pick up the book he had dropped at Lily's approach. The latter's eyes widened charmingly and she broke into a light laugh.

"But I have no engagement with Mr. Selden! My engagement was to go to church; and I'm afraid the omnibus has started without me. *Has* it started, do you know?"

She turned to Selden, who replied that he had heard it drive away some time since.

"Ah, then I shall have to walk; I promised Hilda and Muriel to go to church with them. It's too late to walk there, you say? Well, I shall have the credit of trying, at any rate—and the advantage of escaping part of the service. I'm not so sorry for myself, after all!"

And with a bright nod to the couple on whom she had intruded, Miss Bart strolled through the glass doors and carried her rustling grace down the long perspective of the garden walk.

She was taking her way churchward, but at no very quick pace; a fact not lost on one of her observers, who stood in the doorway looking after her with an air of puzzled amusement. The truth is that she was conscious of a somewhat keen shock of disappointment. All her plans for the day had been built on the assumption that it was to see her that Selden had come to Bellomont. She had expected, when she came downstairs, to find him on the watch for her; and she had found him, instead, in a situation which might well denote that he had been on the watch for another lady. Was it possible, after all, that he had come for Bertha Dorset? The latter had acted on the assumption to the extent of appearing at an hour when she never showed herself to ordinary mortals, and Lily, for the moment, saw no way of putting her in the wrong. It did not occur to her that Selden might have been actuated merely by the desire to spend a Sunday out of town: women never learn to dispense with the sentimental motive in their judgments of men. But Lily was not easily disconcerted; competition put her on her mettle, and she reflected that Selden's coming, if it did not declare him to be still in

Mrs. Dorset's toils, showed him to be so completely free from them that he was not afraid of her proximity.

These thoughts so engaged her that she fell into a gait hardly likely to carry her to church before the sermon, and at length, having passed from the gardens to the wood-path beyond, so far forgot her intention as to sink into a rustic seat at a bend of the walk. The spot was charming, and Lily was not insensible to the charm, or to the fact that her presence enhanced it; but she was not accustomed to taste the joys of solitude except in company, and the combination of a handsome girl and a romantic scene struck her as too good to be wasted. No one, however, appeared to profit by the opportunity; and after a half hour of fruitless waiting she rose and wandered on. She felt a stealing sense of fatigue as she walked; the sparkle had died out of her, and the taste of life was stale on her lips. She hardly knew what she had been seeking, or why the failure to find it had so blotted the light from her sky: she was only aware of a vague sense of failure, of an inner isolation deeper than the loneliness about her.

Her footsteps flagged, and she stood gazing listlessly ahead, digging the ferny edge of the path with the tip of her sunshade. As she did so a step sounded behind her, and she saw Selden at her side.

"How fast you walk!" he remarked. "I thought I should never catch up with you."

She answered gaily: "You must be quite breathless! I've been sitting under that tree for an hour."

"Waiting for me, I hope?" he rejoined; and she said with a vague laugh:

"Well—waiting to see if you would come."

"I seize the distinction, but I don't mind it, since doing the one involved doing the other. But weren't you sure that I should come?"

"If I waited long enough—but you see I had only a limited time to give to the experiment."

"Why limited? Limited by luncheon?"

"No; by my other engagement."

"Your engagement to go to church with Muriel and Hilda?"

"No; but to come home from church with another person."

"Ah, I see; I might have known you were fully provided with alternatives. And is the other person coming home this way?"

Lily laughed again. "That's just what I don't know; and to find out, it is my business to get to church before the service is over."

"Exactly; and it is my business to prevent your doing so; in which case the other person, piqued by your absence, will form the desperate resolve of driving back in the omnibus."

Lily received this with fresh appreciation; his nonsense was like the bubbling of her inner mood. "Is that what you would do in such an emergency?" she enquired.

Selden looked at her with solemnity. "I am here to prove to you," he cried, "what I am capable of doing in an emergency!"

"Walking a mile in an hour—you must own that the omnibus would be quicker!"

"Ah—but will he find you in the end? That's the only test of success."

They looked at each other with the same luxury of enjoyment that they had felt in exchanging absurdities over his tea-table; but suddenly Lily's face changed, and she said: "Well, if it is, he has succeeded."

Selden, following her glance, perceived a party of people advancing toward them from the farther bend of the path. Lady Cressida had evidently insisted on walking home, and the rest of the church-goers had thought it their duty to accompany her. Lily's companion looked rapidly from one to the other of the two men of the party; Wetherall walking respectfully at Lady Cressida's side with his little sidelong look of nervous attention, and Percy Gryce bringing up the rear with Mrs. Wetherall and the Trenors.

"Ah—now I see why you were getting up your Americana!" Selden exclaimed with a note of the freest admiration; but the blush with which the sally was received checked whatever amplifications he had meant to give it.

That Lily Bart should object to being bantered about her suitors, or even about her means of attracting them, was so new to Selden that he had a momentary flash of surprise, which lit up a number of possibilities; but she rose gallantly to the defence of her confusion, by saying, as its object approached: "That was why I was waiting for you—to thank you for having given me so many points!"

"Ah, you can hardly do justice to the subject in such a short time," said Selden, as the Trenor girls caught sight of Miss Bart; and while she signalled a response to their boisterous greeting, he added quickly: "Won't you devote your afternoon to it? You know I must be off tomorrow morning. We'll take a walk, and you can thank me at your leisure."

§ 6

The afternoon was perfect. A deeper stillness possessed the air, and the glitter of the American autumn was tempered by a haze which diffused the brightness without dulling it.

In the woody hollows of the park there was already a faint chill; but as the ground rose the air grew lighter, and ascending the long slopes beyond the high-road, Lily and her companion reached a zone of lingering summer. The path wound across a meadow with scattered trees; then it dipped into a lane plumed with asters and purpling sprays of bramble, whence, through the light quiver of ash-leaves, the country unrolled itself in pastoral distances.

Higher up, the lane showed thickening tufts of fern and of the creeping glossy verdure of shaded slopes; trees began to overhang it, and the shade deepened to the checkered dusk of a beech-grove. The boles of the trees stood well apart, with only a light feathering of undergrowth; the path wound along the edge of the wood, now and then looking out on a sunlit pasture or on an orchard spangled with fruit.

Lily had no real intimacy with nature, but she had a passion for the appropriate and could be keenly sensitive to a scene which was the fitting background of her own sensations. The landscape outspread below her seemed an enlargement of her present mood, and she found something of herself in its calmness, its breadth, its long free reaches. On the nearer slopes the sugar-maples wavered like pyres of light; lower down was a massing of grey orchards, and here and there the lingering green of an oak-grove. Two or three red farm-houses dozed under the apple-trees, and the white wooden spire of a village church showed beyond the shoulder of the hill; while far below, in a haze of dust, the high-road ran between the fields.

"Let us sit here," Selden suggested, as they reached an open ledge of rock above which the beeches rose steeply between mossy boulders.

Lily dropped down on the rock, glowing with her long climb. She sat quiet, her lips parted by the stress of the ascent, her eyes wandering peacefully over the broken ranges of the landscape. Selden stretched himself on the grass at her feet, tilting his hat against the level sun-rays, and clasping his hands behind his head, which rested against the side of the rock. He had no wish to make her talk; her quick-breathing silence seemed a part of the general hush and harmony of things. In his own mind there was only a lazy sense of pleasure, veiling the sharp edges of sensation as the September haze veiled the scene at their feet. But Lily, though her attitude was as calm as his, was throbbing inwardly with a rush of thoughts. There were in her at the moment two beings, one drawing deep breaths of freedom and exhilaration, the other gasping for air in a little black prison-house of fears. But gradually the captive's gasps grew fainter, or the other paid less heed to them: the horizon expanded, the air grew stronger, and the free spirit quivered for flight.

She could not herself have explained the sense of buoyancy which seemed to lift and swing her above the sun-suffused world at her feet. Was it love, she wondered, or a mere fortuitous combination of happy thoughts and sensations? How much of it was owing to the spell of the perfect afternoon, the scent of the fading woods, the thought of the dulness she had fled from? Lily had no definite experience by which to test the quality of her feelings. She had several times been in love with fortunes or careers, but only once with a man. That was years ago, when she first came out, and had been smitten with a romantic passion for a young gentleman named Herbert Melson, who had blue eyes and a little wave in his hair. Mr. Melson, who was possessed of no other negotiable securities, had hastened to employ these in capturing the eldest Miss Van Osburgh: since then he had grown stout and wheezy, and was given to telling anecdotes about his children. If Lily recalled this early emotion it was not to compare it with that which now possessed her; the only point of comparison was the sense of lightness, of emancipation, which she remembered feeling, in the whirl of a waltz or the seclusion of a conservatory, during the brief course of her youthful romance. She had not known again till today that lightness, that glow of freedom; but now it was something more than a blind groping of the blood. The peculiar charm of her feeling for Selden was that she understood it; she could put her finger on every link of the chain that was drawing them together. Though his popularity was of the quiet kind, felt rather than actively expressed among his friends, she had never mistaken his inconspicuousness for obscurity. His reputed cultivation was generally regarded as a slight obstacle to easy intercourse, but Lily, who prided herself on her broad-minded recognition of literature, and always carried an Omar Khayyám in her travelling-bag, was attracted by this attribute, which she felt would have had its distinction in an older society. It was, moreover, one of his gifts to look his part; to have a height which lifted his head above the crowd, and the keenly-modelled dark features which, in a land of amorphous types, gave him the air of belonging to a more specialized race, of carrying the impress of a concentrated past. Expansive persons found him a little dry, and very young girls thought him sarcastic; but this air of friendly aloofness, as far removed as possible from any assertion of personal advantage, was the quality which piqued Lily's interest. Everything about him accorded with the fastidious element in her taste, even to the light irony with which he surveyed what seemed to her most sacred. She admired him most of all, perhaps, for being able to convey as distinct a sense of superiority as the richest man she had ever met.

It was the unconscious prolongation of this thought which led her to say presently, with a laugh: "I have broken two engagements for you today. How many have you broken for me?"

"None," said Selden calmly. "My only engagement at Bellomont was with you."

She glanced down at him, faintly smiling.

"Did you really come to Bellomont to see me?"

"Of course I did."

Her look deepened meditatively. "Why?" she murmured, with an accent which took all tinge of coquetry from the question.

"Because you're such a wonderful spectacle: I always like to see what you are doing."

"How do you know what I should be doing if you were not here?"

Selden smiled. "I don't flatter myself that my coming has deflected your course of action by a hair's breadth."

"That's absurd—since, if you were not here, I could obviously not be taking a walk with you."

"No, but your taking a walk with me is only another way of making use of your material. You are an artist and I happen to be the bit of colour you are using today. It 's a part of your cleverness to be able to produce premeditated effects extemporaneously."

Lily smiled also: his words were too acute not to strike her sense of humour. It was true that she meant to use the accident of his presence as part of a very definite effect; or that, at least, was the secret pretext she had found for breaking her promise to walk with Mr. Gryce. She had sometimes been accused of being too eager—even Judy Trenor had warned her to go slowly. Well, she would not be too eager in this case; she would give her suitor a longer taste of suspense. Where duty and inclination jumped together, it was not in Lily's nature to hold them asunder. She had excused herself from the walk on the plea of a headache: the horrid headache which, in the morning, had prevented her venturing to church. Her appearance at luncheon justified the excuse. She looked languid, full of a suffering sweetness; she carried a scent-bottle in her hand. Mr. Gryce was new to such manifestations; he wondered rather nervously if she were delicate, having far-reaching fears about the future of his progeny. But sympathy won the day, and he besought her not to expose herself: he always connected the outer air with ideas of exposure.

Lily had received his sympathy with languid gratitude, urging him, since she should be such poor company, to join the rest of the party who, after luncheon, were starting in automobiles on a visit to the Van Osburghs at Peekskill. Mr. Gryce was touched by her disinterestedness, and, to escape from the threatened vacuity of the afternoon, had taken her advice and departed mournfully, in a dust-hood and goggles: as the motor-car plunged down the avenue she smiled at his resemblance to a baffled beetle.

Selden had watched her manœuvres with lazy amusement. She had made no reply to his suggestion that they should spend the afternoon together, but as her plan unfolded itself he felt fairly confident of being included in it. The house was empty when at length he heard her step on the stair and strolled out of the billiard-room to join her. She had on a hat and walking-dress, and the dogs were bounding at her feet.

"I thought, after all, the air might do me good," she explained; and he agreed that so simple a remedy was worth trying.

The excursionists would be gone at least four hours; Lily and Selden had the whole afternoon before them, and the sense of leisure and safety gave the last touch of lightness to her spirit. With so much time to talk, and no definite object to be led up to, she could taste the rare joys of mental vagrancy.

She felt so free from ulterior motives that she took up his charge with a touch of resentment.

"I don't know," she said, "why you are always accusing me of premeditation."

"I thought you confessed to it: you told me the other day that you had to follow a certain line—and if one does a thing at all it is a merit to do it thoroughly."

"If you mean that a girl who has no one to think for her is obliged to think for herself, I am quite willing to accept the imputation. But you must find me a dismal kind of person if you suppose that I never yield to an impulse."

"Ah, but I don't suppose that: haven't I told you that your genius lies in converting impulses into intentions?"

"My genius?" she echoed with a sudden note of weariness. "Is there any final test of genius but success? And I certainly haven't succeeded."

Selden pushed his hat back and took a side-glance at her. "Success—what is success? I shall be interested to have your definition."

"Success?" She hesitated. "Why, to get as much as one can out of life, I suppose. It's a relative quality, after all. Isn't that your idea of it?"

"My idea of it? God forbid!" He sat up with sudden energy, resting his elbows on his knees and staring out upon the mellow fields. "My idea of success," he said, "is personal freedom."

"Freedom? Freedom from worries?"

"From everything— from money, from poverty, from ease and anxiety, from all the material accidents. To keep a kind of republic of the spirit—that's what I call success."

She leaned forward with a responsive flash. "I know—I know—it's strange; but that's just what I've been feeling today."

He met her eyes with the latent sweetness of his. "Is the feeling so rare with you?" he said.

She blushed a little under his gaze. "You think me horribly sordid, don't you? But perhaps it's rather that I never had any choice. There was no one, I mean, to tell me about the republic of the spirit."

"There never is—it's a country one has to find the way to one's self."

"But I should never have found my way there if you hadn't told me.

"Ah, there are sign-posts—but one has to know how to read them."

"Well, I have known, I have known!" she cried with a glow of eagerness. "Whenever I see you, I find myself spelling out a letter of the sign—and yesterday—last evening at dinner—I suddenly saw a little way into your republic."

Selden was still looking at her, but with a changed eye. Hitherto he had found, in her presence and her talk, the æsthetic amusement which a reflective man is apt to seek in desultory intercourse with pretty women. His attitude had been one of admiring spectatorship, and he would have been almost sorry to detect in her any emotional weakness which should interfere with the fulfilment of her aims. But now the hint of this weakness had become the most interesting thing about her. He had come on her that morning in a moment of disarray; her face had been pale and altered, and the diminution of her beauty had lent her a poignant charm. *That is how she looks when she is alone!* had been his first thought; and the second was to note in her the change which his coming produced. It was the danger-point of their intercourse that he could not doubt the spontaneity of her liking. From whatever angle he viewed their dawning intimacy, he could not see it as part of her scheme of life; and to be the unforeseen element in a career so accurately planned was stimulating even to a man who had renounced sentimental experiments.

"Well," he said, "did it make you want to see more? Are you going to become one of us?"

He had drawn out his cigarettes as he spoke, and she reached her hand toward the case.

"Oh, do give me one—I haven't smoked for days!"

"Why such unnatural abstinence? Everybody smokes at Bellomont."

"Yes—but it is not considered becoming in a *jeune fille à marier;* and at the present moment I am a *jeune fille à marier.*"

"Ah, then I'm afraid we can't let you into the republic."

"Why not? Is it a celibate order?"

"Not in the least, though I'm bound to say there are not many married people in it. But you will marry some one very rich, and it's as hard for rich people to get into as the kingdom of heaven."

"That's unjust, I think, because, as I understand it, one of the conditions of citizenship is not to think too much about money, and the only way not to think about money is to have a great deal of it."

"You might as well say that the only way not to think about air is to have enough to breathe. That is true enough in a sense; but your lungs are thinking about the air, if you are not. And so it is with your rich people—they may not be thinking of money, but they 're breathing it all the while; take them into another element and see how they squirm and gasp!"

Lily sat gazing absently through the blue rings of her cigarette-smoke.

"It seems to me," she said at length, "that you spend a good deal of your time in the element you disapprove of."

Selden received this thrust without discomposure. "Yes; but I have tried to remain amphibious: it's all right as long as one's lungs can work in another air. The real alchemy consists in being able to turn gold back again into something else; and that's the secret that most of your friends have lost."

Lily mused. "Don't you think," she rejoined after a moment, "that the people who find fault with society are too apt to regard it as an end and not a means, just as the people who despise money speak as if its only use were to be kept in bags and gloated over? Isn't it fairer to look at them both as opportunities, which may be used either stupidly or intelligently, according to the capacity of the user?"

"That is certainly the sane view; but the queer thing about society is that the people who regard it as an end are those who are in it, and not the critics on the fence. It's just the other way with most shows—the audience may be under the illusion, but the actors know that real life is on the other side of the footlights. The people who take society as an escape from work are putting it to its proper use; but when it becomes the thing worked for it distorts all the relations of life." Selden raised himself on his elbow. "Good heavens!" he went on, "I don't underrate the decorative side of life. It seems to me the sense of splendour has justified itself by what it has produced. The worst of it is that so much human nature is used up in the process. If we're all the raw stuff of the cosmic effects, one would rather be the fire that tempers a sword than the fish that dyes a purple cloak. And a society like ours wastes such good material in producing its little patch of purple! Look at a boy like Ned Silverton—he's really too good to be used to refurbish anybody's social shabbiness. There's a lad just setting out to discover the universe. Isn't it a pity he should end by finding it in Mrs. Fisher's drawing-room?"

"Ned is a dear boy, and I hope he will keep his illusions long enough to write some nice poetry about them; but do you think it is only in society that he is likely to lose them?"

Selden answered her with a shrug. "Why do we call all our generous ideas illusions, and the mean ones truths? Isn't it a sufficient condemnation of society to find one's self accepting such phraseology? I very nearly acquired the jargon at Silverton's age, and I know how names can alter the colour of beliefs."

She had never heard him speak with such energy of affirmation. His habitual touch was that of the eclectic, who lightly turns over and compares; and she was moved by this sudden glimpse into the laboratory where his faiths were formed.

"Ah, you are as bad as the other sectarians," she exclaimed; "why do you call your republic a republic? It is a close corporation, and you create arbitrary objections in order to keep people out."

"It is not *my* republic; if it were, I should have a *coup d'état* and seat you on the throne."

"Whereas, in reality, you think I can never even get my foot across the threshold? Oh, I understand what you mean. You despise my ambitions—you think them unworthy of me!"

Selden smiled, but not ironically. "Well, isn't that a tribute? I think them quite worthy of most of the people who live by them."

She had turned to gaze on him gravely. "But isn't it possible that, if I had the opportunities of these people, I might make a better use of them? Money stands for all kinds of things—its purchasing quality isn't limited to diamonds and motor-cars."

"Not in the least: you might expiate your enjoyment of them by founding a hospital."

"But if you think they are what I should really enjoy, you must think my ambitions are good enough for me."

Selden met this appeal with a laugh. "Ah, my dear Miss Bart, I am not divine Providence, to guarantee your enjoying the things you are trying to get!"

"Then the best you can say for me is, that after struggling to get them I probably shan't like them?" She drew a deep breath. "What a miserable future you foresee for me!"

"Well—have you never foreseen it for yourself?"

The slow colour rose to her cheek, not a blush of excitement but drawn from the deep wells of feeling; it was as if the effort of her spirit had produced it.

"Often and often," she said. "But it looks so much darker when you show it to me!"

He made no answer to this exclamation, and for a while they sat silent, while something throbbed between them in the wide quiet of the air. But suddenly she turned on him with a kind of vehemence.

"Why do you do this to me?" she cried. "Why do you make the things I have chosen seem hateful to me, if you have nothing to give me instead?"

The words roused Selden from the musing fit into which he had fallen. He himself did not know why he had led their talk along such lines; it was the last use he would have imagined himself making of an afternoon's solitude with Miss Bart. But it was one of those moments when neither seemed to speak deliberately, when an indwelling voice in each called to the other across unsounded depths of feeling.

"No, I have nothing to give you instead," he said, sitting up and turning so that he faced her. "If I had, it should be yours, you know."

She received this abrupt declaration in a way even stranger than the manner of its making: she dropped her face on her hands and he saw that for a moment she wept.

It was for a moment only, however; for when he leaned nearer and drew down her hands with a gesture less passionate than grave, she turned on him a face softened but not disfigured by emotion, and he said to himself, somewhat cruelly, that even her weeping was an art.

The reflection steadied his voice as he asked, between pity and irony: "Isn't it natural that I should try to belittle all the things I can't offer you?"

Her face brightened at this, but she drew her hand away, not with a gesture of coquetry, but as though renouncing something to which she had no claim.

"But you belittle *me,* don't you," she returned gently, "in being so sure they are the only things I care for?"

Selden felt an inner start; but it was only the last quiver of his egoism. Almost at once he answered quite simply: "But you do care for them, don't you? And no wishing of mine can alter that."

He had so completely ceased to consider how far this might carry him, that he had a distinct sense of disappointment when she turned on him a face sparkling with derision.

"Ah," she cried, "for all your fine phrases you're really as great a coward as I am, for you wouldn't have made one of them if you hadn't been so sure of my answer."

The shock of this retort had the effect of crystallizing Selden's wavering intentions.

"I am not so sure of your answer," he said quietly. "And I do you the justice to believe that you are not either."

It was her turn to look at him with surprise; and after a moment —"Do you want to marry me?" she asked.

He broke into a laugh. "No, I don't want to—but perhaps I should if you did!"

"That's what I told you—you're so sure of me that you can amuse yourself with experiments." She drew back the hand he had regained, and sat looking down on him sadly.

"I am not making experiments," he returned. "Or if I am it is not on you but on myself. I don't know what effect they are going to have on me—but if marrying you is one of them, I will take the risk."

She smiled faintly. "It would be a great risk, certainly—I have never concealed from you how great."

"Ah, it's you who are the coward!" he exclaimed.

She had risen, and he stood facing her with his eyes on hers. The soft isolation of the falling day enveloped them: they seemed lifted into a finer air. All the exquisite influences of the hour trembled in their veins, and drew them to each other as the loosened leaves were drawn to the earth.

"It's you who are the coward," he repeated, catching her hands in his.

She leaned on him for a moment, as if with a drop of tired wings: he felt as though her heart were beating rather with the stress of a long flight than the thrill of new distances. Then, drawing back with a little smile of warning—"I shall look hideous in dowdy clothes; but I can trim my own hats," she declared.

They stood silent for a while after this, smiling at each other like adventurous children who have climbed to a forbidden height from which they discover a new world. The actual world at their feet was veiling itself in dimness, and across the valley a clear moon rose in the denser blue.

Suddenly they heard a remote sound, like the hum of a giant insect, and following the high-road, which wound whiter through the surrounding twilight, a black object rushed across their vision.

Lily started from her attitude of absorption; her smile faded and she began to move toward the lane.

"I had no idea it was so late. We shall not be back till after dark," she said, almost impatiently.

Selden was looking at her with surprise: it took him a moment to regain his usual view of her; then he said, with an uncontrollable note of dryness: "That was not one of our party; the motor was going the other way."

"I know—I know—" She paused, and he saw her redden through the twilight. "But I told them I was not well—that I should not go out. Let us go down!" she murmured.

Selden continued to look at her; then he drew his cigarette-case from his pocket and slowly lit a cigarette. It seemed to him necessary, at that moment, to proclaim, by some habitual gesture of this sort, his recovered hold on the actual: he had an almost puerile wish to let his companion see that, their flight over, he had landed on his feet.

She waited while the spark flickered under his curved palm; then he held out the cigarettes to her.

She took one with an unsteady hand, and putting it to her lips, leaned forward to draw her light from his. In the indistinctness the little red gleam lit up the lower part of her face, and he saw her mouth tremble into a smile.

"Were you serious?" she asked, with an odd thrill of gaiety which she might have caught up, in haste, from a heap of stock inflections, without having time to select the just note.

Selden's voice was under better control. "Why not?" he returned. "You see I took no risks in being so." And as she continued to stand before him, a little pale under the retort, he added quickly: "Let us go down."

§ 7

It spoke much for the depth of Mrs. Trenor's friendship that her voice, in admonishing Miss Bart, took the same note of personal despair as if she had been lamenting the collapse of a house-party.

"All I can say is, Lily, that I can't make you out!" She leaned back, sighing, in the morning abandon of lace and muslin, turning an indifferent shoulder to the heaped-up importunities of her desk, while she considered, with the eye of a physician who has given up the case, the erect exterior of the patient confronting her.

"If you hadn't told me you were going in for him seriously—but I'm sure you made that plain enough from the beginning! Why else did you ask me to let you off bridge, and to keep away Carry and Kate Corby? I don't suppose you did it because he amused you; we could none of us imagine your putting up with him for a moment unless you meant to marry him. And I'm sure everybody played fair! They all wanted to help it along. Even Bertha kept her hands off—I will say that—till Lawrence came down and you dragged him away from her. After that she had a right to retaliate—why on earth did you interfere with her? You've known Lawrence Selden for years—why did you behave as if you had just discovered him? If you had a grudge against Bertha it was a stupid time to show it—you could have paid her back just as well after you were married! I told you Bertha was dangerous. She was in an odious mood when she came here, but Lawrence's turning up put her in a good humour, and if you'd only let her think he came for *her* it would have never occurred to her to play this trick. Oh, Lily, you'll never do anything if you're not serious!"

Miss Bart accepted this exhortation in a spirit of the purest impartiality. Why should she have been angry? It was the voice of her own conscience which spoke to her through Mrs. Trenor's reproachful accents. But even to her own conscience she must trump up a semblance of defence.

"I only took a day off—I thought he meant to stay on all this week, and I knew Mr. Selden was leaving this morning."

Mrs. Trenor brushed aside the plea with a gesture which laid bare its weakness.

"He did mean to stay—that's the worst of it. It shows that he's run away from you; that Bertha's done her work and poisoned him thoroughly."

Lily gave a slight laugh. "Oh, if he's running I'll overtake him!"

Her friend threw out an arresting hand. "Whatever you do, Lily, do nothing!"

Miss Bart received the warning with a smile. "I don't mean, literally, to take the next train. There are ways—" But she did not go on to specify them.

Mrs. Trenor sharply corrected the tense. "There *were* ways—plenty of them! I didn't suppose you needed to have them pointed out. But don't deceive yourself—he's thoroughly frightened. He has run straight home to his mother, and she'll protect him!"

"Oh, to the death," Lily agreed, dimpling at the vision.

"How you can *laugh*—" her friend rebuked her; and she dropped back to a soberer perception of things with the question: "What was it Bertha really told him?"

"Don't ask me—horrors! She seemed to have raked up everything. Oh, you know what I mean—of course there isn't anything, *really;* but I suppose she brought in Prince Varigliano—and Lord Hubert—and there was some story of your having borrowed money of old Ned Van Alstyne: did you ever?"

"He is my father's cousin," Miss Bart interposed.

"Well, of course she left *that* out. It seems Ned told Carry Fisher; and she told Bertha, naturally. They're all alike, you know: they hold their tongues for years, and you think you're safe, but when their opportunity comes they remember everything."

Lily had grown pale: her voice had a harsh note in it. "It was some money I lost at bridge at the Van Osburghs'. I repaid it, of course."

"Ah, well, they wouldn't remember that; besides, it was the idea of the gambling debt that frightened Percy. Oh, Bertha knew her man—she knew just what to tell him!"

In this strain Mrs. Trenor continued for nearly an hour to admonish her friend. Miss Bart listened with admirable equanimity. Her naturally good temper had been disciplined by years of enforced compliance, since she had almost always had to attain her ends by the circuitous path of other people's; and, being naturally inclined to face unpleasant facts as soon as they presented themselves, she was not sorry to hear an impartial statement of what her folly was likely to cost, the more so as her own thoughts were still insisting on the other side of the case. Presented in the light of Mrs. Trenor's vigorous comments, the reckoning was certainly a formidable one, and Lily, as she listened, found herself gradually reverting to her friend's view of the situation. Mrs. Trenor's words were moreover emphasized for her hearer by anxieties which she herself could scarcely guess. Affluence, unless stimulated by a keen imagination, forms but the vaguest notion of the practical strain of poverty. Judy knew it must be "horrid" for poor Lily to have to stop to consider whether she could afford real lace on her petticoats, and not to have a motor-car and a steam-yacht at her orders; but the daily friction of unpaid bills, the daily nibble of small temptations to expenditure, were trials as far out of her experience as the domestic problems of the char-woman. Mrs. Trenor's unconsciousness of the real stress of the situation had the effect of making it more galling to Lily. While her friend reproached her for missing the opportunity to eclipse her rivals, she was once more battling in imagination with the mounting tide of indebtedness from which she had so nearly escaped. What wind of folly had driven her out again on those dark seas?

If anything was needed to put the last touch to her self-abasement it was the sense of the way her old life was opening its ruts again to receive her. Yesterday her fancy had fluttered free pinions above a choice of occupations; now she had to drop to the level of the familiar routine, in which moments of seeming brilliancy and freedom alternated with long hours of subjection.

She laid a deprecating hand on her friend's. "Dear Judy! I'm sorry to have been such a bore, and you are very good to me. But you must have some letters for me to answer—let me at least be useful."

She settled herself at the desk, and Mrs. Trenor accepted her resumption of the morning's task with a sigh which implied that, after all, she had proved herself unfit for higher uses.

The luncheon table showed a depleted circle. All the men but Jack Stepney and Dorset had returned to town (it seemed to Lily a last touch of irony that Selden and Percy Gryce should have gone in the same train), and Lady Cressida and the attendant Wetheralls had been despatched by motor to lunch at a distant country-house. At such moments of diminished interest it was usual for Mrs. Dorset to keep her room till the afternoon; but on this occasion she drifted in when luncheon was half over, hollow-eyed and drooping, but with an edge of malice under her indifference.

She raised her eyebrows as she looked about the table. "How few of us are left! I do so enjoy the quiet—don't you, Lily? I wish the men would always stop away—it's really much nicer without them. Oh, you don't count, George: one doesn't have to talk to one's husband. But I thought Mr. Gryce was to stay for the rest of the week?" she added enquiringly. "Didn't he intend to, Judy? He's such a nice boy—I wonder what drove him away? He is rather shy, and I'm afraid we may have shocked him: he has been brought up in such an old-fashioned way. Do you know, Lily, he told me he had never seen a girl play cards for money till he saw you doing it the other night? And he lives on the interest of his income, and always has a lot left over to invest!"

Mrs. Fisher leaned forward eagerly. "I do believe it is some one's duty to educate that young man. It is shocking that he has never been made to realize his duties as a citizen. Every wealthy man should be compelled to study the laws of his country."

Mrs. Dorset glanced at her quietly. "I think he has studied the divorce laws. He told me he had promised the Bishop to sign some kind of a petition against divorce."

Mrs. Fisher reddened under her powder, and Stepney said with a laughing glance at Miss Bart: "I suppose he is thinking of marriage, and wants to tinker up the old ship before he goes aboard."

His betrothed looked shocked at the metaphor, and George Dorset exclaimed with a sardonic growl: "Poor devil! It isn't the ship that will do for him, it's the crew."

"Or the stowaways," said Miss Corby brightly. "If I contemplated a voyage with him I should try to start with a friend in the hold."

Miss Van Osburgh's vague feeling of pique was struggling for appropriate expression. "I'm sure I don't see why you laugh at him; I think he's very nice," she exclaimed; "and, at any rate, a girl who married him would always have enough to be comfortable."

She looked puzzled at the redoubled laughter which hailed her words, but it might have consoled her to know how deeply they had sunk into the breast of one of her hearers.

Comfortable! At that moment the word was more eloquent to Lily Bart than any other in the language. She could not even pause to smile over the heiress's view of a colossal fortune as a mere shelter against want: her mind was filled with the vision of what that shelter might have been to her. Mrs. Dorset's pin-pricks did not smart, for her own irony cut deeper: no one could hurt her as much as she was hurting herself, for no one else—not even Judy Trenor—knew the full magnitude of her folly.

She was roused from these unprofitable considerations by a whispered request from her hostess, who drew her apart as they left the luncheon-table.

"Lily, dear, if you've nothing special to do, may I tell Carry Fisher that you intend to drive to the station and fetch Gus? He will be back at four, and I know she has it in her mind to meet him. Of course I'm very glad to have him amused, but I happen to know that she has bled him rather severely since she's been here, and she is so keen about going to fetch him that I fancy she must have got a lot more bills this morning. It seems to me," Mrs. Trenor feelingly concluded, "that most of her alimony is paid by other women's husbands!"

Miss Bart, on her way to the station, had leisure to muse over her friend's words, and their peculiar application to herself. Why should she have to suffer for having once, for a few hours, borrowed money of an elderly cousin, when a woman like Carry Fisher could make a living unrebuked from the good-nature of her men friends and the tolerance of their wives? It all turned on the tiresome distinction between what a married woman might, and a girl might not, do. Of course it was shocking for a married woman to borrow money—and Lily was expertly aware of the implication involved—but still, it was the mere *malum prohibitum* which the world decries but condones, and which, though it may be punished by private vengeance, does not provoke the collective disapprobation of society. To Miss Bart, in short, no such opportunities were possible. She could of course borrow from her women friends—a hundred here or there, at the utmost—but they were more ready to give a gown or a trinket, and looked a little askance when she hinted her preference for a cheque. Women are not generous lenders, and those among whom her lot was cast were either in the same case as herself, or else too far removed from it to understand its necessities. The result of her meditations was the decision to join her aunt at Richfield. She could not remain at Bellomont without playing bridge, and being involved in other expenses; and to continue her usual series of autumn visits would merely prolong the same difficulties. She had reached a point where abrupt retrenchment was necessary, and the only cheap life was a dull life. She would start the next morning for Richfield.

At the station she thought Gus Trenor seemed surprised, and not wholly unrelieved, to see her. She yielded up the reins of the light runabout in which she had driven over, and as he climbed heavily to her side, crushing her into a scant third of the seat, he said: "Halloo! It isn't often you honour me. You must have been uncommonly hard up for something to do."

The afternoon was warm, and propinquity made her more than usually conscious that he was red and massive, and that beads of moisture had caused the dust of the train to adhere unpleasantly to the broad expanse of cheek and neck which he turned to her; but she was aware also, from the look in his small dull eyes, that the contact with her freshness and slenderness was as agreeable to him as the sight of a cooling beverage.

The perception of this fact helped her to answer gaily: "It's not often I have the chance. There are too many ladies to dispute the privilege with me."

"The privilege of driving me home? Well, I'm glad you won the race, anyhow. But I know what really happened—my wife sent you. Now didn't she?"

He had the dull man's unexpected flashes of astuteness, and Lily could not help joining in the laugh with which he had pounced on the truth.

"You see, Judy thinks I'm the safest person for you to be with; and she's quite right," she rejoined.

"Oh, is she, though? If she is, it's because you wouldn't waste your time on an old hulk like me. We married men have to put up with what we can get: all the prizes are for the clever chaps who've kept a free foot. Let me light a cigar, will you? I've had a beastly day of it."

He drew up in the shade of the village street, and passed the reins to her while he held a match to his cigar. The little flame under his hand cast a deeper crimson on his puffing face, and Lily averted her eyes with a momentary feeling of repugnance. And yet some women thought him handsome!

As she handed back the reins, she said sympathetically: "Did you have such a lot of tiresome things to do?"

"I should say so—rather!" Trenor, who was seldom listened to, either by his wife or her friends, settled down into the rare enjoyment of a confidential talk. "You don't know how a fellow has to hustle to keep this kind of thing going." He waved his whip in the direction of the Bellomont acres, which lay out-spread before them in opulent undulations. "Judy has no idea of what she spends—not that there isn't plenty to keep the thing going," he interrupted himself, "but a man has got to keep his eyes open and pick up all the tips he can. My father and mother used to live like fighting-cocks on their income, and put by a good bit of it too—luckily for me—but at the pace we go now, I don't know where I should be if it weren't for taking a flyer now and then. The women all think—I mean Judy thinks—I've nothing to do but to go down town once a month and cut off coupons, but the truth is it takes a devilish lot of hard work to keep the machinery running. Not that I ought to complain today, though," he went on after a moment, "for I did a very neat stroke of business, thanks to Stepney's friend Rosedale: by the way, Miss Lily, I wish you'd try to persuade Judy to be decently civil to that chap. He's going to be rich enough to buy us all out one of these days, and if she'd only ask him to dine now and then I could get almost anything out of him. The man is mad to know the people who don't want to know him, and when a fellow's in that state there is nothing he won't do for the first woman who takes him up."

Lily hesitated a moment. The first part of her companion's discourse had started an interesting train of thought, which was rudely interrupted by the mention of Mr. Rosedale's name. She uttered a faint protest.

"But you know Jack did try to take him about, and he was impossible."

"Oh, hang it—because he's fat and shiny, and has a shoppy manner! Well, all I can say is that the people who are clever enough to be civil to him now will make a mighty good thing of it. A few years from now he'll be in it whether we want him or not, and then he won't be giving away a half-a-million tip for a dinner."

Lily's mind had reverted from the intrusive personality of Mr. Rosedale to the train of thought set in motion by Trenor's first words. This vast mysterious Wall Street world of "tips" and "deals" —might she not find in it the means of escape from her dreary predicament? She had often heard of women making money in this way through their friends: she had no more notion than most of her sex of the exact nature of the transaction, and its vagueness seemed to diminish its indelicacy. She could not, indeed, imagine herself, in any extremity, stooping to extract a "tip" from Mr. Rosedale; but at her side was a man in possession of that precious commodity, and who, as the husband of her dearest friend, stood to her in a relation of almost fraternal intimacy.

In her inmost heart Lily knew it was not by appealing to the fraternal instinct that she was likely to move Gus Trenor; but this way of explaining the situation helped to drape its crudity, and she was always scrupulous about keeping up appearances to herself. Her personal fastidiousness had a moral equivalent, and when she made a tour of inspection in her own mind there were certain closed doors she did not open.

As they reached the gates of Bellomont she turned to Trenor with a smile.

"The afternoon is so perfect—don't you want to drive me a little farther? I've been rather out of spirits all day, and it's so restful to be away from people, with some one who won't mind if I'm a little dull."

She looked so plaintively lovely as she proffered the request, so trustfully sure of his sympathy and understanding, that Trenor felt himself wishing that his wife could see how other women treated him—not battered wire-pullers like Mrs. Fisher, but a girl that most men would have given their boots to get such a look from.

"Out of spirits? Why on earth should you ever be out of spirits? Is your last box of Doucet dresses a failure, or did Judy rook you out of everything at bridge last night?"

Lily shook her head with a sigh. "I have had to give up Doucet; and bridge too—I can't afford it. In fact I can't afford any of the things my friends do, and I am afraid Judy often thinks me a bore because I don't play cards any longer, and because I am not as smartly dressed as the other women. But you will think me a bore too if I talk to you about my worries, and I only mention them because I want you to do me a favour—the very greatest of favours."

Her eyes sought his once more, and she smiled inwardly at the tinge of apprehension that she read in them.

"Why, of course—if it's anything I can manage———" He broke off, and she guessed that his enjoyment was disturbed by the remembrance of Mrs. Fisher's methods.

"The greatest of favours," she rejoined gently. "The fact is, Judy is angry with me, and I want you to make my peace."

"Angry with you? Oh, come, nonsense———" his relief broke through in a laugh. "Why, you know she's devoted to you."

"She is the best friend I have, and that is why I mind having to vex her. But I daresay you know what she has wanted me to do. She has set her heart—poor dear—on my marrying—marrying a great deal of money."

She paused with a slight falter of embarrassment, and Trenor, turning abruptly, fixed on her a look of growing intelligence.

"A great deal of money? Oh, by Jove—you don't mean Gryce? What—you do? Oh, no, of course I won't mention it—you can trust me to keep my mouth shut—but Gryce—good Lord, *Gryce!* Did Judy really think you could bring yourself to marry that portentous little ass? But you couldn't, eh? And so you gave him the sack, and that's the reason why he lit out by the first train this morning?" He leaned back, spreading himself farther across the seat, as if dilated by the joyful sense of his own discernment. "How on earth could Judy think you would do such a thing? *I* could have told her you'd never put up with such a little milksop!"

Lily sighed more deeply. "I sometimes think," she murmured, "that men understand a woman's motives better than other women do."

"Some men—I'm certain of it! I could have *told* Judy," he repeated, exulting in the implied superiority over his wife.

"I thought you would understand; that's why I wanted to speak to you," Miss Bart rejoined. "I *can't* make that kind of marriage; it's impossible. But neither can I go on living as all the women in my set do. I am almost entirely dependent on my aunt, and though she is very kind to me she makes me no regular allowance, and lately I've lost money at cards, and I don't dare tell her about it. I have paid my card debts, of course, but there is hardly anything left for my other expenses, and if I go on with my present life I shall be in horrible difficulties. I have a tiny income of my own, but I'm afraid it's badly invested, for it seems to bring in less every year, and I am so ignorant of money matters that I don't know if my aunt's agent, who looks after it, is a good adviser." She paused a moment, and added in a lighter tone: "I didn't mean to bore you with all this, but I want your help in making Judy understand that I can't, at present, go on living as one must live among you all. I am going away tomorrow to join my aunt at Richfield, and I shall stay there for the rest of the autumn, and dismiss my maid and learn how to mend my own clothes."

At this picture of loveliness in distress, the pathos of which was heightened by the light touch with which it was drawn, a murmur of indignant sympathy broke from Trenor. Twenty-four hours earlier, if his wife had consulted him on the subject of Miss Bart's future, he would have said that a girl with extravagant tastes and no money had better marry the first rich man she could get; but with the subject of discussion at his side, turning to him for sympathy, making him feel that he understood her better than her dearest friends, and confirming the assurance by the appeal of her exquisite nearness, he was ready to swear that such a marriage was a desecration, and that, as a man of honour, he was bound to do all he could to protect her from the results of her disinterestedness. This impulse was reinforced by the reflection that if she had married Gryce she would have been surrounded by flattery and approval, whereas, having refused to sacrifice herself to expediency, she was left to bear the whole cost of her resistance. Hang it, if he could find a way out of such difficulties for a professional sponge like Carry Fisher, who was simply a mental habit corresponding to the physical titillations of the cigarette or the cock-tail, he could surely do as much for a girl who appealed to his highest sympathies, and who brought her troubles to him with the trustfulness of a child.

Trenor and Miss Bart prolonged their drive till long after sunset; and before it was over he had tried, with some show of success, to prove to her that, if she would only trust him, he could make a handsome sum of money for her without endangering the small amount she possessed. She was too genuinely ignorant of the manipulations of the stock-market to understand his technical explanations, or even perhaps to perceive that certain points in them were slurred; the haziness enveloping the transaction served as a veil for her embarrassment, and through the general blur her hopes dilated like lamps in a fog. She understood only that her modest investments were to be mysteriously multiplied without risk to herself; and the assurance that this miracle would take place within a short time, that there would be no tedious interval for suspense and reaction, relieved her of her lingering scruples.

Again she felt the lightening of her load, and with it the release of repressed activities. Her immediate worries conjured, it was easy to resolve that she would never again find herself in such straits, and as the need of economy and self-denial receded from her foreground she felt herself ready to meet any other demand which life might make. Even the immediate one of letting Trenor, as they drove homeward, lean a little nearer and rest his hand reassuringly on hers, cost her only a momentary shiver of reluctance. It was part of the game to make him feel that her appeal had been an uncalculated impulse, provoked by the liking he inspired; and the renewed sense of power in handling men, while it consoled her wounded vanity, helped also to obscure the thought of the claim at which his manner hinted. He was a coarse dull man who, under all his show of authority, was a mere supernumerary in the costly show for which his money paid: surely, to a clever girl, it would be easy to hold him by his vanity, and so keep the obligation on his side.

§ 8

The first thousand dollar cheque which Lily received with a blotted scrawl from Gus Trenor strengthened her self-confidence in the exact degree to which it effaced her debts.

The transaction had justified itself by its results: she saw now how absurd it would have been to let any primitive scruple deprive her of this easy means of appeasing her creditors. Lily felt really virtuous as she dispensed the sum in sops to her tradesmen, and the fact that a fresh order accompanied each payment did not lessen her sense of disinterestedness. How many women, in her place, would have given the orders without making the payment!

She had found it reassuringly easy to keep Trenor in a good humour. To listen to his stories, to receive his confidences and laugh at his jokes, seemed for the moment all that was required of her, and the complacency with which her hostess regarded these attentions freed them of the least hint of ambiguity. Mrs. Trenor evidently assumed that Lily's growing intimacy with her husband was simply an indirect way of returning her own kindness.

"I'm so glad you and Gus have become such good friends," she said approvingly. "It's too delightful of you to be so nice to him, and put up with all his tiresome stories. I know what they are, because I had to listen to him when we were engaged—I'm sure he is telling the same ones still. And now I shan't always have to be asking Carry Fisher here to keep him in a good humour. She's a perfect vulture, you know; and she hasn't the least moral sense. She is always getting Gus to speculate for her, and I'm sure she never pays when she loses."

Miss Bart could shudder at this state of things without the embarrassment of a personal application. Her own position was surely quite different. There could be no question of her not paying when she lost, since Trenor had assured her that she was certain not to lose. In sending her the cheque he had explained that he had made five thousand for her out of Rosedale's "tip," and put four thousand back in the same venture, as there was the promise of another "big rise"; she understood therefore that he was now speculating with her own money, and that she consequently owed him no more than the gratitude which such a trifling service demanded. She vaguely supposed that, to raise the first sum, he had borrowed on her securities; but this was a point over which her curiosity did not linger. It was concentrated, for the moment, on the probable date of the next "big rise."

The news of this event was received by her some weeks later, on the occasion of Jack Stepney's marriage to Miss Van Osburgh. As a cousin of the bridegroom, Miss Bart had been asked to act as bridesmaid; but she had declined on the plea that, since she was much taller than the other attendant virgins, her presence might mar the symmetry of the group. The truth was, she had attended too many brides to the altar: when next seen there she meant to be the chief figure in the ceremony. She knew the pleasantries made at the expense of young girls who have been too long before the public, and she was resolved to avoid such assumptions of youthfulness as might lead people to think her older than she really was.

The Van Osburgh marriage was celebrated in the village church near the paternal estate on the Hudson. It was the "simple country wedding" to which guests are conveyed in special trains, and from which the hordes of the uninvited have to be fended off by the intervention of the police. While these sylvan rites were taking place, in a church packed with fashion and festooned with orchids, the representatives of the press were threading their way, note-book in hand, through the labyrinth of wedding presents, and the agent of a cinematograph syndicate was setting up his apparatus at the church door. It was the kind of scene in which Lily had often pictured herself as taking the principal part, and on this occasion the fact that she was once more merely a casual spectator, instead of the mystically veiled figure occupying the centre of attention, strengthened her resolve to assume the latter part before the year was over. The fact that her immediate anxieties were relieved did not blind her to a possibility of their recurrence; it merely gave her enough buoyancy to rise once more above her doubts and feel a renewed faith in her beauty, her power, and her general fitness to attract a brilliant destiny. It could not be that one conscious of such aptitudes for mastery and enjoyment was doomed to a perpetuity of failure; and her mistakes looked easily reparable in the light of her restored self-confidence.

A special appositeness was given to these reflections by the discovery, in a neighbouring pew, of the serious profile and neatly-trimmed beard of Mr. Percy Gryce. There was something almost bridal in his own aspect: his large white gardenia had a symbolic air that struck Lily as a good omen. After all, seen in an assemblage of his kind he was not ridiculous-looking: a friendly critic might have called his heaviness weighty, and he was at his best in the attitude of vacant passivity which brings out the oddities of the restless. She fancied he was the kind of man whose sentimental associations would be stirred by the conventional imagery of a wedding, and she pictured herself, in the seclusion of the Van Osburgh conservatories, playing skilfully upon sensibilities thus prepared for her touch. In fact, when she looked at the other women about her, and recalled the image she had brought away from her own glass, it did not seem as though any special skill would be needed to repair her blunder and bring him once more to her feet.

The sight of Selden's dark head, in a pew almost facing her, disturbed for a moment the balance of her complacency. The rise of her blood as their eyes met was succeeded by a contrary motion, a wave of resistance and withdrawal. She did not wish to see him again, not because she feared his influence, but because his presence always had the effect of cheapening her aspirations, of throwing her whole world out of focus. Besides, he was a living reminder of the worst mistake in her career, and the fact that he had been its cause did not soften her feelings toward him. She could still imagine an ideal state of existence in which, all else being superadded, intercourse with Selden might be the last touch of luxury; but in the world as it was, such a privilege was likely to cost more than it was worth.

"Lily, dear, I never saw you look so lovely! You look as if something delightful had just happened to you!"

The young lady who thus formulated her admiration of her brilliant friend did not, in her own person, suggest such happy possibilities. Miss Gertrude Farish, in fact, typified the mediocre and the ineffectual. If there were compensating qualities in her wide frank glance and the freshness of her smile, these were qualities which only the sympathetic observer would perceive before noticing that her eyes were of a workaday grey and her lips without haunting curves. Lily's own view of her wavered between pity for her limitations and impatience at her cheerful acceptance of them. To Miss Bart, as to her mother, acquiescence in dinginess was evidence of stupidity; and there were moments when, in the consciousness of her own power to look and to be so exactly what the occasion required, she almost felt that other girls were plain and inferior from choice. Certainly no one need have confessed such acquiescence in her lot as was revealed in the "useful" colour of Gerty Farish's gown and the subdued lines of her hat: it is almost as stupid to let your clothes betray that you know you are ugly as to have them proclaim that you think you are beautiful.

Of course, being fatally poor and dingy, it was wise of Gerty to have taken up philanthropy and symphony concerts; but there was something irritating in her assumption that existence yielded no higher pleasures, and that one might get as much interest and excitement out of life in a cramped flat as in the splendours of the Van Osburgh establishment. Today, however, her chirping enthusiasms did not irritate Lily. They seemed only to throw her own exceptionalness into becoming relief, and give a soaring vastness to her scheme of life.

"Do let us go and take a peep at the presents before every one else leaves the dining-room!" suggested Miss Farish, linking her arm in her friend's. It was characteristic of her to take a sentimental and unenvious interest in all the details of a wedding: she was the kind of person who always kept her handkerchief out during the service, and departed clutching a box of wedding-cake.

"Isn't everything beautifully done?" she pursued, as they entered the distant drawing-room assigned to the display of Miss Van Osburgh's bridal spoils. "I always say no one does things better than cousin Grace! Did you ever taste anything more delicious than that *mousse* of lobster with champagne sauce? I made up my mind weeks ago that I wouldn't miss this wedding, and just fancy how delightfully it all came about. When Lawrence Selden heard I was coming, he insisted on fetching me himself and driving me to the station, and when we go back this evening I am to dine with him at Sherry's. I really feel as excited as if I were getting married myself!"

Lily smiled: she knew that Selden had always been kind to his dull cousin, and she had sometimes wondered why he wasted so much time in such an unremunerative manner; but now the thought gave her a vague pleasure.

"Do you see him often?" she asked.

"Yes; he is very good about dropping in on Sundays. And now and then we do a play together; but lately I haven't seen much of him. He doesn't look well, and he seems nervous and unsettled. The dear fellow! I do wish he would marry some nice girl. I told him so today, but he said he didn't care for the really nice ones, and the other kind didn't care for him—but that was just his joke, of course. He could never marry a girl who *wasn't* nice. Oh, my dear, did you ever see such pearls?"

They had paused before the table on which the bride's jewels were displayed, and Lily's heart gave an envious throb as she caught the refraction of light from their surfaces—the milky gleam of perfectly matched pearls, the flash of rubies relieved against contrasting velvet, the intense blue rays of sapphires kindled into light by surrounding diamonds: all these precious tints enhanced and deepened by the varied art of their setting. The glow of the stones warmed Lily's veins like wine. More completely than any other expression of wealth they symbolized the life she longed to lead, the life of fastidious aloofness and refinement in which every detail should have the finish of a jewel, and the whole form a harmonious setting to her own jewel-like rareness.

"Oh, Lily, do look at this diamond pendant—it's as big as a dinner-plate! Who can have given it?" Miss Farish bent short-sightedly over the accompanying card. *"Mr. Simon Rosedale.* What, that horrid man? Oh, yes—I remember he's a friend of Jack's, and I suppose Cousin Grace had to ask him here today; but she must rather hate having to let Gwen accept such a present from him."

Lily smiled. She doubted Mrs. Van Osburgh's reluctance, but was aware of Miss Farish's habit of ascribing her own delicacies of feeling to the persons least likely to be encumbered by them.

"Well, if Gwen doesn't care to be seen wearing it she can always exchange it for something else," she remarked.

"Ah, here is something so much prettier," Miss Farish continued. "Do look at this exquisite white sapphire. I'm sure the person who chose it must have taken particular pains. What is the name? Percy Gryce? Ah, then I'm not surprised!" She smiled significantly as she replaced the card. "Of course you've heard that he's perfectly devoted to Evie Van Osburgh? Cousin Grace is so pleased about it—it's quite a romance! He met her first at the George Dorsets', only about six weeks ago, and it's just the nicest possible marriage for dear Evie. Oh, I don't mean the money—of course she has plenty of her own—but she's such a quiet stay-at-home kind of girl, and it seems he has just the same tastes; so they are exactly suited to each other."

Lily stood staring vacantly at the white sapphire on its velvet bed. Evie Van Osburgh and Percy Gryce? The names rang derisively through her brain. *Evie Van Osburgh?* The youngest, dumpiest, dullest of the four dull and dumpy daughters whom Mrs. Van Osburgh, with unsurpassed astuteness, had "placed" one by one in enviable niches of existence. Ah, lucky girls who grow up in the shelter of a mother's love—a mother who knows how to contrive opportunities without conceding favours, how to take advantage of propinquity without allowing appetite to be dulled by habit! The cleverest girl may miscalculate where her own interests are concerned, may yield too much at one moment and withdraw too far at the next: it takes a mother's unerring vigilance and foresight to land her daughters safely in the arms of wealth and suitability.

Lily's passing light-heartedness sank beneath a renewed sense of failure. Life was too stupid, too blundering! Why should Percy Gryce's millions be joined to another great fortune, why should this clumsy girl be put in possession of powers she would never know how to use?

She was roused from these speculations by a familiar touch on her arm, and turning saw Gus Trenor beside her. She felt a thrill of vexation: what right had he to touch her? Luckily Gerty Farish had wandered off to the next table, and they were alone.

Trenor, looking stouter than ever in his tight frock-coat, and unbecomingly flushed by the bridal libations, gazed at her with undisguised approval.

"By Jove, Lily, you do look a stunner!" He had slipped insensibly into the use of her Christian name, and she had never found the right moment to correct him. Besides, in her set all the men and women called each other by their Christian names; it was only on Trenor's lips that the familiar address had an unpleasant significance.

"Well," he continued, still jovially impervious to her annoyance, "have you made up your mind which of these little trinkets you mean to duplicate at Tiffany's tomorrow? I've got a cheque for you in my pocket that will go a long way in that line!"

Lily gave him a startled look: his voice was louder than usual, and the room was beginning to fill with people. But as her glance assured her that they were still beyond ear-shot a sense of pleasure replaced her apprehension.

"Another dividend?" she asked, smiling and drawing near him in the desire not be be overheard.

"Well, not exactly: I sold out on the rise and I've pulled off four thou' for you. Not so bad for a beginner, eh? I suppose you'll begin to think you're a pretty knowing speculator. And perhaps you won't think poor old Gus such an awful ass as some people do."

"I think you the kindest of friends; but I can't thank you properly now."

She let her eyes shine into his with a look that made up for the hand-clasp he would have claimed if they had been alone—and how glad she was that they were not! The news filled her with the glow produced by a sudden cessation of physical pain. The world was not so stupid and blundering after all: now and then a stroke of luck came to the unluckiest. At the thought her spirits began to rise: it was characteristic of her that one trifling piece of good fortune should give wings to all her hopes. Instantly came the reflection that Percy Gryce was not irretrievably lost; and she smiled to think of the excitement of recapturing him from Evie Van Osburgh. What chance could such a simpleton have against her if she chose to exert herself? She glanced about hoping to catch a glimpse of Gryce; but her eyes lit instead on the glossy countenance of Mr. Rosedale, who was slipping through the crowd with an air half obsequious, half obtrusive, as though, the moment his presence was recognized, it would swell to the dimensions of the room.

Not wishing to be the means of effecting this enlargement, Lily quickly transferred her glance to Trenor, to whom the expression of her gratitude seemed not to have brought the complete gratification she had meant it to give.

"Hang thanking me—I don't want to be thanked, but I *should* like the chance to say two words to you now and then," he grumbled. "I thought you were going to spend the whole autumn with us, and I've hardly laid eyes on you for the last month. Why can't you come back to Bellomont this evening? We're all alone, and Judy is as cross as two sticks. Do come and cheer a fellow up. If you say yes I'll run you over in the motor, and you can telephone your maid to bring your traps from town by the next train."

Lily shook her head with a charming semblance of regret. "I wish I could—but it's quite impossible. My aunt has come back to town, and I must be with her for the next few days."

"Well, I've seen a good deal less of you since we've got to be such pals than I used to when you were Judy's friend," he continued with unconscious penetration.

"When I was Judy's friend? Am I not her friend still? Really, you say the most absurd things! If I were always at Bellomont you would tire of me much sooner than Judy—but come and see me at my aunt's the next afternoon you are in town; then we can have a nice quiet talk, and you can tell me how I had better invest my fortune."

It was true that, during the last three or four weeks, she had absented herself from Bellomont on the pretext of having other visits to pay; but she now began to feel that the reckoning she had thus contrived to evade had rolled up interest in the interval.

The prospect of the nice quiet talk did not appear as all-sufficing to Trenor as she had hoped, and his brows continued to lower as he said: "Oh, I don't know that I can promise you a fresh tip every day. But there's one thing you might do for me; and that is, just to be a little civil to Rosedale. Judy has promised to ask him to dine when we get to town, but I can't induce her to have him at Bellomont, and if you would let me bring him up now it would make a lot of difference. I don't believe two women have spoken to him this afternoon, and I can tell you he's a chap it pays to be decent to."

Miss Bart made an impatient movement, but suppressed the words which seemed about to accompany it. After all, this was an unexpectedly easy way of acquitting her debt; and had she not reasons of her own for wishing to be civil to Mr. Rosedale?

"Oh, bring him by all means," she said smiling; "perhaps I can get a tip out of him on my own account."

Trenor paused abruptly, and his eyes fixed themselves on hers with a look which made her change colour.

"I say, you know—you'll please remember he's a blooming bounder," he said; and with a slight laugh she turned toward the open window near which they had been standing.

The throng in the room had increased, and she felt a desire for space and fresh air. Both of these she found on the terrace, where only a few men were lingering over cigarettes and liqueur, while scattered couples strolled across the lawn to the autumn-tinted borders of the flower-garden.

As she emerged, a man moved toward her from the knot of smokers, and she found herself face to face with Selden. The stir of the pulses which his nearness always caused was increased by a slight sense of constraint. They had not met since their Sunday afternoon walk at Bellomont, and that episode was still so vivid to her that she could hardly believe him to be less conscious of it. But his greeting expressed no more than the satisfaction which every pretty woman expects to see reflected in masculine eyes; and the discovery, if distasteful to her vanity, was reassuring to her nerves. Between the relief of her escape from Trenor, and the vague apprehension of her meeting with Rosedale, it was pleasant to rest a moment on the sense of complete understanding which Lawrence Selden's manner always conveyed.

"This is luck," he said smiling. "I was wondering if I should be able to have a word with you before the special snatches us away. I came with Gerty Farish, and promised not to let her miss the train, but I am sure she is still extracting sentimental solace from the wedding presents. She appears to regard their number and value as evidence of the disinterested affection of the contracting parties."

There was not the least trace of embarrassment in his voice, and as he spoke, leaning slightly against the jamb of the window, and letting his eyes rest on her in the frank enjoyment of her grace, she felt with a faint chill of regret that he had gone back without an effort to the footing on which they had stood before their last talk together. Her vanity was stung by the sight of his unscathed smile. She longed to be to him something more than a piece of sentient prettiness, a passing diversion to his eye and brain; and the longing betrayed itself in her reply.

"Ah," she said, "I envy Gerty that power she has of dressing up with romance all our ugly and prosaic arrangements! I have never recovered my self-respect since you showed me how poor and unimportant my ambitions were."

The words were hardly spoken when she realizd their infelicity. It seemed to her her fate to appear at her worst to Selden.

"I thought, on the contrary," he returned lightly, "that I had been the means of proving they were more important to you than anything else."

It was as if the eager current of her being had been checked by a sudden obstacle which drove it back upon itself. She looked at him helplessly, like a hurt or frightened child: this real self of hers, which he had the faculty of drawing out of the depths, was so little accustomed to go alone!

The appeal of her helplessness touched in him, as it always did, a latent chord of inclination. It would have meant nothing to him to discover that his nearness made her more brilliant, but this glimpse of a twilight mood to which he alone had the clue seemed once more to set him in a world apart with her.

"At least you can't think worse things of me than you say!" she exclaimed with a trembling laugh; but before he could answer, the flow of comprehension between them was abruptly stayed by the reappearance of Gus Trenor, who advanced with Mr. Rosedale in his wake.

"Hang it, Lily, I thought you'd given me the slip: Rosedale and I have been hunting all over for you!"

His voice had a note of conjugal familiarity: Miss Bart fancied she detected in Rosedale's eye a twinkling perception of the fact, and the idea turned her dislike of him to repugnance.

She returned his profound bow with a slight nod, made more disdainful by the sense of Selden's surprise that she should number Rosedale among her acquaintances. Trenor had turned away, and his companion continued to stand before Miss Bart, alert and expectant, his lips parted in a smile at whatever she might be about to say, and his very back conscious of the privilege of being seen with her.

It was the moment for tact; for the quick bridging over of gaps; but Selden still leaned against the window, a detached observer of the scene, and under the spell of his observation Lily felt herself powerless to exert her usual arts. The dread of Selden's suspecting that there was any need for her to propitiate such a man as Rosedale checked the trivial phrases of politeness. Rosedale still stood before her in an expectant attitude, and she continued to face him in silence, her glance just level with his polished baldness. The look put the finishing touch to what her silence implied.

He reddened slowly, shifting from one foot to the other, fingered the plump black pearl in his tie, and gave a nervous twist to his moustache; then, running his eye over her, he drew back, and said, with a side-glance at Selden: "Upon my soul, I never saw a more ripping get-up. Is that the last creation of the dress-maker you go to see at the Benedick? If so, I wonder all the other women don't go to her too!"

The words were projected sharply against Lily's silence, and she saw in a flash that her own act had given them their emphasis. In ordinary talk they might have passed unheeded; but following on her prolonged pause they acquired a special meaning. She felt, without looking, that Selden had immediately seized it, and would inevitably connect the allusion with her visit to himself. The consciousness increased her irritation against Rosedale, but also her feeling that now, if ever, was the moment to propitiate him, hateful as it was to do so in Selden's presence.

"How do you know the other women don't go to my dressmaker?" she returned. "You see I'm not afraid to give her address to my friends!"

Her glance and accent so plainly included Rosedale in this privileged circle that his small eyes puckered with gratification, and a knowing smile drew up his moustache.

"By Jove, you needn't be!" he declared. "You could give 'em the whole outfit and win at a canter!"

"Ah, that's nice of you; and it would be nicer still if you would carry me off to a quiet corner, and get me a glass of lemonade or some innocent drink before we all have to rush for the train."

She turned away as she spoke, letting him strut at her side through the gathering groups on the terrace, while every nerve in her throbbed with the consciousness of what Selden must have thought of the scene.

But under her angry sense of the perverseness of things, and the light surface of her talk with Rosedale, a third idea persisted: she did not mean to leave without an attempt to discover the truth about Percy Gryce. Chance, or perhaps his own resolve, had kept them apart since his hasty withdrawal from Bellomont; but Miss Bart was an expert in making the most of the unexpected, and the distasteful incidents of the last few minutes—the revelation to Selden of precisely that part of her life which she most wished to ignore—increased her longing for shelter, for escape from such humiliating contingencies. Any definite situation would be more tolerable than this buffeting of chances, which kept her in an attitude of uneasy alertness toward every possibility of life.

Indoors there was a general sense of dispersal in the air, as of an audience gathering itself up for departure after the principal actors had left the stage; but among the remaining groups, Lily could discover neither Gryce nor the youngest Miss Van Osburgh. That both should be missing struck her with foreboding; and she charmed Mr. Rosedale by proposing that they should make their way to the conservatories at the farther end of the house. There were just enough people left in the long suite of rooms to make their progress conspicuous, and Lily was aware of being followed by looks of amusement and interrogation, which glanced off as harmlessly from her indifference as from her companion's self-satisfaction. She cared very little at that moment about being seen with Rosedale: all her thoughts were centred on the object of her search. The latter, however, was not discoverable in the conservatories, and Lily, oppressed by a sudden conviction of failure, was casting about for a way to rid herself of her now superfluous companion, when they came upon Mrs. Van Osburgh, flushed and exhausted, but beaming with the consciousness of duty performed.

She glanced at them a moment with the benign but vacant eye of the tired hostess, to whom her guests have become mere whirling spots in a kaleidoscope of fatigue; then her attention became suddenly fixed, and she seized on Miss Bart with a confidential gesture.

"My dear Lily, I haven't had time for a word with you, and now

I suppose you are just off. Have you seen Evie? She's been looking everywhere for you: she wanted to tell you her little secret; but I daresay you have guessed it already. The engagement is not to be announced till next week—but you are such a friend of Mr. Gryce's that they both wished you to be the first to know of their happiness."

§ 9

In Mrs. Peniston's youth, fashion had returned to town in October; therefore on the tenth day of the month the blinds of her Fifth Avenue residence were drawn up, and the eyes of the Dying Gladiator in bronze who occupied the drawing-room window resumed their survey of that deserted thoroughfare.

The first two weeks after her return represented to Mrs. Peniston the domestic equivalent of a religious retreat. She "went through" the linen and blankets in the precise spirit of the penitent exploring the inner folds of conscience; she sought for moths as the stricken soul seeks for lurking infirmities. The topmost shelf of every closet was made to yield up its secret, cellar and coalbin were probed to their darkest depths and, as a final stage in the lustral rites, the entire house was swathed in penitential white and deluged with expiatory soapsuds.

It was on this phase of the proceedings that Miss Bart entered on the afternoon of her return from the Van Osburgh wedding. The journey back to town had not been calculated to soothe her nerves. Though Evie Van Osburgh's engagement was still officially a secret, it was one of which the innumerable intimate friends of the family were already possessed; and the trainful of returning guests buzzed with allusions and anticipations. Lily was acutely aware of her own part in this drama of innuendo: she knew the exact quality of the amusement the situation evoked. The crude forms in which her friends took their pleasure included a loud enjoyment of such complications: the zest of surprising destiny in the act of playing a practical joke. Lily knew well enough how to bear herself in difficult situations. She had, to a shade, the exact manner between victory and defeat: every insinuation was shed without an effort by the bright indifference of her manner. But she was beginning to feel the strain of the attitude; the reaction was more rapid, and she lapsed to a deeper self-disgust.

As was always the case with her, this moral repulsion found a physical outlet in a quickened distaste for her surroundings. She revolted from the complacent ugliness of Mrs. Peniston's black walnut, from the slippery gloss of the vestibule tiles, and the mingled odour of sapolio and furniture-polish that met her at the door.

The stairs were still carpetless, and on the way up to her room she was arrested on the landing by an encroaching tide of soapsuds. Gathering up her skirts, she drew aside with an impatient gesture; and as she did so she had the odd sensation of having already found herself in the same situation but in different surroundings. It seemed to her that she was again descending the staircase from Selden's rooms; and looking down to remonstrate with the dispenser of the soapy flood, she found herself met by a lifted stare which had once before confronted her under similar circumstances. It was the char-woman of the Benedick who, resting on crimson elbows, examined her with the same unflinching curiosity, the same apparent reluctance to let her pass. On this occasion, however, Miss Bart was on her own ground.

"Don't you see that I wish to go by? Please move your pail," she said sharply.

The woman at first seemed not to hear; then, without a word of excuse, she pushed back her pail and dragged a wet floor-cloth across the landing, keeping her eyes fixed on Lily while the latter swept by. It was insufferable that Mrs. Peniston should have such creatures about the house; and Lily entered her room resolved that the woman should be dismissed that evening.

Mrs. Peniston, however, was at the moment inaccessible to remonstrance: since early morning she had been shut up with her maid, going over her furs, a process which formed the culminating episode in the drama of household renovation. In the evening also Lily found herself alone, for her aunt, who rarely dined out, had responded to the summons of a Van Alstyne cousin who was passing through town. The house, in its state of unnatural immaculateness and order, was a dreary as a tomb, and as Lily, turning from her brief repast between shrouded sideboards, wandered into the newly-uncovered glare of the drawing-room she felt as though she were buried alive in the stifling limits of Mrs. Peniston's existence.

She usually contrived to avoid being at home during the season of domestic renewal. On the present occasion, however, a variety of reasons had combined to bring her to town; and foremost among them was the fact that she had fewer invitations than usual for the autumn. She had so long been accustomed to pass from one country-house to another, till the close of the holidays brought her friends to town, that the unfilled gaps of time confronting her produced a sharp sense of waning popularity. It was as she had said to Selden—people were tired of her. They would welcome her in a new character, but as Miss Bart they knew her by heart. She knew herself by heart too, and was sick of the old story. There were moments when she longed blindly for anything different, anything strange, remote and untried; but the utmost reach of her imagination did not go beyond picturing her usual life in a new setting. She could not figure herself as anywhere but in a drawing-room, diffusing elegance as a flower sheds perfume.

Meanwhile, as October advanced she had to face the alternative of returning to the Trenors or joining her aunt in town. Even the desolating dulness of New York in October, and the soapy discomforts of Mrs. Peniston's interior, seemed preferable to what might await her at Bellomont; and with an air of heroic devotion she announced her intention of remaining with her aunt till the holidays.

Sacrifices of this nature are sometimes received with feelings as mixed as those which actuate them; and Mrs. Peniston remarked to her confidential maid that, if any of the family were to be with her at such a crisis (though for forty years she had been thought competent to see to the hanging of her own curtains), she would certainly have preferred Miss Grace to Miss Lily. Grace Stepney was an obscure cousin, of adaptable manners and vicarious interests, who "ran in" to sit with Mrs. Peniston when Lily dined out too continuously; who played bézique, picked up dropped stitches, read out the deaths from the *Times,* and sincerely admired the purple satin drawing-room curtains, the Dying Gladiator in the window, and the seven-by-five painting of Niagara which represented the one artistic excess of Mr. Peniston's temperate career.

Mrs. Peniston, under ordinary circumstances, was as much bored by her excellent cousin as the recipient of such services usually is by the person who performs them. She greatly preferred the brilliant and unreliable Lily, who did not know one end of a crochet-needle from the other, and had frequently wounded her susceptibilities by suggesting that the drawing-room should be "done over." But when it came to hunting for missing napkins, or helping to decide whether the backstairs needed recarpeting, Grace's judgment was certainly sounder than Lily's: not to mention the fact that the latter resented the smell of beeswax and brown soap, and behaved as though she thought a house ought to keep clean of itself, without extraneous assistance.

Seated under the cheerless blaze of the drawing-room chandelier —Mrs. Peniston never lit the lamps unless there was "company"— Lily seemed to watch her own figure retreating down vistas of neutral-tinted dulness to a middle age like Grace Stepney's. When she ceased to amuse Judy Trenor and her friends she would have to fall back on amusing Mrs. Peniston; whichever way she looked she saw only a future of servitude to the whims of others, never the possibility of asserting her own eager individuality.

A ring at the door-bell, sounding emphatically through the empty house, roused her suddenly to the extent of her boredom. It was as though all the weariness of the past months had culminated in the vacuity of that interminable evening. If only the ring meant a summons from the outer world—a token that she was still remembered and wanted!

After some delay a parlour-maid presented herself with the announcement that there was a person outside who was asking to see Miss Bart; and on Lily's pressing for a more specific description, she added:

"It's Mrs. Haffen, Miss; she won't say what she wants."

Lily, to whom the name conveyed nothing, opened the door upon a woman in a battered bonnet, who stood firmly planted under the hall-light. The glare of the unshaded gas shone familiarly on her pock-marked face and the reddish baldness visible through thin strands of straw-coloured hair. Lily looked at the char-woman in surprise.

"Do you wish to see me?" she asked.

"I should like to say a word to you, Miss." The tone was neither aggressive nor conciliatory: it revealed nothing of the speaker's errand. Nevertheless, some precautionary instinct warned Lily to withdraw beyond earshot of the hovering parlour-maid.

She signed to Mrs. Haffen to follow her into the drawing-room, and closed the door when they had entered.

"What is it that you wish?" she enquired.

The char-woman, after the manner of her kind, stood with her arms folded in her shawl. Unwinding the latter, she produced a small parcel wrapped in dirty newspaper.

"I have something here that you might like to see, Miss Bart." She spoke the name with an unpleasant emphasis, as though her knowing it made a part of her reason for being there. To Lily the intonation sounded like a threat.

"You have found something belonging to me?" she asked, extending her hand.

Mrs. Haffen drew back. "Well, if it comes to that, I guess it's mine as much as anybody's," she returned.

Lily looked at her perplexedly. She was sure, now, that her visitor's manner conveyed a threat; but, expert as she was in certain directions, there was nothing in her experience to prepare her for the exact significance of the present scene. She felt, however, that it must be ended as promptly as possible.

"I don't understand; if this parcel is not mine, why have you asked for me?"

The woman was unabashed by the question. She was evidently prepared to answer it, but like all her class she had to go a long way back to make a beginning, and it was only after a pause that she replied: "My husband was janitor to the Benedick till the first of the month; since then he can't get nothing to do."

Lily remained silent and she continued: "It wasn't no fault of our own, neither: the agent had another man he wanted the place for, and we was put out, bag and baggage, just to suit his fancy. I had a long sickness last winter, and an operation that ate up all we'd put by; and it's hard for me and the children, Haffen being so long out of a job."

After all, then, she had come only to ask Miss Bart to find a place for her husband; or, more probably, to seek the young lady's intervention with Mrs. Peniston. Lily had such an air of always getting what she wanted that she was used to being appealed to as an intermediary, and, relieved of her vague apprehension, she took refuge in the conventional formula.

"I am sorry you have been in trouble," she said.

"Oh, that we have, Miss, and it's on'y just beginning. If on'y we'd 'a got another situation—but the agent, he's dead against us. It ain't no fault of ours, neither, but——"

At this point Lily's impatience overcame her. "If you have anything to say to me——" she interposed.

The woman's resentment of the rebuff seemed to spur her lagging ideas.

"Yes, Miss; I'm coming to that," she said. She paused again, with her eyes on Lily, and then continued, in a tone of diffuse narrative: "When we was at the Benedick I had charge of some of the gentlemen's rooms; leastways, I swep' 'em out on Saturdays. Some of the gentlemen got the greatest sight of letters: I never saw the like of it. Their waste-paper baskets 'd be fairly brimming, and papers falling over on the floor. Maybe havin' so many is how they get so careless. Some of 'em is worse than others. Mr. Selden, Mr. Lawrence Selden, he was always one of the carefullest: burnt his letters in winter, and tore 'em in little bits in summer. But sometimes he'd have so many he'd just bunch 'em together, the way the others did, and tear the lot through once—like this."

While she spoke she had loosened the string from the parcel in her hand, and now she drew forth a letter which she laid on the table between Miss Bart and herself. As she had said, the letter was torn in two; but with a rapid gesture she laid the torn edges together and smoothed out the page.

A wave of indignation swept over Lily. She felt herself in the presence of something vile, as yet but dimly conjectured—the kind of vileness of which people whispered, but which she had never thought of as touching her own life. She drew back with a motion of disgust, but her withdrawal was checked by a sudden discovery: under the glare of Mrs. Peniston's chandelier she had recognized the hand-writing of the letter. It was a large disjointed hand, with a flourish of masculinity which but slightly disguised its rambling weakness, and the words, scrawled in heavy ink on pale-tinted note-paper, smote on Lily's ear as though she had heard them spoken.

At first she did not grasp the full import of the situation. She understood only that before her lay a letter written by Bertha Dorset, and addressed, presumably, to Lawrence Selden. There was no date, but the blackness of the ink proved the writing to be comparatively recent. The packet in Mrs. Haffen's hand doubtless contained more letters of the same kind—a dozen, Lily conjectured from its thickness. The letter before her was short, but its few words, which had leapt into her brain before she was conscious of reading them, told a long history—a history over which, for the last four years, the friends of the writer had smiled and shrugged, viewing it merely as one among the countless "good situations" of the mundane comedy. Now the other side presented itself to Lily, the volcanic nether side of the surface over which conjecture and innuendo glide so lightly till the first fissure turns their whisper to a shriek. Lily knew that there is nothing society resents so much as having given its protection to those who have not known how to profit by it: it is for having betrayed its connivance that the body social punishes the offender who is found out. And in this case there was no doubt of the issue. The code of Lily's world decreed that a woman's husband should be the only judge of her conduct: she was technically above suspicion while she had the shelter of his approval, or even of his indifference. But with a man of George Dorset's temper there could be no thought of condonation—the possessor of his wife's letters could overthrow with a touch the whole structure of her existence. And into what hands Bertha Dorset's secret had been delivered! For a moment the irony of the coincidence tinged Lily's disgust with a confused sense of triumph. But the disgust prevailed—all her instinctive resistances, of taste, of training, of blind inherited scruples, rose against the other feeling. Her strongest sense was one of personal contamination.

She moved away, as though to put as much distance as possible between herself and her visitor. "I know nothing of these letters," she said; "I have no idea why you have brought them here."

Mrs. Haffen faced her steadily. "I'll tell you why, Miss. I brought 'em to you to sell, because I ain't got no other way of raising money, and if we don't pay our rent by tomorrow night we'll be put out. I never done anythin' of the kind before, and if you'd speak to Mr. Selden or to Mr. Rosedale about getting Haffen taken on again at the Benedick—I seen you talking to Mr. Rosedale on the steps that day you come out of Mr. Selden's rooms——"

The blood rushed to Lily's forehead. She understood now—Mrs. Haffen supposed her to be the writer of the letters. In the first leap of her anger she was about to ring and order the woman out; but an obscure impulse restrained her. The mention of Selden's name had started a new train of thought. Bertha Dorset's letters were nothing to her—they might go where the current of chance carried them! But Selden was inextricably involved in their fate. Men do not, at worst, suffer much from such exposure; and in this instance the flash of divination which had carried the meaning of the letters to Lily's brain had revealed also that they were appeals—repeated and therefore probably unanswered—for the renewal of a tie which time had evidently relaxed. Nevertheless, the fact that the correspondence had been allowed to fall into strange hands would convict Selden of negligence in a matter where the world holds it least pardonable; and there were graver risks to consider where a man of Dorset's ticklish balance was concerned.

If she weighed all these things it was unconsciously: she was aware only of feeling that Selden would wish the letters rescued, and that therefore she must obtain possession of them. Beyond that her mind did not travel. She had, indeed, a quick vision of returning the packet to Bertha Dorset, and of the opportunities the restitution offered; but this thought lit up abysses from which she shrank back ashamed.

Meanwhile Mrs. Haffen, prompt to perceive her hesitation, had already opened the packet and ranged its contents on the table. All the letters had been pieced together with strips of thin paper. Some were in small fragments, the others merely torn in half. Though there were not many, thus spread out they nearly covered the table. Lily's glance fell on a word here and there—then she said in a low voice: "What do you wish me to pay you?"

Mrs. Haffen's face reddened with satisfaction. It was clear that the young lady was badly frightened, and Mrs. Haffen was the woman to make the most of such fears. Anticipating an easier victory than she had foreseen, she named an exorbitant sum.

But Miss Bart showed herself a less ready prey than might have been expected from her imprudent opening. She refused to pay the price named, and after a moment's hesitation, met it by a counter-offer of half the amount.

Mrs. Haffen immediately stiffened. Her hand travelled toward the outspread letters, and folding them slowly, she made as though to restore them to their wrapping.

"I guess they're worth more to you than to me, Miss, but the poor has got to live as well as the rich," she observed sententiously.

Lily was throbbing with fear, but the insinuation fortified her resistance.

"You are mistaken," she said indifferently. "I have offered all I am willing to give for the letters; but there may be other ways of getting them."

Mrs. Haffen raised a suspicious glance: she was too experienced not to know that the traffic she was engaged in had perils as great as its rewards, and she had a vision of the elaborate machinery of revenge which a word of this commanding young lady's might set in motion.

She applied the corner of her shawl to her eyes, and murmured through it that no good came of bearing too hard on the poor, but that for her part she had never been mixed up in such a business before, and that on her honour as a Christian all she and Haffen had thought of was that the letters mustn't go any farther.

Lily stood motionless, keeping between herself and the char-woman the greatest distance compatible with the need of speaking in low tones. The idea of bargaining for the letters was intolerable to her, but she knew that, if she appeared to weaken, Mrs. Haffen would at once increase her original demand.

She could never afterward recall how long the duel lasted, or what was the decisive stroke which finally, after a lapse of time recorded in minutes by the clock, in hours by the precipitate beat of her pulses, put her in possession of the letters; she knew only that the door had finally closed, and that she stood alone with the packet in her hand.

She had no idea of reading the letters; even to unfold Mrs. Haffen's dirty newspaper would have seemed degrading. But what did she intend to do with its contents? The recipient of the letters had meant to destroy them, and it was her duty to carry out his intention. She had no right to keep them—to do so was to lessen whatever merit lay in having secured their possession. But how destroy them so effectually that there should be no second risk of their falling in such hands? Mrs. Peniston's icy drawing-room grate shone with a forbidding lustre: the fire, like the lamps, was never lit except when there was company.

Miss Bart was turning to carry the letters upstairs when she heard the opening of the outer door, and her aunt entered the drawing-room. Mrs. Peniston was a small plump woman, with a colourless skin lined with trivial wrinkles. Her grey hair was arranged with precision, and her clothes looked excessively new and yet slightly old-fashioned. They were always black and tightly fitting, with an expensive glitter: she was the kind of woman who wore jet at breakfast. Lily had never seen her when she was not cuirassed in shining black, with small tight boots, and an air of being packed and ready to start; yet she never started.

She looked about the drawing-room with an expression of minute scrutiny. "I saw a streak of light under one of the blinds as I drove up: it's extraordinary that I can never teach that woman to draw them down evenly."

Having corrected the irregularity, she seated herself on one of the glossy purple arm-chairs; Mrs. Peniston always sat on a chair, never in it. Then she turned her glance to Miss Bart.

"My dear, you look tired; I suppose it's the excitement of the wedding. Cornelia Van Alstyne was full of it: Molly was there, and Gerty Farish ran in for a minute to tell us about it. I think it was odd, their serving melons before the *consommé:* a wedding breakfast should always begin with *consommé.* Molly didn't care for the bridesmaids' dresses. She had it straight from Julia Melson that they cost three hundred dollars apiece at Céleste's, but she says they didn't look it. I'm glad you decided not to be a bridesmaid; that shade of salmon-pink wouldn't have suited you."

Mrs. Peniston delighted in discussing the minutest details of festivities in which she had not taken part. Nothing would have induced her to undergo the exertion and fatigue of attending the Van Osburgh wedding, but so great was her interest in the event that, having heard two versions of it, she now prepared to extract a third from her niece. Lily, however, had been deplorably careless in noting the particulars of the entertainment. She had failed to observe the colour of Mrs. Van Osburgh's gown, and could not even say whether the old Van Osburgh Sèvres had been used at the bride's table: Mrs. Peniston, in short, found that she was of more service as a listener than as a narrator.

"Really, Lily, I don't see why you took the trouble to go to the wedding, if you don't remember what happened or whom you saw there. When I was a girl I used to keep the *menu* of every dinner I went to, and write the names of the people on the back; and I never threw away my cotillion favours till after your uncle's death, when it seemed unsuitable to have so many coloured things about the house. I had a whole closet-full, I remember; and I can tell to this day what balls I got them at. Molly Van Alstyne reminds me of what I was at that age; it 's wonderful how she notices. She was able to tell her mother exactly how the wedding-dress was cut, and we knew at once, from the fold in the back, that it must have come from Paquin."

Mrs. Peniston rose abruptly, and, advancing to the ormulu clock surmounted by a helmeted Minerva, which throned on the chimney-piece between two malachite vases, passed her lace handkerchief between the helmet and its visor.

"I knew it—the parlour-maid never dusts there!" she exclaimed, triumphantly displaying a minute spot on the handkerchief; then, reseating herself, she went on: "Molly thought Mrs. Dorset the best-dressed woman at the wedding. I've no doubt her dress *did* cost more than any one else's, but I can't quite like the idea—a combination of sable and *point de Milan*. It seems she goes to a new man in Paris, who won't take an order till his client has spent a day with him at his villa at Neuilly. He says he must study his subject's home life—a most peculiar arrangement, I should say! But Mrs. Dorset told Molly about it herself: she said the villa was full of the most exquisite things and she was really sorry to leave. Molly said she never saw her looking better; she was in tremendous spirits, and said she had made a match between Evie Van Osburgh and Percy Gryce. She really seems to have a very good influence on young men. I hear she is interesting herself now in that silly Silverton boy, who has had his head turned by Carry Fisher, and has been gambling so dreadfully. Well, as I was saying, Evie is really engaged: Mrs. Dorset had her to stay with Percy Gryce, and managed it all, and Grace Van Osburgh is in the seventh heaven—she had almost despaired of marrying Evie."

Mrs. Peniston again paused, but this time her scrutiny addressed itself, not to the furniture, but to her niece.

"Cornelia Van Alystyne was so surprised: she had heard that you were to marry young Gryce. She saw the Wetheralls just after they had stopped with you at Bellomont, and Alice Wetherall was quite sure there was an engagement. She said that when Mr. Gryce left unexpectedly one morning, they all thought he had rushed to town for the ring."

Lily rose and moved toward the door.

"I believe I *am* tired: I think I will go to bed," she said; and Mrs. Peniston, suddenly distracted by the discovery that the easel sustaining the late Mr. Peniston's crayon-portrait was not exactly in line with the sofa in front of it, presented an absent-minded brow to her kiss.

In her own room Lily turned up the gas-jet and glanced toward the grate. It was as brilliantly polished as the one below, but here at least she could burn a few papers with less risk of incurring her aunt's disapproval. She made no immediate motion to do so, however, but dropping into a chair looked wearily about her. Her room was large and comfortably-furnished—it was the envy and admiration of poor Grace Stepney, who boarded; but, contrasted with the light tints and luxurious appointments of the guest-rooms where so many weeks of Lily's existence were spent, it seemed as dreary as a prison. The monumental wardrobe and bedstead of black walnut had migrated from Mr. Peniston's bedroom, and the magenta "flock" wall-paper, of a pattern dear to the early 'sixties, was hung with large steel engravings of an anecdotic character. Lily had tried to mitigate this charmless background by a few frivolous touches, in the shape of a lace-decked toilet table and a little painted desk surmounted by photographs; but the futility of the attempt struck her as she looked about the room. What a contrast to the subtle elegance of the setting she had pictured for herself—an apartment which should surpass the complicated luxury of her friends' surroundings by the whole extent of that artistic sensibility which made her feel herself their superior; in which every tint and line should combine to enhance her beauty and give distinction to her leisure. Once more the haunting sense of physical ugliness was intensified by her mental depression, so that each piece of the offending furniture seemed to thrust forth its most aggressive angle.

Her aunt's words had told her nothing new; but they had revived the vision of Bertha Dorset, smiling, flattered, victorious, holding her up to ridicule by insinuations intelligible to every member of their little group. The thought of the ridicule struck deeper than any other sensation: Lily knew every turn of the allusive jargon which could flay its victims without the shedding of blood. Her cheek burned at the recollection, and she rose and caught up the letters. She no longer meant to destroy them: that intention had been effaced by the quick corrosion of Mrs. Peniston's words.

Instead, she approached her desk, and lighting a taper, tied and sealed the packet; then she opened the wardrobe, drew out a despatch-box, and deposited the letters within it. As she did so, it struck her with a flash of irony that she was indebted to Gus Trenor for the means of buying them.

§ 10

The autumn dragged on monotonously. Miss Bart had received one or two notes from Judy Trenor, reproaching her for not returning to Bellomont; but she replied evasively, alleging the obligation to remain with her aunt. In truth, however, she was fast wearying of her solitary existence with Mrs. Peniston, and only the excitement of spending her newly-acquired money lightened the dulness of the days.

All her life Lily had seen money go out as quickly as it came in, and whatever theories she cultivated as to the prudence of setting aside a part of her gains, she had unhappily no saving vision of the risks of the opposite course. It was a keen satisfaction to feel that, for a few months at least, she would be independent of her friends' bounty, that she could show herself abroad without wondering whether some penetrating eye would detect in her dress the traces of Judy Trenor's refurbished splendour. The fact that the money freed her temporarily from all minor obligations obscured her sense of the greater one it represented, and having never before known what it was to command so large a sum, she lingered delectably over the amusement of spending it.

It was on one of these occasions that, leaving a shop where she had spent an hour of deliberation over a dressing-case of the most complicated elegance, she ran across Miss Farish, who had entered the same establishment with the modest object of having her watch repaired. Lily was feeling unusually virtuous. She had decided to defer the purchase of the dressing-case till she should receive the bill for her new opera-cloak, and the resolve made her feel much richer than when she had entered the shop. In this mood of self-approval she had a sympathetic eye for others, and she was struck by her friend's air of dejection.

Miss Farish, it appeared, had just left the committee-meeting of a struggling charity in which she was interested. The object of the association was to provide comfortable lodgings, with a reading-room and other modest distractions, where young women of the class employed in down town offices might find a home when out of work, or in need of rest, and the first year's financial report showed so deplorably small a balance that Miss Farish, who was convinced of the urgency of the work, felt proportionately discouraged by the small amount of interest it aroused. The other-regarding sentiments had not been cultivated in Lily, and she was often bored by the relation of her friend's philanthropic efforts, but today her quick dramatizing fancy seized on the contrast between her own situation and that represented by some of Gerty's "cases." These were young girls, like herself: some perhaps pretty, some not without a trace of her finer sensibilities. She pictured herself leading such a life as theirs—a life in which achievement seemed as squalid as failure—and the vision made her shudder sympathetically. The price of the dressing-case was still in her pocket; and drawing out her little gold purse she slipped a liberal fraction of the amount into Miss Farish's hand.

The satisfaction derived from this act was all that the most ardent moralist could have desired. Lily felt a new interest in herself as a person of charitable instincts: she had never before thought of doing good with the wealth she had so often dreamed of possessing, but now her horizon was enlarged by the vision of a prodigal philanthropy. Moreover, by some obscure process of logic, she felt that her momentary burst of generosity had justified all previous extravagances, and excused any in which she might subsequently indulge. Miss Farish's surprise and gratitude confirmed this feeling, and Lily parted from her with a sense of self-esteem which she naturally mistook for the fruits of altruism.

About this time she was farther cheered by an invitation to spend the Thanksgiving week at a camp in the Adirondacks. The invitation was one which, a year earlier, would have provoked a less ready response, for the party, though organzied by Mrs. Fisher, was ostensibly given by a lady of obscure origin and indomitable social ambitions, whose acquaintance Lily had hitherto avoided. Now, however, she was disposed to coincide with Mrs. Fisher's view, that it didn't matter who gave the party, as long as things were well done; and doing things well (under competent direction) was Mrs. Wellington Bry's strong point. The lady (whose consort was known as "Welly" Bry on the Stock Exchange and in sporting circles) had already sacrificed one husband, and sundry minor considerations, to her determination to get on; and, having obtained a hold on Carry Fisher, she was astute enough to perceive the wisdom of committing herself entirely to that lady's guidance. Everything, accordingly, was well done, for there was no limit to Mrs. Fisher's prodigality when she was not spending her own money, and as she remarked to her pupil, a good cook was the best introduction to society. If the company was not as select as the *cuisine,* the Welly Brys at least had the satisfaction of figuring for the first time in the society columns in company with one or two noticeable names; and foremost among these was of course Miss Bart's. The young lady was treated by her hosts with corresponding deference; and she was in the mood when such attentions are acceptable, whatever their source. Mrs. Bry's admiration was a mirror in which Lily's self-complacency recovered its lost outline. No insect hangs its nest on threads as frail as those which will sustain the weight of human vanity: and the sense of being of importance among the insignificant was enough to restore to Miss Bart the gratifying consciousness of power. If these people paid court to her it proved that she was still conspicuous in the world to which they aspired; and she was not above a certain enjoyment in dazzling them by her fineness, in developing their puzzled perception of her superiorities.

Perhaps, however, her enjoyment proceeded more than she was aware from the physical stimulus of the excursion, the challenge of crisp cold and hard exercise, the responsive thrill of her body to the influences of the winter woods. She returned to town in a glow of rejuvenation, conscious of a clearer colour in her cheeks, a fresh elasticity in her muscles. The future seemed full of a vague promise, and all her apprehensions were swept out of sight on the buoyant current of her mood.

A few days after her return to town she had the unpleasant surprise of a visit from Mr. Rosedale. He came late, at the confidential hour when the tea-table still lingers by the fire in friendly expectancy; and his manner showed a readiness to adapt itself to the intimacy of the occasion.

Lily, who had a vague sense of his being somehow connected with her lucky speculations, tried to give him the welcome he expected; but there was something in the quality of his geniality which chilled her own, and she was conscious of marking each step in their acquaintance by a fresh blunder.

Mr. Rosedale—making himself promptly at home in an adjoining easy-chair, and sipping his tea critically, with the comment: "You ought to go to my man for something really good"—appeared totally unconscious of the repugnance which kept her in frozen erectness behind the urn. It was perhaps her very manner of holding herself aloof that appealed to his collector's passion for the rare and unattainable. He gave, at any rate, no sign of resenting it and seemed prepared to supply in his own manner all the ease that was lacking in hers.

His object in calling was to ask her to go to the opera in his box on the opening night, and seeing her hesitate he said persuasively: "Mrs. Fisher is coming, and I've secured a tremendous admirer of yours, who'll never forgive me if you don't accept."

As Lily's silence left him with this allusion on his hands, he added with a confidential smile: "Gus Trenor has promised to come to town on purpose. I fancy he'd go a good deal farther for the pleasure of seeing you."

Miss Bart felt an inward motion of annoyance: it was distasteful enough to hear her name coupled with Trenor's, and on Rosedale's lips the allusion was peculiarly unpleasant.

"The Trenors are my best friends—I think we should all go a

long way to see each other," she said, absorbing herself in the preparation of fresh tea.

Her visitor's smile grew increasingly intimate. "Well, I wasn't thinking of Mrs. Trenor at the moment—they say Gus doesn't always, you know." Then, dimly conscious that he had not struck the right note, he added, with a well-meant effort at diversion: "How's your luck been going in Wall Street, by the way? I hear Gus pulled off a nice little pile for you last month."

Lily put down the tea-caddy with an abrupt gesture. She felt that her hands were trembling, and clasped them on her knee to steady them; but her lip trembled too, and for a moment she was afraid the tremor might communicate itself to her voice. When she spoke, however, it was in a tone of perfect lightness.

"Ah, yes—I had a little bit of money to invest, and Mr. Trenor, who helps me about such matters, advised my putting it in stocks instead of a mortgage, as my aunt's agent wanted me to do; and as it happened, I made a lucky 'turn'—is that what you call it? For you make a great many yourself, I believe."

She was smiling back at him now, relaxing the tension of her attitude, and admitting him, by imperceptible gradations of glance and manner, a step farther toward intimacy. The protective instinct always nerved her to successful dissimulation, and it was not the first time she had used her beauty to divert attention from an inconvenient topic.

When Mr. Rosedale took leave, he carried with him, not only her acceptance of his invitation, but a general sense of having comported himself in a way calculated to advance his cause. He had always believed he had a light touch and a knowing way with women, and the prompt manner in which Miss Bart (as he would have phrased it) had "come into line," confirmed his confidence in his powers of handling the skittish sex. Her way of glossing over the transaction with Trenor he regarded at once as a tribute to his own acuteness, and a confirmation of his suspicions. The girl was evidently nervous, and Mr. Rosedale, if he saw no other means of advancing his acquaintance with her, was not above taking advantage of her nervousness.

He left Lily to a passion of disgust and fear. It seemed incredible that Gus Trenor should have spoken of her to Rosedale. With all his faults, Trenor had the safeguard of his traditions, and was the less likely to overstep them because they were so purely instinctive. But Lily recalled with a pang that there were convivial moments when, as Judy had confided to her, Gus "talked foolishly": in one of these, no doubt, the fatal word had slipped from him. As for Rosedale, she did not, after the first shock, greatly care what conclusions he had drawn. Though usually adroit enough where her own interests were concerned, she made the mistake, not uncommon to persons in whom the social habits are instinctive, of supposing that the inability to acquire them quickly implies a general dulness. Because a blue-bottle bangs irrationally against a window-pane, the drawing-room naturalist may forget that under less artificial conditions it is capable of measuring distances and drawing conclusions with all the accuracy needful to its welfare; and the fact that Mr. Rosedale's drawing-room manner lacked perspective made Lily class him with Trenor and the other dull men she knew, and assume that a little flattery, and the occasional acceptance of his hospitality, would suffice to render him innocuous. However, there could be no doubt of the expediency of showing herself in his box on the opening night of the opera; and after all, since Judy Trenor had promised to take him up that winter, it was as well to reap the advantage of being first in the field.

For a day or two after Rosedale's visit, Lily's thoughts were dogged by the consciousness of Trenor's shadowy claim, and she wished she had a clearer notion of the exact nature of the transaction which seemed to have put her in his power; but her mind shrank from any unusual application, and she was always helplessly puzzled by figures. Moreover she had not seen Trenor since the day of the Van Osburgh wedding, and in his continued absence the trace of Rosedale's words was soon effaced by other impressions.

When the opening night of the opera came, her apprehensions had so completely vanished that the sight of Trenor's ruddy countenance in the back of Mr. Rosedale's box filled her with a sense of pleasant reassurance. Lily had not quite reconciled herself to the necessity of appearing as Rosedale's guest on so conspicuous an occasion, and it was a relief to find herself supported by any one of her own set—for Mrs. Fisher's social habits were too promiscuous for her presence to justify Miss Bart's.

To Lily, always inspirited by the prospect of showing her beauty in public, and conscious tonight of all the added enhancements of dress, the insistency of Trenor's gaze merged itself in the general stream of admiring looks of which she felt herself the centre. Ah, it was good to be young, to be radiant, to glow with the sense of slenderness, strength and elasticity, of well-poised lines and happy tints, to feel one's self lifted to a height apart by that incommunicable grace which is the bodily counterpart of genius!

All means seemed justifiable to attain such an end, or rather, by a happy shifting of lights with which practice had familiarized Miss Bart, the cause shrank to a pin-point in the general brightness of the effect. But brilliant young ladies, a little blinded by their own effulgence, are apt to forget that the modest satellite drowned in their light is still performing its own revolutions and generating heat at its own rate. If Lily's poetic enjoyment of the moment was undisturbed by the base thought that her gown and opera cloak had been indirectly paid for by Gus Trenor, the latter had not sufficient poetry in his composition to lose sight of these prosaic facts. He knew only that he had never seen Lily look smarter in her life, that there wasn't a woman in the house who showed off good clothes as she did, and that hitherto he, to whom she owed the opportunity of making this display, had reaped no return beyond that of gazing at her in company with several hundred other pairs of eyes.

It came to Lily therefore as a disagreeable surprise when, in the back of the box, where they found themselves alone between two acts, Trenor said, without preamble, and in a tone of sulky authority: "Look here, Lily, how is a fellow ever to see anything of you? I'm in town three or four days in the week, and you know a line to the club will always find me, but you don't seem to remember my existence nowadays unless you want to get a tip out of me."

The fact that the remark was in distinctly bad taste did not make it any easier to answer, for Lily was vividly aware that it was not the moment for that drawing up of her slim figure and surprised lifting of the brows by which she usually quelled incipient signs of familiarity.

"I'm very much flattered by your wanting to see me," she returned, essaying lightness instead, "but, unless you have mislaid my address, it would have been easy to find me any afternoon at my aunt's—in fact, I rather expected you to look me up there."

If she hoped to mollify him by this last concession the attempt was a failure, for he only replied, with the familiar lowering of the brows that made him look his dullest when he was angry: "Hang going to your aunt's, and wasting the afternoon listening to a lot of other chaps talking to you! You know I'm not the kind to sit in a crowd and jaw—I'd always rather clear out when that sort of circus is going on. But why can't we go off somewhere on a little lark together—a nice quiet little expedition like that drive at Bellomont, the day you met me at the station?"

He leaned unpleasantly close in order to convey this suggestion, and she fancied she caught a significant aroma which explained the dark flush on his face and the glistening dampness of his forehead.

The idea that any rash answer might provoke an unpleasant outburst tempered her disgust with caution, and she answered with a laugh: "I don't see how one can very well take country drives in town, but I am not always surrounded by an admiring throng, and if you will let me know what afternoon you are coming I will arrange things so that we can have a nice quiet talk."

"Hang talking! That's what you always say," returned Trenor, whose expletives lacked variety. "You put me off with that at the Van Osburgh wedding—but the plain English of it is that, now you've got what you wanted out of me, you'd rather have any other fellow about."

His voice had risen sharply with the last words, and Lily flushed with annoyance, but she kept command of the situation and laid a persuasive hand on his arm.

"Don't be foolish, Gus; I can't let you talk to me in that ridiculous way. If you really want to see me, why shouldn't we take a walk in the Park some afternoon? I agree with you that it's amusing to be rustic in town, and if you like I'll meet you there, and we'll go and feed the squirrels, and you shall take me out on the lake in the steam-gondola."

She smiled as she spoke, letting her eyes rest on his in a way that took the edge from her banter and made him suddenly malleable to her will.

"All right, then: that's a go. Will you come tomorrow? Tomorrow at three o'clock, at the end of the Mall? I'll be there sharp, remember; you won't go back on me, Lily?"

But to Miss Bart's relief the repetition of her promise was cut short by the opening of the box door to admit George Dorset.

Trenor sulkily yielded his place, and Lily turned a brilliant smile on the newcomer. She had not talked with Dorset since their visit at Bellomont, but something in his look and manner told her that he recalled the friendly footing on which they had last met. He was not a man to whom the expression of admiration came easily: his long sallow face and distrustful eyes seemed always barricaded against the expansive emotions. But, where her own influence was concerned, Lily's intuitions sent out threadlike feelers, and as she made room for him on the narrow sofa she was sure he found a dumb pleasure in being near her. Few women took the trouble to make themselves agreeable to Dorset, and Lily had been kind to him at Bellomont, and was now smiling on him with a divine renewal of kindness.

"Well, here we are, in for another six months of caterwauling," he began complainingly. "Not a shade of difference between this year and last, except that the women have got new clothes and the singers haven't got new voices. My wife's musical, you know—puts me through a course of this every winter. It isn't so bad on Italian nights—then she comes late, and there's time to digest. But when they give Wagner we have to rush dinner, and I pay up for it. And the draughts are damnable—asphyxia in front and pleurisy in the back. There's Trenor leaving the box without drawing the curtain! With a hide like that draughts don't make any difference. Did you ever watch Trenor eat? If you did, you'd wonder why he's alive; I suppose he's leather inside too.—But I came to say that my wife wants you to come down to our place next Sunday. Do for heaven's sake say yes. She's got a lot of bores coming—intellectual ones, I mean; that's her new line, you know, and I'm not sure it ain't worse than the music. Some of 'em have long hair, and they start an argument with the soup, and don't notice when things are handed to them. The consequence is the dinner gets cold, and I have dyspepsia. That silly ass Silverton brings them to the house—he writes poetry, you know, and Bertha and he are getting tremendously thick. She could write better than any of 'em if she chose, and I don't blame her for wanting clever fellows about; all I say is: 'Don't let me see 'em eat!' "

The gist of this strange communication gave Lily a distinct thrill of pleasure. Under ordinary circumstances, there would have been nothing surprising in an invitation from Bertha Dorset; but since the Bellomont episode an unavowed hostility had kept the two women apart. Now, with a start of inner wonder, Lily felt that her thirst for retaliation had died out. *If you would forgive your enemy,* says the Malay proverb, *first inflict a hurt on him;* and Lily was experiencing the truth of the apothegm. If she had destroyed Mrs. Dorset's letters, she might have continued to hate her; but the fact that they remained in her possession had fed her resentment to satiety.

She uttered a smiling acceptance, hailing in the renewal of the tie an escape from Trenor's importunities.

§ 11

Meanwhile the holidays had gone by and the season was beginning. Fifth Avenue had become a nightly torrent of carriages surging upward to the fashionable quarters about the Park, where illuminated windows and outspread awnings betokened the usual routine of hospitality. Other tributary currents crossed the main stream, bearing their freight to the theatres, restaurants or opera; and Mrs. Peniston, from the secluded watch-tower of her upper window, could tell to a nicety just when the chronic volume of sound was increased by the sudden influx setting toward a Van Osburgh ball, or when the multiplication of wheels meant merely that the opera was over, or that there was a big supper at Sherry's.

Mrs. Peniston followed the rise and culmination of the season as keenly as the most active sharer in its gaieties; and, as a looker-on, she enjoyed opportunities of comparison and generalization such as those who take part must proverbially forego. No one could have kept a more accurate record of social fluctuations, or have put a more unerring finger on the distinguishing features of each season: its dulness, its extravagance, its lack of balls or excess of divorces. She had a special memory for the vicissitudes of the "new people" who rose to the surface with each recurring tide, and were either submerged beneath its rush or landed triumphantly beyond the reach of envious breakers; and she was apt to display a remarkable retrospective insight into their ultimate fate, so that, when they had fulfilled their destiny, she was almost always able to say to Grace Stepney—the recipient of her prophecies—that she had known exactly what would happen.

This particular season Mrs. Peniston would have characterized as that in which everybody "felt poor" except the Welly Brys and Mr. Simon Rosedale. It had been a bad autumn in Wall Street, where prices fell in accordance with that peculiar law which proves railway stocks and bales of cotton to be more sensitive to the allotment of executive power than many estimable citizens trained to all the advantages of self-government. Even fortunes supposed to be independent of the market either betrayed a secret dependence on it, or suffered from a sympathetic affection: fashion sulked in its country-houses, or came to town incognito, general entertainments were discountenanced, and informality and short dinners became the fashion.

But society, amused for a while at playing Cinderella, soon wearied of the hearthside rôle, and welcomed the Fairy Godmother in the shape of any magician powerful enough to turn the shrunken pumpkin back again into the golden coach. The mere fact of growing richer at a time when most people's investments are shrinking, is calculated to attract envious attention; and according to Wall Street rumours, Welly Bry and Rosedale had found the secret of performing this miracle.

Rosedale, in particular, was said to have doubled his fortune, and there was talk of his buying the newly-finished house of one of the victims of the crash, who, in the space of twelve short months, had made the same number of millions, built a house in Fifth Avenue, filled a picture-gallery with old masters, entertained all New York in it, and been smuggled out of the country between a trained nurse and a doctor, while his creditors mounted guard over the old masters, and his guests explained to each other that they had dined with him only because they wanted to see the pictures. Mr. Rosedale meant to have a less meteoric career. He knew he should have to go slowly, and the instincts of his race fitted him to suffer rebuffs and put up with delays. But he was prompt to perceive that the general dulness of the season afforded him an unusual opportunity to shine, and he set about with patient industry to form a background for his growing glory. Mrs. Fisher was of immense service to him at this period. She had set off so many newcomers on the social stage that she was like one of those pieces of stock scenery which tell the experienced spectator exactly what is going to take place. But Mr. Rosedale wanted, in the long run, a more individual environment. He was sensitive to shades of difference which Miss Bart would never have credited him with perceiving, because he had no corresponding variations of manner; and it was becoming more and more clear to him that Miss Bart herself possessed precisely the complementary qualities needed to round off his social personality.

Such details did not fall within the range of Mrs. Peniston's vision. Like many minds of panoramic sweep, hers was apt to overlook the *minutiæ* of the foreground, and she was much more likely to know where Carry Fisher had found the Welly Brys' *chef* for them, than what was happening to her own niece. She was not, however, without purveyors of information ready to supplement her deficiencies. Grace Stepney's mind was like a kind of moral fly-paper, to which the buzzing items of gossip were drawn by a fatal attraction, and where they hung fast in the toils of an inexorable memory. Lily would have been surprised to know how many trivial facts concerning herself were lodged in Miss Stepney's head. She was quite aware that she was of interest to dingy people, but she assumed that there is only one form of dinginess, and that admiration for brilliancy is the natural expression of its inferior state. She knew that Gerty Farish admired her blindly, and therefore supposed that she inspired the same sentiments in Grace Stepney, whom she classified as a Gerty Farish without the saving traits of youth and enthusiasm.

In reality, the two differed from each other as much as they differed from the object of their mutual contemplation. Miss Farish's heart was a fountain of tender illusions, Miss Stepney's a precise register of facts as manifested in their relation to herself. She had sensibilities which, to Lily, would have seemed comic in a person with a freckled nose and red eye-lids, who lived in a boarding-house and admired Mrs. Peniston's drawing-room; but poor Grace's limitations gave them a more concentrated inner life, as poor soil starves certain plants into intenser efflorescence. She had in truth no abstract propensity to malice: she did not dislike Lily because the latter was brilliant and predominant, but because she thought that Lily disliked her. It is less mortifying to believe one's self unpopular than insignificant, and vanity prefers to assume that indifference is a latent form of unfriendliness. Even such scant civilities as Lily accorded to Mr. Rosedale would have made Miss Stepney her friend for life; but how could she foresee that such a friend was worth cultivating? How, moreover, can a young woman who has never been ignored measure the pang which this injury inflicts? And, lastly, how could Lily, accustomed to choose between a pressure of engagements, guess that she had mortally offended Miss Stepney by causing her to be excluded from one of Mrs. Peniston's infrequent dinner-parties?

Mrs. Peniston disliked giving dinners, but she had a high sense of family obligation, and on the Jack Stepneys' return from their honeymoon she felt it incumbent upon her to light the drawing-room lamps and extract her best silver from the Safe Deposit vaults. Mrs. Peniston's rare entertainments were preceded by days of heart-rending vacillation as to every detail of the feast, from the seating of the guests to the pattern of the table-cloth, and in the course of one of these preliminary discussions she had imprudently suggested to her cousin Grace that, as the dinner was a family affair, she might be included in it. For a week the prospect had lighted up Miss Stepney's colourless existence; then she had been given to understand that it would be more convenient to have her another day. Miss Stepney knew exactly what had happened. Lily, to whom family reunions were occasions of unalloyed dulness, had persuaded her aunt that a dinner of "smart" people would be much more to the taste of the young couple, and Mrs. Peniston, who leaned helplessly on her niece in social matters, had been prevailed upon to pronounce Grace's exile. After all, Grace could come any other day; why should she mind being put off?

It was precisely because Miss Stepney could come any other day—and because she knew her relations were in the secret of her unoccupied evenings—that this incident loomed gigantically on her horizon. She was aware that she had Lily to thank for it; and dull resentment was turned to active animosity.

Mrs. Peniston, on whom she had looked in a day or two after the dinner, laid down her crochet-work and turned abruptly from her oblique survey of Fifth Avenue.

"Gus Trenor?—Lily and Gus Trenor?" she said, growing so suddenly pale that her visitor was almost alarmed.

"Oh, cousin Julia . . . of course I don't mean . . ."

"I don't know what you *do* mean," said Mrs. Peniston, with a frightened quiver in her small fretful voice. "Such things were never heard of in my day. And my own niece! I'm not sure I understand you. Do people say he's in love with her?"

Mrs. Peniston's horror was genuine. Though she boasted an unequalled familiarity with the secret chronicles of society, she had the innocence of the school-girl who regards wickedness as a part of "history," and to whom it never occurs that the scandals she reads of in lesson-hours may be repeating themselves in the next street. Mrs. Peniston had kept her imagination shrouded, like the drawing-room furniture. She knew, of course, that society was "very much changed," and that many women her mother would have thought "peculiar" were now in a position to be critical about their visiting-lists; she had discussed the perils of divorce with her rector, and had felt thankful at times that Lily was still unmarried; but the idea that any scandal could attach to a young girl's name, above all that it could be lightly coupled with that of a married man, was so new to her that she was as much aghast as if she had been accused of leaving her carpets down all summer, or of violating any of the other cardinal laws of house-keeping.

Miss Stepney, when her first fright had subsided, began to feel the superiority that greater breadth of mind confers. It was really pitiable to be as ignorant of the world as Mrs. Peniston!

She smiled at the latter's question: "People always say unpleasant things—and certainly they're a great deal together. A friend of mine met them the other afternoon in the Park—quite late, after the lamps were lit. It's a pity Lily makes herself so conspicuous."

"Conspicuous!" gasped Mrs. Peniston. She bent forward, lowering her voice to mitigate the horror. "What sort of things do they say? That he means to get a divorce and marry her?"

Grace Stepney laughed outright. "Dear me, no! He would hardly do that. It—it's a flirtation—nothing more."

"A flirtation? Between my niece and a married man? Do you mean to tell me that, with Lily's looks and advantages, she could find no better use for her time than to waste it on a fat stupid man almost old enough to be her father?" This argument had such a convincing ring that it gave Mrs. Peniston sufficient reassurance to pick up her work, while she waited for Grace Stepney to rally her scattered forces.

But Miss Stepney was on the spot in an instant. "That's the worst of it—people say she isn't wasting her time! Every one knows, as you say, that Lily is too handsome and—and charming—to devote herself to a man like Gus Trenor unless——"

"Unless?" echoed Mrs. Peniston.

Her visitor drew breath nervously. It was agreeable to shock Mrs. Peniston, but not to shock her to the verge of anger. Miss Stepney was not sufficiently familiar with the classic drama to have recalled in advance how bearers of bad tidings are proverbially received, but she now had a rapid vision of forfeited dinners and a reduced wardrobe as the possible consequence of her disinterestedness. To the honour of her sex, however, hatred of Lily prevailed over more personal considerations. Mrs. Peniston had chosen the wrong moment to boast of her niece's charms.

"Unless," said Grace, leaning forward to speak with low-toned emphasis, "unless there are material advantages to be gained by making herself agreeable to him."

She felt that the moment was tremendous, and remembered suddenly that Mrs. Peniston's black brocade, with the cut jet fringe, would have been hers at the end of the season.

Mrs. Peniston put down her work again. Another aspect of the same idea had presented itself to her, and she felt that it was beneath her dignity to have her nerves racked by a dependent relative who wore her old clothes.

"If you take pleasure in annoying me by mysterious insinuations," she said coldly, "you might at least have chosen a more suitable time than just as I am recovering from the strain of giving a large dinner."

The mention of the dinner dispelled Miss Stepney's last scruples. "I don't know why I should be accused of taking pleasure in telling you about Lily. I was sure I shouldn't get any thanks for it," she returned with a flare of temper. "But I have some family feeling left, and as you are the only person who has any authority over Lily, I thought you ought to know what is being said of her."

"Well," said Mrs. Peniston, "what I complain of is that you haven't told me yet what *is* being said."

"I didn't suppose I should have to put it so plainly. People say that Gus Trenor pays her bills."

"Pays her bills—her bills?" Mrs. Peniston broke into a laugh. "I can't imagine where you can have picked up such rubbish. Lily has her own income—and I provide for her very handsomely——"

"Oh, we all know that," interposed Miss Stepney drily. "But Lily wears a great many smart gowns——"

"I like her to be well-dressed—it's only suitable!"

"Certainly; but then there are her gambling debts besides."

Miss Stepney, in the beginning, had not meant to bring up this point; but Mrs. Peniston had only her own incredulity to blame. She was like the stiff-necked unbelievers of Scripture, who must be annihilated to be convinced.

"Gambling debts? Lily?" Mrs. Peniston's voice shook with anger and bewilderment. She wondered whether Grace Stepney had gone out of her mind. "What do you mean by her gambling debts?"

"Simply that if one plays bridge for money in Lily's set one is liable to lose a great deal—and I don't suppose Lily always wins."

"Who told you that my niece played cards for money?"

"Mercy, cousin Julia, don't look at me as if I were trying to turn you against Lily! Everybody knows she is crazy about bridge. Mrs. Gryce told me herself that it was her gambling that frightened Percy Gryce—it seems he was really taken with her at first. But, of course, among Lily's friends, it's quite the custom for girls to play for money. In fact, people are inclined to excuse her on that account——"

"To excuse her for what?"

"For being hard up—and accepting attentions from men like Gus Trenor—and George Dorset——"

Mrs. Peniston gave another cry. "George Dorset? Is there any one else? I should like to know the worst, if you please."

"Don't put it in that way, cousin Julia. Lately Lily has been a good deal with the Dorsets, and he seems to admire her—but of course that's only natural. And I'm sure there is no truth in the horrid things people say; but she *has* been spending a great deal of money this winter. Evie Van Osburgh was at Céleste's ordering her trousseau the other day—yes, the marriage takes place next month—and she told me that Céleste showed her the most exquisite things she was just sending home to Lily. And people say that Judy Trenor has quarrelled with her on account of Gus; but I'm sure I'm sorry I spoke, though I only meant it as a kindness."

Mrs. Peniston's genuine incredulity enabled her to dismiss Miss Stepney with a disdain which boded ill for that lady's prospect of succeeding to the black brocade; but minds impenetrable to reason have generally some crack through which suspicion filters, and her visitor's insinuations did not glide off as easily as she had expected. Mrs. Peniston disliked scenes, and her determination to avoid them had always led her to hold herself aloof from the details of Lily's life. In her youth, girls had not been supposed to require close supervision. They were generally assumed to be taken up with the legitimate business of courtship and marriage, and interference in such affairs on the part of their natural guardians was considered as unwarrantable as a spectator's suddenly joining in a game. There had of course been "fast" girls even in Mrs. Peniston's early experience; but their fastness, at worst, was understood to be a mere excess of animal spirits, against which there could be no graver charge than that of being "unladylike." The modern fastness appeared synonymous with immorality, and the mere idea of immorality was as offensive to Mrs. Peniston as a smell of cooking in the drawing-room: it was one of the conceptions her mind refused to admit.

She had no immediate intention of repeating to Lily what she had heard, or even of trying to ascertain its truth by means of discreet interrogation. To do so might be to provoke a scene; and a scene, in the shaken state of Mrs. Peniston's nerves, with the effects of her dinner not worn off, and her mind still tremulous with new impressions, was a risk she deemed it her duty to avoid. But there remained in her thoughts a settled deposit of resentment against her niece, all the denser because it was not to be cleared by explanation or discussion. It was horrible of a young girl to let herself be talked about; however unfounded the charges against her, she must be to blame for their having been made. Mrs. Peniston felt as if there had been a contagious illness in the house, and she was doomed to sit shivering among her contaminated furniture.

§ 12

Miss Bart had in fact been treading a devious way, and none of her critics could have been more alive to the fact than herself; but she had a fatalistic sense of being drawn from one wrong turning to another, without ever perceiving the right road till it was too late to take it.

Lily, who considered herself above narrow prejudices, had not imagined that the fact of letting Gus Trenor make a little money for her would ever disturb her self-complacency. And the fact in itself still seemed harmless enough; only it was a fertile source of harmful complications. As she exhausted the amusement of spending the money these complications became more pressing, and Lily, whose mind could be severely logical in tracing the causes of her ill-luck to others, justified herself by the thought that she owed all her troubles to the enmity of Bertha Dorset. This enmity, however, had apparently expired in a renewal of friendliness between the two women. Lily's visit to the Dorsets had resulted, for both, in the discovery that they could be of use to each other; and the civilized instinct finds a subtler pleasure in making use of its antagonist than in confounding him. Mrs. Dorset was, in fact, engaged in a new sentimental experiment, of which Mrs. Fisher's late property, Ned Silverton, was the rosy victim; and at such moments, as Judy Trenor had once remarked, she felt a peculiar need of distracting her husband's attention. Dorset was as difficult to amuse as a savage; but even his self-engrossment was not proof against Lily's arts, or rather these were especially adapted to soothe an uneasy egoism. Her experience with Percy Gryce stood her in good stead in ministering to Dorset's humours, and if the incentive to please was less urgent, the difficulties of her situation were teaching her to make much of minor opportunities.

Intimacy with the Dorsets was not likely to lessen such difficulties on the material side. Mrs. Dorset had none of Judy Trenor's lavish impulses, and Dorset's admiration was not likely to express itself in financial "tips," even had Lily cared to renew her experiences in that line. What she required, for the moment, of the Dorsets' friendship, was simply its social sanction. She knew that people were beginning to talk of her; but this fact did not alarm her as it had alarmed Mrs. Peniston. In her set such gossip was not unusual, and a handsome girl who flirted with a married man was merely assumed to be pressing to the limit of her opportunities. It was Trenor himself who frightened her. Their walk in the Park had not been a success. Trenor had married young, and since his marriage his intercourse with women had not taken the form of the sentimental small-talk which doubles upon itself like the paths in a maze. He was first puzzled and then irritated to find himself always led back to the same starting-point, and Lily felt that she was gradually losing control of the situation. Trenor was in truth in an unmanageable mood. In spite of his understanding with Rosedale he had been somewhat heavily "touched" by the fall in stocks; his household expenses weighed on him, and he seemed to be meeting, on all sides, a sullen opposition to his wishes, instead of the easy good luck he had hitherto encountered.

Mrs. Trenor was still at Bellomont, keeping the townhouse open, and descending on it now and then for a taste of the world, but preferring the recurrent excitement of week-end parties to the restrictions of a dull season. Since the holidays she had not urged Lily to return to Bellomont, and the first time they met in town Lily fancied there was a shade of coldness in her manner. Was it merely the expression of her displeasure at Miss Bart's neglect, or had disquieting rumours reached her? The latter contingency seemed improbable, yet Lily was not without a sense of uneasiness. If her roaming sympathies had struck root anywhere, it was in her friendship with Judy Trenor. She believed in the sincerity of her friend's affection, though it sometimes showed itself in self-interested ways, and she shrank with peculiar reluctance from any risk of estranging it. But, aside from this, she was keenly conscious of the way in which such an estrangement would react on herself. The fact that Gus Trenor was Judy's husband was at times Lily's strongest reason for disliking him, and for resenting the obligation under which he had placed her.

To set her doubts at rest, Miss Bart, soon after the New Year, "proposed" herself for a week-end at Bellomont. She had learned in advance that the presence of a large party would protect her from too great assiduity on Trenor's part, and his wife's telegraphic "come by all means" seemed to assure her of her usual welcome.

Judy received her amicably. The cares of a large party always prevailed over personal feelings, and Lily saw no change in her hostess's manner. Nevertheless, she was soon aware that the experiment of coming to Bellomont was destined not to be successful. The party was made up of what Mrs. Trenor called "poky people"—her generic name for persons who did not play bridge—and, it being her habit to group all such obstructionists in one class, she usually invited them together, regardless of their other characteristics. The result was apt to be an irreducible combination of persons having no other quality in common than their abstinence from bridge, and the antagonisms developed in a group lacking the one taste which might have amalgamated them, were in this case aggravated by bad weather, and by the ill-concealed boredom of their host and hostess. In such emergencies, Judy would usually have turned to Lily to fuse the discordant elements; and Miss Bart, assuming that such a service was expected of her, threw herself into it with her accustomed zeal. But at the outset she perceived a subtle resistance to her efforts. If Mrs. Trenor's manner toward her was unchanged, there was certainly a faint coldness in that of the other ladies. An occasional caustic allusion to "your friends the Wellington Brys," or to "the little Jew who has bought the Greiner house—some one told us you knew him, Miss Bart,"—showed Lily that she was in disfavour with that portion of society which, while contributing least to its amusement, has assumed the right to decide what forms that amusement shall take. The indication was a slight one, and a year ago Lily would have smiled at it, trusting to the charm of her personality to dispel any prejudice against her. But now she had grown more sensitive to criticism and less confident in her power of disarming it. She knew, moreover, that if the ladies at Bellomont permitted themselves to criticize her friends openly, it was a proof that they were not afraid of subjecting her to the same treatment behind her back. The nervous dread lest anything in Trenor's manner should seem to justify their disapproval made her seek every pretext for avoiding him, and she left Bellomont conscious of having failed in every purpose which had taken her there.

In town she returned to preoccupations which, for the moment, had the happy effect of banishing troublesome thoughts. The Welly Brys, after much debate, and anxious counsel with their newly acquired friends, had decided on the bold move of giving a general entertainment. To attack society collectively, when one's means of approach are limited to a few acquaintances, is like advancing into a strange country with an insufficient number of scouts; but such rash tactics have sometimes led to brilliant victories, and the Brys had determined to put their fate to the touch. Mrs. Fisher, to whom they had entrusted the conduct of the affair, had decided that *tableaux vivants* and expensive music were the two baits most likely to attract the desired prey, and after prolonged negotiations, and the kind of wirepulling in which she was known to excel, she had induced a dozen fashionable women to exhibit themselves in a series of pictures which, by a farther miracle of persuasion, the distinguished portrait painter, Paul Morpeth, had been prevailed upon to organize.

Lily was in her element on such occasions. Under Morpeth's guidance her vivid plastic sense, hitherto nurtured on no higher food than dress-making and upholstery, found eager expression in the disposal of draperies, the study of attitudes, the shifting of lights and shadows. Her dramatic instinct was roused by the choice of subjects, and the gorgeous reproductions of historic dress stirred an imagination which only visual impressions could reach. But keenest of all was the exhilaration of displaying her own beauty under a new aspect: of showing that her loveliness was no more fixed quality, but an element shaping all emotions to fresh forms of grace.

Mrs. Fisher's measures had been well-taken, and society, surprised in a dull moment, succumbed to the temptation of Mrs. Bry's hospitality. The protesting minority were forgotten in the throng which abjured and came; and the audience was almost as brilliant as the show.

Lawrence Selden was among those who had yielded to the proffered inducements. If he did not often act on the accepted social axiom that a man may go where he pleases, it was because he had long since learned that his pleasures were mainly to be found in a small group of the like-minded. But he enjoyed spectacular effects, and was not insensible to the part money plays in their production: all he asked was that the very rich should live up to their calling as stage-managers, and not spend their money in a dull way. This the Brys could certainly not be charged with doing. Their recently built house, whatever it might lack as a frame for domesticity, was almost as well-designed for the display of a festal assemblage as one of those airy pleasure-halls which the Italian architects improvised to set off the hospitality of princes. The air of improvisation was in fact strikingly present: so recent, so rapidly-evoked was the whole *mise-en-scène* that one had to touch the marble columns to learn they were not of cardboard, to seat one's self in one of the damask-and-gold arm-chairs to be sure it was not painted against the wall.

Selden, who had put one of these seats to the test, found himself, from an angle of the ball-room, surveying the scene with frank enjoyment. The company, in obedience to the decorative instinct which calls for fine clothes in fine surroundings, had dressed rather with an eye to Mrs. Bry's background than to herself. The seated throng, filling the immense room without undue crowding, presented a surface of rich tissues and jewelled shoulders in harmony with the festooned and gilded walls, and the flushed splendours of the Venetian ceiling. At the farther end of the room a stage had been constructed behind a proscenium arch curtained with folds of old damask; but in the pause before the parting of the folds there was little thought of what they might reveal, for every woman who had accepted Mrs. Bry's invitation was engaged in trying to find out how many of her friends had done the same.

Gerty Farish, seated next to Selden, was lost in that indiscriminate and uncritical enjoyment so irritating to Miss Bart's finer perceptions. It may be that Selden's nearness had something to do with the quality of his cousin's pleasure; but Miss Farish was so little accustomed to refer her enjoyment of such scenes to her own share in them, that she was merely conscious of a deeper sense of contentment.

"Wasn't it dear of Lily to get me an invitation? Of course it would never have occurred to Carry Fisher to put me on the list, and I should have been so sorry to miss seeing it all—and especially Lily herself. Some one told me the ceiling was by Veronese—you would know, of course, Lawrence. I suppose it's very beautiful, but his women are so dreadfully fat. Goddesses? Well, I can only say that if they'd been mortals and had to wear corsets, it would have been better for them. I think our women are much handsomer. And this room is wonderfully becoming—every one looks so well! Did you ever see such jewels? Do look at Mrs. George Dorset's pearls—I suppose the smallest of them would pay the rent of our Girls' Club for a year. Not that I ought to complain about the club; every one has been so wonderfully kind. Did I tell you that Lily had given us three hundred dollars? Wasn't it splendid of her? And then she collected a lot of money from her friends—Mrs. Bry gave us five hundred, and Mr. Rosedale a thousand. I wish Lily were not so nice to Mr. Rosedale, but she says it's no use being rude to him, because he doesn't see the difference. She really can't bear to hurt people's feelings—it makes me so angry when I hear her called cold and conceited! The girls at the club don't call her that. Do you know she has been there with me twice?—yes, Lily! And you should have seen their eyes! One of them said it was as good as a day in the country just to look at her. And she sat there, and laughed and talked with them—not a bit as if she were being *charitable,* you know, but as if she liked it as much as they did. They 've been asking ever since when she's coming back; and she's promised me——oh!"

Miss Farish's confidences were cut short by the parting of the curtain on the first *tableau*—a group of nymphs dancing across flower-strewn sward in the rhythmic postures of Botticelli's Spring. *Tableaux vivants* depend for their effect not only on the happy disposal of lights and the delusive interposition of layers of gauze, but on a corresponding adjustment of the mental vision. To unfurnished minds they remain, in spite of every enhancement of art, only a superior kind of wax-works; but to the responsive fancy they may give magic glimpses of the boundary world between fact and imagination. Selden's mind was of this order: he could yield to vision-making influences as completely as a child to the spell of a fairy-tale. Mrs. Bry's *tableaux* wanted none of the qualities which go to the producing of such illusions, and under Morpeth's organizing hand the pictures succeeded each other with the rhythmic march of some splendid frieze, in which the fugitive curves of living flesh and the wandering light of young eyes have been subdued to plastic harmony without losing the charm of life.

The scenes were taken from old pictures, and the participators had been cleverly fitted with characters suited to their types. No one, for instance, could have made a more typical Goya than Carry Fisher, with her short dark-skinned face, the exaggerated glow of her eyes, the provocation of her frankly-painted smile. A brilliant Miss Smedden from Brooklyn showed to perfection the sumptuous curves of Titian's Daughter, lifting her gold salver laden with grapes above the harmonizing gold of rippled hair and rich brocade, and a young Mrs. Van Alstyne, who showed the frailer Dutch type, with high blue-veined forehead and pale eyes and lashes, made a characteristic Vandyck, in black satin, against a curtained archway. Then there were Kauffmann nymphs garlanding the altar of Love; a Veronese supper, all sheeny textures, pearl-woven heads and marble architecture; and a Watteau group of lute-playing comedians, lounging by a fountain in a sunlit glade.

Each evanescent picture touched the vision-building faculty in Selden, leading him so far down the vistas of fancy that even Gerty Farish's running commentary—"Oh, how lovely Lulu Melson looks!" or: "That must be Kate Corby, to the right there, in purple"—did not break the spell of the illusion. Indeed, so skilfully had the personality of the actors been subdued to the scenes they figured in that even the least imaginative of the audience must have felt a thrill of contrast when the curtain suddenly parted on a picture which was simply and undisguisedly the portrait of Miss Bart.

Here there could be no mistaking the predominance of personality—the unanimous "Oh!" of the spectators was a tribute, not to the brush-work of Reynolds's "Mrs. Lloyd" but to the flesh and blood loveliness of Lily Bart. She had shown her artistic intelligence in selecting a type so like her own that she could embody the person represented without ceasing to be herself. It was as though she had stepped, not out of, but into, Reynolds's canvas, banishing the phantom of his dead beauty by the beams of her living grace. The impulse to show herself in a splendid setting—she had thought for a moment of representing Tiepolo's Cleopatra—had yielded to the truer instinct of trusting to her unassisted beauty, and she had purposely chosen a picture without distracting accessories of dress or surroundings. Her pale draperies, and the background of foliage against which she stood, served only to relieve the long dryad-like curves that swept upward from her poised foot to her lifted arm.

The noble buoyancy of her attitude, its suggestion of soaring grace, revealed the touch of poetry in her beauty that Selden always felt in her presence, yet lost the sense of when he was not with her. Its expression was now so vivid that for the first time he seemed to see before him the real Lily Bart, divested of the trivialities of her little world, and catching for a moment a note of that eternal harmony of which her beauty was a part.

"Deuced bold thing to show herself in that get-up; but, gad, there isn't a break in the lines anywhere, and I suppose she wanted us to know it!"

These words, uttered by that experienced connoisseur, Mr. Ned Van Alstyne, whose scented white moustache had brushed Selden's shoulder whenever the parting of the curtains presented any exceptional opportunity for the study of the female outline, affected their hearer in an unexpected way. It was not the first time that Selden had heard Lily's beauty lightly remarked on, and hitherto the tone of the comments had imperceptibly coloured his view of her. But now it woke only a motion of indignant contempt. This was the world she lived in, these were the standards by which she was fated to be measured! Does one go to Caliban for a judgment on Miranda?

In the long moment before the curtain fell, he had time to feel the whole tragedy of her life. It was as though her beauty, thus detached from all that cheapened and vulgarized it, had held out suppliant hands to him from the world in which he and she had once met for a moment, and where he felt an overmastering longing to be with her again.

He was roused by the pressure of ecstatic fingers. "Wasn't she too beautiful, Lawrence? Don't you like her best in that simple dress? It makes her look like the real Lily—the Lily I know."

He met Gerty Farish's brimming gaze. "The Lily *we* know," he corrected; and his cousin, beaming at the implied understanding, exclaimed joyfully: "I'll tell her that! She always says you dislike her."

The performance over, Selden's first impulse was to seek Miss Bart. During the interlude of music which succeeded the *tableaux,* the actors had seated themselves here and there in the audience, diversifying its conventional appearance by the varied picturesqueness of their dress. Lily, however, was not among them, and her absence served to protract the effect she had produced on Selden: it would have broken the spell to see her too soon in the surroundings from which accident had so happily detached her. They had not met since the day of the Van Osburgh wedding, and on his side the avoidance had been intentional. Tonight, however, he knew that, sooner or later, he should find himself at her side; and though he let the dispersing crowd drift him whither it would, without making an immediate effort to reach her, his procrastination was not due to any lingering resistance, but to the desire to luxuriate a moment in the sense of complete surrender.

Lily had not an instant's doubt as to the meaning of the murmur greeting her appearance. No other *tableau* had been received with that precise note of approval: it had obviously been called forth by herself, and not by the picture she impersonated. She had feared at the last moment that she was risking too much in dispensing with the advantages of a more sumptuous setting, and the completeness of her triumph gave her an intoxicating sense of recovered power. Not caring to diminish the impression she had produced, she held herself aloof from the audience till the movement of dispersal before supper, and thus had a second opportunity of showing herself to advantage, as the throng poured slowly into the empty drawing-room where she was standing.

She was soon the centre of a group which increased and renewed itself as the circulation became general, and the individual comments on her success were a delightful prolongation of the collective applause. At such moments she lost something of her natural fastidiousness, and cared less for the quality of the admiration received than for its quantity. Differences of personality were merged in a warm atmosphere of praise, in which her beauty expanded like a flower in sunlight; and if Selden had approached a moment or two sooner he would have seen her turning on Ned Van Alstyne and George Dorset the look he had dreamed of capturing for himself.

Fortune willed, however, that the hurried approach of Mrs. Fisher, as whose aide-de-camp Van Alstyne was acting, should break up the group before Selden reached the threshold of the room. One or two of the men wandered off in search of their partners for supper, and the others, noticing Selden's approach, gave way to him in accordance with the tacit free-masonry of the ball-room. Lily was therefore standing alone when he reached her; and finding the expected look in her eye, he had the satisfaction of supposing he had kindled it. The look did indeed deepen as it rested on him, for even in that moment of self-intoxication Lily felt the quicker beat of life that his nearness always produced. She read, too, in his answering gaze the delicious confirmation of her triumph, and for the moment it seemed to her that it was for him only she cared to be beautiful.

Selden had given her his arm without speaking. She took it in silence, and they moved away, not toward the supper-room, but against the tide which was setting thither. The faces about her flowed by like the streaming images of sleep: she hardly noticed where Selden was leading her, till they passed through a glass doorway at the end of the long suite of rooms and stood suddenly in the fragrant hush of a garden. Gravel grated beneath their feet, and about them was the transparent dimness of a midsummer night. Hanging lights made emerald caverns in the depths of foliage, and whitened the spray of a fountain falling among lilies. The magic place was deserted: there was no sound but the plash of the water on the lily-pads, and a distant drift of music that might have been blown across a sleeping lake.

Selden and Lily stood still, accepting the unreality of the scene as a part of their own dream-like sensations. It would not have surprised them to feel a summer breeze on their faces, or to see the lights among the boughs reduplicated in the arch of a starry sky. The strange solitude about them was no stranger than the sweetness of being alone in it together.

At length Lily withdrew her hand, and moved away a step, so that her white-robed slimness was outlined against the dusk of the branches. Selden followed her, and still without speaking they seated themselves on a bench beside the fountain.

Suddenly she raised her eyes with the beseeching earnestness of a child. "You never speak to me—you think hard things of me," she murmured.

"I think of you at any rate, God knows!" he said.

"Then why do we never see each other? Why can't we be friends? You promised once to help me," she continued in the same tone, as though the words were drawn from her unwillingly.

"The only way I can help you is by loving you," Selden said in a low voice.

She made no reply, but her face turned to him with the soft motion of a flower. His own met it slowly, and their lips touched.

She drew back and rose from her seat. Selden rose too, and they stood facing each other. Suddenly she caught his hand and pressed it a moment against her cheek.

"Ah, love me, love me—but don't tell me so!" she sighed with her eyes in his; and before he could speak she had turned and slipped through the arch of boughs, disappearing in the brightness of the room beyond.

Selden stood where she had left him. He knew too well the transiency of exquisite moments to attempt to follow her; but presently he reëntered the house and made his way through the deserted rooms to the door. A few sumptuously-cloaked ladies were already gathered in the marble vestibule, and in the coatroom he found Van Alstyne and Gus Trenor.

The former, at Selden's approach, paused in the careful selection of a cigar from one of the silver boxes invitingly set out near the door.

"Hallo, Selden, going too? You're an Epicurean like myself, I see: you don't want to see all those goddesses gobbling terrapin. Gad, what a show of good-looking women; but not one of 'em could touch that little cousin of mine. Talk of jewels—what's a woman want with jewels when she's got herself to show? The trouble is that all these fal-bals they wear cover up their figures when they've got 'em. I never knew till tonight what an outline Lily has."

"It's not her fault if everybody don't know it now," growled Trenor, flushed with the struggle of getting into his fur-lined coat. "Damned bad taste, I call it—no, no cigar for me. You can't tell what you 're smoking in one of these new houses—likely as not the *chef* buys the cigars. Stay for supper? Not if I know it! When people crowd their rooms so that you can't get near any one you want to speak to, I'd as soon sup in the elevated at the rush hour. My wife was dead right to stay away: she says life's too short to spend it in breaking in new people."

§ 13

Lily woke from happy dreams to find two notes at her bedside.

One was from Mrs. Trenor, who announced that she was coming

to town that afternoon for a flying visit, and hoped Miss Bart would be able to dine with her. The other was from Selden. He wrote briefly that an important case called him to Albany, whence he would be unable to return till the evening, and asked Lily to let him know at what hour on the following day she would see him.

Lily, leaning back among her pillows, gazed musingly at his letter. The scene in the Brys' conservatory had been like a part of her dreams; she had not expected to wake to such evidence of its reality. Her first movement was one of annoyance: this unforeseen act of Selden's added another complication to life. It was so unlike him to yield to such an irrational impulse! Did he really mean to ask her to marry him? She had once shown him the impossibility of such a hope, and his subsequent behaviour seemed to prove that he had accepted the situation with a reasonableness somewhat mortifying to her vanity. It was all the more agreeable to find that this reasonableness was maintained only at the cost of not seeing her; but, though nothing in life was as sweet as the sense of her power over him, she saw the danger of allowing the episode of the previous night to have a sequel. Since she could not marry him, it would be kinder to him, as well as easier for herself, to write a line amicably evading his request to see her: he was not the man to mistake such a hint, and when next they met it would be on their usual friendly footing.

Lily sprang out of bed, and went straight to her desk. She wanted to write at once, while she could trust to the strength of her resolve. She was still languid from her brief sleep and the exhilaration of the evening, and the sight of Selden's writing brought back the culminating moment of her triumph: the moment when she had read in his eyes that no philosophy was proof against her power. It would be pleasant to have that sensation again . . . no one else could give it to her in its fulness; and she could not bear to mar her mood of luxurious retrospection by an act of definite refusal. She took up her pen and wrote hastily: *"Tomorrow at four";* murmuring to herself, as she slipped the sheet into its envelope: "I can easily put him off when tomorrow comes."

Judy Trenor's summons was very welcome to Lily. It was the first time she had received a direct communication from Bellomont since the close of her last visit there, and she was still visited by the dread of having incurred Judy's displeasure. But this characteristic command seemed to reëstablish their former relations; and Lily smiled at the thought that her friend had probably summoned her in order to hear about the Brys' entertainment. Mrs. Trenor had absented herself from the feast, perhaps for the reason so frankly enunciated by her husband, perhaps because, as Mrs. Fisher somewhat differently put it, she "couldn't bear new people when she hadn't discovered them herself." At any rate, though she remained haughtily at Bellomont, Lily suspected in her a devouring eagerness to hear of what she had missed, and to learn exactly in which measure Mrs. Wellington Bry had surpassed all previous competitors for social recognition. Lily was quite ready to gratify this curiosity, but it happened that she was dining out. She determined, however, to see Mrs. Trenor for a few moments, and ringing for her maid she despatched a telegram to say that she would be with her friend that evening at ten.

She was dining with Mrs. Fisher, who had gathered at an informal feast a few of the performers of the previous evening. There was to be plantation music in the studio after dinner—for Mrs. Fisher, despairing of the republic, had taken up modelling, and annexed to her small crowded house a spacious apartment, which, whatever its uses in her hours of plastic inspiration, served at other times for the exercise of an indefatigable hospitality. Lily was reluctant to leave, for the dinner was amusing, and she would have liked to lounge over a cigarette and hear a few songs; but she could not break her engagement with Judy, and shortly after ten she asked her hostess to ring for a hansom, and drove up Fifth Avenue to the Trenors'.

She waited long enough on the doorstep to wonder that Judy's presence in town was not signalized by a greater promptness in admitting her; and her surprise was increased when, instead of the expected footman, pushing his shoulders into a tardy coat, a shabby caretaking person in calico let her into the shrouded hall. Trenor, however, appeared at once on the threshold of the drawing-room, welcoming her with unusual volubility while he relieved her of her cloak and drew her into the room.

"Come along to the den; it's the only comfortable place in the house. Doesn't this room look as if it was waiting for the body to be brought down? Can't see why Judy keeps the house wrapped up in this awful slippery white stuff—it's enough to give a fellow pneumonia to walk through these rooms on a cold day. You look a little pinched yourself, by the way: it's rather a sharp night out. I noticed it walking up from the club. Come along, and I'll give you a nip of brandy, and you can toast yourself over the fire and try some of my new Egyptians—that little Turkish chap at the Embassy put me on to a brand that I want you to try, and if you like 'em I'll get out a lot for you: they don't have 'em here yet, but I'll cable."

He led her through the house to the large room at the back, where Mrs. Trenor usually sat, and where, even in her absence, there was an air of occupancy. Here, as usual, were flowers, newspapers, a littered writing-table, and a general aspect of lamp-lit familiarity, so that it was a surprise not to see Judy's energetic figure start up from the arm-chair near the fire.

It was apparently Trenor himself who had been occupying the seat in question, for it was overhung by a cloud of cigar smoke, and near it stood one of those intricate folding tables which British ingenuity has devised to facilitate the circulation of tobacco and spirits. The sight of such appliances in a drawing-room was not unusual in Lily's set, where smoking and drinking were unrestricted by considerations of time and place, and her first movement was to help herself to one of the cigarettes recommended by Trenor, while she checked his loquacity by asking, with a surprised glance: "Where's Judy?"

Trenor, a little heated by his unusual flow of words, and perhaps by prolonged propinquity with the decanters, was bending over the latter to decipher their silver labels.

"Here, now, Lily, just a drop of cognac in a little fizzy water—you do look pinched, you know: I swear the end of your nose is red. I'll take another glass to keep you company—Judy?—Why, you see, Judy's got a devil of a headache—quite knocked out with it, poor thing—she asked me to explain—make it all right, you know—Do come up to the fire, though; you look dead-beat, really. Now do let me make you comfortable, there's a good girl."

He had taken her hand, half-banteringly, and was drawing her toward a low seat by the hearth; but she stopped and freed herself quietly.

"Do you mean to say that Judy's not well enough to see me? Doesn't she want me to go upstairs?"

Trenor drained the glass he had filled for himself, and paused to set it down before he answered.

"Why, no—the fact is, she's not up to seeing anybody. It came on suddenly, you know, and she asked me to tell you how awfully sorry she was—if she'd known where you were dining she'd have sent you word."

"She did know where I was dining; I mentioned it in my telegram. But it doesn't matter, of course. I suppose if she's so poorly she won't go back to Bellomont in the morning, and I can come and see her then."

"Yes, exactly—that's capital. I'll tell her you'll pop in tomorrow morning. And now do sit down a minute, there's a dear, and let's have a nice quiet jaw together. You won't take a drop, just for sociability? Tell me what you think of that cigarette. Why, don't you like it? What are you chucking it away for?"

"I am chucking it away because I must go, if you'll have the goodness to call a cab for me," Lily returned with a smile.

She did not like Trenor's unusual excitability, with its too evident explanation, and the thought of being alone with him, with her friend out of reach upstairs, at the other end of the great empty house, did not conduce to a desire to prolong their *tête-à-tête.*

But Trenor, with a promptness which did not escape her, had moved between herself and the door.

"Why must you go, I should like to know? If Judy'd been here you'd have sat gossiping till all hours—and you can't even give me five minutes! It's always the same story. Last night I couldn't get near you—I went to that damned vulgar party just to see you, and there was everybody talking about you, and asking me if I'd ever seen anything so stunning, and when I tried to come up and say a word, you never took any notice, but just went on laughing and joking with a lot of asses who only wanted to be able to swagger about afterward, and look knowing when you were mentioned."

He paused, flushed by his diatribe, and fixing on her a look in which resentment was the ingredient she least disliked. But she had regained her presence of mind, and stood composedly in the middle of the room, while her slight smile seemed to put an ever increasing distance between herself and Trenor.

Across it she said: "Don't be absurd, Gus. It's past eleven, and I must really ask you to ring for a cab."

He remained immovable, with the lowering forehead she had grown to detest.

"And supposing I won't ring for one—what'll you do then?"

"I shall go upstairs to Judy if you force me to disturb her."

Trenor drew a step nearer and laid his hand on her arm. "Look here, Lily: won't you give me five minutes of your own accord?"

"Not tonight, Gus: you——"

"Very good, then: I'll take 'em. And as many more as I want." He had squared himself on the threshold, his hands thrust deep in his pockets. He nodded toward the chair on the hearth.

"Go and sit down there, please: I've got a word to say to you."

Lily's quick temper was getting the better of her fears. She drew herself up and moved toward the door.

"If you have anything to say to me, you must say it another time. I shall go up to Judy unless you call a cab for me at once."

He burst into a laugh. "Go upstairs and welcome, my dear; but you won't find Judy. She ain't there."

Lily cast a startled look upon him. "Do you mean that Judy is not in the house—not in town?" she exclaimed.

"That's just what I do mean," returned Trenor, his bluster sinking to sullenness under her look.

"Nonsense—I don't believe you. I am going upstairs," she said impatiently.

He drew unexpectedly aside, letting her reach the threshold unimpeded.

"Go up and welcome; but my wife is at Bellomont."

But Lily had a flash of reassurance. "If she hadn't come she would have sent me word——"

"She did; she telephoned me this afternoon to let you know."

"I received no message."

"I didn't send any."

The two measured each other for a moment, but Lily still saw her opponent through a blur of scorn that made all other considerations indistinct.

"I can't imagine your object in playing such a stupid trick on me; but if you have fully gratified your peculiar sense of humour I must again ask you to send for a cab."

It was the wrong note, and she knew it as she spoke. To be stung by irony it is not necessary to understand it, and the angry streaks on Trenor's face might have been raised by an actual lash.

"Look here, Lily, don't take that high and mighty tone with me." He had again moved toward the door, and in her instinctive shrinking from him she let him regain command of the threshold. "I *did* play a trick on you; I own up to it; but if you think I'm ashamed you're mistaken. Lord knows I've been patient enough—I've hung round and looked like an ass. And all the while you were letting a lot of other fellows make up to you . . . letting 'em make fun of me, I daresay . . . I'm not sharp, and can't dress my friends up to look funny, as you do . . . but I can tell when it's being done to me . . . I can tell fast enough when I'm made a fool of . . ."

"Ah, I shouldn't have thought that!" flashed from Lily; but her laugh dropped to silence under his look.

"No; you wouldn't have thought it; but you'll know better now. That's what you're here for tonight. I've been waiting for a quiet time to talk things over, and now I've got it I mean to make you hear me out."

His first rush of inarticulate resentment had been followed by a steadiness and concentration of tone more disconcerting to Lily than the excitement preceding it. For a moment her presence of mind forsook her. She had more than once been in situations where a quick sword-play of wit had been needful to cover her retreat; but her frightened heart-throbs told her that here such skill would not avail.

To gain time she repeated: "I don't understand what you want."

Trenor had pushed a chair between herself and the door. He threw himself in it, and leaned back, looking up at her.

"I'll tell you what I want: I want to know just where you and I stand. Hang it, the man who pays for the dinner is generally allowed to have a seat at table."

She flamed with anger and abasement, and the sickening need of having to conciliate where she longed to humble.

"I don't know what you mean—but you must see, Gus, that I can't stay here talking to you at this hour——"

"Gad, you go to men's houses fast enough in broad daylight—strikes me you 're not always so deuced careful of appearances."

The brutality of the thrust gave her the sense of dizziness that follows on a physical blow. Rosedale had spoken then—this was the way men talked of her— She felt suddenly weak and defenceless: there was a throb of self-pity in her throat. But all the while another self was sharpening her to vigilance, whispering the terrified warning that every word and gesture must be measured.

"If you have brought me here to say insulting things——" she began.

Trenor laughed. "Don't talk stage-rot. I don't want to insult you. But a man's got his feelings—and you've played with mine too long. I didn't begin this business—kept out of the way, and left the track clear for the other chaps, till you rummaged me out and set to work to make an ass of me—and an easy job you had of it, too. That's the trouble—it was too easy for you—you got reckless—thought you could turn me inside out, and chuck me in the gutter like an empty purse. But, by gad, that ain't playing fair: that's dodging the rules of the game. Of course I know now what you wanted—it wasn't my beautiful eyes you were after—but I tell you what, Miss Lily, you've got to pay up for making me think so——"

He rose, squaring his shoulders aggressively, and stepped toward her with a reddening brow; but she held her footing, though every nerve tore at her to retreat as he advanced.

"Pay up?" she faltered. "Do you mean that I owe you money?"

He laughed again. "Oh, I'm not asking for payment in kind. But there's such a thing as fair play—and interest on one's money—and hang me if I've had as much as a look from you——"

"Your money? What have I to do with your money? You advised me how to invest mine . . . you must have seen I knew nothing of business . . . you told me it was all right——"

"It *was* all right—it is, Lily: you're welcome to all of it, and ten times more. I'm only asking for a word of thanks from you." He was closer still, with a hand that grew formidable; and the frightened self in her was dragging the other down.

"I *have* thanked you; I've shown I was grateful. What more have you done than any friend might do, or any one accept from a friend?"

Trenor caught her up with a sneer. "I don't doubt you've accepted as much before—and chucked the other chaps as you'd like to chuck me. I don't care how you settled your score with them—if you fooled 'em I'm that much to the good. Don't stare at me like that—I know I'm not talking the way a man is supposed to talk to a girl—but, hang it, if you don't like it you can stop me quick enough—you know I'm mad about you—damn the money, there's plenty more of it—if *that* bothers you . . . I was a brute, Lily—Lily!—just look at me——"

Over and over her the sea of humiliation broke—wave crashing on wave so close that the moral shame was one with the physical dread. It seemed to her that self-esteem would have made her invulnerable—that it was her own dishonour which put a fearful solitude about her.

His touch was a shock to her drowning consciousness. She drew back from him with a desperate assumption of scorn.

"I've told you I don't understand—but if I owe you money you shall be paid——"

Trenor's face darkened to rage: her recoil of abhorrence had called out the primitive man.

"Ah—you'll borrow from Selden or Rosedale—and take your chances of fooling them as you've fooled me! Unless—unless you've settled your other scores already—and I'm the only one left out in the cold!"

She stood silent, frozen to her place. The words—the words were worse than the touch! Her heart was beating all over her body—in her throat, her limbs, her helpless useless hands. Her eyes travelled despairingly about the room—they lit on the bell, and she remembered that help was in call. Yes, but scandal with it—a hideous mustering of tongues. No, she must fight her way out alone. It was enough that the servants knew her to be in the house with Trenor—there must be nothing to excite conjecture in her way of leaving it.

She raised her head, and achieved a last clear look at him.

"I am here alone with you," she said. "What more have you to say?"

To her surprise, Trenor answered the look with a speechless stare. With his last gust of words the flame had died out, leaving him chill and humbled. It was as though a cold air had dispersed the fumes of his libations, and the situation loomed before him black and naked as the ruins of a fire. Old habits, old restraints, the hand of inherited order, plucked back the bewildered mind which passion had jolted from its ruts. Trenor's eye had the haggard look of the sleep-walker waked on a deathly ledge.

"Go home! Go away from here"—–he stammered, and turning his back on her walked toward the hearth.

The sharp release from her fears restored Lily to immediate lucidity. The collapse of Trenor's will left her in control, and she heard herself, in a voice that was her own yet outside herself, bidding him ring for the servant, bidding him give the order for a hansom, directing him to put her in it when it came. Whence the strength came to her she knew not; but an insistent voice warned her that she must leave the house openly, and nerved her, in the hall before the hovering care-taker, to exchange light words with Trenor, and charge him with the usual messages for Judy, while all the while she shook with inward loathing. On the doorstep, with the street before her, she felt a mad throb of liberation, intoxicating as the prisoner's first draught of free air; but the clearness of brain continued, and she noted the mute aspect of Fifth Avenue, guessed at the lateness of the hour, and even observed a man's figure—was there something half-familiar in its outline?—which, as she entered the hansom, turned from the opposite corner and vanished in the obscurity of the side street.

But with the turn of the wheels reaction came, and shuddering darkness closed on her. "I can't think—I can't think," she moaned, and leaned her head against the rattling side of the cab. She seemed a stranger to herself, or rather there were two selves in her, the one she had always known, and a new abhorrent being to which it found itself chained. She had once picked up, in a house where she was staying, a translation of the *Eumenides,* and her imagination had been seized by the high terror of the scene where Orestes, in the cave of the oracle, finds his implacable huntresses asleep, and snatches an hour's repose. Yes, the Furies might sometimes sleep, but they were there, always there in the dark corners, and now they were awake and the iron clang of their wings was in her brain . . . She opened her eyes and saw the streets passing—the familiar alien streets. All she looked on was the same and yet changed. There was a great gulf fixed between today and yesterday. Everything in the past seemed simple, natural, full of daylight—and she was alone in a place of darkness and pollution.—Alone! It was the loneliness that frightened her. Her eyes fell on an illuminated clock at a street corner, and she saw that the hands marked the half hour after eleven. Only half-past eleven—there were hours and hours left of the night! And she must spend them alone, shuddering sleepless on her bed. Her soft nature recoiled from this ordeal, which had none of the stimulus of conflict to goad her through it. Oh, the slow cold drip of the minutes on her head! She had a vision of herself lying on the black walnut bed—and the darkness would frighten her, and if she left the light burning the dreary details of the room would brand themselves forever on her brain. She had always hated her room at Mrs. Peniston's—its ugliness, its impersonality, the fact that nothing in it was really hers. To a torn heart uncomforted by human nearness a room may open almost human arms, and the being to whom no four walls mean more than any others, is, at such hours, expatriate everywhere.

Lily had no heart to lean on. Her relation with her aunt was as superficial as that of chance lodgers who pass on the stairs. But even had the two been in closer contact, it was impossible to think of Mrs. Peniston's mind as offering shelter or comprehension to such misery as Lily's. As the pain that can be told is but half a pain, so the pity that questions has little healing in its touch. What Lily craved was the darkness made by enfolding arms, the silence which is not solitude, but compassion holding its breath.

. . . .

§ 14

At Mrs. Fisher's, through the cigar-smoke of the studio, a dozen voices greeted Selden. A song was pending as he entered, and he dropped into a seat near his hostess, his eyes roaming in search of Miss Bart. But she was not there, and the discovery gave him a pang out of all proportion to its seriousness; since the note in his breast-pocket assured him that at four the next day they would meet. To his impatience it seemed immeasurably long to wait, and half-ashamed of the impulse, he leaned to Mrs. Fisher to ask, as the music ceased, if Miss Bart had not dined with her.

"Lily? She's just gone. She had to run off, I forget where. Wasn't she wonderful last night?"

"Who's that? Lily?" asked Jack Stepney, from the depths of a neighboring arm-chair. "Really, you know, I'm no prude, but when it comes to a girl standing there as if she was up at auction—I thought seriously of speaking to cousin Julia."

"You didn't know Jack had become our social censor?" Mrs. Fisher said to Selden with a laugh; and Stepney spluttered, amid the general derision: "But she's a cousin, hang it, and when a man's married—*Town Talk* was full of her this morning."

"Yes: lively reading that was," said Mr. Ned Van Alstyne, stroking his moustache to hide the smile behind it. "Buy the dirty sheet? No, of course not; some fellow showed it to me—but I'd heard the stories before. When a girl's as good-looking as that she'd better marry; then no questions are asked. In our imperfectly organized society there is no provision as yet for the young woman who claims the privileges of marriage without assuming its obligations."

"Well, I understand Lily is about to assume them in the shape of Mr. Rosedale," Mrs. Fisher said with a laugh.

"Rosedale—good heavens!" exclaimed Van Alstyne, dropping his eye-glass. "Stepney, that's your fault for foisting the brute on us."

"Oh, confound it, you know, we don't *marry* Rosedale in our family," Stepney languidly protested; but his wife, who sat in oppressive bridal finery at the other side of the room, quelled him with the judicial reflection: "In Lily's circumstances it's a mistake to have too high a standard."

"I hear even Rosedale has been scared by the talk lately," Mrs. Fisher rejoined; "but the sight of her last night sent him off his head. What do you think he said to me after her *tableau?* 'My God, Mrs. Fisher, if I could get Paul Morpeth to paint her like that, the picture'd appreciate a hundred per cent in ten years.' "

"By Jove,—but isn't she about somewhere?" exclaimed Van Alstyne, restoring his glass with an uneasy glance.

"No; she ran off while you were all mixing the punch down stairs. Where was she going, by the way? What's on tonight? I hadn't heard of anything."

"Oh, not a party, I think," said an inexperienced young Farish who had arrived late. "I put her in her cab as I was coming in, and she gave the driver the Trenors' address."

"The Trenors'?" exclaimed Mrs. Jack Stepney. "Why, the house is closed—Judy telephoned me from Bellomont this evening."

"Did she? That's queer. I'm sure I'm not mistaken. Well, come now, Trenor's there, anyhow—I—oh, well—the fact is, I've no head for numbers," he broke off, admonished by the nudge of an adjoining foot, and the smile that circled the room.

In its unpleasant light Selden had risen and was shaking hands with his hostess. The air of the place stifled him, and he wondered why he had stayed in it so long.

On the doorstep he stood still, remembering a phrase of Lily's: "It seems to me you spend a good deal of time in the element you disapprove of."

Well—what had brought him there but the quest of her? It was her element, not his. But he would lift her out of it, take her beyond! That *Beyond!* on her letter was like a cry for rescue. He knew that Perseus's task is not done when he has loosed Andromeda's chains, for her limbs are numb with bondage, and she cannot rise and walk, but clings to him with dragging arms as he beats back to land with his burden. Well, he had strength for both—it was her weakness which had put the strength in him. It was not, alas, a clean rush of waves they had to win through, but a clogging morass of old associations and habits, and for the moment its vapours were in his throat. But he would see clearer, breathe freer in her presence: she was at once the dead weight at his breast and the spar which should float them to safety. He smiled at the whirl of metaphor with which he was trying to build up a defence against the influences of the last hour. It was pitiable that he, who knew the mixed motives on which social judgments depend, should still feel himself so swayed by them. How could he lift Lily to a freer vision of life, if his own view of her was to be coloured by any mind in which he saw her reflected?

The moral oppression had produced a physical craving for air, and he strode on, opening his lungs to the reverberating coldness of the night. At the corner of Fifth Avenue Van Alstyne hailed him with an offer of company.

"Walking? A good thing to blow the smoke out of one's head. Now that women have taken to tobacco we live in a bath of nicotine. It would be a curious thing to study the effect of cigarettes on the relation of the sexes. Smoke is almost as great a solvent as divorce: both tend to obscure the moral issue."

Nothing could have been less consonant with Selden's mood than Van Alstyne's after-dinner aphorisms, but as long as the latter confined himself to generalities his listener's nerves were in control. Happily Van Alstyne prided himself on his summing up of social aspects, and with Selden for audience was eager to show the sureness of his touch. Mrs. Fisher lived in an East side street near the Park, and as the two men walked down Fifth Avenue the new architectural developments of that versatile thoroughfare invited Van Alstyne's comment.

"That Greiner house, now—a typical rung in the social ladder! The man who built it came from a *milieu* where all the dishes are put on the table at once. His façade is a complete architectural meal; if he had omitted a style his friends might have thought the money had given out. Not a bad purchase for Rosedale, though: attracts attention, and awes the Western sightseer. By and bye he'll get out of that phase, and want something that the crowd will pass and the few pause before. Especially if he marries my clever cousin——"

Selden dashed in with the query: "And the Wellington Brys'? Rather clever of its kind, don't you think?"

They were just beneath the wide white facade, with its rich restraint of line, which suggested the clever corseting of a redundant figure.

"That's the next stage: the desire to imply that one has been to Europe, and has a standard. I'm sure Mrs. Bry thinks her house a copy of the *Trianon;* in America every marble house with gilt furniture is thought to be a copy of the *Trianon*. What a clever chap that architect is, though—how he takes his client's measure! He has put the whole of Mrs. Bry in his use of the composite order. Now for the Trenors, you remember, he chose the Corinthian: exuberant, but based on the best precedent. The Trenor house is one of his best things—doesn't look like a banqueting-hall turned inside out. I hear Mrs. Trenor wants to build out a new ball-room, and that divergence from Gus on that point keeps her at Bellomont. The dimensions of the Brys' ball-room must rankle: you may be sure she knows 'em as well as if she'd been there last night with a yard-measure. Who said she was in town, by the way? That Farish boy? She isn't, I know; Mrs. Stepney was right; the house is dark, you see: I suppose Gus lives in the back."

He had halted opposite the Trenors' corner, and Selden perforce stayed his steps also. The house loomed obscure and uninhabited; only an oblong gleam above the door spoke of provisional occupancy.

"They've bought the house at the back: it gives them a hundred and fifty feet in the side street. There's where the ball-room's to be, with a gallery connecting it: billiard-room and so on above. I suggested changing the entrance, and carrying the drawing-room across the whole Fifth Avenue front: you see the front door corresponds with the windows——"

The walking-stick which Van Alstyne swung in demonstration dropped to a startled "Hallo!" as the door opened and two figures were seen silhouetted against the hall-light. At the same moment a hansom halted at the curb-stone, and one of the figures floated down to it in a haze of evening draperies; while the other, black and bulky, remained persistently projected against the light.

For an immeasurable second the two spectators of the incident were silent; then the house-door closed, the hansom rolled off, and the whole scene slipped by as if with the turn of a stereopticon.

Van Alstyne dropped his eye-glass with a low whistle.

"A—hem—nothing of this, eh, Selden? As one of the family, I know I may count on you—appearances are deceptive—and Fifth Avenue is so imperfectly lighted——"

"Good night," said Selden, turning sharply down the side street without seeing the other's extended hand.

. . . .

PREFATORY NOTE TO "THE EYES"

The Eyes, which originally appeared in *Tales of Men and Ghosts* (1910) is Edith Wharton's most effective indictment of a type of man who appears again and again in her fiction: the selfish, cultivated dilettante who tries to warm his cold and arid nature in hotter life-streams than his own. Her attitude to such men, while hostile in *The Eyes,* is elsewhere more ambiguous. Lawrence Selden in *The House of Mirth* is presented as a hero. The ambiguity may be in part explained by Edith Wharton's own relation to Walter Berry, the exquisite bachelor and international lawyer with whom, as recently published portions of her diary show, she was deeply in love. Berry's cooler feelings towards herself may have prompted the antagonism that some of her heroes seem to arouse in their creator. Theodore Roosevelt found him pompous and stuffy and likened him to a ball of worsted "because he is such a nice thing for a kitten to play with," but Percy Lubbock, who observed him more closely, saw him as a dogmatic, snobbish egotist and the evil genius of Edith Wharton's life.

The Eyes

§ 1

WE HAD BEEN put in the mood for ghosts, that evening, after an excellent dinner at our old friend Culwin's, by a tale of Fred Murchard's—the narrative of a strange personal visitation.

Seen through the haze of our cigars, and by the drowsy gleam of a coal fire, Culwin's library, with its oak walls and dark old bindings, made a good setting for such evocations; and ghostly experiences at first hand being, after Murchard's opening, the only kind acceptable to us, we proceeded to take stock of our group and tax each member for a contribution. There were eight of us, and seven contrived, in a manner more or less adequate, to fulfil the condition imposed. It surprised us all to find that we could muster such a show of supernatural impressions, for none of us, excepting Murchard himself and young Phil Frenham—whose story was the slightest of the lot—had the habit of sending our souls into the invisible. So that, on the whole, we had every reason to be proud of our seven "exhibits," and none of us would have dreamed of expecting an eighth from our host.

Our old friend, Mr. Andrew Culwin, who had sat back in his armchair, listening and blinking through the smoke circles with the cheerful tolerance of a wise old idol, was not the kind of man likely to be favoured with such contacts, though he had imagination enough to enjoy, without envying, the superior privileges of his guests. By age and by education he belonged to the stout Positivist tradition, and his habit of thought had been formed in the days of the epic struggle between physics and metaphysics. But he had been, then and always, essentially a spectator, a humorous detached observer of the immense muddled variety show of life, slipping out of his seat now and then for a brief dip into the convivialities at the back of the house, but never, as far as one knew, showing the least desire to jump on the stage and do a "turn."

Among his contemporaries there lingered a vague tradition of his having, at a remote period, and in a romantic clime, been wounded in a duel; but this legend no more tallied with what we younger men knew of his character than my mother's assertion that he had once been "a charming little man with nice eyes" corresponded to any possible reconstitution of his physiognomy.

"He never can have looked like anything but a bundle of sticks," Murchard had once said of him. "Or a phosphorescent log, rather," some one else amended; and we recognised the happiness of this description of his small squat trunk, with the red blink of the eyes in a face like mottled bark. He had always been possessed of a leisure which he had nursed and protected, instead of squandering it in vain activities. His carefully guarded hours had been devoted to the cultivation of a fine intelligence and a few judiciously chosen habits; and none of the disturbances common to human experience seemed to have crossed his sky. Nevertheless, his dispassionate survey of the universe had not raised his opinion of that costly experiment, and his study of the human race seemed to have resulted in the conclusion that all men were superfluous, and women necessary only because some one had to do the cooking. On the importance of this point his convictions were absolute, and gastronomy was the only science which he revered as a dogma. It must be owned that his little dinners were a strong argument in favour of this view, besides being a reason—though not the main one—for the fidelity of his friends.

Mentally he exercised a hospitality less seductive but no less stimulating. His mind was like a forum, or some open meeting-place for the exchange of ideas: somewhat cold and draughty, but light, spacious and orderly—a kind of academic grove from which all the leaves have fallen. In this privileged area a dozen of us were wont to stretch our muscles and expand our lungs; and, as if to prolong as much as possible the tradition of what we felt to be a vanishing institution, one or two neophytes were now and then added to our band.

Young Phil Frenham was the last, and the most interesting, of these recruits, and a good example of Murchard's somewhat morbid assertion that our old friend "liked 'em juicy." It was indeed a fact that Culwin, for all his dryness, specially tasted the lyric qualities in youth. As he was far too good an Epicurean to nip the flowers of soul which he gathered for his garden, his friendship was not a disintegrating influence: on the contrary, it forced the young idea to robuster bloom. And in Phil Frenham he had a good subject for experimentation. The boy was really intelligent, and the soundness of his nature was like the pure paste under a fine glaze. Culwin had fished him out of a fog of family dulness, and pulled him up to a peak in Darien; and the adventure hadn't hurt him a bit. Indeed, the skill with which Culwin had contrived to stimulate his curiosities without robbing them of their bloom of awe seemed to me a sufficient answer to Murchard's ogreish metaphor. There was nothing hectic in Frenham's efflorescence, and his old friend had not laid even a finger-tip on the sacred stupidities. One wanted no better proof of that than the fact that Frenham still reverenced them in Culwin.

"There's a side of him you fellows don't see. *I* believe that story about the duel!" he declared; and it was of the very essence of this belief that it should impel him—just as our little party was dispersing—to turn back to our host with the joking demand: "And now you've got to tell us about *your* ghost!"

The outer door had closed on Murchard and the others; only Frenham and I remained; and the devoted servant who presided over Culwin's destinies, having brought a fresh supply of soda-water, had been laconically ordered to bed.

Culwin's sociability was a night-blooming flower, and we knew that he expected the nucleus of his group to tighten around him after midnight. But Frenham's appeal seemed to disconcert him comically, and he rose from the chair in which he had just reseated himself after his farewells in the hall.

"*My* ghost. Do you suppose I'm fool enough to go to the expense of keeping one of my own, when there are so many charming ones in my friends' closets?—Take another cigar," he said, revolving toward me with a laugh.

Frenham laughed too, pulling up his slender height before the chimney-piece as he turned to face his short bristling friend.

"Oh," he said, "you'd never be content to share if you met one you really liked."

Culwin had dropped back into his arm-chair, his shock head embedded in the hollow of worn leather, his little eyes glimmering over a fresh cigar.

"Liked—*liked?* Good Lord!" he growled.

"Ah, you *have,* then!" Frenham pounced on him in the same instant, with a side-glance of victory at me; but Culwin cowered gnomelike among his cushions, dissembling himself in a protective cloud of smoke.

"What's the use of denying it? You've seen everything, so of course you've seen a ghost!" his young friend persisted, talking intrepidly into the cloud. "Or, if you haven't seen one, it's only because you've seen two!"

The form of the challenge seemed to strike our host. He shot his head out of the mist with a queer tortoise-like motion he sometimes had, and blinked approvingly at Frenham.

"That's it," he flung at us on a shrill jerk of laughter; "it's only because I've seen two!"

The words were so unexpected that they dropped down and down into a deep silence, while we continued to stare at each other over Culwin's head, and Culwin stared at his ghosts. At length Frenham, without speaking, threw himself into the chair on the other side of the hearth, and leaned forward with his listening smile . . .

§ 2

"Oh, of course they're not show ghosts—a collector wouldn't think anything of them . . . Don't let me raise your hopes . . . their one merit is their numerical strength: the exceptional fact of their being *two.* But, as against this, I'm bound to admit that at any moment I could probably have exorcised them both by asking my doctor for a prescription, or my oculist for a pair of spectacles. Only, as I never could make up my mind whether to go to the doctor or the oculist—whether I was afflicted by an optical or a digestive delusion—I left them to pursue their interesting double life, though at times they made mine exceedingly uncomfortable . . .

"Yes—uncomfortable; and you know how I hate to be uncomfortable! But it was part of my stupid pride, when the thing began, not to admit that I could be disturbed by the trifling matter of seeing two——

"And then I'd no reason, really, to suppose I was ill. As far as I knew I was simply bored—horribly bored. But it was part of my boredom—I remember—that I was feeling so uncommonly well, and didn't know how on earth to work off my surplus energy. I had come back from a long journey—down in South America and Mexico—and had settled down for the winter near New York, with an old aunt who had known Washington Irving and corresponded with N. P. Willis. She lived, not far from Irvington, in a damp Gothic villa, overhung by Norway spruces, and looking exactly like a memorial emblem done in hair. Her personal appearance was in keeping with this image, and her own hair—of which there was little left—might have been sacrificed to the manufacture of the emblem.

"I had just reached the end of an agitated year, with considerable arrears to make up in money and emotion; and theoretically it seemed as though my aunt's mild hospitality would be as beneficial to my nerves as to my purse. But the deuce of it was that as soon as I felt myself safe and sheltered my energy began to revive; and how was I to work it off inside of a memorial emblem? I had, at that time, the illusion that sustained intellectual effort could engage a man's whole activity; and I decided to write a great book—I forget about what. My aunt, impressed by my plan, gave up to me her Gothic library, filled with classics bound in black cloth and daguerreotypes of faded celebrities; and I sat down at my desk to win myself a place among their number. And to facilitate my task she lent me a cousin to copy my manuscript.

"The cousin was a nice girl, and I had an idea that a nice girl was just what I needed to restore my faith in human nature, and principally in myself. She was neither beautiful nor intelligent—poor Alice Nowell!—but it interested me to see any woman content to be so uninteresting, and I wanted to find out the secret of her content. In doing this I handled it rather rashly, and put it out of joint—oh, just for a moment! There's no fatuity in telling you this, for the poor girl had never seen any one but cousins . . .

"Well, I was sorry for what I'd done, of course, and confoundedly bothered as to how I should put it straight. She was staying in the house, and one evening, after my aunt had gone to bed, she came down to the library to fetch a book she'd mislaid, like any artless heroine on the shelves behind us. She was pink-nosed and flustered, and it suddenly occurred to me that her hair, though it was fairly thick and pretty, would look exactly like my aunt's when she grew older. I was glad I had noticed this, for it made it easier for me to decide to do what was right; and when I had found the book she hadn't lost I told her I was leaving for Europe that week.

"Europe was terribly far off in those days, and Alice knew at once what I meant. She didn't take it in the least as I'd expected—it would have been easier if she had. She held her book very tight, and turned away a moment to wind up the lamp on my desk—it had a ground glass shade with vine leaves, and glass drops around the edge, I remember. Then she came back, held out her hand, and said: 'Good-bye.' And as she said it she looked straight at me and kissed me. I had never felt anything as fresh and shy and brave as her kiss. It was worse than any reproach, and it made me ashamed to deserve a reproach from her. I said to myself: 'I'll marry her, and when my aunt dies she'll leave us this house, and I'll sit here at the desk and go on with my book; and Alice will sit over there with her embroidery and look at me as she's looking now. And life will go on like that for any number of years.' The prospect frightened me a little, but at the time it didn't frighten me as much as doing anything to hurt her; and ten minutes later she had my seal ring on her finger, and my promise that when I went abroad she should go with me.

"You'll wonder why I'm enlarging on this incident. It's because the evening on which it took place was the very evening on which I first saw the queer sight I've spoken of. Being at that time an ardent believer in a necessary sequence between cause and effect I naturally tried to trace some kind of link between what had just happened to me in my aunt's library, and what was to happen a few hours later on the same night; and so the coincidence between the two events always remained in my mind.

"I went up to bed with rather a heavy heart, for I was bowed under the weight of the first good action I had ever consciously committed; and young as I was, I saw the gravity of my situation.

Don't imagine from this that I had hitherto been an instrument of destruction. I had been merely a harmless young man, who had followed his bent and declined all collaboration with Providence. Now I had suddenly undertaken to promote the moral order of the world, and I felt a good deal like the trustful spectator who has given his gold watch to the conjurer, and doesn't know in what shape he'll get it back when the trick is over . . . Still, a glow of self-righteousness tempered my fears, and I said to myself as I undressed that when I'd got used to being good it probably wouldn't make me as nervous as it did at the start. And by the time I was in bed, and had blown out my candle, I felt that I really *was* getting used to it, and that, as far as I'd got, it was not unlike sinking down into one of my aunt's very softest wool mattresses.

"I closed my eyes on this image, and when I opened them it must have been a good deal later, for my room had grown cold, and intensely still. I was waked by the queer feeling we all know—the feeling that there was something in the room that hadn't been there when I fell asleep. I sat up and strained my eyes into the darkness. The room was pitch black, and at first I saw nothing; but gradually a vague glimmer at the foot of the bed turned into two eyes staring back at me. I couldn't distinguish the features attached to them, but as I looked the eyes grew more and more distinct: they gave out a light of their own.

"The sensation of being thus gazed at was far from pleasant, and you might suppose that my first impulse would have been to jump out of bed and hurl myself on the invisible figure attached to the eyes. But it wasn't—my impulse was simply to lie still . . . I can't say whether this was due to an immediate sense of the uncanny nature of the apparition—to the certainty that if I did jump out of bed I should hurl myself on nothing—or merely to the benumbing effect of the eyes themselves. They were the very worst eyes I've ever seen: a man's eyes—but what a man! My first thought was that he must be frightfully old. The orbits were sunk, and the thick red-lined lids hung over the eyeballs like blinds of which the cords are broken. One lid drooped a little lower than the other, with the effect of a crooked leer; and between these folds of flesh, with their scant bristle of lashes, the eyes themselves, small glassy disks with an agate-like rim, looked like sea-pebbles in the grip of a star-fish.

"But the age of the eyes was not the most unpleasant thing about them. What turned me sick was their expression of vicious security. I don't know how else to describe the fact that they seemed to belong to a man who had done a lot of harm in his life, but had always kept just inside the danger lines. They were not the eyes of a coward, but of some one much too clever to take risks; and my gorge rose at their look of base astuteness. Yet even that wasn't the worst; for as we continued to scan each other I saw in them a tinge of derision, and felt myself to be its object.

"At that I was seized by an impulse of rage that jerked me to my feet and pitched me straight at the unseen figure. But of course there wasn't any figure there, and my fists struck at emptiness. Ashamed and cold, I groped about for a match and lit the candles. The room looked just as usual—as I had known it would; and I crawled back to bed, and blew out the lights.

"As soon as the room was dark again the eyes reappeared; and I now applied myself to explaining them on scientific principles. At first I thought the illusion might have been caused by the glow of the last embers in the chimney; but the fireplace was on the other side of my bed, and so placed that the fire could not be reflected in my toilet glass, which was the only mirror in the room. Then it struck me that I might have been tricked by the reflection of the embers in some polished bit of wood or metal; and though I couldn't discover any object of the sort in my line of vision, I got up again, groped my way to the hearth, and covered what was left of the fire. But as soon as I was back in bed the eyes were back at its foot.

"They were an hallucination, then: that was plain. But the fact that they were not due to any external dupery didn't make them a bit pleasanter. For if they were a projection of my inner consciousness, what the deuce was the matter with that organ? I had gone deeply enough into the mystery of morbid pathological states to picture the conditions under which an exploring mind might lay itself open to such a midnight admonition; but I couldn't fit it to my present case. I had never felt more normal, mentally and physically; and the only unusual fact in my situation—that of having assured the happiness of an amiable girl—did not seem of a kind to summon unclean spirits about my pillow. But there were the eyes still looking at me . . .

"I shut mine, and tried to evoke a vision of Alice Nowell's. They were not remarkable eyes, but they were as wholesome as fresh water, and if she had had more imagination—or longer lashes—their expression might have been interesting. As it was, they did not prove very efficacious, and in a few moments I perceived that they had mysteriously changed into the eyes at the foot of the bed. It exasperated me more to feel these glaring at me through my shut lids than to see them, and I opened my eyes again and looked straight into their hateful stare . . .

"And so it went on all night. I can't tell you what that night was like, nor how long it lasted. Have you ever lain in bed, hoplessly wide awake, and tried to keep your eyes shut, knowing that if you opened 'em you'd see something you dreaded and loathed? It sounds easy, but it's devilish hard. Those eyes hung there and drew me. I had the *vertige de l'abîme,* and their red lids were the edge of my abyss . . . I had known nervous hours before: hours when I'd felt the wind of danger in my neck; but never this kind of strain. It wasn't that the eyes were awful; they hadn't the majesty of the powers of darkness. But they had—how shall I say?—a physical effect that was the equivalent of a bad smell: their look left a smear like a snail's. And I didn't see what business they had with me, anyhow—and I stared and stared, trying to find out . . .

"I don't know what effect they were trying to produce; but the effect they *did* produce was that of making me pack my portmanteau and bolt to town early the next morning. I left a note for my aunt, explaining that I was ill and had gone to see my doctor; and as a matter of fact I did feel uncommonly ill—the night seemed to have pumped all the blood out of me. But when I reached town I didn't go to the doctor's. I went to a friend's rooms, and threw myself on a bed, and slept for ten heavenly hours. When I woke it was the middle of the night, and I turned cold at the thought of what might be waiting for me. I sat up, shaking, and stared into the darkness; but there wasn't a break in its blessed surface, and when I saw that the eyes were not there I dropped back into another long sleep.

"I had left no word for Alice when I fled, because I meant to go back the next morning. But the next morning I was too exhausted to stir. As the day went on the exhaustion increased, instead of wearing off like the fatigue left by an ordinary night of insomnia: the effect of the eyes seemed to be cumulative, and the thought of seeing them again grew intolerable. For two days I fought my dread; and on the third evening I pulled myself together and decided to go back the next morning. I felt a good deal happier as soon as I'd decided, for I knew that my abrupt disappearance, and the strangeness of my not writing, must have been very distressing to poor Alice. I went to bed with an easy mind, and fell asleep at once; but in the middle of the night I woke, and there were the eyes . . .

"Well, I simply couldn't face them; and instead of going back to my aunt's I bundled a few things into a trunk and jumped aboard the first steamer for England. I was so dead tired when I got on board that I crawled straight into my berth, and slept most of the way over; and I can't tell you the bliss it was to wake from those long dreamless stretches and look fearlessly into the dark, *knowing* that I shouldn't see the eyes . . .

"I stayed abroad for a year, and then I stayed for another; and during that time I never had a glimpse of them. That was enough reason for prolonging my stay if I'd been on a desert island. Another was, of course, that I had perfectly come to see, on the voyage over, the complete impossiblity of my marrying Alice Nowell. The fact that I had been so slow in making this discovery annoyed me, and made me want to avoid explanations. The bliss of escaping at one stroke from the eyes, and from this other embarrasment, gave my freedom an extraordinary zest; and the longer I savoured it the better I liked its taste.

"The eyes had burned such a hole in my consciousness that for a long time I went on puzzling over the nature of the apparition, and wondering if it would ever come back. But as time passed I lost this dread, and retained only the precision of the image. Then that faded in its turn.

"The second year found me settled in Rome, where I was planning, I believe, to write another great book—a definitive work on Etruscan influences in Italian art. At any rate, I'd found some pretext of the kind for taking a sunny apartment in the Piazza di Spagna and dabbling about in the Forum; and there, one morning, a charming youth came to me. As he stood there in the warm light, slender and smooth and hyacinthine, he might have stepped from a ruined altar—one to Antinous, say; but he'd come instead from New York, with a letter (of all people) from Alice Nowell. The letter—the first I'd had from her since our break—was simply a line introducing her young cousin, Gilbert Noyes, and appealing to me to befriend him. It appeared, poor lad, that he 'had talent,' and 'wanted to write'; and, an obdurate family having insisted that his calligraphy should take the form of double entry, Alice had intervened to win him six months' respite, during which he was to travel abroad on a meagre pittance, and somehow prove his ability to increase it by his pen. The quaint conditions of the test struck me first: it seemed about as conclusive as a mediæval 'ordeal.' Then I was touched by her having sent him to me. I had always wanted to do her some service, to justify myself in my own eyes rather than hers; and here was a beautiful occasion.

"I imagine it's safe to lay down the general principle that predestined geniuses don't, as a rule, appear before one in the spring sunshine of the Forum looking like one of its banished gods. At any rate, poor Noyes wasn't a predestined genius. But he *was* beautiful to see, and charming as a comrade. It was only when he began to talk literature that my heart failed me. I knew all the symptoms so well—the things he had 'in him,' and the things outside him that impinged! There's the real test, after all. It was always—punctually, inevitably, with the inexorableness of a mechanical law—it was *always* the wrong thing that struck him. I grew to find a certain fascination in deciding in advance exactly which wrong thing he'd select; and I acquired an astonishing skill at the game . . .

"The worst of it was that his *bêtise* wasn't of the too obvious sort. Ladies who met him at picnics thought him intellectual; and even at dinners he passed for clever. I, who had him under the microscope, fancied now and then that he might develop some kind of a slim talent, something that he could make 'do' and be happy on; and wasn't that, after all, what I was concerned with? He was so charming—he continued to be so charming—that he called forth all my charity in support of this argument; and for the first few months I really believed there was a chance for him . . .

"Those months were delightful. Noyes was constantly with me, and the more I saw of him the better I liked him. His stupidity was a natural grace—it was as beautiful, really, as his eyelashes. And he was so gay, so affectionate, and so happy with me, that telling him the truth would have been about as pleasant as slitting the throat of some gentle animal. At first I used to wonder what had put into that radiant head the detestable delusion that it held a brain. Then I began to see that it was simply protective mimicry—an instinctive ruse to get away from family life and an office desk. Not that Gilbert didn't—dear lad!—believe in himself. There wasn't a trace of hypocrisy in him. He was sure that his 'call' was irresistible, while to me it was the saving grace of his situation that it *wasn't,* and that a little money, a little leisure, a little pleasure would have turned him into an inoffensive idler. Unluckily, however, there was no hope of money, and with the alternative of the office desk before him he couldn't postpone his attempt at literature. The stuff he turned out was deplorable, and I see now that I knew it from the first. Still, the absurdity of deciding a man's whole future on a first trial seemed to justify me in withholding my verdict, and perhaps even in encouraging him a little, on the ground that the human plant generally needs warmth to flower.

"At any rate, I proceeded on that principle, and carried it to the point of getting his term of probation extended. When I left Rome he went with me, and we idled away a delicious summer between Capri and Venice. I said to myself: 'If he has anything in him, it will come out now, and it *did.* He was never more enchanting and enchanted. There were moments of our pilgrimage when beauty born of murmuring sound seemed actually to pass into his face—but only to issue forth in a flood of the palest ink . . .

"Well, the time came to turn off the tap; and I knew there was no hand but mine to do it. We were back in Rome, and I had taken him to stay with me, not wanting him to be alone in his *pension* when he had to face the necessity of renouncing his ambition. I hadn't, of course, relied solely on my own judgment in deciding to advise him to drop literature. I had sent his stuff to various people —editors and critics—and they had always sent it back with the same chilling lack of comment. Really there was nothing on earth to say——

"I confess I never felt more shabbily than I did on the day when I decided to have it out with Gilbert. It was well enough to tell myself that it was my duty to knock the poor boy's hopes into splinters—but I'd like to know what act of gratuitous cruelty hasn't been justified on that plea? I've always shrunk from usurping the functions of Providence, and when I have to exercise them I decidedly prefer that it shouldn't be on an errand of destruction. Besides, in the last issue, who was I to decide, even after a year's trial, if poor Gilbert had it in him or not?

"The more I looked at the part I'd resolved to play, the less I liked it; and I liked it still less when Gilbert sat opposite me, with his head thrown back in the lamplight, just as Phil's is now . . . I'd been going over his last manuscript, and he knew it, and he knew that his future hung on my verdict—we'd tacitly agreed to that. The manuscript lay between us, on my table—a novel, his first novel, if you please!—and he reached over and laid his hand on it, and looked up at me with all his life in the look.

"I stood up and cleared my throat, trying to keep my eyes away from his face and on the the manuscript.

" 'The fact is, my dear Gilbert,' I began——

"I saw him turn pale, but he was up and facing me in an instant.

" 'Oh, look here, don't take on so, my dear fellow! I'm not so awfully cut up as all that!' His hands were on my shoulders, and he was laughing down on me from his full height, with a kind of mortally-stricken gaiety that drove the knife into my side.

"He was too beautifully brave for me to keep up any humbug about my duty. And it came over me suddenly how I should hurt others in hurting him: myself first, since sending him home meant losing him; but more particularly poor Alice Nowell, to whom I had so longed to prove my good faith and my desire to serve her. It really seemed like failing her twice to fail Gilbert——

"But my intuition was like one of those lightning flashes that encircle the whole horizon, and in the same instant I saw what I might be letting myself in for if I didn't tell the truth. I said to myself: 'I shall have him for life'—and I'd never yet seen any one, man or woman, whom I was quite sure of wanting on those terms. Well, this impulse of egotism decided me. I was ashamed of it, and to get away from it I took a leap that landed me straight in Gilbert's arms.

" 'The thing's all right, and you're all wrong!' I shouted up at him; and as he hugged me, and I laughed and shook in his clutch, I had for a minute the sense of self-complacency that is supposed to attend the footsteps of the just. Hang it all, making people happy *has* its charms——

"Gilbert, of course, was for celebrating his emancipation in some spectacular manner; but I sent him away alone to explode his emotions, and went to bed to sleep off mine. As I undressed I began to wonder what their after-taste would be—so many of the finest don't keep! Still, I wasn't sorry, and I meant to empty the bottle, even if it *did* turn a trifle flat.

"After I got into bed I lay for a long time smiling at the memory of his eyes—his blissful eyes . . . Then I fell asleep, and when I woke the room was deathly cold, and I sat up with a jerk—and there were *the other eyes* . . .

"It was three years since I'd seen them, but I'd thought of them so often that I fancied they could never take me unawares again. Now, with their red sneer on me, I knew that I had never really believed they would come back, and that I was as defenceless as ever against them . . . As before, it was the insane irrelevance of their coming that made it so horrible. What the deuce were they after, to leap out at me at such a time? I had lived more or less carelessly in the years since I'd seen them, though my worst indiscretions were not dark enough to invite the searchings of their infernal glare; but at this particular moment I was really in what might have been called a state of grace; and I can't tell you how the fact added to their horror . . .

"But it's not enough to say they were as bad as before: they were worse. Worse by just so much as I'd learned of life in the interval; by all the damnable implications my wider experience read into them. I saw now what I hadn't seen before: that they were eyes which had grown hideous gradually, which had built up their baseness coral-wise, bit by bit, out of a series of small turpitudes slowly accumulated through the industrious years. Yes—it came to me that what made them so bad was that they'd grown bad so slowly . . .

"There they hung in the darkness, their swollen lids dropped across the little watery bulbs rolling loose in the orbits, and the puff of flesh making a muddy shadow underneath—and as their stare moved with my movements, there came over me a sense of their tacit complicity, of a deep hidden understanding between us that was worse than the first shock of their strangeness. Not that I understood them; but that they made it so clear that some day I should . . . Yes, that was the worst part of it, decidedly; and it was the feeling that became stronger each time they came back . . .

"For they got into the damnable habit of coming back. They reminded me of vampires with a taste for young flesh, they seemed so to gloat over the taste of a good conscience. Every night for a month they came to claim their morsel of mine: since I'd made Gilbert happy they simply wouldn't loosen their fangs. The coincidence almost made me hate him, poor lad, fortuitous as I felt it to be. I puzzled over it a good deal, but couldn't find any hint of an explanation except in the chance of his association with Alice Nowell. But then the eyes had let up on me the moment I had abandoned her, so they could hardly be the emissaries of a woman scorned, even if one could have pictured poor Alice charging such spirits to avenge her. That set me thinking, and I began to wonder if they would let up on me if I abandoned Gilbert. The temptation was insidious, and I had to stiffen myself against it; but really, dear boy! he was too charming to be sacrificed to such demons. And so, after all, I never found out what they wanted . . ."

§ 3

The fire crumbled, sending up a flash which threw into relief the narrator's gnarled face under its grey-black stubble. Pressed into the hallow of the chairback, it stood out an instant like an intaglio of yellowish red-veined stone, with spots of enamel for the eyes; then the fire sank and it became once more a dim Rembrandtish blur.

Phil Frenham, sitting in a low chair on the opposite side of the hearth, one long arm propped on the table behind him, one hand supporting his thrown-back head, and his eyes fixed on his old friend's face, had not moved since the tale began. He continued to maintain his silent immobility after Culwin had ceased to speak, and it was I who, with a vague sense of disappointment at the sudden drop of the story, finally asked: "But how long did you keep on seeing them?"

Culwin, so sunk into his chair that he seemed like a heap of his own empty clothes, stirred a little, as if in surprise at my question. He appeared to have half-forgotten what he had been telling us.

"How long? Oh, off and on all that winter. It was infernal. I never got used to them. I grew really ill."

Frenham shifted his attitude, and as he did so his elbow struck against a small mirror in a bronze frame standing on the table behind him. He turned and changed its angle slightly; then he resumed his former attitude, his dark head thrown back on his lifted palm, his eyes intent on Culwin's face. Something in his silent gaze embarrassed me, and as if to divert attention from it I pressed on with another question:

"And you never tried sacrificing Noyes?"

"Oh, no. The fact is I didn't have to. He did it for me, poor boy!'

"Did it for you? How do you mean?"

"He wore me out—wore everybody out. He kept on pouring out his lamentable twaddle, and hawking it up and down the place till he became a thing of terror. I tried to wean him from writing—oh, ever so gently, you understand, by throwing him with agreeable people, giving him a chance to make himself felt, to come to a sense of what he *really* had to give. I'd foreseen this solution from the beginning—felt sure that, once the first ardour of authorship was quenched, he'd drop into his place as a charming parasitic thing, the kind of chronic Cherubino for whom, in old societies, there's always a seat at table, and a shelter behind the ladies' skirts. I saw him take his place as 'the poet': The poet who doesn't write. One knows the type in every drawing-room. Living in that way doesn't cost much—I'd worked it all out in my mind, and felt sure that, with a little help, he could manage it for the next few years: and meanwhile he'd be sure to marry. I saw him married to a widow, rather older, with a good cook and a well-run house. And I actually had my eye on the widow . . . Meanwhile I did everything to help the transition—lent him money to ease his conscience, introduced him to pretty women to make him forget his vows. But nothing would do him: he had but one idea in his beautiful obstinate head. He wanted the laurel and not the rose, and he kept on repeating Gautier's axiom, and battering and filing at his limp prose till he'd spread it out over Lord knows how many hundred pages. Now and then he would send a barrelful to a publisher, and of course it would always come back.

"At first it didn't matter—he thought he was 'misunderstood.' He took the attitudes of genius, and whenever an opus came home he wrote another to keep it company. Then he had a reaction of despair, and accused me of deceiving him, and Lord knows what. I got angry at that, and told him it was he who had deceived himself. He'd come to me determined to write, and I'd done my best to help him. That was the extent of my offence, and I'd done it for his cousin's sake, not his.

"That seemed to strike home, and he didn't answer for a minute. Then he said: 'My time's up and my money's up. What do you think I'd better do?'

" 'I think you'd better not be an ass,' I said.

" 'What do you mean by being an ass?' he asked.

"I took a letter from my desk and held it out to him.

" 'I mean refusing this offer of Mrs. Ellinger's: to be her secretary at a salary of five thousand dollars. There may be a lot more in it than that.'

"He flung out his hand with a violence that struck the letter from mine. 'Oh, I know well enough what's in it!' he said, red to the roots of his hair.

" 'And what's the answer, if you know?' I asked.

"He made none at the minute, but turned away slowly to the door. There, with his hand on the threshold, he stopped to say, almost under his breath: 'Then you really think my stuff's no good?'

"I was tired and exasperated, and I laughed. I don't defend my laugh—it was in wretched taste. But I must plead in extenuation that the boy was a fool, and that I'd done my best for him—I really had.

"He went out of the room, shutting the door quietly after him. That afternoon I left for Frascati, where I'd promised to spend the Sunday with some friends. I was glad to escape from Gilbert, and by the same token, as I learned that night, I had also escaped from the eyes. I dropped into the same lethargic sleep that had come to me before when I left off seeing them; and when I woke the next morning, in my peaceful room above the ilexes, I felt the utter weariness and deep relief that always followed on that sleep. I put in two blessed nights at Frascati, and when I got back to my rooms in Rome I found that Gilbert had gone . . . Oh, nothing tragic had happened—the episode never rose to *that*. He'd simply packed his manuscripts and left for America—for his family and the Wall Street desk. He left a decent enough note to tell me of his decision, and behaved altogether, in the circumstances, as little like a fool as it's possible for a fool to behave . . ."

§ 4

Culwin paused again, and Frenham still sat motionless, the dusky contour of his young head reflected in the mirror at his back.

"And what became of Noyes afterward?" I finally asked, still disquieted by a sense of incompleteness, by the need of some connecting thread between the parallel lines of the tale.

Culwin twitched his shoulders. "Oh, nothing became of him—because he became nothing. There could be no question of 'becoming' about it. He vegetated in an office, I believe, and finally got a clerkship in a consulate, and married drearily in China. I saw him once in Hong Kong, years afterward. He was fat and hadn't shaved. I was told he drank. He didn't recognise me."

"And the eyes?" I asked, after another pause which Frenham's continued silence made oppressive.

Culwin, stroking his chin, blinked at me meditatively through the shadows. "I never saw them after my last talk with Gilbert. Put two and two together if you can. For my part, I haven't found the link."

He rose, his hands in his pockets, and walked stiffly over to the table on which reviving drinks had been set out.

"You must be parched after this dry tale. Here, help yourself, my dear fellow. Here, Phil——" He turned back to the hearth.

Frenham made no response to his host's hospitable summons. He still sat in his low chair without moving, but as Culwin advanced toward him, their eyes met in a long look; after which the young man, turning suddenly, flung his arms across the table behind him, and dropped his face upon them.

Culwin, at the unexpected gesture, stopped short, a flush on his face.

"Phil—what the deuce? Why, have the eyes scared *you?* My dear boy—my dear fellow—I never had such a tribute to my literary ability, never!"

He broke into a chuckle at the thought, and halted on the hearth-rug, his hands still in his pockets, gazing down at the youth's bowed head. Then, as Frenham still made no answer, he moved a step or two nearer.

"Cheer up, my dear Phil! It's years since I've seen them—apparently I've done nothing lately bad enough to call them out of chaos. Unless my present evocation of them has made *you* see them; which would be their worst stroke yet!"

His bantering appeal quivered off into an uneasy laugh, and he moved still nearer, bending over Frenham, and laying his gouty hands on the lad's shoulders.

"Phil, my dear boy, really—what's the matter? Why don't you answer? *Have* you seen the eyes?"

Frenham's face was still hidden, and from where I stood behind Culwin I saw the latter, as if under the rebuff of this unaccountable attitude, draw back slowly from his friend. As he did so, the light of the lamp on the table fell full on his congested face, and I caught its reflection in the mirror behind Frenham's head.

Culwin saw the reflection also. He paused, his face level with the mirror, as if scarcely recognising the countenance in it as his own. But as he looked his expression gradually changed, and for an appreciable space of time he and the image in the glass confronted each other with a glare of slowly gathering hate. Then Culwin let go on Frenham's shoulders, and drew back a step . . .

Frenham, his face still hidden, did not stir.

PREFATORY NOTE TO "ETHAN FROME" AND "BUNNER SISTERS"

It has always aroused comment that the author of *Ethan Frome* should have been a rich and fashionable New Yorker who viewed her Massachusetts subject material from the great formal house that the architect Ogden Codman designed for her summers in Lenox. The final joke of the *tour de force* seems to be that Edith Wharton wrote the story initially in French. But a trained eye should be able to observe from any position. Mrs. Wharton, incompatibly married and complaining from Lenox that "this grim New England country, for all its beauty, gives nothing to compensate for the complete mental starvation," had more in common with Ethan Frome, shackled to an acidulous valitudinarian than might at first appear. Zeena Frome, with her implacability, her egotism, her naiveté and her ultimate strength, is a blend of the New England virtues and vices.

Mrs. Wharton in later years came to resent the fact that *Ethan Frome* preempted so large a part of her literary reputation, and it is certainly true that she did subtler and more complex work, but none that was more powerful. The stunning finale is far more than an O. Henry twist, for it contains the essence of the tale and reveals the spiritual core of each of the three main characters.

Bunner Sisters was published in *Xingu* (1916), five years after *Ethan Frome*. Its dramatic impact depends on the contrast between the gentle mood of its opening pages about two old maids who keep a Manhattan notions shop, and the terrible things that happen to them. It is as if Tennessee Williams came to visit in Cranford. The Misses Bunner live poorly but adequately with a strict economy; their diversions consist of a tiny bit of steak on Sunday and a thimbleful of cherry brandy with a rare visitor. All they lack is life and love, and these overdue and dangerous twins come knocking at last at their door in the shape of a middle-aged German clock-dealer who is also a dope addict. The ensuing devastation of their little barricaded corner makes a grim and tragic tale.

Introduction

I HAD KNOWN something of New England village life long before I made my home in the same county as my imaginary Starkfield; though, during the years spent there, certain of its aspects became much more familiar to me.

Even before that final initiation, however, I had had an uneasy sense that the New England of fiction bore little—except a vague botanical and dialectical—resemblance to the harsh and beautiful land as I had seen it. Even the abundant enumeration of sweet-fern, asters and mountain-laurel, and the conscientious reproduction of the vernacular, left me with the feeling that the outcropping granite had in both cases been overlooked. I give the impression merely as a personal one; it accounts for "Ethan Frome," and may, to some readers, in a measure justify it.

So much for the origin of the story; there is nothing else of interest to say of it, except as concerns its construction.

The problem before me, as I saw in the first flash, was this: I had to deal with a subject of which the dramatic climax, or rather the anti-climax, occurs a generation later than the first acts of the tragedy. This enforced lapse of time would seem to anyone persuaded—as I have always been—that every subject (in the novelist's sense of the term) implicitly *contains its own form and dimensions,* to mark Ethan Frome as the subject for a novel. But I never thought this for a moment, for I had felt, at the same time, that the theme of my tale was not one on which many variations could be played. It must be treated as starkly and summarily as life had always presented itself to my protagonists; any attempt to elaborate and complicate their sentiments would necessarily have falsified the whole. They were, in truth, these figures, my *granite outcroppings;* but half-emerged from the soil, and scarcely more articulate.

This incompatibility between subject and plan would perhaps have seemed to suggest that my "situation" was after all one to be rejected. Every novelist has been visited by the insinuating wraiths of false "good situations," siren-subjects luring his cockle-shell to the rocks; their voice is oftenest heard, and their mirage-sea beheld, as he traverses the waterless desert which awaits him half-way through whatever work is actually in hand. I knew well enough what song those sirens sang, and had often tied myself to my dull job until they were out of hearing—perhaps carrying a lost masterpiece in their rainbow veils. But I had no such fear of them in the case of Ethan Frome. It was the first subject I had ever approached with full confidence in its value, for my own purpose, and a relative faith in my power to render at least a part of what I saw in it.

Every novelist, again, who "intends upon" his art, has lit upon such subjects, and been fascinated by the difficulty of presenting them in the fullest relief, yet without an added ornament, or a trick of drapery or lighting. This was my task, if I were to tell the story of Ethan Frome; and my scheme of construction—which met with the immediate and unqualified disapproval of the few friends to whom I tentatively outlined it—I still think justified in the given case. It appears to me, indeed, that, while an air of artificiality is lent to a tale of complex and sophisticated people which the novelist causes to be guessed at and interpreted by any mere looker-on, there need be no such drawback if the looker-on is sophisticated, and the people he interprets are simple. If he is capable of seeing all around them, no violence is done to probability in allowing him to exercise this faculty; it is natural enough that he should act as the sympathizing intermediary between his rudimentary characters and the more complicated minds to whom he is trying to present them. But this is all self-evident, and needs explaining only to those who have never thought of fiction as an art of composition.

The real merit of my construction seems to me to lie in a minor detail. I had to find means to bring my tragedy, in a way at once natural and picture-making, to the knowledge of its narrator. I might have sat him down before a village gossip who would have poured out the whole affair to him in a breath, but in doing this I should have been false to two essential elements of my picture: first, the deep-rooted reticence and inarticulateness of the people I was trying to draw, and secondly the effect of "roundness" (in the plastic sense) produced by letting their case be seen through eyes as different as those of Harmon Gow and Mrs. Ned Hale. Each of my chroniclers contributes to the narrative *just so much as he or she is capable of understanding* of what, to them, is a complicated and mysterious case; and only the narrator of the tale has scope enough to see it all, to resolve it back into simplicity, and to put it in its rightful place among his larger categories.

I make no claim for originality in following a method of which "La Grande Bretêche" and "The Ring and the Book" had set me the magnificent example; my one merit is, perhaps, to have guessed that the proceeding there employed was also applicable to my small tale.

I have written this brief analysis—the first I have ever published of any of my books—because, as an author's introduction to his work, I can imagine nothing of any value to his readers except a statement as to why he decided to attempt the work in question, and why he selected one form rather than another for its embodiment. These primary aims, the only ones that can be explicitly stated, must, by the artist, be almost instinctively felt and acted upon before there can pass into his creation that imponderable something more which causes life to circulate in it, and preserves it for a little from decay.

EDITH WHARTON

Ethan Frome

I HAD THE STORY, bit by bit, from various people, and, as generally happens in such cases, each time it was a different story.

If you know Starkfield, Massachusetts, you know the post-office. If you know the post-office you must have seen Ethan Frome drive up to it, drop the reins on his hollow-backed bay and drag himself across the brick pavement to the white colonnade: and you must have asked who he was.

It was there that, several years ago, I saw him for the first time; and the sight pulled me up sharp. Even then he was the most striking figure in Starkfield, though he was but the ruin of a man. It was not so much his great height that marked him, for the "natives" were easily singled out by their lank longitude from the stockier foreign breed: it was the careless powerful look he had, in spite of a lameness checking each step like the jerk of a chain. There was something bleak and unapproachable in his face, and he was so stiffened and grizzled that I took him for an old man and was surprised to hear that he was not more than fifty-two. I had this from Harmon Gow, who had driven the stage from Bettsbridge to Starkfield in pre-trolley days and knew the chronicle of all the families on his line.

"He's looked that way ever since he had his smash-up; and that's twenty-four years ago come next February," Harmon threw out between reminiscent pauses.

The "smash-up" it was—I gathered from the same informant—which, besides drawing the red gash across Ethan Frome's forehead, had so shortened and warped his right side that it cost him a visible effort to take the few steps from his buggy to the post-office window. He used to drive in from his farm every day at about noon, and as that was my own hour for fetching my mail I often passed him in the porch or stood beside him while we waited on the motions of the distributing hand behind the grating. I noticed that, though he came so punctually, he seldom received anything but a copy of the *Bettsbridge Eagle,* which he put without a glance into his sagging pocket. At intervals, however, the post-master would hand him an envelope addressed to Mrs. Zenobia—or Mrs. Zeena—Frome, and usually bearing conspicuously in the upper left-hand corner the address of some manufacturer of patent medicine and the name of his specific. These documents my neighbour would also pocket without a glance, as if too much used to them to wonder at their number and variety, and would then turn away with a silent nod to the post-master.

Every one in Starkfield knew him and gave him a greeting tempered to his own grave mien; but his taciturnity was respected and it was only on rare occasions that one of the older men of the place detained him for a word. When this happened he would listen quietly, his blue eyes on the speaker's face, and answer in so low a tone that his words never reached me; then he would climb stiffly into his buggy, gather up the reins in his left hand and drive slowly away in the direction of his farm.

"It was a pretty bad smash-up?" I questioned Harmon, looking after Frome's retreating figure, and thinking how gallantly his lean brown head, with its shock of light hair, must have sat on his strong shoulders before they were bent out of shape.

"Wust kind," my informant assented. "More'n enough to kill most men. But the Fromes are tough. Ethan'll likely touch a hundred."

"Good God!" I exclaimed. At the moment Ethan Frome, after climbing to his seat, had leaned over to assure himself of the security of a wooden box—also with a druggist's label on it—which he had placed in the back of the buggy, and I saw his face as it probably looked when he thought himself alone. "*That* man touch a hundred? He looks as if he was dead and in hell now!"

Harmon drew a slab of tobacco from his pocket, cut off a wedge and pressed it into the leather pouch of his cheek. "Guess he's been in Starkfield too many winters. Most of the smart ones get away."

"Why didn't *he?*"

"Somebody had to stay and care for the folks. There warn't ever anybody but Ethan. Fust his father—then his mother—then his wife."

"And then the smash-up?"

Harmon chuckled sardonically. "That's so. He *had* to stay then."

"I see. And since then they've had to care for him?"

Harmon thoughtfully passed his tobacco to the other cheek. "Oh, as to that: I guess it's always Ethan done the caring."

Though Harmon Gow developed the tale as far as his mental and moral reach permitted there were perceptible gaps between his facts, and I had the sense that the deeper meaning of the story was in the gaps. But one phrase stuck in my memory and served as the nucleus about which I grouped my subsequent inferences: "Guess he's been in Starkfield too many winters."

Before my own time there was up I had learned to know what that meant. Yet I had come in the degenerate day of trolley, bicycle and rural delivery, when communication was easy between the scattered mountain villages, and the bigger towns in the valleys, such as Bettsbridge and Shadd's Falls, had libraries, theatres and Y. M. C. A. halls to which the youth of the hills could descend for recreation. But when winter shut down on Starkfield, and the village lay under a sheet of snow perpetually renewed from the pale skies, I began to see what life there—or rather its negation—must have been in Ethan Frome's young manhood.

I had been sent up by my employers on a job connected with the big power-house at Corbury Junction, and a long-drawn carpenters' strike had so delayed the work that I found myself anchored at Starkfield—the nearest habitable spot—for the best part of the winter. I chafed at first, and then, under the hypnotising effect of routine, gradually began to find a grim satisfaction in the life. During the early part of my stay I had been struck by the contrast between the vitality of the climate and the deadness of the community. Day by day, after the December snows were over, a blazing blue sky poured down torrents of light and air on the white landscape, which gave them back in an intenser glitter. One would have supposed that such an atmosphere must quicken the emotions as well as the blood; but it seemed to produce no change except that of retarding still more the sluggish pulse of Starkfield. When I had been there a little longer, and had seen this phase of crystal clearness followed by long stretches of sunless cold; when the storms of February had pitched their white tents about the devoted village and the wild cavalry of March winds had charged down to their support; I began to understand why Starkfield emerged from its six months' siege like a starved garrison capitulating without quarter. Twenty years earlier the means of resistance must have been far fewer, and the enemy in command of almost all the lines of access between the beleaguered villages; and, considering these things, I felt the sinister force of Harmon's phrase: "Most of the smart ones get away." But if that were the case, how could any combination of obstacles have hindered the flight of a man like Ethan Frome?

During my stay at Starkfield I lodged with a middle-aged widow colloquially known as Mrs. Ned Hale. Mrs. Hale's father had been the village lawyer of the previous generation, and "lawyer Varnum's house," where my landlady still lived with her mother, was the most considerable mansion in the village. It stood at one end of the main street, its classic portico and small-paned windows looking down a flagged path between Norway spruces to the slim white steeple of the Congregational church. It was clear that the Varnum fortunes were at the ebb, but the two women did what they could to preserve a decent dignity; and Mrs. Hale, in particular, had a certain wan refinement not out of keeping with her pale old-fashioned house.

In the "best parlour," with its black horse-hair and mahogany weakly illuminated by a gurgling Carcel lamp, I listened every evening to another and more delicately shaded version of the Starkfield chronicle. It was not that Mrs. Ned Hale felt, or affected, any social superiority to the people about her; it was only that the accident of a finer sensibility and a little more education had put just enough distance between herself and her neighbours to enable her to judge them with detachment. She was not unwilling to exercise this faculty, and I had great hopes of getting from her the missing facts of Ethan Frome's story, or rather such a key to his character as should co-ordinate the facts I knew. Her mind was a store-house of innocuous anecdote and any question about her acquaintances brought forth a volume of detail; but on the subject of Ethan Frome I found her unexpectedly reticent. There was no hint of disapproval in her reserve; I merely felt in her an insurmountable reluctance to speak of him or his affairs, a low "Yes, I knew them both . . . it was awful . . ." seeming to be the utmost concession that her distress could make to my curiosity.

So marked was the change in her manner, such depths of sad initiation did it imply, that, with some doubts as to my delicacy, I put the case anew to my village oracle, Harmon Gow; but got for my pains only an uncomprehending grunt.

"Ruth Varnum was always as nervous as a rat; and, come to think of it, she was the first one to see 'em after they was picked up. It happened right below lawyer Varnum's, down at the bend of the Corbury road, just round about the time that Ruth got engaged to Ned Hale. The young folks was all friends, and I guess she just can't bear to talk about it. She's had troubles enough of her own."

All the dwellers in Starkfield, as in more notable communities, had had troubles enough of their own to make them comparatively indifferent to those of their neighbours; and though all conceded that Ethan Frome's had been beyond the common measure, no one gave me an explanation of the look in his face which, as I persisted in thinking, neither poverty nor physical suffering could have put there. Nevertheless, I might have contented myself with the story pieced together from these hints had it not been for the provocation of Mrs. Hale's silence, and—a little later—for the accident of personal contact with the man.

On my arrival at Starkfield, Denis Eady, the rich Irish grocer, who was the proprietor of Starkfield's nearest approach to a livery stable, had entered into an agreement to send me over daily to Corbury Flats, where I had to pick up my train for the Junction. But about the middle of the winter Eady's horses fell ill of a local epidemic. The illness spread to the other Starkfield stables and for a day or two I was put to it to find a means of transport. Then Harmon Gow suggested that Ethan Frome's bay was still on his legs and that his owner might be glad to drive me over.

I stared at the suggestion. "Ethan Frome? But I've never even spoken to him. Why on earth should he put himself out for me?"

Harmon's answer surprised me still more. "I don't know as he would; but I know he wouldn't be sorry to earn a dollar."

I had been told that Frome was poor, and that the saw-mill and the arid acres of his farm yielded scarcely enough to keep his household through the winter; but I had not supposed him to be in such want as Harmon's words implied, and I expressed my wonder.

"Well, matters ain't gone any too well with him," Harmon said. "When a man's been setting round like a hulk for twenty years or more, seeing things that want doing, it eats inter him, and he loses his grit. That Frome farm was always 'bout as bare's a milkpan when the cat's been round; and you know what one of them old water-mills is wuth nowadays. When Ethan could sweat over 'em both from sun-up to dark he kinder choked a living out of 'em; but his folks ate up most everything, even then, and I don't see how he makes out now. Fust his father got a kick, out haying, and went soft in the brain, and gave away money like Bible texts afore he died. Then his mother got queer and dragged along for years as weak as a baby; and his wife Zeena, she's always been the greatest hand at doctoring in the county. Sickness and trouble: that's what Ethan's had his plate full up with, ever since the very first helping."

The next morning, when I looked out, I saw the hollow-backed bay between the Varnum spruces, and Ethan Frome, throwing back his worn bearskin, made room for me in the sleigh at his side. After that, for a week, he drove me over every morning to Corbury Flats, and on my return in the afternoon met me again and carried me back through the icy night to Starkfield. The distance each way was barely three miles, but the old bay's pace was slow, and even with firm snow under the runners we were nearly an hour on the way. Ethan Frome drove in silence, the reins loosely held in his left hand, his brown seamed profile, under the helmet-like peak of the cap, relieved against the banks of snow like the bronze image of a hero. He never turned his face to mine, or answered, except in monosyllables, the questions I put, or such slight pleasantries as I ventured. He seemed a part of the mute melancholy landscape, an incarnation of its frozen woe, with all that was warm and sentient in him fast bound below the surface; but there was nothing unfriendly in his silence. I simply felt that he lived in a depth of moral isolation too remote for casual access, and I had the sense that his loneliness was not merely the result of his personal plight, tragic as I guessed that to be, but had in it, as Harmon Gow had hinted, the profound accumulated cold of many Starkfield winters.

Only once or twice was the distance between us bridged for a moment; and the glimpses thus gained confirmed my desire to know more. Once I happened to speak of an engineering job I had been on the previous year in Florida, and of the contrast between the winter landscape about us and that in which I had found myself the year before; and to my surprise Frome said suddenly: "Yes: I was down there once, and for a good while afterward I could call up the sight of it in winter. But now it's all snowed under."

He said no more, and I had to guess the rest from the inflection of his voice and his sharp relapse into silence.

Another day, on getting into my train at the Flats, I missed a volume of popular science—I think it was on some recent discoveries in bio-chemistry—which I had carried with me to read on the way. I thought no more about it till I got into the sleigh again that evening, and saw the book in Frome's hand.

"I found it after you were gone," he said.

I put the volume into my pocket and we dropped back into our usual silence; but as we began to crawl up the long hill from Corbury Flats to the Starkfield ridge I became aware in the dusk that he had turned his face to mine.

"There are things in that book that I didn't know the first word about," he said.

I wondered less at his words than at the queer note of resentment in his voice. He was evidently surprised and slightly aggrieved at his own ignorance.

"Does that sort of thing interest you?" I asked.

"It used to."

"There are one or two rather new things in the book: there have been some big strides lately in that particular line of research." I waited a moment for an answer that did not come; then I said: "If you'd like to look the book through I'd be glad to leave it with you."

He hesitated, and I had the impression that he felt himself about to yield to a stealing tide of inertia; then, "Thank you—I'll take it," he answered shortly.

I hoped that this incident might set up some more direct communication between us. Frome was so simple and straightforward that I was sure his curiosity about the book was based on a genuine interest in its subject. Such tastes and acquirements in a man of his condition made the contrast more poignant between his outer situation and his inner needs, and I hoped that the chance of giving expression to the latter might at least unseal his lips. But something in his past history, or in his present way of living, had apparently driven him too deeply into himself for any casual impulse to draw him back to his kind. At our next meeting he made no allusion to the book, and our intercouse seemed fated to remain as negative and one-sided as if there had been no break in his reserve.

Frome had been driving me over to the Flats for about a week when one morning I looked out of my window into a thick snowfall. The height of the white waves massed against the garden-fence and along the wall of the church showed that the storm must have been going on all night, and that the drifts were likely to be heavy in the open. I thought it probable that my train would be delayed; but I had to be at the power-house for an hour or two that afternoon, and I decided, if Frome turned up, to push through to the Flats and wait there till my train came in. I don't know why I put it in the conditional, however, for I never doubted that Frome would appear. He was not the kind of man to be turned from his business by any commotion of the elements; and at the appointed hour his sleigh glided up through the snow like a stage-apparition behind thickening veils of gauze.

I was getting to know him too well to express either wonder or gratitude at his keeping his appointment; but I exclaimed in surprise as I saw him turn his horse in a direction opposite to that of the Corbury road.

"The railroad's blocked by a freight-train that got stuck in a drift below the Flats," he explained, as we jogged off into the stinging whiteness.

"But look here—where are you taking me, then?"

"Straight to the Junction, by the shortest way," he answered, pointing up School House Hill with his whip.

"To the Junction—in this storm? Why, it's a good ten miles!"

"The bay'll do it if you give him time. You said you had some business there this afternoon. I'll see you get there."

He said it so quietly that I could only answer: "You're doing me the biggest kind of a favour."

"That's all right," he rejoined.

Abreast of the schoolhouse the road forked, and we dipped down a lane to the left, between hemlock boughs bent inward to their trunks by the weight of the snow. I had often walked that way on Sundays, and knew that the solitary roof showing through bare branches near the bottom of the hill was that of Frome's saw-mill. It looked exanimate enough, with its idle wheel looming above the black stream dashed with yellow-white spume, and its cluster of sheds sagging under their white load. Frome did not even turn his head as we drove by, and still in silence we began to mount the next slope. About a mile farther, on a road I had never travelled, we came to an orchard of starved apple-trees writhing over a hillside among outcroppings of slate that nuzzled up through the snow like animals pushing out their noses to breathe. Beyond the orchard lay a field or two, their boundaries lost under drifts; and above the fields, huddled against the white immensities of land and sky, one of those lonely New England farm-houses that make the landscape lonelier.

"That's my place," said Frome, with a sideway jerk of his lame elbow; and in the distress and oppression of the scene I did not know what to answer. The snow had ceased, and a flash of watery sunlight exposed the house on the slope above us in all its plaintive ugliness. The black wraith of a deciduous creeper flapped from the porch, and the thin wooden walls, under their worn coat of paint, seemed to shiver in the wind that had risen with the ceasing of the snow.

"The house was bigger in my father's time: I had to take down the 'L,' a while back," Frome continued, checking with a twitch of the left rein the bay's evident intention of turning in through the broken-down gate.

I saw then that the unusually forlorn and stunted look of the house was partly due to the loss of what is known in New England as the "L": that long deep-roofed adjunct usually built at right angles to the main house, and connecting it, by way of store-rooms and tool-house, with the wood-shed and cow-barn. Whether because of its symbolic sense, the image it presents of a life linked with the soil, and enclosing in itself the chief sources of warmth and nourishment, or whether merely because of the consolatory thought that it enables the dwellers in that harsh climate to get to their morning's work without facing the weather, it is certain that the "L" rather than the house itself seems to be the centre, the actual hearth-stone of the New England farm. Perhaps this connection of ideas, which had often occurred to me in my rambles about Starkfield, caused me to hear a wistful note in Frome's words, and to see in the diminished dwelling the image of his own shrunken body.

"We're kinder side-tracked here now," he added, "but there was considerable passing before the railroad was carried through to the Flats." He roused the lagging bay with another twitch; then, as if the mere sight of the house had let me too deeply into his confidence for any farther pretence of reserve, he went on slowly: "I've always set down the worst of mother's trouble to that. When she got the rheumatism so bad she couldn't move around she used to sit up there and watch the road by the hour; and one year, when they was six months mending the Bettsbridge pike after the floods, and Harmon Gow had to bring his stage round this way, she picked up so that she used to get down to the gate most days to see him. But after the trains begun running nobody ever come by here to speak of, and mother never could get it through her head what had happened, and it preyed on her right along till she died."

As we turned into the Corbury road the snow began to fall again, cutting off our last glimpse of the house; and Frome's silence fell with it, letting down between us the old veil of reticence. This time the wind did not cease with the return of the snow. Instead, it sprang up to a gale which now and then, from a tattered sky, flung pale sweeps of sunlight over a landscape chaotically tossed. But the bay was as good as Frome's word, and we pushed on to the Junction through the wild white scene.

In the afternoon the storm held off, and the clearness in the west seemed to my inexperienced eye the pledge of a fair evening. I finished my business as quickly as possible, and we set out for Starkfield with a good chance of getting there for supper. But at sunset the clouds gathered again, bringing an earlier night, and the snow began to fall straight and steadily from a sky without wind, in a soft universal diffusion more confusing than the gusts and eddies of the morning. It seemed to be a part of the thickening darkness, to be the winter night itself descending on us layer by layer.

The small ray of Frome's lantern was soon lost in this smothering medium, in which even his sense of direction, and the bay's homing instinct, finally ceased to serve us. Two or three times some ghostly landmark sprang up to warn us that we were astray, and then was sucked back into the mist; and when we finally regained our road the old horse began to show signs of exhaustion. I felt myself to blame for having accepted Frome's offer, and after a short discussion I persuaded him to let me get out of the sleigh and walk along through the snow at the bay's side. In this way we struggled on for another mile or two, and at last reached a point where Frome, peering into what seemed to me formless night, said: "That's my gate down yonder."

The last stretch had been the hardest part of the way. The bitter cold and the heavy going had nearly knocked the wind out of me, and I could feel the horse's side ticking like a clock under my hand.

"Look here, Frome," I began, "there's no earthly use in your going any farther–" but he interrupted me: "Nor you neither. There's been about enough of this for anybody."

I understood that he was offering me a night's shelter at the farm, and without answering I turned into the gate at his side, and followed him to the barn, where I helped him to unharness and bed down the tired horse. When this was done he unhooked the lantern from the sleigh, stepped out again into the night, and called to me over his shoulder: "This way."

Far off above us a square of light trembled through the screen of snow. Staggering along in Frome's wake I floundered toward it, and in the darkness almost fell into one of the deep drifts against the front of the house. Frome scrambled up the slippery steps of the porch, digging a way through the snow with his heavily booted foot. Then he lifted his lantern, found the latch, and led the way into the house. I went after him into a low unlit passage, at the back of which a ladder-like staircase rose into obscurity. On our right a line of light marked the door of the room which had sent its ray across the night; and behind the door I heard a woman's voice droning querulously.

Frome stamped on the worn oil-cloth to shake the snow from his boots, and set down his lantern on a kitchen chair which was the only piece of furniture in the hall. Then he opened the door.

"Come in," he said; and as he spoke the droning voice grew still . . .

It was that night that I found the clue to Ethan Frome, and began to put together this vision of his story. . . .

CHAPTER I

THE VILLAGE lay under two feet of snow, with drifts at the windy corners. In a sky of iron the points of the Dipper hung like icicles and Orion flashed his cold fires. The moon had set, but the night was so transparent that the white house-fronts between the elms looked gray against the snow, clumps of bushes made black stains on it, and the basement windows of the church sent shafts of yellow light far across the endless undulations.

Young Ethan Frome walked at a quick pace along the deserted street, past the bank and Michael Eady's new brick store and Lawyer Varnum's house with the two black Norway spruces at the gate. Opposite the Varnum gate, where the road fell away toward the Corbury valley, the church reared its slim white steeple and narrow peristyle. As the young man walked toward it the upper windows drew a black arcade along the side wall of the building, but from the lower openings, on the side where the ground sloped steeply down to the Corbury road, the light shot its long bars, illuminating many fresh furrows in the track leading to the basement door, and showing, under an adjoining shed, a line of sleighs with heavily blanketed horses.

The night was perfectly still, and the air so dry and pure that it gave little sensation of cold. The effect produced on Frome was rather of a complete absence of atmosphere, as though nothing less tenuous than ether intervened between the white earth under his feet and the metallic dome overhead. "It's like being in an exhausted receiver," he thought. Four or five years earlier he had taken a year's course at a technological college at Worcester, and dabbled in the laboratory with a friendly professor of physics; and the images supplied by that experience still cropped up, at unexpected moments, through the totally different associations of thought in which he had since been living. His father's death, and the misfortunes following it, had put a premature end to Ethan's studies; but though they had not gone far enough to be of much practical use they had fed his fancy and made him aware of huge cloudy meanings behind the daily face of things.

As he strode along through the snow the sense of such meanings glowed in his brain and mingled with the bodily flush produced by his sharp tramp. At the end of the village he paused before the darkened front of the church. He stood there a moment, breathing quickly, and looking up and down the street, in which not another figure moved. The pitch of the Corbury road, below lawyer Varnum's spruces, was the favourite coasting-ground of Starkfield, and on clear evenings the church corner rang till late with the shouts of the coasters; but to-night not a sled darkened the whiteness of the long declivity. The hush of midnight lay on the village, and all its waking life was gathered behind the church windows, from which strains of dance-music flowed with the broad bands of yellow light.

The young man, skirting the side of the building, went down the slope toward the basement door. To keep out of range of the revealing rays from within he made a circuit through the untrodden snow and gradually approached the farther angle of the basement wall. Thence, still hugging the shadow, he edged his way cautiously forward to the nearest window, holding back his straight spare body and craning his neck till he got a glimpse of the room.

Seen thus, from the pure and frosty darkness in which he stood, it seemed to be seething in a mist of heat. The metal reflectors of the gas-jet sent crude waves of light against the whitewashed walls, and the iron flanks of the stove at the end of the hall looked as though they were heaving with volcanic fires. The floor was thronged with girls and young men. Down the side wall facing the window stood a row of kitchen chairs from which the older women had just risen. By this time the music had stopped, and the musicians—a fiddler, and the young lady who played the harmonium on Sundays—were hastily refreshing themselves at one corner of the supper-table which aligned its devastated pie-dishes and ice-cream saucers on the platform at the end of the hall. The guests were preparing to leave, and the tide had already set toward the passage where coats and wraps were hung, when a young man with a sprightly foot and a shock of black hair shot into the middle of the floor and clapped his hands. The signal took instant effect. The musicians hurried to their instruments, the dancers—some already half-muffled for departure—fell into line down each side of the room, the older spectators slipped back to their chairs, and the lively young man, after diving about here and there in the throng, drew forth a girl who had already wound a cherry-coloured "fascinator" about her head, and, leading her up to the end of the floor, whirled her down its length to the bounding tune of a Virginia reel.

Frome's heart was beating fast. He had been straining for a glimpse of the dark head under the cherry-coloured scarf and it vexed him that another eye should have been quicker than his. The leader of the reel, who looked as if he had Irish blood in his veins, danced well, and his partner caught his fire. As she passed down the line, her light figure swinging from hand to hand in circles of increasing swiftness, the scarf flew off her head and stood out behind her shoulders, and Frome, at each turn, caught sight of her laughing panting lips, the cloud of dark hair about her forehead, and the dark eyes which seemed the only fixed points in a maze of flying lines.

The dancers were going faster and faster, and the musicians, to keep up with them, belaboured their instruments like jockeys lashing their mounts on the home-stretch; yet it seemed to the young man at the window that the reel would never end. Now and then he turned his eyes from the girl's face to that of her partner, which, in the exhilaration of the dance, had taken on a look of almost impudent ownership. Denis Eady was the son of Michael Eady, the ambitious Irish grocer, whose suppleness and effrontery had given Starkfield its first notion of "smart" business methods, and whose new brick store testified to the success of the attempt. His son seemed likely to follow in his steps, and was meanwhile applying the same arts to the conquest of the Starkfield maidenhood. Hitherto Ethan Frome had been content to think him a mean fellow; but now he positively invited a horse-whipping. It was strange that the girl did not seem aware of it: that she could lift her rapt face to her dancer's, and drop her hands into his, without appearing to feel the offence of his look and touch.

Frome was in the habit of walking into Starkfield to fetch home his wife's cousin, Mattie Silver, on the rare evenings when some chance of amusement drew her to the village. It was his wife who had suggested, when the girl came to live with them, that such opportunities should be put in her way. Mattie Silver came from Stamford, and when she entered the Fromes' household to act as her cousin Zeena's aid it was thought best, as she came without pay, not to let her feel too sharp a contrast between the life she had left and the isolation of a Starkfield farm. But for this—as Frome sardonically reflected—it would hardly have occurred to Zeena to take any thought for the girl's amusement.

When his wife first proposed that they should give Mattie an occasional evening out he had inwardly demurred at having to do the extra two miles to the village and back after his hard day on the farm; but not long afterward he had reached the point of wishing that Starkfield might give all its nights to revelry.

Mattie Silver had lived under his roof for a year, and from early morning till they met at supper he had frequent chances of seeing her; but no moments in her company were comparable to those when, her arm in his, and her light step flying to keep time with his long stride, they walked back through the night to the farm. He had taken to the girl from the first day, when he had driven over to the Flats to meet her, and she had smiled and waved to him from the train, crying out, "You must be Ethan!" as she jumped down with her bundles, while he reflected, looking over her slight person:"She don't look much on housework, but she ain't a fretter, anyhow." But it was not only that the coming to his house of a bit of hopeful young life was like the lighting of a fire on a cold hearth. The girl was more than the bright serviceable creature he had thought her. She had an eye to see and an ear to hear: he could show her things and tell her things, and taste the bliss of feeling that all he imparted left long reverberations and echoes he could wake at will.

It was during their night walks back to the farm that he felt most intensely the sweetness of this communion. He had always been more sensitive than the people about him to the appeal of natural beauty. His unfinished studies had given form to this sensibility and even in his unhappiest moments field and sky spoke to him with a deep and powerful persuasion. But hitherto the emotion had remained in him as a silent ache, veiling with sadness the beauty that evoked it. He did not even know whether any one else in the world felt as he did, or whether he was the sole victim of this mournful privilege. Then he learned that one other spirit had trembled with the same touch of wonder: that at his side, living under his roof and eating his bread, was a creature to whom he could say: "That's Orion down yonder; the big fellow to the right is Aldebaran, and the bunch of little ones—like bees swarming—they're the Pleiades . . ." or whom he could hold entranced before a ledge of granite thrusting up through the fern while he unrolled the huge panorama of the ice age, and the long dim stretches of succeeding time. The fact that admiration for his learning mingled with Mattie's wonder at what he taught was not the least part of his pleasure. And there were other sensations, less definable but more exquisite, which drew them together with a shock of silent joy: the cold red of sunset behind winter hills, the flight of cloud-flocks over slopes of golden stubble, or the intensely blue shadows of hemlocks on sunlit snow. When she said to him once: "It looks just as if it was painted!" it seemed to Ethan that the art of definition could go no farther, and that words had at last been found to utter his secret soul. . . .

As he stood in the darkness outside the church these memories came back with the poignancy of vanished things. Watching Mattie whirl down the floor from hand to hand he wondered how he could ever have thought that his dull talk interested her. To him, who was never gay but in her presence, her gaiety seemed plain proof of indifference. The face she lifted to her dancers was the same which, when she saw him, always looked like a window that has caught the sunset. He even noticed two or three gestures which, in his fatuity, he had thought she kept for him: a way of throwing her head back when she was amused, as if to taste her laugh before she let it out, and a trick of sinking her lids slowly when anything charmed or moved her.

The sight made him unhappy, and his unhappiness roused his latent fears. His wife had never shown any jealousy of Mattie, but of late she had grumbled increasingly over the house-work and found oblique ways of attracting attention to the girl's inefficiency. Zeena had always been what Starkfield called "sickly," and Frome had to admit that, if she were as ailing as she believed, she needed the help of a stronger arm than the one which lay so lightly in his during the night walks to the farm. Mattie had no natural turn for housekeeping, and her training had done nothing to remedy the defect. She was quick to learn, but forgetful and dreamy, and not disposed to take the matter seriously. Ethan had an idea that if she were to marry a man she was fond of the dormant instinct would wake, and her pies and biscuits become the pride of the county; but domesticity in the abstract did not interest her. At first she was so awkward that he could not help laughing at her; but she laughed with him and that made them better friends. He did his best to supplement her unskilled efforts, getting up earlier than usual to light the kitchen fire, carrying in the wood overnight, and neglecting the mill for the farm that he might help her about the house during the day. He even crept down on Saturday nights to scrub the kitchen floor after the women had gone to bed; and Zeena, one day, had surprised him at the churn and had turned away silently, with one of her queer looks.

Of late there had been other signs of her disfavour, as intangible but more disquieting. One cold winter morning, as he dressed in the dark, his candle flickering in the draught of the ill-fitting window, he had heard her speak from the bed behind him.

"The doctor don't want I should be left without anybody to do for me," she said in her flat whine.

He had supposed her to be asleep, and the sound of her voice had startled him, though she was given to abrupt explosions of speech after long intervals of secretive silence.

He turned and looked at her where she lay indistinctly outlined under the dark calico quilt, her high-boned face taking a grayish tinge from the whiteness of the pillow.

"Nobody to do for you?" he repeated.

"If you say you can't afford a hired girl when Mattie goes."

Frome turned away again, and taking up his razor stooped to catch the reflection of his stretched cheek in the blotched looking-glass above the wash-stand.

"Why on earth should Mattie go?"

"Well, when she gets married, I mean," his wife's drawl came from behind him.

"Oh, she'd never leave us as long as you needed her," he returned, scraping hard at his chin.

"I wouldn't ever have it said that I stood in the way of a poor girl like Mattie marrying a smart fellow like Denis Eady," Zeena answered in a tone of plaintive self-effacement.

Ethan, glaring at his face in the glass, threw his head back to draw the razor from ear to chin. His hand was steady, but the attitude was an excuse for not making an immediate reply.

"And the doctor don't want I should be left without anybody," Zeena continued. "He wanted I should speak to you about a girl he's heard about, that might come——"

Ethan laid down the razor and straightened himself with a laugh.

"Denis Eady! If that's all, I guess there's no such hurry to look round for a girl."

"Well, I'd like to talk to you about it," said Zeena obstinately.

He was getting into his clothes in fumbling haste. "All right. But I haven't got the time now; I'm late as it is," he returned, holding his old silver turnip-watch to the candle.

Zeena, apparently accepting this as final, lay watching him in silence while he pulled his suspenders over his shoulders and jerked his arms into his coat; but as he went toward the door she said, suddenly and incisively: "I guess you're always late, now you shave every morning."

That thrust had frightened him more than any vague insinuations about Denis Eady. It was a fact that since Mattie Silver's coming he had taken to shaving every day; but his wife always seemed to be asleep when he left her side in the winter darkness, and he had stupidly assumed that she would not notice any change in his appearance. Once or twice in the past he had been faintly disquieted by Zenobia's way of letting things happen without seeming to remark them, and then, weeks afterward, in a casual phrase, revealing that she had all along taken her notes and drawn her inferences. Of late, however, there had been no room in his thoughts for such vague apprehensions. Zeena herself, from an oppressive reality, had faded into an insubstantial shade. All his life was lived in the sight and sound of Mattie Silver, and he could no longer conceive of its being otherwise. But now, as he stood outside the church, and saw Mattie spinning down the floor with Denis Eady, a throng of disregarded hints and menaces wove their cloud about his brain. . . .

CHAPTER II

As THE DANCERS poured out of the hall Frome, drawing back behind the projecting storm-door, watched the segregation of the grotesquely muffled groups, in which a moving lantern ray now and then lit up a face flushed with food and dancing. The villagers, being afoot, were the first to climb the slope to the main street, while the country neighbours packed themselves more slowly into the sleighs under the shed.

"Ain't you riding, Mattie?" a woman's voice called back from the throng about the shed, and Ethan's heart gave a jump. From where he stood he could not see the persons coming out of the hall till they had advanced a few steps beyond the wooden sides of the storm-door; but through its cracks he heard a clear voice answer: "Mercy no! Not on such a night."

She was there, then, close to him, only a thin board between. In another moment she would step forth into the night, and his eyes, accustomed to the obscurity, would discern her as clearly as though she stood in daylight. A wave of shyness pulled him back into the dark angle of the wall, and he stood there in silence instead of making his presence known to her. It had been one of the wonders of their intercourse that from the first, she, the quicker, finer, more expressive, instead of crushing him by the contrast, had given him something of her own ease and freedom; but now he felt as heavy and loutish as in his student days, when he had tried to "jolly" the Worcester girls at a picnic.

He hung back, and she came out alone and paused within a few yards of him. She was almost the last to leave the hall, and she stood looking uncertainly about her as if wondering why he did not show himself. Then a man's figure approached, coming so close to her that under their formless wrappings they seemed merged in one dim outline.

"Gentleman friend gone back on you? Say, Matt, that's tough! No, I wouldn't be mean enough to tell the other girls. I ain't as low-down as that." (How Frome hated his cheap banter!) "But look a here, ain't it lucky I got the old man's cutter down there waiting for us?"

Frome heard the girl's voice, gaily incredulous:

"What on earth's your father's cutter doin' down there?"

"Why, waiting for me to take a ride. I got the roan colt too. I kinder knew I'd want to take a ride to-night," Eady, in his triumph, tried to put a sentimental note into his bragging voice.

The girl seemed to waver, and Frome saw her twirl the end of her scarf irresolutely about her fingers. Not for the world would he have made a sign to her, though it seemed to him that his life hung on her next gesture.

"Hold on a minute while I unhitch the colt," Denis called to her, springing toward the shed.

She stood perfectly still, looking after him, in an attitude of tranquil expectancy torturing to the hidden watcher. Frome noticed that she no longer turned her head from side to side, as though peering through the night for another figure. She let Denis Eady lead out the horse, climb into the cutter and fling back the bearskin to make room for her at his side; then, with a swift motion of flight, she turned about and darted up the slope toward the front of the church.

"Good-bye! Hope you'll have a lovely ride!" she called back to him over her shoulder.

Denis laughed, and gave the horse a cut that brought him quickly abreast of her retreating figure.

"Come along! Get in quick! It's as slippery as thunder on this turn," he cried, leaning over to reach out a hand to her.

She laughed back at him: "Good-night! I'm not getting in."

By this time they had passed beyond Frome's earshot and he could only follow the shadowy pantomime of their silhouettes as they continued to move along the crest of the slope above him. He saw Eady, after a moment, jump from the cutter and go toward the girl with the reins over one arm. The other he tried to slip through hers; but she eluded him nimbly, and Frome's heart, which had swung out over a black void, trembled back to safety. A moment later he heard the jingle of departing sleigh bells and discerned a figure advancing alone toward the empty expanse of snow before the church.

In the black shade of the Varnum spruces he caught up with her and she turned with a quick "Oh!"

"Think I'd forgotten you, Matt?" he asked with sheepish glee.

She answered seriously: "I thought maybe you couldn't come back for me."

"Couldn't? What on earth could stop me?"

"I knew Zeena wasn't feeling any too good to-day."

"Oh, she's in bed long ago." He paused, a question struggling in him. "Then you meant to walk home all alone?"

"Oh, I ain't afraid!" she laughed.

They stood together in the gloom of the spruces, an empty world glimmering about them wide and grey under the stars. He brought his question out.

"If you thought I hadn't come, why didn't you ride back with Denis Eady?"

"Why, where *were* you? How did you know? I never saw you!"

Her wonder and his laughter ran together like spring rills in a thaw. Ethan had the sense of having done something arch and ingenious. To prolong the effect he groped for a dazzling phrase, and brought out, in a growl of rapture: "Come along."

He slipped an arm through hers, as Eady had done, and fancied it was faintly pressed against her side; but neither of them moved. It was so dark under the spruces that he could barely see the shape of her head beside his shoulder. He longed to stoop his cheek and rub it against her scarf. He would have liked to stand there with her all night in the blackness. She moved forward a step or two and then paused again above the dip of the Corbury road. Its icy slope, scored by innumerable runners, looked like a mirror scratched by travellers at an inn.

"There was a whole lot of them coasting before the moon set," she said.

"Would you like to come in and coast with them some night?" he asked.

"Oh, *would* you, Ethan? It would be lovely!"

"We'll come to-morrow if there's a moon."

She lingered, pressing closer to his side. "Ned Hale and Ruth Varnum came just as *near* running into the big elm at the bottom. We were all sure they were killed." Her shiver ran down his arm. "Wouldn't it have been too awful? They're so happy!"

"Oh, Ned ain't much at steering. I guess I can take you down all right!" he said disdainfully.

He was aware that he was "talking big," like Denis Eady; but his reaction of joy had unsteadied him, and the inflection with which she had said of the engaged couple "They're so happy!" made the words sound as if she had been thinking of herself and him.

"The elm *is* dangerous, though. It ought to be cut down," she insisted.

"Would you be afraid of it, with me?"

"I told you I ain't the kind to be afraid," she tossed back, almost indifferently; and suddenly she began to walk on with a rapid step.

These alterations of mood were the despair and joy of Ethan Frome. The motions of her mind were as incalculable as the flit of a bird in the branches. The fact that he had no right to show his feelings, and thus provoke the expression of hers, made him attach a fantastic importance to every change in her look and tone. Now he thought she understood him, and feared; now he was sure she did not, and despaired. To-night the pressure of accumulated misgivings sent the scale drooping toward despair, and her indifference was the more chilling after the flush of joy into which she had plunged him by dismissing Denis Eady. He mounted School House Hill at her side and walked on in silence till they reached the lane leading to the saw-mill; then the need of some definite assurance grew too strong for him.

"You'd have found me right off if you hadn't gone back to have that last reel with Denis," he brought out awkwardly. He could not pronounce the name without a stiffening of the muscles of his throat.

"Why, Ethan, how could I tell you were there?"

"I suppose what folks say is true," he jerked out at her, instead of answering.

She stopped short, and he felt, in the darkness, that her face was lifted quickly to his. "Why, what do folks say?"

"It's natural enough you should be leaving us," he floundered on, following his thought.

"Is that what they say?" she mocked back at him; then, with a sudden drop of her sweet treble: "You mean that Zeena—ain't suited with me any more?" she faltered.

Their arms had slipped apart and they stood motionless, each seeking to distinguish the other's face.

"I know I ain't anything like as smart as I ought to be," she went on, while he vainly struggled for expression. "There's lots of things a hired girl could do that come awkward to me still—and I haven't got much strength in my arms. But if she'd only tell me I'd try. You know she hardly ever says anything, and sometimes I can see she ain't suited, and yet I don't know why." She turned on him with a sudden flash of indignation. "You'd ought to tell me, Ethan Frome—you'd ought to! Unless *you* want me to go too——"

Unless he wanted her to go too! The cry was balm to his raw wound. The iron heavens seemed to melt and rain down sweetness. Again he struggled for the all-expressive word, and again, his arm in hers, found only a deep "Come along."

They walked on in silence through the blackness of the hemlock-shaded lane, where Ethan's saw-mill gloomed through the night, and out again into the comparative clearness of the fields. On the farther side of the hemlock belt the open country rolled away before them grey and lonely under the stars. Sometimes their way led them under the shade of an overhanging bank or through the thin obscurity of a clump of leafless trees. Here and there a farmhouse stood far back among the fields, mute and cold as a grave-stone. The night was so still that they heard the frozen snow crackle under their feet. The crash of a loaded branch falling far off in the woods reverberated like a musket-shot, and once a fox barked, and Mattie shrank closer to Ethan, and quickened her steps.

At length they sighted the group of larches at Ethan's gate, and as they drew near it the sense that the walk was over brought back his words.

"Then you don't want to leave us, Matt?"

He had to stoop his head to catch her stifled whisper: "Where'd I go, if I did?"

The answer sent a pang through him but the tone suffused him with joy. He forgot what else he had meant to say and pressed her against him so closely that he seemed to feel her warmth in his veins.

"You ain't crying are you, Matt?"

"No, of course I'm not," she quavered.

They turned in at the gate and passed under the shaded knoll where, enclosed in a low fence, the Frome grave-stones slanted at crazy angles through the snow. Ethan looked at them curiously. For years that quiet company had mocked his restlessness, his desire for change and freedom. "We never got away—how should you?" seemed to be written on every headstone; and whenever he went in or out of his gate he thought with a shiver: "I shall just go on living here till I join them." But now all desire for change had vanished, and the sight of the little enclosure gave him a warm sense of continuance and stability.

"I guess we'll never let you go, Matt," he whispered, as though even the dead, lovers once, must conspire with him to keep her; and brushing by the graves, he thought: "We'll always go on living here together, and some day she'll lie there beside me."

He let the vision possess him as they climbed the hill to the house. He was never so happy with her as when he abandoned himself to these dreams. Half-way up the slope Mattie stumbled against some unseen obstruction and clutched his sleeve to steady herself. The wave of warmth that went through him was like the prolongation of his vision. For the first time he stole his arm about her, and she did not resist. They walked on as if they were floating on a summer stream.

Zeena always went to bed as soon as she had had her supper, and the shutterless windows of the house were dark. A dead cucumber-vine dangled from the porch like the crape streamer tied to the door for a death, and the thought flashed through Ethan's brain: "If it was there for Zeena—" Then he had a distinct sight of his wife lying in their bedroom asleep, her mouth slightly open, her false teeth in a tumbler by the bed . . .

They walked around to the back of the house, between the rigid gooseberry bushes. It was Zeena's habit, when they came back late from the village to leave the key of the kitchen door under the mat. Ethan stood before the door, his head heavy with dreams, his arm still about Mattie. "Matt—" he began, not knowing what he meant to say.

She slipped out of his hold without speaking, and he stooped down and felt for the key.

"It's not there!" he said, straightening himself with a start.

They strained their eyes at each other through the icy darkness. Such a thing had never happened before.

"Maybe she's forgotten it," Mattie said in a tremulous whisper; but both of them knew that it was not like Zeena to forget.

"It might have fallen off into the snow," Mattie continued, after a pause during which they had stood intently listening.

"It must have been pushed off, then," he rejoined in the same tone. Another wild thought tore through him. What if tramps had been there—what if . . .

Again he listened, fancying he heard a distant sound in the house; then he felt in his pocket for a match, and kneeling down, passed its light slowly over the rough edges of snow about the door-step.

He was still kneeling when his eyes, on a level with the lower panel of the door, caught a faint ray beneath it. Who could be stirring in that silent house? He heard a step on the stairs, and again for an instant the thought of tramps tore through him. Then the door opened and he saw his wife.

Against the dark background of the kitchen she stood up tall and angular, one hand drawing a quilted counterpane to her flat breast, while the other held a lamp. The light, on a level with her chin, drew out of the darkness her puckered throat and the projecting wrist of the hand that clutched the quilt, and deepened fantastically the hollows and prominences of her high-boned face under its ring of crimping-pins. To Ethan, still in the rosy haze of his hour with Mattie, the sight came with the intense precision of the last dream before waking. He felt as if he had never before known what his wife looked like.

She drew aside without speaking, and Mattie and Ethan passed into the kitchen, which had the deadly chill of a vault after the dry cold of the night.

"Guess you forgot about us, Zeena," Ethan joked, stamping the snow from his boots.

"No. I just felt so mean I couldn't sleep."

Mattie came forward, unwinding her wraps, the colour of the cherry scarf in her fresh lips and cheeks. "I'm so sorry, Zeena! Isn't there anything I can do?"

"No; there's nothing." Zeena turned away from her. "You might 'a' shook off that snow outside," she said to her husband.

She walked out of the kitchen ahead of them and pausing in the hall raised the lamp at arm's-length, as if to light them up the stairs.

Ethan paused also, affecting to fumble for the peg on which he hung his coat and cap. The doors of the two bedrooms faced each other across the narrow upper landing, and to-night it was peculiarly repugnant to him that Mattie should see him follow Zeena.

"I guess I won't come up yet awhile," he said, turning as if to go back to the kitchen.

Zeena stopped short and looked at him. "For the land's sake—what you going to do down here?"

"I've got the mill accounts to go over."

She continued to stare at him, the flame of the unshaded lamp bringing out with microscopic cruelty the fretful lines of her face.

"At this time o' night? You'll ketch your death. The fire's out long ago."

Without answering he moved away toward the kitchen. As he did so his glance crossed Mattie's and he fancied that a fugitive warning gleamed through her lashes. The next moment they sank to her flushed cheeks and she began to mount the stairs ahead of Zeena.

"That's so. It *is* powerful cold down here," Ethan assented; and with lowered head he went up in his wife's wake, and followed her across the threshold of their room.

CHAPTER III

THERE WAS some hauling to be done at the lower end of the wood-lot, and Ethan was out early the next day.

The winter morning was as clear as crystal. The sunrise burned red in a pure sky, the shadows on the rim of the wood-lot were darkly blue, and beyond the white and scintillating fields patches of far-off forest hung like smoke.

It was in the early morning stillness, when his muscles were swinging to their familiar task and his lungs expanding with long draughts of mountain air, that Ethan did his clearest thinking. He and Zeena had not exchanged a word after the door of their room had closed on them. She had measured out some drops from a medicine-bottle on a chair by the bed and, after swallowing them, and wrapping her head in a piece of yellow flannel, had lain down with her face turned away. Ethan undressed hurriedly and blew out the light so that he should not see her when he took his place at her side. As he lay there he could hear Mattie moving about in her room, and her candle, sending its small ray across the landing, drew a scarcely perceptible line of light under his door. He kept his eyes fixed on the light till it vanished. Then the room grew perfectly black, and not a sound was audible but Zeena's asthmatic breathing. Ethan felt confusedly that there were many things he ought to think about, but through his tingling veins and tired brain only one sensation throbbed: the warmth of Mattie's shoulder against his. Why had he not kissed her when he held her there? A few hours earlier he would not have asked himself the question. Even a few minutes earlier, when they had stood alone outside the house, he would not have dared to think of kissing her. But since he had seen her lips in the lamplight he felt that they were his.

Now, in the bright morning air, her face was still before him. It was part of the sun's red and of the pure glitter on the snow. How the girl had changed since she had come to Starkfield! He remembered what a colourless slip of a thing she had looked the day he had met her at the station. And all the first winter, how she had shivered with cold when the northerly gales shook the thin clapboards and the snow beat like hail against the loose-hung windows!

He had been afraid that she would hate the hard life, the cold and loneliness; but not a sign of discontent escaped her. Zeena took the view that Mattie was bound to make the best of Starkfield since she hadn't any other place to go to; but this did not strike Ethan as conclusive. Zeena, at any rate, did not apply the principle in her own case.

He felt all the more sorry for the girl because misfortune had, in a sense, indentured her to them. Mattie Silver was the daughter of a cousin of Zenobia Frome's, who had inflamed his clan with mingled sentiments of envy and admiration by descending from the hills to Connecticut, where he had married a Stamford girl and succeeded to her father's thriving "drug" business. Unhappily Orin Silver, a man of far-reaching aims, had died too soon to prove that the end justifies the means. His accounts revealed merely what the means had been; and these were such that it was fortunate for his wife and daughter that his books were examined only after his impressive funeral. His wife died of the disclosure, and Mattie, at twenty, was left alone to make her way on the fifty dollars obtained from the sale of her piano. For this purpose her equipment, though varied, was inadequate. She could trim a hat, make molasses candy, recite "Curfew shall not ring to-night," and play "The Lost Chord" and a pot-pourri from "Carmen." When she tried to extend the field of her activities in the direction of stenography and book-keeping her health broke down, and six months on her feet behind the counter of a department store did not tend to restore it. Her nearest relations had been induced to place their savings in her father's hands, and though, after his death, they ungrudgingly acquitted themselves of the Christian duty of returning good for evil by giving his daughter all the advice at their disposal, they could hardly be expected to supplement it by material aid. But when Zenobia's doctor recommended her looking about for some one to help her with the house-work the clan instantly saw the chance of exacting a compensation from Mattie. Zenobia, though doubtful of the girl's efficiency, was tempted by the freedom to find fault without much risk of losing her; and so Mattie came to Starkfield.

Zenobia's fault-finding was of the silent kind, but not the less penetrating for that. During the first months Ethan alternately burned with the desire to see Mattie defy her and trembled with fear of the result. Then the situation grew less strained. The pure air, and the long summer hours in the open, gave back life and elasticity to Mattie, and Zeena, with more leisure to devote to her complex ailments, grew less watchful of the girl's omissions; so that Ethan, struggling on under the burden of his barren farm and failing saw-mill, could at least imagine that peace reigned in his house.

There was really, even now, no tangible evidence to the contrary; but since the previous night a vague dread had hung on his sky-line. It was formed of Zeena's obstinate silence, of Mattie's sudden look of warning, of the memory of just such fleeting imperceptible signs as those which told him, on certain stainless mornings, that before night there would be rain.

His dread was so strong that, man-like, he sought to postpone certainty. The hauling was not over till mid-day, and as the lumber was to be delivered to Andrew Hale, the Starkfield builder, it was really easier for Ethan to send Jotham Powell, the hired man, back to the farm on foot, and drive the load down to the village himself. He had scrambled up on the logs, and was sitting astride of them, close over his shaggy grays, when, coming between him and their streaming necks, he had a vision of the warning look that Mattie had given him the night before.

"If there's going to be any trouble I want to be there," was his vague reflection, as he threw to Jotham the unexpected order to unhitch the team and lead them back to the barn.

It was a slow trudge home through the heavy fields, and when the two men entered the kitchen Mattie was lifting the coffee from the stove and Zeena was already at the table. Her husband stopped short at sight of her. Instead of her usual calico wrapper and knitted shawl she wore her best dress of brown merino, and above her thin strands of hair, which still preserved the tight undulations of the crimping-pins, rose a hard perpendicular bonnet, as to which Ethan's clearest notion was that he had to pay five dollars for it at the Bettsbridge Emporium. On the floor beside her stood his old valise and a bandbox wrapped in newspapers.

"Why, where are you going, Zeena?" he exclaimed.

"I've got my shooting pains so bad that I'm going over to Bettsbridge to spend the night with Aunt Martha Pierce and see that new doctor," she answered in a matter-of-fact tone, as if she had said she was going into the store-room to take a look at the preserves, or up to the attic to go over the blankets.

In spite of her sedentary habits such abrupt decisions were not without precedent in Zeena's history. Twice or thrice before she had suddenly packed Ethan's valise and started off to Bettsbridge, or even Springfield, to seek the advice of some new doctor, and her husband had grown to dread these expeditions because of their cost.

Zeena always came back laden with expensive remedies, and her last visit to Springfield had been commemorated by her paying twenty dollars for an electric battery of which she had never been able to learn the use. But for the moment his sense of relief was so great as to preclude all other feelings. He had now no doubt that Zeena had spoken the truth in saying, the night before, that she had sat up because she felt "too mean" to sleep: her abrupt resolve to seek medical advice showed that, as usual, she was wholly absorbed in her health.

As if expecting a protest, she continued plaintively; "If you're too busy with the hauling I presume you can let Jotham Powell drive me over with the sorrel in time to ketch the train at the Flats."

Her husband hardly heard what she was saying. During the winter months there was no stage between Starkfield and Bettsbridge, and the trains which stopped at Corbury Flats were slow and infrequent. A rapid calculation showed Ethan that Zeena could not be back at the farm before the following evening. . . .

"If I'd supposed you'd 'a' made any objection to Jotham Powell's driving me over—" she began again, as though his silence had implied refusal. On the brink of departure she was always seized with a flux of words. "All I know is," she continued, "I can't go on the way I am much longer. The pains are clear away down to my ankles now, or I'd 'a' walked in to Starkfield on my own feet, sooner'n put you out, and asked Michael Eady to let me ride over on his wagon to the Flats, when he sends to meet the train that brings his groceries. I'd 'a' had two hours to wait in the station, but I'd sooner 'a' done it, even with this cold, than to have you say——"

"Of course Jotham'll drive you over," Ethan roused himself to answer. He became suddenly conscious that he was looking at Mattie while Zeena talked to him, and with an effort he turned his eyes to his wife. She sat opposite the window, and the pale light reflected from the banks of snow made her face look more than usually drawn and bloodless, sharpened the three parallel creases between ear and cheek, and drew querulous lines from her thin nose to the corners of her mouth. Though she was but seven years her husband's senior, and he was only twenty-eight, she was already an old woman.

Ethan tried to say something befitting the occasion, but there was only one thought in his mind: the fact that, for the first time since Mattie had come to live with them, Zeena was to be away for a night. He wondered if the girl were thinking of it too. . . .

He knew that Zeena must be wondering why he did not offer to drive her to the Flats and let Jotham Powell take the lumber to Starkfield, and at first he could not think of a pretext for not doing so; then he said: "I'd take you over myself, only I've got to collect the cash for the lumber."

As soon as the words were spoken he regretted them, not only because they were untrue—there being no prospect of his receiving cash payment from Hale—but also because he knew from experience the imprudence of letting Zeena think he was in funds on the eve of one of her therapeutic excursions. At the moment, however, his one desire was to avoid the long drive with her behind the ancient sorrel who never went out of a walk.

Zeena made no reply: she did not seem to hear what he had said. She had already pushed her plate aside, and was measuring out a draught from a large bottle at her elbow.

"It ain't done me a speck of good, but I guess I might as well use it up," she remarked; adding, as she pushed the empty bottle toward Mattie: "If you can get the taste out it'll do for pickles."

CHAPTER IV

As SOON as his wife had driven off Ethan took his coat and cap from the peg. Mattie was washing up the dishes, humming one of the dance tunes of the night before. He said "So long, Matt," and she answered gaily "So long, Ethan"; and that was all.

It was warm and bright in the kitchen. The sun slanted through the south window on the girl's moving figure, on the cat dozing in a chair, and on the geraniums brought in from the door-way, where Ethan had planted them in the summer to "make a garden" for Mattie. He would have liked to linger on, watching her tidy up and then settle down to her sewing; but he wanted still more to get the hauling done and be back at the farm before night.

All the way down to the village he continued to think of his return to Mattie. The kitchen was a poor place, not "spruce" and shining as his mother had kept it in his boyhood; but it was surprising what a homelike look the mere fact of Zeena's absence gave it. And he pictured what it would be like that evening, when he and Mattie were there after supper. For the first time they would be alone together indoors, and they would sit there, one on each side of the stove, like a married couple, he in his stocking feet and smoking his pipe, she laughing and talking in that funny way she had, which was always as new to him as if he had never heard her before.

The sweetness of the picture, and the relief of knowing that his fears of "trouble" with Zeena were unfounded, sent up his spirits with a rush, and he, who was usually so silent, whistled and sang aloud as he drove through the snowy fields. There was in him a slumbering spark of sociability which the long Starkfield winters had not yet extinguished. By nature grave and inarticulate, he admired recklessness and gaiety in others and was warmed to the marrow by friendly human intercourse. At Worcester, though he had the name of keeping to himself and not being much of a hand at a good time, he had secretly gloried in being clapped on the back and hailed as "Old Ethe" or "Old Stiff"; and the cessation of such familiarities had increased the chill of his return to Starkfield.

There the silence had deepened about him year by year. Left alone, after his father's accident, to carry the burden of farm and mill, he had had no time for convivial loiterings in the village; and when his mother fell ill the loneliness of the house grew more oppressive than that of the fields. His mother had been a talker in her day, but after her "trouble" the sound of her voice was seldom heard, though she had not lost the power of speech. Sometimes, in the long winter evenings, when in desperation her son asked her why she didn't "say something," she would lift a finger and answer: "Because I'm listening"; and on stormy nights, when the loud wind was about the house, she would complain, if he spoke to her: "They're talking so out there that I can't hear you."

It was only when she drew toward her last illness, and his cousin Zenobia Pierce came over from the next valley to help him nurse her, that human speech was heard again in the house. After the mortal silence of his long imprisonment Zeena's volubility was music in his ears. He felt that he might have "gone like his mother" if the sound of a new voice had not come to steady him. Zeena seemed to understand his case at a glance. She laughed at him for not knowing the simplest sick-bed duties and told him to "go right along out" and leave her to see to things. The mere fact of obeying her orders, of feeling free to go about his business again and talk with other men, restored his shaken balance and magnified his sense of what he owed her. Her efficiency shamed and dazzled him. She seemed to possess by instinct all the household wisdom that his long apprenticeship had not instilled in him. When the end came it was she who had to tell him to hitch up and go for the undertaker, and she thought it "funny" that he had not settled beforehand who was to have his mother's clothes and the sewing-machine. After the funeral, when he saw her preparing to go away, he was seized with an unreasoning dread of being left alone on the farm; and before he knew what he was doing he had asked her to stay there with him. He had often thought since that it would not have happened if his mother had died in spring instead of winter . . .

When they married it was agreed that, as soon as he could straighten out the difficulties resulting from Mrs. Frome's long illness, they would sell the farm and saw-mill and try their luck in a large town. Ethan's love of nature did not take the form of a taste for agriculture. He had always wanted to be an engineer, and to live in towns, where there were lectures and big libraries and "fellows doing things." A slight engineering job in Florida, put in his way during his period of study at Worcester, increased his faith in his ability as well as his eagerness to see the world; and he felt sure that, with a "smart" wife like Zeena, it would not be long before he had made himself a place in it.

Zeena's native village was slightly larger and nearer to the railway than Starkfield, and she had let her husband see from the first that life on an isolated farm was not what she had expected when she married. But purchasers were slow in coming, and while he waited for them Ethan learned the impossibility of transplanting her. She chose to look down on Starkfield, but she could not have lived in a place which looked down on her. Even Bettsbridge or Shadd's Falls would not have been sufficiently aware of her, and in the greater cities which attracted Ethan she would have suffered a complete loss of identity. And within a year of their marriage she developed the "sickliness" which had since made her notable even in a community rich in pathological instances. When she came to take care of his mother she had seemed to Ethan like the very genius of health, but he soon saw that her skill as a nurse had been acquired by the absorbed observation of her own symptoms.

Then she too fell silent. Perhaps it was the inevitable effect of life on the farm, or perhaps, as she sometimes said, it was because Ethan "never listened." The charge was not wholly unfounded. When she spoke it was only to complain, and to complain of things not in his power to remedy; and to check a tendency to impatient retort he had first formed the habit of not answering her, and finally of thinking of other things while she talked. Of late, however, since he had had reasons for observing her more closely, her silence had begun to trouble him. He recalled his mother's growing taciturnity, and wondered if Zeena were also turning "queer." Women did, he knew. Zeena, who had at her fingers' ends the pathological chart of the whole region, had cited many cases of the kind while she was nursing his mother; and he himself knew of certain lonely farmhouses in the neighbourhood where stricken creatures pined, and of others where sudden tragedy had come of their presence. At times, looking at Zeena's shut face, he felt the chill of such forebodings. At other times her silence seemed deliberately assumed to conceal far-reaching intentions, mysterious conclusions drawn from suspicions and resentments impossible to guess. That supposition was even more disturbing than the other; and it was the one which had come to him the night before, when he had seen her standing in the kitchen door.

Now her departure for Bettsbridge had once more eased his mind, and all his thoughts were on the prospect of his evening with Mattie. Only one thing weighed on him, and that was his having told Zeena that he was to receive cash for the lumber. He foresaw so clearly the consequences of this imprudence that with considerable reluctance he decided to ask Andrew Hale for a small advance on his load.

When Ethan drove into Hale's yard the builder was just getting out of his sleigh.

"Hello, Ethe!" he said. "This comes handy."

Andrew Hale was a ruddy man with a big grey moustache and a stubbly double-chin unconstrained by a collar; but his scrupulously clean shirt was always fastened by a small diamond stud. This display of opulence was misleading, for though he did a fairly good business it was known that his easy-going habits and the demands of his large family frequently kept him what Starkfield called "behind." He was an old friend of Ethan's family, and his house one of the few to which Zeena occasionally went, drawn there by the fact that Mrs. Hale, in her youth, had done more "doctoring" than any other woman in Starkfield, and was still a recognised authority on symptoms and treatment.

Hale went up to the greys and patted their sweating flanks.

"Well, sir," he said, "you keep them two as if they was pets."

Ethan set about unloading the logs and when he had finished his job he pushed open the glazed door of the shed which the builder used as his office. Hale sat with his feet up on the stove, his back propped against a battered desk strewn with papers: the place, like the man, was warm, genial and untidy.

"Sit right down and thaw out," he greeted Ethan.

The latter did not know how to begin, but at length he managed to bring out his request for an advance of fifty dollars. The blood rushed to his thin skin under the sting of Hale's astonishment. It was the builder's custom to pay at the end of three months, and there was no precedent between the two men for a cash settlement.

Ethan felt that if he had pleaded an urgent need Hale might have made shift to pay him; but pride, and an instinctive prudence, kept him from resorting to this argument. After his father's death it had taken time to get his head above water, and he did not want Andrew Hale, or any one else in Starkfield, to think he was going under again. Besides, he hated lying; if he wanted the money he wanted it, and it was nobody's business to ask why. He therefore made his demand with the awkwardness of a proud man who will not admit to himself that he is stooping; and he was not much surprised at Hale's refusal.

The builder refused genially, as he did everything else: he treated the matter as something in the nature of a practical joke, and wanted to know if Ethan meditated buying a grand piano or adding a "cupolo" to his house; offering, in the latter case, to give his services free of cost.

Ethan's arts were soon exhausted, and after an embarrassed pause he wished Hale good day and opened the door of the office. As he passed out the builder suddenly called after him: "See here—you ain't in a tight place, are you?"

"Not a bit," Ethan's pride retorted before his reason had time to intervene.

"Well, that's good! Because I *am,* a shade. Fact is, I was going to ask you to give me a little extra time on that payment. Business is pretty slack, to begin with, and then I'm fixing up a little house for Ned and Ruth when they're married. I'm glad to do it for 'em, but it costs." His look appealed to Ethan for sympathy. "The young people like things nice. You know how it is yourself: it's not so long ago since you fixed up your own place for Zeena."

Ethan left the greys in Hale's stable and went about some other business in the village. As he walked away the builder's last phrase lingered in his ears, and he reflected grimly that his seven years with Zeena seemed to Starkfield "not so long."

The afternoon was drawing to an end, and here and there a lighted pane spangled the cold grey dusk and made the snow look whiter. The bitter weather had driven every one indoors and Ethan had the long rural street to himself. Suddenly he heard the brisk play of sleigh-bells and a cutter passed him, drawn by a free-going horse. Ethan recognised Michael Eady's roan colt, and young Denis Eady, in a handsome new fur cap, leaned forward and waved a greeting. "Hello, Ethe!" he shouted and spun on.

The cutter was going in the direction of the Frome farm, and Ethan's heart contracted as he listened to the dwindling bells. What more likely than that Denis Eady had heard of Zeena's departure for Bettsbridge, and was profiting by the opportunity to spend an hour with Mattie? Ethan was ashamed of the storm of jealousy in his breast. It seemed unworthy of the girl that his thoughts of her should be so violent.

He walked on to the church corner and entered the shade of the Varnum spruces, where he had stood with her the night before. As he passed into their gloom he saw an indistinct outline just ahead of him. At his approach it melted for an instant into two separate shapes and then conjoined again, and he heard a kiss, and a half-laughing "Oh!" provoked by the discovery of his presence. Again the outline hastily disunited and the Varnum gate slammed on one half while the other hurried on ahead of him. Ethan smiled at the discomfiture he had caused. What did it matter to Ned Hale and Ruth Varnum if they were caught kissing each other? Everybody in Starkfield knew they were engaged. It pleased Ethan to have surprised a pair of lovers on the spot where he and Mattie had stood with such a thirst for each other in their hearts; but he felt a pang at the thought that these two need not hide their happiness.

He fetched the greys from Hale's stable and started on his long climb back to the farm. The cold was less sharp than earlier in the day and a thick fleecy sky threatened snow for the morrow. Here and there a star pricked through, showing behind it a deep well of blue. In an hour or two the moon would push over the ridge behind the farm, burn a gold-edged rent in the clouds, and then be swallowed by them. A mournful peace hung on the fields, as though they felt the relaxing grasp of the cold and stretched themselves in their long winter sleep.

Ethan's ears were alert for the jingle of sleighbells, but not a sound broke the silence of the lonely road. As he drew near the farm he saw, through the thin screen of larches at the gate, a light twinkling in the house above him. "She's up in her room," he said to himself, "fixing herself up for supper"; and he remembered Zeena's sarcastic stare when Mattie, on the evening of her arrival, had come down to supper with smoothed hair and a ribbon at her neck.

He passed by the graves on the knoll and turned his head to glance at one of the older headstones, which had interested him deeply as a boy because it bore his name.

SACRED TO THE MEMORY OF
ETHAN FROME AND ENDURANCE HIS WIFE,
WHO DWELLED TOGETHER IN PEACE
FOR FIFTY YEARS.

He used to think that fifty years sounded like a long time to live together, but now it seemed to him that they might pass in a flash.

Then, with a sudden dart of irony, he wondered if, when their turn came, the same epitaph would be written over him and Zeena.

He opened the barn-door and craned his head into the obscurity, half-fearing to discover Denis Eady's roan colt in the stall beside the sorrel. But the old horse was there alone, mumbling his crib with toothless jaws, and Ethan whistled cheerfully while he bedded down the greys and shook an extra measure of oats into their mangers. His was not a tuneful throat, but harsh melodies burst from it as he locked the barn and sprang up the hill to the house. He reached the kitchen-porch and turned the door-handle; but the door did not yield to his touch.

Startled at finding it locked he rattled the handle violently; then he reflected that Mattie was alone and that it was natural she should barricade herself at nightfall. He stood in the darkness expecting to hear her step. It did not come, and after vainly straining his ears he called out in a voice that shook with joy: "Hello, Matt!"

Silence answered; but in a minute or two he caught a sound on the stairs and saw a line of light about the door-frame, as he had seen it the night before. So strange was the precision with which the incidents of the previous evening were repeating themselves that he half expected, when he heard the key turn, to see his wife before him on the threshold; but the door opened, and Mattie faced him.

She stood just as Zeena had stood, a lifted lamp in her hand, against the black background of the kitchen. She held the light at the same level, and it drew out with the same distinctness her slim young throat and the brown wrist no bigger than a child's. Then, striking upward, it threw a lustrous fleck on her lips, edged her eyes with velvet shade, and laid a milky whiteness above the black curve of her brows.

She wore her usual dress of darkish stuff, and there was no bow at her neck; but through her hair she had run a streak of crimson ribbon. This tribute to the unusual transformed and glorified her. She seemed to Ethan taller, fuller, more womanly in shape and motion. She stood aside, smiling silently, while he entered, and then moved away from him with something soft and flowing in her gait. She set the lamp on the table, and he saw that it was carefully laid for supper, with fresh doughnuts, stewed blueberries and his favourite pickles in a dish of gay red glass. A bright fire glowed in the stove and the cat lay stretched before it, watching the table with a drowsy eye.

Ethan was suffocated with the sense of well-being. He went out into the passage to hang up his coat and pull off his wet boots. When he came back Mattie had set the teapot on the table and the cat was rubbing itself persuasively against her ankles.

"Why, Puss! I nearly tripped over you," she cried, the laughter sparkling through her lashes.

Again Ethan felt a sudden twinge of jealousy. Could it be his coming that gave her such a kindled face?

"Well, Matt, any visitors?" he threw off, stooping down carelessly to examine the fastening of the stove.

She nodded and laughed "Yes, one," and he felt a blackness settling on his brows.

"Who was that?" he questioned, raising himself up to slant a glance at her beneath his scowl.

Her eyes danced with malice. "Why, Jotham Powell. He came in after he got back, and asked for a drop of coffee before he went down home."

The blackness lifted and light flooded Ethan's brain. "That all? Well, I hope you made out to let him have it." And after a pause he felt it right to add: "I suppose he got Zeena over to the Flats all right?"

"Oh, yes; in plenty of time."

The name threw a chill between them, and they stood a moment looking sideways at each other before Mattie said with a shy laugh. "I guess it's about time for supper."

They drew their seats up to the table, and the cat, unbidden, jumped between them into Zeena's empty chair. "Oh, Puss!" said Mattie, and they laughed again.

Ethan, a moment earlier, had felt himself on the brink of eloquence; but the mention of Zeena had paralysed him. Mattie seemed to feel the contagion of his embarrassment, and sat with downcast lids, sipping her tea, while he feigned an insatiable appetite for doughnuts and sweet pickles. At last, after casting about for an effective opening, he took a long gulp of tea, cleared his throat, and said: "Looks as if there'd be more snow."

She feigned great interest. "Is that so? Do you suppose it'll interfere with Zeena's getting back?" She flushed red as the question escaped her, and hastily set down the cup she was lifting.

Ethan reached over for another helping of pickles. "You never can tell, this time of year, it drifts so bad on the Flats." The name had benumbed him again, and once more he felt as if Zeena were in the room between them.

"Oh, Puss, you're too greedy!" Mattie cried.

The cat, unnoticed, had crept up on muffled paws from Zeena's seat to the table, and was stealthily elongating its body in the direction of the milk-jug, which stood between Ethan and Mattie. The two leaned forward at the same moment and their hands met on the handle of the jug. Mattie's hand was underneath, and Ethan kept his clasped on it a moment longer than was necessary. The cat, profiting by this unusual demonstration, tried to effect an unnoticed retreat, and in doing so backed into the pickle-dish, which fell to the floor with a crash.

Mattie, in an instant, had sprung from her chair and was down on her knees by the fragments.

"Oh, Ethan, Ethan—it's all to pieces! What will Zeena say?"

But this time his courage was up. "Well, she'll have to say it to the cat, any way!" he rejoined with a laugh, kneeling down at Mattie's side to scrape up the swimming pickles.

She lifted stricken eyes to him. "Yes, but, you see, she never meant it should be used, not even when there was company; and I had to get up on the step-ladder to reach it down from the top shelf of the china-closet, where she keeps it with all her best things, and of course she'll want to know why I did it——"

The case was so serious that it called forth all of Ethan's latent resolution.

"She needn't know anything about it if you keep quiet. I'll get another just like it to-morrow. Where did it come from? I'll go to Shadd's Falls for it if I have to!"

"Oh, you'll never get another even there! It was a wedding present—don't you remember? It came all the way from Philadelphia, from Zeena's aunt that married the minister. That's why she wouldn't ever use it. Oh, Ethan, Ethan, what in the world shall I do?"

She began to cry, and he felt as if every one of her tears were pouring over him like burning lead. "Don't, Matt, don't—oh, *don't!*" he implored her.

She struggled to her feet, and he rose and followed her helplessly while she spread out the pieces of glass on the kitchen dresser. It seemed to him as if the shattered fragments of their evening lay there.

"Here, give them to me," he said in a voice of sudden authority.

She drew aside, instinctively obeying his tone. "Oh, Ethan, what are you going to do?"

Without replying he gathered the pieces of glass into his broad palm and walked out of the kitchen to the passage. There he lit a candle-end, opened the china-closet, and, reaching his long arm up to the highest shelf, laid the pieces together with such accuracy of touch that a close inspection convinced him of the impossibility of detecting from below that the dish was broken. If he glued it together the next morning months might elapse before his wife noticed what had happened, and meanwhile he might after all be able to match the dish at Shadd's Falls or Bettsbridge. Having satisfied himself that there was no risk of immediate discovery he went back to the kitchen with a lighter step, and he found Mattie disconsolately removing the last scraps of pickle from the floor.

"It's all right, Matt. Come back and finish supper," he commanded her.

Completely reassured, she shone on him through tear-hung lashes, and his soul swelled with pride as he saw how his tone subdued her. She did not even ask what he had done. Except when he was steering a big log down the mountain to his mill he had never known such a thrilling sense of mastery.

CHAPTER V

THEY FINISHED supper, and while Mattie cleared the table Ethan went to look at the cows and then took a last turn about the house. The earth lay dark under a muffled sky and the air was so still that now and then he heard a lump of snow come thumping down from a tree far off on the edge of the wood-lot.

When he returned to the kitchen Mattie had pushed up his chair to the stove and seated herself near the lamp with a bit of sewing. The scene was just as he had dreamed of it that morning. He sat down, drew his pipe from his pocket and stretched his feet to the glow. His hard day's work in the keen air made him feel at once lazy and light of mood, and he had a confused sense of being in another world, where all was warmth and harmony and time could bring no change. The only draw-back to his complete well-being was the fact that he could not see Mattie from where he sat; but he was too indolent to move and after a moment he said: "Come over here and sit by the stove."

Zeena's empty rocking-chair stood facing him. Mattie rose obediently, and seated herself in it. As her young brown head detached itself against the patch-work cushion that habitually framed his wife's gaunt countenance, Ethan had a momentary shock. It was almost as if the other face, the face of the superseded woman, had obliterated that of the intruder. After a moment Mattie seemed to be affected by the same sense of constraint. She changed her position, leaning forward to bend her head above her work, so that he saw only the foreshortened tip of her nose and the streak of red in her hair; then she slipped to her feet, saying "I can't see to sew," and went back to her chair by the lamp.

Ethan made a pretext of getting up to replenish the stove, and when he returned to his seat he pushed it sideways that he might get a view of her profile and of the lamplight falling on her hands. The cat, who had been a puzzled observer of these unusual movements, jumped up into Zeena's chair, rolled itself into a ball, and lay watching them with narrowed eyes.

Deep quiet sank on the room. The clock ticked above the dresser, a piece of charred wood fell now and then in the stove, and the faint sharp scent of the geraniums mingled with the odour of Ethan's smoke, which began to throw a blue haze about the lamp and to hang its greyish cobwebs in the shadowy corners of the room.

All constraint had vanished between the two, and they began to talk easily and simply. They spoke of every-day things, of the prospect of snow, of the next church sociable, of the loves and quarrels of Starkfield. The commonplace nature of what they said produced in Ethan an illusion of long-established intimacy which no outburst of emotion could have given, and he set his imagination adrift on the fiction that they had always spent their evenings thus and would always go on doing so . . .

"This is the night we were to have gone coasting, Matt," he said at length, with the rich sense, as he spoke, that they could go on any other night they chose, since they had all time before them.

She smiled back at him. "I guess you forgot!"

"No, I didn't forget; but it's as dark as Egypt outdoors. We might go to-morrow if there's a moon."

She laughed with pleasure, her head tilted back, the lamplight sparkling on her lips and teeth. "That would be lovely, Ethan!"

He kept his eyes fixed on her, marvelling at the way her face changed with each turn of their talk, like a wheat-field under a summer breeze. It was intoxicating to find such magic in his clumsy words, and he longed to try new ways of using it.

"Would you be scared to go down the Corbury road with me on a night like this?" he asked.

Her cheeks burned redder. "I ain't any more scared than you are!"

"Well, *I'd* be scared, then; I wouldn't do it. That's an ugly corner down by the big elm. If a fellow didn't keep his eyes open he'd go plumb into it." He luxuriated in the sense of protection and authority which his words conveyed. To prolong and intensify the feeling he added: "I guess we're well enough here."

She let her lids sink slowly, in the way he loved. "Yes, we're well enough here," she sighed.

Her tone was so sweet that he took the pipe from his mouth and drew his chair up to the table. Leaning forward, he touched the farther end of the strip of brown stuff that she was hemming. "Say, Matt," he began with a smile, "what do you think I saw under the Varnum spruces, coming along home just now? I saw a friend of yours getting kissed."

The words had been on his tongue all the evening, but now that he had spoken them they struck him as inexpressibly vulgar and out of place.

Mattie blushed to the roots of her hair and pulled her needle rapidly twice or thrice through her work, insensibly drawing the end of it away from him. "I suppose it was Ruth and Ned," she said in a low voice, as though he had suddenly touched on something grave.

Ethan had imagined that his allusion might open the way to the accepted pleasantries, and these perhaps in turn to a harmless caress, if only a mere touch on her hand. But now he felt as if her blush had set a flaming guard about her. He supposed it was his natural awkwardness that made him feel so. He knew that most young men made nothing at all of giving a pretty girl a kiss, and he remembered that the night before, when he had put his arm about Mattie, she had not resisted. But that had been out-of-doors, under the open irresponsible night. Now, in the warm lamp-lit room, with all its ancient implications of conformity and order, she seemed infinitely farther away from him and more unapproachable.

To ease his constraint he said: "I suppose they'll be setting a date before long."

"Yes. I shouldn't wonder if they got married some time along in the summer." She pronounced the word *married* as if her voice caressed it. It seemed a rustling covert leading to enchanted glades. A pang shot through Ethan, and he said, twisting away from her in his chair: "It'll be your turn next, I wouldn't wonder."

She laughed a little uncertainly. "Why do you keep on saying that?"

He echoed her laugh. "I guess I do it to get used to the idea."

He drew up to the table again and she sewed on in silence, with dropped lashes, while he sat in fascinated contemplation of the way in which her hands went up and down above the strip of stuff, just as he had seen a pair of birds make short perpendicular flights over a nest they were building. At length, without turning her head or lifting her lids, she said in a low tone: "It's not bcause you think Zeena's got anything against me, is it?"

His former dread started up full-armed at the suggestion. "Why, what do you mean?" he stammered.

She raised distressed eyes to his, her work dropping on the table between them. "I don't know. I thought last night she seemed to have."

"I'd like to know what," he growled.

"Nobody can tell with Zeena." It was the first time they had ever spoken so openly of her attitude toward Mattie, and the repetition of the name seemed to carry it to the farther corners of the room and send it back to them in long repercussions of sound. Mattie waited, as if to give the echo time to drop, and then went on: "She hasn't said anything to *you?*"

He shook his head. "No, not a word."

She tossed the hair back from her forehead with a laugh. "I guess I'm just nervous, then. I'm not going to think about it any more."

"Oh, no—don't let's think about it, Matt!"

The sudden heat of his tone made her colour mount again, not with a rush, but gradually, delicately, like the reflection of a thought stealing slowly across her heart. She sat silent, her hands clasped on her work, and it seemed to him that a warm current flowed toward him along the strip of stuff that still lay unrolled between them. Cautiously he slid his hand palm-downward along the table till his finger-tips touched the end of the stuff. A faint vibration of her lashes seemed to show that she was aware of his gesture, and that it had sent a counter-current back to her; and she let her hands lie motionless on the other end of the strip.

As they sat thus he heard a sound behind him and turned his head. The cat had jumped from Zeena's chair to dart at a mouse in the wainscot, and as a result of the sudden movement the empty chair had set up a spectral rocking.

"She'll be rocking in it herself this time to-morrow," Ethan thought. "I've been in a dream, and this is the only evening we'll ever have together." The return to reality was as painful as the return to consciousness after taking an anæsthetic. His body and brain ached with indescribable weariness, and he could think of nothing to say or to do that should arrest the mad flight of the moments.

His alteration of mood seemed to have communicated itself to Mattie. She looked up at him languidly, as though her lids were weighted with sleep and it cost her an effort to raise them. Her glance fell on his hand, which now completely covered the end of her work and grasped it as if it were a part of herself. He saw a scarcely perceptible tremor cross her face, and without knowing what he did he stooped his head and kissed the bit of stuff in his hold. As his lips rested on it he felt it glide slowly from beneath them, and saw that Mattie had risen and was silently rolling up her work. She fastened it with a pin, and then, finding her thimble and scissors, put them with the roll of stuff into the box covered with fancy paper which he had once brought to her from Bettsbridge.

He stood up also, looking vaguely about the room. The clock above the dresser struck eleven.

"Is the fire all right?" she asked in a low voice.

He opened the door of the stove and poked aimlessly at the embers. When he raised himself again he saw that she was dragging toward the stove the old soap-box lined with carpet in which the cat made its bed. Then she recrossed the floor and lifted two of the geranium pots in her arms, moving them away from the cold window. He followed her and brought the other geraniums, the hyacinth bulbs in a cracked custard bowl and the German ivy trained over an old croquet hoop.

When these nightly duties were performed there was nothing left to do but to bring in the tin candlestick from the passage, light the candle and blow out the lamp. Ethan put the candlestick in Mattie's hand and she went out of the kitchen ahead of him, the light that she carried before her making her dark hair look like a drift of mist on the moon.

"Good night, Matt," he said as she put her foot on the first step of the stairs.

She turned and looked at him a moment. "Good night, Ethan," she answered, and went up.

When the door of her room had closed on her he remembered that he had not even touched her hand.

CHAPTER VI

THE NEXT MORNING at breakfast Jotham Powell was between them, and Ethan tried to hide his joy under an air of exaggerated indifference, lounging back in his chair to throw scraps to the cat, growling at the weather, and not so much as offering to help Mattie when she rose to clear away the dishes.

He did not know why he was so irrationally happy, for nothing was changed in his life or hers. He had not even touched the tip of her fingers or looked her full in the eyes. But their evening together had given him a vision of what life at her side might be, and he was glad now that he had done nothing to trouble the sweetness of the picture. He had a fancy that she knew what had restrained him . . .

There was a last load of lumber to be hauled to the village, and Jotham Powell—who did not work regularly for Ethan in winter—had "come round" to help with the job. But a wet snow, melting to sleet, had fallen in the night and turned the roads to glass. There was more wet in the air and it seemed likely to both men that the weather would "milden" toward afternoon and make the going safer. Ethan therefore proposed to his assistant that they should load the sledge at the wood-lot, as they had done on the previous morning, and put off the "teaming" to Starkfield till later in the day. This plan had the advantage of enabling him to send Jotham to the Flats after dinner to meet Zenobia, while he himself took the lumber down to the village.

He told Jotham to go out and harness up the greys, and for a moment he and Mattie had the kitchen to themselves. She had plunged the breakfast dishes into a tin dish-pan and was bending above it with her slim arms bared to the elbow, the steam from the hot water beading her forehead and tightening her rough hair into little brown rings like the tendrils on the traveller's joy.

Ethan stood looking at her, his heart in his throat. He wanted to say: "We shall never be alone again like this." Instead, he reached down his tobacco-pouch from a shelf of the dresser, put it into his pocket and said: "I guess I can make out to be home for dinner."

She answered "All right, Ethan," and he heard her singing over the dishes as he went.

As soon as the sledge was loaded he meant to send Jotham back to the farm and hurry on foot into the village to buy the glue for the pickle-dish. With ordinary luck he should have had time to carry out this plan; but everything went wrong from the start. On the way over to the wood-lot one of the greys slipped on a glare of ice and cut his knee; and when they got him up again Jotham had to go back to the barn for a strip of rag to bind the cut. Then, when the loading finally began, a sleety rain was coming down once more, and the tree trunks were so slippery that it took twice as long as usual to lift them and get them in place on the sledge. It was what Jotham called a sour morning for work, and the horses, shivering and stamping under their wet blankets, seemed to like it as little as the men. It was long past the dinner-hour when the job was done, and Ethan had to give up going to the village because he wanted to lead the injured horse home and wash the cut himself.

He thought that by starting out again with the lumber as soon as he had finished his dinner he might get back to the farm with the glue before Jotham and the old sorrel had had time to fetch Zenobia from the Flats; but he knew the chance was a slight one. It turned on the state of the roads and on the possible lateness of the Bettsbridge train. He remembered afterward, with a grim flash of self-derision, what importance he had attached to the weighing of these probabilities . . .

As soon as dinner was over he set out again for the wood-lot, not daring to linger till Jotham Powell left. The hired man was still drying his wet feet at the stove, and Ethan could only give Mattie a quick look as he said beneath his breath: "I'll be back early."

He fancied that she nodded her comprehension; and with that scant solace he had to trudge off through the rain.

He had driven his load half-way to the village when Jotham Powell overtook him, urging the reluctant sorrel toward the Flats. "I'll have to hurry up to do it," Ethan mused, as the sleigh dropped down ahead of him over the dip of the school-house hill. He worked like ten at the unloading, and when it was over hastened on to Michael Eady's for the glue. Eady and his assistant were both "down street," and young Denis, who seldom deigned to take their place, was lounging by the stove with a knot of the golden youth of Starkfield. They hailed Ethan with ironic compliment and offers of conviviality; but no one knew where to find the glue. Ethan, consumed with the longing for a last moment alone with Mattie, hung about impatiently while Denis made an ineffectual search in the obscurer corners of the store.

"Looks as if we were all sold out. But if you'll wait around till the old man comes along maybe he can put his hand on it."

"I'm obliged to you, but I'll try if I can get it down at Mrs. Homan's," Ethan answered, burning to be gone.

Denis's commercial instinct compelled him to aver on oath that what Eady's store could not produce would never be found at the widow Homan's; but Ethan, heedless of this boast, had already climbed to the sledge and was driving on to the rival establishment. Here, after considerable search, and sympathetic questions as to what he wanted it for, and whether ordinary flour paste wouldn't do as well if she couldn't find it, the widow Homan finally hunted down her solitary bottle of glue to its hiding-place in a medley of cough-lozenges and corset-laces.

"I hope Zeena ain't broken anything she sets store by," she called after him as he turned the greys toward home.

The fitful bursts of sleet had changed into a steady rain and the horses had heavy work even without a load behind them. Once or twice, hearing sleigh-bells, Ethan turned his head, fancying that Zeena and Jotham might overtake him; but the old sorrel was not in sight, and he set his face against the rain and urged on his ponderous pair.

The barn was empty when the horses turned into it and, after giving them the most perfunctory ministrations they had ever received from him, he strode up to the house and pushed open the kitchen door.

Mattie was there alone, as he had pictured her. She was bending over a pan on the stove; but at the sound of his step she turned with a start and sprang to him.

"See, here, Matt, I've got some stuff to mend the dish with! Let me get at it quick," he cried, waving the bottle in one hand while he put her lightly aside; but she did not seem to hear him.

"Oh, Ethan—Zeena's come," she said in a whisper, clutching his sleeve.

They stood and stared at each other, pale as culprits.

"But the sorrel's not in the barn!" Ethan stammered.

"Jotham Powell brought some goods over from the Flats for his wife, and he drove right on home with them," she explained.

He gazed blankly about the kitchen, which looked cold and squalid in the rainy winter twilight.

"How is she?" he asked, dropping his voice to Mattie's whisper.

She looked away from him uncertainly. "I don't know. She went right up to her room."

"She didn't say anything?"

"No."

Ethan let out his doubts in a low whistle and thrust the bottle back into his pocket. "Don't fret; I'll come down and mend it in the night," he said. He pulled on his wet coat again and went back to the barn to feed the greys.

While he was there Jotham Powell drove up with the sleigh, and when the horses had been attended to Ethan said to him: "You might as well come back up for a bite." He was not sorry to assure himself of Jotham's neutralising presence at the supper table, for Zeena was always "nervous" after a journey. But the hired man, though seldom loth to accept a meal not included in his wages, opened his stiff jaws to answer slowly: "I'm obliged to you, but I guess I'll go along back."

Ethan looked at him in surprise. "Better come up and dry off. Looks as if there'd be something hot for supper."

Jotham's facial muscles were unmoved by this appeal and, his vocabulary being limited, he merely repeated: "I guess I'll go along back."

To Ethan there was something vaguely ominous in this stolid rejection of free food and warmth, and he wondered what had happened on the drive to nerve Jotham to such stoicism. Perhaps Zeena had failed to see the new doctor or had not liked his counsels: Ethan knew that in such cases the first person she met was likely to be held responsible for her grievance.

When he re-entered the kitchen the lamp lit up the same scene of shining comfort as on the previous evening. The table had been as carefully laid, a clear fire glowed in the stove, the cat dozed in its warmth, and Mattie came forward carrying a plate of doughnuts.

She and Ethan looked at each other in silence; then she said, as she had said the night before: "I guess it's about time for supper."

CHAPTER VII

ETHAN WENT OUT into the passage to hang up his wet garments. He listened for Zeena's step and, not hearing it, called her name up the stairs. She did not answer, and after a moment's hesitation he went up and opened her door. The room was almost dark, but in the obscurity he saw her sitting by the window, bolt upright, and knew by the rigidity of the outline projected against the pane that she had not taken off her travelling dress.

"Well, Zeena," he ventured from the threshold.

She did not move, and he continued: "Supper's about ready. Ain't you coming?"

She replied: "I don't feel as if I could touch a morsel."

It was the consecrated formula, and he expected it to be followed, as usual, by her rising and going down to supper. But she remained seated, and he could think of nothing more felicitous than: "I presume you're tired after the long ride."

Turning her head at this, she answered solemnly: "I'm a great deal sicker than you think."

Her words fell on his ear with a strange shock of wonder. He had often heard her pronounce them before—what if at last they were true?

He advanced a step or two into the dim room. "I hope that's not so, Zeena," he said.

She continued to gaze at him through the twilight with a mien of wan authority, as of one consciously singled out for a great fate. "I've got complications," she said.

Ethan knew the word for one of exceptional import. Almost everybody in the neighbourhood had "troubles," frankly localized and specified; but only the chosen had "complications." To have them was in itself a distinction, though it was also, in most cases, a death-warrant. People struggled on for years with "troubles," but they almost always succumbed to "complications."

Ethan's heart was jerking to and fro between two extremities of feeling, but for the moment compassion prevailed. His wife looked so hard and lonely, sitting there in the darkness with such thoughts.

"Is that what the new doctor told you?" he asked, instinctively lowering his voice.

"Yes. He says any regular doctor would want me to have an operation."

Ethan was aware that, in regard to the important question of surgical intervention, the female opinion of the neighbourhood was divided, some glorying in the prestige conferred by operations while others shunned them as indelicate. Ethan, from motives of economy, had always been glad that Zeena was of the latter faction.

In the agitation caused by the gravity of her announcement he sought a consolatory short cut. "What do you know about this doctor anyway? Nobody ever told you that before."

He saw his blunder before she could take it up: she wanted sympathy, not consolation.

"I didn't need to have anybody tell me I was losing ground every day. Everybody but you could see it. And everybody in Bettsbridge knows about Dr. Buck. He has his office in Worcester, and comes over once a fortnight to Shadd's Falls and Bettsbridge for consultations. Eliza Spears was wasting away with kidney trouble before she went to him, and now she's up and around, and singing in the choir."

"Well, I'm glad of that. You must do just what he tells you," Ethan answered sympathetically.

She was still looking at him. "I mean to," she said. He was struck by a new note in her voice. It was neither whining nor reproachful, but drily resolute.

"What does he want you should do?" he asked, with a mounting vision of fresh expenses.

"He wants I should have a hired girl. He says I oughtn't to have to do a single thing around the house."

"A hired girl?" Ethan stood transfixed.

"Yes. And Aunt Martha found me one right off. Everybody said I was lucky to get a girl to come away out here, and I agreed to give her a dollar extry to make sure. She'll be over to-morrow afternoon."

Wrath and dismay contended in Ethan. He had foreseen an immediate demand for money, but not a permanent drain on his scant resources. He no longer believed what Zeena had told him of the supposed seriousness of her state: he saw in her expedition to Bettsbridge only a plot hatched between herself and her Pierce relations to foist on him the cost of a servant; and for the moment wrath predominated.

"If you meant to engage a girl you ought to have told me before you started," he said.

"How could I tell you before I started? How did I know what Dr. Buck would say?"

"Oh, Dr. Buck–" Ethan's incredulity escaped in a short laugh. "Did Dr. Buck tell you how I was to pay her wages?"

Her voice rose furiously with his. "No, he didn't. For I'd 'a' been ashamed to tell *him* that you grudged me the money to get back my health, when I lost it nursing your own mother!"

"*You* lost your health nursing mother?"

"Yes; and my folks all told me at the time you couldn't do no less than marry me after––"

"Zeena!"

Through the obscurity which hid their faces their thoughts seemed to dart at each other like serpents shooting venom. Ethan was seized with horror of the scene and shame at his own share in it. It was as senseless and savage as a physical fight between two enemies in the darkness.

He turned to the shelf above the chimney, groped for matches and lit the one candle in the room. At first its weak flame made no impression on the shadows; then Zeena's face stood grimly out against the uncurtained pane, which had turned from grey to black.

It was the first scene of open anger between the couple in their sad seven years together, and Ethan felt as if he had lost an irretrievable advantage in descending to the level of recrimination. But the practical problem was there and had to be dealt with.

"You know I haven't got the money to pay for a girl, Zeena. You'll have to send her back: I can't do it."

"The doctor says it'll be my death if I go on slaving the way I've had to. He doesn't understand how I've stood it as long as I have."

"Slaving!–" He checked himself again, "You sha'n't lift a hand, if he says so. I'll do everything round the house myself––"

She broke in: "You're neglecting the farm enough already," and this being true, he found no answer, and left her time to add ironically: "Better send me over to the almshouse and done with it . . . I guess there's been Fromes there afore now."

The taunt burned into him, but he let it pass. "I haven't got the money. That settles it."

There was a moment's pause in the struggle, as though the combatants were testing their weapons. Then Zeena said in a level voice: "I thought you were to get fifty dollars from Andrew Hale for that lumber."

"Andrew Hale never pays under three months." He had hardly spoken when he remembered the excuse he had made for not accompanying his wife to the station the day before; and the blood rose to his frowning brows.

"Why, you told me yesterday you'd fixed it up with him to pay cash down. You said that was why you couldn't drive me over to the Flats."

Ethan had no suppleness in deceiving. He had never before been convicted of a lie, and all the resources of evasion failed him. "I guess that was a misunderstanding," he stammered.

"You ain't got the money?"

"No."

"And you ain't going to get it?"

"No."

"Well, I couldn't know that when I engaged the girl, could I?"

"No." He paused to control his voice. "But you know it now. I'm sorry, but it can't be helped. You're a poor man's wife, Zeena; but I'll do the best I can for you."

For a while she sat motionless, as if reflecting, her arms stretched along the arms of her chair, her eyes fixed on vacancy. "Oh, I guess we'll make out," she said mildly.

The change in her tone reassured him. "Of course we will! There's a whole lot more I can do for you, and Mattie——"

Zeena, while he spoke, seemed to be following out some elaborate mental calculation. She emerged from it to say: "There'll be Mattie's board less, anyhow——"

Ethan, supposing the discussion to be over, had turned to go down to supper. He stopped short, not grasping what he heard. "Mattie's board less—?" he began.

Zeena laughed. It was an odd unfamiliar sound—he did not remember ever having heard her laugh before. "You didn't suppose I was going to keep two girls, did you? No wonder you were scared at the expense!"

He still had but a confused sense of what she was saying. From the beginning of the discussion he had instinctively avoided the mention of Mattie's name, fearing he hardly knew what: criticism, complaints, or vague allusions to the imminent probability of her marrying. But the thought of a definite rupture had never come to him, and even now could not lodge itself in his mind.

"I don't know what you mean," he said. "Mattie Silver's not a hired girl. She's your relation."

"She's a pauper that's hung onto us all after her father'd done his best to ruin us. I've kep' her here a whole year: it's somebody else's turn now."

As the shrill words shot out Ethan heard a tap on the door, which he had drawn shut when he turned back from the threshold.

"Ethan—Zeena!" Mattie's voice sounded gaily from the landing, "do you know what time it is? Supper's been ready half an hour."

Inside the room there was a moment's silence; then Zeena called out from her seat: "I'm not coming down to supper."

"Oh, I'm sorry! Aren't you well? Sha'n't I bring you up a bite of something?"

Ethan roused himself with an effort and opened the door. "Go along down, Matt. Zeena's just a little tired. I'm coming."

He heard her "All right!" and her quick step on the stairs; then he shut the door and turned back into the room. His wife's attitude was unchanged, her face inexorable, and he was seized with the despairing sense of his helplessness.

"You ain't going to do it, Zeena?"

"Do what?" she emitted between flattened lips.

"Send Mattie away—like this?"

"I never bargained to take her for life!"

He continued with rising vehemence: "You can't put her out of the house like a thief—a poor girl without friends or money. She's done her best for you and she's got no place to go to. You may forget she's your kin but everybody else'll remember it. If you do a thing like that what do you suppose folks'll say of you?"

Zeena waited a moment, as if giving him time to feel the full force of the contrast between his own excitement and her composure. Then she replied in the same smooth voice: "I know well enough what they say of my having kep' her here as long as I have."

Ethan's hand dropped from the door-knob, which he had held clenched since he had drawn the door shut on Mattie. His wife's retort was like a knife-cut across the sinews and he felt suddenly weak and powerless. He had meant to humble himself, to argue that Mattie's keep didn't cost much, after all, that he could make out to buy a stove and fix up a place in the attic for the hired girl—but Zeena's words revealed the peril of such pleadings.

"You mean to tell her she's got to go—at once?" he faltered out, in terror of letting his wife complete her sentence.

As if trying to make him see reason she replied impartially: "The girl will be over from Bettsbridge to-morrow, and I presume she's got to have somewheres to sleep."

Ethan looked at her with loathing. She was no longer the listless creature who had lived at his side in a state of sullen self-absorption, but a mysterious alien presence, an evil energy secreted from the long years of silent brooding. It was the sense of his helplessness that sharpened his antipathy. There had never been anything in her that one could appeal to; but as long as he could ignore and command he had remained indifferent. Now she had mastered him and he abhorred her. Mattie was her relation, not his: there were no means by which he could compel her to keep the girl under her roof. All the long misery of his baffled past, of his youth of failure, hardship and vain effort, rose up in his soul in bitterness and seemed to take shape before him in the woman who at every turn had barred his way. She had taken everything else from him; and now she meant to take the one thing that made up for all the others. For a moment such a flame of hate rose in him that it ran down his arm and clenched his fist against her. He took a wild step forward and then stopped.

"You're—you're not coming down?" he said in a bewildered voice.

"No. I guess I'll lay down on the bed a little while," she answered mildly; and he turned and walked out of the room.

In the kitchen Mattie was sitting by the stove, the cat curled up on her knees. She sprang to her feet as Ethan entered and carried the covered dish of meat-pie to the table.

"I hope Zeena isn't sick?" she asked.

"No."

She shone at him across the table. "Well, sit right down then. You must be starving." She uncovered the pie and pushed it over to him.

So they were to have one more evening together, her happy eyes seemed to say!

He helped himself mechanically and began to eat; then disgust took him by the throat and he laid down his fork.

Mattie's tender gaze was on him and she marked the gesture.

"Why, Ethan, what's the matter? Don't it taste right?"

"Yes—it's first-rate. Only I—" He pushed his plate away, rose from his chair, and walked around the table to her side. She started up with frightened eyes.

"Ethan, there's something wrong! I *knew* there was!"

She seemed to melt against him in her terror, and he caught her in his arms, held her fast there, felt her lashes beat his cheek like netted butterflies.

"What is it—what is it?" she stammered; but he had found her lips at last and was drinking unconsciousness of everything but the joy they gave him.

She lingered a moment, caught in the same strong current; then she slipped from him and drew back a step or two, pale and troubled. Her look smote him with compunction, and he cried out, as if he saw her drowning in a dream: "You can't go, Matt! I'll never let you!"

"Go—go?" she stammered. "Must I go?"

The words went on sounding between them as though a torch of warning flew from hand to hand through a black landscape.

Ethan was overcome with shame at his lack of self-control in flinging the news at her so brutally. His head reeled and he had to support himself against the table. All the while he felt as if he were still kissing her, and yet dying of thirst for her lips.

"Ethan, what has happened? Is Zeena mad with me?"

Her cry steadied him, though it deepened his wrath and pity. "No, no," he assured her, "it's not that. But this new doctor has scared her about herself. You know she believes all they say the first time she sees them. And this one's told her she won't get well unless she lays up and don't do a thing about the house—not for months——"

He paused, his eyes wandering from her miserably. She stood silent a moment, drooping before him like a broken branch. She was so small and weak-looking that it wrung his heart; but suddenly she lifted her head and looked straight at him. "And she wants somebody handier in my place? Is that it?"

"That's what she says to-night."

"If she says it to-night she'll say it to-morrow."

Both bowed to the inexorable truth: they knew that Zeena never changed her mind, and that in her case a resolve once taken was equivalent to an act performed.

There was a long silence between them; then Mattie said in a low voice: "Don't be too sorry, Ethan."

"Oh, God—oh, God," he groaned. The glow of passion he had felt for her had melted to an aching tenderness. He saw her quick lids beating back the tears, and longed to take her in his arms and soothe her.

"You're letting your supper get cold," she admonished him with a pale gleam of gaiety.

"Oh, Matt—Matt—where'll you go to?"

Her lids sank and a tremor crossed her face. He saw that for the first time the thought of the future came to her distinctly. "I might get something to do over at Stamford," she faltered, as if knowing that he knew she had no hope.

He dropped back into his seat and hid his face in his hands. Despair seized him at the thought of her setting out alone to renew the weary quest for work. In the only place where she was known she was surrounded by indifference or animosity; and what chance had she, inexperienced and untrained, among the million bread-seekers of the cities? There came back to him miserable tales he had heard at Worcester, and the faces of girls whose lives had begun as hopefully as Mattie's. . . . It was not possible to think of such things without a revolt of his whole being. He sprang up suddenly.

"You can't go, Matt! I won't let you! She's always had her way, but I mean to have mine now——"

Mattie lifted her hand with a quick gesture, and he heard his wife's step behind him.

Zeena came into the room with her dragging down-at-the-heel step, and quietly took her accustomed seat between them.

"I felt a little mite better, and Dr. Buck says I ought to eat all I can to keep my strength up, even if I ain't got any appetite," she said in her flat whine, reaching across Mattie for the teapot. Her "good" dress had been replaced by the black calico and brown knitted shawl which formed her daily wear, and with them she had put on her usual face and manner. She poured out her tea, added a great deal of milk to it, helped herself largely to pie and pickles, and made the familiar gesture of adjusting her false teeth before she began to eat. The cat rubbed itself ingratiatingly against her, and she said "Good Pussy," stooped to stroke it and gave it a scrap of meat from her plate.

Ethan sat speechless, not pretending to eat, but Mattie nibbled valiantly at her food and asked Zeena one or two questions about her visit to Bettsbridge. Zeena answered in her every-day tone and, warming to the theme, regaled them with several vivid descriptions of intestinal disturbances among her friends and relatives. She looked straight at Mattie as she spoke, a faint smile deepening the vertical lines between her nose and chin.

When supper was over she rose from her seat and pressed her hand to the flat surface over the region of her heart. "That pie of yours always sets a mite heavy, Matt," she said, not ill-naturedly. She seldom abbreviated the girl's name, and when she did so it was always a sign of affability.

"I've a good mind to go and hunt up those stomach powders I got last year over in Springfield," she continued. "I ain't tried them for quite a while, and maybe they'll help the heartburn."

Mattie lifted her eyes. "Can't I get them for you, Zeena?" she ventured.

"No. They're in a place you don't know about," Zeena answered darkly, with one of her secret looks.

She went out of the kitchen and Mattie, rising, began to clear the dishes from the table. As she passed Ethan's chair their eyes met and clung together desolately. The warm still kitchen looked as peaceful as the night before. The cat had sprung to Zeena's rocking-chair, and the heat of the fire was beginning to draw out the faint sharp scent of the geraniums. Ethan dragged himself wearily to his feet.

"I'll go out and take a look around," he said, going toward the passage to get his lantern.

As he reached the door he met Zeena coming back into the room, her lips twitching with anger, a flush of excitement on her sallow face. The shawl had slipped from her shoulders and was dragging at her down-trodden heels, and in her hands she carried the fragments of the red glass pickle-dish.

"I'd like to know who done this," she said, looking sternly from Ethan to Mattie.

There was no answer, and she continued in a trembling voice: "I went to get those powders I'd put away in father's old spectacle-case, top of the china-closet, where I keep the things I set store by, so's folks sha'n't meddle with them—" Her voice broke, and two small tears hung on her lashless lids and ran slowly down her cheeks. "It takes the stepladder to get at the top shelf, and I put Aunt Philura Maple's pickle-dish up there o' purpose when we was married, and it's never been down since, 'cept for the spring cleaning, and then I always lifted it with my own hands, so's 't shouldn't get broke." She laid the fragments reverently on the table. "I want to know who done this," she quavered.

At the challenge Ethan turned back into the room and faced her. "I can tell you, then. The cat done it."

"The *cat?*"

"That's what I said."

She looked at him hard, and then turned her eyes to Mattie, who was carrying the dish-pan to the table.

"I'd like to know how the cat got into my china-closet," she said.

"Chasin' mice, I guess," Ethan rejoined. "There was a mouse round the kitchen all last evening."

Zeena continued to look from one to the other; then she emitted her small strange laugh. "I knew the cat was a smart cat," she said in a high voice, "but I didn't know he was smart enough to pick up the pieces of my pickle-dish and lay 'em edge to edge on the very shelf he knocked 'em off of."

Mattie suddenly drew her arms out of the steaming water. "It wasn't Ethan's fault, Zeena! The cat *did* break the dish; but I got it down from the china-closet, and I'm the one to blame for its getting broken."

Zeena stood beside the ruin of her treasure, stiffening into a stony image of resentment, "*You* got down my pickle-dish—what for?"

A bright flush flew to Mattie's cheeks. "I wanted to make the supper-table pretty," she said.

"You wanted to make the supper-table pretty; and you waited till my back was turned, and took the thing I set most store by of anything I've got, and wouldn't never use it, not even when the minister come to dinner, or Aunt Martha Pierce come over from Bettsbridge—" Zeena paused with a gasp, as if terrified by her own evocation of the sacrilege. "You're a bad girl, Mattie Silver, and I always known it. It's the way your father begun, and I was warned of it when I took you, and I tried to keep my things where you couldn't get at 'em—and now you've took from me the one I cared for most of all—" She broke off in a short spasm of sobs that passed and left her more than ever like a shape of stone.

"If I'd 'a' listened to folks, you'd 'a' gone before now, and this wouldn't 'a' happened," she said; and gathering up the bits of broken glass she went out of the room as if she carried a dead body . . .

CHAPTER VIII

WHEN ETHAN was called back to the farm by his father's illness his mother gave him, for his own use, a small room behind the untenanted "best parlour." Here he had nailed up shelves for his books, built himself a box-sofa out of boards and a mattress, laid out his papers on a kitchen-table, hung on the rough plaster wall an engraving of Abraham Lincoln and a calender with "Thoughts from the Poets," and tried, with these meagre properties, to produce some likeness to the study of a "minister" who had been kind to him and lent him books when he was at Worcester. He still took refuge there in summer, but when Mattie came to live at the farm he had had to give her his stove, and consequently the room was uninhabitable for several months of the year.

To this retreat he descended as soon as the house was quiet, and Zeena's steady breathing from the bed had assured him that there was to be no sequel to the scene in the kitchen. After Zeena's departure he and Mattie had stood speechless, neither seeking to approach the other. Then the girl had returned to her task of clearing up the kitchen for the night and he had taken his lantern and gone on his usual round outside the house. The kitchen was empty when he came back to it; but his tobacco-pouch and pipe had been laid on the table, and under them was a scrap of paper torn from the back of a seedsman's catalogue, on which three words were written: "Don't trouble, Ethan."

Going into his cold dark "study" he placed the lantern on the table and, stooping to its light, read the message again and again. It was the first time that Mattie had ever written to him, and the possession of the paper gave him a strange new sense of her nearness; yet it deepened his anguish by reminding him that henceforth they would have no other way of communicating with each other. For the life of her smile, the warmth of her voice, only cold paper and dead words!

Confused motions of rebellion stormed in him. He was too young, too strong, too full of the sap of living, to submit so easily to the destruction of his hopes. Must he wear out all his years at the side of a bitter querulous woman? Other possibilities had been in him, possibilities sacrificed, one by one, to Zeena's narrow-mindedness and ignorance. And what good had come of it? She was a hundred times bitterer and more discontented than when he had married her: the one pleasure left her was to inflict pain on him. All the healthy instincts of self-defence rose up in him against such waste . . .

He bundled himself into his old coon-skin coat and lay down on the box-sofa to think. Under his cheek he felt a hard object with strange protuberances. It was a cushion which Zeena had made for him when they were engaged—the only piece of needlework he had ever seen her do. He flung it across the floor and propped his head against the wall . . .

He knew a case of a man over the mountain—a young fellow of about his own age—who had escaped from just such a life of misery by going West with the girl he cared for. His wife had divorced him, and he had married the girl and prospered. Ethan had seen the couple the summer before at Shadd's Falls, where they had come to visit relatives. They had a little girl with fair curls, who wore a gold locket and was dressed like a princess. The deserted wife had not done badly either. Her husband had given her the farm and she had managed to sell it, and with that and the alimony she had started a lunch-room at Bettsbridge and bloomed into activity and importance. Ethan was fired by the thought. Why should he not leave with Mattie the next day, instead of letting her go alone? He would hide his valise under the seat of the sleigh, and Zeena would suspect nothing till she went upstairs for her afternoon nap and found a letter on the bed . . .

His impulses were still near the surface, and he sprang up, re-lit the lantern, and sat down at the table. He rummaged in the drawer for a sheet of paper, found one, and began to write.

"Zeena, I've done all I could for you, and I don't see as it's been any use. I don't blame you, nor I don't blame myself. Maybe both of us will do better separate. I'm going to try my luck West, and you can sell the farm and mill, and keep the money——"

His pen paused on the word, which brought home to him the relentless conditions of his lot. If he gave the farm and mill to Zeena what would be left him to start his own life with? Once in the West he was sure of picking up work—he would not have feared to try his chance alone. But with Mattie depending on him the case was different. And what of Zeena's fate? Farm and mill were mortgaged to the limit of their value, and even if she found a purchaser —in itself an unlikely chance—it was doubtful if she could clear a thousand dollars on the sale. Meanwhile, how could she keep the farm going? It was only by incessant labour and personal supervision that Ethan drew a meagre living from his land, and his wife, even if she were in better health than she imagined, could never carry such a burden alone.

Well, she could go back to her people, then, and see what they would do for her. It was the fate she was forcing on Mattie—why not let her try it herself? By the time she had discovered his whereabouts, and brought suit for divorce, he would probably—wherever he was—be earning enough to pay her a sufficient alimony. And the alternative was to let Mattie go forth alone, with far less hope of ultimate provision . . .

He had scattered the contents of the table-drawer in his search for a sheet of paper, and as he took up his pen his eye fell on an old copy of the *Bettsbridge Eagle.* The advertising sheet was folded uppermost, and he read the seductive words: "Trips to the West: Reduced Rates."

He drew the lantern nearer and eagerly scanned the fares; then the paper fell from his hand and he pushed aside his unfinished letter. A moment ago he had wondered what he and Mattie were to live on when they reached the West; now he saw that he had not even the money to take her there. Borrowing was out of the question: six months before he had given his only security to raise funds for necessary repairs to the mill, and he knew that without security no one at Starkfield would lend him ten dollars. The inexorable facts closed in on him like prison-warders handcuffing a convict. There was no way out—none. He was a prisoner for life, and now his one ray of light was to be extinguished.

He crept back heavily to the sofa, stretching himself out with limbs so leaden that he felt as if they would never move again. Tears rose in his throat and slowly burned their way to his lids.

As he lay there, the window-pane that faced him, growing gradually lighter, inlaid upon the darkness a square of moon-suffused sky. A crooked tree-branch crossed it, a branch of the apple-tree under which, on summer evenings, he had sometimes found Mattie sitting when he came up from the mill. Slowly the rim of the rainy vapours caught fire and burnt away, and a pure moon swung into the blue. Ethan, rising on his elbow, watched the landscape whiten and shape itself under the sculpture of the moon. This was the night on which he was to have taken Mattie coasting, and there hung the lamp to light them! He looked out at the slopes bathed in lustre, the silver-edged darkness of the woods, the spectral purple of the hills against the sky, and it seemed as though all the beauty of the night had been poured out to mock his wretchedness . . .

He fell asleep, and when he woke the chill of the winter dawn was in the room. He felt cold and stiff and hungry, and ashamed of being hungry. He rubbed his eyes and went to the window. A red sun stood over the grey rim of the fields, behind trees that looked black and brittle. He said to himself: "This is Matt's last day," and tried to think what the place would be without her.

As he stood there he heard a step behind him and she entered.

"Oh, Ethan—were you here all night?"

She looked so small and pinched, in her poor dress, with the red scarf wound about her, and the cold light turning her paleness sallow, that Ethan stood before her without speaking.

"You must be frozen," she went on, fixing lustreless eyes on him.

He drew a step nearer. "How did you know I was here?"

"Because I heard you go down stairs again after I went to bed, and I listened all night, and you didn't come up."

All his tenderness rushed to his lips. He looked at her and said: "I'll come right along and make up the kitchen fire."

They went back to the kitchen, and he fetched the coal and kindlings and cleared out the stove for her, while she brought in the milk and the cold remains of the meat-pie. When warmth began to radiate from the stove, and the first ray of sunlight lay on the kitchen floor, Ethan's dark thoughts melted in the mellower air. The sight of Mattie going about her work as he had seen her on so many mornings made it seem impossible that she should ever cease to be a part of the scene. He said to himself that he had doubtless exaggerated the significance of Zeena's threats, and that she too, with the return of daylight, would come to a saner mood.

He went up to Mattie as she bent above the stove, and laid his hand on her arm. "I don't want you should trouble either," he said, looking down into her eyes with a smile.

She flushed up warmly and whispered back: "No, Ethan, I ain't going to trouble."

"I guess things'll straighten out," he added.

There was no answer but a quick throb of her lids, and he went on: "She ain't said anything this morning?"

"No. I haven't seen her yet."

"Don't you take any notice when you do."

With this injunction he left her and went out to the cow-barn. He saw Jotham Powell walking up the hill through the morning mist, and the familiar sight added to his growing conviction of security.

As the two men were clearing out the stalls Jotham rested on his pitch-fork to say: "Dan'l Byrne's goin' over to the Flats to-day noon, an' he c'd take Mattie's trunk along, and make it easier ridin' when I take her over in the sleigh."

Ethan looked at him blankly, and he continued: "Mis' Frome said the new girl'd be at the Flats at five, and I was to take Mattie then, so's 't she could ketch the six o'clock train for Stamford."

Ethan felt the blood drumming in his temples. He had to wait a moment before he could find voice to say: "Oh, it ain't so sure about Mattie's going——"

"That so?" said Jotham indifferently; and they went on with their work.

When they returned to the kitchen the two women were already at breakfast. Zeena had an air of unusual alertness and activity. She drank two cups of coffee and fed the cat with the scraps left in the pie-dish; then she rose from her seat and, walking over to the window, snipped two or three yellow leaves from the geraniums. "Aunt Martha's ain't got a faded leaf on 'em; but they pine away when they ain't cared for," she said reflectively. Then she turned to Jotham and asked: "What time'd you say Dan'l Byrne'd be along?"

The hired man threw a hesitating glance at Ethan. "Round about noon," he said.

Zeena turned to Mattie. "That trunk of yours is too heavy for the sleigh, and Dan'l Byrne'll be round to take it over to the Flats," she said.

"I'm much obliged to you, Zeena," said Mattie.

"I'd like to go over things with you first," Zeena continued in an unperturbed voice. "I know there's a huckaback towel missing; and I can't make out what you done with that match-safe 't used to stand behind the stuffed owl in the parlour."

She went out, followed by Mattie, and when the men were alone Jotham said to his employer: "I guess I better let Dan'l come round, then."

Ethan finished his usual morning tasks about the house and barn; then he said to Jotham: "I'm going down to Starkfield. Tell them not to wait dinner."

The passion of rebellion had broken out in him again. That which had seemed incredible in the sober light of day had really come to pass, and he was to assist as a helpless spectator at Mattie's banishment. His manhood was humbled by the part he was compelled to play and by the thought of what Mattie must think of him. Confused impulses struggled in him as he strode along to the village. He had made up his mind to do something, but he did not know what it would be.

The early mist had vanished and the fields lay like a silver shield under the sun. It was one of the days when the glitter of winter shines through a pale haze of spring. Every yard of the road was alive with Mattie's presence, and there was hardly a branch against the sky or tangle of brambles on the bank in which some bright shred of memory was not caught. Once, in the stillness, the call of a bird in a mountain ash was so like her laughter that his heart tightened and then grew large; and all these things made him see that something must be done at once.

Suddenly it occurred to him that Andrew Hale, who was a kind-hearted man, might be induced to reconsider his refusal and advance a small sum on the lumber if he were told that Zeena's ill-health made it necessary to hire a servant. Hale, after all, knew enough of Ethan's situation to make it possible for the latter to renew his appeal without too much loss of pride; and, moreover, how much did pride count in the ebullition of passions in his breast?

The more he considered his plan the more hopeful it seemed. If he could get Mrs. Hale's ear he felt certain of success, and with fifty dollars in his pocket nothing could keep him from Mattie . . .

His first object was to reach Starkfield before Hale had started for his work; he knew the carpenter had a job down the Corbury road and was likely to leave his house early. Ethan's long strides grew more rapid with the accelerated beat of his thoughts, and as he reached the foot of School House Hill he caught sight of Hale's sleigh in the distance. He hurried forward to meet it, but as it drew nearer he saw that it was driven by the carpenter's youngest boy and that the figure at his side, looking like a large upright cocoon in spectacles, was that of Mrs. Hale. Ethan signed to them to stop, and Mrs. Hale leaned forward, her pink wrinkles twinkling with benevolence.

"Mr. Hale? Why, yes, you'll find him down home now. He ain't going to his work this forenoon. He woke up with a touch o' lumbago, and I just made him put on one of old Dr. Kidder's plasters and set right up into the fire."

Beaming maternally on Ethan, she bent over to add: "I on'y just heard from Mr. Hale 'bout Zeena's going over to Bettsbridge to see that new doctor. I'm real sorry she's feeling so bad again! I hope he thinks he can do something for her. I don't know anybody round here's had more sickness than Zeena. I always tell Mr. Hale I don't know what she'd 'a' done if she hadn't 'a' had you to look after her; and I used to say the same thing 'bout your mother. You've had an awful mean time, Ethan Frome."

She gave him a last nod of sympathy while her son chirped to the horse; and Ethan, as she drove off, stood in the middle of the road and stared after the retreating sleigh.

It was a long time since any one had spoken to him as kindly as Mrs. Hale. Most people were either indifferent to his troubles, or disposed to think it natural that a young fellow of his age should have carried without repining the burden of three crippled lives. But Mrs. Hale had said, "You've had an awful mean time, Ethan Frome," and he felt less alone with his misery. If the Hales were sorry for him they would surely respond to his appeal . . .

He started down the road toward their house, but at the end of a few yards he pulled up sharply, the blood in his face. For the first time, in the light of the words he had just heard, he saw what he was about to do. He was planning to take advantage of the Hales' sympathy to obtain money from them on false pretences. That was a plain statement of the cloudy purpose which had driven him in headlong to Starkfield.

With the sudden perception of the point to which his madness had carried him, the madness fell and he saw his life before him as it was. He was a poor man, the husband of a sickly woman, whom his desertion would leave alone and destitute; and even if he had had the heart to desert her he could have done so only by deceiving two kindly people who had pitied him.

He turned and walked slowly back to the farm.

CHAPTER IX

AT THE KITCHEN DOOR Daniel Byrne sat in his sleigh behind a big-boned grey who pawed the snow and swung his long head restlessly from side to side.

Ethan went into the kitchen and found his wife by the stove. Her head was wrapped in her shawl, and she was reading a book called "Kidney Troubles and Their Cure" on which he had had to pay extra postage only a few days before.

Zeena did not move or look up when he entered, and after a moment he asked: "Where's Mattie?"

Without lifting her eyes from the page she replied: "I presume she's getting down her trunk."

The blood rushed to his face. "Getting down her trunk–alone?"

"Jotham Powell's down in the wood-lot, and Dan'l Byrne says he darsn't leave that horse," she returned.

Her husband, without stopping to hear the end of the phrase, had left the kitchen and sprung up the stairs. The door of Mattie's room was shut, and he wavered a moment on the landing. "Matt," he said in a low voice; but there was no answer, and he put his hand on the door-knob.

He had never been in her room except once, in the early summer, when he had gone there to plaster up a leak in the eaves, but he remembered exactly how everything had looked: the red-and-white quilt on her narrow bed, the pretty pin-cushion on the chest of drawers, and over it the enlarged photograph of her mother, in an oxydized frame, with a bunch of dyed grasses at the back. Now these and all other tokens of her presence had vanished and the room looked as bare and comfortless as when Zeena had shown her into it on the day of her arrival. In the middle of the floor stood her trunk, and on the trunk she sat in her Sunday dress, her back turned to the door and her face in her hands. She had not heard Ethan's call because she was sobbing and she did not hear his step till he stood close behind her and laid his hands on her shoulders.

"Matt–oh, don't–oh, *Matt!*"

She started up, lifting her wet face to his. "Ethan–I thought I wasn't ever going to see you again!"

He took her in his arms, pressing her close, and with a trembling hand smoothed away the hair from her forehead.

"Not see me again? What do you mean?"

She sobbed out: "Jotham said you told him we wasn't to wait dinner for you, and I thought––"

"You thought I meant to cut it?" he finished for her grimly.

She clung to him without answering, and he laid his lips on her hair, which was soft yet springy, like certain mosses on warm slopes, and had the faint woody fragrance of fresh sawdust in the sun.

Through the door they heard Zeena's voice calling out from below: "Dan'l Byrne says you better hurry up if you want him to take that trunk."

They drew apart with stricken faces. Words of resistance rushed to Ethan's lips and died there. Mattie found her handkerchief and dried her eyes; then, bending down, she took hold of a handle of the trunk.

Ethan put her aside. "You let go, Matt," he ordered her.

She answered: "It takes two to coax it round the corner"; and submitting to this argument he grasped the other handle, and together they manœuvered the heavy trunk out to the landing.

"Now let go," he repeated; then he shouldered the trunk and carried it down the stairs and across the passage to the kitchen. Zeena, who had gone back to her seat by the stove, did not lift her head from her book as he passed. Mattie followed him out of the door and helped him to lift the trunk into the back of the sleigh. When it was in place they stood side by side on the door-step, watching Daniel Byrne plunge off behind his fidgety horse.

It seemed to Ethan that his heart was bound with cords which an unseen hand was tightening with every tick of the clock. Twice he opened his lips to speak to Mattie and found no breath. At length, as she turned to re-enter the house, he laid a detaining hand on her.

"I'm going to drive you over, Matt," he whispered.

She murmured back: "I think Zeena wants I should go with Jotham."

"I'm going to drive you over," he repeated; and she went into the kitchen without answering.

At dinner Ethan could not eat. If he lifted his eyes they rested on Zeena's pinched face, and the corners of her straight lips seemed to quiver away into a smile. She ate well, declaring that the mild weather made her feel better, and pressed a second helping of beans on Jotham Powell, whose wants she generally ignored.

Mattie, when the meal was over, went about her usual task of clearing the table and washing up the dishes. Zeena, after feeding the cat, had returned to her rocking-chair by the stove, and Jotham Powell, who always lingered last, reluctantly pushed back his chair and moved toward the door.

On the threshold he turned back to say to Ethan: "What time'll I come round for Mattie?"

Ethan was standing near the window, mechanically filling his pipe while he watched Mattie move to and fro. He answered: "You needn't come round; I'm going to drive her over myself."

He saw the rise of the colour in Mattie's averted cheek, and the quick lifting of Zeena's head.

"I want you should stay here this afternoon, Ethan," his wife said. "Jotham can drive Mattie over."

Mattie flung an imploring glance at him, but he repeated curtly: "I'm going to drive her over myself."

Zeena continued in the same even tone: "I wanted you should stay and fix up that stove in Mattie's room afore the girl gets here. It ain't been drawing right for nigh on a month now."

Ethan's voice rose indignantly. "If it was good enough for Mattie I guess it's good enough for a hired girl."

"That girl that's coming told me she was used to a house where they had a furnace," Zeena persisted with the same monotonous mildness.

"She'd better ha' stayed there then," he flung back at her; and turning to Mattie he added in a hard voice: "You be ready by three, Matt; I've got business at Corbury."

Jotham Powell had started for the barn, and Ethan strode down after him aflame with anger. The pulses in his temples throbbed and a fog was in his eyes. He went about his task without knowing what force directed him, or whose hands and feet were fulfilling its orders. It was not till he led out the sorrel and backed him between the shafts of the sleigh that he once more became conscious of what he was doing. As he passed the bridle over the horse's head, and wound the traces around the shafts, he remembered the day when he had made the same preparations in order to drive over and meet his wife's cousin at the Flats. It was little more than a year ago, on just such a soft afternoon, with a "feel" of spring in the air. The sorrel, turning the same big ringed eye on him, nuzzled the palm of his hand in the same way; and one by one all the days between rose up and stood before him . . .

He flung the bearskin into the sleigh, climbed to the seat, and drove up to the house. When he entered the kitchen it was empty, but Mattie's bag and shawl lay ready by the door. He went to the foot of the stairs and listened. No sound reached him from above, but presently he thought he heard some one moving about in his deserted study, and pushing open the door he saw Mattie, in her hat and jacket, standing with her back to him near the table.

She started at his approach and turning quickly said: "Is it time?"

"What are you doing here, Matt?" he asked her.

She looked at him timidly. "I was just taking a look round—that's all," she answered, with a wavering smile.

They went back into the kitchen without speaking, and Ethan picked up her bag and shawl.

"Where's Zeena?" he asked.

"She went upstairs right after dinner. She said she had those shooting pains again, and didn't want to be disturbed."

"Didn't she say good-bye to you?"

"No. That was all she said."

Ethan, looking slowly about the kitchen, said to himself with a shudder that in a few hours he would be returning to it alone. Then the sense of unreality overcame him once more, and he could not bring himself to believe that Mattie stood there for the last time before him.

"Come on," he said almost gaily, opening the door and putting her bag into the sleigh. He sprang to his seat and bent over to tuck the rug about her as she slipped into the place at his side. "Now then, go 'long," he said, with a shake of the reins that sent the sorrel placidly jogging down the hill.

"We got lots of time for a good ride, Matt!" he cried seeking her hand beneath the fur and pressing it in his. His face tingled and he felt dizzy, as if he had stopped in at the Starkfield saloon on a zero day for a drink.

At the gate, instead of making for Starkfield, he turned the sorrel to the right, up the Bettsbridge road. Mattie sat silent, giving no sign of surprise; but after a moment she said: "Are you going round by Shadow Pond?"

He laughed and answered: "I knew you'd know!"

She drew closer under the bearskin, so that, looking sideways around his coat-sleeve, he could just catch the tip of her nose and a blown brown wave of hair. They drove slowly up the road between fields glistening under the pale sun, and then bent to the right down a lane edged with spruce and larch. Ahead of them, a long way off, a range of hills stained by mottlings of black forest flowed away in round white curves against the sky. The lane passed into a pine-wood with boles reddening in the afternoon sun and delicate blue shadows on the snow. As they entered it the breeze fell and a warm stillness seemed to drop from the branches with the dropping needles. Here the snow was so pure that the tiny tracks of wood-animals had left on it intricate lace-like patterns, and the bluish cones caught in its surface stood out like ornaments of bronze.

Ethan drove on in silence till they reached a part of the wood where the pines were more widely spaced, then he drew up and helped Mattie to get out of the sleigh. They passed between the aromatic trunks, the snow breaking crisply under their feet, till they came to a small sheet of water with steep wooded sides. Across its frozen surface, from the farther bank, a single hill rising against the western sun threw the long conical shadow which gave the lake its name. It was a shy secret spot, full of the same dumb melancholy that Ethan felt in his heart.

He looked up and down the little pebbly beach till his eye lit on a fallen tree-trunk half submerged in snow.

"There's where we sat at the picnic," he reminded her.

The entertainment of which he spoke was one of the few that they had taken part in together: a "church picnic" which, on a long afternoon of the preceding summer, had filled the retired place with merry-making. Mattie had begged him to go with her but he had refused. Then, toward sunset, coming down from the mountain where he had been felling timber, he had been caught by some strayed revellers and drawn into the group by the lake, where Mattie, encircled by facetious youths, and bright as a blackberry under her spreading hat, was brewing coffee over a gipsy fire. He remembered the shyness he had felt at approaching her in his uncouth clothes, and then the lighting up of her face, and the way she had broken through the group to come to him with a cup in her hand. They had sat for a few minutes on the fallen log by the pond, and she had missed her gold locket, and set the young men searching for it; and it was Ethan who had spied it in the moss. . . . That was all; but all their intercourse had been made up of just such inarticulate flashes, when they seemed to come suddenly upon happiness as if they had surprised a butterfly in the winter woods . . .

"It was right there I found your locket," he said, pushing his foot into a dense tuft of blueberry bushes.

"I never saw anybody with such sharp eyes!" she answered.

She sat down on the tree-trunk in the sun and he sat down beside her.

"You were as pretty as a picture in that pink hat," he said.

She laughed with pleasure. "Oh, I guess it was the hat!" she rejoined.

They had never before avowed their inclination so openly, and Ethan, for a moment, had the illusion that he was a free man, wooing the girl he meant to marry. He looked at her hair and longed to touch it again, and to tell her that it smelt of the woods; but he had never learned to say such things.

Suddenly she rose to her feet and said: "We mustn't stay here any longer."

He continued to gaze at her vaguely, only half-roused from his dream. "There's plenty of time," he answered.

They stood looking at each other as if the eyes of each were straining to absorb and hold fast the other's image. There were things he had to say to her before they parted, but he could not say them in that place of summer memories, and he turned and followed her in silence to the sleigh. As they drove away the sun sank behind the hill and the pine-boles turned from red to grey.

By a devious track between the fields they wound back to the Starkfield road. Under the open sky the light was still clear, with a reflection of cold red on the eastern hills. The clumps of trees in the snow seemed to draw together in ruffled lumps, like birds with their heads under their wings; and the sky, as it paled, rose higher, leaving the earth more alone.

As they turned into the Starkfield road Ethan said: "Matt, what do you mean to do?"

She did not answer at once, but at length she said: "I'll try to get a place in a store."

"You know you can't do it. The bad air and the standing all day nearly killed you before."

"I'm a lot stronger than I was before I came to Starkfield."

"And now you're going to throw away all the good it's done you!"

There seemed to be no answer to this, and again they drove on for a while without speaking. With every yard of the way some spot where they had stood, and laughed together or been silent, clutched at Ethan and dragged him back.

"Isn't there any of your father's folks could help you?"

"There isn't any of 'em I'd ask."

He lowered his voice to say: "You know there's nothing I wouldn't do for you if I could."

"I know there isn't."

"But I can't—"

She was silent, but he felt a slight tremor in the shoulder against his.

"Oh, Matt," he broke out, "if I could ha' gone with you now I'd ha' done it—"

She turned to him, pulling a scrap of paper from her breast. "Ethan—I found this," she stammered. Even in the failing light he saw it was the letter to his wife that he had begun the night before and forgotten to destroy. Through his astonishment there ran a fierce thrill of joy. "Matt—" he cried; "if I could ha' done it, would you?"

"Oh, Ethan, Ethan—what's the use?" With a sudden movement she tore the letter in shreds and sent them fluttering off into the snow.

"Tell me, Matt! Tell me!" he adjured her.

She was silent for a moment; then she said, in such a low tone that he had to stoop his head to hear her: "I used to think of it sometimes, summer nights, when the moon was so bright I couldn't sleep."

His heart reeled with the sweetness of it. "As long ago as that?"

She answered, as if the date had long been fixed for her: "The first time was at Shadow Pond."

"Was that why you gave me my coffee before the others?"

"I don't know. Did I? I was dreadfully put out when you wouldn't go to the picnic with me; and then, when I saw you coming down the road, I thought maybe you'd gone home that way o' purpose; and that made me glad."

They were silent again. They had reached the point where the road dipped to the hollow by Ethan's mill and as they descended the darkness descended with them, dropping down like a black veil from the heavy hemlock boughs.

"I'm tied hand and foot, Matt. There isn't a thing I can do," he began again.

"You must write to me sometimes, Ethan."

"Oh, what good'll writing do? I want to put my hand out and touch you. I want to do for you and care for you. I want to be there when you're sick and when you're lonesome."

"You mustn't think but what I'll do all right."

"You won't need me, you mean? I suppose you'll marry!"

"Oh, Ethan!" she cried.

"I don't know how it is you make me feel, Matt. I'd a'most rather have you dead than that!"

"Oh, I wish I was, I wish I was!" she sobbed.

The sound of her weeping shook him out of his dark anger, and he felt ashamed.

"Don't let's talk that way," he whispered.

"Why shouldn't we, when it's true? I've been wishing it every minute of the day."

"Matt! You be quiet! Don't you say it."

"There's never anybody been good to me but you."

"Don't say that either, when I can't lift a hand for you!"

"Yes; but it's true just the same."

They had reached the top of School House Hill and Starkfield lay below them in the twilight. A cutter, mounting the road from the village, passed them by in a joyous flutter of bells, and they straightened themselves and looked ahead with rigid faces. Along the main street lights had begun to shine from the house-fronts and stray figures were turning in here and there at the gates. Ethan, with a touch of his whip, roused the sorrel to a languid trot.

As they drew near the end of the village the cries of children reached them, and they saw a knot of boys, with sleds behind them, scattering across the open space before the church.

"I guess this'll be their last coast for a day or two," Ethan said, looking up at the mild sky.

Mattie was silent, and he added: "We were to have gone down last night."

Still she did not speak and, prompted by an obscure desire to help himself and her through their miserable last hour, he went on discursively: "Ain't it funny we haven't been down together but just that once last winter?"

She answered: "It wasn't often I got down to the village."

"That's so," he said.

They had reached the crest of the Corbury road, and between the indistinct white glimmer of the church and the black curtain of the Varnum spruces the slope stretched away below them without a sled on its length. Some erratic impulse prompted Ethan to say: "How'd you like me to take you down now?"

She forced a laugh. "Why, there isn't time!"

"There's all the time we want. Come along!" His one desire now was to postpone the moment of turning the sorrel toward the Flats.

"But the girl," she faltered. "The girl'll be waiting at the station."

"Well, let her wait. You'd have to if she didn't. Come!"

The note of authority in his voice seemed to subdue her, and when he had jumped from the sleigh she let him help her out, saying only, with a vague feint of reluctance: "But there isn't a sled round anywheres."

"Yes, there is! Right over there under the spruces."

He threw the bearskin over the sorrel, who stood passively by the roadside, hanging a meditative head. Then he caught Mattie's hand and drew her after him toward the sled.

She seated herself obediently and he took his place behind her, so close that her hair brushed his face. "All right, Matt?" he called out, as if the width of the road had been between them.

She turned her head to say: "It's dreadfully dark. Are you sure you can see?"

He laughed contemptuously: "I could go down this coast with my eyes tied!" and she laughed with him, as if she liked his audacity. Nevertheless he sat still a moment, straining his eyes down the long hill, for it was the most confusing hour of the evening, the hour when the last clearness from the upper sky is merged with the rising night in a blur that disguises landmarks and falsifies distances.

"Now!" he cried.

The sled started with a bound, and they flew on through the dusk, gathering smoothness and speed as they went, with the hollow night opening out below them and the air singing by like an organ. Mattie sat perfectly still, but as they reached the bend at the foot of the hill, where the big elm thrust out a deadly elbow, he fancied that she shrank a little closer.

"Don't be scared, Matt!" he cried exultantly, as they spun safely past it and flew down the second slope; and when they reached the level ground beyond, and the speed of the sled began to slacken, he heard her give a little laugh of glee.

They sprang off and started to walk back up the hill. Ethan dragged the sled with one hand and passed the other through Mattie's arm.

"Were you scared I'd run you into the elm?" he asked with a boyish laugh.

"I told you I was never scared with you," she answered.

The strange exaltation of his mood had brought on one of his rare fits of boastfulness. "It *is* a tricky place, though. The least swerve, and we'd never ha' come up again. But I can measure distances to a hair's-breadth—always could."

She murmured: "I always say you've got the surest eye . . ."

Deep silence had fallen with the starless dusk, and they leaned on each other without speaking; but at every step of their climb Ethan said to himself: "It's the last time we'll ever walk together."

They mounted slowly to the top of the hill. When they were abreast of the church he stooped his head to her to ask: "Are you tired?" and she answered, breathing quickly: "It was splendid!"

With a pressure of his arm he guided her toward the Norway spruces. "I guess this sled must be Ned Hale's. Anyhow I'll leave it where I found it." He drew the sled up to the Varnum gate and rested it against the fence. As he raised himself he suddenly felt Mattie close to him among the shadows.

"Is this where Ned and Ruth kissed each other?" she whispered breathlessly, and flung her arms about him. Her lips, groping for his, swept over his face, and he held her fast in a rapture of surprise.

"Good-bye—good-bye," she stammered, and kissed him again.

"Oh, Matt, I can't let you go!" broke from him in the same old cry.

She freed herself from his hold and he heard her sobbing. "Oh, I can't go either!" she wailed.

"Matt! What'll we do? What'll we do?"

They clung to each others' hands like children, and her body shook with desperate sobs.

Through the stillness they heard the church clock striking five.

"Oh, Ethan, it's time!" she cried.

He drew her back to him. "Time for what? You don't suppose I'm going to leave you now?"

"If I missed my train where'd I go?"

"Where are you going if you catch it?"

She stood silent, her hands lying cold and relaxed in his.

"What's the good of either of us going anywheres without the other one now?" he said.

She remained motionless, as if she had not heard him. Then she snatched her hands from his, threw her arms about his neck, and pressed a sudden drenched cheek against his face. "Ethan! Ethan! I want you to take me down again!"

"Down where?"

"The coast. Right off," she panted. "So 't we'll never come up any more."

"Matt! What on earth do you mean?"

She put her lips close against his ear to say: "Right into the big elm. You said you could. So 't we'd never have to leave each other any more."

"Why, what are you talking of? You're crazy!"

"I'm not crazy; but I will be if I leave you."

"Oh, Matt, Matt—" he groaned.

She tightened her fierce hold about his neck. Her face lay close to his face.

"Ethan, where'll I go if I leave you? I don't know how to get along alone. You said so yourself just now. Nobody but you was ever good to me. And there'll be that strange girl in the house . . . and she'll sleep in my bed, where I used to lay nights and listen to hear you come up the stairs . . ."

The words were like fragments torn from his heart. With them came the hated vision of the house he was going back to—of the stairs he would have to go up every night, of the woman who would wait for him there. And the sweetness of Mattie's avowal, the wild wonder of knowing at last that all that had happened to him had happened to her too, made the other vision more abhorrent, the other life more intolerable to return to . . .

Her pleadings still came to him between short sobs, but he no longer heard what she was saying. Her hat had slipped back and he was stroking her hair. He wanted to get the feeling of it into his hand, so that it would sleep there like a seed in winter. Once he found her mouth again, and they seemed to be by the pond together in the burning August sun. But his cheek touched hers, and it was cold and full of weeping, and he saw the road to the Flats under the night and heard the whistle of the train up the line.

The spruces swathed them in blackness and silence. They might have been in their coffins underground. He said to himself: "Perhaps it'll feel like this . . ." and then again: "After this I sha'n't feel anything . . ."

Suddenly he heard the old sorrel whinny across the road, and thought: "He's wondering why he doesn't get his supper . . ."

"Come," Mattie whispered, tugging at his hand.

Her sombre violence constrained him: she seemed the embodied instrument of fate. He pulled the sled out, blinking like a night-bird as he passed from the shade of the spruces into the transparent dusk of the open. The slope below them was deserted. All Starkfield was at supper, and not a figure crossed the open space before the church. The sky, swollen with the clouds that announce a thaw, hung as low as before a summer storm. He strained his eyes through the dimness, and they seemed less keen, less capable than usual.

He took his seat on the sled and Mattie instantly placed herself in front of him. Her hat had fallen into the snow and his lips were in her hair. He stretched out his legs, drove his heels into the road to keep the sled from slipping forward, and bent her head back between his hands. Then suddenly he sprang up again.

"Get up," he ordered her.

It was the tone she always heeded, but she cowered down in her seat, repeating vehemently: "No, no, no!"

"Get up!"

"Why?"

"I want to sit in front."

"No, no! How can you steer in front?"

"I don't have to. We'll follow the track."

They spoke in smothered whispers, as though the night were listening.

"Get up! Get up!" he urged her; but she kept on repeating: "Why do you want to sit in front?"

"Because I—because I want to feel you holding me," he stammered, and dragged her to her feet.

The answer seemed to satisfy her, or else she yielded to the power of his voice. He bent down, feeling in the obscurity for the glassy slide worn by preceding coasters, and placed the runners carefully between its edges. She waited while he seated himself with crossed legs in the front of the sled; then she crouched quickly down at his back and clasped her arms about him. Her breath in his neck set him shuddering again, and he almost sprang from his seat. But in a flash he remembered the alternative. She was right: this was better than parting. He leaned back and drew her mouth to his . . .

Just as they started he heard the sorrel's whinney again, and the familiar wistful call, and all the confused images it brought with it, went with him down the first reach of the road. Half-way down there was a sudden drop, then a rise, and after that another long delirious descent. As they took wing for this it seemed to him that they were flying indeed, flying far up into the cloudy night, with Starkfield immeasurably below them, falling away like a speck in space . . . Then the big elm shot up ahead, lying in wait for them at the bend of the road, and he said between his teeth: "We can fetch it; I know we can fetch it——"

As they flew toward the tree Mattie pressed her arms tighter, and her blood seemed to be in his veins. Once or twice the sled swerved a little under them. He slanted his body to keep it headed for the elm, repeating to himself again and again: "I know we can fetch it"; and little phrases she had spoken ran through his head and danced before him on the air. The big tree loomed bigger and closer, and as they bore down on it he thought: "It's waiting for us: it seems to know." But suddenly his wife's face, with twisted monstrous lineaments, thrust itself between him and his goal, and he made an instinctive movement to brush it aside. The sled swerved in response, but he righted it again, kept it straight, and drove down on the black projecting mass. There was a last instant when the air shot past him like millions of fiery wires; and then the elm . . .

The sky was still thick, but looking straight up he saw a single star, and tried vaguely to reckon whether it were Sirius, or—or— The effort tired him too much, and he closed his heavy lids and thought that he would sleep . . . The stillness was so profound that he heard a little animal twittering somewhere near by under the snow. It made a small frightened *cheep* like a field mouse, and he wondered languidly if it were hurt. Then he understood that it must be in pain: pain so excruciating that he seemed, mysteriously, to feel it shooting through his own body. He tried in vain to roll over in the direction of the sound, and stretched his left arm out across the snow. And now it was as though he felt rather than heard the twittering; it seemed to be under his palm, which rested on something soft and springy. The thought of the animal's suffering was intolerable to him and he struggled to raise himself, and could not because a rock, or some huge mass, seemed to be lying on him. But he continued to finger about cautiously with his left hand, thinking he might get hold of the little creature and help it; and all at once he knew that the soft thing he had touched was Mattie's hair and that his hand was on her face.

He dragged himself to his knees, the monstrous load on him moving with him as he moved, and his hand went over and over her face, and he felt that the twittering came from her lips . . .

He got his face down close to hers, with his ear to her mouth, and in the darkness he saw her eyes open and heard her say his name.

"Oh, Matt, I thought we'd fetched it," he moaned; and far off, up the hill, he heard the sorrel whinny, and thought: "I ought to be getting him his feed . . ."

CHAPTER X

THE QUERULOUS DRONE ceased as I entered Frome's kitchen, and of the two women sitting there I could not tell which had been the speaker.

One of them, on my appearing, raised her tall bony figure from her seat, not as if to welcome me—for she threw me no more than a brief glance of surprise—but simply to set about preparing the meal which Frome's absence had delayed. A slatternly calico wrapper hung from her shoulders and the wisps of her thin grey hair were drawn away from a high forehead and fastened at the back by a broken comb. She had pale opaque eyes which revealed nothing and reflected nothing, and her narrow lips were of the same sallow colour as her face.

The other woman was much smaller and slighter. She sat huddled in an arm-chair near the stove, and when I came in she turned her head quickly toward me, without the least corresponding movement of her body. Her hair was as grey as her companion's, her face as bloodless and shrivelled, but amber-tinted, with swarthy shadows sharpening the nose and hollowing the temples. Under her shapeless dress her body kept its limp immobility, and her dark eyes had the bright witch-like stare that disease of the spine sometimes gives.

Even for that part of the country the kitchen was a poor-looking place. With the exception of the dark-eyed woman's chair, which looked like a soiled relic of luxury bought at a country auction, the furniture was of the roughest kind. Three coarse china plates and a broken-nosed milk-jug had been set on a greasy table scored with knife-cuts, and a couple of straw-bottomed chairs and a kitchen dresser of unpainted pine stood meagrely against the plaster walls.

"My, it's cold here! The fire must be 'most out," Frome said, glancing about him apologetically as he followed me in.

The tall woman, who had moved away from us toward the dresser, took no notice; but the other, from her cushioned niche, answered complainingly, in a high thin voice. "It's on'y just been made up this very minute. Zeena fell asleep and slep' ever so long, and I thought I'd be frozen stiff before I could wake her up and get her to 'tend to it."

I knew then that it was she who had been speaking when we entered.

Her companion, who was just coming back to the table with the remains of a cold mince-pie in a battered pie-dish, set down her unappetising burden without appearing to hear the accusation brought against her.

Frome stood hesitatingly before her as she advanced; then he looked at me and said: "This is my wife, Mis' Frome." After another interval he added, turning toward the figure in the arm-chair: "And this is Miss Mattie Silver . . ."

. . . .

Mrs. Hale, tender soul, had pictured me as lost in the Flats and buried under a snow-drift; and so lively was her satisfaction on seeing me safely restored to her the next morning that I felt my peril had caused me to advance several degrees in her favour.

Great was her amazement, and that of old Mrs. Varnum, on learning that Ethan Frome's old horse had carried me to and from Corbury Junction through the worst blizzard of the winter; greater still their surprise when they heard that his master had taken me in for the night.

Beneath their wondering exclamations I felt a secret curiosity to know what impressions I had received from my night in the Frome household, and divined that the best way of breaking down their reserve was to let them try to penetrate mine. I therefore confined myself to saying, in a matter-of-fact tone, that I had been received with great kindness, and that Frome had made a bed for me in a room on the ground-floor which seemed in happier days to have been fitted up as a kind of writing-room or study.

"Well," Mrs. Hale mused, "in such a storm I suppose he felt he couldn't do less than take you in—but I guess it went hard with Ethan. I don't believe but what you're the only stranger has set foot in that house for over twenty years. He's that proud he don't even like his oldest friends to go there; and I don't know as any do, any more, except myself and the doctor . . ."

"You still go there, Mrs. Hale?" I ventured.

"I used to go a good deal after the accident, when I was first married; but after awhile I got to think it made 'em feel worse to see us. And then one thing and another came, and my own troubles . . . But I generally make out to drive over there round about New Year's, and once in the summer. Only I always try to pick a day when Ethan's off somewheres. It's bad enough to see the two women sitting there—but *his* face, when he looks round that bare place, just kills me . . . You see, I can look back and call it up in his mother's day, before their troubles."

Old Mrs. Varnum, by this time, had gone up to bed, and her daughter and I were sitting alone, after supper, in the austere seclusion of the horsehair parlour. Mrs. Hale glanced at me tentatively, as though trying to see how much footing my conjectures gave her; and I guessed that if she had kept silence till now it was because she had been waiting, through all the years, for some one who should see what she alone had seen.

I waited to let her trust in me gather strength before I said: "Yes, it's pretty bad, seeing all three of them there together."

She drew her mild brows into a frown of pain. "It was just awful from the beginning. I was here in the house when they were carried up—they laid Mattie Silver in the room you're in. She and I were great friends, and she was to have been my bridesmaid in the spring . . . When she came to I went up to her and stayed all night. They gave her things to quiet her, and she didn't know much till to'rd morning, and then all of a sudden she woke up just like herself, and looked straight at me out of her big eyes, and said . . . Oh, I don't know why I'm telling you all this," Mrs. Hale broke off, crying.

She took off her spectacles, wiped the moisture from them, and put them on again with an unsteady hand. "It got about the next day," she went on, "that Zeena Frome had sent Mattie off in a hurry because she had a hired girl coming, and the folks here could never rightly tell what she and Ethan were doing that night coasting, when they'd ought to have been on their way to the Flats to ketch the train . . . I never knew myself what Zeena thought—I don't to this day. Nobody knows Zeena's thoughts. Anyhow, when she heard o' the accident she came right in and stayed with Ethan over to the minister's, where they'd carried him. And as soon as the doctors said that Mattie could be moved, Zeena sent for her and took her back to the farm."

"And there she's been ever since?"

Mrs. Hale answered simply: "There was nowhere else for her to go"; and my heart tightened at the thought of the hard compulsions of the poor.

"Yes, there she's been," Mrs. Hale continued, "and Zeena's done for her, and done for Ethan, as good as she could. It was a miracle, considering how sick she was—but she seemed to be raised right up just when the call came to her. Not as she's ever given up doctoring, and she's had sick spells right along; but she's had the strength given her to care for those two for over twenty years, and before the accident came she thought she couldn't even care for herself."

Mrs. Hale paused a moment, and I remained silent, plunged in the vision of what her words evoked. "It's horrible for them all," I murmured.

"Yes: it's pretty bad. And they ain't any of 'em easy people either. Mattie *was*, before the accident; I never knew a sweeter nature. But she's suffered too much—that's what I always say when folks tell me how she's soured. And Zeena, she was always cranky. Not but what she bears with Mattie wonderful—I've seen that myself. But sometimes the two of them get going at each other, and then Ethan's face'd break your heart . . . When I see that, I think it's *him* that suffers most . . . anyhow it ain't Zeena, because she ain't got the time . . . It's a pity, though," Mrs. Hale ended, sighing, "that they're all shut up there'n that one kitchen. In the summertime, on pleasant days, they move Mattie into the parlour, or out in the door-yard, and that makes it easier . . . but winters there's the fires to be thought of; and there ain't a dime to spare up at the Fromes'."

Mrs. Hale drew a deep breath, as though her memory were eased of its long burden, and she had no more to say; but suddenly an impulse of complete avowal seized her.

She took off her spectacles again, leaned toward me across the bead-work table-cover, and went on with lowered voice: "There was one day, about a week after the accident, when they all thought Mattie couldn't live. Well, I say it's a pity she *did*. I said it right out to our minister once, and he was shocked at me. Only he wasn't with me that morning when she first came to . . . And I say, if she'd ha' died, Ethan might ha' lived; and the way they are now, I don't see's there's much difference between the Fromes up at the farm and the Fromes down in the graveyard; 'cept that down there they're all quiet, and the women have got to hold their tongues."

Bunner Sisters

§ 1

In the days when New York's traffic moved at the pace of the drooping horse-car, when society applauded Christine Nilsson at the Academy of Music and basked in the sunsets of the Hudson River School on the walls of the National Academy of Design, an inconspicuous shop with a single show-window was intimately and favourably known to the feminine population of the quarter bordering on Stuyvesant Square.

It was a very small shop, in a shabby basement, in a side-street already doomed to decline; and from the miscellaneous display behind the window-pane, and the brevity of the sign surmounting it (merely "Bunner Sisters" in blotchy gold on a black ground) it would have been difficult for the uninitiated to guess the precise nature of the business carried on within. But that was of little consequence, since its fame was so purely local that the customers on whom its existence depended were almost congenitally aware of the exact range of "goods" to be found at Bunner Sisters'.

The house of which Bunner Sisters had annexed the basement was a private dwelling with a brick front, green shutters on weak hinges, and a dress-maker's sign in the window above the shop. On each side of its modest three stories stood higher buildings, with fronts of brown stone, cracked and blistered, cast-iron balconies and cat-haunted grass-patches behind twisted railings. These houses too had once been private, but now a cheap lunchroom filled the basement of one, while the other announced itself, above the knotty wisteria that clasped its central balcony, as the Mendoza Family Hotel. It was obvious from the chronic cluster of refuse-barrels at its area-gate and the blurred surface of its curtainless windows, that the families frequenting the Mendoza Hotel were not exacting in their tastes; though they doubtless indulged in as much fastidiousness as they could afford to pay for, and rather more than their landlord thought they had a right to express.

These three houses fairly exemplified the general character of the street, which, as it stretched eastward, rapidly fell from shabbiness to squalor, with an increasing frequency of projecting sign-boards, and of swinging doors that softly shut or opened at the touch of red-nosed men and pale little girls with broken jugs. The middle of the street was full of irregular depressions, well adapted to retain the long swirls of dust and straw and twisted paper that the wind drove up and down its sad untended length; and toward the end of the day, when traffic had been active, the fissured pavement formed a mosaic of coloured handbills, lids of tomato-cans, old shoes, cigar-stumps and banana skins, cemented together by a layer of mud, or veiled in a powdering dust, as the state of the weather determined.

The sole refuge offered from the contemplation of this depressing waste was the sight of the Bunner Sisters' window. Its panes were always well-washed, and though their display of artificial flowers, bands of scalloped flannel, wire hat-frames, and jars of home-made preserves, had the undefinable greyish tinge of objects long preserved in the show-case of a museum, the window revealed a background of orderly counters and white-washed walls in pleasant contrast to the adjoining dinginess.

The Bunner sisters were proud of the neatness of their shop and content with its humble prosperity. It was not what they had once imagined it would be, but though it presented but a shrunken image of their earlier ambitions it enabled them to pay their rent and keep themselves alive and out of debt; and it was long since their hopes had soared higher.

Now and then, however, among their greyer hours there came one not bright enough to be called sunny, but rather of the silvery twilight hue which sometimes ends a day of storm. It was such an hour that Ann Eliza, the elder of the firm, was soberly enjoying as she sat one January evening in the back room which served as bedroom, kitchen and parlour to herself and her sister Evelina. In the shop the blinds had been drawn down, the counters cleared and the wares in the window lightly covered with an old sheet; but the shop-door remained unlocked till Evelina, who had taken a parcel to the dyer's, should come back.

In the back room a kettle bubbled on the stove, and Ann Eliza had laid a cloth over one end of the centre table, and placed near the green-shaded sewing lamp two tea-cups, two plates, a sugar-bowl and a piece of pie. The rest of the room remained in a greenish shadow which discreetly veiled the outline of an old-fashioned mahogany bedstead surmounted by a chromo of a young lady in a night-gown who clung with eloquently-rolling eyes to a crag described in illuminated letters as the Rock of Ages; and against the unshaded windows two rocking-chairs and a sewing-machine were silhouetted on the dusk.

Ann Eliza, her small and habitually anxious face smoothed to unusual serenity, and the streaks of pale hair on her veined temples shining glossily beneath the lamp, had seated herself at the table, and was tying up, with her usual fumbling deliberation, a knotty object wrapped in paper. Now and then, as she struggled with the string, which was too short, she fancied she heard the click of the shop-door, and paused to listen for her sister; then, as no one came, she straightened her spectacles and entered into renewed conflict with the parcel. In honour of some event of obvious importance, she had put on her double-dyed and triple-turned black silk. Age, while bestowing on this garment a *patine* worthy of a Renaissance bronze, had deprived it of whatever curves the wearer's pre-Raphaelite figure had once been able to impress on it; but this stiffness of outline gave it an air of sacerdotal state which seemed to emphasize the importance of the occasion.

Seen thus, in her sacramental black silk, a wisp of lace turned over the collar and fastened by a mosaic brooch, and her face smoothed into harmony with her apparel, Ann Eliza looked ten years younger than behind the counter, in the heat and burden of the day. It would have been as difficult to guess her approximate age as that of the black silk, for she had the same worn and glossy aspect as her dress; but a faint tinge of pink still lingered on her cheek-bones, like the reflection of sunset which sometimes colours the west long after the day is over.

When she had tied the parcel to her satisfaction, and laid it with furtive accuracy just opposite her sister's plate, she sat down, with an air of obviously-assumed indifference, in one of the rocking-chairs near the window; and a moment later the shop-door opened and Evelina entered.

The younger Bunner sister, who was a little taller than her elder, had a more pronounced nose, but a weaker slope of mouth and chin. She still permitted herself the frivolity of waving her pale hair, and its tight little ridges, stiff as the tresses of an Assyrian statue, were flattened under a dotted veil which ended at the tip of her cold-reddened nose. In her scant jacket and skirt of black cashmere she looked singularly nipped and faded; but it seemed possible that under happier conditions she might still warm into relative youth.

"Why, Ann Eliza," she exclaimed, in a thin voice pitched to chronic fretfulness, "what in the world you got your best silk on for?"

Ann Eliza had risen with a blush that made her steel-bowed spectacles incongruous.

"Why, Evelina, why shouldn't I, I sh'ld like to know? Ain't it your birthday, dear?" She put out her arms with the awkwardness of habitually repressed emotion.

Evelina, without seeming to notice the gesture, threw back the jacket from her narrow shoulders.

"Oh, pshaw," she said, less peevishly. "I guess we'd better give up birthdays. Much as we can do to keep Christmas nowadays."

"You hadn't oughter say that, Evelina. We ain't so badly off as all that. I guess you're cold and tired. Set down while I take the kettle off: it's right on the boil."

She pushed Evelina toward the table, keeping a sideward eye on her sister's listless movements, while her own hands were busy with the kettle. A moment later came the exclamation for which she waited.

"Why, Ann Eliza!" Evelina stood transfixed by the sight of the parcel beside her plate.

Ann Eliza, tremulously engaged in filling the teapot, lifted a look of hypocritical surprise.

"Sakes, Evelina! What's the matter?"

The younger sister had rapidly untied the string, and drawn from its wrappings a round nickel clock of the kind to be bought for a dollar-seventy-five.

"Oh, Ann Eliza, how could you?" She set the clock down, and the sisters exchanged agitated glances across the table.

"Well," the elder retorted, *"ain't* it your birthday?"

"Yes, but—"

"Well, and ain't you had to run round the corner to the Square every morning, rain or shine, to see what time it was, ever since we had to sell mother's watch last July? Ain't you, Evelina?"

"Yes, but—"

"There ain't any buts. We've always wanted a clock and now we've got one: that's all there is about it. Ain't she a beauty, Evelina?" Ann Eliza, putting back the kettle on the stove, leaned over her sister's shoulder to pass an approving hand over the circular rim of the clock. "Hear how loud she ticks. I was afraid you'd hear her soon as you come in."

"No. I wasn't thinking," murmured Evelina.

"Well, ain't you glad now?" Ann Eliza gently reproached her. The rebuke had no acerbity, for she knew that Evelina's seeming indifference was alive with unexpressed scruples.

"I'm real glad, sister; but you hadn't oughter. We could have got on well enough without."

"Evelina Bunner, just you sit down to your tea. I guess I know what I'd oughter and what I'd hadn't oughter just as well as you do—I'm old enough!"

"You're real good, Ann Eliza; but I know you've given up something you needed to get me this clock."

"What do I need, I'd like to know? Ain't I got a best black silk?" the elder sister said with a laugh full of nervous pleasure.

She poured out Evelina's tea, adding some condensed milk from the jug, and cutting for her the largest slice of pie; then she drew up her own chair to the table.

The two women ate in silence for a few moments before Evelina began to speak again. "The clock is perfectly lovely and I don't say it ain't a comfort to have it; but I hate to think what it must have cost you."

"No, it didn't, neither," Ann Eliza retorted. "I got it dirt cheap, if you want to know. And I paid for it out of a little extra work I did the other night on the machine for Mrs. Hawkins."

"The baby-waists?"

"Yes."

"There, I knew it! You swore to me you'd buy a new pair of shoes with that money."

"Well, and s'posin' I didn't want 'em—what then? I've patched up the old ones as good as new—and I do declare, Evelina Bunner, if you ask me another question you'll go and spoil all my pleasure."

"Very well, I won't," said the younger sister.

They continued to eat without further words. Evelina yielded to her sister's entreaty that she should finish the pie, and poured out a second cup of tea, into which she put the last lump of sugar; and between them, on the table, the clock kept up its sociable tick.

"Where'd you get it, Ann Eliza?" asked Evelina, fascinated.

"Where'd you s'pose? Why, right round here, over acrost the Square, in the queerest little store you ever laid eyes on. I saw it in the window as I was passing, and I stepped right in and asked how much it was, and the store-keeper he was real pleasant about it. He was just the nicest man. I guess he's a German. I told him I couldn't give much, and he said, well, he knew what hard times was too. His name's Ramy—Herman Ramy; I saw it written up over the store. And he told me he used to work at Tiff'ny's, oh, for years, in the clock-department, and three years ago he took sick with some kinder fever, and lost his place, and when he got well they'd engaged somebody else and didn't want him, and so he started this little store by himself. I guess he's real smart, and he spoke quite like an educated man—but he looks sick."

Evelina was listening with abosrbed attention. In the narrow lives of the two sisters such an episode was not to be underrated.

"What you say his name was?" she asked as Ann Eliza paused.

"Herman Ramy."

"How old is he?"

"Well, I couldn't exactly tell you, he looked so sick—but I don't b'lieve he's much over forty."

By this time the plates had been cleared and the teapot emptied, and the two sisters rose from the table. Ann Eliza, tying an apron over her black silk, carefully removed all traces of the meal; then, after washing the cups and plates, and putting them away in a cupboard, she drew her rocking-chair to the lamp and sat down to a heap of mending. Evelina, meanwhile, had been roaming about the room in search of an abiding-place for the clock. A rosewood what-not with ornamental fret-work hung on the wall beside the devout young lady in dishabille, and after much weighing of alternatives the sisters decided to dethrone a broken china vase filled with dried grasses which had long stood on the top shelf, and to put the clock in its place; the vase, after further consideration, being relegated to a small table covered with blue and white bead-work, which held a Bible and prayer-book, and an illustrated copy of Longfellow's poems given as a school-prize to their father.

This change having been made, and the effect studied from every angle of the room, Evelina languidly put her pinking-machine on the table, and sat down to the monotonous work of pinking a heap of black silk flounces. The strips of stuff slid slowly to the floor at her side, and the clock, from its commanding altitude, kept time with the dispiriting click of the instrument under her fingers.

§ 2

The purchase of Evelina's clock had been a more important event in the life of Ann Eliza Bunner than her younger sister could divine. In the first place, there had been the demoralizing satisfaction of finding herself in possession of a sum of money which she need not put into the common fund, but could spend as she chose, without consulting Evelina, and then the excitement of her stealthy trips abroad, undertaken on the rare occasions when she could trump up a pretext for leaving the shop; since as a rule, it was Evelina who took the bundles to the dyer's, and delivered the purchases of those among their customers who were too genteel to be seen carrying home a bonnet or a bundle of pinking—so that, had it not been for the excuse of having to see Mrs. Hawkins's teething baby, Ann Eliza would hardly have known what motive to allege for deserting her usual seat behind the counter.

The infrequency of her walks made them the chief events of her life. The mere act of going out from the monastic quiet of the shop into the tumult of the streets filled her with a subdued excitement which grew too intense for pleasure as she was swallowed by the engulfing roar of Broadway or Third Avenue, and began to do timid battle with their incessant cross-currents of humanity. After a glance or two into the great show-windows she usually allowed herself to be swept back into the shelter of a side-street, and finally regained her own roof in a state of breathless bewilderment and fatigue; but gradually, as her nerves were soothed by the familiar quiet of the little shop, and the click of Evelina's pinking-machine, certain sights and sounds would detach themselves from the torrent along which she had been swept, and she would devote the rest of the day to a mental reconstruction of the different episodes of her walk, till finally it took shape in her thought as a consecutive and highly-coloured experience, from which, for weeks afterwards, she would detach some fragmentary recollection in the course of her long dialogues with her sister.

But when, to the unwonted excitement of going out, was added the intenser interest of looking for a present for Evelina, Ann Eliza's agitation, sharpened by concealment, actually preyed upon her rest; and it was not till the present had been given, and she had unbosomed herself of the experiences connected with its purchase, that she could look back with anything like composure to that stirring moment of her life. From that day forward, however, she began to take a certain tranquil pleasure in thinking of Mr. Ramy's small shop, not unlike her own in its countrified obscurity, though the layer of dust which covered its counter and shelves made the comparison only superficially acceptable. Still, she did not judge the state of the shop severely, for Mr. Ramy had told her that he was alone in the world, and lone men, she was aware, did not know how to deal with dust. It gave her a good deal of occupation to wonder why he had never married, or if, on the other hand, he were a widower, and had lost all his dear little children; and she scarcely knew which alternative seemed to make him the more interesting. In either case, his life was assuredly a sad one; and she passed many hours in speculating on the manner in which he probably spent his evenings. She knew he lived at the back of his shop, for she had caught, on entering, a glimpse of a dingy room with a tumbled bed; and the pervading smell of cold fry suggested that he probably did his own cooking. She wondered if he did not often make his tea with water that had not boiled, and asked herself, almost jealously, who looked after the shop while he went to market. Then it occurred to her as likely that he bought his provisions at the same market as Evelina; and she was fascinated by the thought that he and her sister might constantly be meeting in total unconsciousness of the link between them. Whenever she reached this stage in her reflections she lifted a furtive glance to the clock, whose loud staccato tick was becoming a part of her inmost being.

The seed sown by these long hours of meditation germinated at last in the secret wish to go to market some morning in Evelina's stead. As this purpose rose to the surface of Ann Eliza's thoughts she shrank back shyly from its contemplation. A plan so steeped in duplicity had never before taken shape in her crystalline soul. How was it possible for her to consider such a step? And, besides (she did not possess sufficient logic to mark the downward trend of this "besides"), what excuse could she make that would not excite her sister's curiosity? From this second query it was an easy descent to the third: how soon could she manage to go?

It was Evelina herself, who furnished the necessary pretext by awaking with a sore throat on the day when she usually went to market. It was a Saturday, and as they always had their bit of steak on Sunday the expedition could not be postponed, and it seemed natural that Ann Eliza, as she tied an old stocking around Evelina's throat, should announce her intention of stepping round to the butcher's.

"Oh, Ann Eliza, they'll cheat you so," her sister wailed.

Ann Eliza brushed aside the imputation with a smile, and a few minutes later, having set the room to rights, and cast a last glance at the shop, she was tying on her bonnet with a fumbling haste.

The morning was damp and cold, with a sky full of sulky clouds that would not make room for the sun, but as yet dropped only an occasional snow-flake. In the early light the street looked its meanest and most neglected; but to Ann Eliza, never greatly troubled by any untidiness for which she was not responsible, it seemed to wear a singularly friendly aspect.

A few minutes' walk brought her to the market where Evelina made her purchases, and where, if he had any sense of topographical fitness, Mr. Ramy must also deal.

Ann Eliza, making her way through the outskirts of potato-barrels and flabby fish, found no one in the shop but the gory-aproned butcher who stood in the background cutting chops.

As she approached him across the tessellation of fish-scales, blood and saw-dust, he laid aside his cleaver and not unsympathetically asked: "Sister sick?"

"Oh, not very—jest a cold," she answered, as guiltily as if Evelina's illness had been feigned. "We want a steak as usual, please—and my sister said you was to be sure to give me jest as good a cut as if it was her," she added with child-like candour.

"Oh, that's all right." The butcher picked up his weapon with a grin. "Your sister knows a cut as well as any of us," he remarked.

In another moment, Ann Eliza reflected, the steak would be cut and wrapped up, and no choice left her but to turn her disappointed steps toward home. She was too shy to try to delay the butcher by such conversational arts as she possessed, but the approach of a deaf old lady in an antiquated bonnet and mantle gave her her opportunity.

"Wait on her first, please," Ann Eliza whispered. "I ain't in any hurry."

The butcher advanced to his new customer, and Ann Eliza, palpitating in the back of the shop, saw that the old lady's hesitations between liver and pork chops were likely to be indefinitely prolonged. They were still unresolved when she was interrupted by the entrance of a blowsy Irish girl with a basket on her arm. The newcomer caused a momentary diversion, and when she had departed the old lady, who was evidently as intolerant of interruption as a professional story-teller, insisted on returning to the beginning of her complicated order, and weighing anew, with an anxious appeal to the butcher's arbitration, the relative advantages of pork and liver. But even her hesitations, and the intrusion on them of two or three other customers, were of no avail, for Mr. Ramy was not among those who entered the shop; and at last Ann Eliza, ashamed of staying longer, reluctantly claimed her steak, and walked home through the thickening snow.

Even to her simple judgment the vanity of her hopes was plain, and in the clear light that disappointment turns upon our actions she wondered how she could have been foolish enough to suppose that, even if Mr. Ramy *did* go to that particular market, he would hit on the same day and hour as herself.

There followed a colourless week unmarked by farther incident. The old stocking cured Evelina's throat, and Mrs. Hawkins dropped in once or twice to talk of her baby's teeth; some new orders for pinking were received, and Evelina sold a bonnet to the lady with puffed sleeves. The lady with puffed sleeves—a resident of "the Square," whose name they had never learned, because she always carried her own parcels home—was the most distinguished and interesting figure on their horizon. She was youngish, she was elegant (as the title they had given her implied), and she had a sweet sad smile about which they had woven many histories; but even the news of her return to town—it was her first apparition that year—failed to arouse Ann Eliza's interest. All the small daily happenings which had once sufficed to fill the hours now appeared to her in their deadly insignificance; and for the first time in her long years of drudgery she rebelled at the dullness of her life. With Evelina such fits of discontent were habitual and openly proclaimed, and Ann Eliza still excused them as one of the prerogatives of youth. Besides, Evelina had not been intended by Providence to pine in such a narrow life: in the original plan of things, she had been meant to marry and have a baby, to wear silk on Sundays, and take a leading part in a Church circle. Hitherto opportunity had played her false; and for all her superior aspirations and carefully crimped hair she had remained as obscure and unsought as Ann Eliza. But the elder sister, who had long since accepted her own fate, had never accepted Evelina's. Once a pleasant young man who taught in Sunday-school had paid the younger Miss Bunner a few shy visits. That was years since, and he had speedily vanished from their view. Whether he had carried with him any of Evelina's illusions, Ann Eliza had never discovered; but his attentions had clad her sister in a halo of exquisite possibilities.

Ann Eliza, in those days, had never dreamed of allowing herself the luxury of self-pity; it seemed as much a personal right of Evelina's as her elaborately crinkled hair. But now she began to transfer to herself a portion of the sympathy she had so long bestowed on Evelina. She had at last recognized her right to set up some lost opportunities of her own; and once that dangerous precedent established, they began to crowd upon her memory.

It was at this stage of Ann Eliza's transformation that Evelina, looking up one evening from her work, said suddenly: "My! She's stopped."

Ann Eliza, raising her eyes from a brown merino seam, followed her sister's glance across the room. It was a Monday, and they always wound the clock on Sundays.

"Are you sure you wound her yesterday, Evelina?"

"Jest as sure as I live. She must be broke. I'll go and see."

Evelina laid down the hat she was trimming, and took the clock from its shelf.

"There—I knew it! She's wound jest as *tight*—what you suppose's happened to her, Ann Eliza?"

"I dunno, I'm sure," said the elder sister, wiping her spectacles before proceeding to a close examination of the clock.

With anxiously bent heads the two women shook and turned it, as though they were trying to revive a living thing, but it remained unresponsive to their touch, and at length Evelina laid it down with a sigh.

"Seems like somethin' *dead,* don't it, Ann Eliza? How still the room is!"

"Yes, ain't it?"

"Well, I'll put her back where she belongs," Evelina continued, in the tone of one about to perform the last offices for the departed. "And I guess," she added, "you'll have to step round to Mr. Ramy's to-morrow, and see if he can fix her."

Ann Eliza's face burned, "I—yes, I guess I'll have to," she stammered, stooping to pick up a spool of cotton which had rolled to the floor. A sudden heart-throb stretched the seams of her flat alpaca bosom, and a pulse leapt to life in each of her temples.

That night, long after Evelina slept, Ann Eliza lay awake in the unfamiliar silence, more acutely conscious of the nearness of the crippled clock than when it had volubly told out the minutes. The next morning she woke from a troubled dream of having carried it to Mr. Ramy's and found that he and his shop had vanished; and all through the day's occupations the memory of this dream oppressed her.

It had been agreed that Ann Eliza should take the clock to be repaired as soon as they had dined; but while they were still at table a weak-eyed little girl in a black apron stabbed with innumerable pins burst in on them with the cry: "Oh, Miss Bunner, for mercy's sake! Miss Mellins has been took again."

Miss Mellins was the dress-maker upstairs, and the weak-eyed child one of her youthful apprentices.

Ann Eliza started from her seat. "I'll come at once. Quick, Evelina, the cordial!"

By this euphemistic name the sisters designated a bottle of cherry brandy, the last of a dozen inherited from their grandmother, which they kept locked in their cupboard against such emergencies. A moment later, cordial in hand, Ann Eliza was hurrying upstairs behind the weak-eyed child.

Miss Mellins's "turn" was sufficiently serious to detain Ann Eliza for nearly two hours, and dusk had fallen when she took up the depleted bottle of cordial and descended again to the shop. It was empty, as usual, and Evelina sat at her pinking-machine in the back room. Ann Eliza was still agitated by her efforts to restore the dress-maker, but in spite of her preoccupation she was struck, as soon as she entered, by the loud tick of the clock, which still stood on the shelf where she had left it.

"Why, she's going!" she gasped, before Evelina could question her about Miss Mellins. "Did she start up again by herself?"

"Oh, no; but I couldn't stand not knowing what time it was, I've got so accustomed to having her round; and just after you went upstairs Mrs. Hawkins dropped in, so I asked her to tend the store for a minute, and I clapped on my things and ran right round to Mr. Ramy's. It turned out there wasn't anything the matter with her—nothin' on'y a speck of dust in the works—and he fixed her for me in a minute and I brought her right back. Ain't it lovely to hear her going again? But tell me about Miss Mellins, quick!"

For a moment Ann Eliza found no words. Not till she learned that she had missed her chance did she understand how many hopes had hung upon it. Even now she did not know why she had wanted so much to see the clock-maker again.

"I s'pose it's because nothing's ever happened to me," she thought, with a twinge of envy for the fate which gave Evelina every opportunity that came their way. "She had the Sunday-school teacher too," Ann Eliza murmured to herself; but she was well-trained in the arts of renunciation, and after a scarcely perceptible pause she plunged into a detailed description of the dress-maker's "turn."

Evelina, when her curiosity was roused, was an insatiable questioner, and it was supper-time before she had come to the end of her enquiries about Miss Mellins; but when the two sisters had seated themselves at their evening meal Ann Eliza at last found a chance to say: "So she on'y had a speck of dust in her."

Evelina understood at once that the reference was not to Miss Mellins. "Yes—at least he thinks so," she answered, helping herself as a matter of course to the first cup of tea.

"On'y to think!" murmured Ann Eliza.

"But he isn't *sure,*" Evelina continued, absently pushing the teapot toward her sister. "It may be something wrong with the—I forgot what he called it. Anyhow, he said he'd call round and see, day after to-morrow, after supper."

"Who said?" gasped Ann Eliza.

"Why, Mr. Ramy, of course. I think he's real nice, Ann Eliza. And I don't believe he's forty; but he *does* look sick. I guess he's pretty lonesome, all by himself in that store. He as much as told me so, and somehow"—Evelina paused and bridled—"I kinder thought that maybe his saying he'd call round about the clock was on'y just an excuse. He said it just as I was going out of the store. What you think, Ann Eliza?"

"Oh, I don't har'ly know." To save herself, Ann Eliza could produce nothing warmer.

"Well, I don't pretend to be smarter than other folks," said Evelina, putting a conscious hand to her hair, "but I guess Mr. Herman Ramy wouldn't be sorry to pass an evening here, 'stead of spending it all alone in that poky little place of his."

Her self-consciousness irritated Ann Eliza.

"I guess he's got plenty of friends of his own," she said, almost harshly.

"No, he ain't, either. He's got hardly any."

"Did he tell you that too?" Even to her own ears there was a faint sneer in the interrogation.

"Yes, he did," said Evelina, dropping her lids with a smile "He seemed to be just crazy to talk to somebody—somebody agreeable, I mean. I think the man's unhappy, Ann Eliza."

"So do I," broke from the elder sister.

"He seems such an educated man, too. He was reading the paper when I went in. Ain't it sad to think of his being reduced to that little store, after being years at Tiff'ny's, and one of the head men in their clock-department?"

"He told you all that?"

"Why, yes. I think he'd a' told me everything ever happened to him if I'd had the time to stay and listen. I tell you he's dead lonely, Ann Eliza."

"Yes," said Ann Eliza.

§ 3

Two days afterward, Ann Eliza noticed that Evelina, before they sat down to supper, pinned a crimson bow under her collar; and when the meal was finished the younger sister, who seldom concerned herself with the clearing of the table, set about with nervous haste to help Ann Eliza in the removal of the dishes.

"I hate to see food mussing about," she grumbled. "Ain't it hateful having to do everything in one room?"

"Oh, Evelina, I've always thought we was so comfortable," Ann Eliza protested.

"Well, so we are, comfortable enough; but I don't suppose there's any harm in my saying I wisht we had a parlour, is there? Anyway, we might manage to buy a screen to hide the bed."

Ann Eliza coloured. There was something vaguely embarrassing in Evelina's suggestion.

"I always think if we ask for more what we have may be taken from us," she ventured.

"Well, whoever took it wouldn't get much," Evelina retorted with a laugh as she swept up the table-cloth.

A few moments later the back room was in its usual flawless order and the two sisters had seated themselves near the lamp. Ann Eliza had taken up her sewing, and Evelina was preparing to make artificial flowers. The sisters usually relegated this more delicate business to the long leisure of the summer months; but to-night Evelina had brought out the box which lay all winter under the bed, and spread before her a bright array of muslin petals, yellow stamens and green corollas, and a tray of little implements curiously suggestive of the dental art. Ann Eliza made no remark on this unusual proceeding;

perhaps she guessed why for that evening her sister had chosen a graceful task.

Presently a knock on the outer door made them look up; but Evelina, the first on her feet, said promptly: "Sit still. I'll see who it is."

Ann Eliza was glad to sit still: the baby's petticoat that she was stitching shook in her fingers.

"Sister, here's Mr. Ramy come to look at the clock," said Evelina, a moment later, in the high drawl she cultivated before strangers; and a shortish man with a pale bearded face and upturned coat-collar came stiffly into the room.

Ann Eliza let her work fall as she stood up. "You're very welcome, I'm sure, Mr. Ramy. It's real kind of you to call."

"Nod ad all, ma'am." A tendency to illustrate Grimm's law in the interchange of his consonants betrayed the clock-maker's nationality, but he was evidently used to speaking English, or at least the particular branch of the vernacular with which the Bunner sisters were familiar. "I don't like to led any clock go out of my store without being sure it gives satisfaction," he added.

"Oh,—but we were satisfied," Ann Eliza assured him.

"But I wasn't, you see, ma'am," said Mr. Ramy looking slowly about the room, "nor I won't be, not till I see that clock's going all right."

"May I assist you off with your coat, Mr. Ramy?" Evelina interposed. She could never trust Ann Eliza to remember these opening ceremonies.

"Thank you, ma'am," he replied, and taking his thread-bare over-coat and shabby hat she laid them on a chair with the gesture she imagined the lady with the puffed sleeves might make use of on similar occasions. Ann Eliza's social sense was roused, and she felt that the next act of hospitality must be hers. "Won't you suit yourself to a seat?" she suggested. "My sister will reach down the clock; but I'm sure she's all right again. She's went beautiful ever since you fixed her."

"Dat's good," said Mr. Ramy. His lips parted in a smile which showed a row of yellowish teeth with one or two gaps in it; but in spite of this disclosure Ann Eliza thought his smile extremely pleasant: there was something wistful and conciliating in it which agreed with the pathos of his sunken cheeks and prominent eyes. As he took the clock from Evelina and bent toward the lamp, the light fell on his bulging forehead and wide skull thinly covered with grayish hair. His hands were pale and broad, with knotty joints and square finger-tips rimmed with grime; but his touch was as light as a woman's.

"Well, ladies, dat clock's all right," he pronounced.

"I'm sure we're very much obliged to you," said Evelina, throwing a glance at her sister.

"Oh," Ann Eliza murmured, involuntarily answering the admonition. She selected a key from the bunch that hung at her waist with her cutting-out scissors, and fitting it into the lock of the cupboard, brought out the cherry brandy and three old-fashioned glasses engraved with vine wreaths.

"It's a very cold night," she said, "and maybe you'd like a sip of this cordial. It was made a great while ago by our grandmother."

"It looks fine," said Mr. Ramy bowing, and Ann Eliza filled the glasses. In her own and Evelina's she poured only a few drops, but she filled their guest's to the brim. "My sister and I seldom take wine," she explained.

With another bow, which included both his hostesses, Mr. Ramy drank off the cherry brandy and pronounced it excellent.

Evelina meanwhile, with an assumption of industry intended to put their guest at ease, had taken up her instruments and was twisting a rose-petal into shape.

"You make artificial flowers, I see, ma'am," said Mr. Ramy with interest. "It's very pretty work. I had a lady-vriend in Shermany dat used to make flowers." He put out a square finger-tip to touch the petal.

Evelina blushed a little. "You left Germany long ago, I suppose?"

"Dear me yes, a goot while ago, I was only ninedeen when I come to the States."

After this the conversation dragged on intermittently till Mr. Ramy, peering about the room with the short-sighted glance of his race, said with an air of interest: "You're pleasantly fixed here; it looks real cosy." The note of wistfulness in his voice was obscurely moving to Ann Eliza.

"Oh, we live very plainly," said Evelina, with an affectation of grandeur deeply impressive to her sister. "We have very simple tastes."

"You look real comfortable, anyhow," said Mr. Ramy. His bulging eyes seemed to muster the details of the scene with a gentle envy. "I wisht I had as good a store; but I guess no blace seems homelike when you're always alone in it."

For some minutes longer the conversation moved on at this desultory pace, and then Mr. Ramy, who had been obviously nerving himself for the difficult act of departure, took his leave with an abruptness which would have startled anyone used to the subtler gradations of intercourse. But to Ann Eliza and her sister there was nothing surprising in his abrupt retreat. The long-drawn agonies of preparing to leave, and the subsequent dumb plunge through the door, were so usual in their circle that they would have been as much embarrassed as Mr. Ramy if he had tried to put any fluency into his adieux.

After he had left both sisters remained silent for a while; then Evelina, laying aside her unfinished flower, said: "I'll go and lock up."

§ 4

Intolerably monotonous seemed now to the Bunner sisters the treadmill routine of the shop, colourless and long their evenings about the lamp, aimless their habitual interchange of words to the weary accompaniment of the sewing and pinking machines.

It was perhaps with the idea of relieving the tension of their mood that Evelina, the following Sunday, suggested inviting Miss Mellins to supper. The Bunner sisters were not in a position to be lavish of the humblest hospitality, but two or three times in the year they shared their evening meal with a friend; and Miss Mellins, still flushed with the importance of her "turn," seemed the most interesting guest they could invite.

As the three women seated themselves at the supper-table, embellished by the unwonted addition of pound cake and sweet pickles, the dress-maker's sharp swarthy person stood out vividly between the neutral-tinted sisters. Miss Mellins was a small woman with a glossy yellow face and a frizz of black hair bristling with imitation tortoise-shell pins. Her sleeves had a fashionable cut, and half a dozen metal bangles rattled on her wrists. Her voice rattled like her bangles as she poured forth a stream of anecdote and ejaculation; and her round black eyes jumped with acrobatic velocity from one face to another. Miss Mellins was always having or hearing of amazing adventures. She had surprised a burglar in her room at midnight (though how he got there, what he robbed her of, and by what means he escaped had never been quite clear to her auditors); she had been warned by anonymous letters that her grocer (a rejected suitor) was putting poison in her tea; she had a customer who was shadowed by detectives, and another (a very wealthy lady) who had been arrested in a department store for kleptomania; she had been present at a spiritualist seance where an old gentleman had died in a fit on seeing a materialization of his mother-in-law; she had escaped from two fires in her night-gown, and at the funeral of her first cousin the horses attached to the hearse had run away and smashed the coffin, precipitating her relative into an open man-hole before the eyes of his distracted family.

A sceptical observer might have explained Miss Mellins' proneness to adventure by the fact that she derived her chief mental nourishment from the *Police Gazette* and the *Fireside Weekly;* but her lot was cast in a circle where such insinuations were not likely to be heard, and where the title-role in blood-curdling drama had long been her recognized right.

"Yes," she was now saying, her emphatic eyes on Ann Eliza, "you may not believe it, Miss Bunner, and I don't know's I should myself if anybody else was to tell me, but over a year before ever I was born, my mother she went to see a gypsy fortune-teller that was exhibited in a tent on the Battery with the green-headed lady, though her father warned her not to—and what you s'pose she told her? Why, she told her these very words—says she: 'Your next child'll be a girl with jet-black curls, and she'll suffer from spasms.' "

"Mercy!" murmured Ann Eliza, a ripple of sympathy running down her spine.

"D'you ever have spasms before, Miss Mellins?" Evelina asked.

"Yes, ma'am," the dress-maker declared. "And where'd you suppose I had 'em? Why, at my cousin Emma McIntyre's wedding, her that married the apothecary over in Jersey City, though her mother appeared to her in a dream and told her she'd rue the day she done it, but as Emma said, she got more advice than she wanted from the living, and if she was to listen to spectres too she'd never be sure what she'd ought to do and what she'd oughtn't; but I will say her husband took to drink, and she never was the same woman after her fust baby—well, they had an elegant church wedding, and what you s'pose I saw as I was walkin' up the aisle with the wedding percession?"

"Well?" Ann Eliza whispered, forgetting to thread her needle.

"Why, a coffin, to be sure, right on the top step of the chancel—Emma's folks is 'piscopalians and she would have a church wedding, though *his* mother raised a terrible rumpus over it—well, there it set, right in front of where the minister stood that was going to marry 'em, a coffin, covered with a black velvet pall with a gold fringe, and a 'Gates Ajar' in white camellias atop of it."

"Goodness," said Evelina, starting, "there's a knock!"

"Who can it be?" shuddered Ann Eliza, still under the spell of Miss Mellins's hallucination.

Evelina rose and lit a candle to guide her through the shop. They heard her turn the key of the outer door, and a gust of night air stirred the close atmosphere of the back room; then there was a sound of vivacious exclamations, and Evelina returned with Mr. Ramy.

Ann Eliza's heart rocked like a boat in a heavy sea, and the dress-maker's eyes, distended with curiosity, sprang eagerly from face to face.

"I just thought I'd call in again," said Mr. Ramy, evidently somewhat disconcerted by the presence of Miss Mellins. "Just to see how the clock's behaving," he added with his hollow-cheeked smile.

"Oh, she's behaving beautiful," said Ann Eliza; "but we're real glad to see you all the same. Miss Mellins, let me make you acquainted with Mr. Ramy."

The dress-maker tossed back her head and dropped her lids in condescending recognition of the stranger's presence; and Mr. Ramy responded by an awkward bow. After the first moment of constraint a renewed sense of satisfaction filled the consciousness of the three women. The Bunner sisters were not sorry to let Miss Mellins see that they received an occasional evening visit, and Miss

Mellins was clearly enchanted at the opportunity of pouring her latest tale into a new ear. As for Mr. Ramy, he adjusted himself to the situation with greater ease than might have been expected, and Evelina, who had been sorry that he should enter the room while the remains of supper still lingered on the table, blushed with pleasure at his good-humored offer to help her "glear away."

The table cleared, Ann Eliza suggested a game of cards; and it was after eleven o'clock when Mr. Ramy rose to take leave. His adieux were so much less abrupt than on the occasion of his first visit that Evelina was able to satisfy her sense of etiquette by escorting him, candle in hand, to the outer door; and as the two disappeared into the shop Miss Mellins playfully turned to Ann Eliza.

"Well, well, Miss Bunner," she murmured, jerking her chin in the direction of the retreating figures, "I'd no idea your sister was keeping company. On'y to think!"

Ann Eliza, roused from a state of dreamy beatitude turned her timid eyes on the dress-maker.

"Oh, you're mistaken, Miss Mellins. We don't har'ly know Mr. Ramy."

Miss Mellins smiled incredulously. "You go 'long, Miss Bunner. I guess there'll be a wedding somewheres round here before spring, and I'll be real offended if I ain't asked to make the dress. I've always seen her in a gored satin with rooshings."

Ann Eliza made no answer. She had grown very pale, and her eyes lingered searchingly on Evelina as the younger sister reentered the room. Evelina's cheeks were pink, and her blue eyes glittered; but it seemed to Ann Eliza that the coquettish tilt of her head regrettably emphasized the weakness of her receding chin. It was the first time that Ann Eliza had ever seen a flaw in her sister's beauty, and her involuntary criticism startled her like a secret disloyalty.

That night, after the light had been put out, the elder sister knelt longer than usual at her prayers. In the silence of the darkened room she was offering up certain dreams and aspirations whose brief blossoming had lent a transient freshness to her days. She wondered now how she could ever have supposed that Mr. Ramy's visits had another cause than the one Miss Mellins suggested. Had not the sight of Evelina first inspired him with a sudden solicitude for the welfare of the clock? And what charms but Evelina's could have induced him to repeat his visit? Grief held up its torch to the frail fabric of Ann Eliza's illusions, and with a firm heart she watched them shrivel into ashes; then, rising from her knees full of the chill joy of renunciation, she laid a kiss on the crimping pins of the sleeping Evelina and crept under the bedspread at her side.

§ 5

During the months that followed, Mr. Ramy visited the sisters with increasing frequency. It became his habit to call on them every Sunday evening, and occasionally during the week he would find an excuse for dropping in unannounced as they were settling down to their work beside the lamp. Ann Eliza noticed that Evelina now took the precaution of putting on her crimson bow every evening before supper, and that she had refurbished with a bit of carefully washed lace the black silk which they still called new because it had been bought a year after Ann Eliza's.

Mr. Ramy, as he grew more intimate, became less conversational, and after the sisters had blushingly accorded him the privilege of a pipe he began to permit himself long stretches of meditative silence that were not without charm to his hostesses. There was something at once fortifying and pacific in the sense of that tranquil male presence in an atmosphere which had so long quivered with little feminine doubts and distresses; and the sisters fell into the habit of saying to each other, in moments of uncertainty: "We'll ask Mr. Ramy when he comes," and of accepting his verdict, whatever it might be, with a fatalistic readiness that relieved them of all responsibility.

When Mr. Ramy drew the pipe from his mouth and became, in his turn, confidential, the acuteness of their sympathy grew almost painful to the sisters. With passionate participation they listened to the story of his early struggles in Germany, and of the long illness which had been the cause of his recent misfortunes. The name of the Mrs. Hochmüller (an old comrade's widow) who had nursed him through his fever was greeted with reverential sighs and an inward pang of envy whenever it recurred in his biographical monologues, and once when the sisters were alone Evelina called a responsive flush to Ann Eliza's brow by saying suddenly, without the mention of any name: "I wonder what she's like?"

One day toward spring Mr. Ramy, who had by this time become as much a part of their lives as the letter-carrier or the milkman, ventured the suggestion that the ladies should accompany him to an exhibition of stereoptical views which was to take place at Chickering Hall on the following evening.

After their first breathless "Oh!" of pleasure there was a silence of mutual consultation, which Ann Eliza at last broke by saying: "You better go with Mr. Ramy, Evelina. I guess we don't both want to leave the store at night."

Evelina, with such protests as politeness demanded, acquiesced in this opinion, and spent the next day in trimming a white chip bonnet with forget-me-nots of her own making. Ann Eliza brought out her mosaic brooch, a cashmere scarf of their mother's was taken from its linen cerements, and thus adorned Evelina blushingly departed with Mr. Ramy, while the elder sister sat down in her place at the pinking-machine.

It seemed to Ann Eliza that she was alone for hours, and she was surprised, when she heard Evelina tap on the door, to find that the clock marked only half-past ten.

"It must have gone wrong again," she reflected as she rose to let her sister in.

The evening had been brilliantly interesting, and several striking stereopticon views of Berlin had afforded Mr. Ramy the opportunity of enlarging on the marvels of his native city.

"He said he'd love to show it all to me!" Evelina declared as Ann Eliza conned her glowing face. "Did you ever hear anything so silly? I didn't know which way to look."

Ann Eliza received this confidence with a sympathetic murmur.

"My bonnet *is* becoming, isn't it?" Evelina went on irrelevantly, smiling at her reflection in the cracked glass above the chest of drawers.

"You're jest lovely," said Ann Eliza.

Spring was making itself unmistakably known to the distrustful New Yorker by an increased harshness of wind and prevalence of dust, when one day Evelina entered the back room at supper-time with a cluster of jonquils in her hand.

"I was just that foolish," she answered Ann Eliza's wondering glance, "I couldn't help buyin' 'em. I felt as if I must have something pretty to look at right away."

"Oh, sister," said Ann Eliza, in trembling sympathy. She felt that special indulgence must be conceded to those in Evelina's state since she had had her own fleeting vision of such mysterious longings as the words betrayed.

Evelina, meanwhile, had taken the bundle of dried grasses out of the broken china vase, and was putting the jonquils in their place with touches that lingered down their smooth stems and blade-like leaves.

"Ain't they pretty?" she kept repeating as she gathered the flowers into a starry circle. "Seems as if spring was really here, don't it?"

Ann Eliza remembered that it was Mr. Ramy's evening.

When he came, the Teutonic eye for anything that blooms made him turn at once to the jonquils.

"Ain't dey pretty?" he said. "Seems like as if de spring was really here."

"Don't it?" Evelina exclaimed, thrilled by the coincidence of their thought. "It's just what I was saying to my sister."

Ann Eliza got up suddenly and moved away: she remembered that she had not wound the clock the day before. Evelina was sitting at the table; the jonquils rose slenderly between herself and Mr. Ramy.

"Oh," she murmured with vague eyes, "how I'd love to get away somewheres into the country this very minute—somewheres where it was green and quiet. Seems as if I couldn't stand the city another day." But Ann Eliza noticed that she was looking at Mr. Ramy, and not at the flowers.

"I guess we might go to Central Park some Sunday," their visitor suggested. "Do you ever go there, Miss Evelina?"

"No, we don't very often; leastways we ain't been for a good while." She sparkled at the prospect. "It would be lovely, wouldn't it, Ann Eliza?"

"Why, yes," said the elder sister, coming back to her seat.

"Well, why don't we go next Sunday?" Mr. Ramy continued. "And we'll invite Miss Mellins too—that'll make a gosy little party."

That night when Evelina undressed she took a jonquil from the vase and pressed it with a certain ostentation between the leaves of her prayer-book. Ann Eliza, covertly observing her, felt that Evelina was not sorry to be observed, and that her own acute consciousness of the act was somehow regarded as magnifying its significance.

The following Sunday broke blue and warm. The Bunner sisters were habitual church-goers, but for once they left their prayer-books on the what-not, and ten o'clock found them, gloved and bonneted, awaiting Miss Mellins's knock. Miss Mellins presently appeared in a glitter of jet sequins and spangles, with a tale of having seen a strange man prowling under her windows till he was called off at dawn by a confederate's whistle; and shortly afterward came Mr. Ramy, his hair brushed with more than usual care, his broad hands encased in gloves of olive-green kid.

The little party set out for the nearest street-car, and a flutter of mingled gratification and embarrassment stirred Ann Eliza's bosom when it was found that Mr. Ramy intended to pay their fares. Nor did he fail to live up to this opening liberality; for after guiding them through the Mall and the Ramble he led the way to a rustic restaurant where, also at his expense, they fared idyllically on milk and lemon-pie.

After this they resumed their walk, strolling on with the slowness of unaccustomed holiday-makers from one path to another—through budding shrubberies, past grass-banks sprinkled with lilac crocuses, and under rocks on which the forsythia lay like sudden sunshine. Everything about her seemed new and miraculously lovely to Ann Eliza; but she kept her feelings to herself, leaving it to Evelina to exclaim at the hepaticas under the shady ledges, and to Miss Mellins, less interested in the vegetable than in the human world, to remark significantly on the probable history of the persons they met. All the alleys were thronged with promenaders and obstructed by perambulators; and Miss Mellins's running commentary threw a glare of lurid possibilities over the placid family groups and their romping progeny.

Ann Eliza was in no mood for such interpretations of life; but, knowing that Miss Mellins had been invited for the sole purpose of keeping her company she continued to cling to the dress-maker's side, letting Mr. Ramy lead the way with Evelina. Miss Mellins, stimulated by the excitement of the occasion, grew more and more discursive, and her ceaseless talk, and the kaleidoscopic whirl of the crowd, were unspeakably bewildering to Ann Eliza. Her feet, accustomed to the slippered ease of the shop, ached with the unfamiliar effort of walking, and her ears with the din of the dress-maker's anecdotes; but every nerve in her was aware of Evelina's enjoyment, and she was determined that no weariness of hers should curtail it. Yet even her heroism shrank from the significant glances which Miss Mellins presently began to cast at the couple in front of them: Ann Eliza could bear to connive at Evelina's bliss, but not to acknowledge it to others.

At length Evelina's feet also failed her, and she turned to suggest that they ought to be going home. Her flushed face had grown pale with fatigue, but her eyes were radiant.

The return lived in Ann Eliza's memory with the persistence of an evil dream. The horse-cars were packed with the returning throng, and they had to let a dozen go by before they could push their way into one that was already crowded. Ann Eliza had never before felt so tired. Even Miss Mellins's flow of narrative ran dry, and they sat silent, wedged between a Negro woman and a pock-marked man with a bandaged head, while the car rumbled slowly down a squalid avenue to their corner. Evelina and Mr. Ramy sat together in the forward part of the car, and Ann Eliza could catch only an occasional glimpse of the forget-me-not bonnet and the clock-maker's shiny coat-collar; but when the little party got out at their corner the crowd swept them together again, and they walked back in the effortless silence of tired children to the Bunner sisters' basement. As Miss Mellins and Mr. Ramy turned to go their various ways Evelina mustered a last display of smiles; but Ann Eliza crossed the threshold in silence, feeling the stillness of the little shop reach out to her like consoling arms.

That night she could not sleep; but as she lay cold and rigid at her sister's side, she suddenly felt the pressure of Evelina's arms, and heard her whisper: "Oh, Ann Eliza, warn't it heavenly?"

§ 6

For four days after their Sunday in the Park the Bunner sisters had no news of Mr. Ramy. At first neither one betrayed her disappointment and anxiety to the other; but on the fifth morning Evelina, always the first to yield to her feelings, said, as she turned from her untasted tea: "I thought you'd oughter take that money out by now, Ann Eliza."

Ann Eliza understood and reddened. The winter had been a fairly prosperous one for the sisters, and their slowly accumulated savings had now reached the handsome sum of two hundred dollars; but the satisfaction they might have felt in this unwonted opulence had been clouded by a suggestion of Miss Mellins's that there were dark rumours concerning the savings bank in which their funds were deposited. They knew Miss Mellins was given to vain alarms; but her words, by the sheer force of repetition, had so shaken Ann Eliza's peace that after long hours of midnight counsel the sisters had decided to advise with Mr. Ramy; and on Ann Eliza, as the head of the house, this duty had devolved. Mr. Ramy, when consulted, had not only confirmed the dress-maker's report, but had offered to find some safe investment which should give the sisters a higher rate of interest than the suspected savings bank; and Ann Eliza knew that Evelina alluded to the suggested transfer.

"Why, yes, to be sure," she agreed. "Mr. Ramy said if he was us he wouldn't want to leave his money there any longer'n he could help."

"It was over a week ago he said it," Evelina reminded her.

"I know; but he told me to wait till he'd found out for sure about that other investment; and we ain't seen him since then."

Ann Eliza's words released their secret fear. "I wonder what's happened to him," Evelina said. "You don't suppose he could be sick?"

"I was wondering too," Ann Eliza rejoined; and the sisters looked down at their plates.

"I should think you'd oughter do something about that money pretty soon," Evelina began again.

"Well, I know I'd oughter. What would you do if you was me?"

"If I was *you,*" said her sister, with perceptible emphasis and a rising blush, "I'd go right round and see if Mr. Ramy was sick. *You* could."

The words pierced Ann Eliza like a blade. "Yes, that's so," she said.

"It would only seem friendly, if he really *is* sick. If I was you I'd go to-day," Evelina continued; and after dinner Ann Eliza went.

On the way she had to leave a parcel at the dyer's, and having performed that errand she turned toward Mr. Ramy's shop. Never before had she felt so old, so hopeless and humble. She knew she was bound on a love-errand of Evelina's, and the knowledge seemed to dry the last drop of young blood in her veins. It took from her, too, all her faded virginal shyness; and with a brisk composure she turned the handle of the clock-maker's door.

But as she entered her heart began to tremble, for she saw Mr. Ramy, his face hidden in his hands, sitting behind the counter in an attitude of strange dejection. At the click of the latch he looked up slowly, fixing a lustreless stare on Ann Eliza. For a moment she thought he did not know her.

"Oh, you're sick!" she exclaimed; and the sound of her voice seemed to recall his wandering senses.

"Why, if it ain't Miss Bunner!" he said, in low thick tone; but he made no attempt to move, and she noticed that his face was the colour of yellow ashes.

"You *are* sick," she persisted, emboldened by his evident need of help. "Mr. Ramy, it was real unfriendly of you not to let us know."

He continued to look at her with dull eyes. "I ain't been sick," he said. "Leastways not very: only one of my old turns." He spoke in a slow laboured way, as if he had difficulty in getting his words together.

"Rheumatism?" she ventured, seeing how unwillingly he seemed to move.

"Well—somethin' like, maybe. I couldn't hardly put a name to it."

"If it *was* anything like rheumatism, my grandmother used to make a tea—" Ann Eliza began: she had forgotten, in the warmth of the moment, that she had only come as Evelina's messenger.

At the mention of tea an expression of uncontrollable repugnance passed over Mr. Ramy's face. "Oh, I guess I'm getting on all right. I've just got a headache to-day."

Ann Eliza's courage dropped at the note of refusal in his voice.

"I'm sorry," she said gently. "My sister and me'd have been glad to do anything we could for you."

"Thank you kindly," said Mr. Ramy wearily; then, as she turned to the door, he added with an effort: "Maybe I'll step round to-morrow."

"We'll be real glad," Ann Eliza repeated. Her eyes were fixed on a dusty bronze clock in the window. She was unaware of looking at it at the time, but long afterward she remembered that it represented a Newfoundland dog with his paw on an open book.

When she reached home there was a purchaser in the shop, turning over hooks and eyes and under Evelina's absent-minded supervision. Ann Eliza passed hastily into the back room, but in an instant she heard her sister at her side.

"Quick! I told her I was goin' to look for some smaller hooks—how is he?" Evelina gasped.

"He ain't been very well," said Ann Eliza slowly, her eyes on Evelina's eager face; "but he says he'll be sure to be round to-morrow night."

"He will? Are you telling me the truth?"

"Why, Evelina Bunner!"

"Oh, I don't care!" cried the younger recklessly, rushing back into the shop.

Ann Eliza stood burning with the shame of Evelina's self-exposure. She was shocked that, even to her, Evelina should lay bare the nakedness of her emotion; and she tried to turn her thoughts from it as though its recollection made her a sharer in her sister's debasement.

The next evening, Mr. Ramy reappeared, still somewhat sallow and red-lidded, but otherwise like his usual self. Ann Eliza consulted him about the investment he had recommended, and after it had been settled that he should attend to the matter for her he took up the illustrated volume of Longfellow—for, as the sisters had learned, his culture soared beyond the newspapers—and read aloud, with a fine confusion of consonants, the poem on "Maidenhood." Evelina lowered her lids while he read. It was a very beautiful evening, and Ann Eliza thought afterward how different life might have been with a companion who read poetry like Mr. Ramy.

§ 7

During the ensuing weeks Mr. Ramy, though his visits were as frequent as ever, did not seem to regain his usual spirits. He complained frequently of headache, but rejected Ann Eliza's tentatively proffered remedies, and seemed to shrink from any prolonged investigation of his symptoms. July had come, with a sudden ardour of heat, and one evening, as the three sat together by the open window in the back room, Evelina said: "I dunno what I wouldn't give, a night like this, for a breath of real country air."

"So would I," said Mr. Ramy, knocking the ashes from his pipe. "I'd like to be setting in an arbour with you dis very minute."

"Oh, wouldn't it be lovely?"

"I always think it's real cool here—we'd be heaps hotter up where Miss Mellins is," said Ann Eliza.

"Oh, I daresay—but we'd be heaps cooler somewhere else," her sister snapped: she was not infrequently exasperated by Ann Eliza's furtive attempts to mollify Providence.

A few days later Mr. Ramy appeared with a suggestion which enchanted Evelina. He had gone the day before to see his friend, Mrs. Hochmüller, who lived in the outskirts of Hoboken, and Mrs. Hochmüller had proposed that on the following Sunday he should bring the Bunner sisters to spend the day with her.

"She's got a real garden, you know," Mr. Ramy explained, "wid trees and a real summer-house to set in; and hens and chickens too. And it's an elegant sail over on de ferry-boat."

The proposal drew no response from Ann Eliza. She was still oppressed by the recollection of her interminable Sunday in the Park; but, obedient to Evelina's imperious glance, she finally faltered out an acceptance.

The Sunday was a very hot one, and once on the ferry-boat Ann Eliza revived at the touch of the salt breeze, and the spectacle of the crowded waters; but when they reached the other shore, and stepped out on the dirty wharf, she began to ache with anticipated weariness. They got into a street-car, and were jolted from one mean street to another, till at length Mr. Ramy pulled the conductor's sleeve and they got out again; then they stood in the blazing sun, near the door of a crowded beer-saloon, waiting for another car to come; and that carried them out to a thinly settled district, past vacant lots and narrow brick houses standing in unsupported solitude, till they finally reached an almost rural region of scattered cottages and low wooden buildings that looked like village "stores." Here the car finally stopped of its own accord, and they walked along a rutty road, past a stonecutter's yard with a high fence tapestried with theatrical advertisements, to a little red house with green blinds and a garden paling. Really, Mr. Ramy had not deceived them. Clumps of dielytra and day-lilies bloomed behind the paling, and a crooked elm hung romantically over the gable of the house.

At the gate Mrs. Hochmüller, a broad woman in brick-brown merino, met them with nods and smiles, while her daughter Linda, a flaxen-haired girl with mottled red cheeks and a side-long stare, hovered inquisitively behind her. Mrs. Hochmüller, leading the way into the house, conducted the Bunner sisters the way to her bedroom. Here they were invited to spread out on a mountainous white feather-bed the cashmere mantles under which the solemnity of the occasion had compelled them to swelter, and when they had given their black silks the necessary twitch of readjustment, and Evelina had fluffed out her hair before a looking-glass framed in pink-shell work, their hostess led them to a stuffy parlour smelling of ginger-bread. After another ceremonial pause, broken by polite enquires and shy ejaculations, they were shown into the kitchen, where the table was already spread with strange-looking spice-cakes and stewed fruits, and where they presently found themselves seated between Mrs. Hochmüller and Mr. Ramy, while the staring Linda bumped back and forth from the stove with steaming dishes.

To Ann Eliza the dinner seemed endless, and the rich fare strangely unappetizing. She was abashed by the easy intimacy of her hostess's voice and eye. With Mr. Ramy Mrs. Hochmüller was almost flippantly familiar, and it was only when Ann Eliza pictured her generous form bent above his sick-bed that she could forgive her for tersely addressing him as "Ramy." During one of the pauses of the meal Mrs. Hochmüller laid her knife and fork against the edges of her plate, and, fixing her eyes on the clock-maker's face, said accusingly: "You hat one of dem turns again, Ramy."

"I dunno as I had," he returned evasively.

Evelina glanced from one to the other. "Mr. Ramy *has* been sick," she said at length, as though to show that she also was in a position to speak with authority. "He's complained very frequently of headaches."

"Ho!—I know him," said Mrs. Hochmüller with a laugh, her eyes still on the clock-maker. "Ain't you ashamed of yourself, Ramy?"

Mr. Ramy, who was looking at his plate, said suddenly one word which the sisters could not understand; it sounded to Ann Eliza like "Shwike."

Mrs. Hochmüller laughed again. "My, my," she said, "wouldn't you think he'd be ashamed to go and be sick and never dell me, me that nursed him troo dat awful fever?"

"Yes, I *should,*" said Evelina, with a spirited glance at Ramy; but he was looking at the sausages that Linda had just put on the table.

When dinner was over Mrs. Hochmüller invited her guests to step out of the kitchen-door, and they found themselves in a green enclosure, half garden, half orchard. Grey hens followed by golden broods clucked under the twisted apple-boughs, a cat dozed on the edge of an old well, and from tree to tree ran the network of clothes-line that denoted Mrs. Hochmüller's calling. Beyond the apple trees stood a yellow summer-house festooned with scarlet runners; and below it, on the farther side of a rough fence, the land dipped down, holding a bit of woodland in its hollow. It was all strangely sweet and still on that hot Sunday afternoon, and as she moved across the grass under the apple-boughs Ann Eliza thought of quiet afternoons in church, and of the hymns her mother had sung to her when she was a baby.

Evelina was more restless. She wandered from the well to the summer-house and back, she tossed crumbs to the chickens and disturbed the cat with arch caresses; and at last she expressed a desire to go down into the wood.

"I guess you got to go round by the road, then," said Mrs. Hochmüller. "My Linda she goes troo a hole in de fence, but I guess you'd tear your dress if you was to dry."

"I'll help you," said Mr. Ramy; and guided by Linda the pair walked along the fence till they reached a narrow gap in its boards. Through this they disappeared, watched curiously in their descent by the grinning Linda, while Mrs. Hochmüller and Ann Eliza were left alone in the summer-house.

Mrs. Hochmüller looked at her guest with a confidential smile. "I guess dey'll be gone quite a while," she remarked, jerking her double chin toward the gap in the fence. "Folks like dat don't never remember about de dime." And she drew out her knitting.

Ann Eliza could think of nothing to say.

"Your sister she thinks a great lot of him, don't she?" her hostess continued.

Ann Eliza's cheeks grew hot. "Ain't you a teeny bit lonesome away out here sometimes?" she asked. "I should think you'd be scared nights, all alone with your daughter."

"Oh, no, I ain't," said Mrs. Hochmüller. "You see I take in washing—dat's my business—and it's a lot cheaper doing it out here dan in de city: where'd I get a drying-ground like dis in Hobucken? And den it's safer for Linda too; it geeps her outer de streets."

"Oh," said Ann Eliza, shrinking. She began to feel a distinct aversion for her hostess, and her eyes turned with involuntary annoyance to the square-backed form of Linda, still inquisitively suspended on the fence. It seemed to Ann Eliza that Evelina and her companion would never return from the wood; but they came at length, Mr. Ramy's brow pearled with perspiration, Evelina pink and self-conscious, a drooping bunch of ferns in her hand; and it was clear that, to her at least, the moments had been winged.

"D'you suppose they'll revive?" she asked, holding up the ferns; but Ann Eliza, rising at her approach, said stiffly: "We'd better be getting home, Evelina."

"Mercy me! Ain't you going to take your coffee first?" Mrs. Hochmüller protested; and Ann Eliza found to her dismay that another long gastronomic ceremony must intervene before politeness permitted them to leave. At length, however, they found themselves again on the ferry-boat. Water and sky were grey, with a dividing gleam of sunset that sent sleek opal waves in the boat's wake. The wind had a cool tarry breath, as though it had travelled over miles of shipping, and the hiss of the water about the paddles was as delicious as though it had been splashed into their tired faces.

Ann Eliza sat apart, looking away from the others. She had made up her mind that Mr. Ramy had proposed to Evelina in the wood, and she was silently preparing herself to receive her sister's confidence that evening.

But Evelina was apparently in no mood for confidences. When they reached home she put her faded ferns in water, and after supper, when she had laid aside her silk dress and the forget-me-not bonnet, she remained silently seated in her rocking-chair near the open window. It was long since Ann Eliza had seen her in so uncommunicative a mood.

The following Saturday Ann Eliza was sitting alone in the shop when the door opened and Mr. Ramy entered. He had never before called at that hour, and she wondered a little anxiously what had brought him.

"Has anything happened?" she asked, pushing aside the basketful of buttons she had been sorting.

"Not's I know of," said Mr. Ramy tranquilly. "But I always close up the store at two o'clock Saturdays at this season, so I thought I might as well call round and see you."

"I'm real glad, I'm sure," said Ann Eliza; "but Evelina's out."

"I know dat," Mr. Ramy answered. "I met her round de corner. She told me she got to go to dat new dyer's up in Forty-eighth Street. She won't be back for a couple of hours, har'ly, will she?"

Ann Eliza looked at him with rising bewilderment. "No, I guess not," she answered; her instinctive hospitality prompting her to add: "Won't you set down jest the same?"

Mr. Ramy sat down on the stool beside the counter, and Ann Eliza returned to her place behind it.

"I can't leave the store," she explained.

"Well, I guess we're very well here." Ann Eliza had become suddenly aware that Mr. Ramy was looking at her with unusual intentness. Involuntarily her hand strayed to the thin streaks of hair on her temples, and thence descended to straighten the brooch beneath her collar.

"You're looking very well to-day, Miss Bunner," said Mr. Ramy, following her gesture with a smile.

"Oh," said Ann Eliza nervously. "I'm always well in health," she added.

"I guess you're healthier than your sister, even if you are less sizeable."

"Oh, I don't know. Evelina's a mite nervous sometimes, but she ain't a bit sickly."

"She eats heartier than you do; but that don't mean nothing," said Mr. Ramy.

Ann Eliza was silent. She could not follow the trend of his thought, and she did not care to commit herself farther about Evelina before she had ascertained if Mr. Ramy considered nervousness interesting or the reverse.

But Mr. Ramy spared her all farther indecision.

"Well, Miss Bunner," he said, drawing his stool closer to the counter, "I guess I might as well tell you fust as last what I come here for to-day. I want to get married."

Ann Eliza, in many a prayerful midnight hour, had sought to strengthen herself for the hearing of this avowal, but now that it had come she felt pitifully frightened and unprepared. Mr. Ramy was leaning with both elbows on the counter, and she noticed that his nails were clean and that he had brushed his hat; yet even these signs had not prepared her!

At last she heard herself say, with a dry throat in which her heart was hammering: "Mercy me, Mr. Ramy!"

"I want to get married," he repeated. "I'm too lonesome. It ain't good for a man to live all alone, and eat noding but cold meat every day."

"No," said Ann Eliza softly.

"And the dust fairly beats me."

"Oh, the dust—I know!"

Mr. Ramy stretched one of his blunt-fingered hands toward her. "I wisht you'd take me."

Still Ann Eliza did not understand. She rose hesitatingly from her seat, pushing aside the basket of buttons which lay between them; then she perceived that Mr. Ramy was trying to take her hand, and as their fingers met a flood of joy swept over her. Never afterward, though every other word of their interview was stamped on her memory beyond all possible forgetting, could she recall what he said while their hands touched; she only knew that she seemed to be floating on a summer sea, and that all its waves were in her ears.

"Me—me?" she gasped.

"I guess so," said her suitor placidly. "You suit me right down to the ground, Miss Bunner. Dat's the truth."

A woman passing along the street paused to look at the shop-window, and Ann Eliza half hoped she would come in; but after a desultory inspection she went on.

"Maybe you don't fancy me?" Mr. Ramy suggested, discountenanced by Ann Eliza's silence.

A word of assent was on her tongue, but her lips refused it. She must find some other way of telling him.

"I don't say that."

"Well, I always kinder thought we was suited to one another," Mr. Ramy continued, eased of his momentary doubt. "I always liked de quiet style—no fuss and airs, and not afraid of work." He spoke as though dispassionately cataloguing her charms.

Ann Eliza felt that she must make an end. "But, Mr. Ramy, you don't understand. I've never thought of marrying."

Mr. Ramy looked at her in surprise. "Why not?"

"Well, I don't know, har'ly." She moistened her twitching lips. "The fact is, I ain't as active as I look. Maybe I couldn't stand the care. I ain't as spry as Evelina—nor as young," she added, with a last great effort.

"But you do most of de work here, anyways," said her suitor doubtfully.

"Oh, well, that's because Evelina's busy outside; and where there's only two women the work don't amount to much. Besides, I'm the oldest; I have to look after things," she hastened on, half pained that her simple ruse should so readily deceive him.

"Well, I guess you're active enough for me," he persisted. His calm determination began to frighten her; she trembled lest her own should be less staunch.

"No, no," she repeated, feeling the tears on her lashes. "I couldn't, Mr. Ramy, I couldn't marry. I'm so surprised. I always thought it was Evelina—always. And so did everybody else. She's so bright and pretty—it seemed so natural."

"Well, you was all mistaken," said Mr. Ramy obstinately.

"I'm so sorry."

He rose, pushing back his chair.

"You'd better think it over," he said, in the large tone of a man who feels he may safely wait.

"Oh, no, no. It ain't any sorter use, Mr. Ramy. I don't never mean to marry. I get tired so easily—I'd be afraid of the work. And I have such awful headaches." She paused, racking her brain for more convincing infirmities.

"Headaches, do you?" said Mr. Ramy, turning back.

"My, yes, awful ones, that I have to give right up to. Evelina has to do everything when I have one of them headaches. She has to bring me my tea in the mornings."

"Well, I'm sorry to hear it," said Mr. Ramy.

"Thank you kindly all the same," Ann Eliza murmured. "And please don't—don't—" She stopped suddenly, looking at him through her tears.

"Oh, that's all right," he answered. "Don't you fret, Miss Bunner. Folks have got to suit themselves." She thought his tone had grown more resigned since she had spoken of her headaches.

For some moments he stood looking at her with a hesitating eye, as though uncertain how to end their conversation; and at length she found courage to say (in the words of a novel she had once read): "I don't want this should make any difference between us."

"Oh, my, no," said Mr. Ramy, absently picking up his hat.

"You'll come in just the same?" she continued, nerving herself to the effort. "We'd miss you awfully if you didn't. Evelina, she—" She paused, torn between her desire to turn his thoughts to Evelina, and the dread of prematurely disclosing her sister's secret.

"Don't Miss Evelina have no headaches?" Mr. Ramy suddenly asked.

"My, no, never—well, not to speak of, anyway. She ain't had one for ages, and when Evelina *is* sick she won't never give into it," Ann Eliza declared, making some hurried adjustments with her conscience.

"I wouldn't have thought that," said Mr. Ramy.

"I guess you don't know us as well as you thought you did."

"Well, no, that's so; maybe I don't. I'll wish you good day, Miss Bunner"; and Mr. Ramy moved toward the door.

"Good day, Mr. Ramy," Ann Eliza answered.

She felt unutterably thankful to be alone. She knew the crucial moment of her life had passed, and she was glad that she had not fallen below her own ideals. It had been a wonderful experience, full of undreamed-of fear and fascination; and in spite of the tears on her cheeks she was not sorry to have known it. Two facts, however, took the edge from its perfection: that it had happened in the shop, and that she had not had on her black silk.

She passed the next hour in a state of dreamy ecstasy. Something had entered into her life of which no subsequent empoverishment could rob it: she glowed with the same rich sense of possessorship that once, as a little girl, she had felt when her mother had given her a gold locket and she had sat up in bed in the dark to draw it from its hiding-place beneath her nightgown.

At length a dread of Evelina's return began to mingle with these musings. How could she meet her younger sister's eye without betraying what had happened? She felt as though a visible glory lay on her, and she was glad that dusk had fallen when Evelina entered. But her fears were superfluous. Evelina, always self-absorbed, had of late lost all interest in the simple happenings of the shop, and Ann Eliza, with mingled mortification and relief, perceived that she was in no danger of being cross-questioned as to the events of the afternoon. She was glad of this; yet there was a touch of humiliation in finding that the portentous secret in her bosom did not visibly shine forth. It struck her as dull, and even slightly absurd, of Evelina not to know at last that they were equals.

§ 8

Mr. Ramy, after a decent interval, returned to the shop; and Ann Eliza, when they met, was unable to detect whether the emotions which seethed under her black alpaca found an echo in his bosom. Outwardly he made no sign. He lit his pipe as placidly as ever and seemed to relapse without effort into the unruffled intimacy of old. Yet to Ann Eliza's initiated eye a change became gradually perceptible. She saw that he was beginning to look at her sister as he had looked at her on that momentous afternoon: she even discerned a secret significance in the turn of his talk with Evelina. Once he asked her abruptly if she should like to travel, and Ann Eliza saw that the flush on Evelina's cheek was reflected from the same fire which had scorched her own.

So they drifted on through the sultry weeks of July. At that season the business of the little shop almost ceased, and one Saturday morning Mr. Ramy proposed that the sisters should lock up early and go with him for a sail down the bay in one of the Coney Island boats.

Ann Eliza saw the light in Evelina's eye and her resolve was instantly taken.

"I guess I won't go, thank you kindly; but I'm sure my sister will be happy to."

She was pained by the perfunctory phrase with which Evelina urged her to accompany them; and still more by Mr. Ramy's silence.

"No, I guess I won't go," she repeated, rather in answer to herself than to them. "It's dreadfully hot and I've got a kinder headache."

"Oh, well, I wouldn't then," said her sister hurriedly. "You'd better jest set here quietly and rest."

"Yes, I'll rest," Ann Eliza assented.

At two o'clock Mr. Ramy returned, and a moment later he and Evelina left the shop. Evelina had made herself another new bonnet for the occasion, a bonnet, Ann Eliza thought, almost too youthful in shape and colour. It was the first time it had ever occurred to her to criticise Evelina's taste, and she was frightened at the insidious change in her attitude toward her sister.

When Ann Eliza, in later days, looked back on that afternoon she felt that there had been something prophetic in the quality of its solitude; it seemed to distill the triple essence of loneliness in which all her after-life was to be lived. No purchasers came; not a hand fell on the door-latch; and the tick of the clock in the back room ironically emphasized the passing of the empty hours.

Evelina returned late and alone. Ann Eliza felt the coming crisis in the sound of her footstep, which wavered along as if not knowing on what it trod. The elder sister's affection had so passionately projected itself into her junior's fate that at such moments she seemed to be living two lives, her own and Evelina's; and her private longings shrank into silence at the sight of the other's hungry bliss. But it was evident that Evelina, never acutely alive to the emotional atmosphere about her, had no idea that her secret was suspected; and with an assumption of unconcern that would have made Ann Eliza smile if the pang had been less piercing, the younger sister prepared to confess herself.

"What are you so busy about?" she said impatiently, as Ann Eliza, beneath the gas-jet, fumbled for the matches. "Ain't you even got time to ask me if I'd had a pleasant day?"

Ann Eliza turned with a quiet smile. "I guess I don't have to. Seems to me it's pretty plain you have."

"Well, I don't know. I don't know *how* I feel—it's all so queer. I almost think I'd like to scream."

"I guess you're tired."

"No, I ain't. It's not that. But it all happened so suddenly, and the boat was so crowded I thought everybody'd hear what he was saying.—Ann Eliza," she broke out, "why on earth don't you ask me what I'm talking about?"

Ann Eliza, with a last effort of heroism, feigned a fond incomprehension.

"What *are* you?"

"Why, I'm engaged to be married—so there! Now it's out! And it happened right on the boat; only to think of it! Of course I wasn't exactly surprised—I've known right along he was going to sooner or later—on'y somehow I didn't think of its happening to-day. I thought he'd never get up his courage. He said he was so 'fraid I'd say no—that's what kep' him so long from asking me. Well, I ain't said yes *yet*—leastways I told him I'd have to think it over; but I guess he knows. Oh, Ann Eliza, I'm so happy!" She hid the blinding brightness of her face.

Ann Eliza, just then, would only let herself feel that she was glad. She drew down Evelina's hands and kissed her, and they held each other. When Evelina regained her voice she had a tale to tell which carried their vigil far into the night. Not a syllable, not a glance or gesture of Ramy's, was the elder sister spared; and with unconscious irony she found herself comparing the details of his proposal to her with those which Evelina was imparting with merciless prolixity.

The next few days were taken up with the embarrassed adjustment of their new relation to Mr. Ramy and to each other. Ann Eliza's ardour carried her to new heights of self-effacement, and she invented late duties in the shop in order to leave Evelina and her suitor longer alone in the back room. Later on, when she tried to remember the details of those first days, few came back to her: she knew only that she got up each morning with the sense of having to push the leaden hours up the same long steep of pain.

Mr. Ramy came daily now. Every evening he and his betrothed

went out for a stroll around the Square, and when Evelina came in her cheeks were always pink. "He's kissed her under that tree at the corner, away from the lamp-post," Ann Eliza said to herself, with sudden insight into unconjectured things. On Sundays they usually went for the whole afternoon to the Central Park, and Ann Eliza, from her seat in the mortal hush of the back room, followed step by step their long slow beatific walk.

There had been, as yet, no allusion to their marriage, except that Evelina had once told her sister that Mr. Ramy wished them to invite Mrs. Hochmüller and Linda to the wedding. The mention of the laundress raised a half-forgotten fear in Ann Eliza, and she said in a tone of tentative appeal: "I guess if I was you I wouldn't want to be very great friends with Mrs. Hochmüller."

Evelina glanced at her compassionately. "I guess if you was me you'd want to do everything you could to please the man you loved. It's lucky," she added with glacial irony, "that I'm not too grand for Herman's friends."

"Oh," Ann Eliza protested, "that ain't what I mean—and you know it ain't. Only somehow the day we saw her I didn't think she seemed like the kinder person you'd want for a friend."

"I guess a married woman's the best judge of such matters," Evelina replied, as though she already walked in the light of her future state.

Ann Eliza, after that, kept her own counsel. She saw that Evelina wanted her sympathy as little as her admonitions, and that already she counted for nothing in her sister's scheme of life. To Ann Eliza's idolatrous acceptance of the cruelties of fate this exclusion seemed both natural and just; but it caused her the most lively pain. She could not divest her love for Evelina of its passionate motherliness; no breath of reason could lower it to the cool temperature of sisterly affection.

She was then passing, as she thought, through the novitiate of her pain; preparing, in a hundred experimental ways, for the solitude awaiting her when Evelina left. It was true that it would be a tempered loneliness. They would not be far apart. Evelina would "run in" daily from the clock-maker's; they would doubtless take supper with her on Sundays. But already Ann Eliza guessed with what growing perfunctoriness her sister would fulfill these obligations; she even foresaw the day when, to get news of Evelina, she should have to lock the shop at nightfall and go herself to Mr. Ramy's door. But on that contingency she would not dwell. "They can come to me when they want to—they'll always find me here," she simply said to herself.

One evening Evelina came in flushed and agitated from her stroll around the Square. Ann Eliza saw at once that something had happened; but the new habit of reticence checked her question.

She had not long to wait. "Oh, Ann Eliza, on'y to think what he says—" (the pronoun stood exclusively for Mr. Ramy). "I declare I'm so upset I thought the people in the Square would notice me. Don't I look queer? He wants to get married right off—this very next week."

"Next week?"

"Yes. So's we can move out to St. Louis right away."

"Him and you—move out to St. Louis?"

"Well, I don't know as it would be natural for him to want to go out there without me," Evelina simpered. "But it's all so sudden I don't know what to think. He only got the letter this morning. *Do* I look queer, Ann Eliza?" Her eye was roving for the mirror.

"No, you don't," said Ann Eliza almost harshly.

"Well, it's a mercy," Evelina pursued with a tinge of disappointment. "It's a regular miracle I didn't faint right out there in the Square. Herman's so thoughtless—he just put the letter into my hand without a word. It's from a big firm out there—the Tiff'ny of St. Louis, he says it is—offering him a place in their clock-department. Seems they heard of him through a German friend of his that's settled out there. It's a splendid opening, and if he gives satisfaction they'll raise him at the end of the year."

She paused, flushed with the importance of the situation, which seemed to lift her once for all above the dull level of her former life.

"Then you'll have to go?" came at last from Ann Eliza.

Evelina stared. "You wouldn't have me interfere with his prospects, would you?"

"No—no. I on'y meant—has it got to be so soon?"

"Right away, I tell you—next week. Ain't it awful?" blushed the bride.

Well, this was what happened to mothers. They bore it, Ann

Eliza mused; so why not she? Ah, but they had their own chance first; she had had no chance at all. And now this life which she had made her own was going from her forever; had gone, already, in the inner and deeper sense, and was soon to vanish in even its outward nearness, its surface-communion of voice and eye. At that moment even the thought of Evelina's happiness refused her its consolatory ray; or its light, if she saw it, was too remote to warm her. The thirst for a personal and inalienable tie, for pangs and problems of her own, was parching Ann Eliza's soul: it seemed to her that she could never again gather strength to look her loneliness in the face.

The trivial obligations of the moment came to her aid. Nursed in idleness her grief would have mastered her; but the needs of the shop and the back room, and the preparations for Evelina's marriage, kept the tyrant under.

Miss Mellins, true to her anticipations, had been called on to aid in the making of the wedding dress, and she and Ann Eliza were bending one evening over the breadths of pearl-grey cashmere which, in spite of the dress-maker's prophetic vision of gored satin, had been judged most suitable, when Evelina came into the room alone.

Ann Eliza had already had occasion to notice that it was a bad sign when Mr. Ramy left his affianced at the door. It generally meant that Evelina had something disturbing to communicate, and Ann Eliza's first glance told her that this time the news was grave.

Miss Mellins, who sat with her back to the door and her head bent over her sewing, started as Evelina came around to the opposite side of the table.

"Mercy, Miss Evelina! I declare I thought you was a ghost, the way you crep' in. I had a customer once up in Forty-ninth Street—a lovely young woman with a thirty-six bust and a waist you could ha' put into her wedding ring—and her husband, he crep' up behind her that way jest for a joke, and frightened her into a fit, and when she come to she was a raving maniac, and had to be taken to Bloomingdale with two doctors and a nurse to hold her in the carriage, and a lovely baby on'y six weeks old—and there she is to this day, poor creature."

"I didn't mean to startle you," said Evelina.

She sat down on the nearest chair, and as the lamplight fell on her face Ann Eliza saw that she had been crying.

"You do look dead-beat," Miss Mellins resumed, after a pause of soul-probing scrutiny. "I guess Mr. Ramy lugs you round that Square too often. You'll walk your legs off if you ain't careful. Men don't never consider—they're all alike. Why, I had a cousin once that was engaged to a book-agent—"

"Maybe we'd better put away the work for to-night, Miss Mellins," Ann Eliza interposed. "I guess what Evelina wants is a good night's rest."

"That's so," assented the dress-maker. "Have you got the back breadths run together, Miss Bunner? Here's the sleeves. I'll pin 'em together." She drew a cluster of pins from her mouth, in which she seemed to secrete them as squirrels stow away nuts. "There," she said, rolling up her work, "you go right away to bed, Miss Evelina, and we'll set up a little later to-morrow night. I guess you're a mite nervous, ain't you? I know when my turn comes I'll be scared to death."

With this arch forecast she withdrew, and Ann Eliza, returning to the back room, found Evelina still listlessly seated by the table. True to her new policy of silence, the elder sister set about folding up the bridal dress; but suddenly Evelina said in a harsh unnatural voice: "There ain't any use in going on with that."

The folds slipped from Ann Eliza's hands.

"Evelina Bunner—what you mean?"

"Jest what I say. It's put off."

"Put off—what's put off?"

"Our getting married. He can't take me to St. Louis. He ain't got money enough." She brought the words out in the monotonous tone of a child reciting a lesson.

Ann Eliza picked up another breadth of cashmere and began to smooth it out. "I don't understand," she said at length.

"Well, it's plain enough. The journey's fearfully expensive, and we've got to have something left to start with when we get out there. We've counted up, and he ain't got the money to do it—that's all."

"But I thought he was going right into a splendid place."

"So he is; but the salary's pretty low the first year, and board's very high in St. Louis. He's jest got another letter from his German friend. and he's been figuring it out, and he's afraid to chance it. He'll have to go alone."

"But there's your money—have you forgotten that? The hundred dollars in the bank."

Evelina made an impatient movement. "Of course I ain't forgotten it. On'y it ain't enough. It would all have to go into buying furniture, and if he was took sick and lost his place again we wouldn't have a cent left. He says he's got to lay by another hundred dollars before he'll be willing to take me out there."

For a while Ann Eliza pondered this surprising statement; then she ventured: "Seems to me he might have thought of it before."

In an instant Evelina was aflame. "I guess he knows what's right as well as you or me. I'd sooner die than be a burden to him."

Ann Eliza made no answer. The clutch of an unformulated doubt had checked the words on her lips. She had meant, on the day of her sister's marriage, to give Evelina the other half of their common savings; but something warned her not to say so now.

The sisters undressed without farther words. After they had gone to bed, and the light had been put out, the sound of Evelina's weeping came to Ann Eliza in the darkness, but she lay motionless on her own side of the bed, out of contact with her sister's shaken body. Never had she felt so coldly remote from Evelina.

The hours of the night moved slowly, ticked off with wearisome insistence by the clock which had played so prominent a part in their lives. Evelina's sobs still stirred the bed at gradually lengthening intervals, till at length Ann Eliza thought she slept. But with the dawn the eyes of the sisters met, and Ann Eliza's courage failed her as she looked in Evelina's face.

She sat up in bed and put out a pleading hand.

"Don't cry so, dearie. Don't."

"Oh, I can't bear it, I can't bear it," Evelina moaned.

Ann Eliza stroked her quivering shoulder. "Don't, don't," she repeated. "If you take the other hundred, won't that be enough? I always meant to give it to you. On'y I didn't want to tell you till your wedding day."

§ 9

Evelina's marriage took place on the appointed day. It was celebrated in the evening, in the chantry of the church which the sisters attended, and after it was over the few guests who had been present repaired to the Bunner Sisters' basement, where a wedding supper awaited them. Ann Eliza, aided by Miss Mellins and Mrs. Hawkins, and consciously supported by the sentimental interest of the whole street, had expended her utmost energy on the decoration of the shop and the back room. On the table a vase of white chrysanthemums stood between a dish of oranges and bananas and an iced wedding-cake wreathed with orange-blossoms of the bride's own making. Autumn leaves studded with paper roses festooned the what-not and the chromo of the Rock of Ages, and a wreath of yellow immortelles was twined about the clock which Evelina revered as the mysterious agent of her happiness.

At the table sat Miss Mellins, profusely spangled and bangled, her head sewing-girl, a pale young thing who had helped with Evelina's outfit, Mr. and Mrs. Hawkins, with Johnny, their eldest boy, and Mrs. Hochmüller and her daughter.

Mrs. Hochmüller's large blonde personality seemed to pervade the room to the effacement of the less amply-proportioned guests. It was rendered more impressive by a dress of crimson poplin that stood out from her in organ-like folds; and Linda, whom Ann Eliza had remembered as an uncouth child with a sly look about the eyes, surprised her by a sudden blossoming into feminine grace such as sometimes follows on a gawky girlhood. The Hochmüllers, in fact, struck the dominant note in the entertainment. Beside them Evelina, unusually pale in her grey cashmere and white bonnet, looked like a faintly washed sketch beside a brilliant chromo; and Mr. Ramy, doomed to the traditional insignificance of the bridegroom's part, made no attempt to rise above his situation. Even Miss Mellins sparkled and jingled in vain in the shadow of Mrs. Hochmüller's crimson bulk; and Ann Eliza, with a sense of vague foreboding, saw that the wedding feast centred about the two guests she had most wished to exclude from it. What was said or done while they all sat about the table she never afterward recalled: the long hours remained in her memory as a whirl of high colours and loud voices, from which the pale presence of Evelina now and then emerged like a drowned face on a sunset-dabbled sea.

The next morning Mr. Ramy and his wife started for St. Louis, and Ann Eliza was left alone. Outwardly the first strain of parting was tempered by the arrival of Miss Mellins, Mrs. Hawkins and Johnny, who dropped in to help in the ungarlanding and tidying up of the back room. Ann Eliza was duly grateful for their kindness, but the "talking over" on which they had evidently counted was Dead Sea fruit on her lips; and just beyond the familiar warmth of their presences she saw the form of Solitude at her door.

Ann Eliza was but a small person to harbour so great a guest, and a trembling sense of insufficiency possessed her. She had no high musings to offer to the new companion of her hearth. Every one of her thoughts had hitherto turned to Evelina and shaped itself in homely easy words; of the mighty speech of silence she knew not the earliest syllable.

Everything in the back room and the shop, on the second day after Evelina's going, seemed to have grown coldly unfamiliar. The whole aspect of the place had changed with the changed conditions of Ann Eliza's life. The first customer who opened the shop-door startled her like a ghost; and all night she lay tossing on her side of the bed, sinking now and then into an uncertain doze from which she would suddenly wake to reach out her hand for Evelina. In the new silence surrounding her the walls and furniture found voice, frightening her at dusk and midnight with strange sighs and stealthy whispers. Ghostly hands shook the window shutters or rattled at the outer latch, and once she grew cold at the sound of a step like Evelina's stealing through the dark shop to die out on the threshold. In time, of course, she found an explanation for these noises, telling herself that the bedstead was warping, that Miss Mellins trod heavily overhead, or that the thunder of passing beer-waggons shook the door-latch; but the hours leading up to these conclusions were full of the floating terrors that harden into fixed foreboding. Worst of all were the solitary meals, when she absently continued to set aside the largest slice of pie for Evelina, and to let the tea grow cold while she waited for her sister to help herself to the first cup. Miss Mellins, coming in on one of these sad repasts, suggested the acquisition of a cat; but Ann Eliza shook her head. She had never been used to animals, and she felt the vague shrinking of the pious from creatures divided from her by the abyss of soullessness.

At length, after ten empty days, Evelina's first letter came.

"My dear Sister," she wrote, in her pinched Spencerian hand, "it seems strange to be in this great City so far from home alone with him I have chosen for life, but marriage has its solemn duties which those who are not can never hope to understand, and happier perhaps for this reason, life for them has only simple tasks and pleasures, but those who must take thought for others must be prepared to do their duty in whatever station it has pleased the Almighty to call them. Not that I have cause to complain, my dear Husband is all love and devotion, but being absent all day at his business how can I help but feel lonesome at times, as the poet says it is hard for they that love to live apart, and I often wonder, my dear Sister, how you are getting along alone in the store, may you never experience the feelings of solitude I have underwent since I came here. We are boarding now, but soon expect to find rooms and change our place of Residence. then I shall have all the care of a household to bear, but such is the fate of those who join their Lot with others, they cannot hope to escape from the burdens of Life, nor would I ask it, I would not live alway, but while I live would always pray for strength to do my duty. This city is not near as large or handsome as New York, but had my lot been cast in a Wilderness I hope I should not repine, such never was my nature, and they who exchange their independence for the sweet name of Wife must be prepared to find all is not gold that glitters, nor I would not expect like you to drift down the stream of Life unfettered and serene as a Summer cloud, such is not my fate, but come what may will always find in me a resigned and prayerful Spirit, and hoping this finds you as well as it leaves me, I remain, my dear Sister,

"Yours truly,
"EVELINA B. RAMY."

Ann Eliza had always secretly admired the oratorical and impersonal tone of Evelina's letters; but the few she had previously read, having been addressed to schoolmates or distant relatives, had appeared in the light of literary compositions rather than as records of personal experience. Now she could not but wish that Evelina had laid aside her swelling periods for a style more suited to the chronicling of homely incidents. She read the letter again and again, seeking for a clue to what her sister was really doing and thinking; but after each reading she emerged impressed but unenlightened from the labyrinth of Evelina's eloquence.

During the early winter she received two or three more letters of the same kind, each enclosing in its loose husk of rhetoric a smaller kernel of fact. By dint of patient interlinear study, Ann Eliza gathered from them that Evelina and her husband, after various costly experiments in boarding, had been reduced to a tenement-house flat; that living in St. Louis was more expensive than they had supposed, and that Mr. Ramy was kept out late at night (why, at a jeweller's, Ann Eliza wondered?) and found his position less satisfactory than he had been led to expect. Toward February the letters fell off; and finally they ceased to come.

At first Ann Eliza wrote, shyly but persistently, entreating for more frequent news; then, as one appeal after another was swallowed up in the mystery of Evelina's protracted silence, vague fears began to assail the elder sister. Perhaps Evelina was ill, and with no one to nurse her but a man who could not even make himself a cup of tea! Ann Eliza recalled the layer of dust in Mr. Ramy's shop, and pictures of domestic disorder mingled with the more poignant vision of her sister's illness. But surely if Evelina were ill Mr. Ramy would have written. He wrote a small neat hand, and epistolary communication was not an insuperable embarrassment to him. The too probable alternative was that both the unhappy pair had been prostrated by some disease which left them powerless to summon her—for summon her they surely would, Ann Eliza with unconscious cynicism reflected, if she or her small economies could be of use to them! The more she strained her eyes into the mystery, the darker it grew; and her lack of initiative, her inability to imagine what steps might be taken to trace the lost in distant places, left her benumbed and helpless.

At last there floated up from some depth of troubled memory the name of the firm of St. Louis jewellers by whom Mr. Ramy was employed. After much hesitation, and considerable effort, she addressed to them a timid request for news of her brother-in-law; and sooner than she could have hoped the answer reached her.

"Dear Madam,

"In reply to yours of the 29th ult. we beg to state that the party you refer to was discharged from our employ a month ago. We are sorry we are unable to furnish you with his address.

"Yours respectfully,

"Ludwig and Hammerbusch."

Ann Eliza read and re-read the curt statement in a stupor of distress. She had lost her last trace of Evelina. All that night she lay awake, revolving the stupendous project of going to St. Louis in search of her sister; but though she pieced together her few financial possibilities with the ingenuity of a brain used to fitting odd scraps into patch-work quilts, she woke to the cold daylight fact that she could not raise the money for her fare. Her wedding gift to Evelina had left her without any resources beyond her daily earnings, and these had steadily dwindled as the winter passed. She had long since renounced her weekly visit to the butcher, and had reduced her other expenses to the narrowest measure; but the most systematic frugality had not enabled her to put by any money. In spite of her dogged efforts to maintain the prosperity of the little shop, her sister's absence had already told on its business. Now that Ann Eliza had to carry the bundles to the dyer's herself, the customers who called in her absence, finding the shop locked, too often went elsewhere. Moreover, after several stern but unavailing efforts, she had had to give up the trimming of bonnets, which in Evelina's hands had been the most lucrative as well as the most interesting part of the business. This change, to the passing female eye, robbed the shop window of its chief attraction; and when painful experience had convinced the regular customers of the Bunner Sisters of Ann Eliza's lack of millinery skill they began to lose faith in her ability to curl a feather or even "freshen up" a bunch of flowers. The time came when Ann Eliza had almost made up her mind to speak to the lady with puffed sleeves, who had always looked at her so kindly, and had once ordered a hat of Evelina. Perhaps the lady with puffed sleeves would be able to get her a little plain sewing to do; or she might recommend the shop to friends. Ann Eliza, with this possibility in view, rummaged out of a drawer the fly-blown remainder of the business cards which the sisters had ordered in the first flush of their commercial adventure; but when the lady with puffed sleeves finally appeared she was in deep mourning, and wore so sad a look that Ann Eliza dared not speak. She came in to buy some spools of black thread and silk, and in the doorway she turned back to say: "I am going away to-morrow for a long time. I hope you will have a pleasant winter." And the door shut on her.

One day not long after this it occurred to Ann Eliza to go to Hoboken in quest of Mrs. Hochmüller. Much as she shrank from pouring her distress into that particular ear, her anxiety had carried her beyond such reluctances; but when she began to think the matter over she was faced by a new difficulty. On the occasion of her only visit to Mrs. Hochmüller, she and Evelina had suffered themselves to be led there by Mr. Ramy; and Ann Eliza now perceived that she did not even know the name of the laundress's suburb, much less that of the street in which she lived. But she must have news of Evelina, and no obstacle was great enough to thwart her.

Though she longed to turn to some one for advice she disliked to expose her situation to Miss Mellins's searching eye, and at first she could think of no other confidante. Then she remembered Mrs. Hawkins, or rather her husband, who, though Ann Eliza had always thought him a dull uneducated man, was probably gifted with the mysterious masculine faculty of finding out people's addresses. It went hard with Ann Eliza to trust her secret even to the mild ear of Mrs. Hawkins, but at least she was spared the cross-examination to which the dress-maker would have subjected her. The accumulating pressure of domestic cares had so crushed in Mrs. Hawkins any curiosity concerning the affairs of others that she received her visitor's confidence with an almost masculine indifference, while she rocked her teething baby on one arm and with the other tried to check the acrobatic impulses of the next in age.

"My, my," she simply said as Ann Eliza ended. "Keep still now, Arthur: Miss Bunner don't want you to jump up and down on her foot to-day. And what are you gaping at, Johnny? Run right off and play," she added, turning sternly to her eldest, who, because he was the least naughty, usually bore the brunt of her wrath against the others.

"Well, perhaps Mr. Hawkins can help you," Mrs. Hawkins continued meditatively, while the children, after scattering at her bidding, returned to their previous pursuits like flies settling down on the spot from which an exasperated hand has swept them. "I'll send him right round the minute he comes in, and you can tell him the whole story. I wouldn't wonder but what he can find that Mrs. Hochmüller's address in the d'rectory. I know they've got one where he works."

"I'd be real thankful if he could," Ann Eliza murmured, rising from her seat with the factitious sense of lightness that comes from imparting a long-hidden dread.

§ 10

Mr. Hawkins proved himself worthy of his wife's faith in his capacity. He learned from Ann Eliza as much as she could tell him about Mrs. Hochmüller and returned the next evening with a scrap of paper bearing her address, beneath which Johnny (the family scribe) had written in a large round hand the names of the streets that led there from the ferry.

Ann Eliza lay awake all that night, repeating over and over again the directions Mr. Hawkins had given her. He was a kind man, and she knew he would willingly have gone with her to Hoboken; indeed she read in his timid eye the half-formed intention of offering to accompany her—but on such an errand she preferred to go alone.

The next Sunday, accordingly, she set out early, and without much trouble found her way to the ferry. Nearly a year had passed since her previous visit to Mrs. Hochmüller, and a chilly April breeze smote her face as she stepped on the boat. Most of the passengers were huddled together in the cabin, and Ann Eliza shrank into its obscurest corner, shivering under the thin black mantle which had seemed so hot in July. She began to feel a little bewildered as she stepped ashore, but a paternal policeman put her into the right car, and as in a dream she found herself retracing the way to Mrs. Hochmüller's door. She had told the conductor the name of the street at which she wished to get out, and presently she stood in the biting wind at the corner near the beer-saloon, where the sun had once beat down on her so fiercely. At length an empty car appeared, its yellow flank emblazoned with the name of Mrs. Hochmüller's suburb, and Ann Eliza was presently jolting past the narrow brick houses islanded between vacant lots like giant piles in a desolate lagoon. When the car reached the end of its journey she got out and stood for some time trying to remember which turn Mr. Ramy had taken. She had just made up her mind to ask the cab-driver when he shook the reins on the backs of his lean horses, and the car, still empty, jogged away toward Hoboken.

Ann Eliza, left alone by the roadside, began to move cautiously forward, looking about for a small red house with a gable overhung by an elm-tree; but everything about her seemed unfamiliar and forbidding. One or two surly looking men slouched past with inquisitive glances, and she could not make up her mind to stop and speak to them.

At length a tow-headed boy came out of a swinging door suggestive of illicit conviviality, and to him Ann Eliza ventured to confide her difficulty. The offer of five cents fired him with an instant willingness to lead her to Mrs. Hochmüller, and he was soon trotting past the stone-cutter's yard with Ann Eliza in his wake.

Another turn in the road brought them to the little red house, and having rewarded her guide, Ann Eliza unlatched the gate and walked up to the door. Her heart was beating violently, and she had to lean against the door-post to compose her twitching lips: she had not known till that moment how much it was going to hurt her to speak of Evelina to Mrs. Hochmüller. As her agitation subsided she began to notice how much the appearance of the house had changed. It was not only that winter had stripped the elm, and blackened the flower-borders: the house itself had a debased and deserted air. The window-panes were cracked and dirty, and one or two shutters swung dismally on loosened hinges.

She rang several times before the door was opened. At length an Irish woman with a shawl over her head and a baby in her arms appeared on the threshold, and glancing past her into the narrow passage Ann Eliza saw that Mrs. Hochmüller's neat abode had deteriorated as much within as without.

At the mention of the name the woman stared. "Mrs. who, did ye say?"

"Mrs. Hochmüller. This is surely her house?"

"No, it ain't neither," said the woman turning away.

"Oh, but wait, please," Ann Eliza entreated. "I can't be mistaken. I mean the Mrs. Hochmüller who takes in washing. I came out to see her last June."

"Oh, the Dutch washerwoman is it—her that used to live here?

She's been gone two months and more. It's Mike McNulty lives here now. Whisht!" to the baby, who had squared his mouth for a howl.

Ann Eliza's knees grew weak. "Mrs. Hochmüller gone? But where has she gone? She must be somewhere round here. Can't you tell me?"

"Sure an' I can't," said the woman. "She wint away before iver we come."

"Dalia Geoghegan, will ye bring the choild in out av the cowld?" cried an irate voice from within.

"Please wait—oh, please wait," Ann Eliza insisted. "You see I must find Mrs. Hochmüller."

"Why don't ye go and look for her thin?" the woman returned, slamming the door in her face.

She stood motionless on the door-step dazed by the immensity of her disappointment, till a burst of loud voices inside the house drove her down the path and out of the gate.

Even then she could not grasp what had happened, and pausing in the road she looked back at the house, half hoping that Mrs. Hochmüller's once detested face might appear at one of the grimy windows.

She was roused by an icy wind that seemed to spring up suddenly from the desolate scene, piercing her thin dress like gauze; and turning away she began to retrace her steps. She thought of enquiring for Mrs. Hochmüller at some of the neighbouring houses, but their look was so unfriendly that she walked on without making up her mind at which door to ring. When she reached the horse-car terminus a car was just moving off toward Hoboken, and for nearly an hour she had to wait on the corner in the bitter wind. Her hands and feet were stiff with cold when the car at length loomed into sight again, and she thought of stopping somewhere on the way to the ferry for a cup of tea; but before the region of lunch-rooms was reached she had grown so sick and dizzy that the thought of food was repulsive. At length she found herself on the ferry-boat, in the soothing stuffiness of the crowded cabin; then came another interval of shivering on a street-corner, another long jolting journey in a "cross-town" car that smelt of damp straw and tobacco; and lastly, in the cold spring dusk, she unlocked her door and groped her way through the shop to her fireless bedroom.

The next morning Mrs. Hawkins, dropping in to hear the result of the trip, found Ann Eliza sitting behind the counter wrapped in an old shawl.

"Why, Miss Bunner, you're sick! You must have fever—your face is just as red!"

"It's nothing. I guess I caught cold yesterday on the ferry-boat," Ann Eliza acknowledged.

"And it's jest like a vault in here!" Mrs. Hawkins rebuked her. "Let me feel your hand—it's burning. Now, Miss Bunner, you've got to go right to bed this very minute."

"Oh, but I can't, Mrs. Hawkins." Ann Eliza attempted a wan smile. "You forget there ain't nobody but me to tend the store."

"I guess you won't tend it long neither, if you ain't careful," Mrs. Hawkins grimly rejoined. Beneath her placid exterior she cherished a morbid passion for disease and death, and the sight of Ann Eliza's suffering had roused her from her habitual indifference. "There ain't so many folks comes to the store anyhow," she went on with unconscious cruelty, "and I'll go right up and see if Miss Mellins can't spare one of her girls."

Ann Eliza, too weary to resist, allowed Mrs. Hawkins to put her to bed and make a cup of tea over the stove, while Miss Mellins, always good-naturedly responsive to any appeal for help, sent down the weak-eyed little girl to deal with hypothetical customers.

Ann Eliza, having so far abdicated her independence, sank into sudden apathy. As far as she could remember, it was the first time in her life that she had been taken care of instead of taking care, and there was a momentary relief in the surrender. She swallowed the tea like an obedient child, allowed a poultice to be applied to her aching chest and uttered no protest when a fire was kindled in the rarely used grate; but as Mrs. Hawkins bent over to "settle" her pillows she raised herself on her elbow to whisper: "Oh, Mrs. Hawkins, Mrs. Hochmüller warn't there." The tears rolled down her cheeks.

"She warn't there? Has she moved?"

"Over two months ago—and they don't know where she's gone. Oh what'll I do, Mrs. Hawkins?"

"There, there, Miss Bunner. You lay still and don't fret. I'll ask Mr. Hawkins soon as ever he comes home."

Ann Eliza murmured her gratitude, and Mrs. Hawkins, bending down, kissed her on the forehead. "Don't you fret," she repeated, in the voice with which she soothed her children.

For over a week Ann Eliza lay in bed, faithfully nursed by her two neighbours, while the weak-eyed child, and the pale sewing girl who had helped to finish Evelina's wedding dress, took turns in minding the shop. Every morning, when her friends appeared, Ann Eliza lifted her head to ask: "Is there a letter?" and at their gentle negative sank back in silence. Mrs. Hawkins, for several days, spoke no more of her promise to consult her husband as to the best way of tracing Mrs. Hochmüller; and dread of fresh disappointment kept Ann Eliza from bringing up the subject.

But the following Sunday evening, as she sat for the first time bolstered up in her rocking-chair near the stove, while Miss Mellins studied the *Police Gazette* beneath the lamp, there came a knock on the shop-door and Mr. Hawkins entered.

Ann Eliza's first glance at his plain friendly face showed her he had news to give, but though she no longer attempted to hide her anxiety from Miss Mellins, her lips trembled too much to let her speak.

"Good evening, Miss Bunner," said Mr. Hawkins in his dragging voice. "I've been over to Hoboken all day looking round for Mrs. Hochmüller."

"Oh, Mr. Hawkins—you *have?*"

"I made a through search, but I'm sorry to say it was no use. She's left Hoboken—moved clear away, and nobody seems to know where."

"It was real good of you, Mr. Hawkins." Ann Eliza's voice struggled up in a faint whisper through the submerging tide of her disappointment.

Mr. Hawkins, in his embarrassed sense of being the bringer of bad news, stood before her uncertainly; then he turned to go. "No trouble at all," he paused to assure her from the doorway.

She wanted to speak again, to detain him, to ask him to advise her; but the words caught in her throat and she lay back silent.

The next day she got up early, and dressed and bonneted herself with twitching fingers. She waited till the weak-eyed child appeared, and having laid on her minute instructions as to the care of the shop, she slipped out into the street. It had occurred to her in one of the weary watches of the previous night that she might go to Tiffany's and make enquiries about Ramy's past. Possibly in that way she might obtain some information that would suggest a new way of reaching Evelina. She was guiltily aware that Mrs. Hawkins and Miss Mellins would be angry with her for venturing out of doors, but she knew she should never feel any better till she had news of Evelina.

The morning air was sharp, and as she turned to face the wind she felt so weak and unsteady that she wondered if she should ever get as far as Union Square; but by walking very slowly, and standing still now and then when she could do so without being noticed, she found herself at last before the jeweller's great glass doors.

It was still so early that there were no purchasers in the shop, and she felt herself the centre of innumerable unemployed eyes as she moved forward between long lines of show-cases glittering with diamonds and silver.

She was glancing about in the hope of finding the clock-department without having to approach one of the impressive gentlemen who paced the empty aisles, when she attracted the attention of one of the most impressive of the number.

The formidable benevolence with which he enquired what he could do for her made her almost despair of explaining herself; but she finally disentangled from a flurry of wrong beginnings the request to be shown to the clock-department.

The gentleman considered her thoughtfully. "May I ask what style of clock you are looking for? Would it be for a wedding-present, or—"

The irony of the illusion filled Ann Eliza's veins with sudden strength. "I don't want to buy a clock at all. I want to see the head of the department."

"Mr. Loomis?" His stare still weighed her—then he seemed to brush aside the problem she presented as beneath his notice. "Oh, certainly. Take the elevator to the second floor. Next aisle to the left." He waved her down the endless perspective of show-cases.

Ann Eliza followed the line of his lordly gesture, and a swift ascent brought her to a great hall full of the buzzing and booming of thousands of clocks. Whichever way she looked, clocks stretched away from her in glittering interminable vistas: clocks of all sizes and voices, from the bell-throated giant of the hallway to the chirping dressing-table toy; tall clocks of mahogany and brass with cathedral chimes; clocks of bronze, glass, porcelain, of every possible size, voice and configuration; and between their serried ranks, along the polished floor of the aisles, moved the languid forms of other gentlemanly floor-walkers, waiting for their duties to begin.

One of them soon approached, and Ann Eliza repeated her request. He received it affably.

"Mr. Loomis? Go right down to the office at the other end." He pointed to a kind of box of ground glass and highly polished panelling.

As she thanked him he turned to one of his companions and said something in which she caught the name of Mr. Loomis, and which was received with an appreciative chuckle. She suspected herself of being the object of the pleasantry, and straightened her thin shoulders under her mantle.

The door of the office stood open, and within sat a gray-bearded man at a desk. He looked up kindly, and again she asked for Mr. Loomis.

"I'm Mr. Loomis. What can I do for you?"

He was much less portentous than the others, though she guessed him to be above them in authority; and encouraged by his tone she seated herself on the edge of the chair he waved her to.

"I hope you'll excuse my troubling you, sir. I came to ask if you could tell me anything about Mr. Herman Ramy. He was employed here in the clock-department two or three years ago."

Mr. Loomis showed no recognition of the name.

"Ramy? When was he discharged?"

"I don't har'ly know. He was very sick, and when he got well his place had been filled. He married my sister last October and they went to St. Louis, I ain't had any news of them for over two months, and she's my only sister, and I'm most crazy worrying about her."

"I see." Mr. Loomis reflected. "In what capacity was Ramy employed here?" he asked after a moment.

"He—he told us that he was one of the heads of the clock-department," Ann Eliza stammered, overswept by a sudden doubt.

"That was probably a slight exaggeration. But I can tell you about him by referring to our books. The name again?"

"Ramy—Herman Ramy."

There ensued a long silence, broken only by the flutter of leaves as Mr. Loomis turned over his ledgers. Presently he looked up, keeping his finger between the pages.

"Here it is—Herman Ramy. He was one of our ordinary workmen, and left us three years and a half ago last June."

"On account of sickness?" Ann Eliza faltered.

Mr. Loomis appeared to hesitate; then he said: "I see no mention of sickness." Ann Eliza felt his compassionate eyes on her again. "Perhaps I'd better tell you the truth. He was discharged for drug-taking. A capable workman, but we couldn't keep him straight. "I'm sorry to have to tell you this, but it seems fairer, since you say you're anxious about your sister."

The polished sides of the office vanished from Ann Eliza's sight, and the cackle of the innumerable clocks came to her like the yell of waves in a storm. She tried to speak but could not; tried to get to her feet, but the floor was gone.

"I'm very sorry," Mr. Loomis repeated, closing the ledger. "I remember the man perfectly now. He used to disappear every now and then, and turn up again in a state that made him useless for days."

As she listened, Ann Eliza recalled the day when she had come on Mr. Ramy sitting in abject dejection behind his counter. She saw again the blurred unrecognizing eyes he had raised to her, the layer of dust over everything in the shop, and the green bronze clock in the window representing a Newfoundland dog with his paw on a book. She stood up slowly.

"Thank you. I'm sorry to have troubled you."

"It was no trouble. You say Ramy married your sister last October?"

"Yes, sir; and they went to St. Louis right afterward. I don't know how to find her. I thought maybe somebody here might know about him."

"Well, possibly some of the workmen might. Leave me your name and I'll send you word if I get on his track."

He handed her a pencil, and she wrote down her address; then she walked away blindly between the clocks.

§ 11

Mr. Loomis, true to his word, wrote a few days later that he had enquired in vain in the work-shop for any news of Ramy; and as she folded this letter and laid it between the leaves of her Bible, Ann Eliza felt that her last hope was gone. Miss Mellins, of course, had long since suggested the mediation of the police, and cited from her favourite literature convincing instances of the supernatural ability of the Pinkerton detective; but Mr. Hawkins, when called in council, dashed this project by remarking that detectives cost something like twenty dollars a day; and a vague fear of the law, some half-formed vision of Evelina in the clutch of a blue-coated "officer," kept Ann Eliza from invoking the aid of the police.

After the arrival of Mr. Loomis's note the weeks followed each other uneventfully. Ann Eliza's cough clung to her till late in the spring, the reflection in her looking-glass grew more bent and meagre, and her forehead sloped back farther toward the twist of hair that was fastened above her parting by a comb of black India-rubber.

Toward spring a lady who was expecting a baby took up her abode at the Mendoza Family Hotel, and through the friendly intervention of Miss Mellins the making of some of the baby-clothes was entrusted to Ann Eliza. This eased her of anxiety for the immediate future; but she had to rouse herself to feel any sense of relief. Her personal welfare was what least concerned her. Sometimes she thought of giving up the shop altogether; and only the fear that, if she changed her address, Evelina might not be able to find her, kept her from carrying out this plan.

Since she had lost her last hope of tracing her sister, all the activities of her lonely imagination had been concentrated on the possibility of Evelina's coming back to her. The discovery of Ramy's secret filled her with dreadful fears. In the solitude of the shop and the back room she was tortured by vague pictures of Evelina's sufferings. What horrors might not be hidden beneath her silence? Ann Eliza's great dread was that Miss Mellins should worm out of her what she had learned from Mr. Loomis. She was sure Miss Mellins must have abominable things to tell about drug-fiends—things she did not have the strength to hear. "Drug-fiend"—the very word was Satanic: she could hear Miss Mellins roll it on her tongue. But Ann Eliza's own imagination, left to itself, had begun to people the long hours with evil visions. Sometimes, in the night, she thought she heard herself called: the voice was her sister's, but faint with a nameless terror. Her most peaceful moments were those in which she managed to convince herself that Evelina was dead. She thought of her then, mournfully but more calmly, as thrust away under the neglected mound of some unknown cemetery, where no headstone marked her name, no mourner with flowers for another grave paused in pity to lay a blossom on hers. But this vision did not often give Ann Eliza its negative relief: and always, beneath its hazy lines, lurked the dark conviction that Evelina was alive, in misery and longing for her.

So the summer wore on. Ann Eliza was conscious that Mrs. Hawkins and Miss Mellins were watching her with affectionate anxiety, but the knowledge brought no comfort. She no longer cared what they felt or thought about her. Her grief lay far beyond touch of human healing, and after a while she became aware that they knew they could not help her. They still came in as often as their busy lives permitted, but their visits grew shorter, and Mrs. Hawkins always brought Arthur or the baby, so that there should be something to talk about, and some one whom she could scold.

The autumn came, and the winter. Business had fallen off again, and but few purchasers came to the little shop in the basement. In January Ann Eliza pawned her mother's cashmere scarf, her mosaic brooch, and the rosewood what-not on which the clock had always stood; she would have sold the bedstead too, but for the persistent vision of Evelina returning weak and weary, and not knowing where to lay her head.

The winter passed in its turn, and March reappeared with its galaxies of yellow jonquils at the windy street corners, reminding Ann Eliza of the spring day when Evelina had come home with a bunch of jonquils in her hand. In spite of the flowers which lent such a premature brightness to the streets the month was fierce and stormy, and Ann Eliza could get no warmth into her bones. Nevertheless, she was insensibly beginning to take up the healing routine of life. Little by little she had grown used to being alone, she had begun to take a languid interest in the one or two new purchasers the season had brought, and though the thought of Evelina was as poignant as ever, it was less persistently in the foreground of her mind.

Late one afternoon she was sitting behind the counter, wrapped in her shawl, and wondering how soon she might draw down the blinds and retreat into the comparative cosiness of the back room. She was not thinking of anything in particular, except perhaps in a hazy way of the lady with the puffed sleeves, who after her long eclipse had reappeared the day before in sleeves of a new cut, and bought some tape and needles. The lady still wore mourning, but she was evidently lightening it, and Ann Eliza saw in this the hope of future orders. The lady had left the shop about an hour before, walking away with her graceful step toward Fifth Avenue. She had wished Ann Eliza good day in her usual affable way, and Ann Eliza thought how odd it was that they should have been acquainted so long, and yet that she should not know the lady's name. From this consideration her mind wandered to the cut of the lady's new sleeves, and she was vexed with herself for not having noted it more carefully. She felt Miss Mellins might have liked to know about it. Ann Eliza's powers of observation had never been as keen as Evelina's, when the latter was not too self-absorbed to exert them. As Miss Mellins always said, Evelina could "take patterns with her eyes": she could have cut that new sleeve out of a folded newspaper in a trice! Musing on these things, Ann Eliza wished the lady would come back and give her another look at the sleeve. It was not unlikely that she might pass that way, for she certainly lived in or about the Square. Suddenly Ann Eliza remarked a small neat handkerchief on the counter: it must have dropped from the lady's purse, and she would probably come back to get it. Ann Eliza, pleased at the idea, sat on behind the counter and watched the darkening street. She always lit the gas as late as possible, keeping the box of matches at her elbow, so that if any one came she could apply a quick flame to the gas-jet. At length through the deepening dusk she distinguished a slim dark figure coming down the steps to the shop. With a little warmth of pleasure about her heart she reached up to light the gas. "I do believe I'll ask her name this time," she thought. She raised the flame to its full height, and saw her sister standing in the door.

There she was at last, the poor pale shade of Evelina, her thin face blanched of its faint pink, the stiff ripples gone from her hair, and a mantle shabbier than Ann Eliza's drawn about her narrow shoulders. The glare of the gas beat full on her as she stood and looked at Ann Eliza.

"Sister—oh, Evelina! I knowed you'd come!"

Ann Eliza had caught her close with a long moan of triumph. Vague words poured from her as she laid her cheek against Evelina's —trivial inarticulate endearments caught from Mrs. Hawkins's long discourses to her baby.

For a while Evelina let herself be passively held; then she drew back from her sister's clasp and looked about the shop. "I'm dead tired. Ain't there any fire?" she asked.

"Of course there is!" Ann Eliza, holding her hand fast, drew her into the back room. She did not want to ask any questions yet: she simply wanted to feel the emptiness of the room brimmed full again by the one presence that was warmth and light to her.

She knelt down before the grate, scraped some bits of coal and kindling from the bottom of the coal-scuttle, and drew one of the rocking-chairs up to the weak flame. "There—that'll blaze up in a minute," she said. She pressed Evelina down on the faded cushions of the rocking-chair, and kneeling beside her, began to rub her hands.

"You're stone-cold, ain't you? Just sit still and warm yourself while I run and get the kettle. I've got something you always used to fancy for supper." She laid her hand on Evelina's shoulder. "Don't talk—oh, don't talk yet!" she implored. She wanted to keep that one frail second of happiness between herself and what she knew must come.

Evelina, without a word, bent over the fire, stretching her thin hands to the blaze and watching Ann Eliza fill the kettle and set the supper table. Her gaze had the dreamy fixity of a half-awakened child's.

Ann Eliza, with a smile of triumph, brought a slice of custard pie from the cupboard and put it by her sister's plate.

"You do like that, don't you? Miss Mellins sent it down to me this morning. She had her aunt from Brooklyn to dinner. Ain't it funny it just so happened?"

"I ain't hungry," said Evelina, rising to approach the table.

She sat down in her usual place, looked about her with the same wondering stare, and then, as of old, poured herself out the first cup of tea.

"Where's the what-not gone to?" she suddenly asked.

Ann Eliza set down the teapot and rose to get a spoon from the cupboard. With her back to the room she said: "The what-not? Why, you see, dearie, living here all alone by myself it only made one more thing to dust; so I sold it."

Evelina's eyes were still travelling about the familiar room. Though it was against all the traditions of the Bunner family to sell any household possession, she showed no surprise at her sister's answer.

"And the clock? The clock's gone too."

"Oh, I gave that away—I gave it to Mrs. Hawkins. She's kep' awake so nights with that last baby."

"I wish you'd never bought it," said Evelina harshly.

Ann Eliza's heart grew faint with fear. Without answering, she crossed over to her sister's seat and poured her out a second cup of tea. Then another thought struck her, and she went back to the cupboard and took out the cordial. In Evelina's absence considerable draughts had been drawn from it by invalid neighbours; but a glassful of the precious liquid still remained.

"Here, drink this right off—it'll warm you up quicker than anything," Ann Eliza said.

Evelina obeyed, and a slight spark of colour came into her cheeks. She turned to the custard pie and began to eat with a silent voracity distressing to watch. She did not even look to see what was left for Ann Eliza.

"I ain't hungry," she said at last as she laid down her fork. "I'm only so dead tired—that's the trouble."

"Then you'd better get right into bed. Here's my old plaid dressing-gown—you remember it, don't you?" Ann Eliza laughed, recalling Evelina's ironies on the subject of the antiquated garment. With trembling fingers she began to undo her sister's cloak. The dress beneath it told a tale of poverty that Ann Eliza dared not pause to note. She drew it gently off, and as it slipped from Evelina's shoulders it revealed a tiny black bag hanging on a ribbon about her neck. Evelina lifted her hand as though to screen the bag from Ann Eliza; and the elder sister, seeing the gesture, continued her task with lowered eyes. She undressed Evelina as quickly as she could, and wrapping her in the plaid dressing-gown put her to bed, and spread her own shawl and her sister's cloak above the blanket.

"Where's the old red comfortable?" Evelina asked, as she sank down on the pillow.

"The comfortable? Oh, it was so hot and heavy I never used it after you went—so I sold that too. I never could sleep under much clothes."

She became aware that her sister was looking at her more attentively.

"I guess you've been in trouble too," Evelina said.

"Me? In trouble? What do you mean, Evelina?"

"You've had to pawn the things, I suppose," Evelina continued in a weary unmoved tone. "Well, I've been through worse than that. I've been to hell and back."

"Oh, Evelina—don't say it, sister!" Ann Eliza implored, shrinking from the unholy word. She knelt down and began to rub her sister's feet beneath the bed-clothes.

"I've been to hell and back—if I *am* back," Evelina repeated. She lifted her head from the pillow and began to talk with a sudden feverish volubility. "It began right away, less than a month after we were married. I've been in hell all that time, Ann Eliza." She fixed her eyes with passionate intentness on Ann Eliza's face. "He took opium. I didn't find it out till long afterward—at first, when he acted so strange, I thought he drank. But it was worse, much worse than drinking."

"Oh, sister, don't say it—don't say it yet! It's so sweet just to have you here with me again."

"I must say it," Evelina insisted, her flushed face burning with a kind of bitter cruelty. "You don't know what life's like—you don't know anything about it—setting here safe all the while in this peaceful place."

"Oh, Evelina—why didn't you write and send for me if it was like that?"

"That's why I couldn't write. Didn't you guess I was ashamed?"

"How could you be? Ashamed to write to Ann Eliza?"

Evelina raised herself on her thin elbow, while Ann Eliza, bending over, drew a corner of the shawl about her shoulder.

"Do lay down again. You'll catch your death."

"My death? That don't frighten me! You don't know what I've been through." And sitting upright in the old mahogany bed, with flushed cheeks and chattering teeth, and Ann Eliza's trembling arm clasping the shawl about her neck, Evelina poured out her story. It was a tale of misery and humiliation so remote from the elder sister's innocent experiences that much of it was hardly intelligible to her. Evelina's dreadful familiarity with it all, her fluency about things which Ann Eliza half-guessed and quickly shuddered back from, seemed even more alien and terrible than the actual tale she told. It was one thing—and heaven knew it was bad enough!—to learn that one's sister's husband was a drug-fiend; it was another, and much worse thing, to learn from that sister's pallid lips what vileness lay behind the word.

Evelina, unconscious of any distress but her own, sat upright, shivering in Ann Eliza's hold, while she piled up, detail by detail, her dreary narrative.

"The minute we got out there, and he found the job wasn't as good as he expected, he changed. At first I thought he was sick—I used to try to keep him home and nurse him. Then I saw it was something different. He used to go off for hours at a time, and when he came back his eyes kinder had a fog over them. Sometimes he didn't har'ly know me, and when he did he seemed to hate me. Once he hit me here," She touched her breast. "Do you remember, Ann Eliza, that time he didn't come to see us for a week—the time after we all went to Central Park together—and you and I thought he must be sick?"

Ann Eliza nodded.

"Well, that was the trouble—he'd been at it then. But nothing like as bad. After we'd been out there about a month he disappeared for a whole week. They took him back at the store, and gave him another chance; but the second time they discharged him, and he drifted round for ever so long before he could get another job. We spent all our money and had to move to a cheaper place. Then he got something to do, but they hardly paid him anything, and he didn't stay there long. When he found out about the baby—"

"The baby?" Ann Eliza faltered.

"It's dead—it only lived a day. When he found out about it, he got mad, and said he hadn't any money to pay doctors' bills, and I'd better write to you to help us. He had an idea you had money hidden away that I didn't know about." She turned to her sister with remorseful eyes. "It was him that made me get that hundred dollars out of you."

"Hush, hush. I always meant it for you anyhow."

"Yes, but I wouldn't have taken it if he hadn't been at me the whole time. He used to make me do just what he wanted. Well, when I said I wouldn't write to you for more money he said I'd better try and earn some myself. That was when he struck me. . . . Oh, you don't know what I'm talking about yet! . . . I tried to get work at a milliner's, but I was so sick I couldn't stay. I was sick all the time. I wisht I'd ha' died, Ann Eliza."

"No, no, Evelina."

"Yes, I do. It kept getting worse and worse. We pawned the furniture, and they turned us out because we couldn't pay the rent; and so then we went to board with Mrs. Hochmüller."

Ann Eliza pressed her closer to dissemble her own tremor. "Mrs. Hochmüller?"

"Didn't you know she was out there? She moved out a month after we did. She wasn't bad to me, and I think she tried to keep him straight—but Linda—"

"Linda—?"

"Well, when I kep' getting worse, and he was always off, for days at a time, the doctor had me sent to a hospital."

"A hospital? Sister—sister!"

"It was better than being with him; and the doctors were real kind to me. After the baby was born I was very sick and had to stay there a good while. And one day when I was laying there Mrs. Hochmüller came in as white as a sheet, and told me him and Linda had gone off together and taken all her money. That's the last I ever saw of him." She broke off with a laugh and began to cough again.

Ann Eliza tried to persuade her to lie down and sleep, but the rest of her story had to be told before she could be soothed into consent. After the news of Ramy's flight she had had brain fever, and had been sent to another hospital where she stayed a long time—how long she couldn't remember. Dates and days meant nothing to her in the shapeless ruin of her life. When she left the hospital she found that Mrs. Hochmüller had gone too. She was penniless, and had no one to turn to. A lady visitor at the hospital was kind, and found her a place where she did housework; but she was so weak they couldn't keep her. Then she got a job as waitress in a down-town lunch-room, but one day she fainted while she was handing a dish, and that evening when they paid her they told her she needn't come again.

"After that I begged in the streets"—(Ann Eliza's grasp again grew tight)—"and one afternoon last week, when the matinées was coming out, I met a man with a pleasant face, something like Mr. Hawkins, and he stopped and asked me what the trouble was. I told him if he'd give me five dollars I'd have money enough to buy a ticket back to New York, and he took a good look at me and said, well, if that was what I wanted he'd go straight to the station with me and give me the five dollars there. So he did—and he bought the ticket, and put me in the cars."

Evelina sank back, her face a sallow wedge in the white cleft of the pillow. Ann Eliza leaned over her, and for a long time they held each other without speaking.

They were still clasped in this dumb embrace when there was a step in the shop and Ann Eliza, starting up, saw Miss Mellins in the doorway.

"My sakes, Miss Bunner! What in the land are you doing? Miss Evelina—Mrs. Ramy—it ain't you?"

Miss Mellins's eyes, bursting from their sockets, sprang from Evelina's pallid face to the disordered supper table and the heap of worn clothes on the floor; then they turned back to Ann Eliza, who had placed herself on the defensive between her sister and the dressmaker.

"My sister Evelina has come back—come back on a visit. She was taken sick in the cars on the way home—I guess she caught cold—so I made her go right to bed as soon as ever she got here."

Ann Eliza was surprised at the strength and steadiness of her voice. Fortified by its sound she went on, her eyes on Miss Mellins's baffled countenance: "Mr. Ramy has gone west on a trip—a trip connected with his business; and Evelina is going to stay with me till he comes back."

§ 12

What measure of belief her explanation of Evelina's return obtained in the small circle of her friends Ann Eliza did not pause to enquire. Though she could not remember ever having told a lie before, she adhered with rigid tenacity to the consequences of her first lapse from truth, and fortified her original statement with additional details whenever a questioner sought to take her unawares.

But other and more serious burdens lay on her startled conscience. For the first time in her life she dimly faced the awful problem of the inutility of self-sacrifice. Hitherto she had never thought of questioning the inherited principles which had guided her life. Self-effacement for the good of others had always seemed to her both natural and necessary; but then she had taken it for granted that it implied the securing of that good. Now she perceived that to refuse the gifts of life does not ensure their transmission to those for whom they have been surrendered; and her familiar heaven was unpeopled. She felt she could no longer trust in the goodness of God, and that if he was not good he was not God, and there was only a black abyss above the roof of Bunner Sisters.

But there was little time to brood upon such problems. The care of Evelina filled Ann Eliza's days and nights. The hastily summoned doctor had pronounced her to be suffering from pneumonia, and under his care the first stress of the disease was relieved. But her recovery was only partial, and long after the doctor's visits had ceased she continued to lie in bed, too weak to move, and seemingly indifferent to everything about her.

At length one evening, about six weeks after her return, she said to her sister: "I don't feel's if I'd ever get up again."

Ann Eliza turned from the kettle she was placing on the stove. She was startled by the echo the words woke in her own breast.

"Don't you talk like that, Evelina! I guess you're on'y tired out—and disheartened."

"Yes, I'm disheartened," Evelina murmured.

A few months earlier Ann Eliza would have met the confession with a word of pious admonition; now she accepted it in silence.

"Maybe you'll brighten up when your cough gets better," she suggested.

"Yes—or my cough'll get better when I brighten up," Evelina retorted with a touch of her old tartness.

"Does your cough keep on hurting you jest as much?"

"I don't see's there's much difference."

"Well, I guess I'll get the doctor to come round again," Ann Eliza said, trying for the matter-of-course tone in which one might speak of sending for the plumber or the gas-fitter.

"It ain't any use sending for the doctor—and who's going to pay him?"

"I am," answered the elder sister. "Here's your tea, and a mite of toast. Don't that tempt you?"

Already, in the watches of the night, Ann Eliza had been tormented by that same question—who was to pay the doctor?—and a few days before she had temporarily silenced it by borrowing twenty dollars of Miss Mellins. The transaction had cost her one of the bitterest struggles of her life. She had never borrowed a penny of any one before, and the possiblity of having to do so had always been classed in her mind among those shameful extremities to which Providence does not let decent people come. But nowadays she no longer believed in the personal supervision of Providence; and had she been compelled to steal the money instead of borrowing it, she would have felt that her conscience was the only tribunal before which she had to answer. Nevertheless, the actual humiliation of having to ask for the money was no less bitter; and she could hardly hope that Miss Mellins would view the case with the same detachment as herself. Miss Mellins was very kind; but she not unnaturally felt that her kindness should be rewarded by according her the right to ask questions; and bit by bit Ann Eliza saw Evelina's miserable secret slipping into the dress-maker's possession.

When the doctor came she left him alone with Evelina, busying herself in the shop that she might have an opportunity of seeing him alone on his way out. To steady herself she began to sort a trayful of buttons, and when the doctor appeared she was reciting under her breath: "Twenty-four horn, two and a half cards fancy pearl. . . ." She saw at once that his look was grave.

He sat down on the chair beside the counter, and her mind travelled miles before he spoke.

"Miss Bunner, the best thing you can do is to let me get a bed for your sister at St. Luke's."

"The hospital?"

"Come now, you're above that sort of prejudice, aren't you?" The doctor spoke in the tone of one who coaxes a spoiled child. "I know how devoted you are—but Mrs. Ramy can be much better cared for there than here. You really haven't time to look after her and attend to your business as well. There'll be no expense, you understand—"

Ann Eliza made no answer. "You think my sister's going to be sick a good while, then?" she asked.

"Well, yes—possibly."

"You think she's very sick?"

"Well, yes. She's very sick."

His face had grown still graver; he sat there as though he had never known what it was to hurry.

Ann Eliza continued to separate the pearl and horn buttons. Suddenly she lifted her eyes and looked at him. "Is she going to die?"

The doctor laid a kindly hand on hers. "We never say that, Miss Bunner. Human skill works wonders—and at the hospital Mrs. Ramy would have every chance."

"What is it? What's she dying of?"

The doctor hesitated, seeking to substitute a popular phrase for the scientific terminology which rose to his lips.

"I want to know," Ann Eliza persisted.

"Yes, of course; I understand. Well, your sister has had a hard time lately, and there is a complication of causes, resulting in consumption—rapid consumption. At the hospital—"

"I'll keep her here," said Ann Eliza quietly.

After the doctor had gone she went on for some time sorting the buttons; then she slipped the tray into its place on a shelf behind the counter and went into the back room. She found Evelina propped upright against the pillows, a flush of agitation on her cheeks. Ann Eliza pulled up the shawl which had slipped from her sister's shoulders.

"How long you've been! What's he been saying?"

"Oh, he went long ago—he on'y stopped to give me a prescription. I was sorting out that tray of buttons. Miss Mellins's girl got them all mixed up."

She felt Evelina's eyes upon her.

"He must have said something: what was it?"

"Why, he said you'd have to be careful—and stay in bed—and take this new medicine he's given you."

"Did he say I was going to get well?"

"Why, Evelina!"

"What's the use, Ann Eliza? You can't deceive me. I've just been up to look at myself in the glass; and I saw plenty of 'em in the hospital that looked like me. They didn't get well, and I ain't going to." Her head dropped back. "It don't much matter—I'm about tired. On'y there's one thing—Ann Eliza—"

The elder sister drew near to the bed.

"There's one thing I ain't told you. I didn't want to tell you yet because I was afraid you might be sorry—but if he says I'm going to die I've got to say it." She stopped to cough, and to Ann Eliza it now seemed as though every cough struck a minute from the hours remaining to her.

"Don't talk now—you're tired."

"I'll be tireder to-morrow, I guess. And I want you should know. Sit down close to me—there."

Ann Eliza sat down in silence, stroking her shrunken hand.

"I'm a Roman Catholic, Ann Eliza."

"Evelina—oh, Evelina Bunner! A Roman Catholic—*you?* Oh, Evelina, did *he* make you?"

Evelina shook her head. "I guess he didn't have no religion; he never spoke of it. But you see Mrs. Hochmüller was a Catholic, and so when I was sick she got the doctor to send me to a Roman Catholic hospital, and the sisters was so good to me there—and the priest used to come and talk to me; and the things he said kep' me from going crazy. He seemed to make everything easier."

"Oh, sister, how could you?" Ann Eliza wailed. She knew little of the Catholic religion except that "Papists" believed in it—in itself a sufficient indictment. Her spiritual rebellion had not freed her from the formal part of her religious belief, and apostasy had always seemed to her one of the sins from which the pure in mind avert their thoughts.

"And then when the baby was born," Evelina continued, "he christened it right away, so it could go to heaven; and after that, you see, I had to be a Catholic."

"I don't see—"

"Don't I have to be where the baby is? I couldn't ever ha' gone there if I hadn't been made a Catholic. Don't you understand that?"

Ann Eliza sat speechless, drawing her hand away. Once more she found herself shut out of Evelina's heart, an exile from her closest affections.

"I've got to go where the baby is," Evelina feverishly insisted.

Ann Eliza could think of nothing to say; she could only feel that Evelina was dying, and dying as a stranger in her arms. Ramy and the day-old baby had parted her forever from her sister.

Evelina began again. "If I get worse I want you to send for a priest. Miss Mellins'll know where to send—she's got an aunt that's a Catholic. Promise me faithful you will."

"I promise," said Ann Eliza.

After that they spoke no more of the matter; but Ann Eliza now understood that the little black bag about her sister's neck, which she had innocently taken for a memento of Ramy, was some kind of sacrilegious amulet, and her fingers shrank from its contact when she bathed and dressed Evelina. It seemed to her the diabolical instrument of the estrangement.

§ 13

Spring had really come at last. There were leaves on the ailanthus-tree that Evelina could see from her bed, gentle clouds floated over it in the blue, and now and then the cry of a flower-seller sounded from the street.

One day there was a shy knock on the back-room door, and Johnny Hawkins came in with two yellow jonquils in his fist. He was getting bigger and squarer, and his round freckled face was growing into a smaller copy of his father's. He walked up to Evelina and held out the flowers.

"They blew off the cart and the fellow said I could keep 'em. But you can have 'em," he announced.

Ann Eliza rose from her seat at the sewing-machine and tried to take the flowers from him.

"They ain't for you; they're for her," he sturdily objected; and Evelina held out her hand for the jonquils.

After Johnny had gone she lay and looked at them without speaking. Ann Eliza, who had gone back to the machine, bent her head over the seam she was stitching; the click, click, click of the machine sounded in her ear like the tick of Ramy's clock, and it seemed to her that life had gone backward, and that Evelina, radiant and foolish, had just come into the room with the yellow flowers in her hand.

When at last she ventured to look up, she saw that her sister's head had drooped against the pillow, and that she was sleeping quietly. Her relaxed hand still held the jonquils, but it was evident that they had awakened no memories; she had dozed off almost as soon as Johnny had given them to her. The discovery gave Ann Eliza a startled sense of the ruins that must be piled upon her past. "I don't believe I could have forgotten that day, though," she said to herself. But she was glad that Evelina had forgotten.

Evelina's disease moved on along the usual course, now lifting her on a brief wave of elation, now sinking her to new depths of weakness. There was little to be done, and the doctor came only at lengthening intervals. On his way out he always repeated his first friendly suggestion about sending Evelina to the hospital; and Ann Eliza always answered: "I guess we can manage."

The hours passed for her with the fierce rapidity that great joy or anguish lends them. She went through the days with a sternly smiling precision, but she hardly knew what was happening, and when night-fall released her from the shop, and she could carry her work to Evelina's bedside, the same sense of unreality accompanied her, and she still seemed to be accomplishing a task whose object had escaped her memory.

Once, when Evelina felt better, she expressed a desire to make some artificial flowers, and Ann Eliza, deluded by this awakening interest, got out the faded bundles of stems and petals and the little tools and spools of wire. But after a few minutes the work dropped from Evelina's hands and she said: "I'll wait till to-morrow."

She never again spoke of the flower-making, but one day, after watching Ann Eliza's laboured attempt to trim a spring hat for Mrs.

Hawkins, she demanded impatiently that the hat should be brought to her, and in a trice had galvanized the lifeless bow and given the brim the twist it needed.

These were rare gleams; and more frequent were the days of speechless lassitude, when she lay for hours silently staring at the window, shaken only by the hard incessant cough that sounded to Ann Eliza like the hammering of nails into a coffin.

At length one morning Ann Eliza, starting up from the mattress at the foot of the bed, hastily called Miss Mellins down, and ran through the smoky dawn for the doctor. He came back with her and did what he could to give Evelina momentary relief; then he went away, promising to look in again before night. Miss Mellins, her head still covered with curl-papers, disappeared in his wake, and when the sisters were alone Evelina beckoned to Ann Eliza.

"You promised," she whispered, grasping her sister's arm; and Ann Eliza understood. She had not yet dared to tell Miss Mellins of Evelina's change of faith; it had seemed even more difficult than borrowing the money; but now it had to be done. She ran upstairs after the dress-maker and detained her on the landing.

"Miss Mellins, can you tell me where to send for a priest—a Roman Catholic priest?"

"A priest, Miss Bunner?"

"Yes. My sister became a Roman Catholic while she was away. They were kind to her in her sickness—and now she wants a priest." Ann Eliza faced Miss Mellins with unflinching eyes.

"My aunt Dugan'll know. I'll run right round to her the minute I get my papers off," the dress-maker promised; and Ann Eliza thanked her.

An hour or two later the priest appeared. Ann Eliza, who was watching, saw him coming down the steps to the shop-door and went to meet him. His expression was kind, but she shrank from his peculiar dress, and from his pale face with its bluish chin and enigmatic smile. Ann Eliza remained in the shop. Miss Mellins's girl had mixed the buttons again and she set herself to sort them. The priest stayed a long time with Evelina. When he again carried his enigmatic smile past the counter, and Ann Eliza rejoined her sister, Evelina was smiling with something of the same mystery; but she did not tell her secret.

After that it seemed to Ann Eliza that the shop and the back room no longer belonged to her. It was as though she were there on sufferance, indulgently tolerated by the unseen power which hovered over Evelina even in the absence of its minister. The priest came almost daily; and at last a day arrived when he was called to administer some rite of which Ann Eliza but dimly grasped the sacramental meaning. All she knew was that it meant that Evelina was going, and going, under this alien guidance, even farther from her than to the dark places of death.

When the priest came, with something covered in his hands, she crept into the shop, closing the door of the back room to leave him alone with Evelina.

It was a warm afternoon in May, and the crooked ailanthus-tree rooted in a fissure of the opposite pavement was a fountain of tender green. Women in light dresses passed with the languid step of spring; and presently there came a man with a hand-cart full of pansy and geranium plants who stopped outside the window, signalling to Ann Eliza to buy.

An hour went by before the door of the back room opened and the priest reappeared with that mysterious covered something in his hands. Ann Eliza had risen, drawing back as he passed. He had doubtless divined her antipathy, for he had hitherto only bowed in going in and out; but to-day he paused and looked at her compassionately.

"I have left your sister in a very beautiful state of mind," he said in a low voice like a woman's. "She is full of spiritual consolation."

Ann Eliza was silent, and he bowed and went out. She hastened back to Evelina's bed, and knelt down beside it. Evelina's eyes were very large and bright; she turned them on Ann Eliza with a look of inner illumination.

"I shall see the baby," she said; then her eyelids fell and she dozed.

The doctor came again at nightfall, administering some last palliatives; and after he had gone Ann Eliza, refusing to have her vigil shared by Miss Mellins or Mrs. Hawkins, sat down to keep watch alone.

It was a very quiet night. Evelina never spoke or opened her eyes, but in the still hour before dawn Ann Eliza saw that the restless hand outside the bed-clothes had stopped its twitching. She stooped over and felt no breath on her sister's lips.

The funeral took place three days later. Evelina was buried in Calvary Cemetery, the priest assuming the whole care of the necessary arrangements, while Ann Eliza, a passive spectator, beheld with stony indifference this last negation of her past.

A week afterward she stood in her bonnet and mantle in the doorway of the little shop. Its whole aspect had changed. Counter and shelves were bare, the window was stripped of its familiar miscellany of artificial flowers, note-paper, wire hat-frames, and limp garments from the dyer's; and against the glass pane of the doorway hung a sign: "This store to let."

Ann Eliza turned her eyes from the sign as she went out and locked the door behind her. Evelina's funeral had been very expensive, and Ann Eliza, having sold her stock-in-trade and the few articles of furniture that remained to her, was leaving the shop for the last time. She had not been able to buy any mourning, but Miss Mellins had sewed some crape on her old black mantle and bonnet, and having no gloves she slipped her bare hands under the folds of the mantle.

It was a beautiful morning, and the air was full of a warm sunshine that had coaxed open nearly every window in the street, and summoned to the window-sills the sickly plants nurtured indoors in winter. Ann Eliza's way lay westward, toward Broadway; but at the corner she paused and looked back down the familiar length of the street. Her eyes rested a moment on the blotched "Bunner Sisters" above the empty window of the shop; then they travelled on to the overflowing foliage of the Square, above which was the church tower with the dial that had marked the hours for the sisters before Ann Eliza had bought the nickel clock. She looked at it all as though it had been the scene of some unknown life, of which the vague report had reached her: she felt for herself only the remote pity that busy people accord to the misfortunes which come to them by hearsay.

She walked to Broadway and down to the office of the house-agent to whom she had entrusted the sub-letting of the shop. She left the key with one of his clerks, who took it from her as if it had been any one of a thousand others, and remarked that the weather looked as if spring was really coming; then she turned and began to move up the great thoroughfare, which was just beginning to wake to its multitudinous activities.

She walked less rapidly now, studying each shop window as she passed, but not with the desultory eye of enjoyment: the watchful fixity of her gaze overlooked everything but the object of its quest. At length she stopped before a small window wedged between two mammoth buildings, and displaying, behind its shining plate-glass festooned with muslin, a varied assortment of sofa-cushions, tea-cloths, pen-wipers, painted calendars and other specimens of feminine industry. In a corner of the window she had read, on a slip of paper pasted against the pane: "Wanted, a Saleslady," and after studying the display of fancy articles beneath it, she gave her mantle a twitch, straightened her shoulders and went in.

Behind a counter crowded with pin-cushions, watch-holders and other needle-work trifles, a plump young woman with smooth hair sat sewing bows of ribbon on a scrap basket. The little shop was about the size of the one on which Ann Eliza had just closed the door; and it looked as fresh and gay and thriving as she and Evelina had once dreamed of making Bunner Sisters. The friendly air of the place made her pluck up courage to speak.

"Saleslady? Yes, we do want one. Have you any one to recommend?" the young woman asked, not unkindly.

Ann Eliza hesitated, disconcerted by the unexpected question; and the other, cocking her head on one side to study the effect of the bow she had just sewed on the basket, continued: "We can't afford more than thirty dollars a month, but the work is light. She would be expected to do a little fancy sewing between times. We want a bright girl: stylish, and pleasant manners. You know what I mean. Not over thirty, anyhow; and nice-looking. Will you write down the name?"

Ann Eliza looked at her confusedly. She opened her lips to explain, and then, without speaking, turned toward the crisply-curtained door.

"Ain't you going to leave the *ad*-dress?" the young woman called out after her. Ann Eliza went out into the thronged street. The great city, under the fair spring sky, seemed to throb with the stir of innumerable beginnings. She walked on, looking for another shop window with a sign in it.

PREFATORY NOTE TO "WITH THE TIDE"

Theodore Roosevelt and Edith Wharton were born within a few years of each other into the same New York social milieu that was, in her opinion, so stultifying to any impulse towards the unusual or the exciting. That both managed to transcend it, that both, as one observer was to put it, were "self-made men," was always a bond between them. His opinion that *The Valley of Decision* should have ended democratically with a marriage between duke and commoner amused her, but how many presidents, she must have speculated, would have read her at all? Two days after his death on January 5, 1919 she wrote this tribute.

With the Tide

Somewhere I read, in an old book whose name
Is gone from me, I read that when the days
Of a man are counted, and his business done,
There comes up the shore at evening, with the tide,
To the place where he sits, a boat—
And in the boat, from the place where he sits, he sees,
Dim in the dusk, dim and yet so familiar,
The faces of his friends long dead; and knows,
They come for him, brought in upon the tide,
To take him where men go at set of day.
Then rising, with his hands in theirs, he goes
Between them his last steps, that are the first
Of the new life—and with the ebb they pass,
Their shaken sail grown small upon the moon.

Often I thought of this, and pictured me
How many a man who lives with throngs about him,
Yet straining through the twilight for that boat
Shall scarce make out one figure in the stern,
And that so faint its features shall perplex him
With doubtful memories—and his heart hang back
But others, rising as they see the sail
Increase upon the sunset, hasten down,
Hands out and eyes elated; for they see
Head over head crowding from bow to stern,
Repeopling their loneliness with smiles,
The faces of their friends; and such go forth
Content upon the ebb tide, with safe hearts.

But never
To worker summoned when his day was done
Did mounting tide bring in such freight of friends
As stole to you up the white wintry shingle
That night while they that watched you thought you slept.
Softly they came, and beached the boat, and gathered
In the still cove under the icy stars,
Your last-born, and the dear loves of your heart,
And all men that have loved right more than ease,
And honor above honors; all who gave
Free-handed of their best for other men,
And thought their giving taking: they who knew
Man's natural state is effort, up and up—
All these were there, so great a company
Perchance you marveled, wondering what great ship
Had brought that throng unnumbered to the cove
Where the boys used to beach their light canoe
After old happy picnics—

But these, your friends and children, to whose hands
Committed, in the silent night you rose
And took your last faint steps—
These led you down, O great American,
Down to the Winter night and the white beach,
And there you saw that the huge hull that waited
Was not as are the boats of other dead,
Frail craft for a brief passage; no, for this
Was first of a long line of towering transports,
Storm-worn and ocean-weary every one,
The ships you launched, the ships you manned, the ships
That now, returning from their sacred quest
With the thrice-sacred burden of their dead,
Lay waiting there to take you forth with them,
Out with the ebb tide, on some farther quest.

Hyères, January 7, 1919.

PREFATORY NOTE TO
"THE AGE OF INNOCENCE"

The Age of Innocence could almost be called an historical novel, for it is set in the early 1870s when Mrs. Wharton was still a child. Half a century afterwards, even a memory as sharp as her own had to be bolstered by research, for she wanted every detail of her bright, vivid canvas to be exact. Her industry was fruitful. In no other pages is the social life of the period more surely or vividly evoked. Mrs. Wharton had the skill to delineate characters with the very props that she used for their settings, as Mrs. Archer and her maiden daughter who "cultivated ferns in Wardian cases, made macramé lace and wool embroidery on linen, collected American revolutionary glazed ware, subscribed to 'Good Words,' and read Ouida's novels for the sake of the Italian atmosphere."

Ellen Olenska, in the first half of the novel here included, Book I, has fled from Europe and a vicious titled husband to what seems to her the dear quaint heaven of her native New York. She soon discovers that its knives are as sharp as any in Europe. Newland Archer, the stuffy young man who is engaged to her cousin and who acts as her somewhat compromising champion, learns in his turn that the society which he has admired as brilliant is really provincial. Yet both find that there is integrity under its staidness and loyalty beneath its caution. Newland and Ellen renounce each other at the end of Book I, and Newland marries his fiancée. In Book II the married Newland returns to the pursuit of Ellen, but again renounces her when he discovers that his wife is pregnant. It is simply a variation on the original theme.

FROM *The Age of Innocence*, BOOK I

§ 1

ON A January evening of the early seventies, Christine Nilsson was singing in Faust at the Academy of Music in New York.

Though there was already talk of the erection, in remote metropolitan distances "above the Forties," of a new Opera House which should compete in costliness and splendour with those of the great European capitals, the world of fashion was still content to reassemble every winter in the shabby red and gold boxes of the sociable old Academy. Conservatives cherished it for being small and inconvenient, and thus keeping out the "new people" whom New York was beginning to dread and yet be drawn to; and the sentimental clung to it for its historic associations, and the musical for its excellent acoustics, always so problematic a quality in halls built for the hearing of music.

It was Madame Nilsson's first appearance that winter, and what the daily press had already learned to describe as "an exceptionally brilliant audience" had gathered to hear her, transported through the slippery, snowy streets in private broughams, in the spacious family landau, or in the humbler but more convenient "Brown *coupé*." To come to the Opera in a Brown *coupé* was almost as honourable a way of arriving as in one's own carriage; and departure by the same means had the immense advantage of enabling one (with a playful allusion to democratic principles) to scramble into the first Brown conveyance in the line, instead of waiting till the cold-and-gin congested nose of one's own coachman gleamed under the portico of the Academy. It was one of the great livery-stableman's most masterly intuitions to have discovered that Americans want to get away from amusement even more quickly than they want to get to it.

When Newland Archer opened the door at the back of the club box the curtain had just gone up on the garden scene. There was no reason why the young man should not have come earlier, for he had dined at seven, alone with his mother and sister, and had lingered afterward over a cigar in the Gothic library with glazed black-walnut bookcases and finial-topped chairs which was the only room in the house where Mrs. Archer allowed smoking. But, in the first place, New York was a metropolis, and perfectly aware that in metropolises it was "not the thing" to arrive early at the opera; and what was or was not "the thing" played a part as important in Newland Archer's New York as the inscrutable totem terrors that had ruled the destinies of his forefathers thousands of years ago.

The second reason for his delay was a personal one. He had dawdled over his cigar because he was at heart a dilettante, and thinking over a pleasure to come often gave him a subtler satisfaction than its realisation. This was especially the case when the pleasure was a delicate one, as his pleasures mostly were; and on this occasion the moment he looked forward to was so rare and exquisite in quality that—well, if he had timed his arrival in accord with the prima donna's stage-manager he could not have entered the Academy at a more significant moment than just as she was singing: "He loves me—he loves me not—*he loves me!*" and sprinkling the falling daisy petals with notes as clear as dew.

She sang, of course, *"M'ama!"* and not "he loves me," since an unalterable and unquestioned law of the musical world required that the German text of French operas sung by Swedish artists should be translated into Italian for the clearer understanding of English-speaking audiences. This seemed as natural to Newland Archer as all the other conventions on which his life was moulded: such as the duty of using two silver-backed brushes with his monogram in blue enamel to part his hair, and of never appearing in society without a flower (preferably a gardenia) in his buttonhole.

"M'ama . . . non m'ama . . ." the prima donna sang, and *"M'ama!"*, with a final burst of love triumphant, as she pressed the dishevelled daisy to her lips and lifted her large eyes to the sophisticated countenance of the little brown Faust-Capoul, who was vainly

trying, in a tight purple velvet doublet and plumed cap, to look as pure and true as his artless victim.

Newland Archer, leaning against the wall at the back of the club box, turned his eyes from the stage and scanned the opposite side of the house. Directly facing him was the box of old Mrs. Manson Mingott, whose monstrous obesity had long since made it impossible for her to attend the Opera, but who was always represented on fashionable nights by some of the younger members of the family. On this occasion, the front of the box was filled by her daughter-in-law, Mrs. Lovell Mingott, and her daughter, Mrs. Welland; and slightly withdrawn behind these brocaded matrons sat a young girl in white with eyes ecstatically fixed on the stage-lovers. As Madame Nilsson's *"M'ama!"* thrilled out above the silent house (the boxes always stopped talking during the Daisy Song) a warm pink mounted to the girl's cheek, mantled her brow to the roots of her fair braids, and suffused the young slope of her breast to the line where it met a modest tulle tucker fastened with a single gardenia. She dropped her eyes to the immense bouquet of lilies-of-the-valley on her knee, and Newland Archer saw her white-gloved finger-tips touch the flowers softly. He drew a breath of satisfied vanity and his eyes returned to the stage.

No expense had been spared on the setting, which was acknowledged to be very beautiful even by people who shared his acquaintance with the Opera houses of Paris and Vienna. The foreground, to the footlights, was covered with emerald green cloth. In the middle distance symmetrical mounds of woolly green moss bounded by croquet hoops formed the base of shrubs shaped like orange-trees but studded with large pink and red roses. Gigantic pansies, considerably larger than the roses, and closely resembling the floral penwipers made by female parishioners for fashionable clergymen, sprang from the moss beneath the rose-trees; and here and there a daisy grafted on a rose-branch flowered with a luxuriance prophetic of Mr. Luther Burbank's far-off prodigies.

In the centre of this enchanted garden Madame Nilsson, in white cashmere slashed with pale blue satin, a reticule dangling from a blue girdle, and large yellow braids carefully disposed on each side of her muslin chemisette, listened with downcast eyes to M. Capoul's impassioned wooing, and affected a guileless incomprehension of his designs whenever, by word or glance, he persuasively indicated the ground floor window of the neat brick villa projecting obliquely from the right wing.

"The darling!" thought Newland Archer, his glance flitting back to the young girl with the lilies-of-the-valley. "She doesn't even guess what it's all about." And he contemplated her absorbed young face with a thrill of possessorship in which pride in his own masculine initiation was mingled with a tender reverence for her abysmal purity. "We'll read Faust together . . . by the Italian lakes . . ." he thought, somewhat hazily confusing the scene of his projected honey-moon with the masterpieces of literature which it would be his manly privilege to reveal to his bride. It was only that afternoon that May Welland had let him guess that she "cared" (New York's consecrated phrase of maiden avowal), and already his imagination, leaping ahead of the engagement ring, the betrothal kiss and the march from Lohengrin, pictured her at his side in some scene of old European witchery.

He did not in the least wish the future Mrs. Newland Archer to be a simpleton. He meant her (thanks to his enlightening companionship) to develop a social tact and readiness of wit enabling her to hold her own with the most popular married women of the "younger set," in which it was the recognised custom to attract masculine homage while playfully discouraging it. If he had probed to the bottom of his vanity (as he sometimes nearly did) he would have found there the wish that his wife should be as worldly-wise and as eager to please as the married lady whose charms had held his fancy through two mildly agitated years; without, of course, any hint of the frailty which had so nearly marred that unhappy being's life, and had disarranged his own plans for a whole winter.

How this miracle of fire and ice was to be created, and to sustain itself in a harsh world, he had never taken the time to think out; but he was content to hold his view without analysing it, since he knew it was that of all the carefully-brushed, white-waistcoated, buttonhole-flowered gentlemen who succeeded each other in the club box, exchanged friendly greetings with him, and turned their opera-glasses critically on the circle of ladies who were the product of the system. In matters intellectual and artistic Newland Archer felt himself distinctly the superior of these chosen specimens of old

New York gentility; he had probably read more, thought more, and even seen a good deal more of the world, than any other man of the number. Singly they betrayed their inferiority; but grouped together they represented "New York," and the habit of masculine solidarity made him accept their doctrine on all the issues called moral. He instinctively felt that in this respect it would be troublesome—and also rather bad form—to strike out for himself.

"Well—upon my soul!" exclaimed Lawrence Lefferts, turning his opera-glass abruptly away from the stage. Lawrence Lefferts was, on the whole, the foremost authority on "form" in New York. He had probably devoted more time than any one else to the study of this intricate and fascinating question; but study alone could not account for his complete and easy competence. One had only to look at him, from the slant of his bald forehead and the curve of his beautiful fair moustache to the long patent-leather feet at the other end of his lean and elegant person, to feel that the knowledge of "form" must be congenital in any one who knew how to wear such good clothes so carelessly and carry such height with so much lounging grace. As a young admirer had once said of him: "If anybody can tell a fellow just when to wear a black tie with evening clothes and when not to, it's Larry Lefferts." And on the question of pumps versus patent-leather "Oxfords" his authority had never been disputed.

"My God!" he said; and silently handed his glass to old Sillerton Jackson.

Newland Archer, following Lefferts's glance, saw with surprise that his exclamation had been occasioned by the entry of a new figure into old Mrs. Mingott's box. It was that of a slim young woman, a little less tall than May Welland, with brown hair growing in close curls about her temples and held in place by a narrow band of diamonds. The suggestion of this headdress, which gave her what was then called a "Josephine look," was carried out in the cut of the dark blue velvet gown rather theatrically caught up under her bosom by a girdle with a large old-fashioned clasp. The wearer of this unusual dress, who seemed quite unconscious of the attention it was attracting, stood a moment in the centre of the box, discussing with Mrs. Welland the propriety of taking the latter's place in the front right-hand corner; then she yielded with a slight smile, and seated herself in line with Mrs. Welland's sister-in-law, Mrs. Lovell Mingott, who was installed in the opposite corner.

Mr. Sillerton Jackson had returned the opera-glass to Lawrence Lefferts. The whole of the club turned instinctively, waiting to hear what the old man had to say; for old Mr. Jackson was as great an authority on "family" as Lawrence Lefferts was on "form." He knew all the ramifications of New York's cousinships; and could not only elucidate such complicated questions as that of the connection between the Mingotts (through the Thorleys) with the Dallases of South Carolina, and that of the relationship of the elder branch of Philadelphia Thorleys to the Albany Chiverses (on no account to be confused with the Manson Chiverses of University Place), but could also enumerate the leading characteristics of each family; as, for instance, the fabulous stinginess of the younger lines of Leffertses (the Long Island ones); or the fatal tendency of the Rushworths to make foolish matches; or the insanity recurring in every second generation of the Albany Chiverses, with whom their New York cousins had always refused to intermarry—with the disastrous exception of poor Medora Manson, who, as everybody knew . . . but then her mother was a Rushworth.

In addition to this forest of family trees, Mr. Sillerton Jackson carried between his narrow hollow temples, and under his soft thatch of silver hair, a register of most of the scandals and mysteries that had smouldered under the unruffled surface of New York society within the last fifty years. So far indeed did his information extend, and so acutely retentive was his memory, that he was supposed to be the only man who could have told you who Julius Beaufort, the banker, really was, and what had become of handsome Bob Spicer, old Mrs. Manson Mingott's father, who had disappeared so mysteriously (with a large sum of trust money) less than a year after his marriage, on the very day that a beautiful Spanish dancer who had been delighting thronged audiences in the old Opera-house on the Battery had taken ship for Cuba. But these mysteries, and many others, were closely locked in Mr. Jackson's breast; for not only did his keen sense of honour forbid his repeating anything privately imparted, but he was fully aware that his reputation for discretion increased his opportunities of finding out what he wanted to know.

The club box, therefore, waited in visible suspense while Mr. Sillerton Jackson handed back Lawrence Lefferts's opera-glass. For a moment he silently scrutinised the attentive group out of his filmy blue eyes overhung by old veined lids; then he gave his moustache a thoughtful twist, and said simply: "I didn't think the Mingotts would have tried it on."

§ 2

Newland Archer, during this brief episode had been thrown into a strange state of embarrassment.

It was annoying that the box which was thus attracting the undivided attention of masculine New York should be that in which his betrothed was seated between her mother and aunt; and for a moment he could not identify the lady in the Empire dress, nor imagine why her presence created such excitement among the initiated. Then light dawned on him, and with it came a momentary rush of indignation. No, indeed; no one would have thought the Mingotts would have tried it on!

But they had; they undoubtedly had; for the low-toned comments behind him left no doubt in Archer's mind that the young woman was May Welland's cousin, the cousin always referred to in the family as "poor Ellen Olenska." Archer knew that she had suddenly arrived from Europe a day or two previously; he had even heard from Miss Welland (not disapproving) that she had been to see poor Ellen, who was staying with old Mrs. Mingott. Archer entirely approved of family solidarity, and one of the qualities he most admired in the Mingotts was their resolute championship of the few black sheep that their blameless stock had produced. There was nothing mean or ungenerous in the young man's heart, and he was glad that his future wife should not be restrained by false prudery from being kind (in private) to her unhappy cousin; but to receive Countess Olenska in the family circle was a different thing from producing her in public, at the Opera of all places, and in the very box with the young girl whose engagement to him, Newland Archer, was to be announced within a few weeks. No, he felt as old Sillerton Jackson felt; he did not think the Mingotts would have tried it on!

He knew, of course, that whatever man dared (within Fifth Avenue's limits) that old Mrs. Manson Mingott, the Matriarch of the line, would dare. He had always admired the high and mighty old lady, who, in spite of having been only Catherine Spicer of Staten Island, with a father mysteriously discredited, and neither money nor position enough to make people forget it, had allied herself with the head of the wealthy Mingott line, married two of her daughters to "foreigners" (an Italian Marquis and an English banker), and put the crowning touch to her audacities by building a large house of pale cream-coloured stone (when brown sandstone seemed as much the only wear as a frock-coat in the afternoon) in an inaccessible wilderness near the Central Park.

Old Mrs. Mingott's foreign daughters had become a legend. They never came back to see their mother, and the latter being, like many persons of active mind and dominating will, sedentary and corpulent in her habit, had philosophically remained at home. But the cream-coloured house (supposed to be modelled on the private hotels of the Parisian aristocracy) was there as a visible proof of her moral courage; and she throned in it, among pre-Revolutionary furniture and souvenirs of the Tuileries of Louis Napoleon (where she had shone in her middle age), as placidly as if there were nothing peculiar in living above Thirty-fourth Street, or in having French windows that opened like doors instead of sashes that pushed up.

Every one (including Mr. Sillerton Jackson) was agreed that old Catherine had never had beauty—a gift which, in the eyes of New York, justified every success, and excused a certain number of failings. Unkind people said that, like her Imperial namesake, she had won her way to success by strength of will and hardness of heart, and a kind of haughty effrontery that was somehow justified by the extreme decency and dignity of her private life. Mr. Manson Mingott had died when she was only twenty-eight, and had "tied up" the money with an additional caution born of the general distrust of the Spicers; but his bold young widow went her way fearlessly, mingled freely in foreign society, married her daughters in heaven knew what corrupt and fashionable circles, hobnobbed with Dukes and Ambassadors, associated familiarly with Papists, entertained Opera singers, and was the intimate friend of Mme. Taglioni; and all the while (as Sillerton Jackson was the first to proclaim) there had never been a breath on her reputation; the only respect, he always added, in which she differed from the earlier Catherine.

Mrs. Manson Mingott had long since succeeded in untying her husband's fortune, and had lived in affluence for half a century; but memories of her early straits had made her excessively thrifty, and though, when she bought a dress or a piece of furniture, she took care that it should be of the best, she could not bring herself to spend much on the transient pleasures of the table. Therefore, for totally different reasons, her food was as poor as Mrs. Archer's, and her wines did nothing to redeem it. Her relatives considered that the penury of her table discredited the Mingott name, which had always been associated with good living; but people continued to come to her in spite of the "made dishes" and flat champagne, and in reply to the remonstrances of her son Lovell (who tried to retrieve the family credit by having the best *chef* in New York) she used to say laughingly: "What's the use of two good cooks in one family, now that I've married the girls and can't eat sauces?"

Newland Archer, as he mused on these things, had once more turned his eyes toward the Mingott box. He saw that Mrs. Welland and her sister-in-law were facing their semi-circle of critics with the Mingottian *aplomb* which old Catherine had inculcated in all her tribe, and that only May Welland betrayed, by a heightened colour (perhaps due to the knowledge that he was watching her) a sense of the gravity of the situation. As for the cause of the commotion, she sat gracefully in her corner of the box, her eyes fixed on the stage, and revealing, as she leaned forward, a little more shoulder and bosom than New York was accustomed to seeing, at least in ladies who had reasons for wishing to pass unnoticed.

Few things seemed to Newland Archer more awful than an offence against "Taste," that far-off divinity of whom "Form" was the mere visible representative and viceregent. Madame Olenska's pale and serious face appealed to his fancy as suited to the occasion and to her unhappy situation; but the way her dress (which had no tucker) sloped away from her thin shoulders shocked and troubled him. He hated to think of May Welland's being exposed to the influence of a young woman so careless of the dictates of Taste.

"After all," he heard one of the younger men begin behind him (everybody talked through the Mephistopheles-and-Martha scenes), "after all, just *what* happened?"

"Well—she left him; nobody attempts to deny that."

"He's an awful brute, isn't he?" continued the young enquirer, a candid Thorley, who was evidently preparing to enter the lists as the lady's champion.

"The very worse; I knew him at Nice," said Lawrence Lefferts with authority. "A half-paralysed white sneering fellow—rather handsome head, but eyes with a lot of lashes. Well, I'll tell you the sort: when he wasn't with women he was collecting china. Paying any price for both, I understand."

There was a general laugh, and the young champion said: "Well, then——?"

"'Well, then; she bolted with his secretary."

"Oh, I see." The champion's face fell.

"It didn't last long, though: I heard of her a few months later living alone in Venice. I believe Lovell Mingott went out to get her. He said she was desperately unhappy. That's all right—but this parading her at the Opera's another thing."

"Perhaps," young Thorley hazarded, "she's too unhappy to be left at home."

This was greeted with an irreverent laugh, and the youth blushed deeply, and tried to look as if he had meant to insinuate what knowing people called a *"double entendre."*

"Well—it's queer to have brought Miss Welland, anyhow," some one said in a low tone, with a side-glance at Archer.

"Oh, that's part of the campaign; Granny's orders, no doubt," Lefferts laughed. "When the old lady does a thing she does it thoroughly."

The act was ending, and there was a general stir in the box. Suddenly Newland Archer felt himself impelled to decisive action. The desire to be the first man to enter Mrs. Mingott's box, to proclaim to the waiting world his engagement to May Welland, and to see her through whatever difficulties her cousin's anomalous situation might involve her in; this impulse had abruptly overruled all scruples and hesitations, and sent him hurrying through the red corridors to the farther side of the house.

As he entered the box his eyes met Miss Welland's, and he saw that she had instantly understood his motive, though the family dignity which both considered so high a virtue would not permit her to tell him so. The persons of their world lived in an atmosphere of faint implications and pale delicacies, and the fact that he and she understood each other without a word seemed to the young man to bring them nearer than any explanation would have done. Her eyes said: "You see why Mamma brought me," and his answered: "I would not for the world have had you stay away."

"You know my niece Countess Olenska?" Mrs. Welland enquired as she shook hands with her future son-in-law. Archer bowed without extending his hand, as was the custom on being introduced to a lady; and Ellen Olenska bent her head slightly, keeping her own pale-gloved hands clasped on her huge fan of eagle feathers. Having greeted Mrs. Lovell Mingott, a large blonde lady in creaking satin, he sat down beside his betrothed, and said in a low tone: "I hope you've told Madame Olenska that we're engaged? I want everybody to know—I want you to let me announce it this evening at the ball."

Miss Welland's face grew rosy as the dawn, and she looked at him with radiant eyes. "If you can persuade Mamma," she said; "but why should we change what is already settled?" He made no answer but that which his eyes returned, and she added, still more confidently smiling: "Tell my cousin yourself: I give you leave. She says she used to play with you when you were children."

She made way for him by pushing back her chair, and promptly, and a little ostentatiously, with the desire that the whole house should see what he was doing, Archer seated himself at the Countess Olenska's side.

"We *did* use to play together, didn't we?" she asked, turning her grave eyes to his. "You were a horrid boy, and kissed me once behind a door; but it was your cousin Vandie Newland, who never looked at me, that I was in love with." Her glance swept the horseshoe curve of boxes. "Ah, how this brings it all back to me—I see everybody here in knickerbockers and pantalettes," she said, with her trailing slightly foreign accent, her eyes returning to his face.

Agreeable as their expression was, the young man was shocked that they should reflect so unseemly a picture of the august tribunal before which, at that very moment, her case was being tried. Nothing could be in worse taste than misplaced flippancy; and he answered somewhat stiffly: "Yes, you have been away a very long time."

"Oh, centuries and centuries; so long," she said, "that I'm sure I'm dead and buried, and this dear old place is heaven"; which, for reasons he could not define, struck Newland Archer as an even more disrespectful way of describing New York society.

§ 3

It invariably happened in the same way.

Mrs. Julius Beaufort, on the night of her annual ball, never failed to appear at the Opera; indeed, she always gave her ball on an Opera night in order to emphasise her complete superiority to household cares, and her possession of a staff of servants competent to organize every detail of the entertainment in her absence.

The Beauforts' house was one of the few in New York that possessed a ball-room (it antedated even Mrs. Manson Mingott's and the Headly Chiverses); and at a time when it was beginning to be thought "provincial" to put a "crash" over the drawing-room floor and move the furniture upstairs, the possession of a ballroom that was used for no other purpose, and left for three-hundred-and-sixty-four days of the year to shuttered darkness, with its gilt chairs stacked in a corner and its chandelier in a bag; this undoubted superiority was felt to compensate for whatever was regrettable in the Beaufort past.

Mrs. Archer, who was fond of coining her social philosophy into axioms, had once said: "We all have our pet common people—" and though the phrase was a daring one, its truth was secretly admitted in many an exclusive bosom. But the Beauforts were not exactly common; some people said they were even worse. Mrs. Beaufort belonged indeed to one of America's most honoured families; she had been the lovely Regina Dallas (of the South Carolina branch), a penniless beauty introduced to New York society by her cousin, the imprudent Medora Manson, who was always doing the wrong thing from the right motive. When one was related to the Mansons and the Rushworths one had a *"droit de cité"* (as Mr. Sillerton Jackson, who had frequented the Tuileries, called it) in

New York society; but did one not forfeit it in marrying Julius Beaufort?

The question was: who *was* Beaufort? He passed for an Englishman, was agreeable, handsome, ill-tempered, hospitable and witty. He had come to America with letters of recommendation from old Mrs. Manson Mingott's English son-in-law, the banker, and had speedily made himself an important position in the world of affairs; but his habits were dissipated, his tongue was bitter, his antecedents were mysterious; and when Medora Manson announced her cousin's engagement to him it was felt to be one more act of folly in poor Medora's long record of imprudences.

But folly is as often justified of her children as wisdom, and two years after young Mrs. Beaufort's marriage it was admitted that she had the most distinguished house in New York. No one knew exactly how the miracle was accomplished. She was indolent, passive, the caustic even called her dull; but dressed like an idol, hung with pearls, growing younger and blonder and more beautiful each year, she throned in Mr. Beaufort's heavy brown-stone palace, and drew all the world there without lifting her jewelled little finger. The knowing people said it was Beaufort himself who trained the servants, taught the *chef* new dishes, told the gardeners what hot-house flowers to grow for the dinner-table and the drawing-rooms, selected the guests, brewed the after-dinner punch and dictated the little notes his wife wrote to her friends. If he did, these domestic activities were privately performed, and he presented to the world the appearance of a careless and hospitable millionaire strolling into his own drawing-room with the detachment of an invited guest, and saying: "My wife's gloxinias are a marvel, aren't they? I believe she gets them out from Kew."

Mr. Beaufort's secret, people were agreed, was the way he carried things off. It was all very well to whisper that he had been "helped" to leave England by the international banking-house in which he had been employed; he carried off that rumour as easily as the rest—though New York's business conscience was no less sensitive than its moral standard—he carried everything before him, and all New York into his drawing-rooms, and for over twenty years now people had said they were "going to the Beauforts' " with the same tone of security as if they had said they were going to Mrs. Manson

Mingott's, and with the added satisfaction of knowing they would get hot canvas-back ducks and vintage wines, instead of tepid Veuve Clicquot without a year and warmed-up croquettes from Philadelphia.

Mrs. Beaufort, then, had as usual appeared in her box just before the Jewel Song; and when, again as usual, she rose at the end of the third act, drew her opera cloak about her lovely shoulders, and disappeared, New York knew that meant that half an hour later the ball would begin.

The Beaufort house was one that New Yorkers were proud to show to foreigners, especially on the night of the annual ball. The Beauforts had been among the first people in New York to own their own red velvet carpet and have it rolled down the steps by their own footmen, under their own awning, instead of hiring it with the supper and the ball-room chairs. They had also inaugurated the custom of letting the ladies take their cloaks off in the hall, instead of shuffling up to the hostess's bedroom and recurling their hair with the aid of the gas-burner; Beaufort was understood to have said that he supposed all his wife's friends had maids who saw to it that they were properly *coiffées* when they left home.

Then the house had been boldly planned with a ball-room so that, instead of squeezing through a narrow passage to get to it (as at the Chiverses') one marched solemnly down a vista of enfiladed drawing-rooms (the sea-green, the crimson and the *bouton d'or*), seeing from afar the many-candled lustres reflected in the polished parquetry, and beyond that the depths of a conservatory where camellias and tree-ferns arched their costly foliage over seats of black and gold bamboo.

Newland Archer, as became a young man of his position, strolled in somewhat late. He had left his overcoat with the silk-stockinged footmen (the stockings were one of Beaufort's few fatuities), had dawdled a while in the library hung with Spanish leather and furnished with Buhl and malachite, where a few men were chatting and putting on their dancing-gloves, and had finally joined the line of guests whom Mrs. Beaufort was receiving on the threshold of the crimson drawing-room.

Archer was distinctly nervous. He had not gone back to his club after the Opera (as the young bloods usually did), but, the night being fine, had walked for some distance up Fifth Avenue before turning back in the direction of the Beauforts' house. He was definitely afraid that the Mingotts might be going too far; that, in fact they might have Granny Mingott's orders to bring the Countess Olenska to the ball.

From the tone of the club box he had preceived how grave a mistake that would be; and, though he was more than ever determined to "see the thing through," he felt less chivalrously eager to champion his betrothed's cousin than before their brief talk at the Opera.

Wandering on to the *bouton d'or* drawing-room (where Beaufort had had the audacity to hang "Love Victorious," the much-discussed nude of Bouguereau) Archer found Mrs. Welland and her daughter standing near the ball-room door. Couples were already gliding over the floor beyond: the light of the wax candles fell on revolving tulle skirts, on girlish heads wreathed with modest blossoms, on the dashing aigrettes and ornaments of the young married women's *coiffures,* and on the glitter of highly glazed shirt-fronts and fresh glacé gloves.

Miss Welland, evidently about to join the dancers, hung on the threshold, her lilies-of-the-valley in her hand (she carried no other bouquet), her face a little pale, her eyes burning with a candid excitement. A group of young men and girls were gathered about her, and there was much hand-clasping, laughing and pleasantry on which Mrs. Welland, standing slightly apart, shed the beam of a qualified approval. It was evident that Miss Welland was in the act of announcing her engagement, while her mother affected the air of parental reluctance considered suitable to the occasion.

Archer paused a moment. It was at his express wish that the announcement had been made, and yet it was not thus that he would have wished to have his happiness known. To proclaim it in the heat and noise of a crowded ball-room was to rob it of the fine bloom of privacy which should belong to things nearest the heart. His joy was so deep that this blurring of the surface left its essence untouched; but he would have liked to keep the surface pure too. It was something of a satisfaction to find that May Welland shared this feeling. Her eyes fled to his beseechingly, and their look said: "Remember, we're doing this because it's right."

No appeal could have found a more immediate response in Archer's breast; but he wished that the necessity of their action had been represented by some ideal reason, and not simply by poor Ellen Olenska. The group about Miss Welland made way for him with significant smiles, and after taking his share of the felicitations he drew his betrothed into the middle of the ball-room floor and put his arm about her waist.

"Now we shan't have to talk," he said, smiling into her candid eyes, as they floated away on the soft waves of the Blue Danube.

She made no answer. Her lips trembled into a smile, but the eyes remained distant and serious, as if bent on some ineffable vision. "Dear," Archer whispered, pressing her to him: it was borne in on him that the first hours of being engaged, even if spent in a ball-room, had in them something grave and sacramental. What a new life it was going to be, with this whiteness, radiance, goodness at one's side!

The dance over, the two, as became an affianced couple, wandered into the conservatory; and sitting behind a tall screen of tree-ferns and camellias Newland pressed her gloved hand to his lips.

"You see I did as you asked me to," she said.

"Yes: I couldn't wait," he answered smiling. After a moment he added: "Only I wish it hadn't had to be at a ball."

"Yes, I know." She met his glance comprehendingly. "But after all—even here we're alone together, aren't we?"

"Oh, dearest—always!" Archer cried.

Evidently she was always going to understand; she was always going to say the right thing. The discovery made the cup of his bliss overflow, and he went on gaily: "The worst of it is that I want to kiss you and I can't." As he spoke he took a swift glance about the conservatory, assured himself of their momentary privacy and catching her to him laid a fugitive pressure on her lips. To counteract the audacity of this proceeding he led her to a bamboo sofa in a less secluded part of the conservatory, and sitting down beside her broke a lily-of-the-valley from her bouquet. She sat silent, and the world lay like a sunlit valley at their feet.

"Did you tell my cousin Ellen?" she asked presently, as if she spoke through a dream.

He roused himself, and remembered that he had not done so.

Some invincible repugnance to speak of such things to the strange foreign woman had checked the words on his lips.

"No—I hadn't the chance after all," he said, fibbing hastily.

"Ah." She looked disappointed, but gently resolved on gaining her point. "You must, then, for I didn't either; and I shouldn't like her to think—"

"Of course not. But aren't you, after all, the person to do it?"

She pondered on this. "If I'd done it at the right time, yes: but now that there's been a delay I think you must explain that I'd asked you to tell her at the Opera, before our speaking about it to everybody here. Otherwise she might think I had forgotten her. You see, she's one of the family, and she's been away so long that she's rather—sensitive."

Archer looked at her glowingly. "Dear and great angel! Of course I'll tell her." He glanced a trifle apprehensively toward the crowded ball-room. "But I haven't seen her yet. Has she come?"

"No; at the last minute she decided not to."

"At the last minute?" he echoed, betraying his surprise that she should ever have considered the alternative possible.

"Yes. She's awfully fond of dancing," the young girl answered simply. "But suddenly she made up her mind that her dress wasn't smart enough for a ball, though we thought it so lovely; and so my aunt had to take her home."

"Oh, well—" said Archer with happy indifference. Nothing about his betrothed pleased him more than her resolute determination to carry to its utmost limit that ritual of ignoring the "unpleasant" in which they had both been brought up.

"She knows as well as I do," he reflected, "the real reason of her cousin's staying away; but I shall never let her see by the least sign that I am conscious of there being a shadow of a shade on poor Ellen Olenska's reputation."

§ 4

In the course of the next day the first of the usual betrothal visits were exchanged. The New York ritual was precise and inflexible in such matters; and in conformity with it Newland Archer first went with his mother and sister to call on Mrs. Welland, after which he and Mrs. Welland and May drove out to old Mrs. Manson Mingott's to receive that venerable ancestress's blessing.

A visit to Mrs. Manson Mingott was always an amusing episode to the young man. The house in itself was already an historic document, though not, of course, as venerable as certain other old family houses in University Place and lower Fifth Avenue. Those were of the purest 1830, with a grim harmony of cabbage-rose-garlanded carpets, rosewood consoles, round-arched fireplaces with black marble mantels, and immense glazed book-cases of mahogany; whereas old Mrs. Mingott, who had built her house later, had bodily cast out the massive furniture of her prime, and mingled with the Mingott heirlooms the frivolous upholstery of the Second Empire. It was her habit to sit in a window of her sitting-room on the ground floor, as if watching calmly for life and fashion to flow northward to her solitary doors. She seemed in no hurry to have them come, for her patience was equalled by her confidence. She was sure that presently the hoardings, the quarries, the one-story saloons, the wooden green-houses in ragged gardens, and the rocks from which goats surveyed the scene, would vanish before the advance of residences as stately as her own—perhaps (for she was an impartial woman) even statelier; and that the cobblestones over which the old clattering omnibuses bumped would be replaced by smooth asphalt, such as people reported having seen in Paris. Meanwhile, as every one she cared to see came to *her* (and she could fill her rooms as easily as the Beauforts, and without adding a single item to the *menu* of her suppers), she did not suffer from her geographic isolation.

The immense accretion of flesh which had descended on her in middle life like a flood of lava on a doomed city had changed her from a plump active little woman with a neatly-turned foot and ankle into something as vast and august as a natural phenomenon. She had accepted this submergence as philosophically as all her other trials, and now, in extreme old age, was rewarded by presenting to her mirror an almost unwrinkled expanse of firm pink and white flesh, in the centre of which the traces of a small face survived as if awaiting excavation. A flight of smooth double chins led down to the dizzy depths of a still-snowy bosom veiled in snowy muslins that were held in place by a miniature portrait of the late Mr.

Mingott; and around and below, wave after wave of black silk surged away over the edges of a capacious armchair, with two tiny white hands poised like gulls on the surface of the billows.

The burden of Mrs. Manson Mingott's flesh had long since made it impossible for her to go up and down stairs, and with characteristic independence she had made her reception rooms upstairs and established herself (in flagrant violation of all the New York proprieties) on the ground floor of her house; so that, as you sat in her sitting-room window with her, you caught (through a door that was always open, and a looped-back yellow damask portière) the unexpected vista of a bedroom with a huge low bed upholstered like a sofa, and a toilet-table with frivolous lace flounces and a gilt-framed mirror.

Her visitors were startled and fascinated by the foreignness of this arrangement, which recalled scenes in French fiction, and architectural incentives to immorality such as the simple American had never dreamed of. That was how women with lovers lived in the wicked old societies, in apartments with all the rooms on one floor, and all the indecent propinquities that their novels described. It amused Newland Archer (who had secretly situated the love-scenes of "Monsieur de Camors" in Mrs. Mingott's bedroom) to picture her blameless life led in the stage-setting of adultery; but he said to himself, with considerable admiration, that if a lover had been what she wanted, the intrepid woman would have had him too.

To the general relief the Countess Olenska was not present in her grandmother's drawing-room during the visit of the betrothed couple. Mrs. Mingott said she had gone out; which, on a day of such glaring sunlight, and at the "shopping hour," seemed in itself an indelicate thing for a compromised woman to do. But at any rate it spared them the embarrassment of her presence, and the faint shadow that her unhappy past might seem to shed on their radiant future. The visit went off successfully, as was to have been expected. Old Mrs. Mingott was delighted with the engagement, which, being long foreseen by watchful relatives, had been carefully passed upon in family council; and the engagement ring, a large thick sapphire set in invisible claws, met with her unqualified admiration.

"It's the new setting: of course it shows the stone beautifully, but it looks a little bare to old-fashioned eyes," Mrs. Welland had explained, with a conciliatory side glance at her future son-in-law.

"Old-fashioned eyes? I hope you don't mean mine, my dear? I like all the novelties," said the ancestress, lifting the stone to her small bright orbs, which no glasses had ever disfigured. "Very handsome," she added, returning the jewel; "very liberal. In my time a cameo set in pearls was thought sufficient. But it's the hand that sets off the ring, isn't it, my dear Mr. Archer?" and she waved one of her tiny hands, with small pointed nails and rolls of aged fat encircling the wrist like ivory bracelets. "Mine was modelled in Rome by the great Ferrigiani. You should have May's done: no doubt he'll have it done, my child. Her hand is large—it's these modern sports that spread the joints—but the skin is white.—And when's the wedding to be?" she broke off, fixing her eyes on Archer's face.

"Oh—" Mrs. Welland murmured, while the young man, smiling at his betrothed, replied: "As soon as ever it can, if only you'll back me up, Mrs. Mingott."

"We must give them time to get to know each other a little better, mamma," Mrs. Welland interposed with the proper affection of reluctance; to which the ancestress rejoined: "Know each other? Fiddlesticks! Everybody in New York has always known everybody. Let the young man have his way, my dear; don't wait till the bubble's off the wine. Marry them before Lent; I may catch pneumonia any winter now, and I want to give the wedding-breakfast."

These successive statements were received with the proper expressions of amusement, incredulity and gratitude; and the visit was breaking up in a vein of mild pleasantry when the door opened to admit the Countess Olenska, who entered in bonnet and mantle followed by the unexpected figure of Julius Beaufort.

There was a cousinly murmur of pleasure between the ladies, and Mrs. Mingott held out Ferrigiani's model to the banker. "Ha! Beaufort, this is a rare favour!" (She had an odd foreign way of addressing men by their surnames.)

"Thanks. I wish it might happen oftener," said the visitor in his easy arrogant way. "I'm generally so tied down; but I met the Countess Ellen in Madison Square, and she was good enough to let me walk home with her."

"Ah—I hope the house will be gayer, now that Ellen's here!"

cried Mrs. Mingott with a glorious effrontery. "Sit down—sit down, Beaufort: push up the yellow armchair; now I've got you I want a good gossip. I hear your ball was magnificent; and I understand you invited Mrs. Lemuel Struthers? Well—I've a curiosity to see the woman myself."

She had forgotten her relatives, who were drifting out into the hall under Ellen Olenska's guidance. Old Mrs. Mingott had always professed a great admiration for Julius Beaufort, and there was a kind of kinship in their cool domineering way and their short-cuts through the conventions. Now she was eagerly curious to know what had decided the Beauforts to invite (for the first time) Mrs. Lemuel Struthers, the widow of Struthers's Shoe-polish, who had returned the previous year from a long initiatory sojourn in Europe to lay siege to the tight little citadel of New York. "Of course if you and Regina invite her the thing is settled. Well, we need new blood and new money—and I hear she's still very good looking," the carnivorous old lady declared.

In the hall, while Mrs. Welland and May drew on their furs, Archer saw that the Countess Olenska was looking at him with a faintly questioning smile.

"Of course you know already—about May and me," he said, answering her look with a shy laugh. "She scolded me for not giving you the news last night at the Opera: I had her orders to tell you that we were engaged—but I couldn't, in that crowd."

The smile passed from Countess Olenska's eyes to her lips: she looked younger, more like the bold brown Ellen Mingott of his boyhood. "Of course I know; yes. And I'm so glad. But one doesn't tell such things first in a crowd." The ladies were on the threshold and she held out her hand.

"Good-bye; come and see me some day," she said, still looking at Archer.

In the carriage, on the way down Fifth Avenue, they talked pointedly of Mrs. Mingott, of her age, her spirit, and all her wonderful attributes. No one alluded to Ellen Olenska; but Archer knew that Mrs. Welland was thinking: "It's a mistake for Ellen to be seen, the very day after her arrival, parading up Fifth Avenue at the crowded hour with Julius Beaufort—" and the young man himself mentally added: "And she ought to know that a man who's just engaged doesn't spend his time calling on married women. But I daresay in the set she's lived in they do—they never do anything else." And, in spite of the cosmopolitan views on which he prided himself, he thanked heaven that he was a New Yorker, and about to ally himself with one of his own kind.

§ 5

The next evening old Mr. Sillerton Jackson came to dine with the Archers.

Mrs. Archer was a shy woman and shrank from society; but she liked to be well-informed as to its doings. Her old friend Mr. Sillerton Jackson applied to the investigation of his friends' affairs the patience of a collector and the science of a naturalist; and his sister, Miss Sophy Jackson, who lived with him, and was entertained by all the people who could not secure her much-sought-after brother, brought home bits of minor gossip that filled out usefully the gaps in his picture.

Therefore, whenever anything happened that Mrs. Archer wanted to know about, she asked Mr. Jackson to dine; and as she honoured few people with her invitations, and as she and her daughter Janey were an excellent audience, Mr. Jackson usually came himself instead of sending his sister. If he could have dictated all the conditions, he would have chosen the evenings when Newland was out; not because the young man was uncongenial to him (the two got on capitally at their club) but because the old anecdotist sometimes felt, on Newland's part, a tendency to weigh his evidence that the ladies of the family never showed.

Mr. Jackson, if perfection had been attainable on earth, would also have asked that Mrs. Archer's food should be a little better. But then New York, as far back as the mind of man could travel, had been divided into the two great fundamental groups of the Mingotts and Mansons and all their clan, who cared about eating and clothes and money, and the Archer-Newland-van-der-Luyden tribe, who were devoted to travel, horticulture and the best fiction, and looked down on the grosser forms of pleasure.

You couldn't have everything, after all. If you dined with the Lovell Mingotts you got canvas-back and terrapin and vintage wines; at Adeline Archer's you could talk about Alpine scenery and "The Marble Faun"; and luckily the Archer Madeira had gone round the Cape. Therefore when a friendly summons came from Mrs. Archer, Mr. Jackson, who was a true eclectic, would usually say to his sister: "I've been a little gouty since my last dinner at the Lovell Mingotts'—it will do me good to diet at Adeline's."

Mrs. Archer, who had long been a widow, lived with her son and daughter in West Twenty-eighth Street. An upper floor was dedicated to Newland, and the two women squeezed themselves into narrower quarters below. In an unclouded harmony of tastes and interests they cultivated ferns in Wardian cases, made macramé lace and wool embroidery on linen, collected American revolutionary glazed ware, subscribed to "Good Words," and read Ouida's novels for the sake of the Italian atmosphere. (They preferred those about peasant life, because of the descriptions of scenery and the pleasanter sentiments, though in general they liked novels about people in society, whose motives and habits were more comprehensible, spoke severely of Dickens, who "had never drawn a gentleman," and considered Thackeray less at home in the great world than Bulwer—who, however, was beginning to be thought old-fashioned.)

Mrs. and Miss Archer were both great lovers of scenery. It was what they prinicipally sought and admired on their occasional travels abroad; considering architecture and painting as subjects for men, and chiefly for learned persons who read Ruskin. Mrs. Archer had been born a Newland, and mother and daughter, who were as like as sisters, were both, as people said, "true Newlands"; tall, pale, and slightly round-shouldered, with long noses, sweet smiles and a kind of drooping distinction like that in certain faded Reynolds portraits. Their physical resemblance would have been complete if an elderly *embonpoint* had not stretched Mrs. Archer's black brocade, while Miss Archer's brown and purple poplins hung, as the years went on, more and more slackly on her virgin frame.

Mentally, the likeness between them, as Newland was aware, was less complete than their identical mannerisms often made it appear. The long habit of living together in mutually dependent intimacy had given them the same vocabulary, and the same habit of beginning their phrases "Mother thinks" or "Janey thinks," according as one or the other wished to advance an opinion of her own; but in reality, while Mrs. Archer's serene unimaginativeness rested easily in the accepted and familiar, Janey was subject to starts and aberrations of fancy welling up from springs of suppressed romance.

Mother and daughter adored each other and revered their son and brother; and Archer loved them with a tenderness made compunctious and uncritical by the sense of their exaggerated admiration, and by his secret satisfaction in it. After all, he thought it a good thing for a man to have his authority respected in his own house, even if his sense of humour sometimes made him question the force of his mandate.

On this occasion the young man was very sure that Mr. Jackson would rather have had him dine out; but he had his own reasons for not doing so.

Of course old Jackson wanted to talk about Ellen Olenska, and of course Mrs. Archer and Janey wanted to hear what he had to tell. All three would be slightly embarrassed by Newland's presence, now that his prospective relation to the Mingott clan had been made known; and the young man waited with an amused curiosity to see how they would turn the difficulty.

They began, obliquely, by talking about Mrs. Lemuel Struthers.

"It's a pity the Beauforts asked her," Mrs. Archer said gently. "But then Regina always does what he tells her; and *Beaufort*—"

"Certain *nuances* escape Beaufort," said Mr. Jackson, cautiously inspecting the broiled shad, and wondering for the thousandth time why Mrs. Archer's cook always burnt the roe to a cinder. (Newland, who had long shared his wonder, could always detect it in the older man's expression of melancholy disapproval.)

"Oh, necessarily; Beaufort is a vulgar man," said Mrs. Archer. "My grandfather Newland always used to say to my mother: 'Whatever you do, don't let that fellow Beaufort be introduced to the girls.' But at least he's had the advantage of associating with gentlemen; in England too, they say. It's all very mysterious—" She glanced at Janey and paused. She and Janey knew every fold of the Beaufort mystery, but in public Mrs. Archer continued to assume that the subject was not one for the unmarried.

"But this Mrs. Struthers," Mrs. Archer continued; "what did you say *she* was, Sillerton?"

"Out of a mine: or rather out of the saloon at the head of the pit. Then with Living Wax-Works, touring New England. After the police broke *that* up, they say she lived—" Mr. Jackson in his turn glanced at Janey, whose eyes began to bulge from under her prominent lids. There were still hiatuses for her in Mrs. Struthers's past.

"Then," Mr. Jackson continued (and Archer saw he was wondering why no one had told the butler never to slice cucumbers with a steel knife), "then Lemuel Struthers came along. They say his advertiser used the girl's head for the shoe-polish posters; her hair's intensely black, you know—the Egyptian style. Anyhow, he—eventually—married her." There were volumes of innuendo in the way the "eventually" was spaced, and each syllable given its due stress.

"Oh, well—at the pass we've come to nowadays, it doesn't matter," said Mrs. Archer indifferently. The ladies were not really interested in Mrs. Struthers just then; the subject of Ellen Olenska was too fresh and too absorbing to them. Indeed, Mrs. Struthers's name had been introduced by Mrs. Archer only that she might presently be able to say: "And Newland's new cousin—Countess Olenska? Was *she* at the ball too?"

There was a faint touch of sarcasm in the reference to her son, and Archer knew it and had expected it. Even Mrs. Archer, who was seldom unduly pleased with human events, had been altogether glad of her son's engagement. ("Especially after that silly business with Mrs. Rushworth," as she had remarked to Janey, alluding to what had once seemed to Newland a tragedy of which his soul would always bear the scar.) There was no better match in New York than May Welland, look at the question from whatever point you chose. Of course such a marriage was only what Newland was entitled to; but young men are so foolish and incalculable—and some women so ensnaring and unscrupulous—that it was nothing short of a miracle to see one's only son safe past the Siren Isle and in the haven of a blameless domesticity.

All this Mrs. Archer felt, and her son knew she felt; but he knew also that she had been perturbed by the premature announcement of his engagement, or rather by its cause; and it was for that reason —because on the whole he was a tender and indulgent master—that he had stayed at home that evening. "It's not that I don't approve of the Mingotts' *esprit de corps;* but why Newland's engagement should be mixed up with that Olenska woman's comings and goings I don't see," Mrs. Archer grumbled to Janey, the only witness of her slight lapses from perfect sweetness.

She had behaved beautifully—and in beautiful behaviour she was unsurpassed—during the call on Mrs. Welland; but Newland knew (and his betrothed doubtless guessed) that all through the visit she and Janey were nervously on the watch for Madame Olenska's possible intrusion; and when they left the house together she had permitted herself to say to her son: "I'm thankful that Augusta Welland received us alone."

These indications of inward disturbance moved Archer the more that he too felt that the Mingotts had gone a little too far. But, as it was against all the rules of their code that the mother and son should ever allude to what was uppermost in their thoughts, he simply replied: "Oh, well, there's always a phase of family parties to be gone through when one gets engaged, and the sooner it's over the better." At which his mother merely pursed her lips under the lace veil that hung down from her grey velvet bonnet trimmed with frosted grapes.

Her revenge, he felt—her lawful revenge—would be to "draw" Mr. Jackson that evening on the Countess Olenska; and, having publicly done his duty as a future member of the Mingott clan, the young man had no objection to hearing the lady discussed in private—except that the subject was already beginning to bore him.

Mr. Jackson had helped himself to a slice of the tepid *filet* which the mournful butler had handed him with a look as sceptical as his own, and had rejected the mushroom sauce after a scarcely perceptible sniff. He looked baffled and hungry, and Archer reflected that he would probably finish his meal on Ellen Olenska.

Mr. Jackson leaned back in his chair, and glanced up at the candlelit Archers, Newlands and van der Luydens hanging in dark frames on the dark walls.

"Ah, how your grandfather Archer loved a good dinner, my dear Newland!" he said, his eyes on the portrait of a plump full-chested young man in a stock and a blue coat, with a view of a white-columned country-house behind him. "Well—well—well . . . I wonder what he would have said to all these foreign marriages!"

Mrs. Archer ignored the allusion to the ancestral *cuisine* and Mr. Jackson continued with deliberation: "No, she was *not* at the ball."

"Ah—" Mrs. Archer murmured, in a tone that implied: "She had that decency."

"Perhaps the Beauforts don't know her," Janey suggested, with her artless malice.

Mr. Jackson gave a faint sip, as if he had been tasting invisible Madeira. "Mrs. Beaufort may not—but Beaufort certainly does, for she was seen walking up Fifth Avenue this afternoon with him by the whole of New York."

"Mercy—" moaned Mrs. Archer, evidently perceiving the uselessness of trying to ascribe the actions of foreigners to a sense of delicacy.

"I wonder if she wears a round hat or a bonnet in the afternoon," Janey speculated. "At the Opera I know she had on dark blue velvet, perfectly plain and flat—like a night-gown."

"Janey!" said her mother; and Miss Archer blushed and tried to look audacious.

"It was, at any rate, in better taste not to go to the ball," Mrs. Archer continued.

A spirit of perversity moved her son to rejoin: "I don't think it was a question of taste with her. May said she meant to go, and then decided that the dress in question wasn't smart enough."

Mrs. Archer smiled at this confirmation of her inference. "Poor Ellen," she simply remarked; adding compassionately: "We must always bear in mind what an eccentric bringing-up Medora Manson gave her. What can you expect of a girl who was allowed to wear black satin at her coming-out ball?"

"Ah—don't I remember her in it!" said Mr. Jackson; adding: "Poor girl!" in the tone of one who, while enjoying the memory, had fully understood at the time what the sight portended.

"It's odd," Janey remarked, "that she should have kept such an ugly name as Ellen. I should have changed it to Elaine." She glanced about the table to see the effect of this.

Her brother laughed. "Why Elaine?"

"I don't know; it sounds more—more Polish," said Janey, blushing.

"It sounds more conspicuous; and that can hardly be what she wishes," said Mrs. Archer distantly.

"Why not?" broke in her son, growing suddenly argumentative. "Why shouldn't she be conspicuous if she chooses? Why should she slink about as if it were she who had disgraced herself? She's 'poor Ellen' certainly, because she had the bad luck to make a wretched marriage; but I don't see that that's a reason for hiding her head as if she were the culprit."

"That, I suppose," said Mr. Jackson, speculatively, "is the line the Mingotts mean to take."

The young man reddened. "I didn't have to wait for their cue, if that's what you mean, sir. Madame Olenska has had an unhappy life: that doesn't make her an outcast."

"There are rumours," began Mr. Jackson, glancing at Janey.

"Oh, I know: the secretary," the young man took him up. "Nonsense, mother; Janey's grown-up. They say, don't they," he went on, "that the secretary helped her to get away from her brute of a husband, who kept her practically a prisoner? Well, what if he did? I hope there isn't a man among us who wouldn't have done the same in such a case."

Mr. Jackson glanced over his shoulder to say to the sad butler: "Perhaps . . . that sauce . . . just a little, after all—"; then, having helped himself, he remarked: "I'm told she's looking for a house. She means to live here."

"I hear she means to get a divorce," said Janey boldly.

"I hope she will!" Archer exclaimed.

The word had fallen like a bombshell in the pure and tranquil atmosphere of the Archer dining-room. Mrs. Archer raised her delicate eye-brows in the particular curve that signified: "The butler —" and the young man, himself mindful of the bad taste of discussing such intimate matters in public, hastily branched off into an account of his visit to old Mrs. Mingott.

After dinner, according to immemorial custom, Mrs. Archer and Janey trailed their long silk draperies up to the drawing-room, where, while the gentlemen smoked below stairs, they sat beside a Carcel lamp with an engraved globe, facing each other across a rosewood work-table with a green silk bag under it, and stitched at the two ends of a tapestry band of field-flowers destined to adorn an "occasional" chair in the drawing-room of young Mrs. Newland Archer.

While this rite was in progress in the drawing-room, Archer settled Mr. Jackson in an armchair near the fire in the Gothic library and handed him a cigar. Mr. Jackson sank into the armchair with satisfaction, lit his cigar with perfect confidence (it was Newland who bought them), and stretching his thin old ankles to the coals, said: "You say the secretary merely helped her to get away, my dear fellow? Well, he was still helping her a year later, then; for somebody met 'em living at Lausanne together."

Newland reddened. "Living together? Well, why not? Who had the right to make her life over if she hadn't? I'm sick of the hypocrisy that would bury alive a woman of her age if her husband prefers to live with harlots."

He stopped and turned away angrily to light his cigar. "Women ought to be free—as free as we are," he declared, making a discovery of which he was too irritated to measure the terrific consequences.

Mr. Sillerton Jackson stretched his ankles nearer the coals and emitted a sardonic whistle.

"Well," he said after a pause, "apparently Count Olenski takes your view; for I never heard of his having lifted a finger to get his wife back."

§ 6

That evening, after Mr. Jackson had taken himself away, and the ladies had retired to their chintz-curtained bedroom, Newland Archer mounted thoughtfully to his own study. A vigilant hand had, as usual, kept the fire alive and the lamp trimmed; and the room, with its rows and rows of books, its bronze and steel statuettes of "The Fencers" on the mantelpiece and its many photographs of famous pictures, looked singularly home-like and welcoming.

As he dropped into his armchair near the fire his eyes rested on a large photograph of May Welland, which the young girl had given him in the first days of their romance, and which had now displaced all the other portraits on the table. With a new sense of awe he looked at the frank forehead, serious eyes and gay innocent mouth of the young creature whose soul's custodian he was to be. That terrifying product of the social system he belonged to and believed in, the young girl who knew nothing and expected everything, looked back at him like a stranger through May Welland's familiar features; and once more it was borne in on him that marriage was not the safe anchorage he had been taught to think, but a voyage on uncharted seas.

The case of the Countess Olenska had stirred up old settled convictions and set them drifting dangerously through his mind. His own exclamation: "Women should be free—as free as we are," struck to the root of a problem that it was agreed in his world to regard as non-existent. "Nice" women, however wronged, would never claim the kind of freedom he meant, and generous-minded men like himself were therefore—in the heat of argument—the more chivalrously ready to concede it to them. Such verbal generosities were in fact only a humbugging disguise of the inexorable conventions that tied things together and bound people down to the old pattern. But here he was pledged to defend, on the part of his betrothed's cousin, conduct that, on his own wife's part, would justify him in calling down on her all the thunders of Church and State. Of course the dilemma was purely hypothetical; since he wasn't a blackguard Polish nobleman, it was absurd to speculate what his wife's rights would be if he *were*. But Newland Archer was too imaginative not to feel that, in his case and May's, the tie might gall for reasons far less gross and palpable. What could he and she really know of each other, since it was his duty, as a "decent" fellow, to conceal his past from her, and hers, as a marriageable girl, to have no past to conceal? What if, for some one of the subtler reasons that would tell with both of them, they should tire of each other, misunderstand or irritate each other? He reviewed his friends' marriages—the supposedly happy ones—and saw none that answered, even remotely, to the passionate and tender comradeship which he pictured as his permanent relation with May Welland. He perceived that such a picture presupposed, on her part, the experience, the versatility, the freedom of judgment, which she had been carefully trained not to possess; and with a shiver of foreboding he saw his marriage becoming what most of the other marriages about him were: a dull association of material and social interests held together by ignorance on the one side and hypocrisy on the other. Lawrence Lefferts occurred to him as the husband who had most completely realised this enviable ideal. As became the high-priest of form, he had formed a wife so completely to his own convenience that, in the most conspicuous moments of his frequent love-affairs with other men's wives, she went about in smiling unconsciousness, saying that "Lawrence was so frightfully strict"; and had been known to blush indignantly, and avert her gaze, when some one alluded in her presence to the fact that Julius Beaufort (as became a "foreigner" of doubtful origin) had what was known in New York as "another establishment."

Archer tried to console himself with the thought that he was not quite such an ass as Larry Lefferts, nor May such a simpleton as poor Gertrude; but the difference was after all one of intelligence and not of standards. In reality they all lived in a kind of hieroglyphic world, where the real thing was never said or done or even thought, but only represented by a set of arbitrary signs; as when Mrs. Welland, who knew exactly why Archer had pressed her to announce her daughter's engagement at the Beaufort ball (and had indeed expected him to do no less), yet felt obliged to simulate reluctance, and the air of having had her hand forced, quite as, in the books on Primitive Man that people of advanced culture were beginning to read, the savage bride is dragged with shrieks from her parents' tent.

The result, of course, was that the young girl who was the centre of this elaborate system of mystification remained the more inscrutable for her very frankness and assurance. She was frank, poor darling, because she had nothing to conceal, assured because she knew of nothing to be on her guard against; and with no better preparation than this, she was to be plunged overnight into what people evasively called "the facts of life."

The young man was sincerely but placidly in love. He delighted in the radiant good looks of his betrothed, in her health, her horsemanship, her grace and quickness at games, and the shy interest in books and ideas that she was beginning to develop under his guidance. (She had advanced far enough to join him in ridiculing the Idylls of the King, but not to feel the beauty of Ulysses and the Lotus Eaters.) She was straightforward, loyal and brave; she had a sense of humour (chiefly proved by her laughing at *his* jokes); and he suspected, in the depths of her innocently-gazing soul, a glow of feeling that it would be a joy to waken. But when he had gone the brief round of her he returned discouraged by the thought that all this frankness and innocence were only an artificial product. Untrained human nature was not frank and innocent; it was full of the twists and defences of an instinctive guile. And he felt himself oppressed by this creation of factitious purity, so cunningly manufactured by a conspiracy of mothers and aunts and grandmothers and long-dead ancestresses, because it was supposed to be what he wanted, what he had a right to, in order that he might exercise his lordly pleasure in smashing it like an image made of snow.

There was a certain triteness in these reflections: they were those habitual to young men on the approach of their wedding day. But they were generally accompanied by a sense of compunction and self-abasement of which Newland Archer felt no trace. He could not deplore (as Thackeray's heroes so often exasperated him by doing) that he had not a blank page to offer his bride in exchange for the unblemished one she was to give to him. He could not get away from the fact that if he had been brought up as she had they would have been no more fit to find their way about than the Babes in the Wood; nor could he, for all his anxious cogitations, see any honest reason (any, that is, unconnected with his own momentary pleasure, and the passion of masculine vanity) why his bride should not have been allowed the same freedom of experience as himself.

Such questions, at such an hour, were bound to drift through his mind; but he was conscious that their uncomfortable persistence and precision were due to the inopportune arrival of the Countess Olenska. Here he was, at the very moment of his betrothal—a moment for pure thoughts and cloudless hopes—pitchforked into a coil of scandal which raised all the special problems he would have preferred to let lie. "Hang Ellen Olenska!" he grumbled, as he covered his fire and began to undress. He could not really see why her fate should have the least bearing on his; yet he dimly felt that he had only just begun to measure the risks of the championship which his engagement had forced upon him.

A few days later the bolt fell.

The Lovell Mingotts had sent out cards for what was known as "a formal dinner" (that is, three extra footmen, two dishes for each course, and a Roman punch in the middle), and had headed their invitations with the words "To meet the Countess Olenska," in accordance with the hospitable American fashion, which treats strangers as if they were royalties, or at least as their ambassadors.

The guests had been selected with a boldness and discrimination in which the initiated recognized the firm hand of Catherine the Great. Associated with such immemorial standbys as the Selfridge Merrys, who were asked everywhere because they always had been, the Beauforts, on whom there was a claim of relationship, and Mr. Sillerton Jackson and his sister Sophy (who went wherever her brother told her to), were some of the most fashionable and yet most irreproachable of the dominant "young married" set; the Lawrence Leffertses, Mrs. Lefferts Rushworth (the lovely widow), the Harry Thorleys, the Reggie Chiverses and young Morris Dagonet and his wife (who was a van der Luyden). The company indeed was perfectly assorted, since all the members belonged to the little inner group of people who, during the long New York season, disported themselves together daily and nightly with apparently undiminished zest.

Forty-eight hours later the unbelievable had happened; every one had refused the Mingotts' invitation except the Beauforts and old Mr. Jackson and his sister. The intended slight was emphasised by the fact that even the Reggie Chiverses, who were of the Mingott clan, were among those inflicting it; and by the uniform wording of the notes, in all of which the writers "regretted that they were unable to accept," without the mitigating plea of a "previous engagement" that ordinary courtesy prescribed.

New York society was, in those days, far too small, and too scant in its resources, for every one in it (including livery-stable-keepers, butlers and cooks) not to know exactly on which evenings people were free; and it was thus possible for the recipients of Mrs. Lovell Mingott's invitations to make cruelly clear their determination not to meet the Countess Olenska.

The blow was unexpected; but the Mingotts, as their way was, met it gallantly. Mrs. Lovell Mingott confided the case to Mrs. Welland, who confided it to Newland Archer; who, aflame at the outrage, appealed passionately and authoritatively to his mother; who, after a painful period of inward resistance and outward temporising, succumbed to his instances (as she always did), and immediately embracing his cause with an energy redoubled by her previous hesitations, put on her grey velvet bonnet and said: "I'll go and see Louisa van der Luyden."

The New York of Newland Archer's day was a small and slippery pyramid, in which, as yet, hardly a fissure had been made or a foothold gained. At its base was a firm foundation of what Mrs. Archer called "plain people"; an honourable but obscure majority of respectable families who (as in the case of the Spicers or the Leffertses or the Jacksons) had been raised above their level by marriage with one of the ruling clans. People, Mrs. Archer always said, were not as particular as they used to be; and with old Catherine Spicer ruling one end of Fifth Avenue, and Julius Beaufort the other, you couldn't expect the old traditions to last much longer.

Firmly narrowing upward from this wealthy but inconspicuous substratum was the compact and dominant group which the Mingotts, Newlands, Chiverses and Mansons so actively represented. Most people imagined them to be the very apex of the pyramid; but they themselves (at least those of Mrs. Archer's generation) were aware that, in the eyes of the professional genealogist, only a still smaller number of families could lay claim to that eminence.

"Don't tell me," Mrs. Archer would say to her children, "all this modern newspaper rubbish about a New York aristocracy. If there is one, neither the Mingotts nor the Mansons belong to it; no, nor the Newlands or the Chiverses either. Our grandfathers and great-grandfathers were just respectable English or Dutch merchants, who came to the colonies to make their fortune, and stayed here because they did so well. One of your great-grandfathers signed the Declaration, and another was a general on Washington's staff, and received General Burgoyne's sword after the battle of Saratoga. These are things to be proud of, but they have nothing to do with rank or class. New York has always been a commercial community, and there are not more than three families in it who can claim an aristocratic origin in the real sense of the word."

Mrs. Archer and her son and daughter, like every one else in New York, knew who these privileged beings were: the Dagonets of Washington Square, who came of an old English county family allied with the Pitts and Foxes; the Lannings, who had intermarried with the descendants of Count de Grasse, and the van der Luydens, direct descendants of the first Dutch governor of Manhattan, and related by pre-revolutionary marriages to several members of the French and British aristocracy.

The Lannings survived only in the person of two very old but lively Miss Lannings, who lived cheerfully and reminiscently among family portraits and Chippendale; the Dagonets were a considerable clan, allied to the best names in Baltimore and Philadelphia; but the van der Luydens, who stood above all of them, had faded into a kind of super-terrestrial twilight, from which only two figures impressively emerged; those of Mr. and Mrs. Henry van der Luyden.

Mrs. Henry van der Luyden had been Louisa Dagonet, and her mother had been the granddaughter of Colonel du Lac, of an old Channel Island family, who had fought under Cornwallis and had settled in Maryland, after the war, with his bride, Lady Angelica Trevenna, fifth daughter of the Earl of St. Austrey. The tie between the Dagonets, the du Lacs of Maryland, and their aristocratic Cornish kinsfolk, the Trevennas, had always remained close and cordial. Mr. and Mrs. van der Luyden had more than once paid long visits to the present head of the house of Trevenna, the Duke of St. Austrey, at his country-seat in Cornwall and at St. Austrey in Gloucestershire; and his Grace had frequently announced his intention of some day returning their visit (without the Duchess, who feared the Atlantic).

Mr. and Mrs. van der Luyden divided their time between Trevenna, their place in Maryland, and Skuytercliff, the great estate on the Hudson which had been one of the colonial grants of the Dutch government to the famous first Governor, and of which Mr. van der Luyden was still "Patroon." Their large solemn house in Madison Avenue was seldom opened, and when they came to town they received in it only their most intimate friends.

"I wish you would go with me, Newland," his mother said, suddenly pausing at the door of the Brown *coupé.* "Louisa is fond of you; and of course it's on account of dear May that I'm taking this step—and also because, if we don't all stand together, there'll be no such thing as Society left."

§ 7

Mrs. Henry van der Luyden listened in silence to her cousin Mrs. Archer's narrative.

It was all very well to tell yourself in advance that Mrs. van der Luyden was always silent, and that, though noncommittal by nature and training, she was very kind to the people she really liked. Even personal experience of these facts was not always a protection from the chill that descended on one in the high-ceilinged white-walled Madison Avenue drawing-room, with the pale brocaded armchairs so obviously uncovered for the occasion, and the gauze still veiling the ormolu mantel ornaments and the beautiful old carved frame of Gainsborough's "Lady Angelica du Lac."

Mrs. van der Luyden's portrait by Huntington (in black velvet and Venetian point) faced that of her lovely ancestress. It was generally considered "as fine as a Cabanel," and, though twenty years had elapsed since its execution, was still "a perfect likeness." Indeed the Mrs. van der Luyden who sat beneath it listening to Mrs. Archer might have been the twin-sister of the fair and still youngish woman drooping against a gilt armchair before a green rep curtain. Mrs. van der Luyden still wore black velvet and Venetian point when she went into society—or rather (since she never dined out) when she threw open her own doors to receive it. Her fair hair, which had faded without turning grey, was still parted in flat overlapping points on her forehead, and the straight nose that divided her pale blue eyes was only a little more pinched about the nostrils than when the portrait had been painted. She always, indeed, struck Newland Archer as having been rather gruesomely preserved in the airless atmosphere of a perfectly irreproachable existence, as bodies caught in glaciers keep for years a rosy life-in-death.

Like all his family, he esteemed and admired Mrs. van der Luyden; but he found her gentle bending sweetness less approachable than the grimness of some of his mother's old aunts, fierce spinsters who said "No" on principle before they knew what they were going to be asked.

Mrs. van der Luyden's attitude said neither yes nor no, but always appeared to incline to clemency till her thin lips, wavering into the shadow of a smile, made the almost invariable reply: "I shall first have to talk this over with my husband."

She and Mr. van der Luyden were so exactly alike that Archer often wondered how, after forty years of the closest conjugality, two such merged identities ever separated themselves enough for anything as controversial as a talking-over. But as neither had ever reached a decision without prefacing it by this mysterious conclave, Mrs. Archer and her son, having set forth their case, waited resignedly for the familiar phrase.

Mrs. van der Luyden, however, who had seldom surprised any one, now surprised them by reaching her long hand toward the bell-rope.

"I think," she said, "I should like Henry to hear what you have told me."

A footman appeared, to whom she gravely added: "If Mr. van der Luyden has finished reading the newspaper, please ask him to be kind enough to come."

She said "reading the newspaper" in the tone in which a Minister's wife might have said: "Presiding at a Cabinet meeting"—not from any arrogance of mind, but because the habit of a life-time, and the attitude of her friends and relations, had led her to consider Mr. van der Luyden's least gesture as having an almost sacerdotal importance.

Her promptness of action showed that she considered the case as pressing as Mrs. Archer; but, lest she should be thought to have committed herself in advance, she added, with the sweetest look: "Henry always enjoys seeing you, dear Adeline; and he will wish to congratulate Newland."

The double doors had solemnly reopened and between them appeared Mr. Henry van der Luyden, tall, spare and frock-coated, with faded fair hair, a straight nose like his wife's and the same look of frozen gentleness in eyes that were merely pale grey instead of pale blue.

Mr. van der Luyden greeted Mrs. Archer with cousinly affability, proffered to Newland low-voiced congratulations couched in the same language as his wife's, and seated himself in one of the brocade armchairs with the simplicity of a reigning sovereign.

"I had just finished reading the Times," he said, laying his long finger-tips together. "In town my mornings are so much occupied that I find it more convenient to read the newspapers after luncheon."

"Ah, there's a great deal to be said for that plan—indeed I think my uncle Egmont used to say he found it less agitating not to read the morning papers till after dinner," said Mrs. Archer responsively.

"Yes: my good father abhorred hurry. But now we live in a constant rush," said Mr. van der Luyden in measured tones, looking with pleasant deliberation about the large shrouded room which to Archer was so complete an image of its owners.

"But I hope you *had* finished your reading, Henry?" his wife interposed.

"Quite—quite," he reassured her.

"Then I should like Adeline to tell you—"

"Oh, it's really Newland's story," said his mother smiling; and proceeded to rehearse once more the monstrous tale of the affront inflicted on Mrs. Lovell Mingott.

"Of course," she ended, "Augusta Welland and Mary Mingott both felt that, especially in view of Newland's engagement, you and Henry *ought to know.*"

"Ah—" said Mr. van der Luyden, drawing a deep breath.

There was a silence during which the tick of the monumental ormolu clock on the white marble mantel piece grew as loud as the boom of a minute-gun. Archer contemplated with awe the two slender faded figures, seated side by side in a kind of viceregal rigidity, mouth-pieces of some remote ancestral authority which fate compelled them to wield, when they would so much rather have lived in simplicity and seclusion, digging invisible weeds out of the perfect lawns of Skuytercliff, and playing Patience together in the evenings.

Mr. van der Luyden was the first to speak.

"You really think this is due to some—some intentional interference of Lawrence Lefferts's?" he enquired, turning to Archer.

"I'm certain of it, sir. Larry has been going it rather harder than usual lately—if cousin Louisa won't mind my mentioning it—having rather a stiff affair with the postmaster's wife in their village, or some one of that sort; and whenever poor Gertrude Lefferts begins to suspect anything, and he's afraid of trouble, he gets up a fuss of this kind, to show how awfully moral he is, and talks at the top of his voice about the impertinence of inviting his wife to meet people he doesn't wish her to know. He's simply using Madame Olenska as a lightning-rod; I've seen him try the same thing often before."

"The *Leffertses!*—" said Mrs. van der Luyden.

"The *Leffertses!*—" echoed Mrs. Archer. "What would uncle Egmont have said of Lawrence Lefferts's pronouncing on anybody's social position? It shows what Society has come to."

"We'll hope it has not quite come to that," said Mr. van der Luyden firmly.

"Ah, if only you and Louisa went out more!" sighed Mrs. Archer.

But instantly she became aware of her mistake. The van der Luydens were morbidly sensitive to any criticism of their secluded existence. They were the arbiters of fashion, the Court of last Appeal, and they knew it, and bowed to their fate. But being shy and retiring persons, with no natural inclination for their part, they lived as much as possible in the sylvan solitude of Skuytercliff, and when they came to town, declined all invitations on the plea of Mrs. van der Luyden's health.

Newland Archer came to his mother's rescue. "Everybody in New York knows what you and cousin Louisa represent. That's why Mrs. Mingott felt she ought not to allow this slight on Countess Olenska to pass without consulting you."

Mrs. van der Luyden glanced at her husband, who glanced back at her.

"It is the principle that I dislike," said Mr. van der Luyden. "As long as a member of a well-known family is backed up by that family it should be considered—final."

"It seems so to me," said his wife, as if she were producing a new thought.

"I had no idea," Mr. van der Luyden continued, "that things had come to such a pass." He paused, and looked at his wife again. "It occurs to me, my dear, that the Countess Olenska is already a sort of relation—through Medora Manson's first husband. At any rate, she will be when Newland marries." He turned toward the young man. "Have you read this morning's Times, Newland?"

"Why, yes, sir," said Archer, who usually tossed off half a dozen papers with his morning coffee.

Husband and wife looked at each other again. Their pale eyes clung together in prolonged and serious consultation; then a faint smile fluttered over Mrs. van der Luyden's face. She had evidently guessed and approved.

Mr. van der Luyden turned to Mrs. Archer. "If Louisa's health allowed her to dine out—I wish you would say to Mrs. Lovell Mingott—she and I would have been happy to—er—fill the places of the Lawrence Leffertses at her dinner." He paused to let the irony of this sink in. "As you know, this is impossible." Mrs. Archer sounded a sympathetic assent. "But Newland tells me he has read this morning's Times; therefore he has probably seen that Louisa's relative, the Duke of St. Austrey, arrives next week on the Russia. He is coming to enter his new sloop, the Guinevere, in next summer's International Cup Race; and also to have a little canvasback shooting at Trevenna." Mr. van der Luyden paused again, and continued with increasing benevolence: "Before taking him down to Maryland we are inviting a few friends to meet him here—only a little dinner—with a reception afterward. I am sure Louisa will be as glad as I am if Countess Olenska will let us include her among our guests." He got up, bent his long body with a stiff friendliness toward his cousin, and added: "I think I have Louisa's authority for saying that she will herself leave the invitation to dine when she drives out presently: with our cards—of course with our cards."

Mrs. Archer, who knew this to be a hint that the seventeen-hand chestnuts which were never kept waiting were at the door, rose with a hurried murmur of thanks. Mrs. van der Luyden beamed on her with the smile of Esther interceding with Ahasuerus; but her husband raised a protesting hand.

"There is nothing to thank me for, dear Adeline; nothing whatever. This kind of thing must not happen in New York; it shall not, as long as I can help it," he pronounced with sovereign gentleness as he steered his cousins to the door.

Two hours later, every one knew that the great C-spring barouche in which Mrs. van der Luyden took the air at all seasons had been seen at old Mrs. Mingott's door, where a large square envelope was handed in; and that evening at the Opera Mr. Sillerton Jackson was able to state that the envelope contained a card inviting the Countess Olenska to the dinner which the van der Luydens were giving the following week for their cousin, the Duke of St. Austrey.

Some of the younger men in the club box exchanged a smile at this announcement and glanced sideways at Lawrence Lefferts, who sat carelessly in the front of the box, pulling his long fair moustache, and who remarked with authority, as the soprano paused: "No one but Patti ought to attempt the Sonnambula."

§ 8

It was generally agreed in New York that the Countess Olenska had "lost her looks."

She had appeared there first, in Newland Archer's boyhood, as a brilliantly pretty little girl of nine or ten, of whom people said that she "ought to be painted." Her parents had been continental wanderers, and after a roaming babyhood she had lost them both, and been taken in charge by her aunt, Medora Manson, also a wanderer, who was herself returning to New York to "settle down."

Poor Medora, repeatedly widowed, was always coming home to settle down (each time in a less expensive house), and bringing with her a new husband or an adopted child; but after a few months she invariably parted from her husband or quarrelled with her ward, and, having got rid of her house at a loss, set out again on her wanderings. As her mother had been a Rushworth, and her last unhappy marriage had linked her to one of the crazy Chiverses, New York looked indulgently on her eccentricities; but when she returned with her little orphaned niece, whose parents had been popular in spite of their regrettable taste for travel, people thought it a pity that the pretty child should be in such hands.

Every one was disposed to be kind to little Ellen Mingott, though her dusky red cheeks and tight curls gave her an air of gaiety that seemed unsuitable in a child who should still have been in black for her parents. It was one of the misguided Medora's many peculiarities to flout the unalterable rules that regulated American mourning, and when she stepped from the steamer her family were scandalised to see that the crape veil she wore for her own brother was seven inches shorter than those of her sisters-in-law, while little Ellen was in crimson merino and amber beads, like a gipsy foundling.

But New York had so long resigned itself to Medora that only a few old ladies shook their heads over Ellen's gaudy clothes, while her other relations fell under the charm of her high colour and high spirits. She was a fearless and familiar little thing, who asked disconcerting questions, made precocious comments, and possessed outlandish arts, such as dancing a Spanish shawl dance and singing Neapolitan love-songs to a guitar. Under the direction of her aunt (whose real name was Mrs. Thorley Chivers, but who, having received a Papal title, had resumed her first husband's patronymic, and called herself the Marchioness Manson, because in Italy she could turn it into Manzoni) the little girl received an expensive but incoherent education, which included "drawing from the model," a thing never dreamed of before, and playing the piano in quintets with professional musicians.

Of course no good could come of this; and when, a few years later, poor Chivers finally died in a madhouse, his widow (draped in strange weeds) again pulled up stakes and departed with Ellen, who had grown into a tall bony girl with conspicuous eyes. For some time no more was heard of them; then news came of Ellen's marriage to an immensely rich Polish nobleman of legendary fame, whom she had met at a ball at the Tuileries, and who was said to have princely establishments in Paris, Nice and Florence, a yacht at Cowes, and many square miles of shooting in Transylvania. She disappeared in a kind of sulphurous apotheosis, and when a few years later Medora again came back to New York, subdued, impoverished, mourning a third husband, and in quest of a still smaller house, people wondered that her rich niece had not been able to do something for her. Then came the news that Ellen's own marriage had ended in disaster, and that she was herself returning home to seek rest and oblivion among her kinsfolk.

These things passed through Newland Archer's mind a week later as he watched the Countess Olenska enter the van der Luyden drawing-room on the evening of the momentous dinner. The occasion was a solemn one, and he wondered a little nervously how she would carry it off. She came rather late, one hand still ungloved, and fastening a bracelet about her wrist; yet she entered without any appearance of haste or embarrassment the drawing-room in which New York's most chosen company was somewhat awfully assembled.

In the middle of the room she paused, looking about her with a grave mouth and smiling eyes; and in that instant Newland Archer rejected the general verdict on her looks. It was true that her early radiance was gone. The red cheeks had paled; she was thin, worn, a little older-looking than her age, which must have been nearly thirty. But there was about her the mysterious authority of beauty, a sureness in the carriage of the head, the movement of the eyes, which, without being in the least theatrical, struck him as highly trained and full of a conscious power. At the same time she was simpler in manner than most of the ladies present, and many people (as he heard afterward from Janey) were disappointed that her appearance was not more "stylish"—for stylishness was what New York most valued. It was, perhaps, Archer reflected, because her early vivacity had disappeared; because she was so quiet—quiet in her movements, her voice, and the tones of her low-pitched voice. New York had expected something a good deal more resonant in a young woman with such a history.

The dinner was a somewhat formidable business. Dining with the van der Luydens was at best no light matter, and dining there with a Duke who was their cousin was almost a religious solemnity. It pleased Archer to think that only an old New Yorker could perceive the shade of difference (to New York) between being merely a Duke and being the van der Luydens' Duke. New York took stray noblemen calmly, and even (except in the Struthers set) with a certain distrustful *hauteur;* but when they presented such credentials as these they were received with an old-fashioned cordiality that they would have been greatly mistaken in ascribing solely to their standing in Debrett. It was for just such distinctions that the young man cherished his old New York even while he smiled at it.

The van der Luydens had done their best to emphasise the importance of the occasion. The du Lac Sèvres and the Trevenna George II plate were out; so was the van der Luyden "Lowestoft" (East India Company) and the Dagonet Crown Derby. Mrs. van der Luyden looked more than ever like a Cabanel, and Mrs. Archer, in her grandmother's seed-pearls and emeralds, reminded her son of an Isabey miniature. All the ladies had on their handsomest jewels, but it was characteristic of the house and the occasion that these were mostly in rather heavy old-fashioned settings; and old Miss Lanning, who had been persuaded to come, actually wore her mother's cameos and a Spanish blonde shawl.

The Countess Olenska was the only young woman at the dinner; yet, as Archer scanned the smooth plump elderly faces between their diamond necklaces and towering ostrich feathers, they struck him as curiously immature compared with hers. It frightened him to think what must have gone to the making of her eyes.

The Duke of St. Austrey, who sat at his hostess's right, was naturally the chief figure of the evening. But if the Countess Olenska was less conspicuous than had been hoped, the Duke was almost invisible. Being a well-bred man he had not (like another recent ducal visitor) come to the dinner in a shooting-jacket; but his evening clothes were so shabby and baggy, and he wore them with such an air of their being homespun, that (with his stooping way of sitting, and the vast beard spreading over his shirt-front) he hardly gave the appearance of being in dinner attire. He was short, round-shouldered, sunburnt, with a thick nose, small eyes and a sociable smile; but he seldom spoke, and when he did it was in such low tones that, despite the frequent silences of expectation about the table, his remarks were lost to all but his neighbours.

When the men joined the ladies after dinner the Duke went straight up to the Countess Olenska, and they sat down in a corner and plunged into animated talk. Neither seemed aware that the Duke should first have paid his respects to Mrs. Lovell Mingott and Mrs. Headly Chivers, and the Countess have conversed with that amiable hypochondriac, Mr. Urban Dagonet of Washington Square, who, in order to have the pleasure of meeting her, had broken through his fixed rule of not dining out between January and April. The two chatted together for nearly twenty minutes; then the Countess rose and, walking alone across the wide drawing-room, sat down at Newland Archer's side.

It was not the custom in New York drawing-rooms for a lady to get up and walk away from one gentleman in order to seek the company of another. Etiquette required that she should wait, immovable as an idol, while the men who wished to converse with her succeeded each other at her side. But the Countess was apparently unaware of having broken any rule; she sat at perfect ease in a corner of the sofa beside Archer, and looked at him with the kindest eyes.

"I want you to talk to me about May," she said.

Instead of answering her he asked: "You knew the Duke before?"

"Oh, yes—we used to see him every winter at Nice. He's very fond of gambling—he used to come to the house a great deal." She said it in the simplest manner, as if she had said: "He's fond of wild-flowers"; and after a moment she added candidly: "I think he's the dullest man I ever met."

This pleased her companion so much that he forgot the slight shock her previous remark had caused him. It was undeniably exciting to meet a lady who found the van der Luydens' Duke dull, and dared to utter the opinion. He longed to question her, to hear more about the life of which her careless words had given him so illuminating a glimpse; but he feared to touch on distressing memories, and before he could think of anything to say she had strayed back to her original subject.

"May is a darling; I've seen no young girl in New York so handsome and so intelligent. Are you very much in love with her?"

Newland Archer reddened and laughed. "As much as a man can be."

She continued to consider him thoughtfully, as if not to miss any shade of meaning in what he said, "Do you think, then, there is a limit?"

"To being in love? If there is, I haven't found it!"

She glowed with sympathy. "Ah—it's really and truly a romance?"

"The most romantic of romances!"

"How delightful! And you found it all out for yourselves—it was not in the least arranged for you?"

Archer looked at her incredulously. "Have you forgotten," he asked with a smile, "that in our country we don't allow our marriages to be arranged for us?"

A dusky blush rose to her cheek, and he instantly regretted his words.

"Yes," she answered, "I'd forgotten. You must forgive me if I sometimes make these mistakes. I don't always remember that everything here is good that was—that was bad where I've come from." She looked down at her Viennese fan of eagle feathers, and he saw that her lips trembled.

"I'm so sorry," he said impulsively; "but you *are* among friends here, you know."

"Yes—I know. Wherever I go I have that feeling. That's why I came home. I want to forget everything else, to become a complete American again, like the Mingotts and Wellands, and you and your delightful mother, and all the other good people here tonight. Ah, here's May arriving, and you will want to hurry away to her," she added, but without moving; and her eyes turned back from the door to rest on the young man's face.

The drawing-rooms were beginning to fill up with after-dinner guests, and following Madame Olenska's glance Archer saw May Welland entering with her mother. In her dress of white and silver, with a wreath of silver blossoms in her hair, the tall girl looked like a Diana just alight from the chase.

"Oh," said Archer, "I have so many rivals: you see she's already surrounded. There's the Duke being introduced."

"Then stay with me a little longer," Madame Olenska said in a low tone, just touching his knee with her plumed fan. It was the lightest touch, but it thrilled him like a caress.

"Yes, let me stay," he answered in the same tone, hardly knowing what he said; but just then Mr. van der Luyden came up, followed by old Mr. Urban Dagonet. The Countess greeted them with her grave smile, and Archer, feeling his host's admonitory glance on him, rose and surrendered his seat.

Madame Olenska held out her hand as if to bid him good-bye.

"Tomorrow, then, after five—I shall expect you," she said; and then turned back to make room for Mr. Dagonet.

"Tomorrow—" Archer heard himself repeating, though there had been no engagement, and during their talk she had given him no hint that she wished to see him again.

As he moved away he saw Lawrence Lefferts, tall and resplendent, leading his wife up to be introduced; and heard Gertrude Lefferts say, as she beamed on the Countess with her large unperceiving smile: "But I think we used to go to dancing-school together when we were children—." Behind her, waiting their turn to name themselves to the Countess, Archer noticed a number of the recalcitrant couples who had declined to meet her at Mrs. Lovell Mingott's. As Mrs. Archer remarked: when the van der Luydens chose, they knew how to give a lesson. The wonder was that they chose so seldom.

The young man felt a touch on his arm and saw Mrs. van der Luyden looking down on him from the pure eminence of black velvet and the family diamonds. "It was good of you, dear Newland, to devote yourself so unselfishly to Madame Olenska. I told your cousin Henry he must really come to the rescue."

He was aware of smiling at her vaguely, and she added, as if condescending to his natural shyness: "I've never seen May looking lovelier. The Duke thinks her the handsomest girl in the room."

§ 9

The Countess Olenska had said "after five"; and at half after the hour Newland Archer rang the bell of the peeling stucco house with a giant wisteria throttling its feeble cast-iron balcony, which she had hired, far down West Twenty-third Street, from the vagabond Medora.

It was certainly a strange quarter to have settled in. Small dressmakers, bird-stuffers and "people who wrote" were her nearest neighbours; and further down the dishevelled street Archer recognised a dilapidated wooden house, at the end of a paved path, in which a writer and journalist called Winsett, whom he used to come across now and then, had mentioned that he lived. Winsett did not invite people to his house; but he had once pointed it out to Archer in the course of a nocturnal stroll, and the latter had asked himself, with a little shiver, if the humanities were so meanly housed in other capitals.

Madame Olenska's own dwelling was redeemed from the same appearance only by a little more paint about the window-frames; and as Archer mustered its modest front he said to himself that the Polish Count must have robbed her of her fortune as well as of her illusions.

The young man had spent an unsatisfactory day. He had lunched with the Wellands, hoping afterward to carry off May for a walk in the Park. He wanted to have her to himself, to tell her how enchanting she had looked the night before, and how proud he was of her, and to press her to hasten their marriage. But Mrs. Welland had firmly reminded him that the round of family visits was not half over, and, when he hinted at advancing the date of the wedding, had raised reproachful eye-brows and sighed out: "Twelve dozen of everything—hand-embroidered—"

Packed in the family landau they rolled from one tribal doorstep to another, and Archer, when the afternoon's round was over, parted from his betrothed with the feeling that he had been shown off like a wild animal cunningly trapped. He supposed that his readings in anthropology caused him to take such a coarse view of what was after all a simple and natural demonstration of family feeling; but when he remembered that the Wellands did not expect the wedding to take place till the following autumn, and pictured what his life would be till then, a dampness fell upon his spirit.

"Tomorrow," Mrs. Welland called after him, "we'll do the Chiverses and the Dallases"; and he perceived that she was going through their two families alphabetically, and that they were only in the first quarter of the alphabet.

He had meant to tell May of the Countess Olenska's request—her command, rather—that he should call on her that afternoon; but in the brief moments when they were alone he had had more pressing things to say. Besides, it struck him as a little absurd to allude to the matter. He knew that May most particularly wanted him to be kind to her cousin; was it not that wish which had hastened the announcement of their engagement? It gave him an odd sensation to reflect that, but for the Countess's arrival, he might have been, if not still a free man, at least a man less irrevocably pledged. But May had willed it so, and he felt himself somehow relieved of further responsibility—and therefore at liberty, if he chose, to call on her cousin without telling her.

As he stood on Madame Olenska's threshold curiosity was his uppermost feeling. He was puzzled by the tone in which she had summoned him; he concluded that she was less simple than she seemed.

The door was opened by a swarthy foreign-looking maid, with a prominent bosom under a gay neckerchief, whom he vaguely fancied to be Sicilian. She welcomed him with all her white teeth, and answering his enquiries by a head-shake of incomprehension led him through the narrow hall into a low firelit drawing-room. The room was empty, and she left him, for an appreciable time, to wonder whether she had gone to find her mistress, or whether she had not understood what he was there for, and thought it might be to wind the clocks—of which he perceived that the only visible specimen had stopped. He knew that the southern races communicated with each other in the language of pantomime, and was mortified to find her shrugs and smiles so unintelligible. At length she returned with a lamp; and Archer, having meanwhile put together a phrase out of Dante and Petrarch, evoked the answer: *"La signora è fuori; ma verrà subito";* which he took to mean: "She's out—but you'll soon see."

What he saw, meanwhile, with the help of the lamp, was the faded shadowy charm of a room unlike any room he had known. He knew that the Countess Olenska had brought some of her possessions with her—bits of wreckage, she called them—and these, he supposed, were represented by some small slender tables of dark wood, a delicate little Greek bronze on the chimney-piece, and a stretch of red damask nailed on the discoloured wallpaper behind a couple of Italian-looking pictures in old frames.

Newland Archer prided himself on his knowledge of Italian art. His boyhood had been saturated with Ruskin, and he had read all the latest books: John Addington Symonds, Vernon Lee's "Euphorion," the essays of P. G. Hamerton, and a wonderful new volume called "The Renaissance" by Walter Pater. He talked easily of Botticelli, and spoke of Fra Angelico with a faint condescension. But these pictures bewildered him, for they were like nothing that he was accustomed to look at (and therefore able to see) when he travelled in Italy; and perhaps, also, his powers of observation were impaired by the oddness of finding himself in this strange empty house, where apparently no one expected him. He was sorry that he had not told May Welland of Countess Olenska's request, and a little disturbed by the thought that his betrothed might come in to see her cousin. What would she think if she found him sitting there with the air of intimacy implied by waiting alone in the dusk at a lady's fireside?

But since he had come he meant to wait; and he sank into a chair and stretched his feet to the logs.

It was odd to have summoned him in that way, and then forgotten him; but Archer felt more curious than mortified. The atmosphere of the room was so different from any he had ever breathed that self-consciousness vanished in the sense of adventure. He had been before in drawing-rooms hung with red damask, with pictures "of the Italian school"; what struck him was the way in which Medora Manson's shabby hired house, with its blighted background of pampas grass and Rogers statuettes, had, by a turn of the hand, and the skilful use of a few properties, been transformed into something intimate, "foreign," subtly suggestive of old romantic scenes and sentiments. He tried to analyse the trick, to find a clue to it in the way the chairs and tables were grouped, in the fact that only two Jacqueminot roses (of which nobody ever bought less than a dozen) had been placed in the slender vase at his elbow, and in the vague pervading perfume that was not what one put on handkerchiefs, but rather like the scent of some far-off bazaar, a smell made up of Turkish coffee and ambergris and dried roses.

His mind wandered away to the question of what May's drawing-room would look like. He knew that Mr. Welland, who was behaving "very handsomely," already had his eye on a newly built house in East Thirty-ninth Street. The neighbourhood was thought remote and the house was built in a ghastly greenish-yellow stone that the younger architects were beginning to employ as a protest against the brownstone of which the uniform hue coated New York like a cold chocolate sauce; but the plumbing was perfect. Archer would have liked to travel, to put off the housing question; but, though the Wellands approved of an extended European honeymoon (perhaps even a winter in Egypt), they were firm as to the need of a house for the returning couple. The young man felt that his fate was sealed: for the rest of his life he would go up every evening between the cast-iron railings of that greenish-yellow doorstep, and pass through a Pompeian vestibule into a hall with a wainscoting of varnished yellow wood. But beyond that his imagination could not travel. He knew the drawing-room above had a bay window, but he could not fancy how May would deal with it. She submitted cheerfully to the purple satin and yellow tuftings of the Welland drawing-room, to its sham Buhl tables and gilt vitrines full of modern Saxe. He saw no reason to suppose that she would want anything different in her own house; and his only comfort was to reflect that she would probably let him arrange his library as he pleased—which would be, of course, with "sincere" Eastlake furniture, and the plain new book-cases without glass doors.

The round-bosomed maid came in, drew the curtains, pushed back a log, and said consolingly: *"Verrà—verrà."* When she had gone Archer stood up and began to wander about. Should he wait any longer? His position was becoming rather foolish. Perhaps he had misunderstood Madame Olenska—perhaps she had not invited him after all.

Down the cobblestones of the quiet street came the ring of a stepper's hoofs; they stopped before the house, and he caught the opening of a carriage door. Parting the curtains he looked out into the early dusk. A street-lamp faced him, and in its light he saw Julius Beaufort's compact English brougham, drawn by a big roan, and the banker descending from it, and helping out Madame Olenska.

Beaufort stood, hat in hand, saying something which his companion seemed to negative; then they shook hands, and he jumped into his carriage while she mounted the steps.

When she entered the room she showed no surprise at seeing Archer there; surprise seemed the emotion that she was least addicted to.

"How do you like my funny house?" she asked. "To me it's like heaven."

As she spoke she untied her little velvet bonnet and tossing it away with her long cloak stood looking at him with meditative eyes.

"You've arranged it delightfully," he rejoined, alive to the flatness of the words, but imprisoned in the conventional by his consuming desire to be simple and striking.

"Oh, it's a poor little place. My relations despise it. But at any rate it's less gloomy than the van der Luydens'."

The words gave him an electric shock, for few were the rebellious spirits who would have dared to call the stately home of the van der Luydens gloomy. Those privileged to enter it shivered there, and spoke of it as "handsome." But suddenly he was glad that she had given voice to the general shiver.

"It's delicious—what you've done here," he repeated.

"I like the little house," she admitted; "but I suppose what I like is the blessedness of its being here, in my own country and my own town; and then, of being alone in it." She spoke so low that he hardly heard the last phrase; but in his awkwardness he took it up.

"You like so much to be alone?"

"Yes; as long as my friends keep me from feeling lonely." She sat down near the fire, said: "Nastasia will bring the tea presently," and signed to him to return to his armchair, adding: "I see you've already chosen your corner."

Leaning back, she folded her arms behind her head, and looked at the fire under drooping lids.

"This is the hour I like best—don't you?"

A proper sense of his dignity caused him to answer: "I was afraid you'd forgotten the hour. Beaufort must have been very engrossing."

She looked amused. "Why—have you waited long? Mr. Beaufort took me to see a number of houses—since it seems I'm not to be allowed to stay in this one." She appeared to dismiss both Beaufort and himself from her mind, and went on: "I've never been in a city where there seems to be such a feeling against living in *des quartiers excentriques*. What does it matter where one lives? I'm told this street is respectable."

"It's not fashionable."

"Fashionable! Do you all think so much of that? Why not make one's own fashions? But I suppose I've lived too independently; at any rate, I want to do what you all do—I want to feel cared for and safe."

He was touched, as he had been the evening before when she spoke of her need of guidance.

"That's what your friends want you to feel. New York's an awfully safe place," he added with a flash of sarcasm.

"Yes, isn't it? One feels that," she cried, missing the mockery. "Being here is like—like—being taken on a holiday when one has been a good little girl and done all one's lessons."

The analogy was well meant, but did not altogether please him. He did not mind being flippant about New York, but disliked to hear any one else take the same tone. He wondered if she did not begin to see what a powerful engine it was, and how nearly it had crushed her. The Lovell Mingotts' dinner, patched up *in extremis* out of all sorts of social odds and ends, ought to have taught her the narrowness of her escape; but either she had been all along unaware of having skirted disaster, or else she had lost sight of it in the triumph of the van der Luyden evening. Archer inclined to the former theory; he fancied that her New York was still completely undifferentiated, and the conjecture nettled him.

"Last night," he said, "New York laid itself out for you. The van der Luydens do nothing by halves."

"No: how kind they are! It was such a nice party. Every one seems to have such an esteem for them."

The terms were hardly adequate; she might have spoken in that way of a tea-party at the dear old Miss Lannings'.

"The van der Luydens," said Archer, feeling himself pompous as he spoke, "are the most powerful influence in New York society. Unfortunately—owing to her health—they receive very seldom."

She unclasped her hands from behind her head, and looked at him meditatively.

"Isn't that perhaps the reason?"

"The reason—?"

"For their great influence; that they make themselves so rare."

He coloured a little, stared at her—and suddenly felt the penetration of the remark. At a stroke she had pricked the van der Luydens and they collapsed. He laughed, and sacrificed them.

Nastasia brought the tea, with handleless Japanese cups and little covered dishes, placing the tray on a low table.

"But you'll explain these things to me—you'll tell me all I ought to know," Madame Olenska continued, leaning forward to hand him his cup.

"It's you who are telling me; opening my eyes to things I'd looked at so long that I'd ceased to see them."

She detached a small gold cigarette-case from one of her bracelets, held it out to him, and took a cigarette herself. On the chimney were long spills for lighting them.

"Ah, then we can both help each other. But I want help so much more. You must tell me just what to do."

It was on the tip of his tongue to reply: "Don't be seen driving about the streets with Beaufort—" but he was being too deeply drawn into the atmosphere of the room, which was her atmosphere, and to give advice of that sort would have been like telling some one who was bargaining for attar-of-roses in Samarkand that one should always be provided with arctics for a New York winter. New York seemed much farther off than Samarkand, and if they were indeed to help each other she was rendering what might prove the first of their mutual services by making him look at his native city objectively. Viewed thus, as through the wrong end of a telescope, it looked disconcertingly small and distant; but then from Samarkand it would.

A flame darted from the logs and she bent over the fire, stretching her thin hands so close to it that a faint halo shone about the oval nails. The light touched to russet the rings of dark hair escaping from her braids, and made her pale face paler.

"There are plenty of people to tell you what to do," Archer rejoined, obscurely envious of them.

"Oh—all my aunts? And my dear old Granny?" She considered the idea impartially. "They're all a little vexed with me for setting up for myself—poor Granny especially. She wanted to keep me with her; but I had to be free—" He was impressed by this light way of speaking of the formidable Catherine, and moved by the thought of what must have given Madame Olenska this thirst for even the loneliest kind of freedom. But the idea of Beaufort gnawed him.

"I think I understand how you feel," he said. "Still, your family can advise you; explain differences; show you the way."

She lifted her thin black eyebrows. "Is New York such a labyrinth? I thought it so straight up and down—like Fifth Avenue. And with all the cross streets numbered!" She seemed to guess his faint disapproval of this, and added, with the rare smile that enchanted her whole face: "If you knew how I like it for just *that*—the straight-up-and-downness, and the big honest labels on everything!"

He saw his chance. "Everything may be labelled—but everybody is not."

"Perhaps. I may simplify too much—but you'll warn me if I do." She turned from the fire to look at him. "There are only two people here who make me feel as if they understood what I mean and could explain things to me: you and Mr. Beaufort."

Archer winced at the joining of the names, and then, with a quick readjustment, understood, sympathised and pitied. So close to the powers of evil she must have lived that she still breathed more freely in their air. But since she felt that he understood her also, his business would be to make her see Beaufort as he really was, with all he represented—and abhor it.

He answered gently: "I understand. But just at first don't let go of your old friends' hands: I mean the older women, your Granny Mingott, Mrs. Welland, Mrs. van der Luyden. They like and admire you—they want to help you."

She shook her head and sighed. "Oh, I know—I know! But on condition that they don't hear anything unpleasant. Aunt Welland put it in those very words when I tried. . . . Does no one want to know the truth here, Mr. Archer? The real loneliness is living among all these kind people who only ask one to pretend!" She lifted her hands to her face, and he saw her thin shoulders shaken by a sob.

"Madame Olenska!—Oh, don't, Ellen," he cried, starting up and bending over her. He drew down one of her hands, clasping and chafing it like a child's while he murmured reassuring words; but in a moment she freed herself, and looked up at him with wet lashes.

"Does no one cry here, either? I suppose there's no need to, in heaven," she said, straightening her loosened braids with a laugh, and bending over the tea-kettle. It was burnt into his consciousness that he had called her "Ellen"—called her so twice; and that she had not noticed it. Far down the inverted telescope he saw the faint white figure of May Welland—in New York.

Suddenly Nastasia put her head in to say something in her rich Italian.

Madame Olenska, again with a hand at her hair, uttered an exclamation of assent—a flashing *"Già—già"*—and the Duke of St. Austrey entered, piloting a tremendous black-wigged and red-plumed lady in overflowing furs.

"My dear Countess, I've brought an old friend of mine to see you—Mrs. Struthers. She wasn't asked to the party last night, and she wants to know you."

The Duke beamed on the group, and Madame Olenska advanced with a murmur of welcome toward the queer couple. She seemed to have no idea how oddly matched they were, nor what a liberty the

Duke had taken in bringing his companion—and to do him justice, as Archer perceived, the Duke seemed as unaware of it himself.

"Of course I want to know you, my dear," cried Mrs. Struthers in a round rolling voice that matched her bold feathers and her brazen wig. "I want to know everybody who's young and interesting and charming. And the Duke tells me you like music—didn't you, Duke? You're a pianist yourself, I believe? Well, do you want to hear Sarasate play tomorrow evening at my house? You know I've something going on every Sunday evening—it's the day when New York doesn't know what to do with itself, and so I say to it: 'Come and be amused.' And the Duke thought you'd be tempted by Sarasate. You'll find a number of your friends."

Madame Olenska's face grew brilliant with pleasure. "How kind! How good of the Duke to think of me!" She pushed a chair up to the tea-table and Mrs. Struthers sank into it delectably. "Of course I shall be too happy to come."

"That's all right, my dear. And bring your young gentleman with you." Mrs. Struthers extended a hail-fellow hand to Archer. "I can't put a name to you—but I'm sure I've met you—I've met everybody, here, or in Paris or London. Aren't you in diplomacy? All the diplomatists come to me. You like music too? Duke, you must be sure to bring him."

The Duke said "Rather" from the depths of his beard, and Archer withdrew with a stiffly circular bow that made him feel as full of spine as a self-conscious schoolboy among careless and unnoticing elders.

He was not sorry for the *dénouement* of his visit: he only wished it had come sooner and spared him a certain waste of emotion. As he went out into the wintry night, New York again became vast and imminent, and May Welland the loveliest woman in it. He turned into his florist's to send her the daily box of lilies-of-the-valley which, to his confusion, he found he had forgotten that morning.

As he wrote a word on his card and waited for an envelope he glanced about the embowered shop, and his eye lit on a cluster of yellow roses. He had never seen any as sun-golden before, and his first impulse was to send them to May instead of the lilies. But they did not look like her—there was something too rich, too strong in their fiery beauty. In a sudden revulsion of mood and almost without knowing what he did, he signed to the florist to lay the roses in another long box, and slipped his card into a second envelope, on which he wrote the name of the Countess Olenska; then, just as he was turning away, he drew the card out again, and left the empty envelope on the box.

"They'll go at once?" he enquired, pointing to the roses.

The florist assured him that they would.

§ 10

The next day he persuaded May to escape for a walk in the Park after luncheon. As was the custom in old-fashioned Episcopalian New York, she usually accompanied her parents to church on Sunday afternoons; but Mrs. Welland condoned her truancy, having that very morning won her over to the necessity of a long engagement, with time to prepare a hand-embroidered trousseau containing the proper number of dozens.

The day was delectable. The bare vaulting of trees along the Mall was ceiled with lapis lazuli, and arched above snow that shone like splintered crystals. It was the weather to call out May's radiance, and she burned like a young maple in the frost. Archer was proud of the glances turned on her, and the simple joy of possessorship cleared away his underlying perplexities.

"It's so delicious—waking every morning to smell lilies-of-the-valley in one's room!" she said.

"Yesterday they came late. I hadn't time in the morning—"

"But your remembering each day to send them makes me love them so much more than if you'd given a standing order, and they came every morning on the minute, like one's music-teacher—as I know Gertrude Lefferts's did, for instance, when she and Lawrence were engaged."

"Ah—they would!" laughed Archer, amused at her keenness. He looked sideways at her fruit-like cheek and felt rich and secure enough to add: "When I sent your lilies yesterday afternoon I saw some rather gorgeous yellow roses and packed them off to Madame Olenska. Was that right?"

"How dear of you! Anything of that kind delights her. It's odd she didn't mention it: she lunched with us today, and spoke of Mr.

Beaufort's having sent her wonderful orchids, and cousin Henry van der Luyden a whole hamper of carnations from Skuytercliff. She seems so surprised to receive flowers. Don't people send them in Europe? She thinks it such a pretty custom."

"Oh, well, no wonder mine were overshadowed by Beaufort's," said Archer irritably. Then he remembered that he had not put a card with the roses, and was vexed at having spoken of them. He wanted to say: "I called on your cousin yesterday," but hesitated. If Madame Olenska had not spoken of his visit it might seem awkward that he should. Yet not to do so gave the affair an air of mystery that he disliked. To shake off the question he began to talk of their own plans, their future, and Mrs. Welland's insistence on a long engagement.

"If you call it long! Isabel Chivers and Reggie were engaged for two years: Grace and Thorley for nearly a year and a half. Why aren't we very well off as we are?"

It was the traditional maidenly interrogation, and he felt ashamed of himself for finding it singularly childish. No doubt she simply echoed what was said for her; but she was nearing her twenty-second birthday, and he wondered at what age "nice" women began to speak for themselves.

"Never, if we won't let them, I suppose," he mused, and recalled his mad outburst to Mr. Sillerton Jackson: "Women ought to be as free as we are—"

It would presently be his task to take the bandage from this young woman's eyes, and bid her look forth on the world. But how many generations of the women who had gone to her making had descended bandaged to the family vault? He shivered a little, remembering some of the new ideas in his scientific books, and the much-cited instance of the Kentucky cave-fish, which had ceased to develop eyes because they had no use for them. What if, when he had bidden May Welland to open hers, they could only look out blankly at blankness?

"We might be much better off. We might be altogether together—we might travel."

Her face lit up. "That would be lovely," she owned: she would love to travel. But her mother would not understand their wanting to do things so differently.

"As if the mere 'differently' didn't account for it!" the wooer insisted.

"Newland! You're so original!" she exulted.

His heart sank, for he saw that he was saying all the things that young men in the same situation were expected to say, and that she was making the answers that instinct and tradition taught her to make—even to the point of calling him original.

"Original! We're all as like each other as those dolls cut out of the same folded paper. We're like patterns stencilled on a wall. Can't you and I strike out for ourselves, May?"

He had stopped and faced her in the excitement of their discussion, and her eyes rested on him with a bright unclouded admiration.

"Mercy—shall we elope?" she laughed.

"If you would—"

"You *do* love me, Newland! I'm so happy."

"But then—why not be happier?"

"We can't behave like people in novels, though, can we?"

"Why not—why not—why not?"

She looked a little bored by his insistence. She knew very well that they couldn't, but it was troublesome to have to produce a reason. "I'm not clever enough to argue with you. But that kind of thing is rather—vulgar, isn't it?" she suggested, relieved to have hit a word that would assuredly extinguish the whole subject.

"Are you so much afraid, then, of being vulgar?"

She was evidently staggered by this. "Of course I should hate it—so would you," she rejoined, a trifle irritably.

He stood silent, beating his stick nervously against his boot-top; and feeling that she had indeed found the right way of closing the discussion, she went on light-heartedly: "Oh, did I tell you that I showed Ellen my ring? She thinks it the most beautiful setting she ever saw. There's nothing like it in the rue de la Paix, she said. I do love you, Newland, for being so artistic!"

The next afternoon, as Archer, before dinner, sat smoking sullenly in his study, Janey wandered in on him. He had failed to stop at his club on the way up from the office where he exercised the profession of the law in the leisurely manner common to well-to-do

New Yorkers of his class. He was out of spirits and slightly out of temper, and a haunting horror of doing the same thing every day at the same hour besieged his brain.

"Sameness—sameness!" he muttered, the word running through his head like a persecuting tune as he saw the familiar tall-hatted figures lounging behind the plateglass; and because he usually dropped in at the club at that hour he had gone home instead. He knew not only what they were likely to be talking about, but the part each one would take in the discussion. The Duke of course would be their principal theme; though the appearance in Fifth Avenue of a golden-haired lady in a small canary-coloured brougham with a pair of black cobs (for which Beaufort was generally thought responsible) would also doubtless be thoroughly gone into. Such "women" (as they were called) were few in New York, those driving their own carriages still fewer, and the appearance of Miss Fanny Ring in Fifth Avenue at the fashionable hour had profoundly agitated society. Only the day before, her carriage had passed Mrs. Lovell Mingott's, and the latter had instantly rung the little bell at her elbow and ordered the coachman to drive her home. "What if it had happened to Mrs. van der Luyden?" people asked each other with a shudder. Archer could hear Lawrence Lefferts, at that very hour, holding forth on the disintegration of society.

He raised his head irritably when his sister Janey entered, and then quickly bent over his book (Swinburne's "Chastelard"—just out) as if he had not seen her. She glanced at the writing-table heaped with books, opened a volume of the "Contes Drôlatiques," made a wry face over the archaic French, and sighed: "What learned things you read!"

"Well—?" he asked, as she hovered Cassandra-like before him.

"Mother's very angry."

"Angry? With whom? About what?"

"Miss Sophy Jackson has just been here. She brought word that her brother would come in after dinner: she couldn't say very much, because he forbade her to: he wishes to give all the details himself. He's with cousin Louisa van der Luyden now."

"For heaven's sake, my dear girl, try a fresh start. It would take an omniscient Deity to know what you're taking about."

"It's not a time to be profane, Newland. . . . Mother feels badly enough about your not going to church . . ."

With a groan he plunged back into his book.

"Newland! Do listen. Your friend Madame Olenska was at Mrs. Lemuel Struthers's party last night: she went there with the Duke and Mr. Beaufort."

At the last clause of this announcement a senseless anger swelled the young man's breast. To smother it he laughed. "Well, what of it? I knew she meant to."

Janey paled and her eyes began to project. "You knew she meant to—and you didn't try to stop her? To warn her?"

"Stop her? Warn her?" He laughed again. "I'm not engaged to be married to the Countess Olenska!" The words had a fantastic sound in his own ears.

"You're marrying into her family."

"Oh, family—family!" he jeered.

"Newland—don't you care about Family?"

"Not a brass farthing."

"Nor about what cousin Louisa van der Luyden will think?"

"Not the half of one—if she thinks such old maid's rubbish."

"Mother is not an old maid," said his virgin sister with pinched lips.

He felt like shouting back: "Yes, she is, and so are the van der Luydens, and so we all are, when it comes to being so much as brushed by the wing-tip of Reality." But he saw her long gentle face puckering into tears, and felt ashamed of the useless pain he was inflicting.

"Hang Countess Olenska! Don't be a goose, Janey—I'm not her keeper."

"No; but you *did* ask the Wellands to announce your engagement sooner so that we might all back her up; and if it hadn't been for that cousin Louisa would never have invited her to the dinner for the Duke."

"Well—what harm was there in inviting her? She was the best-looking woman in the room; she made the dinner a little less funereal than the usual van der Luyden banquet."

"You know cousin Henry asked her to please you: he persuaded cousin Louisa. And now they're so upset that they're going back to

Skuytercliff tomorrow. I think, Newland, you'd better come down. You don't seem to understand how mother feels."

In the drawing-room Newland found his mother. She raised a troubled brow from her needlework to ask: "Has Janey told you?"

"Yes." He tried to keep his tone as measured as her own. "But I can't take it very seriously."

"Not the fact of having offended cousin Louisa and cousin Henry?"

"The fact that they can be offended by such a trifle as Countess Olenska's going to the house of a woman they consider common."

"Consider—!"

"Well, who is; but who has good music, and amuses people on Sunday evenings, when the whole of New York is dying of inanition."

"Good music? All I know is, there was a woman who got up on a table and sang the things they sing at the places you go to in Paris. There was smoking and champagne."

"Well—that kind of thing happens in other places, and the world still goes on."

"I don't suppose, dear, you're really defending the French Sunday?"

"I've heard you often enough, mother, grumble at the English Sunday when we've been in London."

"New York is neither Paris nor London."

"Oh, no, it's not!" her son groaned.

"You mean, I suppose, that society here is not as brilliant? You're right, I daresay; but we belong here, and people should respect our ways when they come among us. Ellen Olenska especially: she came back to get away from the kind of life people lead in brilliant societies."

Newland made no answer, and after a moment his mother ventured: "I was going to put on my bonnet and ask you to take me to see cousin Louisa for a moment before dinner." He frowned, and she continued: "I thought you might explain to her what you've just said: that society abroad is different . . . that people are not as particular, and that Madame Olenska may not have realised how we feel about such things. It would be, you know, dear," she added with an innocent adroitness, "in Madame Olenska's interest if you did."

"Dearest mother, I really don't see how we're concerned in the matter. The Duke took Madame Olenska to Mrs. Struthers's—in fact he brought Mrs. Struthers to call on her. I was there when they came. If the van der Luydens want to quarrel with anybody, the real culprit is under their own roof."

"Quarrel? Newland, did you ever know of cousin Henry's quarrelling? Besides, the Duke's his guest; and a stranger too. Strangers don't discriminate: how should they? Countess Olenska is a New Yorker, and should have respected the feelings of New York."

"Well, then, if they must have a victim, you have my leave to throw Madame Olenska to them," cried her son, exasperated. "I don't see myself—or you either—offering ourselves up to expiate her crimes."

"Oh, of course you see only the Mingott side," his mother answered, in the sensitive tone that was her nearest approach to anger.

The sad butler drew back the drawing-room portières and announced: "Mr. Henry van der Luyden."

Mrs. Archer dropped her needle and pushed her chair back with an agitated hand.

"Another lamp," she cried to the retreating servant, while Janey bent over to straighten her mother's cap.

Mr. van der Luyden's figure loomed on the threshold, and Newland Archer went forward to greet his cousin.

"We were just talking about you, sir," he said.

Mr. van der Luyden seemed overwhelmed by the announcement. He drew off his glove to shake hands with the ladies, and smoothed his tall hat shyly, while Janey pushed an arm-chair forward, and Archer continued: "And the Countess Olenska."

Mrs. Archer paled.

"Ah—a charming woman. I have just been to see her," said Mr. van der Luyden, complacency restored to his brow. He sank into the chair, laid his hat and gloves on the floor beside him in the old-fashioned way, and went on: "She has a real gift for arranging flowers. I had sent her a few carnations from Skuytercliff, and I was astonished. Instead of massing them in big bunches as our head-gardener does, she had scattered them about loosely, here and there . . . I can't say how. The Duke had told me: he said: 'Go and see how cleverly she's arranged her drawing-room.' And she has. I should really like to take Louisa to see her, if the neighbourhood were not so—unpleasant."

A dead silence greeted this unusual flow of words from Mr. van der Luyden. Mrs. Archer drew her embroidery out of the basket into which she had nervously tumbled it, and Newland, leaning against the chimney-place and twisting a humming-bird-feather screen in his hand, saw Janey's gaping countenance lit up by the coming of the second lamp.

"The fact is," Mr. van der Luyden continued, stroking his long grey leg with a bloodless hand weighed down by the Patroon's great signet-ring, "the fact is, I dropped in to thank her for the very pretty note she wrote me about my flowers; and also—but this is between ourselves, of course—to give her a friendly warning about allowing the Duke to carry her off to parties with him. I don't know if you've heard—"

Mrs. Archer produced an indulgent smile. "Has the Duke been carrying her off to parties?"

"You know what these English grandees are. They're all alike. Louisa and I are very fond of our cousin—but it's hopeless to expect people who are accustomed to the European courts to trouble themselves about our little republican distinctions. The Duke goes where he's amused." Mr. van der Luyden paused, but no one spoke. "Yes—it seems he took her with him last night to Mrs. Lemuel Struthers's. Sillerton Jackson has just been to us with the foolish story, and Louisa was rather troubled. So I thought the shortest way was to go straight to Countess Olenska and explain—by the merest hint, you know—how we feel in New York about certain things. I felt I might, without indelicacy, because the evening she dined with us she rather suggested . . . rather let me see that she would be grateful for guidance. And she *was.*"

Mr. van der Luyden looked about the room with what would have been self-satisfaction on features less purged of the vulgar passions. On his face it became a mild benevolence which Mrs. Archer's countenance dutifully reflected.

"How kind you both are, dear Henry—always! Newland will particularly appreciate what you have done because of dear May and his new relations."

She shot an admonitory glance at her son, who said: "Immensely, sir. But I was sure you'd like Madame Olenska."

Mr. van der Luyden looked at him with extreme gentleness. "I never ask to my house, my dear Newland," he said, "any one whom I do not like. And so I have just told Sillerton Jackson." With a glance at the clock he rose and added: "But Louisa will be waiting. We are dining early, to take the Duke to the Opera."

After the portières had solemnly closed behind their visitor a silence fell upon the Archer family.

"Gracious—how romantic!" at last broke explosively from Janey. No one knew exactly what inspired her elliptic comments, and her relations had long since given up trying to interpret them.

Mrs. Archer shook her head with a sigh. "Provided it all turns out for the best," she said, in the tone of one who knows how surely it will not. "Newland, you must stay and see Sillerton Jackson when he comes this evening: I really shan't know what to say to him."

"Poor mother! But he won't come—" her son laughed, stooping to kiss away her frown.

§ 11

Some two weeks later, Newland Archer, sitting in abstracted idleness in his private compartment of the office of Letterblair, Lamson and Low, attorneys at law, was summoned by the head of the firm.

Old Mr. Letterblair, the accredited legal adviser of three generations of New York gentility, throned behind his mahogany desk in evident perplexity. As he stroked his close-clipped white whiskers and ran his hand through the rumpled grey locks above his jutting brows, his disrespectful junior partner thought how much he looked like the Family Physician annoyed with a patient whose symptoms refuse to be classified.

"My dear sir—" he always addressed Archer as "sir"—"I have sent for you to go into a little matter; a matter which, for the moment, I prefer not to mention either to Mr. Skipworth or Mr. Redwood." The gentlemen he spoke of were the other senior partners of the firm; for, as was always the case with legal associations of old standing in New York, all the partners named on the office letter-head were long since dead; and Mr. Letterblair, for example, was, professionally speaking, his own grandson.

He leaned back in his chair with a furrowed brow. "For family reasons—" he continued.

Archer looked up.

"The Mingott family," said Mr. Letterblair with an explanatory smile and bow. "Mrs. Manson Mingott sent for me yesterday. Her grand-daughter the Countess Olenska wishes to sue her husband for divorce. Certain papers have been placed in my hands." He paused and drummed on his desk. "In view of your prospective alliance with the family I should like to consult you—to consider the case with you—before taking any farther steps."

Archer felt the blood in his temples. He had seen the Countess Olenska only once since his visit to her, and then at the Opera, in the Mingott box. During this interval she had become a less vivid and importunate image, receding from his foreground as May Welland resumed her rightful place in it. He had not heard her divorce spoken of since Janey's first random allusion to it, and had dismissed the tale as unfounded gossip. Theoretically, the idea of divorce was almost as distasteful to him as to his mother; and he was annoyed that Mr. Letterblair (no doubt prompted by old Catherine Mingott) should be so evidently planning to draw him into the affair. After all, there were plenty of Mingott men for such jobs, and as yet he was not even a Mingott by marriage.

He waited for the senior partner to continue. Mr. Letterblair unlocked a drawer and drew out a packet. "If you will run your eye over these papers—"

Archer frowned. "I beg your pardon, sir; but just because of the prospective relationship, I should prefer your consulting Mr. Skipworth or Mr. Redwood."

Mr. Letterblair looked surprised and slightly offended. It was unusual for a junior to reject such an opening.

He bowed. "I respect your scruple, sir; but in this case I believe true delicacy requires you to do as I ask. Indeed, the suggestion is not mine but Mrs. Manson Mingott's and her son's. I have seen Lovell Mingott; and also Mr. Welland. They all named you."

Archer felt his temper rising. He had been somewhat languidly drifting with events for the last fortnight, and letting May's fair looks and radiant nature obliterate the rather importunate pressure of the Mingott claims. But this behest of old Mrs. Mingott's roused him to a sense of what the clan thought they had the right to exact from a prospective son-in-law; and he chafed at the rôle.

"Her uncles ought to deal with this," he said.

"They have. The matter has been gone into by the family. They are opposed to the Countess's idea; but she is firm, and insists on a legal opinion."

The young man was silent: he had not opened the packet in his hand.

"Does she want to marry again?"

"I believe it is suggested; but she denies it."

"Then—"

"Will you oblige me, Mr. Archer, by first looking through these papers? Afterward, when we have talked the case over, I will give you my opinion."

Archer withdrew reluctantly with the unwelcome documents. Since their last meeting he had half-unconsciously collaborated with events in ridding himself of the burden of Madame Olenska. His hour alone with her by the firelight had drawn them into a momentary intimacy on which the Duke of St. Austrey's intrusion with Mrs. Lemuel Struthers, and the Countess's joyous greeting of them, had rather providentially broken. Two days later Archer had assisted at the comedy of her reinstatement in the van der Luydens' favour, and had said to himself, with a touch of tartness, that a lady who knew how to thank all-powerful elderly gentlemen to such good purpose for a bunch of flowers did not need either the private consolations or the public championship of a young man of his small compass. To look at the matter in this light simplified his own case and surprisingly furbished up all the dim domestic virtues. He could not picture May Welland, in whatever conceivable emergency, hawking about her private difficulties and lavishing her confidences on strange men: and she had never seemed to him finer or fairer than in the week that followed. He had even yielded to her wish for a long engagement, since she had found the one disarming answer to his plea for haste.

"You know, when it comes to the point, your parents have always let you have your way ever since you were a little girl," he argued; and she had answered, with her clearest look: "Yes, and that's what makes it so hard to refuse the very last thing they'll ever ask of me as a little girl."

That was the old New York note; that was the kind of answer he would like always to be sure of his wife's making. If one had habitually breathed the New York air there were times when anything less crystalline seemed stifling.

The papers he had retired to read did not tell him much in fact; but they plunged him into an atmosphere in which he choked and spluttered. They consisted mainly of an exchange of letters between Count Olenski's solicitors and a French legal firm to whom the Countess had applied for the settlement of her financial situation. There was also a short letter from the Count to his wife: after reading it, Newland Archer rose, jammed the papers back into their envelope, and reëntered Mr. Letterblair's office.

"Here are the letters, sir. If you wish I'll see Madame Olenska," he said in a constrained voice.

"Thank you—thank you, Mr. Archer. Come and dine with me tonight if you're free, and we'll go into the matter afterward: in case you wish to call on our client tomorrow."

Newland Archer walked straight home again that afternoon. It was a winter evening of transparent clearness, with an innocent young moon above the housetops; and he wanted to fill his soul's lungs with the pure radiance, and not exchange a word with any one till he and Mr. Letterblair were closeted together after dinner. It was impossible to decide otherwise than he had done: he must see Madame Olenska himself rather than let her secrets be bared to other eyes. A great wave of compassion had swept away his indifference and impatience: she stood before him as an exposed and pitiful figure, to be saved at all costs from farther wounding herself in her mad plunges against fate.

He remembered what she had told him of Mrs. Welland's request to be spared whatever was "unpleasant" in her history, and winced at the thought that it was perhaps this attitude of mind which kept the New York air so pure. "Are we only Pharisees after all?" he wondered, puzzled by the effort to reconcile his instinctive disgust at human vileness with his equally instinctive pity for human frailty.

For the first time he perceived how elementary his own principles had always been. He passed for a young man who had not been afraid of risks, and he knew that his secret love-affair with poor silly

Mrs. Thorley Rushworth had not been too secret to invest him with a becoming air of adventure. But Mrs. Rushworth was "that kind of woman"; foolish, vain, clandestine by nature, and far more attracted by the secrecy and peril of the affair than by such charms and qualities as he possessed. When the fact dawned on him it nearly broke his heart, but now it seemed the redeeming feature of the case. The affair, in short, had been of the kind that most of the young men of his age had been through, and emerged from with calm consciences and an undisturbed belief in the abysmal distinction between the women one loved and respected and those one enjoyed—and pitied. In this view they were sedulously abetted by their mothers, aunts and other elderly female relatives, who all shared Mrs. Archer's belief that when "such things happened" it was undoubtedly foolish of the man, but somehow always criminal of the woman. All the elderly ladies whom Archer knew regarded any woman who loved imprudently as necessarily unscrupulous and designing, and mere simple-minded man as powerless in her clutches. The only thing to do was to persuade him, as early as possible, to marry a nice girl, and then trust to her to look after him.

In the complicated old European communities, Archer began to guess, love-problems might be less simple and less easily classified. Rich and idle and ornamental societies must produce many more such situations; and there might even be one in which a woman naturally sensitive and aloof would yet, from the force of circumstances, from sheer defencelessness and loneliness, be drawn into a tie inexcusable by conventional standards.

On reaching home he wrote a line to the Countess Olenska, asking at what hour of the next day she could receive him, and despatched it by a messenger-boy, who returned presently with a word to the effect that she was going to Skuytercliff the next morning to stay over Sunday with the van der Luydens, but that he would find her alone that evening after dinner. The note was written on a rather untidy half-sheet, without date or address, but her hand was firm and free. He was amused at the idea of her week-ending in the stately solitude of Skuytercliff, but immediately afterward felt that there, of all places, she would most feel the chill of minds rigorously averted from the "unpleasant."

He was at Mr. Letterblair's punctually at seven, glad of the pretext for excusing himself soon after dinner. He had formed his own opinion from the papers entrusted to him, and did not especially want to go into the matter with his senior partner. Mr. Letterblair was a widower, and they dined alone, copiously and slowly, in a dark shabby room hung with yellowing prints of "The Death of Chatham" and "The Coronation of Napoleon." On the sideboard, between fluted Sheraton knife-cases stood a decanter of Haut Brion, and another of the old Lanning port (the gift of a client), which the wastrel Tom Lanning had sold off a year or two before his mysterious and discreditable death in San Franciso—an incident less publicly humiliating to the family than the sale of the cellar.

After a velvety oyster soup came shad and cucumbers, then a young broiled turkey with corn fritters, followed by a canvas-back with currant jelly and a celery mayonnaise. Mr. Letterblair, who lunched on a sandwich and tea, dined deliberately and deeply, and insisted on his guest's doing the same. Finally, when the closing rites had been accomplished, the cloth was removed, cigars were lit, and Mr. Letterblair, leaning back in his chair and pushing the port westward, said, spreading his back agreeably to the coal fire behind him: "The whole family are against a divorce. And I think rightly."

Archer instantly felt himself on the other side of the argument. "But why, sir? If there ever was a case—"

"Well—what's the use? *She's* here—he's there; the Atlantic's between them. She'll never get back a dollar more of her money than what he's voluntarily returned to her: their damned heathen marriage settlements take precious good care of that. As things go over there, Olenski's acted generously: he might have turned her out without a penny."

The young man knew this and was silent.

"I understand, though," Mr. Letterblair continued, "that she attaches no importance to the money. Therefore, as the family say, why not let well enough alone?"

Archer had gone to the house an hour earlier in full agreement with Mr. Letterblair's view; but put into words by this selfish, well-fed and supremely indifferent old man it suddenly became the Pharisaic voice of a society wholly absorbed in barricading itself against the unpleasant.

"I think that's for her to decide."

"H'm—have you considered the consequences if she decides for divorce?"

"You mean the threat in her husband's letter? What weight would that carry? It's no more than the vague charge of an angry blackguard."

"Yes; but it might make some unpleasant talk if he really defends the suit."

"Unpleasant—!" said Archer explosively.

Mr. Letterblair looked at him from under enquiring eyebrows, and the young man, aware of the uselessness of trying to explain what was in his mind, bowed acquiescently while his senior continued: "Divorce is always unpleasant."

"You agree with me?" Mr. Letterblair resumed, after a waiting silence.

"Naturally," said Archer.

"Well, then, I may count on you; the Mingotts may count on you; to use your influence against the idea?"

Archer hesitated. "I can't pledge myself till I've seen the Countess Olenska," he said at length.

"Mr. Archer, I don't understand you. Do you want to marry into a family with a scandalous divorce-suit hanging over it?"

"I don't think that has anything to do with the case."

Mr. Letterblair put down his glass of port and fixed on his young partner a cautious and apprehensive gaze.

Archer understood that he ran the risk of having his mandate withdrawn, and for some obscure reason he disliked the prospect. Now that the job had been thrust on him he did not propose to relinquish it; and, to guard against the possibility, he saw that he must reassure the unimaginative old man who was the legal conscience of the Mingotts.

"You may be sure, sir, that I shan't commit myself till I've reported to you; what I meant was that I'd rather not give an opinion till I've heard what Madame Olenska has to say."

Mr. Letterblair nodded approvingly at an excess of caution worthy of the best New York tradition, and the young man, glancing at his watch, pleaded an engagement and took leave.

§ 12

Old-fashioned New York dined at seven, and the habit of after-dinner calls, though derided in Archer's set, still generally prevailed. As the young man strolled up Fifth Avenue from Waverley Place, the long thoroughfare was deserted but for a group of carriages standing before the Reggie Chiverses' (where there was a dinner for the Duke), and the occasional figure of an elderly gentleman in heavy overcoat and muffler ascending a brownstone doorstep and disappearing into a gas-lit hall. Thus, as Archer crossed Washington Square, he remarked that old Mr. du Lac was calling on his cousins the Dagonets, and turning down the corner of West Tenth Street he saw Mr. Skipworth, of his own firm, obviously bound on a visit to the Miss Lannings. A little farther up Fifth Avenue, Beaufort appeared on his doorstep, darkly projected against a blaze of light, descended to his private brougham, and rolled away to a mysterious and probably unmentionable destination. It was not an Opera night, and no one was giving a party, so that Beaufort's outing was undoubtedly of a clandestine nature. Archer connected it in his mind with a little house beyond Lexington Avenue in which beribboned window curtains and flower-boxes had recently appeared, and before whose newly painted door the canary-coloured brougham of Miss Fanny Ring was frequently seen to wait.

Beyond the small and slippery pyramid which composed Mrs. Archer's world lay the almost unmapped quarter inhabited by artists, musicians and "people who wrote." These scattered fragments of humanity had never shown any desire to be amalgamated with the social structure. In spite of odd ways they were said to be, for the most part, quite respectable; but they preferred to keep to themselves. Medora Manson, in her prosperous days, had inaugurated a "literary salon"; but it had soon died out owing to the reluctance of the literary to frequent it.

Others had made the same attempt, and there was a household of Blenkers—an intense and voluble mother, and three blowsy daughters who imitated her—where one met Edwin Booth and Patti and William Winter, and the new Shakespearian actor George Rignold, and some of the magazine editors and musical and literary critics.

Mrs. Archer and her group felt a certain timidity concerning these persons. They were odd, they were uncertain, they had things one didn't know about in the background of their lives and minds. Literature and art were deeply respected in the Archer set, and Mrs. Archer was always at pains to tell her children how much more agreeable and cultivated society had been when it included such figures as Washington Irving, Fitz-Greene Halleck and the poet of "The Culprit Fay." The most celebrated authors of that generation had been "gentlemen"; perhaps the unknown persons who succeeded them had gentlemanly sentiments, but their origin, their appearance, their hair, their intimacy with the stage and the Opera, made any old New York criterion inapplicable to them.

"When I was a girl," Mrs. Archer used to say, "we knew everybody between the Battery and Canal Street; and only the people one knew had carriages. It was perfectly easy to place any one then; now one can't tell, and I prefer not to try."

Only old Catherine Mingott, with her absence of moral prejudices and almost *parvenu* indifference to the subtler distinctions, might have bridged the abyss; but she had never opened a book or looked at a picture, and cared for music only because it reminded her of gala nights at the *Italiens,* in the days of her triumph at the Tuileries. Possibly Beaufort, who was her match in daring, would have succeeded in bringing about a fusion; but his grand house and silk-stockinged footmen were an obstacle to informal sociability. Moreover, he was as illiterate as old Mrs. Mingott, and considered "fellows who wrote" as the mere paid purveyors of rich men's pleasures; and no one rich enough to influence his opinion had ever questioned it.

Newland Archer had been aware of these things ever since he could remember, and had accepted them as part of the structure of his universe. He knew that there were societies where painters and poets and novelists and men of science, and even great actors, were as sought after as Dukes; he had often pictured to himself what it would have been to live in the intimacy of drawing-rooms dominated by the talk of Mérimée (whose "Lettres à une Inconnue" was one of his inseparables), of Thackeray, Browning or William Morris. But such things were inconceivable in New York, and unsettling to think of. Archer knew most of the "fellows who wrote," the musicians and the painters: he met them at the Century, or at the little musical and theatrical clubs that were beginning to come into existence. He enjoyed them there, and was bored with them at the Blenkers', where they were mingled with fervid and dowdy women who passed them about like captured curiosities; and even after his most exciting talks with Ned Winsett he always came away with the feeling that if his world was small, so was theirs, and that the only way to enlarge either was to reach a stage of manners where they would naturally merge.

He was reminded of this by trying to picture the society in which the Countess Olenska had lived and suffered, and also—perhaps—tasted mysterious joys. He remembered with what amusement she had told him that her grandmother Mingott and the Wellands objected to her living in a "Bohemian" quarter given over to "people who wrote." It was not the peril but the poverty that her family disliked; but that shade escaped her, and she supposed they considered literature compromising.

She herself had no fears of it, and the books scattered about her drawing-room (a part of the house in which books were usually supposed to be "out of place"), though chiefly works of fiction, had whetted Archer's interest with such new names as those of Paul Bourget, Huysmans, and the Goncourt brothers. Ruminating on these things as he approached her door, he was once more conscious of the curious way in which she reversed his values, and of the need of thinking himself into conditions incredibly different from any that he knew if he were to be of use in her present difficulty.

Nastasia opened the door, smiling mysteriously. On the bench in the hall lay a sable-lined overcoat, a folded opera hat of dull silk with a gold J. B. on the lining, and a white silk muffler: there was no mistaking the fact that these costly articles were the property of Julius Beaufort.

Archer was angry: so angry that he came near scribbling a word on his card and going away; then he remembered that in writing to Madame Olenska he had been kept by excess of discretion from saying that he wished to see her privately. He had therefore no one but himself to blame if she had opened her doors to other visitors; and he entered the drawing-room with the dogged determination to make Beaufort feel himself in the way, and to outstay him.

The banker stood leaning against the mantelshelf, which was draped with an old embroidery held in place by brass candelabra containing church candles of yellowish wax. He had thrust his chest out, supporting his shoulders against the mantel and resting his weight on one large patent-leather foot. As Archer entered he was smiling and looking down on his hostess, who sat on a sofa placed at right angles to the chimney. A table banked with flowers formed a screen behind it, and against the orchids and azaleas which the young man recognised as tributes from the Beaufort hot-houses, Madame Olenska sat half-reclined, her head propped on a hand and her wide sleeve leaving the arm bare to the elbow.

It was usual for ladies who received in the evening to wear what were called "simple dinner dresses": a close-fitting armour of whale-boned silk, slightly open in the neck, with lace ruffles filling in the crack, and tight sleeves with a flounce uncovering just enough wrist to show an Etruscan gold bracelet or a velvet band. But Madame Olenska, heedless of tradition, was attired in a long robe of red velvet bordered about the chin and down the front with glossy black fur. Archer remembered, on his last visit to Paris, seeing a portrait by the new painter, Carolus Duran, whose pictures were the sensation of the Salon, in which the lady wore one of these bold sheath-like robes with her chin nestling in fur. There was something perverse and provocative in the notion of fur worn in the evening in a heated drawing-room, and in the combination of a muffled throat and bare arms; but the effect was undeniably pleasing.

"Lord love us—three whole days at Skuytercliff!" Beaufort was saying in his loud sneering voice as Archer entered. "You'd better take all your furs, and a hot-water-bottle."

"Why? Is the house so cold?" she asked, holding out her left hand to Archer in a way mysteriously suggesting that she expected him to kiss it.

"No; but the missus is," said Beaufort, nodding carelessly to the young man.

"But I thought her so kind. She came herself to invite me. Granny says I must certainly go."

"Granny would, of course. And *I* say it's a shame you're going to miss the little oyster supper I'd planned for you at Delmonico's next Sunday, with Campanini and Scalchi and a lot of jolly people."

She looked doubtfully from the banker to Archer.

"Ah—that does tempt me! Except the other evening at Mrs. Struthers's I've not met a single artist since I've been here."

"What kind of artists? I know one or two painters, very good fellows, that I could bring to see you if you'd allow me," said Archer boldly.

"Painters? Are there painters in New York?" asked Beaufort, in a tone implying that there could be none since he did not buy their pictures; and Madame Olenska said to Archer, with her grave smile: "That would be charming. But I was really thinking of dramatic artists, singers, actors, musicians. My husband's house was always full of them."

She said the words "my husband" as if no sinister associations were connected with them, and in a tone that seemed almost to sigh over the lost delights of her married life. Archer looked at her perplexedly, wondering if it were lightness or dissimulation that enabled her to touch so easily on the past at the very moment when she was risking her reputation in order to break with it.

"I do think," she went on, addressing both men, "that the *imprévu* adds to one's enjoyment. It's perhaps a mistake to see the same people every day."

"It's confoundedly dull, anyhow; New York is dying of dulness," Beaufort grumbled. "And when I try to liven it up for you, you go back on me. Come—think better of it! Sunday is your last chance, for Campanini leaves next week for Baltimore and Philadelphia; and I've a private room, and a Steinway, and they'll sing all night for me."

"How delicious! May I think it over, and write to you tomorrow morning?"

She spoke amiably, yet with the least hint of dismissal in her voice. Beaufort evidently felt it, and being unused to dismissals, stood staring at her with an obstinate line between his eyes.

"Why not now?"

"It's too serious a question to decide at this late hour."

"Do you call it late?"

She returned his glance coolly. "Yes; because I have still to talk business with Mr. Archer for a little while."

"Ah," Beaufort snapped. There was no appeal from her tone, and with a slight shrug he recovered his composure, took her hand, which he kissed with a practised air, and calling out from the threshold: "I say, Newland, if you can persuade the Countess to stop in town of course you're included in the supper," left the room with his heavy important step.

For a moment Archer fancied that Mr. Letterblair must have told her of his coming; but the irrelevance of her next remark made him change his mind.

"You know painters, then? You live in their *milieu?*" she asked, her eyes full of interest.

"Oh, not exactly. I don't know that the arts have a *milieu* here, any of them; they're more like a very thinly settled outskirt."

"But you care for such things?"

"Immensely. When I'm in Paris or London I never miss an exhibition. I try to keep up."

She looked down at the tip of the little satin boot that peeped from her long draperies.

"I used to care immensely too: my life was full of such things. But now I want to try not to."

"You want to try not to?"

"Yes: I want to cast off all my old life, to become just like everybody else here."

Archer reddened. "You'll never be like everybody else," he said.

She raised her straight eyebrows a little. "Ah, don't say that. If you knew how I hate to be different!"

Her face had grown as sombre as a tragic mask. She leaned forward, clasping her knee in her thin hands, and looking away from him into remote dark distances.

"I want to get away from it all," she insisted.

He waited a moment and cleared his throat. "I know. Mr. Letterblair has told me."

"Ah?"

"That's the reason I've come. He asked me to—you see I'm in the firm."

She looked slightly surprised, and then her eyes brightened. "You mean you can manage it for me? I can talk to you instead of Mr. Letterblair? Oh, that will be so much easier!"

Her tone touched him, and his confidence grew with his self-satisfaction. He perceived that she had spoken of business to Beaufort simply to get rid of him; and to have routed Beaufort was something of a triumph.

"I am here to talk about it," he repeated.

She sat silent, her head still propped by the arm that rested on the back of the sofa. Her face looked pale and extinguished, as if dimmed by the rich red of her dress. She struck Archer, of a sudden, as a pathetic and even pitiful figure.

"Now we're coming to hard facts," he thought, conscious in himself of the same instinctive recoil that he had so often criticised in his mother and her contemporaries. How little practice he had had in dealing with unusual situations! Their very vocabulary was unfamiliar to him, and seemed to belong to fiction and the stage. In face of what was coming he felt as awkward and embarrassed as a boy.

After a pause Madame Olenska broke out with unexpected vehemence: "I want to be free; I want to wipe out all the past."

"I understand that."

Her face warmed. "Then you'll help me?"

"First—" he hesitated—"perhaps I ought to know a little more."

She seemed surprised. "You know about my husband—my life with him?"

He made a sign of assent.

"Well—then—what more is there? In this country are such things tolerated? I'm a Protestant—our church does not forbid divorce in such cases."

"Certainly not."

They were both silent again, and Archer felt the spectre of Count Olenski's letter grimacing hideously between them. The letter filled only half a page, and was just what he had described it to be in speaking of it to Mr. Letterblair: the vague charge of an angry blackguard. But how much truth was behind it? Only Count Olenski's wife could tell.

"I've looked through the papers you gave to Mr. Letterblair," he said at length.

"Well—can there be anything more abominable?"

"No."

She changed her position slightly, screening her eyes with her lifted hand.

"Of course you know," Archer continued, "that if your husband chooses to fight the case—as he threatens to—"

"Yes—?"

"He can say things—things that might be unpl——might be disagreeable to you: say them publicly, so that they would get about, and harm you even if—"

"If—"

"I mean: no matter how unfounded they were."

She paused for a long interval; so long that, not wishing to keep his eyes on her shaded face, he had time to imprint on his mind the exact shape of her other hand, the one on her knee, and every detail of the three rings on her fourth and fifth fingers; among which, he noticed, a wedding ring did not appear.

"What harm could such accusations, even if he made them publicly, do me here?"

It was on his lips to exclaim: "My poor child—far more harm than anywhere else!" Instead, he answered, in a voice that sounded in his ears like Mr. Letterblair's: "New York society is a very small world compared with the one you've lived in. And it's ruled, in spite of appearances, by a few people with—well, rather old-fashioned ideas."

She said nothing, and he continued: "Our ideas about marriage and divorce are particularly old-fashioned. Our legislation favours divorce—our social customs don't."

"Never?"

"Well—not if the woman, however injured, however irreproachable, has appearances in the least degree against her, has exposed herself by any unconventional action to—to offensive insinuations—"

She drooped her head a little lower, and he waited again, intensely hoping for a flash of indignation, or at least a brief cry of denial. None came.

A little travelling clock ticked purringly at her elbow, and a log broke in two and sent up a shower of sparks. The whole hushed and brooding room seemed to be waiting silently with Archer.

"Yes," she murmured at length, "that's what my family tell me."

He winced a little. "It's not unnatural—"

"*Our* family," she corrected herself; and Archer coloured. "For you'll be my cousin soon," she continued gently.

"I hope so."

"And you take their view?"

He stood up at this, wandered across the room, stared with void eyes at one of the pictures against the old red damask, and came back irresolutely to her side. How could he say: "Yes, if what your husband hints is true, or if you've no way of disproving it?"

"Sincerely—" she interjected, as he was about to speak.

He looked down into the fire. "Sincerely, then—what should you gain that would compensate for the possibility—the certainty—of a lot of beastly talk?"

"But my freedom—is that nothing?"

It flashed across him at that instant that the charge in the letter was true, and that she hoped to marry the partner of her guilt. How was he to tell her that, if she really cherished such a plan, the laws of the State were inexorably opposed to it? The mere suspicion that the thought was in her mind made him feel harshly and impatiently toward her. "But aren't you as free as air as it is?" he returned. "Who can touch you? Mr. Letterblair tells me the financial question has been settled—"

"Oh, yes," she said indifferently.

"Well, then: is it worth while to risk what may be infinitely disagreeable and painful? Think of the newspapers—their vileness! It's all stupid and narrow and unjust—but one can't make over society."

"No," she acquiesced; and her tone was so faint and desolate that he felt a sudden remorse for his own hard thoughts.

"The individual, in such cases, is nearly always sacrificed to what is supposed to be the collective interest: people cling to any convention that keeps the family together—protects the children, if there are any," he rambled on, pouring out all the stock phrases that rose to his lips in his intense desire to cover over the ugly reality which her silence seemed to have laid bare. Since she would not or could not say the one word that would have cleared the air, his wish was not to let her feel that he was trying to probe into her secret. Better keep on the surface, in the prudent old New York way, than risk uncovering a wound he could not heal.

"It's my business, you know," he went on, "to help you to see these things as the people who are fondest of you see them. The

Mingotts, the Wellands, the van der Luydens, all your friends and relations: if I didn't show you honestly how they judge such questions, it wouldn't be fair of me, would it?" He spoke insistently, almost pleading with her in his eagerness to cover up that yawning silence.

She said slowly: "No; it wouldn't be fair."

The fire had crumbled down to greyness, and one of the lamps made a gurgling appeal for attention. Madame Olenska rose, wound it up and returned to the fire, but without resuming her seat.

Her remaining on her feet seemed to signify that there was nothing more for either of them to say, and Archer stood up also.

"Very well; I will do what you wish," she said abruptly. The blood rushed to his forehead; and, taken aback by the suddenness of her surrender, he caught her two hands awkardly in his.

"I—I do want to help you," he said.

"You do help me. Good night, my cousin."

He bent and laid his lips on her hands, which were cold and lifeless. She drew them away, and he turned to the door, found his coat and hat under the faint gaslight of the hall, and plunged out into the winter night bursting with the belated eloquence of the inarticulate.

§ 13

It was a crowded night at Wallack's theatre. The play was "The Shaughraun," with Dion Boucicault in the title rôle and Harry Montague and Ada Dyas as the lovers. The popularity of the admirable English company was at its height, and the Shaughraun always packed the house. In the galleries the enthusiasm was unreserved; in the stalls and boxes, people smiled a little at the hackneyed sentiments and claptrap situations, and enjoyed the play as much as the galleries did.

There was one episode, in particular, that held the house from floor to ceiling. It was that in which Harry Montague, after a sad, almost monosyllabic scene of parting with Miss Dyas, bade her goodbye, and turned to go. The actress, who was standing near the mantelpiece and looking down into the fire, wore a gray cashmere dress without fashionable loopings or trimmings, moulded to her tall figure and flowing in long lines about her feet. Around her neck was a narrow black velvet ribbon with the ends falling down her back.

When her wooer turned from her she rested her arms against the mantel-shelf and bowed her face in her hands. On the threshold he paused to look at her; then he stole back, lifted one of the ends of velvet ribbon, kissed it, and left the room without her hearing him or changing her attitude. And on this silent parting the curtain fell.

It was always for the sake of that particular scene that Newland Archer went to see "The Shaughraun." He thought the adieux of Montague and Ada Dyas as fine as anything he had ever seen Croisette and Bressant do in Paris, or Madge Robertson and Kendal in London; in its reticence, its dumb sorrow, it moved him more than the most famous histrionic outpourings.

On the evening in question the little scene acquired an added poignancy by reminding him—he could not have said why—of his leave-taking from Madame Olenska after their confidential talk a week or ten days earlier.

It would have been as difficult to discover any resemblance between the two situations as between the appearance of the persons concerned. Newland Archer could not pretend to anything approaching the young English actor's romantic good looks, and Miss Dyas was a tall red-haired woman of monumental build whose pale and pleasantly ugly face was utterly unlike Ellen Olenska's vivid countenance. Nor were Archer and Madame Olenska two lovers parting in heart-broken silence; they were client and lawyer separating after a talk which had given the lawyer the worst possible impression of the client's case. Wherein, then, lay the resemblance that made the young man's heart beat with a kind of retrospective excitement? It seemed to be in Madame Olenska's mysterious faculty of suggesting tragic and moving possibilities outside the daily run of experience. She had hardly ever said a word to him to produce this impression, but it was a part of her, either a projection of her mysterious and outlandish background or of something inherently dramatic, passionate and unusual in herself. Archer had always been inclined to think that chance and circumstance played a small part in shaping people's lots compared with their innate tendency to have things happen to them. This tendency he had felt from the first in Madame Olenska. The quiet, almost passive young woman struck him as exactly the kind of person to whom things were bound to happen, no matter how much she shrank from them and went out of her way to avoid them. The exciting fact was her having lived in an atmosphere so thick with drama that her own tendency to provoke it had apparently passed unperceived. It was precisely the odd absence of surprise in her that gave him the sense of her having been plucked out of a very maelstrom: the things she took for granted gave the measure of those she had rebelled against.

Archer had left her with the conviction that Count Olenski's accusation was not unfounded. The mysterious person who figured in his wife's past as "the secretary" had probably not been unrewarded for his share in her escape. The conditions from which she had fled were intolerable, past speaking of, past believing: she was young, she was frightened, she was desperate—what more natural than that she should be grateful to her rescuer? The pity was that her gratitude put her, in the law's eyes and the world's, on a par with her abominable husband. Archer had made her understand this, as he was bound to do; he had also made her understand that simple-hearted kindly New York, on whose larger charity she had apparently counted, was precisely the place where she could least hope for indulgence.

To have to make this fact plain to her—and to witness her resigned acceptance of it—had been intolerably painful to him. He felt himself drawn to her by obscure feelings of jealousy and pity, as if her dumbly-confessed error had put her at his mercy, humbling yet endearing her. He was glad it was to him she had revealed her secret, rather than to the cold scrutiny of Mr. Letterblair, or the embarrassed gaze of her family. He immediately took it upon himself to assure them both that she had given up her idea of seeking a divorce, basing her decision on the fact that she had understood the uselessness of the proceeding; and with infinite relief they had all turned their eyes from the "unpleasantness" she had spared them.

"I was sure Newland would manage it," Mrs. Welland had said proudly of her future son-in-law; and old Mrs. Mingott, who had summoned him for a confidential interview, had congratulated him on his cleverness, and added impatiently: "Silly goose! I told her myself what nonsense it was. Wanting to pass herself off as Ellen Mingott and an old maid, when she has the luck to be a married woman and a Countess!"

These incidents had made the memory of his last talk with Madame Olenska so vivid to the young man that as the curtain fell on the parting of the two actors his eyes filled with tears, and he stood up to leave the theatre.

In doing so, he turned to the side of the house behind him, and saw the lady of whom he was thinking seated in a box with the Beauforts, Lawrence Lefferts and one or two other men. He had not spoken with her alone since their evening together, and had tried to avoid being with her in company; but now their eyes met, and as Mrs. Beaufort recognised him at the same time, and made her languid little gesture of invitation, it was impossible not to go into the box.

Beaufort and Lefferts made way for him, and after a few words with Mrs. Beaufort, who always preferred to look beautiful and not have to talk, Archer seated himself behind Madame Olenska. There was no one else in the box but Mr. Sillerton Jackson, who was telling Mrs. Beaufort in a confidential undertone about Mrs. Lemuel Struthers's last Sunday reception (where some people reported that there had been dancing). Under cover of this circumstantial narrative, to which Mrs. Beaufort listened with her perfect smile, and her head at just the right angle to be seen in profile from the stalls, Madame Olenska turned and spoke in a low voice.

"Do you think," she asked, glancing toward the stage, "he will send her a bunch of yellow roses tomorrow morning?"

Archer reddened, and his heart gave a leap of surprise. He had called only twice on Madame Olenska, and each time he had sent her a box of yellow roses, and each time without a card. She had never before made any allusion to the flowers, and he supposed she had never thought of him as the sender. Now her sudden recognition of the gift, and her associating it with the tender leave-taking on the stage, filled him with an agitated pleasure.

"I was thinking of that too—I was going to leave the theatre in order to take the picture away with me," he said.

To his surprise her colour rose, reluctantly and duskily. She looked down at the mother-of-pearl opera-glass in her smoothly gloved hands, and said, after a pause: "What do you do while May is away?"

"I stick to my work," he answered, faintly annoyed by the question.

In obedience to a long-established habit, the Wellands had left the previous week for St. Augustine, where, out of regard for the supposed susceptibility of Mr. Welland's bronchial tubes, they always spent the latter part of the winter. Mr. Welland was a mild and silent man, with no opinions but with many habits. With these habits none might interfere; and one of them demanded that his wife and daughter should always go with him on his annual journey to the south. To preserve an unbroken domesticity was essential to his peace of mind; he would not have known where his hair-brushes were, or how to provide stamps for his letters, if Mrs. Welland had not been there to tell him.

As all the members of the family adored each other, and as Mr. Welland was the central object of their idolatry, it never occurred to his wife and May to let him go to St. Augustine alone; and his sons, who were both in the law, and could not leave New York during the winter, always joined him for Easter and travelled back with him.

It was impossible for Archer to discuss the necessity of May's accompanying her father. The reputation of the Mingotts' family physician was largely based on the attack of pneumonia which Mr. Welland had never had; and his insistence on St. Augustine was therefore inflexible. Originally, it had been intended that May's engagement should not be announced till her return from Florida, and the fact that it had been made known sooner could not be expected to alter Mr. Welland's plans. Archer would have liked to join the travellers and have a few weeks of sunshine and boating with his betrothed; but he too was bound by custom and conventions. Little arduous as his professional duties were, he would have been convicted of frivolity by the whole Mingott clan if he had suggested asking for a holiday in mid-winter; and he accepted May's departure with the resignation which he perceived would have to be one of the principal constituents of married life.

He was conscious that Madame Olenska was looking at him

under lowered lids. "I have done what you wished—what you advised," she said abruptly.

"Ah—I'm glad," he returned, embarrassed by her broaching the subject at such a moment.

"I understand—that you were right," she went on a little breathlessly; "but sometimes life is difficult . . . perplexing . . ."

"I know."

"And I wanted to tell you that I *do* feel you were right; and that I'm grateful to you," she ended, lifting her opera-glass quickly to her eyes as the door of the box opened and Beaufort's resonant voice broke in on them.

Archer stood up, and left the box and the theatre.

Only the day before he had received a letter from May Welland in which, with characteristic candour, she had asked him to "be kind to Ellen" in their absence. "She likes you and admires you so much—and you know, though she doesn't show it, she's still very lonely and unhappy. I don't think Granny understands her, or uncle Lovell Mingott either; they really think she's much worldlier and fonder of society than she is. And I can quite see that New York must seem dull to her, though the family won't admit it. I think she's been used to lots of things we haven't got; wonderful music, and picture shows, and celebrities—artists and authors and all the clever people you admire. Granny can't understand her wanting anything but lots of dinners and clothes—but I can see that you're almost the only person in New York who can talk to her about what she really cares for."

His wise May—how he had loved her for that letter! But he had not meant to act on it; he was too busy, to begin with, and he did not care, as an engaged man, to play too conspicuously the part of Madame Olenska's champion. He had an idea that she knew how to take care of herself a good deal better than the ingenuous May imagined. She had Beaufort at her feet, Mr. van der Luyden hovering above her like a protecting deity, and any number of candidates (Lawrence Lefferts among them) waiting their opportunity in the middle distance. Yet he never saw her, or exchanged a word with her, without feeling that, after all, May's ingenuousness almost amounted to a gift of divination. Ellen Olenska was lonely and she was unhappy.

§ 14

As he came out into the lobby Archer ran across his friend Ned Winsett, the only one among what Janey called his "clever people" with whom he cared to probe into things a little deeper than the average level of club and chop-house banter.

He had caught sight, across the house, of Winsett's shabby round-shouldered back, and had once noticed his eyes turned toward the Beaufort box. The two men shook hands, and Winsett proposed a bock at a little German restaurant around the corner. Archer, who was not in the mood for the kind of talk they were likely to get there, declined on the plea that he had work to do at home; and Winsett said: "Oh, well so have I for that matter, and I'll be the Industrious Apprentice too."

They strolled along together, and presently Winsett said: "Look here, what I'm really after is the name of the dark lady in that swell box of yours—with the Beauforts, wasn't she? The one your friend Lefferts seems so smitten by."

Archer, he could not have said why, was slightly annoyed. What the devil did Ned Winsett want with Ellen Olenska's name? And above all, why did he couple it with Lefferts's? It was unlike Winsett to manifest such curiosity; but after all, Archer remembered, he was a journalist.

"It's not for an interview, I hope?" he laughed.

"Well—not for the press; just for myself," Winsett rejoined. "The fact is she's a neighbour of mine—queer quarter for such a beauty to settle in—and she's been awfully kind to my little boy, who fell down her area chasing his kitten, and gave himself a nasty cut. She rushed in bareheaded, carrying him in her arms, with his knee all beautifully bandaged, and was so sympathetic and beautiful that my wife was too dazzled to ask her name."

A pleasant glow dilated Archer's heart. There was nothing extraordinary in the tale: any woman would have done as much for a neighbour's child. But it was just like Ellen, he felt, to have rushed in bareheaded, carrying the boy in her arms, and to have dazzled poor Mrs. Winsett into forgetting to ask who she was.

"That is the Countess Olenska—a granddaughter of old Mrs. Mingott's."

"Whew—a Countess!" whistled Ned Winsett. "Well, I didn't know Countesses were so neighbourly. Mingotts ain't."

"They would be, if you'd let them."

"Ah, well—" It was their old interminable argument as to the obstinate unwillingness of the "clever people" to frequent the fashionable, and both men knew that there was no use in prolonging it.

"I wonder," Winsett broke off, "how a Countess happens to live in our slum?"

"Because she doesn't care a hang about where she lives—or about any of our little social sign-posts," said Archer, with a secret pride in his own picture of her.

"H'm—been in bigger places, I suppose," the other commented. "Well, here's my corner."

He slouched off across Broadway, and Archer stood looking after him and musing on his last words.

Ned Winsett had those flashes of penetration; they were the most interesting thing about him, and always made Archer wonder why they had allowed him to accept failure so stolidly at an age when most men are still struggling.

Archer had known that Winsett had a wife and child, but he had never seen them. The two men always met at the Century, or at some haunt of journalists and theatrical people, such as the restaurant where Winsett had proposed to go for a bock. He had given Archer to understand that his wife was an invalid; which might be true of the poor lady, or might merely mean that she was lacking in social gifts or in evening clothes, or in both. Winsett himself had a savage abhorrence of social observances: Archer, who dressed in the evening because he thought it cleaner and more comfortable to do so, and who had never stopped to consider that cleanliness and comfort are two of the costliest items in a modest budget, regarded Winsett's attitude as part of the boring "Bohemian" pose that always made fashionable people, who changed their clothes without talking about it, and were not forever harping on the number of servants one kept, seem so much simpler and less self-conscious than the others. Nevertheless, he was always stimulated by Winsett, and whenever he caught sight of the journalist's lean bearded face and melancholy eyes he would rout him out of his corner and carry him off for a long talk.

Winsett was not a journalist by choice. He was a pure man of letters, untimely born in a world that had no need of letters; but after publishing one volume of brief and exquisite literary appreciations, of which one hundred and twenty copies were sold, thirty given away, and the balance eventually destroyed by the publishers (as per contract) to make room for more marketable material, he had abandoned his real calling, and taken a sub-editorial job on a women's weekly, where fashion plates and paper patterns alternated with New England love-stories and advertisements of temperance drinks.

On the subject of "Hearth-fires" (as the paper was called) he was inexhaustibly entertaining; but beneath his fun lurked the sterile bitterness of the still young man who has tried and given up. His conversation always made Archer take the measure of his own life, and feel how little it contained; but Winsett's, after all, contained still less, and though their common fund of intellectual interests and curiosities made their talks exhilarating, their exchange of views usually remained within the limits of a pensive dilettantism.

"The fact is, life isn't much a fit for either of us," Winsett had once said. "I'm down and out; nothing to be done about it. I've got only one ware to produce, and there's no market for it here, and won't be in my time. But you're free and you're well-off. Why don't *you* get into touch? There's only one way to do it: to go into politics."

Archer threw his head back and laughed. There one saw at a flash the unbridgeable difference between men like Winsett and the others—Archer's kind. Every one in polite circles knew that, in America, "a gentleman couldn't go into politics." But, since he could hardly put it in that way to Winsett, he answered evasively: "Look at the career of the honest man in American politics! They don't want us."

"Who's 'they'? Why don't you all get together and be 'they' yourselves?"

Archer's laugh lingered on his lips in a slightly condescending smile. It was useless to prolong the discussion: everybody knew the melancholy fate of the few gentlemen who had risked their clean linen in municipal or state politics in New York. The day was past when that sort of thing was possible: the country was in possession of the bosses and the emigrant, and decent people had to fall back on sport or culture.

"Culture! Yes—if we had it! But there are just a few little local patches, dying out here and there for lack of—well, hoeing and cross-fertilising: the last remnants of the old European tradition that your forebears brought with them. But you're in a pitiful little minority: you've got no centre, no competition, no audience. You're like the pictures on the walls of a deserted house: 'The Portrait of a Gentleman.' You'll never amount to anything, any of you, till you roll up your sleeves and get right down into the muck. That, or emigrate . . . God! If I could emigrate . . ."

Archer mentally shrugged his shoulders and turned the conversation back to books, where Winsett, if uncertain, was always interesting. Emigrate! As if a gentleman could abandon his own country! One could no more do that than one could roll up one's sleeves and go down into the muck. A gentleman simply stayed at home and abstained. But you couldn't make a man like Winsett see that; and that was why the New York of literary clubs and exotic restaurants, though a first shake made it seem more of a kaleidoscope, turned out, in the end, to be a smaller box, with a more monotonous pattern, than the assembled atoms of Fifth Avenue.

The next morning Archer scoured the town in vain for more yellow roses. In consequence of this search he arrived late at the office, perceived that his doing so made no difference whatever to any one, and was filled with sudden exasperation at the elaborate futility of his life. Why should he not be, at that moment, on the sands of St. Augustine with May Welland? No one was deceived by his pretense of professional activity. In old-fashioned legal firms like that of which Mr. Letterblair was the head, and which were mainly engaged in the management of large estates and "conservative" investments, there were always two or three young men fairly well-off, and without professional ambition, who, for a certain number of hours of each day, sat at their desks accomplishing trivial tasks, or simply reading the newspapers. Though it was supposed to be proper for them to have an occupation, the crude fact of money-making was still regarded as derogatory, and the law, being a profession, was accounted a more gentlemanly pursuit than business.

But none of these young men had much hope of really advancing in his profession, or any earnest desire to do so; and over many of them the green mould of the perfunctory was already perceptibly spreading.

It made Archer shiver to think that it might be spreading over him too. He had, to be sure, other tastes and interests; he spent his vacations in European travel, cultivated the "clever people" May spoke of, and generally tried to "keep up," as he had somewhat wistfully put it to Madame Olenska. But once he was married, what would become of this narrow margin of life in which his real experiences were lived? He had seen enough of other young men who had dreamed his dream, though perhaps less ardently, and who had gradually sunk into the placid and luxurious routine of their elders.

From the office he sent a note by messenger to Madame Olenska, asking if he might call that afternoon, and begging her to let him find a reply at his club; but at the club he found nothing, nor did he receive any letter the following day. This unexpected silence mortified him beyond reason, and though the next morning he saw a glorious cluster of yellow roses behind a florist's window-pane, he left it there. It was only on the third morning that he received a line by post from the Countess Olenska. To his surprise it was dated from Skuytercliff, whither the van der Luydens had promptly retreated after putting the Duke on board his steamer.

"I ran away," the writer began abruptly (without the usual preliminaries), "the day after I saw you at the play, and these kind friends have taken me in. I wanted to be quiet, and think things over. You were right in telling me how kind they were; I feel myself so safe here. I wish that you were with us." She ended with a conventional "Yours sincerely," and without any allusion to the date of her return.

The tone of the note surprised the young man. What was Madame Olenska running away from, and why did she feel the need to be safe? His first thought was of some dark menace from abroad; then he reflected that he did not know her epistolary style, and that it might run to picturesque exaggeration. Women always exaggerated; and moreover she was not wholly at her ease in English, which she often spoke as if she were translating from the French. "Je me suis évadée—" put in that way, the opening sentence immediately suggested that she might merely have wanted to escape from a boring round of engagements; which was very likely true, for he judged her to be capricious, and easily wearied of the pleasure of the moment.

It amused him to think of the van der Luydens' having carried her off to Skuytercliff on a second visit, and this time for an indefinite period. The doors of Skuytercliff were rarely and grudgingly opened to visitors, and a chilly week-end was the most ever offered to the few thus privileged. But Archer had seen, on his last visit to Paris, the delicious play of Labiche, "Le Voyage de M. Perrichon," and he remembered M. Perrichon's dogged and undiscouraged attachment to the young man whom he had pulled out of the glacier. The van der Luydens had rescued Madame Olenska from a doom almost as icy; and though there were many other reasons for being attracted to her, Archer knew that beneath them all lay the gentle and obstinate determination to go on rescuing her.

He felt a distinct disappointment on learning that she was away; and almost immediately remembered that, only the day before, he had refused an invitation to spend the following Sunday with the Reggie Chiverses at their house on the Hudson, a few miles below Skuytercliff.

He had had his fill long ago of the noisy friendly parties at Highbank, with coasting, ice-boating, sleighing, long tramps in the snow, and a general flavour of mild flirting and milder practical jokes. He had just received a box of new books from his London bookseller, and had preferred the prospect of a quiet Sunday at home with his spoils. But he now went into the club writing-room, wrote a hurried telegram, and told the servant to send it immediately. He knew that Mrs. Reggie didn't object to her visitors' suddenly changing their minds, and that there was always a room to spare in her elastic house.

§ 15

Newland Archer arrived at the Chiverses' on Friday evening, and on Saturday went conscientiously through all the rites appertaining to a week-end at Highbank.

In the morning he had a spin in the ice-boat with his hostess and a few of the hardier guests; in the afternoon he "went over the farm" with Reggie, and listened, in the elaborately appointed stables, to long and impressive disquisitions on the horse; after tea he talked in a corner of the firelit hall with a young lady who had professed herself broken-hearted when his engagement was announced, but was now eager to tell him of her own matrimonial hopes; and finally, about midnight, he assisted in putting a gold-fish in one visitor's bed, dressed up a burglar in the bath-room of a nervous aunt, and saw in the small hours by joining in a pillow-fight that ranged from the nurseries to the basement. But on Sunday after luncheon he borrowed a cutter, and drove over to Skuytercliff.

People had always been told that the house at Skuytercliff was an Italian villa. Those who had never been to Italy believed it; so did some who had. The house had been built by Mr. van der Luyden in his youth, on his return from the "grand tour," and in anticipation of his approaching marriage with Miss Louisa Dagonet. It was a large square wooden structure, with tongued and grooved walls painted pale green and white, a Corinthian portico, and fluted pilasters between the windows. From the high ground on which it stood a series of terraces bordered by balustrades and urns descended in the steel-engraving style to a small irregular lake with an asphalt edge overhung by rare weeping conifers. To the right and left, the famous weedless lawns studded with "specimen" trees (each of a different variety) rolled away to long ranges of grass crested with elaborate cast-iron ornaments; and below, in a hollow, lay the four-roomed stone house which the first Patroon had built on the land granted him in 1612.

Against the uniform sheet of snow and the greyish winter sky the Italian villa loomed up rather grimly; even in summer it kept its distance, and the boldest coleus bed had never ventured nearer than thirty feet from its awful front. Now, as Archer rang the bell, the long tinkle seemed to echo through a mausoleum; and the surprise of the butler who at length responded to the call was as great as though he had been summoned from his final sleep.

Happily Archer was of the family, and therefore, irregular though his arrival was, entitled to be informed that the Countess Olenska was out, having driven to afternoon service with Mrs. van der Luyden exactly three quarters of a hour earlier.

"Mr. van der Luyden," the butler continued, "is in, sir; but my impression is that he is either finishing his nap or else reading yesterday's Evening Post. I heard him say, sir, on his return from church this morning, that he intended to look through the Evening Post after luncheon; if you like, sir, I might go to the library door and listen—"

But Archer, thanking him, said that he would go and meet the ladies; and the butler, obviously relieved, closed the door on him majestically.

A groom took the cutter to the stables, and Archer struck through the park to the high-road. The village of Skuytercliff was only a mile and a half away, but he knew that Mrs. van der Luyden never walked, and that he must keep to the road to meet the carriage. Presently, however, coming down a foot-path that crossed the highway, he caught sight of a slight figure in a red cloak, with a big dog running ahead. He hurried forward, and Madame Olenska stopped short with a smile of welcome.

"Ah, you've come!" she said, and drew her hand from her muff.

The red cloak made her look gay and vivid, like the Ellen Mingott of old days; and he laughed as he took her hand, and answered: "I came to see what you were running away from."

Her face clouded over, but she answered: "Ah, well—you will see, presently."

The answer puzzled him. "Why—do you mean that you've been overtaken?"

She shrugged her shoulders, with a little movement like Nastasia's, and rejoined in a lighter tone: "Shall we walk on? I'm so cold after the sermon. And what does it matter, now you're here to protect me?"

The blood rose to his temples and he caught a fold of her cloak. "Ellen—what is it? You must tell me."

"Oh, presently—let's run a race first: my feet are freezing to the ground," she cried; and gathering up the cloak she fled away across the snow, the dog leaping about her with challenging barks. For a moment Archer stood watching, his gaze delighted by the flash of the red meteor against the snow; then he started after her, and they met, panting and laughing, at a wicket that led into the park.

She stood up at him and smiled. "I knew you'd come!"

"That shows you wanted me to," he returned, with a disproportionate joy in their nonsense. The white glitter of the trees filled the air with its own mysterious brightness, and as they walked on over the snow the ground seemed to sing under their feet.

"Where did you come from?" Madame Olenska asked.

He told her, and added: "It was because I got your note."

After a pause she said, with a just perceptible chill in her voice: "May asked you to take care of me."

"I didn't need any asking."

"You mean—I'm so evidently helpless and defenceless? What a poor thing you must all think me! But women here seem not—seem never to feel the need: any more than the blessed in heaven."

He lowered his voice to ask: "What sort of a need?"

"Ah, don't ask me! I don't speak your language," she retorted petulantly.

The answer smote him like a blow, and he stood still in the path, looking down at her.

"What did I come for, if I don't speak yours?"

"Oh, my friend—!" She laid her hand lightly on his arm, and he pleaded earnestly: "Ellen—why won't you tell me what's happened?"

She shrugged again. "Does anything ever happen in heaven?"

He was silent, and they walked on a few yards without exchanging a word. Finally she said: "I will tell you—but where, where, where? One can't be alone for a minute in that great seminary of a house, with all the doors wide open, and always a servant bringing tea, or a log for the fire, or the newspaper! Is there nowhere in an American house where one may be by one's self? You're so shy, and yet you're so public. I always feel as if I were in the convent again—or on the stage, before a dreadfully polite audience that never applauds."

"Ah, you don't like us!" Archer exclaimed.

They were walking past the house of the old Patroon, with its squat walls and small square windows compactly grouped about a central chimney. The shutters stood wide, and through one of the newly-washed windows Archer caught the light of a fire.

"Why—the house is open!" he said.

She stood still. "No; only for today, at least. I wanted to see it, and Mr. van der Luyden had the fire lit and the windows opened, so that we might stop there on the way back from church this morning." She ran up the steps and tried the door. "It's still unlocked—what luck! Come in and we can have a quiet talk. Mrs. van der Luyden has driven over to see her old aunts at Rhinebeck and we shan't be missed at the house for another hour."

He followed her into the narrow passage. His spirits, which had dropped at her last words, rose with an irrational leap. The homely little house stood there, its panels and brasses shining in the firelight, as if magically created to receive them. A big bed of embers still gleamed in the kitchen chimney, under an iron pot hung from an ancient crane. Rush-bottomed arm-chairs faced each other across the tiled hearth, and rows of Delft plates stood on shelves against the walls. Archer stooped over and threw a log upon the embers.

Madame Olenska, dropping her cloak, sat down in one of the chairs. Archer leaned against the chimney and looked at her.

"You're laughing now; but when you wrote me you were unhappy," he said.

"Yes." She paused. "But I can't feel unhappy when you're here."

"I shan't be here long," he rejoined, his lips stiffening with the effort to say just so much and no more.

"No; I know. But I'm improvident: I live in the moment when I'm happy."

The words stole through him like a temptation, and to close his senses to it he moved away from the hearth and stood gazing out at the black tree-boles against the snow. But it was as if she too had shifted her place, and he still saw her, between himself and the trees, drooping over the fire with her indolent smile. Archer's heart was beating insubordinately. What if it were from him that she had been running away, and if she had waited to tell him so till they were here alone together in this secret room?

"Ellen, if I'm really a help to you—if you really wanted me to come—tell me what's wrong, tell me what it is you're running away from," he insisted.

He spoke without shifting his position, without even turning to look at her: if the thing was to happen, it was to happen in this way, with the whole width of the room between them, and his eyes still fixed on the outer snow.

For a long moment she was silent; and in that moment Archer

imagined her, almost heard her, stealing up behind him to throw her light arms about his neck. While he waited, soul and body throbbing with the miracle to come, his eyes mechanically received the image of a heavily-coated man with his fur collar turned up who was advancing along the path to the house. The man was Julius Beaufort.

"Ah—!" Archer cried, bursting into a laugh.

Madame Olenska had sprung up and moved to his side, slipping her hand into his; but after a glance through the window her face paled and she shrank back.

"So that was it?" Archer said derisively.

"I didn't know he was here," Madame Olenska murmured. Her hand still clung to Archer's; but he drew away from her, and walking out into the passage threw open the door of the house.

"Hallo, Beaufort—this way! Madame Olenska was expecting you," he said.

During his journey back to New York the next morning, Archer relived with a fatiguing vividness his last moments at Skuytercliff.

Beaufort, though clearly annoyed at finding him with Madame Olenska, had, as usual, carried off the situation high-handedly. His way of ignoring people whose presence inconvenienced him actually gave them, if they were sensitive to it, a feeling of invisibility, of non-existence. Archer, as the three strolled back through the park, was aware of this odd sense of disembodiment; and humbling as it was to his vanity it gave him the ghostly advantage of observing unobserved.

Beaufort had entered the little house with his usual easy assurance; but he could not smile away the vertical line between his eyes. It was fairly clear that Madame Olenska had not known that he was coming, though her words to Archer had hinted at the possiblity; at any rate, she had evidently not told him where she was going when she left New York, and her unexplained departure had exasperated him. The ostensible reason of his appearance was the discovery, the very night before, of a "perfect little house," not in the market, which was really just the thing for her, but would be snapped up instantly if she didn't take it; and he was loud in mock-reproaches for the dance she had led him in running away just as he had found it.

"If only this new dodge for talking along a wire had been a little bit nearer perfection I might have told you all this from town, and been toasting my toes before the club fire at this minute, instead of tramping after you through the snow," he grumbled, disguising a real irritation under the pretence of it; and at this opening Madame Olenska twisted the talk away to the fantastic possibility that they might one day actually converse with each other from street to street, or even—incredible dream!—from one town to another. This struck from all three allusions to Edgar Poe and Jules Verne, and such platitudes as naturally rise to the lips of the most intelligent when they are talking against time, and dealing with a new invention in which it would seem ingenuous to believe too soon; and the question of the telephone carried them safely back to the big house.

Mrs. van der Luyden had not yet returned; and Archer took his leave and walked off to fetch the cutter, while Beaufort followed the Countess Olenska indoors. It was probable that, little as the van der Luydens encouraged unannounced visits, he could count on being asked to dine, and sent back to the station to catch the nine o'clock train; but more than that he would certainly not get, for it would be inconceivable to his hosts that a gentleman travelling without luggage should wish to spend the night, and distasteful to them to propose it to a person with whom they were on terms of such limited cordiality as Beaufort.

Beaufort knew all this, and must have foreseen it; and his taking the long journey for so small a reward gave the measure of his impatience. He was undeniably in pursuit of the Countess Olenska; and Beaufort had only one object in view in his pursuit of pretty women. His dull and childless home had long since palled on him; and in addition to more permanent consolations he was always in quest of amorous adventures in his own set. This was the man from whom Madame Olenska was avowedly flying: the question was whether she had fled because his importunities displeased her, or because she did not wholly trust herself to resist them; unless, indeed, all her talk of flight had been a blind, and her departure no more than a manœuvre.

Archer did not really believe this. Little as he had actually seen of Madame Olenska, he was beginning to think that he could read her face, and if not her face, her voice; and both had betrayed annoyance, and even dismay, at Beaufort's sudden appearance. But, after all, if this were the case, was it not worse than if she had left New York for the express purpose of meeting him? If she had done that, she ceased to be an object of interest, she threw in her lot with the vulgarest of dissemblers: a woman engaged in a love affair with Beaufort "classed" herself irretrievably.

No, it was worse a thousand times if, judging Beaufort, and probably despising him, she was yet drawn to him by all that gave him an advantage over the other men about her: his habit of two continents and two societies, his familiar association with artists and actors and people generally in the world's eye, and his careless contempt for local prejudices. Beaufort was vulgar, he was uneducated, he was purse-proud; but the circumstances of his life, and a certain native shrewdness, made him better worth talking to than many men, morally and socially his betters, whose horizon was bounded by the Battery and the Central Park. How should any one coming from a wider world not feel difference and be attracted by it?

Madame Olenska, in a burst of irritation, had said to Archer that he and she did not talk the same language; and the young man knew that in some respects this was true. But Beaufort understood every turn of her dialect, and spoke it fluently: his view of life, his tone, his attitude, were merely a coarser reflection of those revealed in Count Olenski's letter. This might seem to be to his disadvantage with Count Olenski's wife; but Archer was too intelligent to think that a young woman like Ellen Olenska would necessarily recoil from everything that reminded her of her past. She might believe herself wholly in revolt against it; but what had charmed her in it would still charm her, even though it were against her will.

Thus, with a painful impartiality, did the young man make out the case for Beaufort, and for Beaufort's victim. A longing to enlighten her was strong in him; and there were moments when he imagined that all she asked was to be enlightened.

That evening he unpacked his books from London. The box was full of things he had been waiting for impatiently; a new volume of Herbert Spencer, another collection of the prolific Alphonse Daudet's brilliant tales, and a novel called "Middlemarch," as to which there had lately been interesting things said in the reviews. He had declined three dinner invitations in favour of this feast, but though he turned the pages with the sensuous joy of the book-lover, he did not know what he was reading and one book after another dropped from his hand. Suddenly , among them, he lit on a small volume of verse which he had ordered because the name had attracted him: "The House of Life." He took it up, and found himself plunged in an atmosphere unlike any he had ever breathed in books; so warm, so rich, and yet so ineffably tender, that it gave a new and haunting beauty to the most elementary of human passions. All through the night he pursued through those enchanted pages the vision of a woman who had the face of Ellen Olenska; but when he woke the next morning, and looked out at the brown-stone houses across the street, and thought of his desk in Mr. Letterblair's office, and the family pew in Grace Church, his hour in the park of Skuytercliff became as far outside the pale of probability as the visions of the night.

"Mercy, how pale you look, Newland!" Janey commented over the coffee-cups at breakfast; and his mother added: "Newland, dear, I've noticed lately that you've been coughing; I do hope you're not letting yourself be overworked?" For it was the conviction of both ladies that, under the iron despotism of his senior partners, the young man's life was spent in the most exhausting professional labours—and he had never thought it necessary to undeceive them.

The next two or three days dragged by heavily. The taste of the usual was like cinders in his mouth, and there were moments when he felt as if he were being buried alive under his future. He heard nothing of the Countess Olenska, or of the perfect little house, and though he met Beaufort at the club they merely nodded at each other across the whist-tables. It was not till the fourth evening that he found a note awaiting him on his return home. "Come late tomorrow: I must explain to you. Ellen." These were the only words it contained.

The young man, who was dining out, thrust the note into his pocket, smiling a little at the Frenchness of the "to you." After dinner he went to a play; and it was not until his return home, after midnight, that he drew Madame Olenska's missive out again and re-read it slowly a number of times. There were several ways of answering it, and he gave considerable thought to each one during the watches of an agitated night. That on which, when morning came, he finally decided was to pitch some clothes into a portmanteau and jump on board a boat that was leaving that very afternoon for St. Augustine.

§ 16

When Archer walked down the sandy main street of St. Augustine to the house which had been pointed out to him as Mr. Welland's, and saw May Welland standing under a magnolia with the sun in her hair, he wondered why he had waited so long to come.

Here was truth, here was reality, here was the life that belonged to him; and he, who fancied himself so scornful of arbitrary restraints, had been afraid to break away from his desk because of what people might think of his stealing a holiday!

Her first exclamation was: "Newland—has anything happened?" and it occurred to him that it would have been more "feminine" if she had instantly read in his eyes why he had come. But when he answered: "Yes—I found I had to see you," her happy blushes took the chill from her surprise, and he saw how easily he would be forgiven, and how soon even Mr. Letterblair's mild disapproval would be smiled away by a tolerant family.

Early as it was, the main street was no place for any but formal greetings, and Archer longed to be alone with May, and to pour out all his tenderness and his impatience. It still lacked an hour to the late Welland breakfast-time, and instead of asking him to come in she proposed that they should walk out to an old orange-garden beyond the town. She had just been for a row on the river, and the sun that netted the little waves with gold seemed to have caught her in its meshes. Across the warm brown of her cheek her blown hair glittered like silver wire; and her eyes too looked lighter, almost pale in their youthful limpidity. As she walked beside Archer with her long swinging gait her face wore the vacant serenity of a young marble athlete.

To Archer's strained nerves the vision was as soothing as the sight of the blue sky and the lazy river. They sat down on a bench under the orange-trees and he put his arm about her and kissed her. It was like drinking at a cold spring with the sun on it; but his pressure may have been more vehement than he had intended, for the blood rose to her face and she drew back as if he had startled her.

"What is it?" he asked, smiling; and she looked at him with surprise, and answered: "Nothing."

A slight embarrassment fell on them, and her hand slipped out of his. It was the only time that he had kissed her on the lips except for their fugitive embrace in the Beaufort conservatory, and he saw that she was disturbed, and shaken out of her cool boyish composure.

"Tell me what you do all day," he said, crossing his arms under his tilted-back head, and pushing his hat forward to screen the sun-dazzle. To let her talk about familiar and simple things was the easiest way of carrying on his own independent train of thought; and he sat listening to her simple chronicle of swimming, sailing and riding, varied by an occasional dance at the primitive inn when a man-of-war came in. A few pleasant people from Philadelphia and Baltimore were picknicking at the inn, and the Selfridge Merrys had come down for three weeks because Kate Merry had had bronchitis. They were planning to lay out a lawn tennis court on the sands; but no one but Kate and May had racquets, and most of the people had not even heard of the game.

All this kept her very busy, and she had not had time to do more than look at the little vellum book that Archer had sent her the week before (the "Sonnets from the Portuguese") ; but she was learning by heart "How they brought the Good News from Ghent to Aix," because it was one of the first things he had ever read to her; and it amused her to be able to tell him that Kate Merry had never heard of a poet called Robert Browning.

Presently she started up, exclaiming that they would be late for breakfast; and they hurried back to the tumble-down house with its paintless porch and unpruned hedge of plumbago and pink geraniums where the Wellands were installed for the winter. Mr. Welland's sensitive domesticity shrank from the discomforts of the slovenly southern hotel, and at immense expense, and in face of almost insuperable difficulties, Mrs. Welland was obliged, year after year, to improvise an establishment partly made up of discontented New York servants and partly drawn from the local African supply.

"The doctors want my husband to feel that he is in his own home; otherwise he would be so wretched that the climate would not do him any good," she explained, winter after winter, to the sympathising Philadelphians and Baltimoreans; and Mr. Welland, beaming across a breakfast table miraculously supplied with the most varied delicacies, was presently saying to Archer: "You see, my dear fellow, we camp—we literally camp. I tell my wife and May that I want to teach them how to rough it."

Mr. and Mrs. Welland had been as much surprised as their daughter by the young man's sudden arrival; but it had occurred to him to explain that he had felt himself on the verge of a nasty cold, and this seemed to Mr. Welland an all-sufficient reason for abandoning any duty.

"You can't be too careful, especially toward spring," he said, heaping his plate with straw-coloured griddlecakes and drowning them in golden syrup. "If I'd only been as prudent at your age May would have been dancing at the Assemblies now, instead of spending her winters in a wilderness with an old invalid."

"Oh, but I love it here, Papa; you know I do. If only Newland could stay I should like it a thousand times better than New York."

"Newland must stay till he has quite thrown off his cold," said Mrs. Welland indulgently; and the young man laughed, and said he supposed there was such a thing as one's profession.

He managed, however, after an exchange of telegrams with the firm, to make his cold last a week; and it shed an ironic light on the situation to know that Mr. Letterblair's indulgence was partly due to the satisfactory way in which his brilliant young junior partner had settled the troublesome matter of the Olenski divorce. Mr. Letterblair had let Mrs. Welland know that Mr. Archer had "rendered an invaluable service" to the whole family, and that old Mrs. Manson Mingott had been particularly pleased; and one day when May had gone for a drive with her father in the only vehicle the place produced, Mrs. Welland took occasion to touch on a topic which she always avoided in her daughter's presence.

"I'm afraid Ellen's ideas are not at all like ours. She was barely eighteen when Medora Manson took her back to Europe—you remember the excitement when she appeared in black at her coming-out ball? Another of Medora's fads—really this time it was almost prophetic! That must have been at least twelve years ago; and since then Ellen has never been to America. No wonder she is completely Europeanised."

"But European society is not given to divorce: Countess Olenska thought she would be conforming to American ideas in asking for her freedom." It was the first time that the young man had pronounced her name since he had left Skuytercliff, and he felt the colour rise to his cheek.

Mrs. Welland smiled compassionately. "That is just like the extraordinary things that foreigners invent about us. They think we dine at two o'clock and countenance divorce! That is why it seems to me so foolish to entertain them when they come to New York. They accept our hospitality, and then they go home and repeat the same stupid stories."

Archer made no comment on this, and Mrs. Welland continued: "But we do most thoroughly appreciate your persuading Ellen to give up the idea. Her grandmother and her uncle Lovell could do nothing with her; both of them have written that her changing her mind was entirely due to your influence—in fact she said so to her grandmother. She has an unbounded admiration for you. Poor Ellen—she was always a wayward child. I wonder what her fate will be?"

"What we've all contrived to make it," he felt like answering. "If you'd all of you rather she should be Beaufort's mistress than some decent fellow's wife you've certainly gone the right way about it."

He wondered what Mrs. Welland would have said if he had uttered the words instead of merely thinking them. He could picture the sudden decomposure of her firm placid features, to which a lifelong mastery over trifles had given an air of factitious authority. Traces still lingered on them of a fresh beauty like her daughter's; and he asked himself if May's face was doomed to thicken into the same middle-aged image of invincible innocence.

Ah, no, he did not want May to have that kind of innocence, the innocence that seals the mind against imagination and the heart against experience!

"I verily believe," Mrs. Welland continued, "that if the horrible business had come out in the newspapers it would have been my husband's death-blow. I don't know any of the details; I only ask not to, as I told poor Ellen when she tried to talk to me about it. Having an invalid to care for, I have to keep my mind bright and happy. But Mr. Welland was terribly upset; he had a slight temperature every morning while we were waiting to hear what had been decided. It was the horror of his girl's learning that such things were possible—but of course, dear Newland, you felt that too. We all knew that you were thinking of May."

"I'm always thinking of May," the young man rejoined, rising to cut short the conversation.

He had meant to seize the opportunity of his private talk with Mrs. Welland to urge her to advance the date of his marriage. But he could think of no arguments that would move her, and with a sense of relief he saw Mr. Welland and May driving up to the door.

His only hope was to plead again with May, and on the day before his departure he walked with her to the ruinous garden of the Spanish Mission. The background lent itself to allusions to European scenes; and May, who was looking her loveliest under a wide-brimmed hat that cast a shadow of mystery over her too-clear eyes, kindled into eagerness as he spoke of Granada and the Alhambra.

"We might be seeing it all this spring—even the Easter ceremonies at Seville," he urged, exaggerating his demands in the hope of a larger concession.

"Easter in Seville? And it will be Lent next week!" she laughed.

"Why shouldn't we be married in Lent?" he rejoined; but she looked so shocked that he saw his mistake.

"Of course I didn't mean that, dearest; but soon after Easter—so that we could sail at the end of April. I know I could arrange it at the office."

She smiled dreamily upon the possibility; but he perceived that to dream of it sufficed her. It was like hearing him read aloud out of his poetry books the beautiful things that could not possibly happen in real life.

"Oh, do go on, Newland; I do love your descriptions."

"But why should they be only descriptions? Why shouldn't we make them real?"

"We shall, dearest, of course; next year." Her voice lingered over it.

"Don't you want them to be real sooner? Can't I persuade you to break away now?"

She bowed her head, vanishing from him under her conniving hat-brim.

"Why should we dream away another year? Look at me, dear! Don't you understand how I want you for my wife?"

For a moment she remained motionless; then she raised on him eyes of such despairing clearness that he half-released her waist from his hold. But suddenly her look changed and deepened inscrutably. "I'm not sure if I *do* understand," she said. "Is it—is it because you're not certain of continuing to care for me?"

Archer sprang up from his seat. "My God—perhaps—I don't know," he broke out angrily.

May Welland rose also; as they faced each other she seemed to grow in womanly stature and dignity. Both were silent for a moment, as if dismayed by the unforeseen trend of their words: then she said in a low voice. "If that is it—is there some one else?"

"Some one else—between you and me?" He echoed her words slowly, as though they were only half-intelligible and he wanted time to repeat the question to himself. She seemed to catch the uncertainty of his voice, for she went on in a deepening tone: "Let us talk frankly, Newland. Sometimes I've felt a difference in you; especially since our engagement has been announced."

"Dear—what madness!" he recovered himself to exclaim.

She met his protest with a faint smile. "If it is, it won't hurt us to talk about it." She paused, and added, lifting her head with one of her noble movements: "Or even if it's true: why shouldn't we speak of it? You might so easily have made a mistake."

He lowered his head, staring at the black leaf-pattern on the sunny path at their feet. "Mistakes are always easy to make; but if I had made one of the kind you suggest, is it likely that I should be imploring you to hasten our marriage?"

She looked downward too, disturbing the pattern with the point of her sunshade while she struggled for expression. "Yes," she said at length. "You might want—once for all—to settle the question: it's one way."

Her quiet lucidity startled him, but did not mislead him into thinking her insensible. Under her hat-brim he saw the pallor of her profile, and a slight tremor of the nostril above her resolutely steadied lips.

"Well—" he questioned, sitting down on the bench, and looking up at her with a frown that he tried to make playful.

She dropped back into her seat and went on: "You mustn't think that a girl knows as little as her parents imagine. One hears and one notices—one has one's feelings and ideas. And of course, long before you told me that you cared for me, I'd known that there was some one else you were interested in; every one was talking about it two years ago at Newport. And once I saw you sitting together on the verandah at a dance—and when she came back into the house her face was sad, and I felt sorry for her; I remembered it afterward, when we were engaged."

Her voice had sunk almost to a whisper, and she sat clasping and unclasping her hands about the handle of her sunshade. The young man laid his upon them with a gentle pressure; his heart dilated with an inexpressible relief.

"My dear child—was *that* it? If you only knew the truth!"

She raised her head quickly. "Then there is a truth I don't know?"

He kept his hand over hers. "I meant, the truth about the old story you speak of."

"But that's what I want to know, Newland—what I ought to know. I couldn't have my happiness made out of a wrong—an unfairness—to somebody else. And I want to believe that it would be the same with you. What sort of a life could we build on such foundations?"

Her face had taken on a look of such tragic courage that he felt like bowing himself down at her feet. "I've wanted to say this for a long time," she went on. "I've wanted to tell you that, when two people really love each other, I understand that there may be situations which make it right that they should—should go against public opinion. And if you feel yourself in any way pledged . . . pledged to the person we've spoken of . . . and if there is any way . . . any way in which you can fulfill your pledge . . . even by her getting a divorce . . . Newland, don't give her up because of me!"

His surprise at discovering that her fears had fastened upon an episode so remote and so completely of the past as his love affair with Mrs. Thorley Rushworth gave way to wonder at the generosity of her view. There was something superhuman in an attitude so recklessly unorthodox, and if other problems had not pressed on him he would have been lost in wonder at the prodigy of the Wellands' daughter urging him to marry his former mistress. But he was still dizzy with the glimpse of the precipice they had skirted, and full of a new awe at the mystery of young-girlhood.

For a moment he could not speak; then he said: "There is no pledge—no obligation whatever—of the kind you think. Such cases don't always—present themselves quite as simply as . . . But that's no matter . . . I love your generosity, because I feel as you do about those things . . . I feel that each case must be judged individually, on its own merits . . . irrespective of stupid conventionalities . . . I mean, each woman's right to her liberty—" He pulled himself up, startled by the turn his thoughts had taken, and went on, looking at her with a smile: "Since you understand so many things, dearest, can't you go a little farther, and understand the uselessness of our submitting to another form of the same foolish conventionalities? If there's no one and nothing between us, isn't that an argument for marrying quickly, rather than for more delay?"

She flushed with joy and lifted her face to his; as he bent to it he saw that her eyes were full of happy tears. But in another moment she seemed to have descended from her womanly eminence to helpless and timorous girlhood; and he understood that her courage and initiative were all for others, and that she had none for herself. It was evident that the effort of speaking had been much greater than her studied composure betrayed, and that at his first word of reassurance she had dropped back into the usual, as a too-adventurous child takes refuge in its mother's arms.

Archer had no heart to go on pleading with her; he was too much disappointed at the vanishing of the new being who had cast that one deep look at him from her transparent eyes. May seemed to be aware of his disappointment, but without knowing how to alleviate it; and they stood up and walked silently home.

§ 17

"Your cousin the Countess called on mother while you were away," Janey Archer announced to her brother on the evening of his return.

The young man, who was dining alone with his mother and sister, glanced up in surprise and saw Mrs. Archer's gaze demurely bent on her plate. Mrs. Archer did not regard her seclusion from the world as a reason for being forgotten by it; and Newland guessed that she was slightly annoyed that he should be surprised by Madame Olenska's visit.

"She had on a black velvet polonaise with jet buttons, and a tiny green monkey muff; I never saw her so stylishly dressed," Janey continued. "She came alone, early on Sunday afternoon; luckily the fire was lit in the drawing-room. She had one of those new card-cases. She said she wanted to know us because you'd been so good to her."

Newland laughed. "Madame Olenska always takes that tone about her friends. She's very happy at being among her own people again."

"Yes, so she told us," said Mrs. Archer. "I must say she seems thankful to be here."

"I hope you liked her, mother."

Mrs. Archer drew her lips together. "She certainly lays herself out to please, even when she is calling on an old lady."

"Mother doesn't think her simple," Janey interjected her eyes screwed upon her brother's face.

"It's just my old-fashioned feeling; dear May is my ideal," said Mrs. Archer.

"Ah," said her son, "they're not alike."

Archer had left St. Augustine charged with many messages for old Mrs. Mingott; and a day or two after his return to town he called on her.

The old lady received him with unusual warmth; she was grateful to him for persuading the Countess Olenska to give up the idea of a divorce; and when he told her that he had deserted the office without leave, and rushed down to St. Augustine simply because he wanted to see May, she gave an adipose chuckle and patted his knee with her puff-ball hand.

"Ah, ah—so you kicked over the traces, did you? And I suppose Augusta and Welland pulled long faces, and behaved as if the end of the world had come? But little May—she knew better, I'll be bound?"

"I hoped she did; but after all she wouldn't agree to what I'd gone down to ask for."

"Wouldn't she indeed? And what was that?"

"I wanted to get her to promise that we should be married in April. What's the use of our wasting another year?"

Mrs. Manson Mingott screwed up her little mouth into a grimace of mimic prudery and twinkled at him through malicious lids. " 'Ask Mamma,' I suppose—the usual story. Ah, these Mingotts—all alike! Born in a rut, and you can't root 'em out of it. When I built this house you'd have thought I was moving to California! Nobody ever *had* built above Fortieth Street—no, says I, nor above the Battery either, before Christopher Columbus discovered America. No, no; not one of them wants to be different; they're as scared of it as the small-pox. Ah, my dear Mr. Archer, I thank my stars I'm nothing but a vulgar Spicer; but there's not one of my own children that takes after me but my little Ellen." She broke off, still twinkling at him, and asked, with the casual irrelevance of old age: "Now, why in the world didn't you marry my little Ellen?"

Archer laughed. "For one thing, she wasn't there to be married."

"No—to be sure; more's the pity. And now it's too late; her life is finished." She spoke with the cold-blooded complacency of the aged throwing earth into the grave of young hopes. The young man's heart grew chill, and he said hurriedly: "Can't I persuade you to use your influence with the Wellands, Mrs. Mingott? I wasn't made for long engagements."

Old Catherine beamed on him approvingly. "No; I can see that. You've got a quick eye. When you were a little boy I've no doubt you liked to be helped first." She threw back her head with a laugh that made her chins ripple like little waves. "Ah, here's my Ellen now!" she exclaimed, as the portières parted behind her.

Madame Olenska came forward with a smile. Her face looked

vivid and happy, and she held out her hand gaily to Archer while she stooped to her grandmother's kiss.

"I was just saying to him, my dear: 'Now, why didn't you marry my little Ellen?'"

Madame Olenska looked at Archer, still smiling. "And what did he answer?"

"Oh, my darling, I leave you to find that out! He's been down to Florida to see his sweetheart."

"Yes, I know." She still looked at him. "I went to see your mother, to ask where you'd gone. I sent a note that you never answered, and I was afraid you were ill."

He muttered something about leaving unexpectedly, in a great hurry, and having intended to write to her from St. Augustine.

"And of course once you were there you never thought of me again!" She continued to beam on him with a gaiety that might have been a studied assumption of indifference.

"If she still needs me, she's determined not to let me see it," he thought, stung by her manner. He wanted to thank her for having been to see his mother, but under the ancestress's malicious eye he felt himself tongue-tied and constrained.

"Look at him—in such hot haste to get married that he took French leave and rushed down to implore the silly girl on his knees! That's something like a lover—that's the way handsome Bob Spicer carried off my poor mother; and then got tired of her before I was weaned—though they only had to wait eight months for me! But there—you're not a Spicer, young man; luckily for you and for May. It's only my poor Ellen that has kept any of their wicked blood; the rest of them are all model Mingotts," cried the old lady scornfully.

Archer was aware that Madame Olenska, who had seated herself at her grandmother's side, was still thoughtfully scrutinising him. The gaiety had faded from her eyes, and she said with great gentleness: "Surely, Granny, we can persuade them between us to do as he wishes."

Archer rose to go, and as his hand met Madame Olenska's he felt that she was waiting for him to make some allusion to her unanswered letter.

"When can I see you?" he asked, as she walked with him to the door of the room.

"Whenever you like; but it must be soon if you want to see the little house again. I am moving next week."

A pang shot through him at the memory of his lamplit hours in the low-studded drawing-room. Few as they had been, they were thick with memories.

"Tomorrow evening?"

She nodded. "Tomorrow; yes; but early. I'm going out."

The next day was a Sunday, and if she were "going out" on a Sunday evening it could, of course, be only to Mrs. Lemuel Struthers's. He felt a slight movement of annoyance, not so much at her going there (for he rather liked her going where she pleased in spite of the van der Luydens), but because it was the kind of house at which she was sure to meet Beaufort, where she must have known beforehand that she would meet him—and where she was probably going for that purpose.

"Very well; tomorrow evening," he repeated, inwardly resolved that he would not go early, and that by reaching her door late he would either prevent her from going to Mrs. Struthers's, or else arrive after she had started—which, all things considered, would no doubt be the simplest solution.

It was only half-past eight, after all, when he rang the bell under the wisteria; not as late as he had intended by half an hour—but a singular restlessness had driven him to her door. He reflected, however, that Mrs. Struthers's Sunday evenings were not like a ball, and that her guests, as if to minimise their delinquency, usually went early.

The one thing he had not counted on, in entering Madame Olenska's hall, was to find hats and overcoats there. Why had she bidden him to come early if she was having people to dine? On a closer inspection of the garments besides which Nastasia was laying his own, his resentment gave way to curiosity. The overcoats were in fact the very strangest he had ever seen under a polite roof; and it took but a glance to assure himself that neither of them belonged to Julius Beaufort. One was a shaggy yellow ulster of "reach-me-down" cut, the other a very old and rusty cloak with a cape—something like what the French called a "Macfarlane." This garment, which appeared to be made for a person of prodigious size, had evidently seen long and hard wear, and its greenish-black folds gave out a moist sawdusty smell suggestive of prolonged sessions against bar-room walls. On it lay a ragged grey scarf and an odd felt hat of semi-clerical shape.

Archer raised his eyebrows enquiringly at Nastasia, who raised hers in return with a fatalistic "Già!" as she threw open the drawing-room door.

The young man saw at once that his hostess was not in the room; then, with surprise, he discovered another lady standing by the fire. This lady, who was long, lean and loosely put together, was clad in raiment intricately looped and fringed, with plaids and stripes and bands of plain colour disposed in a design to which the clue seemed missing. Her hair, which had tried to turn white and only succeeded in fading, was surmounted by a Spanish comb and black lace scarf, and silk mittens, visibly darned, covered her rheumatic hands.

Beside her, in a cloud of cigar-smoke, stood the owners of the two overcoats, both in morning clothes that they had evidently not taken off since morning. In one of the two, Archer, to his surprise, recognised Ned Winsett; the other and older, who was unknown to him, and whose gigantic frame declared him to be the wearer of the "Macfarlane," had a feebly leonine head with crumpled grey hair, and moved his arms with large pawing gestures, as though he were distributing lay blessings to a kneeling multitude.

These three persons stood together on the hearth-rug, their eyes fixed on an extraordinarily large bouquet of crimson roses, with a knot of purple pansies at their base, that lay on the sofa where Madame Olenska usually sat.

"What they must have cost at this season—though of course it's the sentiment one cares about!" the lady was saying in a sighing staccato as Archer came in.

The three turned with surprise at his appearance, and the lady, advancing, held out her hand.

"Dear Mr. Archer—almost my nephew Newland!" she said. "I am the Marchioness Manson."

Archer bowed, and she continued: "My Ellen has taken me in for a few days. I came from Cuba, where I have been spending the winter with Spanish friends—such delightful distinguished people: the highest nobility of old Castile—how I wish you could know them! But I was called away by our dear great friend here, Dr. Carver. You don't know Dr. Agathon Carver, founder of the Valley of Love Community?"

Dr. Carver inclined his leonine head, and the Marchioness continued: "Ah, New York—New York—how little the life of the spirit has reached it! But I see you do know Mr. Winsett."

"Oh, yes—*I* reached him some time ago; but not by that route," Winsett said with his dry smile.

The Marchioness shook her head reprovingly. "How do you know, Mr. Winsett? The spirit bloweth where it listeth."

"List—oh, list!" interjected Dr. Carver in a stentorian murmur.

"But do sit down, Mr. Archer. We four have been having a delightful little dinner together, and my child has gone up to dress. She expects you; she will be down in a moment. We were just admiring these marvellous flowers, which will surprise her when she reappears."

Winsett remained on his feet. "I'm afraid I must be off. Please tell Madame Olenska that we shall all feel lost when she abandons our street. This house has been an oasis."

"Ah, but she won't abandon *you*. Poetry and art are the breath of life to her. It *is* poetry you write, Mr. Winsett?"

"Well, no; but I sometimes read it," said Winsett, including the group in a general nod and slipping out of the room.

"A caustic spirit—*un peu sauvage*. But so witty; Dr. Carver, you *do* think him witty?"

"I never think of wit," said Dr. Carver severely.

"Ah—ah—you never think of wit! How merciless he is to us weak mortals, Mr. Archer! But he lives only in the life of the spirit; and tonight he is mentally preparing the lecture he is to deliver presently at Mrs. Blenker's. Dr. Carver, would there be time, before you start for the Blenkers' to explain to Mr. Archer your illuminating discovery of the Direct Contact? But no; I see it is nearly nine o'clock, and we have no right to detain you while so many are waiting for your message."

Dr. Carver looked slightly disappointed at this conclusion, but, having compared his ponderous gold timepiece with Madame Olenska's little travelling-clock, he reluctantly gathered up his mighty limbs for departure.

"I shall see you later, dear friend?" he suggested to the Marchioness, who replied with a smile: "As soon as Ellen's carriage comes I will join you; I do hope the lecture won't have begun."

Dr. Carver looked thoughtfully at Archer. "Perhaps, if this young gentleman is interested in my experiences, Mrs. Blenker might allow you to bring him with you?"

"Oh, dear friend, if it were possible—I am sure she would be too happy. But I fear my Ellen counts on Mr. Archer herself."

"That," said Dr. Carver, "is unfortunate—but here is my card." He handed it to Archer, who read on it, in Gothic characters:

AGATHON CARVER
THE VALLEY OF LOVE
KITTASQUATTAMY, N. Y.

Dr. Carver bowed himself out, and Mrs. Manson, with a sigh that might have been either of regret or relief, again waved Archer to a seat.

"Ellen will be down in a moment; and before she comes, I am so glad of this quiet moment with you."

Archer murmured his pleasure at their meeting, and the Marchioness continued, in her low sighing accents: "I know everything, dear Mr. Archer—my child has told me all you have done for her. Your wise advice: your courageous firmness—thank heaven it was not too late!"

The young man listened with considerable embarrassment. Was there any one, he wondered, to whom Madame Olenska had not proclaimed his intervention in her private affairs?

"Madame Olenska exaggerates; I simply gave her a legal opinion, as she asked me to."

"Ah, but in doing it—in doing it you were the unconscious instrument of—of—what word have we moderns for Providence, Mr. Archer?" cried the lady, tilting her head on one side and drooping her lids mysteriously. "Little did you know that at that very moment I was being appealed to: being approached, in fact—from the other side of the Atlantic!"

She glanced over her shoulder, as though fearful of being overheard, and then, drawing her chair nearer, and raising a tiny ivory fan to her lips, breathed behind it: "By the Count himself—my poor, mad, foolish Olenski; who asks only to take her back on her own terms."

"Good God!" Archer exclaimed, springing up.

"You are horrified? Yes, of course; I understand. I don't defend poor Stanislas, though he has always called me his best friend. He does not defend himself—he casts himself at her feet: in my person." She tapped her emaciated bosom. "I have his letter here."

"A letter?— Has Madame Olenska seen it?" Archer stammered, his brain whirling with the shock of the announcement.

The Marchioness Manson shook her head softly. "Time—time; I must have time. I know my Ellen—haughty, intractable; shall I say, just a shade unforgiving?"

"But, good heavens, to forgive is one thing; to go back into that hell—"

"Ah, yes," the Marchioness acquiesced. "So she describes it—my sensitive child! But on the material side, Mr. Archer, if one may stoop to consider such things; do you know what she is giving up? Those roses there on the sofa—acres like them, under glass and in the open, in his matchless terraced gardens at Nice! Jewels—historic pearls: the Sobieski emeralds—sables—but she cares nothing for all these! Art and beauty, those she does care for, she lives for, as I always have; and those also surrounded her. Pictures, priceless furniture, music, brilliant conversation—ah, that, my dear young man, if you'll excuse me, is what you've no conception of here! And she had it all; and the homage of the greatest. She tells me she is not thought handsome in New York—good heavens! Her portrait has been painted nine times; the greatest artists in Europe have begged for the privilege. Are these things nothing? And the remorse of an adoring husband?"

As the Marchioness Manson rose to her climax her face assumed an expression of ecstatic retrospection which would have moved Archer's mirth had he not been numb with amazement.

He would have laughed if any one had foretold to him that his first sight of poor Medora Manson would have been in the guise of a messenger of Satan; but he was in no mood for laughing now, and she seemed to him to come straight out of the hell from which Ellen Olenska had just escaped.

"She knows nothing yet—of all this?" he asked abruptly.

Mrs. Manson laid a purple finger on her lips. "Nothing directly—but does she suspect? Who can tell? The truth is, Mr. Archer, I have been waiting to see you. From the moment I heard of the firm stand you had taken, and of your influence over her, I hoped it might be possible to count on your support—to convince you . . ."

"That she ought to go back? I would rather see her dead!" cried the young man violently.

"Ah," the Marchioness murmured, without visible resentment. For a while she sat in her arm-chair, opening and shutting the absurd ivory fan between her mittened fingers; but suddenly she lifted her head and listened.

"Here she comes," she said in a rapid whisper; and then, pointing to the bouquet on the sofa: "Am I to understand that you prefer *that,* Mr. Archer? After all, marriage is marriage . . . and my niece is still a wife. . . ."

§ 18

"What are you two plotting together, aunt Medora?" Madame Olenska cried as she came into the room.

She was dressed as if for a ball. Everything about her shimmered and glimmered softly, as if her dress had been woven out of candle-beams; and she carried her head high, like a pretty woman challenging a roomful of rivals.

"We were saying, my dear, that here was something beautiful to surprise you with," Mrs. Manson rejoined, rising to her feet and pointing archly to the flowers.

Madame Olenska stopped short and looked at the bouquet. Her colour did not change, but a sort of white radiance of anger ran over her like summer lightning. "Ah," she exclaimed, in a shrill voice that the young man had never heard, "who is ridiculous enough to send me a bouquet? Why a bouquet? And why tonight of all nights? I am not going to a ball; I am not a girl engaged to be married. But some people are always ridiculous."

She turned back to the door, opened it, and called out: "Nastasia!"

The ubiquitous handmaiden promptly appeared, and Archer

heard Madame Olenska say, in an Italian that she seemed to pronounce with intentional deliberateness in order that he might follow it: "Here—throw this into the dust-bin!" and then, as Nastasia stared protestingly: "But no—it's not the fault of the poor flowers. Tell the boy to carry them to the house three doors away, the house of Mr. Winsett, the dark gentleman who dined here. His wife is ill—they may give her pleasure . . . The boy is out, you say? Then, my dear one, run yourself; here, put my cloak over you and fly. I want the thing out of the house immediately! And, as you live, don't say they come from me!"

She flung her velvet opera cloak over the maid's shoulders and turned back into the drawing-room, shutting the door sharply. Her bosom was rising high under its lace, and for a moment Archer thought she was about to cry; but she burst into a laugh instead, and looking from the Marchioness to Archer, asked abruptly: "And you two—have you made friends?"

"It's for Mr. Archer to say, darling; he has waited patiently while you were dressing."

"Yes—I gave you time enough: my hair wouldn't go," Madame Olenska said, raising her hand to the heaped-up curls of her *chignon*. "But that reminds me: I see Dr. Carver is gone, and you'll be late at the Blenkers'. Mr. Archer, will you put my aunt in the carriage?"

She followed the Marchioness into the hall, saw her fitted into a miscellaneous heap of overshoes, shawls and tippets, and called from the doorstep: "Mind, the carriage is to be back for me at ten!" Then she returned to the drawing-room, where Archer, on re-entering it, found her standing by the mantelpiece, examining herself in the mirror. It was not usual, in New York society, for a lady to address her parlour-maid as "my dear one," and send her out on an errand wrapped in her own opera-cloak; and Archer, through all his deeper feelings, tasted the pleasurable excitement of being in a world where action followed on emotion with such Olympian speed.

Madame Olenska did not move when he came up behind her, and for a second their eyes met in the mirror; then she turned, threw herself into her sofa-corner, and sighed out: "There's time for a cigarette."

He handed her the box and lit a spill for her; and as the flame flashed up into her face she glanced at him with laughing eyes and said: "What do you think of me in a temper?"

Archer paused a moment; then he answered with sudden resolution: "It makes me understand what your aunt has been saying about you."

"I knew she'd been talking about me. Well?"

"She said you were used to all kinds of things—splendours and amusements and excitements—that we could never hope to give you here."

Madame Olenska smiled faintly into the circle of smoke about her lips.

"Medora is incorrigibly romantic. It has made up to her for so many things!"

Archer hesitated again, and again took his risk. "Is your aunt's romanticism always consistent with accuracy?"

"You mean: does she speak the truth?" Her niece considered. "Well, I'll tell you: in almost everything she says, there's something true and something untrue. But why do you ask? What has she been telling you?"

He looked away into the fire, and then back at her shining presence. His heart tightened with the thought that this was their last evening by that fireside, and that in a moment the carriage would come to carry her away.

"She says—she pretends that Count Olenski has asked her to persuade you to go back to him."

Madame Olenska made no answer. She sat motionless, holding her cigarette in her half-lifted hand. The expression of her face had not changed; and Archer remembered that he had before noticed her apparent incapacity for surprise.

"You knew, then?" he broke out.

She was silent for so long that the ash dropped from her cigarette. She brushed it to the floor. "She has hinted about a letter: poor darling! Medora's hints—"

"Is it at your husband's request that she has arrived here suddenly?"

Madame Olenska seemed to consider this question also. "There again: one can't tell. She told me she had had a 'spiritual summons,' whatever that is, from Dr. Carver. I'm afraid she's going to marry

Dr. Carver . . . poor Medora, there's always some one she wants to marry. But perhaps the people in Cuba just got tired of her! I think she was with them as a sort of paid companion. Really, I don't know why she came."

"But you do believe she has a letter from your husband?"

Again Madame Olenska brooded silently; then she said: "After all, it was to be expected."

The young man rose and went to lean against the fireplace. A sudden restlessness possessed him, and he was tongue-tied by the sense that their minutes were numbered, and that at any moment he might hear the wheels of the returning carriage.

"You know that your aunt believes you will go back?"

Madame Olenska raised her head quickly. A deep blush rose to her face and spread over her neck and shoulders. She blushed seldom and painfully, as if it hurt her like a burn.

"Many cruel things have been believed of me," she said.

"Oh, Ellen—forgive me; I'm a fool and a brute!"

She smiled a little. "You are horribly nervous; you have your own troubles. I know you think the Wellands are unreasonable about your marriage, and of course I agree with you. In Europe people don't understand our long American engagements; I suppose they are not as calm as we are." She pronounced the "we" with a faint emphasis that gave it an ironic sound.

Archer felt the irony but did not dare to take it up. After all, she had perhaps purposely deflected the conversation from her own affairs, and after the pain his last words had evidently caused her he felt that all he could do was to follow her lead. But the sense of the waning hour made him desperate: he could not bear the thought that a barrier of words should drop between them again.

"Yes," he said abruptly; "I went south to ask May to marry me after Easter. There's no reason why we shouldn't be married then."

"And May adores you—and yet you couldn't convince her? I thought her too intelligent to be the slave of such absurd superstitions."

"She *is* too intelligent—she's not their slave."

Madame Olenska looked at him. "Well, then—I don't understand."

Archer reddened, and hurried on with a rush. "We had a frank talk—almost the first. She thinks my impatience a bad sign."

"Merciful heavens—a bad sign?"

"She thinks it means that I can't trust myself to go on caring for her. She thinks, in short, I want to marry her at once to get away from some one that I—care for more."

Madame Olenska examined this curiously. "But if she thinks that —why isn't she in a hurry too?"

"Because she's not like that: she's so much nobler. She insists all the more on the long engagement, to give me time—"

"Time to give her up for the other woman?"

"If I want to."

Madame Olenska leaned toward the fire and gazed into it with fixed eyes. Down the quiet street Archer heard the approaching trot of her horses.

"That *is* noble," she said, with a slight break in her voice.

"Yes. But it's ridiculous."

"Ridiculous? Because you don't care for any one else?

"Because I don't mean to marry any one else."

"Ah." There was another long interval. At length she looked up at him and asked: "This other woman—does she love you?"

"Oh, there's no other woman; I mean, the person that May was thinking of is—was never—"

"Then, why, after all, are you in such haste?"

"There's your carriage," said Archer.

She half-rose and looked about her with absent eyes. Her fan and gloves lay on the sofa beside her and she picked them up mechanically.

"Yes; I suppose I must be going."

"You're going to Mrs. Struthers's?"

"Yes." She smiled and added: "I must go where I am invited, or I should be too lonely. Why not come with me?"

Archer felt that at any cost he must keep her beside him, must make her give him the rest of her evening. Ignoring her question, he continued to lean against the chimney-piece, his eyes fixed on the hand in which she held her gloves and fan, as if watching to see if he had the power to make her drop them.

"May guessed the truth," he said. "There is another woman—but not the one she thinks."

Ellen Olenska made no answer, and did not move. After a moment he sat down beside her, and, taking her hand, softly unclasped it, so that the gloves and fan fell on the sofa between them.

She started up, and freeing herself from him moved away to the other side of the hearth. "Ah, don't make love to me! Too many people have done that," she said, frowning.

Archer, changing colour, stood up also: it was the bitterest rebuke she could have given him. "I have never made love to you," he said, "and I never shall. But you are the woman I would have married if it had been possible for either of us."

"Possible for either of us?" She looked at him with unfeigned astonishment. "And you say that—when it's you who've made it impossible?"

He stared at her, groping in a blackness through which a single arrow of light tore its blinding way.

"*I've* made it impossible—?"

"You, you, *you!*" she cried, her lip trembling like a child's on the verge of tears. "Isn't it you who made me give up divorcing—give it up because you showed me how selfish and wicked it was, how one must sacrifice one's self to preserve the dignity of marriage . . . and to spare one's family the publicity, the scandal? And because my family was going to be your family—for May's sake and for yours—I did what you told me, what you proved to me that I ought to do. Ah," she broke out with a sudden laugh, "I've made no secret of having done it for you!"

She sank down on the sofa again, crouching among the festive ripples of her dress like a stricken masquerader; and the young man stood by the fireplace and continued to gaze at her without moving.

"Good God," he groaned. "When I thought—"

"You thought?"

"Ah, don't ask me what I thought!"

Still looking at her, he saw the same burning flush creep up her neck to her face. She sat upright, facing him with a rigid dignity.

"I do ask you."

"Well, then: there were things in that letter you asked me to read—"

"My husband's letter?"

"Yes."

"I had nothing to fear from that letter: absolutely nothing! All I feared was to bring notoriety, scandal, on the family—on you and May."

"Good God," he groaned again, bowing his face in his hands.

The silence that followed lay on them with the weight of things final and irrevocable. It seemed to Archer to be crushing him down like his own grave-stone; in all the wide future he saw nothing that would ever lift that load from his heart. He did not move from his place, or raise his head from his hands; his hidden eyeballs went on staring into utter darkness.

"At least I loved you—" he brought out.

On the other side of the hearth, from the sofa-corner where he supposed that she still crouched, he heard a faint stifled crying like a child's. He started up and came to her side.

"Ellen! What madness! Why are you crying? Nothing's done that can't be undone. I'm still free, and you're going to be." He had her in his arms, her face like a wet flower at his lips, and all their vain terrors shrivelling up like ghosts at sunrise. The one thing that astonished him now was that he should have stood for five minutes arguing with her across the width of the room, when just touching her made everything so simple.

She gave him back all his kiss, but after a moment he felt her stiffening in his arms, and she put him aside and stood up.

"Ah, my poor Newland—I suppose this had to be. But it doesn't in the least alter things," she said, looking down at him in her turn from the hearth.

"It alters the whole of life for me."

"No, no—it mustn't, it can't. You're engaged to May Welland; and I'm married."

He stood up too, flushed and resolute. "Nonsense! It's too late for that sort of thing. We've no right to lie to other people or to ourselves. We won't talk of your marriage; but do you see me marrying May after this?"

She stood silent, resting her thin elbows on the mantelpiece, her profile reflected in the glass behind her. One of the locks of her *chignon* had become loosened and hung on her neck; she looked haggard and almost old.

"I don't see you," she said at length, "putting that question to May. Do you?"

He gave a reckless shrug. "It's too late to do anything else."

"You say that because it's the easiest thing to say at this moment

—not because it's true. In reality it's too late to do anything but what we'd both decided on."

"Ah, I don't understand you!"

She forced a pitiful smile that pinched her face instead of smoothing it. "You don't understand because you haven't yet guessed how you've changed things for me: oh, from the first—long before I knew all you'd done."

"All I'd done?"

"Yes. I was perfectly unconscious at first that people here were shy of me—that they thought I was a dreadful sort of person. It seems they had even refused to meet me at dinner. I found that out afterward; and how you'd made your mother go with you to the van der Luydens', and how you'd insisted on announcing your engagement at the Beaufort ball, so that I might have two families to stand by me instead of one—"

At that he broke into a laugh.

"Just imagine," she said, "how stupid and unobservant I was! I knew nothing of all this till Granny blurted it out one day. New York simply meant peace and freedom to me: it was coming home. And I was so happy at being among my own people that every one I met seemed kind and good, and glad to see me. But from the very beginning," she continued, "I felt there was no one as kind as you; no one who gave me reasons that I understood for doing what at first seemed so hard and—unnecessary. The very good people didn't convince me; I felt they'd never been tempted. But you knew; you understood; you had felt the world outside tugging at one with all its golden hands—and yet you hated the things it asks of one; you hated happiness bought by disloyalty and cruelty and indifference. That was what I'd never known before—and it's better than anything I've known."

She spoke in a low even voice, without tears or visible agitation; and each word, as it dropped from her, fell into his breast like burning lead. He sat bowed over, his head between his hands, staring at the hearth-rug, and at the tip of the satin shoe that showed under her dress. Suddenly he knelt down and kissed the shoe.

She bent over him, laying her hands on his shoulders, and looking at him with eyes so deep that he remained motionless under her gaze.

"Ah, don't let us undo what you've done!" she cried. "I can't go back now to that other way of thinking. I can't love you unless I give you up."

His arms were yearning up to her; but she drew away, and they remained facing each other, divided by the distance that her words had created. Then, abruptly, his anger overflowed.

"And Beaufort? Is he to replace me?"

As the words sprang out he was prepared for an answering flare of anger; and he would have welcomed it as fuel for his own. But Madame Olenska only grew a shade paler, and stood with her arms hanging down before her, and her head slightly bent, as her way was when she pondered a question.

"He's waiting for you now at Mrs. Struthers's; why don't you go to him?" Archer sneered.

She turned to ring the bell. "I shall not go out this evening; tell the carriage to go and fetch the Signora Marchesa," she said when the maid came.

After the door had closed again Archer continued to look at her with bitter eyes. "Why this sacrifice? Since you tell me that you're lonely I've no right to keep you from your friends."

She smiled a little under her wet lashes. "I shan't be lonely now. I *was* lonely; I *was* afraid. But the emptiness and the darkness are gone; when I turn back into myself now I'm like a child going at night into a room where there's always a light."

Her tone and her look still enveloped her in a soft inaccessibility, and Archer groaned out again: "I don't understand you!"

"Yet you understand May!"

He reddened under the retort, but kept his eyes on her. "May is ready to give me up."

"What! Three days after you've entreated her on your knees to hasten your marriage?"

"She's refused; that gives me the right—"

"Ah, you've taught me what an ugly word that is," she said.

He turned away with a sense of utter weariness. He felt as though he had been struggling for hours up the face of a steep precipice, and now, just as he had fought his way to the top, his hold had given way and he was pitching down headlong into darkness.

If he could have got her in his arms again he might have swept away her arguments; but she still held him at a distance by something inscrutably aloof in her look and attitude, and by his own awed sense of her sincerity. At length he began to plead again.

"If we do this now it will be worse afterward—worse for every one—"

"No—no—no!" she almost screamed, as if he frightened her.

At that moment the bell sent a long tinkle through the house. They had heard no carriage stopping at the door, and they stood motionless, looking at each other with startled eyes.

Outside, Nastasia's step crossed the hall, the outer door opened, and a moment later she came in carrying a telegram which she handed to the Countess Olenska.

"The lady was very happy at the flowers," Nastasia said, smoothing her apron. "She thought it was her *signor marito* who had sent them, and she cried a little and said it was a folly."

Her mistress smiled and took the yellow envelope. She tore it open and carried it to the lamp; then, when the door had closed again, she handed the telegram to Archer.

It was dated from St. Augustine, and addressed to the Countess Olenska. In it he read: "Granny's telegram successful. Papa and Mamma agree marriage after Easter. Am telegraphing Newland. Am too happy for words and love you dearly. Your grateful May."

Half an hour later, when Archer unlocked his own front-door, he found a similar envelope on the hall-table on top of his pile of notes and letters. The message inside the envelope was also from May Welland, and ran as follows: "Parents consent wedding Tuesday after Easter at twelve Grace Church eight bridesmaids please see Rector so happy love May."

Archer crumpled up the yellow sheet as if the gesture could annihilate the news it contained. Then he pulled out a small pocket-diary and turned over the pages with trembling fingers; but he did not find what he wanted, and cramming the telegram into his pocket he mounted the stairs.

A light was shining through the door of the little hall-room which served Janey as a dressing-room and boudoir, and her brother rapped impatiently on the panel. The door opened, and his sister stood before him in her immemorial purple flannel dressing-gown, with her hair "on pins." Her face looked pale and apprehensive.

"Newland! I hope there's no bad news in that telegram? I waited on purpose, in case—" (No item of his correspondence was safe from Janey.)

He took no notice of her question. "Look here—what day is Easter this year?"

She looked shocked at such unchristian ignorance "Easter? Newland! Why, of course, the first week in April. Why?"

"The first week?" He turned again to the pages of his diary, calculating rapidly under his breath. "The first week, did you say?" He threw back his head with a long laugh.

"For mercy's sake what's the matter?"

"Nothing's the matter, except that I'm going to be married in a month."

Janey fell upon his neck and pressed him to her purple flannel breast. "Oh Newland, how wonderful! I'm so glad! But, dearest, why do you keep on laughing? Do hush, or you'll wake Mamma."

END OF BOOK

PREFATORY NOTE TO "FALSE DAWN" AND "THE OLD MAID"

Continuing in the nostalgic and historical vein of *The Age of Innocence*, Mrs. Wharton wrote a series of four novelettes entitled *Old New York,* each set in a different decade: the 'forties, the 'fifties, the 'sixties and the 'seventies. The first two are here included: *False Dawn* and *The Old Maid.* Critics have not been inclined to give these tales their just due. Never were Edith Wharton's superb story-telling abilities more happily combined with her vivid accuracy of background. *False Dawn,* the story of the pathetic but perceptive Lewis Raycie with his premature collection of Italian primitives, could have been suggested by the history of the Jarvis collection at Yale. It is a brilliant study of the clash of old and new tastes; one sees behind it the Edith Wharton who was a close friend and devoted admirer of Bernard Berenson.

The Old Maid represents the neatest plotting of any story of Edith Wharton with the exception of *Ethan Frome.* It is not surprising that it should have been successfully dramatized. Delia Ralston, the adoptive, and Charlotte Lovell, the real mother of the illegitimate Tina fight with genteel and usually smothered hatred for eighteen years over the girl and the memory of her father. Delia, with the enormous advantages of wealth, position, family and personality, wins every round, including the last, but Charlotte, the bitter, sad old maid, manages always to poison her victories. The ending, when Delia asks the bride Tina to give her last going-away kiss to Charlotte, thus recognizing Charlotte's ultimate right and at the same time her own power in being able to compel its recognition, beautifully states the relationship of the two women and the argument of the tale.

Old New York, FALSE DAWN

§ 1

HAY, verbena and mignonette scented the languid July day. Large strawberries, crimsoning through sprigs of mint, floated in a bowl of pale yellow cup on the verandah table: an old Georgian bowl, with complex reflections on polygonal flanks, engraved with the Raycie arms between lion's heads. Now and again the gentlemen, warned by a menacing hum, slapped their cheeks, their brows or their bald crowns; but they did so as furtively as possible, for Mr. Halston Raycie, on whose verandah they sat, would not admit that there were mosquitoes at High Point.

The strawberries came from Mr. Raycie's kitchen garden; the Georgian bowl came from his great-grandfather (father of the Signer) ; the verandah was that of his country-house, which stood on a height above the Sound, at a convenient driving distance from his town house in Canal Street.

"Another glass, Commodore," said Mr. Raycie, shaking out a cambric handkerchief the size of a table-cloth, and applying a corner of it to his steaming brow.

Mr. Jameson Ledgely smiled and took another glass. He was known as "the Commodore" among his intimates because of having been in the Navy in his youth, and having taken part, as a midshipman under Admiral Porter, in the war of 1812. This jolly sunburnt bachelor, whose face resembled that of one of the bronze idols he might have brought back with him, had kept his naval air, though long retired from the service; and his white duck trousers, his gold-braided cap and shining teeth, still made him look as if he might be in command of a frigate. Instead of that, he had just sailed over a party of friends from his own place on the Long Island shore; and his trim white sloop was now lying in the bay below the point.

The Halston Raycie house overlooked a lawn sloping to the Sound. The lawn was Mr. Raycie's pride: it was mown with a scythe once a fortnight, and rolled in the spring by an old white horse specially shod for the purpose. Below the verandah the turf was broken by three rounds of rose-geranium, heliotrope and Bengal roses, which Mrs. Raycie tended in gauntlet gloves, under a small hinged sunshade that folded back on its carved ivory handle. The house, remodelled and enlarged by Mr. Raycie on his marriage, had played a part in the Revolutionary war as the settler's cottage where Benedict Arnold had had his headquarters. A contemporary print of it hung in Mr. Raycie's study; but no one could have detected the humble outline of the old house in the majestic stone-coloured dwelling built of tongued-and-grooved boards, with an angle tower, tall narrow windows, and a verandah on chamfered posts, that figured so confidently as a "Tuscan Villa" in Downing's "Landscape Gardening in America." There was the same difference between the rude lithograph of the earlier house and the fine steel engraving of its successor (with a "specimen" weeping beech on the lawn) as between the buildings themselves. Mr. Raycie had reason to think well of his architect.

He thought well of most things related to himself by ties of blood or interest. No one had ever been quite sure that he made Mrs. Raycie happy, but he was known to have the highest opinion of her. So it was with his daughters, Sarah Anne and Mary Adeline, fresher replicas of the lymphatic Mrs. Raycie; no one would have sworn that they were quite at ease with their genial parent, yet every one knew how loud he was in their praises. But the most remarkable object within the range of Mr. Raycie's self-approval was his son Lewis. And yet, as Jameson Ledgely, who was given to speaking his mind, had once observed, you wouldn't have supposed young Lewis was exactly the kind of craft Halston would have turned out if he'd had the designing of his son and heir.

Mr. Raycie was a monumental man. His extent in height, width and thickness was so nearly the same that whichever way he was turned one had an almost equally broad view of him; and every inch of that mighty circumference was so exquisitely cared for that to a farmer's eye he might have suggested a great agricultural estate of which not an acre is untilled. Even his baldness, which was in proportion to the rest, looked as if it received a special daily polish; and on a hot day his whole person was like some wonderful example of the costliest irrigation. There was so much of him, and he had so many planes, that it was fascinating to watch each runnel of moisture follow its own particular watershed. Even on his large fresh-looking hands the drops divided, trickling in different ways from the ridges of the fingers; and as for his forehead and temples, and the raised cushion of cheek beneath each of his lower lids, every one of these slopes had its own particular stream, its hollow pools and sudden cataracts; and the sight was never unpleasant, because his whole vast bubbling surface was of such a clean and hearty pink, and the exuding moisture so perceptibly flavoured with expensive eau de Cologne and the best French soap.

Mrs. Raycie, though built on a less heroic scale, had a pale amplitude which, when she put on her best watered silk (the kind that stood alone), and framed her countenance in the innumerable blonde lace ruffles and clustered purple grapes of her newest Paris cap, almost balanced her husband's bulk. Yet from this full-rigged pair, as the Commodore would have put it, had issued the lean little runt of a Lewis, a shrimp of a baby, a shaver of a boy, and now a youth as scant as an ordinary man's midday shadow.

All these things, Lewis himself mused, dangling his legs from the verandah rail, were undoubtedly passing through the minds of the four gentlemen grouped about his father's bowl of cup.

Mr. Robert Huzzard, the banker, a tall broad man, who looked big in any company but Mr. Raycie's, leaned back, lifted his glass, and bowed to Lewis.

"Here's to the Grand Tour!"

"Don't perch on that rail like a sparrow, my boy," Mr. Raycie said reprovingly; and Lewis dropped to his feet, and returned Mr. Huzzard's bow.

"I wasn't thinking," he stammered. It was his too frequent excuse.

Mr. Ambrose Huzzard, the banker's younger brother, Mr. Ledgely and Mr. Donaldson Kent, all raised their glasses and cheerily echoed: "The Grand Tour!"

Lewis bowed again, and put his lips to the glass he had forgotten. In reality, he had eyes only for Mr. Donaldson Kent, his father's cousin, a silent man with a lean hawklike profile, who looked like a retired Revolutionary hero, and lived in daily fear of the most trifling risk or responsibility.

To this prudent and circumspect citizen had come, some years earlier, the unexpected and altogether inexcusable demand that he should look after the daughter of his only brother, Julius Kent. Julius had died in Italy—well, that was his own business, if he chose to live there. But to let his wife die before him, and to leave a minor daughter, and a will entrusting her to the guardianship of his esteemed elder brother, Donaldson Kent Esquire, of Kent's Point, Long Island, and Great Jones Street, New York—well, as Mr. Kent himself said, as his wife said for him, there had never been anything, anything whatever in Mr. Kent's attitude or behaviour, to justify the ungrateful Julius (whose debts he had more than once paid) in laying on him this final burden.

The girl came. She was fourteen, she was considered plain, she was small and black and skinny. Her name was Beatrice, which was bad enough, and made worse by the fact that it had been shortened by ignorant foreigners to Treeshy. But she was eager, serviceable and good-tempered, and as Mr. and Mrs. Kent's friends pointed out, her plainness made everything easy. There were two Kent boys growing up, Bill and Donald; and if this penniless cousin had been compounded of cream and roses—well, she would have taken more watching, and might have rewarded the kindness of her uncle and aunt by some act of wicked ingratitude. But this risk being obviated by her appearance, they could be goodnatured to her without afterthought, and to be goodnatured was natural to them. So, as the years passed, she gradually became the guardian of her guardians; since it was equally natural to Mr. and Mrs. Kent to throw themselves in helpless reliance on every one whom they did not nervously fear or mistrust.

"Yes, he's off on Monday," Mr. Raycie said, nodding sharply at Lewis, who had set down his glass after one sip. "Empty it, you shirk!" the nod commanded; and Lewis, throwing back his head, gulped down the draught, though it almost stuck in his lean throat. He had already had to take two glasses, and even this scant conviviality was too much for him, and likely to result in a mood of excited volubility, followed by a morose evening and a head the next morning. And he wanted to keep his mind clear that day, and to think steadily and lucidly of Treeshy Kent.

Of course he couldn't marry her—yet. He was twenty-one that very day, and still entirely dependent on his father. And he wasn't altogether sorry to be going first on this Grand Tour. It was what he had always dreamed of, pined for, from the moment when his infant eyes had first been drawn to the prints of European cities in the long upper passage that smelt of matting. And all that Treeshy had told him about Italy had confirmed and intensified the longing. Oh, to have been going there with her—with her as his guide, his Beatrice! (For she had given him a little Dante of her father's, with a steel-engraved frontispiece of Beatrice; and his sister Mary Adeline, who had been taught Italian by one of the romantic Milanese exiles, had helped her brother out with the grammar.)

The thought of going to Italy with Treeshy was only a dream; but later, as man and wife, they would return there, and by that time, perhaps, it was Lewis who would be her guide, and reveal to her the historic marvels of her birthplace, of which after all she knew so little, except in minor domestic ways that were quaint but unimportant.

The prospect swelled her suitor's bosom, and reconciled him to the idea of their separation. After all, he secretly felt himself to be still a boy, and it was as a man that he would return: he meant to tell her that when they met the next day. When he came back his character would be formed, his knowledge of life (which he already thought considerable) would be complete; and then no one could keep them apart. He smiled in advance to think how little his father's shouting and booming would impress a man on his return from the Grand Tour . . .

The gentlemen were telling anecdotes about their own early experience in Europe. None of them—not even Mr. Raycie—had travelled as extensively as it was intended that Lewis should; but the two Huzzards had been twice to England on banking matters, and Commodore Ledgely, a bold man, to France and Belgium as well—not to speak of his early experience in the Far East. All three had kept a vivid and amused recollection, slightly tinged with disapprobation, of what they had seen— "Oh, those French wenches," the Commodore chuckled through his white teeth—but poor Mr.

Kent, who had gone abroad on his honeymoon, had been caught in Paris by the revolution of 1830, had had the fever in Florence, and had nearly been arrested as a spy in Vienna; and the only satisfactory episode in this disastrous, and never repeated, adventure, had been the fact of his having been mistaken for the Duke of Wellington (as he was trying to slip out of a Viennese hotel in his courier's blue surtout) by a crowd who had been— "Well, very gratifying in their enthusiasm," Mr. Kent admitted.

"How my poor brother Julius could have lived in Europe! Well, look at the consequences—" he used to say, as if poor Treeshy's plainness gave an awful point to his moral.

"There's one thing in Paris, my boy, that you must be warned against: those gambling-hells in the Pally Royle," Mr. Kent insisted. "I never set foot in the places myself; but a glance at the outside was enough."

"I knew a feller that was fleeced of a fortune there," Mr. Henry Huzzard confirmed; while the Commodore, at his tenth glass, chuckled with moist eyes: "The trollops, oh, the trollops—"

"As for Vienna—" said Mr. Kent.

"Even in London," said Mr. Ambrose Huzzard, "a young man must be on his look-out against gamblers. Every form of swindling is practised, and the touts are always on the look-out for greenhorns; a term," he added apologetically, "which they apply to any traveller new to the country."

"In Paris," said Mr. Kent, "I was once within an ace of being challenged to fight a duel." He fetched a sigh of horror and relief, and glanced reassuredly down the Sound in the direction of his own peaceful roof-tree.

"Oh, a duel," laughed the Commodore. "A man can fight duels here. I fought a dozen when I was a young feller in New Erleens." The Commodore's mother had been a southern lady, and after his father's death had spent some years with her parents in Louisiana, so that her son's varied experiences had begun early. "'Bout women," he smiled confidentially, holding out his empty glass to Mr. Raycie.

"The ladies—!" exclaimed Mr. Kent in a voice of warning.

The gentlemen rose to their feet, the Commodore quite as prompt and steadily as the others. The drawing-room window opened, and from it emerged Mrs. Raycie, in a ruffled sarsenet dress and Point de Paris cap, followed by her two daughters in starched organdy with pink spencers. Mr. Raycie looked with proud approval at his womenkind.

"Gentlemen," said Mrs. Raycie, in a perfectly even voice, "supper is on the table, and if you will do Mr. Raycie and myself the favour—"

"The favour, ma'am," said Mr. Ambrose Huzzard, "is on your side, in so amiably inviting us."

Mrs. Raycie curtsied, the gentlemen bowed, and Mr. Raycie said: "Your arm to Mrs. Raycie, Huzzard. This little farewell party is a family affair, and the other gentlemen must content themselves with my two daughters. Sarah Anne, Mary Adeline—"

The Commodore and Mr. John Huzzard advanced ceremoniously toward the two girls, and Mr. Kent, being a cousin, closed the procession between Mr. Raycie and Lewis.

Oh, that supper-table! The vision of it used sometimes to rise before Lewis Raycie's eyes in outlandish foreign places; for though not a large or fastidious eater when he was at home, he was afterward, in lands of chestnut-flour and garlic and queer bearded sea-things, to suffer many pangs of hunger at the thought of that opulent board. In the centre stood the Raycie *épergne* of pierced silver, holding aloft a bunch of June roses surrounded by dangling baskets of sugared almonds and striped peppermints; and grouped about this decorative "motif" were Lowestoft platters heavy with piles of raspberries, strawberries and the first Delaware peaches. An outer flanking of heaped-up cookies, crullers, strawberry short-cake, piping hot corn-bread and deep golden butter in moist blocks still bedewed from the muslin swathings of the dairy, led the eye to the Virginia ham in front of Mr. Raycie, and the twin dishes of scrambled eggs on toast and broiled blue-fish over which his wife presided. Lewis could never afterward fit into this intricate pattern the "side-dishes" of devilled turkeylegs and creamed chicken hash, the sliced cucumbers and tomatoes, the heavy silver jugs of butter-coloured cream, the floating-island, "slips" and lemon jellies that were somehow interwoven with the solider elements of the design; but they were all there, either together or successively, and so were the towering piles of waffles reeling on their foundations, and the slender silver jugs of maple syrup perpetually escorting them about the table as black Dinah replenished the supply.

They ate—oh, how they all ate!—though the ladies were supposed only to nibble; but the good things on Lewis's plate remained untouched until, ever and again, an admonishing glance from Mr. Raycie, or an entreating one from Mary Adeline, made him insert a languid fork into the heap.

And all the while Mr. Raycie continued to hold forth.

"A young man, in my opinion, before setting up for himself, must see the world; form his taste; fortify his judgment. He must study the most famous monuments, examine the organization of foreign societies, and the habits and customs of those older civilizations whose yoke it has been our glory to cast off. Though he may see in them much to deplore and to reprove—" ("Some of the gals, though," Commodore Ledgely was heard to interject)—"much that will make him give thanks for the privilege of having been born and brought up under our own Free Institutions, yet I believe he will also"—Mr. Raycie conceded it with magnanimity—"be able to learn much."

"The Sundays, though," Mr. Kent hazarded warningly; and Mrs. Raycie breathed across to her son: "Ah, that's what *I* say!"

Mr. Raycie did not like interruption; and he met it by growing visibly larger. His huge bulk hung a moment, like an avalanche, above the silence which followed Mr. Kent's interjection and Mrs. Raycie's murmur; then he crashed down on both.

"The Sundays—the Sundays? Well, what of the Sundays? What is there to frighten a good Episcopalian in what we call the Continental Sunday? I presume that we're all Churchmen here, eh? No puling Methodists or atheistical Unitarians at my table tonight, that I'm aware of. Nor will I offend the ladies of my household by assuming that they have secretly lent an ear to the Baptist ranter in the chapel at the foot of our lane. No? I thought not! Well, then, I say, what's all this flutter about the Papists? Far be it from me to approve of their heathenish doctrines—but, damn it, they go to church, don't they? And they have a real service as we do, don't they? And real clergy and not a lot of nondescripts dressed like laymen, and damned badly at that, who chat familiarly with the Almighty in their own vulgar lingo? No, sir"—he swung about on the shrinking Mr. Kent—"it's not the Church I'm afraid of in foreign countries, it's the sewers, sir!"

Mrs. Raycie had grown very pale: Lewis knew that she too was deeply perturbed about the sewers. "And the night-air," she scarce-audibly sighed.

But Mr. Raycie had taken up his main theme again. "In my opinion, if a young man travels at all, he must travel as extensively as his—er—means permit; must see as much of the world as he can. Those are my son's sailing orders, Commodore; and here's to his carrying them out to the best of his powers!"

Black Dinah, removing the Virginia ham, or rather such of its bony structure as alone remained on the dish, had managed to made room for a bowl of punch from which Mr. Raycie poured deep ladlefuls of perfumed fire into the glasses ranged before him on a silver tray. The gentlemen rose, the ladies smiled and wept, and Lewis's health and the success of the Grand Tour were toasted with an eloquence which caused Mrs. Raycie, with a hasty nod to her daughters, and a covering rustle of starched flounces, to shepherd them softly from the room.

"After all," Lewis heard her murmur to them on the threshold, "your father's using such language shows that he's in the best of humour with dear Lewis."

§ 2

In spite of his enforced potations, Lewis Raycie was up the next morning before sunrise.

Unlatching his shutters without noise, he looked forth over the wet lawn merged in a blur of shrubberies, and the waters of the Sound dimly seen beneath a sky full of stars. His head ached but his heart glowed; what was before him was thrilling enough to clear a heavier brain than his.

He dressed quickly and completely (save for his shoes), and then, stripping the flowered quilt from his high mahogany bed, rolled it in a tight bundle under his arm. Thus enigmatically equipped he was feeling his way, shoes in hand, through the darkness of the upper story to the slippery oak stairs, when he was startled by a candle-gleam in the pitch-blackness of the hall below. He held his breath, and leaning over the stair-rail saw with amazement his sister Mary Adeline come forth, cloaked and bonneted, but also in stocking-feet, from the passage leading to the pantry. She too carried a double burden: her shoes and the candle in one hand, in the other a large covered basket that weighed down her bare arm.

Brother and sister stopped and stared at each other in the blue dusk: the upward slant of the candle-light distorted Mary Adeline's mild features, twisting them into a frightened grin as Lewis stole down to join her.

"Oh—" she whispered. "What in the world are you doing here? I was just getting together a few things for that poor young Mrs. Poe down the lane, who's so ill—before mother goes to the storeroom. You won't tell, will you?"

Lewis signalled his complicity, and cautiously slid open the bolt of the front door. They durst not say more till they were out of ear-shot. On the doorstep they sat down to put on their shoes; then they hastened on without a word through the ghostly shrubberies till they reached the gate into the lane.

"But you, Lewis?" the sister suddenly questioned, with an astonished stare at the rolled-up quilt under her brother's arm.

"Oh, I—. Look here, Addy"—he broke off and began to grope in his pocket—"I haven't much about me . . . the old gentleman keeps me as close as ever . . . but here's a dollar, if you think that poor Mrs. Poe could use it . . . I'd be too happy . . . consider it a privilege . . ."

"Oh, Lewis, Lewis, how noble, how generous of you! Of course I can buy a few extra things with it . . . they never see meat unless I can bring them a bit, you know . . . and I fear she's dying of a decline . . . and she and her mother are so fiery-proud . . ." She wept with gratitude, and Lewis drew a breath of relief. He had diverted her attention from the bed-quilt.

"Ah, there's the breeze," he murmured, sniffing the suddenly chilled air.

"Yes; I must be off; I must be back before the sun is up," said Mary Adeline anxiously, "and it would never do if mother knew—"

"She doesn't know of your visits to Mrs. Poe?"

A look of childish guile sharpened Mary Adeline's undeveloped face. "She *does*, of course; but yet she doesn't . . . we've arranged it so. You see, Mr. Poe's an Atheist; and so father—"

"I see," Lewis nodded. 'Well, we part here; I'm off for a swim," he said glibly. But abruptly he turned back and caught his sister's arm. "Sister, tell Mrs. Poe, please, that I heard her husband give a reading from his poems in New York two nights ago–"

("Oh, Lewis–*you?* But father says he's a blasphemer!")

"–And that he's a great poet–a Great Poet. Tell her that from me, will you, please, Mary Adeline?"

"Oh, brother, I couldn't . . . we never speak of him," the startled girl faltered, hurrying away.

In the cove where the Commodore's sloop had ridden a few hours earlier a biggish rowing-boat took the waking ripples. Young Raycie paddled out to her, fastened his skiff to the moorings, and hastily clambered into the boat.

From various recesses of his pockets he produced rope, string, a carpet-layer's needle, and other unexpected and incongruous tackle; then, lashing one of the oars across the top of the other, and jamming the latter upright between the forward thwart and the bow, he rigged the flowered bed-quilt on this mast, knotted a rope to the free end of the quilt, and sat down in the stern, one hand on the rudder, the other on his improvised sheet.

Venus, brooding silverly above a line of pale green sky, made a pool of glory in the sea as the dawn-breeze plumped the lover's sail . . .

On the shelving pebbles of another cove, two or three miles down the Sound, Lewis Raycie lowered his queer sail and beached his boat. A clump of willows on the shingle-edge mysteriously stirred and parted, and Treeshy Kent was in his arms.

The sun was just pushing above a belt of low clouds in the east, spattering them with liquid gold, and Venus blanched as the light spread upward. But under the willows it was still dusk, a watery green dusk in which the secret murmurs of the night were caught.

"Treeshy–Treeshy!" the young man cried, kneeling beside her–and then, a moment later: "My angel, are you sure that no one guesses–?"

The girl gave a faint laugh which screwed up her funny nose. She leaned her head on his shoulder, her round forehead and rough braids pressed against his cheek, her hands in his, breathing quickly and joyfully.

"I thought I should never get here," Lewis grumbled, "with that ridiculous bed-quilt—and it'll be broad day soon! To think that I was of age yesterday, and must come to you in a boat rigged like a child's toy on a duck-pond! If you knew how it humiliates me—"

"What does it matter, dear, since you're of age now, and your own master?"

"But am I, though? He says so—but it's only on his own terms; only while I do what he wants! You'll see . . . I've a credit of ten thousand dollars . . . ten . . . thou . . . sand . . . d'you hear? . . . placed to my name in a London bank; and not a penny here to bless myself with meanwhile . . . Why, Treeshy darling, why, what's the matter?"

She flung her arms about his neck, and through their innocent kisses he could taste her tears. "What *is* it, Treeshy?" he implored her.

"I . . . oh, I'd forgotten it was to be our last day together till you spoke of London—cruel, cruel!" she reproached him; and through the green twilight of the willows her eyes blazed on him like two stormy stars. No other eyes he knew could express such elemental rage as Treeshy's.

"You little spitfire, you!" he laughed back somewhat chokingly. "Yes, it's our last day—but not for long; at our age two years are not so very long, after all, are they? And when I come back to you I'll come as my own master, independent, free—come to claim you in face of everything and everybody! Think of that, darling, and be brave for my sake . . . brave and patient . . . as I mean to be!" he declared heroically.

"Oh, but you—you'll see other girls; heaps and heaps of them; in those wicked old countries where they're so lovely. My uncle Kent says the European countries are all wicked, even my own poor Italy . . ."

"But *you,* Treeshy; you'll be seeing cousins Bill and Donald meanwhile—seeing them all day long and every day. And you know you've a weakness for that great hulk of a Bill. Ah, if only I stood six-foot-one in my stockings I'd go with an easier heart, you fickle child!" he tried to banter her.

"Fickle? Fickle? *Me*—oh, Lewis!"

He felt the premonitory sweep of sobs, and his untried courage failed him. It was delicious, in theory, to hold weeping beauty to one's breast, but terribly alarming, he found, in practice. There came a responsive twitching in his throat.

"No, no; firm as adamant, true as steel; that's what we both mean to be, isn't it, *cara?*"

"Caro, yes," she sighed appeased.

"And you'll write to me regularly, Treeshy—long, long letters? I may count on that, mayn't I, wherever I am? And they must all be numbered, every one of them, so that I shall know at once if I've missed one; remember!"

"And, Lewis, you'll wear them here?" (She touched his breast.) "Oh, not *all,*" she added, laughing "for they'd make such a big bundle that you'd soon have a hump in front like Pulcinella—but always at least the last one, just the last one. Promise!"

"Always, I promise—as long as they're kind," he said, still struggling to take a spirited line.

"Oh, Lewis, they will be, as long as yours are—and long, long afterward . . ."

Venus failed and vanished in the sun's uprising.

§ 3

The crucial moment, Lewis had always known, would be not that of his farewell to Treeshy, but of his final interview with his father.

On that everything hung: his immediate future as well as his more distant prospects. As he stole home in the early sunlight, over the dew-drenched grass, he glanced up apprehensively at Mr. Raycie's windows, and thanked his stars that they were still tightly shuttered.

There was no doubt, as Mrs. Raycie said, that her husband's "using language" before ladies showed him to be in high good humour, relaxed and slippered, as it were—a state his family so seldom saw him in that Lewis had sometimes impertinently wondered to what awful descent from the clouds he and his two sisters owed their timorous being.

It was all very well to tell himself, as he often did, that the bulk of the money was his mother's, and that he could turn her round his little finger. What difference did that make? Mr. Raycie, the day after his marriage, had quietly taken over the management of his wife's property, and deducted, from the very moderate allowance he accorded her, all her little personal expenses, even to the postage-stamps she used, and the dollar she put in the plate every Sunday. He called the allowance her "pin-money," since, as he often reminded her, he paid all the household bills himself, so that Mrs. Raycie's quarterly pittance could be entirely devoted, if she chose, to frills and feathers.

"And will be, if you respect my wishes, my dear," he always added. "I like to see a handsome figure well set-off, and not to have our friends imagine, when they come to dine, that Mrs. Raycie is sick above-stairs, and I've replaced her by a poor relation in *allapacca.*" In compliance with which Mrs. Raycie, at once flattered and terrified, spent her last penny in adorning herself and her daughters, and had to stint their bedroom fires, and the servants' meals, in order to find a penny for any private necessity.

Mr. Raycie had long since convinced his wife that this method of dealing with her, if not lavish, was suitable, and in fact "handsome"; when she spoke of the subject to her relations it was with tears of gratitude for her husband's kindness in assuming the management of her property. As he managed it exceedingly well, her hard-headed brothers (glad to have the responsibility off their hands, and convinced that, if left to herself, she would have muddled her money away in ill-advised charities) were disposed to share her approval of Mr. Raycie; though her old mother sometimes said helplessly: "When I think that Lucy Ann can't as much as have a drop of gruel brought up to her without his weighing the oatmeal . . ." But even that was only whispered, lest Mr. Raycie's mysterious faculty of hearing what was said behind his back should bring sudden reprisals on the venerable lady to whom he always alluded, with a tremor in his genial voice, as "my dear mother-in-law—unless indeed she will allow me to call her, more briefly but more truly, my dear mother."

To Lewis, hitherto, Mr. Raycie had meted the same measure as to the females of the household. He had dressed him well, educated him expensively, lauded him to the skies—and counted every penny of his allowance. Yet there was a difference and Lewis was as well aware of it as any one.

The dream, the ambition, the passion of Mr. Raycie's life, was (as his son knew) to found a Family; and he had only Lewis to found it with. He believed in primogeniture, in heirlooms, in entailed estates, in all the ritual of the English "landed" tradition. No one was louder than he in praise of the democratic institutions under which he lived; but he never thought of them as affecting that more private but more important institution, the Family; and to the Family all his care and all his thoughts were given. The result, as Lewis dimly guessed, was, that upon his own shrinking and inadequate head was centred all the passion contained in the vast expanse of Mr. Raycie's breast. Lewis was his very own, and Lewis represented what was most dear to him; and for both these reasons Mr. Raycie set an inordinate value on the boy (a quite different thing, Lewis thought, from loving him).

Mr. Raycie was particularly proud of his son's taste for letters. Himself not a wholly unread man, he admired intensely what he called the "cultivated gentleman"—and that was what Lewis was evidently going to be. Could he have combined with this tendency a manlier frame, and an interest in the few forms of sport then popular among gentlemen, Mr. Raycie's satisfaction would have been complete; but whose is, in this disappointing world? Meanwhile he flattered himself that, Lewis being still young and malleable, and his health certainly mending, two years of travel and adventure might send him back a very different figure, physically as well as mentally. Mr. Raycie had himself travelled in his youth, and was persuaded that the experience was formative; he secretly hoped for the return of a bronzed and broadened Lewis, seasoned by independence and adventure, and having discreetly sown his wild oats in foreign pastures, where they would not contaminate the home crop.

All this Lewis guessed; and he guessed as well that these two wander-years were intended by Mr. Raycie to lead up to a marriage and an establishment after Mr. Raycie's own heart, but in which Lewis's was not to have even a consulting voice.

"He's going to give me all the advantages—for his own purpose," the young man summed it up as he went down to join the family at the breakfast table.

Mr. Raycie was never more resplendent than at that moment of the day and season. His spotless white duck trousers, strapped under kid boots, his thin kerseymere coat, and drab *piqué* waistcoat crossed below a snowy stock, made him look as fresh as the morning and as appetizing as the peaches and cream banked before him.

Opposite sat Mrs. Raycie, immaculate also, but paler than usual, as became a mother about to part from her only son; and between the two was Sarah Anne, unusually pink, and apparently occupied in trying to screen her sister's empty seat. Lewis greeted them, and seated himself at his mother's right.

Mr. Raycie drew out his *guillochée* repeating watch, and detaching it from its heavy gold chain laid it on the table beside him.

"Mary Adeline is late again. It is a somewhat unusual thing for a sister to be late at the last meal she is to take—for two years—with her only brother."

"Oh, Mr. Raycie!" Mrs. Raycie faltered.

"I say, the idea is peculiar. Perhaps," said Mr. Raycie sarcastically, "I am going to be blessed with a *peculiar* daughter."

"I'm afraid Mary Adeline is beginning a sick headache, sir. She tried to get up, but really could not," said Sarah Anne in a rush.

Mr. Raycie's only reply was to arch ironic eyebrows, and Lewis hastily intervened: "I'm sorry, sir; but it may be my fault—"

Mrs. Raycie paled, Sarah Anne purpled, and Mr. Raycie echoed with punctilious incredulity: "Your—fault?"

"In being the occasion, sir, of last night's too-sumptuous festivity—"

"Ha—ha—ha!" Mr. Raycie laughed, his thunders instantly dispelled.

He pushed back his chair and nodded to his son with a smile; and the two, leaving the ladies to wash up the teacups (as was still the habit in genteel families) betook themselves to Mr. Raycie's study.

What Mr. Raycie studied in this apartment—except the accounts, and ways of making himself unpleasant to his family—Lewis had never been able to discover. It was a small bare formidable room; and the young man, who never crossed the threshold but with a sinking of his heart, felt it sink lower than ever. *"Now!"* he thought.

Mr. Raycie took the only easy-chair, and began.

"My dear fellow, our time is short, but long enough for what I have to say. In a few hours you will be setting out on your great journey: an important event in the life of any young man. Your talents and character—combined with your means of improving the opportunity—make me hope that in your case it will be decisive. I expect you to come home from this trip a man—"

So far, it was all to order, so to speak; Lewis could have recited it beforehand. He bent his head in acquiescence.

"A man," Mr. Raycie repeated, "prepared to play a part, a considerable part, in the social life of the community. I expect you to be a figure in New York; and I shall give you the means to be so." He cleared his throat. "But means are not enough—though you must never forget that they are essential. Education, polish, experience of the world; these are what so many of our men of standing lack. What do they know of Art or Letters? We have had little time here to produce either as yet—you spoke?" Mr. Raycie broke off with a crushing courtesy.

"I—oh, no," his son stammered.

"Ah; I thought you might be about to allude to certain blasphemous penny-a-liners whose poetic ravings are said to have given them a kind of pothouse notoriety."

Lewis reddened at the allusion but was silent, and his father went on:

"Where is our Byron—our Scott—our Shakespeare? And in painting it is the same. Where are our Old Masters? We are not without comtemporary talent; but for works of genius we must still look to the past; we must, in most cases, content ourselves with copies . . . Ah, here, I know, my dear boy, I touch a responsive chord! Your love of the arts has not passed unperceived; and I mean, I desire, to do all I can to encourage it. Your future position in the world—your duties and obligations as a gentleman and a man of fortune—will not permit you to become, yourself, an eminent painter or a famous sculptor; but I shall raise no objection to your dabbling in these arts as an amateur—at least while you are travelling abroad. It will form your taste, strengthen your judgment, and give you, I hope, the discernment necessary to select for me a few masterpieces which shall *not* be copies. Copies," Mr. Raycie pursued with a deepening emphasis, "are for the less discriminating, or for those less blessed with this world's goods. Yes, my dear Lewis, I wish to create a gallery: a gallery of Heirlooms. Your mother participates in this ambition—she desires to see on our walls a few original specimens of the Italian genius. Raphael, I fear, we can hardly aspire to; but a Domenichino, an Albano, a Carlo Dolci, a Guercino, a Carlo Maratta—one or two of Salvator Rosa's noble landscapes . . . you see my idea? There shall be a Raycie Gallery; and it shall be your mission to get together its nucleus." Mr. Raycie paused, and mopped his flowing forehead. "I believe I could have given my son no task more to his liking."

"Oh, no, sir, none indeed!" Lewis cried, flushing and paling. He had in fact never suspected this part of his father's plan, and his heart swelled with the honour of so unforeseen a mission. Nothing, in truth, could have made him prouder or happier. For a moment he forgot love, forgot Treeshy, forgot everything but the rapture of moving among the masterpieces of which he had so long dreamed, moving not as a mere hungry spectator, but as one whose privilege it should at least be to single out and carry away some of the lesser treasures. He could hardly take in what had happened, and the shock of the announcement left him, as usual, inarticulate.

He heard his father booming on, developing the plan, explaining with his usual pompous precision that one of the partners of the London bank in which Lewis's funds were deposited was himself a noted collector, and had agreed to provide the young traveller with letters of introduction to other connoisseurs, both in France and Italy, so that Lewis's acquisitions might be made under the most enlightened guidance.

"It is," Mr. Raycie concluded, "in order to put you on a footing of equality with the best collectors that I have placed such a large sum at your disposal. I reckon that for ten thousand dollars you can travel for two years in the very best style; and I mean to place another five thousand to your credit"—he paused, and let the syllables drop slowly into his son's brain: "five thousand dollars for the purchase of works of art, which eventually—remember—will be yours; and will be handed on, I trust, to your sons' sons as long as the name of Raycie survives"—a length of time, Mr. Raycie's tone seemed to imply, hardly to be measured in periods less extensive than those of the Egyptian dynasties.

Lewis heard him with a whirling brain. *Five thousand dollars!* The sum seemed so enormous, even in dollars, and so incalculably larger when translated into any continental currency, that he wondered why his father, in advance, had given up all hope of a Raphael . . . "If I travel economically," he said to himself, "and deny myself unnecessary luxuries, I may yet be able to surprise him by bringing one back. And my mother—how magnanimous, how splendid! Now I see why she has consented to all the little economies that sometimes seemed so paltry and so humiliating . . ."

The young man's eyes filled with tears, but he was still silent, though he longed as never before to express his gratitude and admiration to his father. He had entered the study expecting a parting sermon on the subject of thrift, coupled with the prospective announcement of a "suitable establishment" (he could even guess the particular Huzzard girl his father had in view); and instead he had been told to spend his princely allowance in a princely manner, and to return home with a gallery of masterpieces. "At least," he murmured to himself, "it shall contain a Correggio."

"Well, sir?" Mr. Raycie boomed.

"Oh, sir—" his son cried, and flung himself on the vast slope of the parental waistcoat.

Amid all these accumulated joys there murmured deep down in him the thought that nothing had been said or done to interfere with his secret plans about Treeshy. It seemed almost as if his father had tacitly accepted the idea of their unmentioned engagement; and Lewis felt half guilty at not confessing to it then and there. But the gods are formidable even when they unbend; never more so, perhaps, than at such moments . . .

§ 4

Lewis Raycie stood on a projecting rock and surveyed the sublime spectacle of Mont Blanc.

It was a brilliant August day, and the air, at that height, was already so sharp that he had had to put on his fur-lined pelisse. Behind him, at a respectful distance, was the travelling servant who, at a signal, had brought it up to him; below, in the bend of the mountain road, stood the light and elegant carriage which had carried him thus far on his travels.

Scarcely more than a year had passed since he had waved a farewell to New York from the deck of the packet-ship headed down the bay; yet, to the young man confidently facing Mont Blanc, nothing seemed left in him of that fluid and insubstantial being, the former Lewis Raycie, save a lurking and abeyant fear of Mr. Raycie senior. Even that, however, was so attenuated by distance and time, so far sunk below the horizon, and anchored on the far side of the globe, that it stirred in its sleep only when a handsomely folded and wafered letter in his parent's writing was handed out across the desk of some continental counting-house. Mr. Raycie senior did not write often, and when he did it was in a bland and stilted strain. He felt at a disadvantage on paper, and his natural sarcasm was swamped in the rolling periods which it cost him hours of labour to bring forth; so that the dreaded quality lurked for his son only in the curve of certain letters, and in a positively awful way of writing out, at full length, the word *Esquire*.

It was not that Lewis had broken with all the memories of his past of a year ago. Many still lingered in him, or rather had been transferred to the new man he had become—as for instance his tenderness for Treeshy Kent, which, somewhat to his surprise, had obstinately resisted all the assaults of English keep-sake beauties and almond-eyed houris of the East. It startled him, at times to find Treeshy's short dusky face, with its round forehead, the widely spaced eyes and the high cheek-bones, starting out at him suddenly in the street of some legendary town, or in a landscape of languid beauty, just as he had now and again been arrested in an exotic garden by the very scent of the verbena under the verandah at home. His travels had confirmed rather than weakened the family view of Treeshy's plainness; she could not be made to fit into any of the patterns of female beauty so far submitted to him; yet there she was, ensconced in his new heart and mind as deeply as in the old, though her kisses seemed less vivid, and the peculiar rough notes of her voice hardly reached him. Sometimes, half irritably, he said to himself that with an effort he could disperse her once for all; yet she lived on in him, unseen yet ineffaceable, like the image on a daguerreotype plate, no less there because so often invisible.

To the new Lewis, however, the whole business was less important than he had once thought it. His suddenly acquired maturity made Treeshy seem a petted child rather than the guide, the Beatrice, he had once considered her; and he promised himself, with an elderly smile, that as soon as he got to Italy he would write her the long letter for which he was now considerably in her debt.

His travels had first carried him to England. There he spent some weeks in collecting letters and recommendations for his tour, in purchasing his travelling-carriage and its numerous appurtenances, and in driving in it from cathedral town to storied castle, omitting nothing, from Abbotsford to Kenilworth, which deserved the attention of a cultivated mind. From England he crossed to Calais, moving slowly southward to the Mediterranean; and there, taking ship for the Piræus, he plunged into pure romance, and the tourist became a Giaour.

It was the East which had made him into a new Lewis Raycie; the East, so squalid and splendid, so pestilent and so poetic, so full of knavery and romance and fleas and nightingales, and so different, alike in its glories and its dirt, from what his studious youth had dreamed. After Smyrna and the bazaars, after Damascus and Palmyra, the Acropolis, Mytilene and Sunium, what could be left in his mind of Canal Street and the lawn above the Sound? Even the mosquitoes, which seemed at first the only connecting link, were different, because he fought with them in scenes so different; and a young gentleman who had journeyed across the desert in Arabian dress, slept under goats'-hair tents, been attacked by robbers in the Peloponnesus and despoiled by his own escort at Baalbek, and by customs' officials everywhere, could not but look with a smile on the terrors that walk New York and the Hudson river. Encased in security and monotony, that other Lewis Raycie, when his little figure bobbed up to the surface, seemed like a new-born babe preserved in alcohol. Even Mr. Raycie senior's thunders were now no more than the far-off murmur of summer lightning on a perfect evening. Had Mr. Raycie ever really frightened Lewis? Why, now he was not even frightened by Mont Blanc!

He was still gazing with a sense of easy equality at its awful pinnacles when another travelling-carriage paused near his own, and a young man, eagerly jumping from it, and also followed by a servant with a cloak, began to mount the slope. Lewis at once recognized the carriage, and the light springing figure of the young man, his blue coat and swelling stock, and the scar slightly distorting his handsome and eloquent mouth. It was the Englishman who had arrived at the Montanvert inn the night before with a valet, a guide, and such a cargo of books, maps and sketching-materials as threatened to overshadow even Lewis's outfit.

Lewis, at first, had not been greatly drawn to the newcomer, who, seated aloof in the dining-room, seemed not to see his fellow-traveller. The truth was that Lewis was dying for a little conversation. His astonishing experiences were so tightly packed in him (with no outlet save the meagre trickle of his nightly diary) that he felt they would soon melt into the vague blur of other people's travels unless he could give them fresh reality by talking them over. And the stranger with the deep-blue eyes that matched his coat, the scarred cheek and eloquent lip, seemed to Lewis a worthy listener. The Englishman appeared to think otherwise. He preserved an air of moody abstraction, which Lewis's vanity imagined him to have put on as the gods becloud themselves for their secret errands; and the curtness of his goodnight was (Lewis flattered himself) surpassed only by the young New Yorker's.

But today all was different. The stranger advanced affably, raised his hat from his tossed statue-like hair, and enquired with a smile: "Are you by any chance interested in the forms of cirrous clouds?"

His voice was as sweet as his smile, and the two were reinforced by a glance so winning that it made the odd question seem not only pertinent but natural. Lewis, though surprised, was not disconcerted. He merely coloured with the unwonted sense of his ignorance, and replied ingenuously: "I believe, sir, I am interested in everything."

"A noble answer!" cried the other, and held out his hand.

"But I must add," Lewis continued with courageous honesty, "that I have never as yet had occasion to occupy myself particularly with the forms of cirrous clouds."

His companion looked at him merrily. "That," said he, "is no reason why you shouldn't begin to do so now!" To which Lewis as merrily agreed. "For in order to be interested in things," the other continued more gravely, "it is only necessary to see them; and I believe I am not wrong in saying that you are one of the privileged beings to whom the seeing eye has been given."

Lewis blushed his agreement, and his interlocutor continued: "You are one of those who have been on the road to Damascus."

"On the road? I've been to the place itself!" the wanderer exclaimed, bursting with the particulars of his travels; and then blushed more deeply at the perception that the other's use of the name had of course been figurative.

The young Englishman's face lit up. "You've been to Damascus—literally been there yourself? But that may be almost as interesting, in its quite different way, as the formation of clouds or lichens. For the present," he continued with a gesture toward the mountain, "I must devote myself to the extremely inadequate rendering of some of these delicate *aiguilles;* a bit of drudgery not likely to interest you in the face of so sublime a scene. But perhaps this evening—if, as I think, we are staying in the same inn—you will give me a few minutes of your society, and tell me something of your travels. My father," he added with his engaging smile, "has had packed with my paint-brushes a few bottles of a wholly trustworthy Madeira; and if you will favour me with your company at dinner . . ."

He signed to his servant to undo the sketching materials, spread his cloak on the rock, and was already lost in his task as Lewis descended to the carriage.

The Madeira proved as trustworthy as his host had promised. Perhaps it was its exceptional quality which threw such a golden lustre over the dinner; unless it were rather the conversation of the blue-eyed Englishman which made Lewis Raycie, always a small drinker, feel that in his company every drop was nectar.

When Lewis joined his host it had been with the secret hope of at last being able to talk; but when the evening was over (and they kept it up to the small hours) he perceived that he had chiefly listened. Yet there had been no sense of suppression, of thwarted volubility; he had been given all the openings he wanted. Only, whenever he produced a little fact it was instantly overflowed by the other's imagination till it burned like a dull pebble tossed into a rushing stream. For whatever Lewis said was seen by his companion from a new angle, and suggested a new train of thought; each commonplace item of experience became a many-faceted crystal flashing with unexpected fires. The young Englishman's mind moved in a world of associations and references far more richly peopled than Lewis's; but his eager communicativeness, his directness of speech and manner, instantly opened its gates to the simpler youth. It was certainly not the Madeira which sped the hours and flooded them with magic; but the magic gave the Madeira—excellent, and reputed of its kind, as Lewis afterward learned—a taste no other vintage was to have for him.

"Oh, but we must meet again in Italy—there are many things there that I could perhaps help you to see," the young Englishman declared as they swore eternal friendship on the stairs of the sleeping inn.

§ 5

It was in a tiny Venetian church, no more than a chapel, that Lewis Raycie's eyes had been unsealed—in a dull-looking little church not even mentioned in the guidebooks. But for his chance encounter with the young Englishman in the shadow of Mont Blanc, Lewis would never have heard of the place; but then what else that was worth knowing would he ever have heard of, he wondered?

He had stood a long time looking at the frescoes, put off at first—he could admit it now—by a certain stiffness in the attitudes of the people, by the childish elaboration of their dress (so different from the noble draperies which Sir Joshua's Discourses on Art had taught him to admire in the great painters), and by the innocent inexpressive look in their young faces—for even the gray-beards seemed young. And then suddenly his gaze had lit on one of these faces in particular: that of a girl with round cheeks, high cheekbones and widely set eyes under an intricate headdress of pearl-woven braids. Why, it was Treeshy—Treeshy Kent to the life! And so far from being thought "plain," the young lady was no other than the peerless princess about whom the tale revolved. And what a fairyland she lived in—full of lithe youths and round-faced pouting maidens, rosy old men and burnished blackamoors, pretty birds and cats and nibbling rabbits—and all involved and enclosed in golden balustrades, in colonnades of pink and blue, laurel-garlands festooned from ivory balconies, and domes and minarets against summer seas! Lewis's imagination lost itself in the scene; he forgot to regret the noble draperies, the exalted sentiments, the fuliginous backgrounds, of the artists he had come to Italy to admire—forgot Sassoferrato, Guido Reni, Carlo Dolce, Lo Spagnoletto, the Carracci, and even the Transfiguration of Raphael, though he knew it to be the greatest picture in the world.

After that he had seen almost everything else that Italian art had to offer; had been to Florence, Naples, Rome; to Bologna to study the Eclectic School, to Parma to examine the Correggios and the Giulio Romanos. But that first vision had laid a magic seed between his lips; the seed that makes you hear what the birds say and the grasses whisper. Even if his English friend had not continued at his side, pointing out, explaining, inspiring, Lewis Raycie flattered himself that the round face of the little Saint Ursula would have led him safely and confidently past all her rivals. She had become his touchstone, his star: how insipid seemed to him all the sheep-faced Virgins draped in red and blue paint after he had looked into her wondering girlish eyes and traced the elaborate pattern of her brocades! He could remember now, quite distinctly, the day when he had given up even Beatrice Cenci . . . and as for that fat naked Magdalen of Carlo Dolce's lolling over the book she was not reading, and ogling the spectator in the good old way . . . faugh! Saint Ursula did not need to rescue him from *her* . . .

His eyes had been opened to a new world of art. And this world it was his mission to reveal to others—he, the insignificant and ignorant Lewis Raycie, as "but for the grace of God," and that chance encounter on Mont Blanc, he might have gone on being to the end! He shuddered to think of the army of Neapolitan beggar-boys, bituminous monks, whirling prophets, languishing Madonnas and pink-rumped *amorini* who might have been travelling home with him in the hold of the fast new steam-packet.

His excitement had something of the apostle's ecstasy. He was not only, in a few hours, to embrace Treeshy, and be reunited to his honoured parents; he was also to go forth and preach the new gospel to them that sat in the darkness of Salvator Rosa and Lo Spagnoletto . . .

The first thing that struck Lewis was the smallness of the house on the Sound, and the largeness of Mr. Raycie.

He had expected to receive the opposite impression. In his recollection the varnished Tuscan villa had retained something of its impressiveness, even when compared to its supposed originals. Perhaps the very contrast between their draughty distances and naked floors, and the expensive carpets and bright fires of High Point, magnified his memory of the latter—there were moments when the thought of its groaning board certainly added to the effect. But the image of Mr. Raycie had meanwhile dwindled. Everything about him, as his son looked back, seemed narrow, juvenile, almost childish. His bluster about Edgar Poe, for instance—true poet still to Lewis, though he had since heard richer notes; his fussy tyranny of his womenkind; his unconscious but total ignorance of most of the things, books, people, ideas, that now filled his son's mind; above all, the arrogance and incompetence of his artistic judgments. Beyond a narrow range of reading—mostly, Lewis suspected, culled in drowsy after-dinner snatches from Knight's "Half-hours with the Best Authors"—Mr. Raycie made no pretence to book-learning; left *that,* as he handsomely said, "to the professors." But on matters of art he was dogmatic and explicit, prepared to justify his opinions by the citing of eminent authorities and of market-prices, and quite clear, as his farewell talk with his son had shown, as to which Old Masters should be privileged to figure in the Raycie collection.

The young man felt no impatience of these judgments. America was a long way from Europe, and it was many years since Mr. Raycie had travelled. He could hardly be blamed for not knowing that the things he admired were no longer admirable, still less for not knowing why. The pictures before which Lewis had knelt in spirit had been virtually undiscovered, even by art-students and critics, in his father's youth. How was an American gentleman, filled with his own self-importance, and paying his courier the highest salary to show him the accredited "Masterpieces"—how was he to guess that whenever he stood rapt before a Sassoferrato or a Carlo Dolce one of those unknown treasures lurked near by under dust and cobwebs?

No; Lewis felt only tolerance and understanding. Such a view was not one to magnify the paternal image; but when the young man entered the study where Mr. Raycie sat immobilized by gout, the swathed leg stretched along his sofa seemed only another reason for indulgence . . .

Perhaps, Lewis thought afterward, it was his father's prone position, the way his great bulk billowed over the sofa, and the lame leg reached out like a mountain-ridge, that made him suddenly seem to fill the room; or else the sound of his voice booming irritably across the threshold, and scattering Mrs. Raycie and the girls with a fierce: "And now, ladies, if the hugging and kissing are over, I should be glad of a moment with my son." But it was odd that, after mother and daughters had withdrawn with all their hoops and flounces, the study seemed to grow even smaller, and Lewis himself to feel more like a David without the pebble.

"Well, my boy," his father cried, crimson and puffing, "here you are at home again, with many adventures to relate, no doubt; and a few masterpieces to show me, as I gather from the drafts on my exchequer."

"Oh, as to the masterpieces, sir, certainly," Lewis simpered, wondering why his voice sounded so fluty, and his smile was produced with such a conscious muscular effort.

"Good—good," Mr. Raycie approved, waving a violet hand which seemed to be ripening for a bandage. "Reedy carried out my orders, I presume? Saw to it that the paintings were deposited with the bulk of your luggage in Canal Street?"

"Oh, yes, sir; Mr. Reedy was on the dock with precise instructions. You know he always carries out your orders," Lewis ventured with a faint irony.

Mr. Raycie stared. "Mr. Reedy," he said, "does what I tell him, if that's what you mean; otherwise he would hardly have been in my employ for over thirty years."

Lewis was silent, and his father examined him critically. "You appear to have filled out: your health is satisfactory? Well . . . well . . . Mr. Robert Huzzard and his daughters are dining here this evening, by the way, and will no doubt be expecting to see the latest French novelties in stocks and waistcoats. Malvina has become a very elegant figure, your sisters tell me." Mr. Raycie chuckled, and Lewis thought: "I *knew* it was the oldest Huzzard girl!" while a slight chill ran down his spine.

"As to the pictures," Mr. Raycie pursued with growing animation, "I am laid low, as you see, by this cursèd affliction, and till the doctors get me up again, here must I lie and try to imagine how your treasures will look in the new gallery. And meanwhile, my dear boy, I need hardly say that no one is to be admitted to see them till they have been inspected by me and suitably hung. Reedy shall begin unpacking at once; and when we move to town next month Mrs. Raycie, God willing, shall give the handsomest evening party New York has yet seen, to show my son's collection, and perhaps . . . eh, well? . . . to celebrate another interesting event in his history."

Lewis met this with a faint but respectful gurgle, and before his blurred eyes rose the wistful face of Treeshy Kent.

"Ah, well, I shall see her tomorrow," he thought, taking heart again as soon as he was out of his father's presence.

§ 6

Mr. Raycie stood silent for a long time after making the round of the room in the Canal Street house where the unpacked pictures had been set out.

He had driven to town alone with Lewis, sternly rebuffing his daughters' timid hints, and Mrs. Raycie's mute but visible yearning to accompany him. Though the gout was over he was still weak and irritable, and Mrs. Raycie, fluttered at the thought of "crossing him," had swept the girls away at his first frown.

Lewis's hopes rose as he followed his parent's limping progress. The pictures, though standing on chairs and tables, and set clumsily askew to catch the light, bloomed out of the half-dusk of the empty house with a new and persuasive beauty. Ah, how right he had been—how inevitable that his father should own it!

Mr. Raycie halted in the middle of the room. He was still silent, and his face, so quick to frown and glare, wore the calm, almost expressionless look known to Lewis as the mask of inward perplexity. "Oh, of course it will take a little time," the son thought, tingling with the eagerness of youth.

At last, Mr. Raycie woke the echoes by clearing his throat; but the voice which issued from it was as inexpressive as his face. "It is singular," he said, "how little the best copies of the Old Masters resemble the originals. For these *are* Originals?" he questioned, suddenly swinging about on Lewis.

"Oh, absolutely, sir! Besides—" The young man was about to add: "No one would ever have taken the trouble to copy them"—but hastily checked himself.

"Besides—?"

"I meant, I had the most competent advice obtainable."

"So I assume; since it was the express condition on which I authorized your purchases."

Lewis felt himself shrinking and his father expanding; but he sent a glance along the wall, and beauty shed her reviving beam on him.

Mr. Raycie's brows projected ominously; but his face remained smooth and dubious. Once more he cast a slow glance about him.

"Let us," he said pleasantly, "begin with the Raphael." And it was evident that he did not know which way to turn.

"Oh, sir, a Raphael nowadays—I warned you it would be far beyond my budget."

Mr. Raycie's face fell slightly. "I had hoped nevertheless . . . for an inferior specimen . . ." Then, with an effort: "The Sassoferrato, then."

Lewis felt more at his ease; he even ventured a respectful smile. "Sassoferrato is *all* inferior, isn't he? The fact is, he no longer stands . . . quite as he used to . . ."

Mr. Raycie stood motionless: his eyes were vacuously fixed on the nearest picture.

"Sassoferrato . . . no longer . . . ?"

"Well, sir, *no;* not for a collection of this quality."

Lewis saw that he had at last struck the right note. Something large and uncomfortable appeared to struggle in Mr. Raycie's throat; then he gave a cough which might almost have been said to cast out Sassoferrato.

There was another pause before he pointed with his stick to a small picture representing a snub-nosed young woman with a high forehead and jewelled coif, against a background of delicately interwoven columbines. "Is *that,*" he questioned, "your Carlo Dolce? The style is much the same, I see; but it seems to me lacking in his peculiar sentiment."

"Oh, but it's not a Carlo Dolce: it's a Piero della Francesca, sir!" burst in triumph from the trembling Lewis.

His father sternly faced him. "It's a *copy,* you mean? I thought so!"

"No, no; not a copy; it's by a great painter . . . a much greater . . ."

Mr. Raycie had reddened sharply at his mistake. To conceal his natural annoyance he assumed a still more silken manner. "In that case," he said, "I think I should like to see the inferior painters first. Where *is* the Carlo Dolce?"

"There *is* no Carlo Dolce," said Lewis, white to the lips.

The young man's next distinct recollection was of standing, he knew not how long afterward, before the armchair in which his father had sunk down, almost as white and shaken as himself.

"This," stammered Mr. Raycie, "this is going to bring back my gout . . ." But when Lewis entreated: "Oh, sir, do let us drive back quietly to the country, and give me a chance later to explain . . . to put my case" . . . the old gentleman had struck through the pleading with a furious wave of his stick.

"Explain later? Put your case later? It's just what I insist upon doing here and now!" And Mr. Raycie added hoarsely, and as if in actual physical anguish: "I understand that young John Huzzard returned from Rome last week with a Raphael."

After that, Lewis heard himself—as if with the icy detachment of a spectator—marshalling his arguments, pleading the cause he hoped his pictures would have pleaded for him, dethroning the old Powers and Principalities, and setting up these new names in their place. It was first of all the names that stuck in Mr. Raycie's throat: after spending a life-time in committing to memory the correct pronunciation of words like Lo Spagnoletto and Giulio Romano, it was bad enough, his wrathful eyes seemed to say, to have to begin a new set of verbal gymnastics before you could be sure of saying to a friend with careless accuracy: "And *this* is my Giotto da Bondone."

But that was only the first shock, soon forgotten in the rush of greater tribulation. For one might conceivably learn how to pronounce Giotto da Bondone, and even enjoy doing so, provided the friend in question recognized the name and bowed to its authority. But to have your effort received by a blank stare, and the playful request: "You'll have to say that over again, please"—to know that, in going the round of the gallery (the Raycie Gallery!) the same stare and the same request were likely to be repeated before each picture; the bitterness of this was so great that Mr. Raycie, without exaggeration, might have likened his case to that of Agag.

"God! God! God! Carpatcher, you say this other fellow's called? Kept him back till the last because it's the gem of the collection, did you? Carpatcher—well he'd have done better to stick to his trade. Something to do with those new European steam-cars, I suppose eh?" Mr. Raycie was so incensed that his irony was less subtle than usual. "And Angelico you say did that kind of Noah's Ark soldier in pink armour on gold-leaf? Well *there* I've caught you tripping, my boy. Not Angelic*o*, Angelic*a*; Angelica Kauffman was a lady. And the damned swindler who foisted that barbarous daub on you as a picture of hers deserves to be drawn and quartered—and shall be, sir, by God, if the law can reach him! He shall disgorge every penny he's rooked you out of, or my name's not Halston Raycie! A bargain . . . you say the thing was a *bargain?* Why, the price of a clean postage stamp would be too dear for it! God—my son; do you realize you had a *trust* to carry out?"

"Yes, sir, yes; and it's just because—"

"You might have written; you might at least have placed your views before me . . ."

How could Lewis say: "If I had, I knew you'd have refused to let me buy the pictures?" He could only stammer: "I *did* allude to the revolution in taste . . . new names coming up . . . you may remember . . ."

"Revolution! New names! Who says so? I had a letter last week from the London dealers to whom I especially recommended you, telling me that an undoubted Guido Reni was coming into the market this summer."

"Oh, the dealers—*they* don't know!"

"The dealers . . . don't? . . . Who does . . . except yourself?" Mr. Raycie pronounced in a white sneer.

Lewis, as white, still held his ground. "I wrote you, sir, about my friends; in Italy, and afterward in England."

"Well, God damn it, I never heard of one of *their* names before, either; no more'n of these painters of yours here. I supplied you with the names of all the advisers you needed, and all the painters, too; I all but made the collection for you myself, before you started . . . I was explicit enough, in all conscience, wasn't I?"

Lewis smiled faintly. "That's what I hoped the pictures would be . . ."

"What? Be what? What'd you mean?"

"Be explicit . . . Speak for themselves . . . make you see that their painters are already superseding some of the better-known . . ."

Mr. Raycie gave an awful laugh. "They are, are they? In whose estimation? Your friends', I suppose. What's the name, again, of that fellow you met in Italy who picked 'em out for you?"

"Ruskin—John Ruskin," said Lewis.

Mr. Raycie's laugh, prolonged, gathered up into itself a fresh shower of expletives. "Ruskin—Ruskin—just plain John Ruskin, eh? And who *is* this great John Ruskin, who sets God A'mighty right in his judgments? Who'd you say John Ruskin's father was, now?"

"A respected wine-merchant in London, sir."

Mr. Raycie ceased to laugh: he looked at his son with an expression of unutterable disgust.

"Retail?"

"I . . . believe so . . ."

"Faugh!" said Mr. Raycie.

"It wasn't only Ruskin, father . . . I told you of those other friends in London, whom I met on the way home. They inspected the pictures, and all of them agreed that . . . that the collection would some day be very valuable."

"*Some day*—did they give you a date . . . the month and the year? Ah, those other friends; yes. You said there was a Mr. Brown and a Mr. Hunt and a Mr. Rossiter, was it? Well, I never heard of any of those names, either—except perhaps in a trades' directory."

"It's not Rossiter, father: Dante Rossetti."

"Excuse me: Rossetti. And what does Mr. Dante Rossetti's father do? Sell macaroni, I presume?"

Lewis was silent, and Mr. Raycie went on, speaking now with a deadly steadiness: "The friends I sent you to were judges of art, sir; men who know what a picture's worth; not one of 'em but could pick out a genuine Raphael. Couldn't you find 'em when you got to England? Or hadn't they the time to spare for you? You'd better not," Mr. Raycie added, "tell me *that,* for I know how they'd have received your father's son."

"Oh, most kindly . . . they did indeed, sir . . ."

"Ay; but that didn't suit you. You didn't *want* to be advised. You wanted to show off before a lot of ignoramuses like yourself. You wanted—how'd I know what you wanted? It's as if I'd never given you an instruction or laid a charge on you! And the money—God! Where'd it go to? Buying *this*? Nonsense—." Mr. Raycie raised himself heavily on his stick and fixed his angry eyes on his son. "Own up, Lewis; tell me they got it out of you at cards. Professional gamblers the lot, I make no doubt; your Ruskin and your Morris and your Rossiter. Make a business to pick up young American greenhorns on their travels, I daresay . . . No? Not that, you say? Then—women? . . . God A'mighty, Lewis," gasped Mr. Raycie, tottering toward his son with outstretched stick, "I'm no blue-nosed Puritan, sir, and I'd a damn sight rather you told me you'd spent it on a woman, every penny of it, than let yourself be fleeced like a simpleton, buying these things that look more like cuts out o' Foxe's Book of Martyrs than Originals of the Old Masters for a Gentleman's Gallery . . . Youth's youth . . . Gad, sir, I've been young myself . . . a fellow's got to go through his apprenticeship . . Own up now: women?"

"Oh, not women—"

"Not even!" Mr. Raycie groaned. "All in pictures, then? Well, say no more to me now . . . I'll get home, I'll get home . . ." He cast a last apoplectic glance about the room. "The Raycie Gallery! That pack of bones and mummers' finery! . . . Why, let alone the rest, there's not a full-bodied female among 'em . . . Do you know what those Madonnas of yours are like, my son? Why, there ain't one of 'em that don't remind me of a bad likeness of poor Treeshy Kent . . . I should say you'd hired half the sign-painters of Europe to do her portrait for you—if I could imagine your wanting it . . . No, sir! I don't need your arm," Mr. Raycie snarled, heaving his great bulk painfully across the hall. He withered Lewis with a last look from the doorstep. "And to buy *that* you overdrew your account?—No, I'll drive home alone."

§ 7

Mr. Raycie did not die till nearly a year later; but New York agreed it was the affair of the pictures that had killed him.

The day after his first and only sight of them he sent for his lawyer, and it became known that he had made a new will. Then he took to his bed with a return of the gout, and grew so rapidly worse that it was thought "only proper" to postpone the party Mrs. Raycie was to have given that autumn to inaugurate the gallery. This enabled the family to pass over in silence the question of the works of art themselves; but outside of the Raycie house, where they were never mentioned, they formed, that winter, a frequent and fruitful topic of discussion.

Only two persons besides Mr. Raycie were known to have seen them. One was Mr. Donaldson Kent, who owed the privilege to the fact of having once been to Italy; the other, Mr. Reedy, the agent, who had unpacked the pictures. Mr. Reedy, beset by Raycie cousins and old family friends, had replied with genuine humility: "Why, the truth is, I never was taught to see any difference between one picture and another, except as regards the size of them; and these struck me as smallish . . . on the small side, I would say . . ."

Mr. Kent was known to have unbosomed himself to Mr. Raycie with considerable frankness—he went so far, it was rumoured, as to declare that he had never seen any pictures in Italy like those brought back by Lewis, and begged to doubt if they really came from there. But in public he maintained that noncommittal attitude which passed for prudence, but proceeded only from timidity; no one ever got anything from him but the guarded statement: "The subjects are wholly inoffensive."

It was believed that Mr. Raycie dared not consult the Huzzards. Young John Huzzard had just brought home a Raphael; it would have been hard not to avoid comparisons which would have been too galling. Neither to them, nor to any one else, did Mr. Raycie ever again allude to the Raycie Gallery. But when his will was opened it was found that he had bequeathed the pictures to his son. The rest of his property was left absolutely to his two daughters. The bulk of the estate was Mrs. Raycie's; but it was known that Mrs. Raycie had had her instructions, and among them, perhaps, was the order to fade away in her turn after six months of widowhood. When she had been laid beside her husband in Trinity church-yard her will (made in the same week as Mr. Raycie's, and obviously at his dictation) was found to allow five thousand dollars a year to Lewis during his lifetime; the residue of the fortune, which Mr. Raycie's thrift and good management had made into one of the largest in New York, was divided between the daughters. Of these, the one promptly married a Kent and the other a Huzzard; and the latter, Sarah Anne (who had never been Lewis's favourite), was wont to say in later years: "Oh, no, I never grudged my poor brother those funny old pictures. You see, we have a Raphael."

The house stood on the corner of Third Avenue and Tenth Street. It had lately come to Lewis Raycie as his share in the property of a distant cousin, who had made an "old New York will" under which all his kin benefited in proportion to their consanguinity. The neighbourhood was unfashionable, and the house in bad repair; but Mr. and Mrs. Lewis Raycie, who, since their marriage, had been living in retirement at Tarrytown, immediately moved into it.

Their arrival excited small attention. Within a year of his father's death, Lewis had married Treeshy Kent. The alliance had not been encouraged by Mr. and Mrs. Kent, who went so far as to say that their niece might have done better; but as that one of their sons who was still unmarried had always shown a lively sympathy for Treeshy, they yielded to the prudent thought that, after all, it was better than having her entangle Bill.

The Lewis Raycies had been four years married, and during that time had dropped out of the memory of New York as completely as if their exile had covered half a century. Neither of them had ever cut a great figure there. Treeshy had been nothing but the Kents' Cinderella, and Lewis's ephemeral importance, as heir to the Raycie millions, had been effaced by the painful episode which resulted in his being deprived of them.

So secluded was their way of living, and so much had it come to be a habit, that when Lewis announced that he had inherited Uncle Ebenezer's house his wife hardly looked up from the baby-blanket she was embroidering.

"Uncle Ebenezer's house in New York?"

He drew a deep breath. "Now I shall be able to show the pictures."

"Oh, Lewis—" She dropped the blanket. "Are we going to live there?"

"Certainly. But the house is so large that I shall turn the two corner rooms on the ground floor into a gallery. They are very suitably lighted. It was there that Cousin Ebenezer was laid out."

"Oh, Lewis—"

If anything could have made Lewis Raycie believe in his own strength of will it was his wife's attitude. Merely to hear that unquestioning murmur of submission was to feel something of his father's tyrannous strength arise in him; but with the wish to use it more humanely.

"You'll like that, Treeshy? It's been dull for you here, I know."

She flushed up. "Dull? With *you,* darling? Besides, I like the country. But I shall like Tenth Street too. Only—you said there were repairs?"

He nodded sternly. "I shall borrow money to make them. If necessary—" he lowered his voice—"I shall mortgage the pictures."

He saw her eyes fill. "Oh, but it won't be! There are so many ways still in which I can economize."

He laid his hand on hers and turned his profile toward her, because he knew it was so much stronger than his full face. He did not feel sure that she quite grasped his intention about the pictures; was not even certain that he wished her to. He went in to New York every week now, occupying himself mysteriously and importantly with plans, specifications and other business transactions with long names; while Treeshy, through the hot summer months, sat in Tarrytown and waited for the baby.

A little girl was born at the end of the summer and christened Louisa; and when she was a few weeks old the Lewis Raycies left the country for New York.

"Now!" thought Lewis, as they bumped over the cobblestones of Tenth Street in the direction of Cousin Ebenezer's house.

The carriage stopped, he handed out his wife, the nurse followed with the baby, and they all stood and looked up at the house-front.

"Oh, Lewis—" Treeshy gasped; and even little Louisa set up a sympathetic wail.

Over the door—over Cousin Ebenezer's respectable, conservative and intensely private front-door—hung a large sign-board bearing, in gold letters on a black ground, the inscription:

GALLERY OF CHRISTIAN ART

Open on Week-Days from 2 to 4

Admission 25 Cents. Children 10 Cents

Lewis saw his wife turn pale, and pressed her arm in his. "Believe me, it's the only way to make the pictures known. And they *must* be made known," he said with a thrill of his old ardour.

"Yes, dear, of course. But . . . to every one? Publicly?"

"If we showed them only to our friends, of what use would it be? Their opinion is already formed."

She sighed her acknowledgment. "But the . . . the entrance fee . . ."

"If we can afford it later, the gallery will be free. But meanwhile—"

"Oh, Lewis, I quite understand!" And clinging to him, the still-protesting baby in her wake, she passed with a dauntless step under the awful sign-board.

"At last I shall see the pictures properly lighted!" she exclaimed, and turned in the hall to fling her arms about her husband.

"It's all they need . . . to be appreciated," he answered, aglow with her encouragement.

Since his withdrawal from the world it had been a part of Lewis's system never to read the daily papers. His wife eagerly conformed to his example, and they lived in a little air-tight circle of aloofness, as if the cottage at Tarrytown had been situated in another and happier planet.

Lewis, nevertheless, the day after the opening of the Gallery of Christian Art, deemed it his duty to derogate from this attitude, and sallied forth secretly to buy the principal journals. When he reentered his house he went straight up to the nursery where he knew that, at that hour, Treeshy would be giving the little girl her bath. But it was later than he supposed. The rite was over, the baby lay asleep in its modest cot, and the mother sat crouched by the fire, her face hidden in her hands. Lewis instantly guessed that she too had seen the papers.

"Treeshy—you mustn't . . . consider this of any consequence . . . ," he stammered.

She lifted a tear-stained face. "Oh, my darling! I thought you never read the papers."

"Not usually. But I thought it my duty—"

"Yes; I see. But, as you say, what earthly consequence—?"

"None whatever; we must just be patient and persist."

She hesitated, and then, her arms about him, her head on his breast: "Only, dearest, I've been counting up again, ever so carefully; and even if we give up fires everywhere but in the nursery, I'm afraid the wages of the doorkeeper and the guardian . . . especially if the gallery's open to the public every day . . ."

"I've thought of that already, too; and I myself shall hereafter act as doorkeeper and guardian."

He kept his eyes on hers as he spoke. "This is the test," he thought. Her face paled under its brown glow, and the eyes dilated in her effort to check her tears. Then she said gaily: "That will be . . . very interesting, won't it, Lewis? Hearing what the people say . . . Because, as they begin to know the pictures better, and to understand them, they can't fail to say very interesting things . . . can they?" She turned and caught up the sleeping Louisa. "Can they . . . oh, you darling—darling?"

Lewis turned away too. Not another woman in New York would have been capable of that. He could hear all the town echoing with this new scandal of his showing the pictures himself—and she, so much more sensitive to ridicule, so much less carried away by apostolic ardour, how much louder must that mocking echo ring in her ears! But his pang was only momentary. The one thought that possessed him for any length of time was that of vindicating himself by making the pictures known; he could no longer fix his attention on lesser matters. The derision of illiterate journalists was not a thing to wince at; once let the pictures be seen by educated and intelligent people, and they would speak for themselves—especially if he were at hand to interpret them.

§ 8

For a week or two a great many people came to the gallery; but, even with Lewis as interpreter, the pictures failed to make themselves heard. During the first days, indeed, owing to the unprecedented idea of holding a paying exhibition in a private house, and to the mockery of the newspapers, the Gallery of Christian Art was thronged with noisy curiosity-seekers; once the astonished metropolitan police had to be invited in to calm their comments and control their movements. But the name of "Christian Art" soon chilled this class of sightseer, and before long they were replaced by a dumb and respectable throng, who roamed vacantly through the rooms and out again, grumbling that it wasn't worth the money. Then these too diminished; and once the tide had turned, the ebb was rapid. Every day from two to four Lewis still sat shivering among his treasures, or patiently measured the length of the deserted gallery: as long as there was a chance of any one coming he would not admit that he was beaten. For the next visitor might always be the one who understood.

One snowy February day he had thus paced the rooms in unbroken solitude for about an hour when carriage-wheels stopped at the door. He hastened to open it, and in a great noise of silks his sister Sarah Anne Huzzard entered.

Lewis felt for a moment as he used to under his father's glance. Marriage and millions had given the moon-faced Sarah something of the Raycie awfulness; but her brother looked into her empty eyes, and his own kept their level.

"Well, Lewis," said Mrs. Huzzard with a simpering sternness, and caught her breath.

"Well, Sarah Anne—I'm happy that you've come to take a look at my pictures."

"I've come to see you and your wife." She gave another nervous gasp, shook out her flounces, and added in a rush: "And to ask you how much longer this . . . this spectacle is to continue . . ."

"The exhibition?" Lewis smiled. She signed a flushed assent.

"Well, there has been a considerable falling-off lately in the number of visitors—"

"Thank heaven!" she interjected.

"But as long as I feel that any one wishes to come . . . I shall be here . . . to open the door, as you see."

She sent a shuddering glance about her. "Lewis—I wonder if you realize . . . ?"

"Oh, fully."

"Then *why* do you go on? Isn't it enough—aren't you satisfied?"

"With the effect they have produced?"

"With the effect *you* have produced—on your family and on the whole of New York. With the slur on poor Papa's memory."

"Papa left me the pictures, Sarah Anne."

"Yes. But not to make yourself a mountebank about them."

Lewis considered this impartially. "Are you sure? Perhaps, on the contrary, he did it for that very reason."

"Oh, don't heap more insults on our father's memory! Things are bad enough without that. How your wife can allow it I can't see. Do you ever consider the humiliation to *her?*"

Lewis gave another dry smile. "She's used to being humiliated. The Kents accustomed her to that."

Sarah Anne reddened. "I don't know why I should stay to be spoken to in this way. But I came with my husband's approval."

"Do you need that to come and see your brother?"

"I need it to—to make the offer I am about to make; and which he authorizes."

Lewis looked at her in surprise, and she purpled up to the lace ruffles inside her satin bonnet.

"Have you come to make an offer for my collection?" he asked her, humorously.

"You seem to take pleasure in insinuating preposterous things. But anything is better than this public slight on our name." Again she ran a shuddering glance over the pictures. "John and I," she announced, "are prepared to double the allowance mother left you on condition that this . . . this ends . . . for good. That that horrible sign is taken down tonight."

Lewis seemed mildly to weigh the proposal. "Thank you very much, Sarah Anne," he said at length. "I'm touched . . . touched and . . . and surprised . . . that you and John should have made this offer. But perhaps, before I decline it, you will accept *mine:* simply to show you my pictures. When once you've looked at them I think you'll understand—"

Mrs. Huzzard drew back hastily, her air of majesty collapsing. "Look at the pictures? Oh, thank you . . . but I can see them very well from here. And besides, I don't pretend to be a judge . . ."

"Then come up and see Treeshy and the baby," said Lewis quietly.

She stared at him, embarrassed. "Oh, thank you," she stammered again; and as she prepared to follow him: "Then it's *no,* really no, Lewis? Do consider, my dear! You say yourself that hardly any one comes. What harm can there be in closing the place?"

"What—when tomorrow the man may come who understands?"

Mrs. Huzzard tossed her plumes despairingly and followed him in silence.

"What—Mary Adeline?" she exclaimed, pausing abruptly on the threshold of the nursery. Treeshy, as usual, sat holding her baby by the fire; and from a low seat opposite her rose a lady as richly furred and feathered as Mrs. Huzzard, but with far less assurance to carry off her furbelows. Mrs. Kent ran to Lewis and laid her plump cheek against his, while Treeshy greeted Sarah Anne.

"I had no idea you were here, Mary Adeline," Mrs. Huzzard murmured. It was clear that she had not imparted her philanthropic project to her sister, and was disturbed at the idea that Lewis might be about to do so. "I just dropped in for a minute," she continued, "to see that darling little pet of an angel child—" and she enveloped the astonished baby in her ample rustlings and flutterings.

"I'm very glad to see you here, Sarah Anne," Mary Adeline answered with simplicity.

"Ah, it's not for want of wishing that I haven't come before! Treeshy knows that, I hope. But the cares of a household like mine . . ."

"Yes; and it's been so difficult to get about in the bad weather," Treeshy suggested sympathetically.

Mrs. Huzzard lifted the Raycie eyebrows. "Has it really? With two pairs of horses one hardly notices the weather . . . Oh, the pretty, pretty, *pretty* baby! . . . Mary Adeline," Sarah Anne continued, turning severely to her sister, "I shall be happy to offer you a seat in my carriage if you're thinking of leaving."

But Mary Adeline was a married woman too. She raised her mild head and her glance crossed her sister's quietly. "My own carriage is at the door, thank you kindly, Sarah Anne," she said; and the baffled Sarah Anne withdrew on Lewis's arm. But a moment later the old habit of subordination reasserted itself. Mary Adeline's gentle countenance grew as timorous as a child's, and she gathered up her cloak in haste.

"Perhaps I was too quick . . . I'm sure she meant it kindly," she exclaimed, overtaking Lewis as he turned to come up the stairs; and with a smile he stood watching his two sisters drive off together in the Huzzard coach.

He returned to the nursery, where Treeshy was still crooning over her daughter.

"Well, my dear," he said, "what do you suppose Sarah Anne came for?" And, in reply to her wondering gaze: "To buy me off from showing the pictures!"

His wife's indignation took just the form he could have wished. She simply went on with her rich cooing laugh and hugged the baby tighter. But Lewis felt the perverse desire to lay a still greater strain upon her loyalty.

"Offered to double my allowance, she and John, if only I'll take down the sign!"

"No one shall touch the sign!" Treeshy flamed.

"Not till I do," said her husband grimly.

She turned about and scanned him with anxious eyes. "Lewis . . . *you?*"

"Oh, my dear . . . they're right . . . It can't go on forever . . ." He went up to her, and put his arm about her and the child. "You've been braver than an army of heroes; but it won't do. The expenses have been a good deal heavier than I was led to expect. And I . . . I can't raise a mortgage on the pictures. Nobody will touch them."

She met this quickly. "No; I know. That was what Mary Adeline came about."

The blood rushed angrily to Lewis's temples. "Mary Adeline—how the devil did *she* hear of it?"

"Through Mr. Reedy, I suppose. But you must not be angry. She was kindness itself: she doesn't want you to close the gallery, Lewis . . . that is, not as long as you really continue to believe in it . . . She and Donald Kent will lend us enough to go on with for a year longer. That is what she came to say."

For the first time since the struggle had begun, Lewis Raycie's throat was choked with tears. His faithful Mary Adeline! He had a sudden vision of her, stealing out of the house at High Point before daylight to carry a basket of scraps to the poor Mrs. Edgar Poe who was dying of a decline down the lane . . . He laughed aloud in his joy.

"Dear old Mary Adeline! How magnificent of her! Enough to give me a whole year more . . ." He pressed his wet cheek against his wife's in a long silence. "Well, dear," he said at length, "it's for you to say—do we accept?"

He held her off, questioningly, at arm's length, and her wan little smile met his own and mingled with it.

"Of course we accept!"

§ 9

Of the Raycie family, which prevailed so powerfully in the New York of the 'forties, only one of the name survived in my boyhood, half a century later. Like so many of the descendants of the proud little Colonial society, the Raycies had totally vanished, forgotten by everyone but a few old ladies, one or two genealogists and the sexton of Trinity Church, who kept the record of their graves.

The Raycie blood was of course still to be traced in various allied families: Kents, Huzzards, Cosbys and many others, proud to claim cousinship with a "Signer," but already indifferent or incurious as to the fate of his progeny. These old New Yorkers, who lived so well and spent their money so liberally, vanished like a pinch of dust when they disappeared from their pews and their dinner-tables.

If I happen to have been familiar with the name since my youth, it is chiefly because its one survivor was a distant cousin of my mother's whom she sometimes took me to see on days when she thought I was likely to be good because I had been promised a treat for the morrow.

Old Miss Alethea Raycie lived in a house I had always heard spoken of as "Cousin Ebenezer's." It had evidently, in its day, been an admired specimen of domestic architecture; but was now regarded as the hideous though venerable relic of a bygone age. Miss Raycie, being crippled by rheumatism, sat above stairs in a large cold room, meagrely furnished with beadwork tables, rosewood étagères and portraits of pale sad-looking people in odd clothes. She herself was large and saturnine, with a battlemented black lace cap, and so deaf that she seemed a survival of forgotten days, a Rosetta Stone to which the clue was lost. Even to my mother, nursed in that vanished tradition, and knowing instinctively to whom Miss Raycie alluded when she spoke of Mary Adeline, Sarah Anne or Uncle Doctor, intercourse with her was difficult and languishing, and my juvenile interruptions were oftener encouraged than reproved.

In the course of one of these visits my eyes, listlessly roaming, singled out among the pallid portraits a three-crayon drawing of a little girl with a large forehead and dark eyes, dressed in a plaid frock and embroidered pantalettes, and sitting on a grass-bank. I pulled my mother's sleeve to ask who she was, and my mother answered: "Ah, that was poor little Louisa Raycie, who died of a decline. How old was little Louisa when she died, Cousin Alethea?"

To batter this simple question into Cousin Alethea's brain was the affair of ten laborious minutes; and when the job was done, and Miss Raycie, with an air of mysterious displeasure, had dropped a deep "Eleven," my mother was too exhausted to continue. So she turned to me to add, with one of the private smiles we kept for each other: "It was the poor child who would have inherited the Raycie Gallery." But to a little boy of my age this item of information lacked interest, nor did I understand my mother's surreptitious amusement.

This far-off scene suddenly came back to me last year, when, on one of my infrequent visits to New York, I went to dine with my old friend, the banker, John Selwyn, and came to an astonished stand before the mantelpiece in his new library.

"Hal*lo!*" I said, looking up at the picture above the chimney.

My host squared his shoulders, thrust his hands into his pockets, and affected the air of modesty which people think it proper to assume when their possessions are admired. "The Macrino d'Alba? Y—yes . . . it was the only thing I managed to capture out of the Raycie collection."

"The only thing? Well—"

"Ah, but you should have seen the Mantegna; *and* the Giotto; *and* the Piero della Francesca—hang it, one of the most beautiful

Piero della Francescas in the world . . . A girl in profile, with her hair in a pearl net, against a background of columbines; *that* went back to Europe—the National Gallery, I believe. And the Carpaccio, the most exquisite little St. George . . . that went to California . . . *Lord!*" He sat down with the sigh of a hungry man turned away from a groaning board. "Well, it nearly broke me buying *this!*" he murmured, as if at least that fact were some consolation.

I was turning over my early memories in quest of a clue to what he spoke of as the Raycie collection, in a tone which implied that he was alluding to objects familiar to all art-lovers.

Suddenly: "They weren't poor little Louisa's pictures, by any chance?" I asked, remembering my mother's cryptic smile.

Selwyn looked at me perplexedly. "Who the deuce is poor little Louisa?" And, without waiting for my answer, he went on: "They were that fool Netta Cosby's until a year ago—and she never even knew it."

We looked at each other interrogatively, my friend perplexed at my ignorance, and I now absorbed in trying to run down the genealogy of Netta Cosby. I did so finally. "Netta Cosby—you don't mean Netta Kent, the one who married Jim Cosby?"

"That's it. They were cousins of the Raycies', and she inherited the pictures."

I continued to ponder. "I wanted awfully to marry her, the year I left Harvard," I said presently, more to myself than to my hearer.

"Well, if you had you'd have annexed a prize fool; *and* one of the most beautiful collections of Italian Primitives in the world."

"In the world?"

"Well—you wait till you see them; if you haven't already. And I seem to make out that you haven't—that you can't have. How long have you been in Japan? Four years? I thought so. Well, it was only last winter that Netta found out."

"Found out what?"

"What there was in old Alethea Raycie's attic. You must remember the old Miss Raycie who lived in that hideous house in Tenth Street when we were children. She was a cousin of your mother's, wasn't she? Well, the old fool lived there for nearly half a century, with five millions' worth of pictures shut up in the attic over her head. It seems they'd been there ever since the death of a poor young Raycie who collected them in Italy years and years ago. I don't know much about the story; I never was strong on genealogy, and the Raycies have always been rather dim to me. They were everybody's cousins, of course; but as far as one can make out that seems to have been their principal if not their only function. Oh—and I suppose the Raycie Building was called after them; only *they* didn't build it!

"But there was this one young fellow—I wish I could find out more about him. All that Netta seems to know (or to care, for that matter) is that when he was very young—barely out of college—he was sent to Italy by his father to buy Old Masters—in the 'forties, it must have been—and came back with this extraordinary, this unbelievable collection . . . a boy of that age! . . . and was disinherited by the old gentleman for bringing home such rubbish. The young fellow and his wife died ever so many years ago, both of them. It seems he was so laughed at for buying such pictures that they went away and lived like hermits in the depths of the country. There were some funny spectral portraits of them that old Alethea had up in her bedroom. Netta showed me one of them the last time I went to see her: a pathetic drawing of the only child, an anæmic little girl with a big forehead. Jove, but that must have been your little Louisa!"

I nodded. "In a plaid frock and embroidered pantalettes?"

"Yes, something of the sort. Well, when Louisa and her parents died, I suppose the pictures went to old Miss Raycie. At any rate, at some time or other—and it must have been longer ago than you or I can remember—the old lady inherited them with the Tenth Street house; and when *she* died, three or four years ago, her relations found she'd never even been upstairs to look at them."

"Well—?"

"Well, she died intestate, and Netta Kent—Netta Cosby—turned out to be the next of kin. There wasn't much to be got out of the estate (or so they thought) and, as the Cosbys are always hard up, the house in Tenth Street had to be sold, and the pictures were very nearly sent off to the auction room with all the rest of the stuff. But nobody supposed they would bring anything, and the auctioneer said that if you tried to sell pictures with carpets and bedding and kitchen furniture it always depreciated the whole thing; and so, as the Cosbys had some bare walls to cover, they sent for the lot—there were about thirty—and decided to have them cleaned and hang them up. 'After all,' Netta said, 'as well as I can make out through the cobwebs, some of them look like rather jolly copies of early Italian things.' But as she was short of cash she decided to clean them at home instead of sending them to an expert; and one day, while she was operating on this very one before you, with her sleeves rolled up, the man called who always *does* call on such occasions; the man who knows. In the given case, it was a quiet fellow connected with the Louvre, who'd brought her a letter from Paris, and whom she'd invited to one of her stupid dinners. He was announced, and she thought it would be a joke to let him see what she was doing; she has pretty arms, you may remember. So he was asked into the dining-room, where he found her with a pail of hot water and soap-suds, and *this* laid out on the table; and the first thing he did was to grab her pretty arm so tight that it was black and blue, while he shouted out: 'God in heaven! Not *hot* water!' "

My friend leaned back with a sigh of mingled resentment and satisfaction, and we sat silently looking up at the lovely "Adoration" above the mantelpiece.

"That's how I got it a little cheaper—most of the old varnish was gone for good. But luckily for her it was the first picture she had attacked; and as for the others—you must see them, that's all I can say . . . Wait; I've got the catalogue somewhere about . . ."

He began to rummage for it, and I asked, remembering how nearly I had married Netta Kent: "Do you mean to say she didn't keep a single one of them?"

"Oh, yes—in the shape of pearls and Rolls-Royces. And you've seen their new house in Fifth Avenue?" He ended with a grin of irony: "The best of the joke is that Jim was just thinking of divorcing her when the pictures were discovered."

"Poor little Louisa!" I sighed.

Old New York, THE OLD MAID

§ 1

IN THE old New York of the 'fifties a few families ruled, in simplicity and affluence. Of these were the Ralstons.

The sturdy English and the rubicund and heavier Dutch had mingled to produce a prosperous, prudent and yet lavish society. To "do things handsomely" had always been a fundamental principle in this cautious world, built up on the fortunes of bankers, India merchants, ship-builders and ship-chandlers. Those well-fed slow-moving people, who seemed irritable and dyspeptic to European eyes only because the caprices of the climate had stripped them of superfluous flesh, and strung their nerves a little tighter, lived in a genteel monotony of which the surface was never stirred by the dumb dramas now and then enacted underground. Sensitive souls in those days were like muted key-boards, on which Fate played without a sound.

In this compact society, built of solidly welded blocks, one of the largest areas was filled by the Ralstons and their ramifications. The Ralstons were of middle-class English stock. They had not come to the colonies to die for a creed but to live for a bank-account. The result had been beyond their hopes, and their religion was tinged by their success. An edulcorated Church of England which, under the conciliatory name of the "Episcopal Church of the United States of America," left out the coarser allusions in the Marriage Service, slid over the comminatory passages in the Athanasian Creed, and thought it more respectful to say "Our Father *who*" than *"which"* in the Lord's Prayer, was exactly suited to the spirit of compromise whereon the Ralstons had built themselves up. There was in all the tribe the same instinctive recoil from new religions as from unaccounted-for people. Institutional to the core, they represented the conservative element that holds new societies together as seaplants bind the seashore.

Compared with the Ralstons, even such traditionalists as the Lovells, the Halseys or the Vandergraves appeared careless, indifferent to money, almost reckless in their impulses and indecisions. Old John Frederick Ralston, the stout founder of the race, had perceived the difference, and emphasized it to his son, Frederick John, in whom he had scented a faint leaning toward the untried and unprofitable.

"You let the Lannings and the Dagonets and the Spenders take risks and fly kites. It's the county-family blood in 'em: we've nothing to do with that. Look how they're petering out already—the men, I mean. Let your boys marry their girls, if you like (they're wholesome and handsome); though I'd sooner see my grandsons take a Lovell or a Vandergrave, or any of our own kind. But don't let your sons go mooning around after their young fellows, horse-racing, and running down south to those d——d Springs, and gambling at New Orleans, and all the rest of it. That's how you'll build up the family, and keep the weather out. The way we've always done it."

Frederick John listened, obeyed, married a Halsey, and passively followed in his father's steps. He belonged to the cautious generation of New York gentlemen who revered Hamilton and served Jefferson, who longed to lay out New York like Washington, and who laid it out instead like a gridiron, lest they should be thought "undemocratic" by people they secretly looked down upon. Shopkeepers to the marrow, they put in their windows the wares there was most demand for, keeping their private opinions for the back-shop, where through lack of use, they gradually lost substance and colour.

The fourth generation of Ralstons had nothing left in the way of convictions save an acute sense of honour in private and business matters; on the life of the community and the state they took their daily views from the newspapers, and the newspapers they already despised. The Ralstons had done little to shape the destiny of their country, except to finance the Cause when it had become safe to do so. They were related to many of the great men who had built the Republic; but no Ralston had so far committed himself as to be great. As old John Frederick said, it was safer to be satisfied with three per cent: they regarded heroism as a form of gambling. Yet by merely being so numerous and so similar they had come to have a weight in the community. People said: "The Ralstons" when they wished to invoke a precedent. This attribution of authority had gradually convinced the third generation of its collective importance, and the fourth, to which Delia Ralston's husband belonged, had the ease and simplicity of a ruling class.

Within the limits of their universal caution, the Ralstons fulfilled their obligations as rich and respected citizens. They figured on the boards of all the old-established charities, gave handsomely to thriving institutions, had the best cooks in New York, and when they travelled abroad ordered statuary of the American sculptors in Rome whose reputation was already established. The first Ralston who had brought home a statue had been regarded as a wild fellow; but when it became known that the sculptor had executed several orders for the British aristocracy it was felt in the family that this too was a three per cent investment.

Two marriages with the Dutch Vandergraves had consolidated these qualities of thrift and handsome living, and the carefully built-up Ralston character was now so congenital that Delia Ralston sometimes asked herself whether, were she to turn her own little boy loose in a wilderness, he would not create a small New York there, and be on all its boards of directors.

Delia Lovell had married James Ralston at twenty. The marriage, which had taken place in the month of September, 1840, had been solemnized, as was then the custom, in the drawing-room of the bride's country home, at what is now the corner of Avenue A and Ninety-first Street, overlooking the Sound. Thence her husband had driven her (in Grandmamma Lovell's canary-coloured coach with a fringed hammer-cloth) through spreading suburbs and untidy elm-shaded streets to one of the new houses in Gramercy Park, which the pioneers of the younger set were just beginning to affect; and there, at five-and-twenty, she was established, the mother of two children, the possessor of a generous allowance of pin-money, and, by common consent, one of the handsomest and most popular "young matrons" (as they were called) of her day.

She was thinking placidly and gratefully of these things as she sat one afternoon in her handsome bedroom in Gramercy Park. She was too near to the primitive Ralstons to have as clear a view of them as, for instance, the son in question might one day command: she lived under them as unthinkingly as one lives under the laws of one's country. Yet that tremor of the muted key-board, that secret questioning which sometimes beat in her like wings, would now and then so divide her from them that for a fleeting moment she could survey them in their relation to other things. The moment was always fleeting; she dropped back from it quickly, breathless and a little pale, to her children, her house-keeping, her new dresses and her kindly Jim.

She thought of him today with a smile of tenderness, remembering how he had told her to spare no expense on her new bonnet. Though she was twenty-five, and twice a mother, her image was still surprisingly fresh. The plumpness then thought seemly in a young wife stretched the grey silk across her bosom, and caused her heavy gold watch-chain—after it left the anchorage of the brooch of St. Peter's in mosaic that fastened her low-cut Cluny collar—to dangle perilously in the void above a tiny waist buckled into a velvet waistband. But the shoulders above sloped youthfully under her Cashmere scarf, and every movement was as quick as a girl's.

Mrs. Jim Ralston approvingly examined the rosy-cheeked oval set in the blonde ruffles of the bonnet on which, in compliance with her husband's instructions, she had spared no expense. It was a cabriolet of white velvet tied with wide satin ribbons and plumed with a crystal-spangled marabout—a wedding bonnet ordered for the marriage of her cousin, Charlotte Lovell, which was to take place that week at St. Mark's-in-the-Bouwerie. Charlotte was making a match exactly like Delia's own: marrying a Ralston, of the Waverly Place branch, than which nothing could be safer, sounder or more—well, usual. Delia did not know why the word had occurred to her, for it could hardly be postulated, even of the young women of her own narrow clan, that they "usually" married Ralstons; but the soundness, safeness, suitability of the arrangement, did make it typical of the kind of alliance which a nice girl in the nicest set would serenely and blushingly forecast for herself.

Yes—and afterward?

Well—what? And what did this new question mean? Afterward:

why, of course, there was the startled puzzled surrender to the incomprehensible exigencies of the young man to whom one had at most yielded a rosy cheek in return for an engagement ring; there was the large double-bed; the terror of seeing him shaving calmly the next morning, in his shirt-sleeves, through the dressing-room door; the evasions, insinuations, resigned smiles and Bible texts of one's Mamma; the reminder of the phrase "to obey" in the glittering blur of the Marriage Service; a week or a month of flushed distress, confusion, embarrassed pleasure; then the growth of habit, the insidious lulling of the matter-of-course, the dreamless double slumbers in the big white bed, the early morning discussions and consultations through that dressing-room door which had once seemed to open into a fiery pit scorching the brow of innocence.

And then, the babies; the babies who were supposed to "make up for everything," and didn't—though they were such darlings, and one had no definite notion as to what it was that one had missed, and that they were to make up for.

Yes: Charlotte's fate would be just like hers. Joe Ralston was so like his second cousin Jim (Delia's James), that Delia could see no reason why life in the squat brick house in Waverly Place should not exactly resemble life in the tall brown-stone house in Gramercy Park. Only Charlotte's bedroom would certainly not be as pretty as hers.

She glanced complacently at the French wall-paper that reproduced a watered silk, with a "valanced" border, and tassels between the loops. The mahogany bedstead, covered with a white embroidered counterpane, was symmetrically reflected in the mirror of a wardrobe which matched it. Coloured lithographs of the "Four Seasons" by Léopold Robert surmounted groups of family daguerreotypes in deeply-recessed gilt frames. The ormolu clock represented a shepherdess sitting on a fallen trunk, a basket of flowers at her feet. A shepherd, stealing up, surprised her with a kiss, while her little dog barked at him from a clump of roses. One knew the profession of the lovers by their crooks and the shape of their hats. This frivolous time-piece had been a wedding-gift from Delia's aunt, Mrs. Manson Mingott, a dashing widow who lived in Paris and was received at the Tuileries. It had been entrusted by Mrs. Mingott to young Clement Spender, who had come back from Italy for a short holiday just after Delia's marriage; the marriage which might never have been, if Clem Spender could have supported a wife, or if he had consented to give up painting and Rome for New York and the law. The young man (who looked, already, so odd and foreign and sarcastic) had laughingly assured the bride that her aunt's gift was "the newest thing in the Palais Royal"; and the family, who admired Mrs. Manson Mingott's taste though they disapproved of her "foreignness," had criticized Delia's putting the clock in her bedroom instead of displaying it on the drawing-room mantel. But she liked, when she woke in the morning to see the bold shepherd stealing his kiss.

Charlotte would certainly not have such a pretty clock in her bedroom; but then she had not been used to pretty things. Her father, who had died at thirty of lung-fever, was one of the "poor Lovells." His widow, burdened with a young family, and living all the year round "up the River," could not do much for her eldest girl; and Charlotte had entered society in her mother's turned garments, and shod with satin sandals handed down from a defunct aunt who had "opened a ball" with General Washington. The old-fashioned Ralston furniture, which Delia already saw herself banishing, would seem sumptuous to Chatty; very likely she would think Delia's gay French time-piece somewhat frivolous, or even not "quite nice." Poor Charlotte had become so serious, so prudish almost, since she had given up balls and taken to visiting the poor! Delia remembered, with ever-recurring wonder, the abrupt change in her: the precise moment at which it had been privately agreed in the family that, after all, Charlotte Lovell was going to be an old maid.

They had not thought so when she came out. Though her mother could not afford to give her more than one new tarlatan dress, and though nearly everything in her appearance was regrettable, from the too bright red of her hair to the too pale brown of her eyes—not to mention the rounds of brick-rose on her cheek-bones, which almost (preposterous thought!) made her look as if she painted—yet these defects were redeemed by a slim waist, a light foot and a gay laugh; and when her hair was well oiled and brushed for an evening party, so that it looked almost brown, and lay smoothly along her delicate cheeks under a wreath of red and white camellias, several eligible young men (Joe Ralston among them) were known to have called her pretty.

Then came her illness. She caught cold on a moonlight sleighing-party, the brick-rose circles deepened, and she began to cough. There was a report that she was "going like her father," and she was hurried off to a remote village in Georgia, where she lived alone for a year with an old family governess. When she came back everyone felt at once that there was a change in her. She was pale, and thinner than ever, but with an exquisitely transparent cheek, darker eyes and redder hair; and the oddness of her appearance was increased by plain dresses of Quakerish cut. She had left off trinkets and watch-chains, always wore the same grey cloak and small close bonnet, and displayed a sudden zeal for visiting the indigent. The family explained that during her year in the south she had been shocked by the hopeless degradation of the "poor whites" and their children, and that this revelation of misery had made it impossible for her to return to the light-hearted life of her young friends. Everyone agreed, with significant glances, that this unnatural state of mind would "pass off in time"; and meanwhile old Mrs. Lovell, Chatty's grandmother, who understood her perhaps better than the others, gave her a little money for her paupers, and lent her a room in the Lovell stables (at the back of the old lady's Mercer Street house) where she gathered about her, in what would afterward have been called a "day-nursery," some of the destitute children of the neighbourhood. There was even, among them, the baby girl whose origin had excited such intense curiosity two or three years earlier, when a veiled lady in a handsome cloak had brought it to the hovel of Cyrus Washington, the Negro handy-man whose wife Jessamine took in Dr. Lanskell's washing. Dr. Lanskell, the chief medical practitioner of the day, was presumably versed in the secret history of every household from the Battery to Union Square; but, though beset by inquisitive patients, he had invariably declared himself unable to identify Jessamine's "veiled lady," or to hazard a guess as to the origin of the hundred dollar bill pinned to the baby's bib.

The hundred dollars were never renewed, the lady never reappeared, but the baby lived healthily and happily with Jessamine's piccaninnies, and as soon as it could toddle was brought to Chatty Lovell's day-nursery, where it appeared (like its fellow paupers) in little garments cut down from her old dresses, and socks knitted by her untiring hands. Delia, absorbed in her own babies, had nevertheless dropped in once or twice at the nursery, and had come away wishing that Chatty's maternal instinct might find its normal outlet in marriage. The married cousin confusedly felt that her own affection for her handsome children was a mild and measured sentiment compared with Chatty's fierce passion for the waifs in Grandmamma Lovell's stable.

And then, to the general surprise, Charlotte Lovell engaged herself to Joe Ralston. It was known that Joe had "admired her" the year she came out. She was a graceful dancer, and Joe, who was tall and nimble, had footed it with her through many a reel and *Schottische*. By the end of the winter all the match-makers were predicting that something would come of it; but when Delia sounded her cousin, the girl's evasive answer and burning brow seemed to imply that her suitor had changed his mind, and no further questions could be asked. Now it was clear that there had, in fact, been an old romance between them, probably followed by that exciting incident, a "misunderstanding"; but at last all was well, and the bells of St. Mark's were preparing to ring in happier days for Charlotte. "Ah, when she has her first baby," the Ralston mothers chorused . . .

"Chatty!" Delia exclaimed, pushing back her chair as she saw her cousin's image reflected in the glass over her shoulder.

Charlotte Lovell had paused in the doorway. "They told me you were here—so I ran up."

"Of course, darling. How handsome you do look in your poplin! I always said you needed rich materials. I'm so thankful to see you out of grey cashmere." Delia, lifting her hands, removed the white bonnet from her dark polished head, and shook it gently to make the crystals glitter.

"I hope you like it? It's for your wedding," she laughed.

Charlotte Lovell stood motionless. In her mother's old dove-coloured poplin, freshly banded with narrow rows of crimson velvet ribbon, an ermine tippet crossed on her bosom, and a new beaver bonnet with a falling feather, she had already something of the assurance and majesty of a married woman.

"And you know your hair certainly *is* darker, darling," Delia added, still hopefully surveying her.

"Darker? It's grey," Charlotte suddenly broke out in her deep voice. She pushed back one of the pommaded bands that framed her face, and showed a white lock on her temple. "You needn't save up your bonnet; I'm not going to be married," she added, with a smile that showed her small white teeth in a fleeting glare.

Delia had just enough presence of mind to lay down the bonnet, marabout-up, before she flung herself on her cousin.

"Not going to be married? Charlotte, are you perfectly crazy?"

"Why is it crazy to do what I think right?"

"But people said you were going to marry him the year you came out. And no one understood what happened then. And now—how can it possibly be right? You simply *can't!*" Delia incoherently cried.

"Oh—people!" said Charlotte Lovell wearily.

Her married cousin looked at her with a start. Something thrilled in her voice that Delia had never heard in it, or in any other human voice, before. Its echo seemed to set their familiar world rocking, and the Axminster carpet actually heaved under Delia's shrinking slippers.

Charlotte Lovell stood staring ahead of her with strained lids. In the pale brown of her eyes Delia noticed the green specks that floated there when she was angry or excited.

"Charlotte—where on earth have you come from?" she questioned, drawing the girl down to the sofa.

"Come from?"

"Yes. You look as if you had seen a ghost—an army of ghosts."

The same snarling smile drew up Charlotte's lip. "I've seen Joe," she said.

"Well?—Oh, Chatty," Delia exclaimed abruptly illuminated, "you don't mean to say that you're going to let any little thing in Joe's past—? Not that I've ever heard the least hint; never. But even if there were . . ." She drew a deep breath, and bravely proceeded to extremities. "Even if you've heard that he's been . . . that he's had a child—of course he would have provided for it before . . ."

The girl shook her head. "I know: you needn't go on. 'Men will be men'; but it's not that."

"Tell me what it is."

Charlotte Lovell looked about the sunny prosperous room as if it were the image of her world, and that world were a prison she must break out of. She lowered her head. "I want—to get away," she panted.

"Get away? From Joe?"

"From his ideas—the Ralston ideas."

Delia bridled—after all, she was a Ralston! "The Ralston ideas? I haven't found them—so unbearably unpleasant to live with," she smiled a little tartly.

"No. But it was different with you: they didn't ask you to give up things."

"What things?" What in the world (Delia wondered) had poor Charlotte that any one could want her to give up? She had always been in the position of taking rather than of having to surrender. "Can't you explain to me, dear?" Delia urged.

"My poor children—he says I'm to give them up," cried the girl in a stricken whisper.

"Give them up? Give up helping them?"

"Seeing them—looking after them. Give them up altogether. He got his mother to explain to me. After—after we have children . . . he's afraid . . . afraid our children might catch things . . . He'll give me money, of course, to pay some one . . . a hired person, to look after them. He thought that handsome," Charlotte broke out with a sob. She flung off her bonnet and smothered her prostrate weeping in the cushions.

Delia sat perplexed. Of all unforeseen complications this was surely the least imaginable. And with all the acquired Ralston that was in her she could not help seeing the force of Joe's objection, could almost find herself agreeing with him. No one in New York had forgotten the death of the poor Henry van der Luydens' only child, who had caught small-pox at the circus to which an unprincipled nurse had surreptitiously taken him. After such a warning as that, parents felt justified in every precaution against contagion. And poor people were so ignorant and careless, and their children, of course, so perpetually exposed to everything catching. No, Joe Ralston was certainly right, and Charlotte almost insanely unreasonable. But it would be useless to tell her so now. Instinctively, Delia temporized.

"After all," she whispered to the prone ear, "if it's only after you have children—you may not have any—for some time."

"Oh, yes, I shall!" came back in anguish from the cushions.

Delia smiled with matronly superiority. "Really, Chatty, I don't quite see how you can know. You don't understand."

Charlotte Lovell lifted herself up. Her collar of Brussels lace had come undone and hung in a wisp on her crumpled bodice, and through the disorder of her hair the white lock glimmered haggardly. In her pale brown eyes the little green specks floated like leaves in a trout-pool.

"Poor girl," Delia thought, "how old and ugly she looks! More than ever like an old maid; and she doesn't seem to realize in the least that she'll never have another chance."

"You must try to be sensible, Chatty dear. After all, one's own babies have the first claim."

"That's just it." The girl seized her fiercely by the wrists. "How can I give up my own baby?"

"Your—your—?" Delia's world again began to waver under her. "Which of the poor little waifs, dearest, do you call your own baby?" she questioned patiently.

Charlotte looked her straight in the eyes. "I call my own baby my own baby."

"Your own—? Take care—you're hurting my wrists, Chatty!" Delia freed herself, forcing a smile. "Your own—?"

"My own little girl. The one that Jessamine and Cyrus—"

"Oh—" Delia Ralston gasped.

The two cousins sat silent, facing each other; but Delia looked away. It came over her with a shudder of repugnance that such things, even if they had to be said, should not have been spoken in her bedroom, so near the spotless nursery across the passage. Mechanically she smoothed the organ-like folds of her silk skirt, which her cousin's embrace had tumbled. Then she looked again at Charlotte's eyes, and her own melted.

"Oh, poor Chatty—my poor Chatty!" She held out her arms to her cousin.

§ 2

The shepherd continued to steal his kiss from the shepherdess, and the clock in the fallen trunk continued to tick out the minutes.

Delia, petrified, sat unconscious of their passing, her cousin clasped to her. She was dumb with the horror and amazement of learning that her own blood ran in the veins of the anonymous foundling, the "hundred dollar baby" about whom New York had so long furtively jested and conjectured. It was her first contact with the nether side of the smooth social surface, and she sickened at the thought that such things were, and that she, Delia Ralston, should be hearing of them in her own house, and from the lips of the victim! For Chatty of course was a victim—but whose? She had spoken no name, and Delia could put no question: the horror of it sealed her lips. Her mind had instantly raced back over Chatty's past; but she saw no masculine figure in it but Joe Ralston's. And to connect Joe with the episode was obviously unthinkable. Some one in the south, then—? But no: Charlotte had been ill when she left—and in a flash Delia understood the real nature of that illness, and of the girl's disappearance. But from such speculations too her mind recoiled, and instinctively she fastened on something she could still grasp: Joe Ralston's attitude about Chatty's paupers. Of course Joe could not let his wife risk bringing contagion into their home—that was safe ground to dwell on. Her own Jim would have felt in the same way; and she would certainly have agreed with him.

Her eyes travelled back to the clock. She always thought of Clem Spender when she looked at the clock, and suddenly she wondered —if things had been different—what *he* would have said if she had made such an appeal to him as Charlotte had made to Joe. The thing was hard to imagine; yet in a flash of mental readjustment Delia saw herself as Clem's wife, she saw her children as his, she pictured herself asking him to let her go on caring for the poor waifs in the Mercer Street stable, and she distinctly heard his laugh and his light answer: "Why on earth did you ask, you little goose? Do you take me for such a Pharisee as that?"

Yes, that was Clem Spender all over—tolerant, reckless, indifferent to consequences, always doing the kind thing at the moment, and too often leaving others to pay the score. "There's something cheap about Clem," Jim had once said in his heavy way. Delia Ralston roused herself and pressed her cousin closer. "Chatty, tell me," she whispered.

"There's nothing more."

"I mean, about yourself . . . this thing . . . this . . ." Clem Spender's voice was still in her ears. "You loved some one," she breathed.

"Yes, that's over—. Now it's only the child . . . And I could love Joe—in another way." Chatty Lovell straightened herself, wan and frowning.

"I need the money—I must have it for my baby. Or else they'll send it to an Institution." She paused. "But that's not all. I want to marry—to be a wife, like all of you. I should have loved Joe's children—our children. Life doesn't stop . . ."

"No; I suppose not. But you speak as if . . . as if . . . the person who took advantage of you . . ."

"No one took advantage of me. I was lonely and unhappy. I met some one who was lonely and unhappy. People don't all have your luck. We were both too poor to marry each other . . . and mother would never have consented. And so one day . . . one day before he said goodbye . . ."

"He said goodbye?"

"Yes. He was going to leave the country."

"He left the country—knowing?"

"How was he to know? He doesn't live here. He'd just come back—come back to see his family—for a few weeks . . ." She broke off, her thin lips pressed together upon her secret.

There was a silence. Blindly Delia stared at the bold shepherd.

"Come back from where?" she asked at length in a low tone.

"Oh, what does it matter? You wouldn't understand," Charlotte broke off, in the very words her married cousin had compassionately addressed to her virginity.

A slow blush rose to Delia's cheek: she felt oddly humiliated by the rebuke conveyed in that contemptuous retort. She seemed to herself shy, ineffectual, as incapable as an ignorant girl of dealing with the abominations that Charlotte was thrusting on her. But suddenly some fierce feminine intuition struggled and woke in her. She forced her eyes upon her cousin's.

"You won't tell me who it was?"

"What's the use? I haven't told anybody."

"Then why have you come to me?"

Charlotte's stony face broke up in weeping. "It's for my baby . . . my baby . . ."

Delia did not heed her. "How can I help you if I don't know?" she insisted in a harsh dry voice: her heart-beats were so violent that they seemed to send up throttling hands to her throat.

Charlotte made no answer.

"Come back from where?" Delia doggedly repeated; and at that, with a long wail, the girl flung her hands up, screening her eyes. "He always thought you'd wait for him," she sobbed out, "and then, when he found you hadn't . . . and that you were marrying Jim . . . He heard it just as he was sailing . . . He didn't know it till Mrs. Mingott asked him to bring the clock back for your wedding . . ."

"Stop—stop," Delia cried, springing to her feet. She had provoked the avowal, and now that it had come she felt that it had been gratuitously and indecently thrust upon her. Was this New York, *her* New York, her safe friendly hypocritical New York, was this James Ralston's house, and this his wife listening to such revelations of dishonour?

Charlotte Lovell stood up in her turn. "I knew it—I knew it! You think worse of my baby now, instead of better . . . Oh, why did you make me tell you? I knew you'd never understand. I'd always cared for him, ever since I came out; that was why I wouldn't marry any one else. But I knew there was no hope for me . . . he never looked at anybody but you. And then, when he came back four years ago, and there was no *you* for him any more, he began to notice me, to be kind, to talk to me about his life and his painting . . ." She drew a deep breath, and her voice cleared. "That's over—all over. It's as if I couldn't either hate him or love him. There's only the child now—my child. He doesn't even know of it—why should he? It's none of his business; it's nobody's business but mine. But surely you must see that I can't give up my baby."

Delia Ralston stood speechless, looking away from her cousin in a growing horror. She had lost all sense of reality, all feeling of safety and self-reliance. Her impulse was to close her ears to the other's appeal as a child buries its head from midnight terrors. At last she drew herself up, and spoke with dry lips.

"But what do you mean to do? Why have you come to me? Why have you told me all this?"

"Because he loved you!" Charlotte Lovell stammered out; and the two women stood and faced each other.

Slowly the tears rose to Delia's eyes and rolled down her cheeks, moistening her parched lips. Through the tears she saw her cousin's haggard countenance waver and droop like a drowning face under water. Things half-guessed, obscurely felt, surged up from unsuspected depths in her. It was almost as if, for a moment, this other woman were telling her of her own secret past, putting into crude words all the trembling silences of her own heart.

The worst of it was, as Charlotte said, that they must act now; there was not a day to lose. Chatty was right—it was impossible that she should marry Joe if to do so meant giving up the child. But, in any case, how could she marry him without telling him the truth? And was it conceivable that, after hearing it, he should repudiate her? All these questions spun agonizingly through Delia's brain, and through them glimmered the persistent vision of the child—Clem Spender's child—growing up on charity in a Negro hovel, or herded in one of the plague-houses they called Asylums. No: the child came first—she felt it in every fibre of her body. But what should she do, of whom take counsel, how advise the wretched creature who had come to her in Clement's name? Delia glanced about her desperately, and then turned back to her cousin.

"You must give me time. I must think. You ought not to marry him—and yet all the arrangements are made; and the wedding presents . . . There would be a scandal . . . it would kill Granny Lovell . . ."

Charlotte answered in a low voice: "There *is* no time. I must decide now."

Delia pressed her hands against her breast. "I tell you I must think. I wish you would go home.—Or, no: stay here: your mother mustn't see your eyes. Jim's not coming home till late; you can wait in this room till I come back." She had opened the wardrobe and was reaching up for a plain bonnet and heavy veil.

"Stay here? But where are you going?"

"I don't know. I want to walk—to get the air. I think I want to be alone." Feverishly, Delia unfolded her Paisley shawl, tied on bonnet and veil, thrust her mittened hands into her muff. Charlotte, without moving, stared at her dumbly from the sofa.

"You'll wait," Delia insisted, on the threshold.

"Yes: I'll wait."

Delia shut the door and hurried down the stairs.

§ 3

She had spoken the truth in saying that she did not know where she was going. She simply wanted to get away from Charlotte's unbearable face, and from the immediate atmosphere of her tragedy. Outside, in the open, perhaps it would be easier to think.

As she skirted the park-rails she saw her rosy children playing, under their nurse's eyes, with the pampered progeny of other square-dwellers. The little girl had on her new plaid velvet bonnet and white tippet, and the boy his Highland cap and broad-cloth spencer. How happy and jolly they looked! The nurse spied her, but she shook her head, waved at the group and hurried on.

She walked and walked through the familiar streets decked with bright winter sunshine. It was early afternoon, an hour when the gentlemen had just returned to their offices, and there were few pedestrians in Irving Place and Union Square. Delia crossed the Square to Broadway.

The Lovell house in Mercer Street was a sturdy old-fashioned brick dwelling. A large stable adjoined it, opening on an alley such as Delia, on her honey-moon trip to England, had heard called a "mews." She turned into the alley, entered the stable court, and pushed open a door. In a shabby white-washed room a dozen children, gathered about a stove, were playing with broken toys. The Irishwoman who had charge of them was cutting out small garments on a broken-legged deal table. She raised a friendly face, recognizing Delia as the lady who had once or twice been to see the children with Miss Charlotte.

Delia paused, embarrassed.

"I—I came to ask if you need any new toys," she stammered.

"That we do, ma'am. And many another thing too, though Miss

Charlotte tells me I'm not to beg of the ladies that comes to see our poor darlin's."

"Oh, you may beg of me, Bridget," Mrs. Ralston answered, smiling. "Let me see your babies—it's so long since I've been here."

The children had stopped playing and, huddled against their nurse, gazed up open-mouthed at the rich rustling lady. One little girl with pale brown eyes and scarlet cheeks was dressed in a plaid alpaca frock trimmed with imitation coral buttons that Delia remembered. Those buttons had been on Charlotte's "best dress" the year she came out. Delia stopped and took up the child. Its curly hair was brown, the exact color of the eyes—thank heaven! But the eyes had the same little green spangles floating in their transparency. Delia sat down, and the little girl, standing on her knee, gravely fingered her watch-chain.

"Oh, ma'am—maybe her shoes'll soil your skirt. The floor here ain't none too clean."

Delia shook her head, and pressed the child against her. She had forgotten the other gazing babies and their wardress. The little creature on her knee was made of different stuff—it had not needed the plaid alpaca and coral buttons to single her out. Her brown curls grew in points on her high forehead, exactly as Clement Spender's did. Delia laid a burning cheek against the forehead.

"Baby want my lovely yellow chain?"

Baby did.

Delia unfastened the gold chain and hung it about the child's neck. The other babies clapped and crowed, but the little girl, gravely dimpling, continued to finger the links in silence.

"Oh, ma'am, you can't leave that fine chain on little Teeny. When she has to go back to those blacks . . ."

"What is her name?"

"Teena they call her, I believe. It don't seem a Christian name, har'ly."

Delia was silent.

"What I say is, her cheeks is too red. And she coughs too easy. Always one cold and another. Here, Teeny, leave the lady go."

Delia stood up, loosening the tender arms.

"She doesn't want to leave go of you, ma'am. Miss Chatty ain't been in today, and the little thing's kinder lonesome without her.

She don't play like the other children, somehow . . . Teeny, you look at that lovely chain you've got . . . there, there now . . ."

"Goodbye, Clementina," Delia whispered below her breath. She kissed the pale brown eyes, the curly crown, and dropped her veil on rushing tears. In the stable-yard she dried them on her large embroidered handkerchief, and stood hesitating. Then with a decided step she turned toward home.

The house was as she had left it, except that the children had come in; she heard them romping in the nursery as she went down the passage to her bedroom. Charlotte Lovell was seated on the sofa, upright and rigid, as Delia had left her.

"Chatty—Chatty, I've thought it out. Listen. Whatever happens, the baby shan't stay with those people. I mean to keep her."

Charlotte stood up, tall and white. The eyes in her thin face had grown so dark that they seemed like spectral hollows in a skull. She opened her lips to speak, and then, snatching at her handkerchief, pressed it to her mouth, and sank down again. A red trickle dripped through the handkerchief onto her poplin skirt.

"Charlotte—Charlotte," Delia screamed, on her knees beside her cousin. Charlotte's head slid back against the cushions and the trickle ceased. She closed her eyes, and Delia, seizing a vinaigrette from the dressing-table, held it to her pinched nostrils. The room was filled with an acrid aromatic scent.

Charlotte's lids lifted. "Don't be frightened. I still spit blood sometimes—not often. My lung is nearly healed. But it's the terror—"

"No, no: there's to be no terror. I tell you I've thought it all out. Jim is going to let me take the baby."

The girl raised herself haggardly. "Jim? Have you told him? Is that where you've been?"

"No, darling. I've only been to see the baby."

"Oh," Charlotte moaned, leaning back again. Delia took her own handkerchief, and wiped away the tears that were raining down her cousin's cheeks.

"You mustn't cry, Chatty; you must be brave. Your little girl and his—how could you think? But you must give me time: I must manage it in my own way . . . Only trust me . . ."

Charlotte's lips stirred faintly.

"The tears . . . don't dry them, Delia . . . I like to feel them . . ."

The two cousins continued to lean against each other without speaking. The ormolu clock ticked out the measure of their mute communion in minutes, quarters, a half-hour, then an hour: the day declined and darkened, the shadows lengthened across the garlands of the Axminster and the broad white bed. There was a knock.

"The children's waiting to say their grace before supper, ma'am."

"Yes, Eliza. Let them say it to you. I'll come later." As the nurse's steps receded Charlotte Lovell disengaged herself from Delia's embrace.

"Now I can go," she said.

"You're not too weak, dear? I can send for a coach to take you home."

"No, no; it would frighten mother. And I shall like walking now, in the darkness. Sometimes the world used to seem all one awful glare to me. There were days when I thought the sun would never set. And then there was the moon at night." She laid her hands on her cousin's shoulders. "Now it's different. Bye and bye I shan't hate the light."

The two women kissed each other, and Delia whispered: "To-morrow."

§ 4

The Ralstons gave up old customs reluctantly, but once they had adopted a new one they found it impossible to understand why everyone else did not immediately do likewise.

When Delia, who came of the laxer Lovells, and was naturally inclined to novelty, had first proposed to her husband to dine at six o'clock instead of two, his malleable young face had become as relentless as that of the old original Ralston in his grim Colonial portrait. But after a two days' resistance he had come round to his wife's view, and now smiled contemptuously at the obstinacy of those who clung to a heavy mid-day meal and high tea.

"There's nothing I hate like narrow-mindedness. Let people eat when they like, for all I care; it's their narrow-mindedness that I can't stand."

Delia was thinking of this as she sat in the drawing-room (her mother would have called it the parlour) waiting for her husband's return. She had just had time to smooth her glossy braids, and slip on the black-and-white striped moiré with cherry pipings which was his favourite dress. The drawing-room, with its Nottingham lace curtains looped back under florid gilt cornices, its marble centre-table on a carved rosewood foot, and its old-fashioned mahogany armchairs covered with one of the new French silk damasks in a tart shade of apple-green, was one for any young wife to be proud of. The rosewood what-nots on each side of the folding doors that led into the dining-room were adorned with tropical shells, feld-spar vases, an alabaster model of the Leaning Tower of Pisa, a pair of obelisks made of scraps of porphyry and serpentine picked up by the young couple in the Roman Forum, a bust of Clytie in chalk-white biscuit de Sèvres, and four old-fashioned figures of the Seasons in Chelsea ware, that had to be left among the newer ornaments because they had belonged to great-grandmamma Ralston. On the walls hung large dark steel-engravings of Cole's "Voyage of Life," and between the windows stood the lifesize statue of "A Captive Maiden" executed for Jim Ralston's father by the celebrated Harriet Hosmer, immortalized in Hawthorne's novel of the Marble Faun. On the table lay handsomely tooled copies of Turner's Rivers of France, Drake's Culprit Fay, Crabbe's Tales, and the Book of Beauty containing portraits of the British peeresses who had participated in the Earl of Eglinton's tournament.

As Delia sat there, before the hard-coal fire in its arched opening of black marble, her citron-wood work-table at her side, and one of the new French lamps shedding a pleasant light on the centre-table from under a crystal-fringed shade, she asked herself how she could have passed, in such a short time, so completely out of her usual circle of impressions and convictions—so much farther than ever before beyond the Ralston horizon. Here it was, closing in on her again, as if the very plaster ornaments of the ceiling, the forms of the furniture, the cut of her dress, had been built out of Ralston prejudices, and turned to adamant by the touch of Ralston hands.

She must have been mad, she thought, to have committed herself so far to Charlotte; yet, turn about as she would in the ever-tightening circle of the problem, she could still find no other issue. Somehow, it lay with her to save Clem Spender's baby.

She heard the sound of the latch-key (her heart had never beat so high at it), and the putting down of a tall hat on the hall console—or of two tall hats, was it? The drawing-room door opened, and two high-stocked and ample-coated young men came in: two Jim Ralstons, so to speak. Delia had never before noticed how much her husband and his cousin Joe were alike; it made her feel how justified she was in always thinking of the Ralstons collectively.

She would not have been young and tender, and a happy wife, if she had not thought Joe but an indifferent copy of her Jim; yet, allowing for defects in the reproduction, there remained a striking likeness between the two tall athletic figures, the short sanguine faces with straight noses, straight whiskers, straight brows, candid blue eyes and sweet selfish smiles. Only, at the present moment, Joe looked like Jim with a tooth-ache.

"Look here, my dear: here's a young man who's asked to take pot-luck with us," Jim smiled, with the confidence of a well-nourished husband who knows that he can always bring a friend home.

"How nice of you, Joe!—Do you suppose he can put up with oyster soup and a stuffed goose?" Delia beamed upon her husband.

"I knew it! I told you so, my dear chap! He said you wouldn't like it—that you'd be fussed about the dinner. Wait till you're married, Joseph Ralston—." Jim brought down a genial paw on his cousin's bottle-green shoulder, and Joe grimaced as if the tooth had stabbed him.

"It's excessively kind of you, cousin Delia, to take me in this evening. The fact is—"

"Dinner first, my boy, if you don't mind! A bottle of Burgundy will brush away the blue devils. Your arm to your cousin, please; I'll just go and see that the wine is brought up."

Oyster soup, broiled bass, stuffed goose, apple fritters and green peppers, followed by one of Grandmamma Ralston's famous caramel custards: through all her mental anguish, Delia was faintly aware of a secret pride in her achievement. Certainly it would serve to confirm the rumour that Jim Ralston could always bring a friend home to dine without notice. The Ralston and Lovell wines rounded off the effect, and even Joe's drawn face had mellowed by the time the Lovell Madeira started westward. Delia marked the change when the two young men rejoined her in the drawing-room.

"And now, my dear fellow, you'd better tell her the whole story," Jim counselled, pushing an armchair toward his cousin.

The young woman, bent above her wool-work, listened with lowered lids and flushed cheeks. As a married woman—as a mother—Joe hoped she would think him justified in speaking to her frankly: he had her husband's authority to do so.

"Oh, go ahead, go ahead," chafed the exuberant after-dinner Jim from the hearth-rug.

Delia listened, considered, let the bridegroom flounder on through his embarrassed exposition. Her needle hung like a sword of Damocles above the canvas; she saw at once that Joe depended on her trying to win Charlotte over to his way of thinking. But he was very much in love: at a word from Delia, she understood that he would yield, and Charlotte gain her point, save the child, and marry him . . .

How easy it was, after all! A friendly welcome, a good dinner, a ripe wine, and the memory of Charlotte's eyes—so much the more expressive for all that they had looked upon. A secret envy stabbed the wife who had lacked this last enlightenment.

How easy it was—and yet it must not be! Whatever happened, she could not let Charlotte Lovell marry Joe Ralston. All the traditions of honour and probity in which she had been brought up forbade her to connive at such a plan. She could conceive—had already conceived—of high-handed measures, swift and adroit defiances of precedent, subtle revolts against the heartlessness of the social routine. But a lie she could never connive at. The idea of Charlotte's marrying Joe Ralston—her own Jim's cousin—without revealing her past to him, seemed to Delia as dishonourable as it would have seemed to any Ralston. And to tell him the truth would at once put an end to the marriage; of that even Chatty was aware. Social tolerance was not dealt in the same measure to men and to women, and neither Delia nor Charlotte had ever wondered why: like all the young women of their class they simply bowed to the ineluctable.

No; there was no escape from the dilemma. As clearly as it was Delia's duty to save Clem Spender's child, so clearly, also, she seemed destined to sacrifice his mistress. As the thought pressed on her she remembered Charlotte's wistful cry: "I want to be married, like all of you," and her heart tightened. But yet it must not be.

"I make every allowance" (Joe was droning on) "for my sweet girl's ignorance and inexperience—for her lovely purity. How could a man wish his future wife to be—to be otherwise? You're with me, Jim? And Delia? I've told her, you understand, that she shall always have a special sum set apart for her poor children—in addition to her pin-money; on that she may absolutely count. God! I'm willing to draw up a deed, a settlement, before a lawyer, if she says so. I admire, I appreciate her generosity. But I ask you, Delia, as a mother—mind you, now, I want your frank opinion. If you think I can stretch a point—can let her go on giving her personal care to these children until . . . until . . ." A flush of pride suffused the potential father's brow . . . "till nearer duties claim her, why, I'm more than ready . . . if you'll tell her so. I undertake," Joe proclaimed, suddenly tingling with the memory of his last glass, "to make it right with my mother, whose prejudices, of course, while I respect them, I can never allow to—to come between me and my own convictions." He sprang to his feet, and beamed on his dauntless double in the chimney-mirror. "My convictions," he flung back at it.

"Hear, hear!" cried Jim emotionally.

Delia's needle gave the canvas a sharp prick, and she pushed her work aside.

"I think I understand you both, Joe. Certainly, in Charlotte's place, I could never give up those children."

"There you are, my dear fellow!" Jim triumphed, as proud of this vicarious courage as of the perfection of the dinner.

"Never," said Delia. "Especially, I mean, the foundlings—there are two, I think. Those children always die if they are sent to asylums. That is what is haunting Chatty."

"Poor innocents! How I love her for loving them! That there should be such scoundrels upon this earth unpunished—. Delia, will you tell her that I'll do whatever—"

"Gently, old man, gently," Jim admonished him, with a flash of Ralston caution.

"Well, that is to say, whatever—in reason—"

Delia lifted an arresting hand. "I'll tell her, Joe: she will be grateful. But it's of no use—"

"No use? What more—?"

"Nothing more: except this. Charlotte has had a return of her old illness. She coughed blood here today. You must not marry her."

There: it was done. She stood up, trembling in every bone, and feeling herself pale to the lips. Had she done right? Had she done wrong? And would she ever know?

Poor Joe turned on her a face as wan as hers: he clutched the back of his armhair, his head drooping forward like an old man's. His lips moved, but made no sound.

"My God!" Jim stammered. "But you know you've got to buck up, old boy."

"I'm—I'm so sorry for you, Joe. She'll tell you herself tomorrow," Delia faltered, while her husband continued to proffer heavy consolations.

"Take it like a man, old chap. Think of yourself—your future. Can't be, you know. Delia's right; she always *is*. Better get it over—better face the music now than later."

"Now than later," Joe echoed with a tortured grin; and it occurred to Delia that never before in the course of his easy good-natured life had he had—any more than her Jim—to give up anything his heart was set on. Even the vocabulary of renunciation, and its conventional gestures, were unfamiliar to him.

"But I don't understand. I can't give her up," he declared, blinking away a boyish tear.

"Think of the children, my dear fellow; it's your duty," Jim insisted, checking a glance of pride at Delia's wholesome comeliness.

In the long conversation that followed between the cousins—argument, counter-argument, sage counsel and hopeless protest—Delia took but an occasional part. She knew well enough what the end would be. The bridegroom who had feared that his bride might bring home contagion from her visits to the poor would not knowingly implant disease in his race. Nor was that all. Too many sad instances of mothers prematurely fading, and leaving their husbands alone with a young flock to rear, must be pressing upon Joe's memory. Ralstons, Lovells, Lannings, Archers, van der Luydens—which one of them had not some grave to care for in a distant cemetery: graves of young relatives "in a decline," sent abroad to be cured by balmy Italy? The Protestant grave-yards of Rome and Pisa were full of New York names; the vision of that familiar pilgrimage with a dying wife was one to turn the most ardent Ralston cold. And all the while, as she listened with bent head, Delia kept repeating to herself: "This is easy; but how am I going to tell Charlotte?"

When poor Joe, late that evening, wrung her hand with a stammered farewell, she called him back abruptly from the threshold.

"You must let me see her first, please; you must wait till she sends for you—" and she winced a little at the alacrity of his acceptance. But no amount of rhetorical bolstering-up could make it easy for a young man to face what lay ahead of Joe; and her final glance at him was one of compassion . . .

The front door closed upon Joe, and she was roused by her husband's touch on her shoulder.

"I never admired you more, darling. My wise Delia!"

Her head bent back, she took his kiss, and then drew apart.The sparkle in his eyes she understood to be as much an invitation to her bloom as a tribute to her sagacity.

She held him at arms' length. "What should you have done, Jim, if I'd had to tell you about myself what I've just told Joe about Chatty?"

A slight frown showed that he thought the question negligible, and hardly in her usual taste. "Come," his strong arm entreated her.

She continued to stand away from him, with grave eyes. "Poor Chatty! Nothing left now—"

His own eyes grew grave, in instant sympathy. At such moments he was still the sentimental boy whom she could manage.

"Ah, poor Chatty, indeed!" He groped for the readiest panacea. "Lucky, now, after all, that she has those paupers, isn't it? I suppose a woman *must* have children to love——somebody else's if not her own." It was evident that the thought of the remedy had already relieved his pain.

"Yes," Delia agreed, "I see no other comfort for her. I'm sure Joe will feel that too. Between us, darling—" and now she let him have her hands—"between us, you and I must see to it that she keeps her babies."

"Her babies?" He smiled at the possessive pronoun. "Of course, poor girl! Unless indeed she's sent to Italy?"

"Oh, she won't be that—where's the money to come from? And, besides, she'd never leave Aunt Lovell. But I thought, dear, if I might tell her tomorrow—you see, I'm not exactly looking forward to my talk with her—if I might tell her that you would let me look after the baby she's most worried about, the poor little foundling girl who has no name and no home—if I might put aside a fixed sum from my pin-money . . ."

Their hands flowed together, she lifted her flushing face to his. Manly tears were in his eyes; ah, how he triumphed in her health, her wisdom, her generosity!

"Not a penny from your pin-money—never!"

She feigned discouragement and wonder. "Think, dear—if I'd had to give you up!"

"Not a penny from your pin-money, I say—but as much more as you need, to help poor Chatty's pauper. There—will that content you?"

"Dearest! When I think of our own, upstairs!" They held each other, awed by that evocation.

§ 5

Charlotte Lovell, at the sound of her cousin's step, lifted a fevered face from the pillow.

The bedroom, dim and close, smelt of eau de Cologne and fresh linen. Delia, blinking in from the bright winter sun, had to feel her way through a twilight obstructed by dark mahogany.

"I want to see your face, Chatty: unless your head aches too much?"

Charlotte signed "No," and Delia drew back the heavy window curtains and let in a ray of light. In it she saw the girl's head, livid against the bed-linen, the brick-rose circles again visible under darkly shadowed lids. Just so, she remembered, poor cousin So-and-so had looked the week before she sailed for Italy!

"Delia!" Charlotte breathed.

Delia drew near the bed, and stood looking down at her cousin with new eyes. Yes: it had been easy enough, the night before, to dispose of Chatty's future as if it were her own. But now?

"Darling—"

"Oh, begin, please," the girl interrupted, "or I shall know that what's coming is too dreadful!"

"Chatty, dearest, if I promised you too much—"

"Jim won't let you take my child? I knew it! Shall I always go on dreaming things that can never be?"

Delia, her tears running down, knelt by the bed and gave her fresh hand into the other's burning clutch.

"Don't think that, dear: think only of what you'd like best . . ."

"Like best?" The girl sat up sharply against her pillows, alive to the hot fingertips.

"You can't marry Joe, dear—can you—and keep little Tina?" Delia continued.

"Not keep her with me, no: but somewhere I could slip off to see her—oh, I had hoped such follies!"

"Give up follies, Charlotte. Keep her where? See your own child in secret? Always in dread of disgrace? Of wrong to your other children? Have you ever thought of that?"

"Oh, my poor head won't think! You're trying to tell me that I must give her up?"

"No, dear; but that you must not marry Joe."

Charlotte sank back on the pillow, her eyes half-closed. "I tell you I must make my child a home. Delia, you're too blest to understand!"

"Think yourself blest too, Chatty. You shan't give up your baby. She shall live with you: you shall take care of her—for me."

"For you?"

"I promised you I'd take her, didn't I? But not that you should marry Joe. Only that I would make a home for your baby. Well, that's done; you two shall be always together."

Charlotte clung to her and sobbed. "But Joe—I can't tell him, I can't!" She put back Delia suddenly. "You haven't told him of my—of my baby? I couldn't bear to hurt him as much as that."

"I told him that you coughed blood yesterday. He'll see you presently: he's dreadfully unhappy. He has been given to understand that, in view of your bad health, the engagement is broken by your wish—and he accepts your decision; but if he weakens, or if you weaken, I can do nothing for you or for little Tina. For heaven's sake remember that!"

Delia released her hold, and Charlotte leaned back silent, with closed eyes and narrowed lips. Almost like a corpse she lay there. On a chair near the bed hung the poplin with red velvet ribbons which had been made over in honour of her betrothal. A pair of new slippers of bronze kid peeped from beneath it. Poor Chatty! She had hardly had time to be pretty . . .

Delia sat by the bed motionless, her eyes on her cousin's closed face. They followed the course of a tear that forced a way between Charlotte's tight lids, hung on the lashes, glittered slowly down the cheeks. As the tear reached the narrowed lips they spoke.

"Shall I live with her somewhere, do you mean? Just she and I together?"

"Just you and she."

"In a little house?"

"In a little house . . ."

"You're sure, Delia?"

"Sure, my dearest."

Charlotte once more raised herself on her elbow and sent a hand groping under the pillow. She drew out a narrow ribbon on which hung a diamond ring.

"I had taken it off already," she said simply, and handed it to Delia.

§ 6

You could always have told, every one agreed afterward, that Charlotte Lovell was meant to be an old maid. Even before her illness it had been manifest: there was something prim about her in spite of her fiery hair. Lucky enough for her, poor girl, considering her wretched health in her youth: Mrs. James Ralston's contemporaries, for instance, remembered Charlotte as a mere ghost, coughing her lungs out—that, of course, had been the reason for her breaking her engagement with Joe Ralston.

True, she had recovered very rapidly, in spite of the peculiar treatment she was given. The Lovells, as every one knew, couldn't afford to send her to Italy; the previous experiment in Georgia had been unsuccessful; and so she was packed off to a farm-house on the Hudson—a little place on the James Ralstons' property—where she lived for five or six years with an Irish servant-woman and a foundling baby. The story of the foundling was another queer episode in Charlotte's history. From the time of her first illness, when she was only twenty-two or three, she had developed an almost morbid tenderness for children, especially for the children of the poor. It was said—Dr. Lanskell was understood to have said—that the baffled instinct of motherhood was peculiarly intense in cases where lung-disease prevented marriage. And so, when it was decided that Chatty must break her engagement to Joe Ralston and go to live in the country, the doctor had told her family that the only hope of saving her lay in not separating her entirely from her pauper children, but in letting her choose one of them, the youngest and most pitiable, and devote herself to its care. So the James Ralstons had lent her their little farm-house, and Mrs. Jim, with her extraordinary gift of taking things in at a glance, had at once arranged everything, and even pledged herself to look after the baby if Charlotte died.

Charlotte did not die. She lived to grow robust and middle-aged, energetic and even tyrannical. And as the transformation in her character took place she became more and more like the typical old maid: precise, methodical, absorbed in trifles, and attaching an exaggerated importance to the smallest social and domestic observances. Such was her reputation as a vigilant house-wife that, when poor Jim Ralston was killed by a fall from his horse, and left Delia, still young, with a boy and girl to bring up, it seemed perfectly natural that the heart-broken widow should take her cousin to live with her and share her task. But Delia Ralston never did things quite like other people. When she took Charlotte she took Charlotte's foundling too: a dark-haired child with pale brown eyes, and the odd incisive manner of children who have lived too much with their elders. The little girl was called Tina Lovell: it was vaguely supposed that Charlotte had adopted her. She grew up on terms of affectionate equality with her young Ralston cousins, and almost as much so—it might be said—with the two women who mothered her. But, impelled by an instinct of imitation which no one took the trouble to correct, she always called Delia Ralston "Mamma" and Charlotte Lovell "Aunt Chatty." She was a brilliant and engaging creature, and people marvelled at poor Chatty's luck in having chosen so interesting a specimen among her foundlings (for she was by this time supposed to have had a whole asylum-full to choose from).

The agreeable elderly bachelor, Sillerton Jackson, returning from a prolonged sojourn in Paris (where he was understood to have been made much of by the highest personages) was immensely struck by Tina's charms when he saw her at her coming-out ball, and asked Delia's permission to come some evening and dine alone with her and her young people. He complimented the widow on the rosy beauty of her own young Delia; but the mother's keen eye perceived that all the while he was watching Tina, and after dinner he confided to the older ladies that there was something "very French" in the girl's way of doing her hair, and that in the capital of all the Elegances she would have been pronounced extremely stylish.

"Oh—" Delia deprecated, beamingly, while Charlotte Lovell sat bent over her work with pinched lips; but Tina, who had been laughing with her cousins at the other end of the room, was around upon her elders in a flash.

"I heard what Mr. Sillerton said! Yes, I did, Mamma: he says I do my hair stylishly. Didn't I always tell you so? I *know* it's more becoming to let it curl as it wants to than to plaster it down with bandoline like Aunty's—"

"Tina, Tina—you always think people are admiring you!" Miss Lovell protested.

"Why shouldn't I, when they do?" the girl laughingly challenged; and, turning her mocking eyes on Sillerton Jackson: "Do tell Aunt Charlotte not to be so dreadfully old-maidish!"

Delia saw the blood rise to Charlotte Lovell's face. It no longer painted two brick-rose circles on her thin cheekbones, but diffused a harsh flush over her whole countenance, from the collar fastened with an old-fashioned garnet brooch to the pepper-and-salt hair (with no trace of red left in it) flattened down over her hollow temples.

That evening, when they went up to bed, Delia called Tina into her room.

"You ought not to speak to your Aunt Charlotte as you did this evening, dear. It's disrespectful—you must see that it hurts her."

The girl overflowed with compunction. "Oh, I'm so sorry! Because I said she was an old maid? But she *is,* isn't she, Mamma? In her inmost soul, I mean. I don't believe she's ever been young—ever thought of fun or admiration or falling in love—do you? That's why she never understands me, and you always do, you darling dear Mamma." With one of her light movements, Tina was in the widow's arms.

"Child, child," Delia softly scolded, kissing the dark curls planted in five points on the girl's forehead.

There was a soft foot-fall in the passage, and Charlotte Lovell stood in the door. Delia, without moving, sent her a glance of welcome over Tina's shoulder.

"Come in, Charlotte, I'm scolding Tina for behaving like a spoilt baby before Sillerton Jackson. What will he think of her?"

"Just what she deserves, probably," Charlotte returned with a cold smile. Tina went toward her, and her thin lips touched the girl's proffered forehead just where Delia's warm kiss had rested. "Goodnight, child," she said in her dry tone of dismissal.

The door closed on the two women, and Delia signed to Charlotte to take the armchair opposite to her own.

"Not so near the fire," Miss Lovell answered. She chose a straight-backed seat, and sat down with folded hands. Delia's eyes rested absently on the thin ringless fingers: she wondered why Charlotte never wore her mother's jewels.

"I overheard what you were saying to Tina, Delia. You were scolding her because she called me an old maid."

It was Delia's turn to colour. "I scolded her for being disrespectful, dear; if you heard what I said you can't think that I was too severe."

"Not too severe: no. I've never thought you too severe with Tina; on the contrary."

"You think I spoil her?"

"Sometimes."

Delia felt an unreasoning resentment. "What was it I said that you object to?"

Charlotte returned her glance steadily. "I would rather she thought me an old maid than—"

"Oh—" Delia murmured. With one of her quick leaps of intuition she had entered into the other's soul, and once more measured its shuddering loneliness.

"What else," Charlotte inexorably pursued, "*can* she possibly be allowed to think me—ever?"

"I see . . . I see . . ." the widow faltered.

"A ridiculous narrow-minded old maid—nothing else," Charlotte Lovell insisted, getting to her feet, "or I shall never feel safe with her."

"Goodnight, my dear," Delia said compassionately. There were moments when she almost hated Charlotte for being Tina's mother, and others, such as this, when her heart was wrung by the tragic spectacle of that unavowed bond.

Charlotte seemed to have divined her thought.

"Oh, but don't pity me! She's mine," she murmured, going.

§ 7

Delia Ralston sometimes felt that the real events of her life did not begin until both her children had contracted—so safely and suitably—their irreproachable New York alliances. The boy had married first, choosing a Vandergrave in whose father's bank at Albany he was to have an immediate junior partnership; and young Delia (as her mother had foreseen she would) had selected John Junius, the safest and soundest of the many young Halseys, and followed him to his parents' house the year after her brother's marriage.

After young Delia had left the house in Gramercy Park it was inevitable that Tina should take the centre front of its narrow stage. Tina had reached the marriageable age, she was admired and sought after; but what hope was there of her finding a husband? The two watchful women did not propound this question to each other; but Delia Ralston, brooding over it day by day, and taking it up with her when she mounted at night to her bedroom, knew that Charlotte Lovell, at the same hour, carried the same problem with her to the floor above.

The two cousins, during their eight years of life together, had seldom openly disagreed. Indeed, it might almost have been said that there was nothing open in their relation. Delia would have had it otherwise: after they had once looked so deeply into each other's souls it seemed unnatural that a veil should fall between them. But she understood that Tina's ignorance of her origin must at all costs be preserved, and that Charlotte Lovell, abrupt, passionate and inarticulate, knew of no other security than to wall herself up in perpetual silence.

So far had she carried this self-imposed reticence that Mrs. Ralston was surprised at her suddenly asking, soon after young Delia's marriage, to be allowed to move down into the small bedroom next to Tina's that had been left vacant by the bride's departure.

"But you'll be so much less comfortable there, Chatty. Have you thought of that? Or is it on account of the stairs?"

"No; it's not the stairs," Charlotte answered with her usual bluntness. How could she avail herself of the pretext Delia offered her, when Delia knew that she still ran up and down the three flights like a girl? "It's because I should be next to Tina," she said, in a low voice that jarred like an untuned string.

"Oh—very well. As you please." Mrs. Ralston could not tell why she felt suddenly irritated by the request, unless it were that she had already amused herself with the idea of fitting up the vacant room as a sitting-room for Tina. She had meant to do it in pink and pale green, like an opening flower.

"Of course, if there is any reason—" Charlotte suggested, as if reading her thought.

"None whatever; except that—well, I'd meant to surprise Tina by doing the room up as a sort of little boudoir where she could have her books and things, and see her girl friends."

"You're too kind, Delia; but Tina mustn't have boudoirs," Miss Lovell answered ironically, the green specks showing in her eyes.

"Very well: as you please," Delia repeated, in the same irritated tone. "I'll have your things brought down tomorrow."

Charlotte paused in the doorway. "You're sure there's no other reason?"

"Other reason? Why should there be?" The two women looked at each other almost with hostility, and Charlotte turned to go.

The talk once over, Delia was annoyed with herself for having yielded to Charlotte's wish. Why must it always be she who gave in, she who, after all, was the mistress of the house, and to whom both

Charlotte and Tina might almost be said to owe their very existence, or at least all that made it worth having? Yet whenever any question arose about the girl it was invariably Charlotte who gained her point, Delia who yielded: it seemed as if Charlotte, in her mute obstinate way, were determined to take every advantage of the dependence that made it impossible for a woman of Delia's nature to oppose her.

In truth, Delia had looked forward more than she knew to the quiet talks with Tina to which the little boudoir would have lent itself. While her own daughter inhabited the room, Mrs. Ralston had been in the habit of spending an hour there every evening, chatting with the two girls while they undressed, and listening to their comments on the incidents of the day. She always knew beforehand exactly what her own girl would say; but Tina's views and opinions were a perpetual delicious shock to her. Not that they were strange or unfamiliar; there were moments when they seemed to well straight up from the dumb depths of Delia's own past. Only they expressed feelings she had never uttered, ideas she had hardly avowed to herself: Tina sometimes said things which Delia Ralston, in far-off self-communions, had imagined herself saying to Clement Spender.

And now there would be an end to these evening talks: if Charlotte had asked to be lodged next to her daughter, might it not conceivably be because she wished them to end? It had never before occurred to Delia that her influence over Tina might be resented; now the discovery flashed a light far down into the abyss which had always divided the two women. But a moment later Delia reproached herself for attributing feelings of jealousy to her cousin. Was it not rather to herself that she should have ascribed them? Charlotte, as Tina's mother, had every right to wish to be near her, near her in all senses of the word; what claim had Delia to oppose to that natural privilege? The next morning she gave the order that Charlotte's things should be taken down to the room next to Tina's.

That evening, when bedtime came, Charlotte and Tina went upstairs together; but Delia lingered in the drawing-room, on the pretext of having letters to write. In truth, she dreaded to pass the threshold where, evening after evening, the fresh laughter of the two girls used to waylay her while Charlotte Lovell already slept her old-maid sleep on the floor above. A pang went through Delia at the thought that henceforth she would be cut off from this means of keeping her hold on Tina.

An hour later, when she mounted the stairs in her turn, she was guiltily conscious of moving as noiselessly as she could along the heavy carpet of the corridor, and of pausing longer than was necessary over the putting out of the gas-jet on the landing. As she lingered she strained her ears for the sound of voices from the adjoining doors behind which Charlotte and Tina slept; she would have been secretly hurt at hearing talk and laughter from within. But none came, nor was there any light beneath the doors. Evidently Charlotte, in her hard methodical way, had said goodnight to her daughter, and gone straight to bed as usual. Perhaps she had never approved of Tina's vigils, of the long undressing punctuated with mirth and confidences; she might have asked for the room next to her daughter's simply because she did not want the girl to miss her "beauty sleep."

Whenever Delia tried to explore the secret of her cousin's actions she returned from the adventure humiliated and abashed by the base motives she found herself attributing to Charlotte. How was it that she, Delia Ralston, whose happiness had been open and avowed to the world, so often found herself envying poor Charlotte the secret of her scanted motherhood? She hated herself for this movement of envy whenever she detected it, and tried to atone for it by a softened manner and a more anxious regard for Charlotte's feelings; but the attempt was not always successful, and Delia sometimes wondered if Charlotte did not resent any show of sympathy as an indirect glance at her misfortune. The worst of suffering such as hers was that it left one sore to the gentlest touch . . .

Delia, slowly undressing before the same lace-draped toilet-glass which had reflected her bridal image, was turning over these thoughts when she heard a light knock. She opened the door, and there stood Tina, in a dressing-gown, her dark curls falling over her shoulders.

With a happy heart-beat Delia held out her arms.

"I had to say goodnight, Mamma," the girl whispered.

"Of course, dear." Delia pressed a long kiss on her lifted forehead. "Run off now, or you might disturb your aunt. You know she sleeps badly, and you must be as quiet as a mouse now she's next to you."

"Yes, I know," Tina acquiesced, with a grave glance that was almost of complicity.

She asked no further question, she did not linger: lifting Delia's hand she held it a moment against her cheek, and then stole out as noiselessly as she had come.

§ 8

"But you must see," Charlotte Lovell insisted, laying aside the *Evening Post,* "that Tina has changed. You do see that?"

The two women were sitting alone by the drawing-room fire in Gramercy Park. Tina had gone to dine with her cousin, young Mrs. John Junius Halsey, and was to be taken afterward to a ball at the Vandergraves', from which the John Juniuses had promised to see her home. Mrs. Ralston and Charlotte, their early dinner finished, had the long evening to themselves. Their custom, on such occasions, was for Charlotte to read the news aloud to her cousin, while the latter embroidered; but tonight, all through Charlotte's conscientious progress from column to column, without a slip or an omission, Delia had felt her, for some special reason, alert to take advantage of her daughter's absence.

To gain time before answering, Mrs. Ralston bent over a stitch in her delicate white embroidery.

"Tina changed? Since when?" she questioned.

The answer flashed out instantly. "Since Lanning Halsey has been coming here so much."

"Lanning? I used to think he came for Delia," Mrs. Ralston mused, speaking at random to gain still more time.

"It's natural you should suppose that every one came for Delia," Charlotte rejoined dryly; "but as Lanning continues to seek every chance of being with Tina—"

Mrs. Ralston raised her head and stole a swift glance at her cousin. She had in truth noticed that Tina had changed, as a flower changes at the mysterious moment when the unopened petals flush from within. The girl had grown handsomer, shyer, more silent, at times more irrelevantly gay. But Delia had not associated these variations of mood with the presence of Lanning Halsey, one of the numerous youths who had haunted the house before young Delia's marriage. There had, indeed, been a moment when Mrs. Ralston's eye had been fixed, with a certain apprehension, on the handsome Lanning. Among all the sturdy and stolid Halsey cousins he was the only one to whom a prudent mother might have hesitated to entrust her daughter; it would have been hard to say why, except that he was handsomer and more conversable than the rest, chronically unpunctual, and totally unperturbed by the fact. Clem Spender had been like that; and what if young Delia—?

But young Delia's mother was speedily reassured. The girl, herself arch and appetizing, took no interest in the corresponding graces except when backed by more solid qualities. A Ralston to the core, she demanded the Ralston virtues, and chose the Halsey most worthy of a Ralston bride.

Mrs. Ralston felt that Charlotte was waiting for her to speak. "It will be hard to get used to the idea of Tina's marrying," she said gently. "I don't know what we two old women shall do, alone in this empty house—for it will be an empty house then. But I suppose we ought to face the idea."

"I *do* face it," said Charlotte Lovell gravely.

"And you dislike Lanning? I mean, as a husband for Tina?"

Miss Lovell folded the evening paper, and stretched out a thin hand for her knitting. She glanced across the citron-wood worktable at her cousin. "Tina must not be too difficult—" she began.

"Oh—" Delia protested, reddening.

"Let us call things by their names," the other evenly pursued. "That's my way, when I speak at all. Usually, as you know, I say nothing."

The widow made a sign of assent, and Charlotte went on: "It's better so. But I've always known a time would come when we should have to talk this thing out."

"Talk this thing out? You and I? What thing?"

"Tina's future."

There was a silence. Delia Ralston, who always responded instantly to the least appeal to her sincerity, breathed a deep sigh of relief. At last the ice in Charlotte's breast was breaking up!

"My dear," Delia murmured, "you know how much Tina's happiness concerns me. If you disapprove of Lanning Halsey as a husband, have you any other candidate in mind?"

Miss Lovell smiled one of her faint hard smiles. "I am not aware that there is a queue at the door. Nor do I disapprove of Lanning Halsey as a husband. Personally, I find him very agreeable; I understand his attraction for Tina."

"Ah—Tina *is* attracted?"

"Yes."

Mrs. Ralston pushed aside her work and thoughtfully considered her cousin's sharp-lined face. Never had Charlotte Lovell more completely presented the typical image of the old maid than as she sat there, upright on her straight-backed chair, with narrowed elbows and clicking needles, and imperturbably discussed her daughter's marriage.

"I don't understand, Chatty. Whatever Lanning's faults are—and I don't believe they're grave—I share your liking for him. After all—" Mrs. Ralston paused—"What is it that people find so reprehensible in him? Chiefly, as far as I can hear, that he can't decide on the choice of a profession. The New York view about that is rather narrow, as we know. Young men may have other tastes . . . artistic . . . literary . . . they may even have difficulty in deciding . . ."

Both women coloured slightly, and Delia guessed that the same reminiscence which shook her own bosom also throbbed under Charlotte's strait bodice.

Charlotte spoke. "Yes: I understand that. But hesitancy about a profession may cause hesitancy about . . . other decisions . . ."

"What do you mean? Surely not that Lanning—?"

"Lanning has not asked Tina to marry him."

Charlotte paused. The steady click of her needles punctuated the silence as once, years before, it had been punctuated by the tick of the Parisian clock on Delia's mantel. As Delia's memory fled back to that scene she felt its mysterious tension in the air.

Charlotte spoke. "Lanning is not hesitating any longer: he has decided *not* to marry Tina. But he has also decided—not to give up seeing her."

Delia flushed abruptly; she was irritated and bewildered by Charlotte's oracular phrases, doled out between parsimonious lips.

"You don't mean that he has offered himself and then drawn back? I can't think him capable of such an insult to Tina."

"He has not insulted Tina. He has simply told her that he can't afford to marry. Until he chooses a profession his father will allow him only a few hundred dollars a year; and that may be suppressed if—if he marries against his parents' wishes."

It was Delia's turn to be silent. The past was too overwhelmingly resuscitated in Charlotte's words. Clement Spender stood before her, irresolute, impecunious, persuasive. Ah, if only she had let herself be persuaded!

"I'm very sorry that this should have happened to Tina. But as Lanning appears to have behaved honourably, and withdrawn without raising false expectations, we must hope . . . we must hope . . ." Delia paused, not knowing what they must hope.

Charlotte Lovell laid down her knitting. "You know as well as I do, Delia, that every young man who is inclined to fall in love with Tina will find as good reasons for not marrying her."

"Then you think Lanning's excuses are a pretext?"

"Naturally. The first of many that will be found by his successors—for of course he will have successors. Tina—attracts."

"Ah," Delia murmured.

Here they were at last face to face with the problem which, through all the years of silence and evasiveness, had lain as close to the surface as a corpse too hastily buried! Delia drew another deep breath, which again was almost one of relief. She had always known that it would be difficult, almost impossible, to find a husband for Tina; and much as she desired Tina's happiness, some inmost selfishness whispered how much less lonely and purposeless the close of her own life would be should the girl be forced to share it. But how say this to Tina's mother?

"I hope you exaggerate, Charlotte. There may be disinterested characters . . . But, in any case, surely Tina need not be unhappy here, with us who love her so dearly."

"Tina an old maid? Never!" Charlotte Lovell rose abruptly, her closed hand crashing down on the slender work-table. "My child shall have her life . . . her own life . . . whatever it costs me . . ."

Delia's ready sympathy welled up. "I understand your feeling. I should want also . . . hard as it will be to let her go. But surely there is no hurry—no reason for looking so far ahead. The child is not twenty. Wait."

Charlotte stood before her, motionless, perpendicular. At such moments she made Delia think of lava struggling through granite: there seemed no issue for the fires within.

"Wait? But if *she* doesn't wait?"

"But if he has withdrawn—what do you mean?"

"He has given up marrying her—but not seeing her."

Delia sprang up in her turn, flushed and trembling.

"Charlotte! Do you know what you're insinuating?"

"Yes: I know."

"But it's too outrageous. No decent girl—"

The words died on Delia's lips. Charlotte Lovell held her eyes inexorably. "Girls are not always what you call decent," she declared.

Mrs. Ralston turned slowly back to her seat. Her tambour frame had fallen to the floor; she stooped heavily to pick it up. Charlotte's gaunt figure hung over her, relentless as doom.

"I can't imagine, Charlotte, what is gained by saying such things—even by hinting them. Surely you trust your own child."

Charlotte laughed. "My mother trusted me," she said.

"How dare you—how dare you?" Delia began; but her eyes fell, and she felt a tremor of weakness in her throat.

"Oh, I dare anything for Tina, even to judging her as she is," Tina's mother murmured.

"As she is? She's perfect!"

"Let us say then that she must pay for my imperfections. All I want is that she shouldn't pay too heavily."

Mrs. Ralston sat silent. It seemed to her that Charlotte spoke with the voice of all the dark destinies coiled under the safe surface of life; and that to such a voice there was no answer but an awed acquiescence.

"Poor Tina!" she breathed.

"Oh, I don't intend that she shall suffer! It's not for that I've waited . . . waited. Only I've made mistakes: mistakes that I understand now, and must remedy. You've been too good to us—and we must go."

"Go?" Delia gasped.

"Yes. Don't think me ungrateful. You saved my child once—do you suppose I can forget? But now it's my turn—it's I who must save her. And it's only by taking her away from everything here—from everything she's known till now—that I can do it. She's lived too long among unrealities: and she's like me. They won't content her."

"Unrealities?" Delia echoed vaguely.

"Unrealities for her. Young men who make love to her and can't marry her. Happy households where she's welcomed till she's suspected of designs on a brother or a husband—or else exposed to their insults. How could we ever have imagined, either of us, that the child could escape disaster? I thought only of her present happiness—of all the advantages, for both of us, of being with you. But this affair with young Halsey has opened my eyes. I must take Tina away. We must go and live somewhere where we're not known, where we shall be among plain people, leading plain lives. Somewhere where she can find a husband, and make herself a home."

Charlotte paused. She had spoken in a rapid monotonous tone, as if by rote; but now her voice broke and she repeated painfully: "I'm not ungrateful."

"Oh, don't let's speak of gratitude! What place has it between you and me?"

Delia had risen and begun to move uneasily about the room. She longed to plead with Charlotte, to implore her not to be in haste, to picture to her the cruelty of severing Tina from all her habits and associations, of carrying her inexplicably away to lead "a plain life among plain people." What chance was there, indeed, that a creature so radiant would tamely submit to such a fate, or find an acceptable husband in such conditions? The change might only precipitate a tragedy. Delia's experience was too limited for her to picture exactly what might happen to a girl like Tina, suddenly cut off from all that sweetened life for her; but vague visions of revolt and flight—of a "fall" deeper and more irretrievable than Charlotte's—flashed through her agonized imagination.

"It's too cruel—it's too cruel," she cried, speaking to herself rather than to Charlotte.

Charlotte, instead of answering, glanced abruptly at the clock.

"Do you know what time it is? Past midnight. I mustn't keep you sitting up for my foolish girl."

Delia's heart contracted. She saw that Charlotte wished to cut the conversation short, and to do so by reminding her that only Tina's mother had a right to decide what Tina's future should be. At that moment, though Delia had just protested that there could be no question of gratitude between them, Charlotte Lovell seemed to her a monster of ingratitude, and it was on the tip of her tongue to cry out: "Have all the years then given me no share in Tina?" But at the same instant she had put herself once more in Charlotte's place, and was feeling the mother's fierce terrors for her child. It was natural enough that Charlotte should resent the faintest attempt to usurp in private the authority she could never assert in public. With a pang of compassion Delia realized that she herself was literally the one being on earth before whom Charlotte could act the mother. "Poor thing—ah, let her!" she murmured inwardly.

"But why should you sit up for Tina? She has the key, and Delia is to bring her home."

Charlotte Lovell did not immediately answer. She rolled up her knitting, looked severely at one of the candelabra on the mantelpiece, and crossed over to straighten it. Then she picked up her work-bag.

"Yes, as you say—why should any one sit up for her?" She moved about the room, putting out the lamps, covering the fire, assuring herself that the windows were bolted, while Delia passively watched her. Then the two cousins lit their bedroom candles and walked upstairs through the darkened house. Charlotte seemed determined to make no further allusion to the subject of their talk. On the landing she paused, bending her head toward Delia's nightly kiss.

"I hope they've kept up your fire," she said, with her capable housekeeping air; and on Delia's hasty reassurance the two murmured a simultaneous "Goodnight," and Charlotte turned down the passage to her room.

§ 9

Delia's fire had been kept up, and her dressing-gown was warming on an arm-chair near the hearth. But she neither undressed nor yet seated herself. Her conversation with Charlotte had filled her with a deep unrest.

For a few moments she stood in the middle of the floor, looking slowly about her. Nothing had ever been changed in the room which, even as a bride, she had planned to modernize. All her dreams of renovation had faded long ago. Some deep central indifference had gradually made her regard herself as a third person, living the life meant for another woman, a woman totally unrelated to the vivid Delia Lovell who had entered that house so full of plans and visions. The fault, she knew, was not her husband's. With a little managing and a little wheedling she would have gained every point as easily as she had gained the capital one of taking the foundling baby under her wing. The difficulty was that, after that victory, nothing else seemed worth trying for. The first sight of little Tina had somehow decentralized Delia Ralston's whole life, making her indifferent to everything else, except indeed the welfare of her own husband and children. Ahead of her she saw only a future full of duties, and these she had gaily and faithfully accomplished. But her own life was over; she felt as detached as a cloistered nun.

The change in her was too deep not to be visible. The Ralstons openly gloried in dear Delia's conformity. Each acquiescence passed for a concession, and the family doctrine was fortified by such fresh proofs of its durability. Now, as Delia glanced about her at the Léopold Robert lithographs, the family daguerreotypes, the rosewood and mahogany, she understood that she was looking at the walls of her own grave.

The change had come on the day when Charlotte Lovell, cowering on that very lounge, had made her terrible avowal. Then for the first time Delia, with a kind of fearful exaltation, had heard the blind forces of life groping and crying underfoot. But on that day also she had known herself excluded from them, doomed to dwell among shadows. Life had passed her by, and left her with the Ralstons.

Very well, then! She would make the best of herself, and of the Ralstons. The vow was immediate and unflinching; and for nearly twenty years she had gone on observing it. Once only had she been not a Ralston but herself; once only had it seemed worth while. And now perhaps the same challenge had sounded again; again, for a moment, it might be worth while to live. Not for the sake of Clement Spender—poor Clement, married years ago to a plain determined cousin, who had hunted him down in Rome, and enclosing him in an unrelenting domesticity, had obliged all New York on the grand tour to buy his pictures with a resigned grimace. No, not for Clement Spender, hardly for Charlotte or even for Tina; but for her own sake, hers, Delia Ralston's, for the sake of her one missed vision, her forfeited reality, she would once more break down the Ralston barriers and reach out into the world.

A faint sound through the silent house disturbed her meditation. Listening, she heard Charlotte Lovell's door open and her stiff petticoats rustle toward the landing. A light glanced under the door and vanished; Charlotte had passed Delia's threshold on her way downstairs.

Without moving, Delia continued to listen. Perhaps the careful Charlotte had gone down to make sure that the front door was not bolted, or that she had really covered up the fire. If that were her object, her step would presently be heard returning. But no step sounded; and it became gradually evident that Charlotte had gone down to wait for her daughter. Why?

Delia's bedroom was at the front of the house. She stole across the heavy carpet, drew aside the curtains and cautiously folded back the inner shutters. Below her lay the empty square, white with moonlight, its tree-trunks patterned on a fresh sprinkling of snow. The houses opposite slept in darkness; not a footfall broke the white surface, not a wheel-track marred the brilliant street. Overhead a heaven full of stars swam in the moonlight.

Of the households around Gramercy Park Delia knew that only two others had gone to the ball: the Petrus Vandergraves and their cousins the young Parmly Ralstons. The Lucius Lannings had just entered on their three years of mourning for Mrs. Lucius's mother (it was hard on their daughter Kate, just eighteen, who would be unable to "come out" till she was twenty-one); young Mrs. Marcy Mingott was "expecting her third," and consequently secluded from the public eye for nearly a year; and the other denizens of the square belonged to the undifferentiated and uninvited.

Delia pressed her forehead against the pane. Before long carriages would turn the corner, the sleeping square ring with hoof-beats, fresh laughter and young farewells mount from the door-steps. But why was Charlotte waiting for her daughter downstairs in the darkness?

The Parisian clock struck one. Delia came back into the room, raked the fire, picked up a shawl, and wrapped in it, returned to her vigil. Ah, how old she must have grown that she should feel the cold at such a moment! It reminded her of what the future held for her: neuralgia, rheumatism, stiffness, accumulating infirmities. And never had she kept a moonlight watch with a lover's arms to warm her . . .

The square still lay silent. Yet the ball must surely be ending: the gayest dances did not last long after one in the morning, and the drive from University Place to Gramercy Park was a short one. Delia leaned in the embrasure and listened.

Hoof-beats, muffled by the snow, sounded in Irving Place, and the Petrus Vandergraves' family coach drew up before the opposite house. The Vandergrave girls and their brother sprang out and mounted the steps; then the coach stopped again a few doors farther on, and the Parmly Ralstons, brought home by their cousins, descended at their own door. The next carriage that rounded the corner must therefore be the John Juniuses', bringing Tina.

The gilt clock struck half-past one. Delia wondered, knowing that young Delia, out of regard for John Junius's business hours, never stayed late at evening parties. Doubtless Tina had delayed her; Mrs. Ralston felt a little annoyed with Tina's thoughtlessness in keeping her cousin up. But the feeling was swept away by an immediate wave of sympathy. "We must go away somewhere, and lead plain lives among plain people." If Charlotte carried out her threat—and Delia knew she would hardly have spoken unless her resolve had been taken—it might be that at that very moment poor Tina was dancing her last *valse*.

Another quarter of an hour passed; then, just as the cold was finding a way through Delia's shawl, she saw two people turn into the deserted square from Irving Place. One was a young man in opera hat and ample cloak. To his arm clung a figure so closely wrapped and muffled that, until the corner light fell on it, Delia hesitated. After that, she wondered that she had not at once recognized Tina's dancing step, and her manner of tilting her head a little sideways to look up at the person she was talking to.

Tina—Tina and Lanning Halsey, walking home alone in the small hours from the Vandergrave ball! Delia's first thought was of an accident: the carriage might have broken down, or else her daughter been taken ill and obliged to return home. But no; in the latter case she would have sent the carriage on with Tina. And if there had been an accident of any sort the young people would have been hastening to apprise Mrs. Ralston; instead of which, through the bitter brilliant night, they sauntered like lovers in a midsummer glade, and Tina's thin slippers might have been falling on daisies instead of snow.

Delia began to tremble like a girl. In a flash she had the answer to a question which had long been the subject of her secret conjectures. How did lovers like Charlotte and Clement Spender contrive to meet? What Latmian solitude hid their clandestine joys? In the exposed compact little society to which they all belonged, how was it possible—literally—for such encounters to take place? Delia would never have dared to put the question to Charlotte; there were moments when she almost preferred not to know, not even to hazard a guess. But now, at a glance, she understood. How often Charlotte Lovell, staying alone in town with her infirm grandmother, must have walked home from evening parties with Clement Spender, how often have let herself and him into the darkened house in Mercer Street, where there was no one to spy upon their coming but a deaf old lady and her aged servants, all securely sleeping overhead! Delia, at the thought, saw the grim drawing-room which had been their moonlit forest, the drawing-room into which old Mrs. Lovell no longer descended, with its swathed chandelier and hard Empire sofas, and the eyeless marble caryatids of the mantel; she pictured the shaft of moonlight falling across the swans and garlands of the faded carpet, and in that icy light two young figures in each other's arms.

Yes: it must have been some such memory that had roused Charlotte's suspicions, excited her fears, sent her down in the darkness to confront the culprits. Delia shivered at the irony of the confrontation. If Tina had but known! But to Tina, of course, Charlotte was still what she had long since resolved to be: the image of prudish spinsterhood. And Delia could imagine how quietly and decently the scene below stairs would presently be enacted: no astonishment, no reproaches, no insinuations, but a smiling and resolute ignoring of excuses.

"What, Tina? You walked home with Lanning? You imprudent child—in this wet snow! Ah, I see: Delia was worried about the baby, and ran off early, promising to send back the carriage—and it never came? Well, my dear, I congratulate you on finding Lanning to see you home . . . Yes—I sat up because I couldn't for the life of me remember whether you'd taken the latch-key—was there ever such a flighty old aunt? But don't tell your Mamma, dear, or she'd scold me for being so forgetful, and for staying downstairs in the cold . . . You're quite sure you have the key? Ah, Lanning has it? Thank you, Lanning; so kind! Goodnight—or one really ought to say, good morning."

As Delia reached this point in her mute representation of Charlotte's monologue the front door slammed below, and young Lanning Halsey walked slowly away across the square. Delia saw him pause on the opposite pavement, look up at the house-front, and then turn lingeringly away. His dismissal had taken exactly as long as Delia had calculated it would. A moment later she saw a passing light under her door, heard the starched rustle of Charlotte's petticoats, and knew that mother and daughter had reached their rooms.

Slowly, with stiff motions, she began to undress, blew out her candles, and knelt by her bedside, her face hidden.

§ 10

Lying awake till morning, Delia lived over every detail of the fateful day when she had assumed the charge of Charlotte's child. At the time she had been hardly more than a child herself, and there had been no one for her to turn to, no one to fortify her resolution, or to advise her how to put it into effect. Since then, the accumulated experiences of twenty years ought to have prepared her for emergencies, and taught her to advise others instead of seeking their guidance. But these years of experience weighed on her like chains binding her down to her narrow plot of life; independent action struck her as more dangerous, less conceivable, than when she had first ventured on it. There seemed to be so many more people to "consider" now ("consider" was the Ralston word): her children, their children, the families into which they had married. What would the Halseys say, and what the Ralstons? Had she then become a Ralston through and through?

A few hours later she sat in old Dr. Lanskell's library, her eyes on his sooty Smyrna rug. For some years now Dr. Lanskell had no longer practised: at most, he continued to go to a few old patients, and to give consultations in "difficult" cases. But he remained a power in his former kingdom, a sort of lay Pope or medical Elder to whom the patients he had once healed of physical ills often returned for moral medicine. People were agreed that Dr. Lanskell's judgments was sound; but what secretly drew them to him was the fact that, in the most totem-ridden of communities, he was known not to be afraid of anything.

Now, as Delia sat and watched his massive silver-headed figure moving ponderously about the room, between rows of medical books in calf bindings and the Dying Gladiators and Young Augustuses of grateful patients, she already felt the reassurance given by his mere bodily presence.

"You see, when I first took Tina I didn't perhaps consider sufficiently—"

The Doctor halted behind his desk and brought his fist down on it with a genial thump. "Thank goodness you didn't! There are considerers enough in this town without you, Delia Lovell."

She looked up quickly. "Why do you call me Delia Lovell?"

"Well, because today I rather suspect you *are,*" he rejoined astutely; and she met this with a wistful laugh.

"Perhaps, if I hadn't been, once before—I mean, if I'd always been a prudent deliberate Ralston it would have been kinder to Tina in the end."

Dr. Lanskell sank his gouty bulk into the armchair behind his desk, and beamed at her through ironic spectacles. "I hate in-the-end kindnesses: they're about as nourishing as the third day of cold mutton."

She pondered. "Of course I realize that if I adopt Tina—"

"Yes?"

"Well, people will say . . ." A deep blush rose to her throat, covered her cheeks and brow, and ran like fire under her decently-parted hair.

He nodded: "Yes."

"Or else—" the blush darkened—"that she's Jim's—"

Again Dr. Lanskell nodded. "That's what they're more likely to think; and what's the harm if they do? I know Jim: he asked you no questions when you took the child—but he knew whose she was."

She raised astonished eyes. "He knew—?"

"Yes: he came to me. And—well—in the baby's interest I violated professional secrecy. That's how Tina got a home. You're not going to denounce me, are you?"

"Oh, Dr. Lanskell—" Her eyes filled with painful tears. "Jim knew? And didn't tell me?"

"No. People didn't tell each other things much in those days, did they? But he admired you enormously for what you did. And if you assume—as I suppose you do—that he's now in a world of completer enlightenment, why not take it for granted that he'll admire you still more for what you're going to do? Presumably," the Doctor concluded sardonically, "people realize in heaven that it's a devilish sight harder, on earth, to do a brave thing at forty-five than at twenty-five."

"Ah, that's what I was thinking this morning," she confessed.

"Well, you're going to prove the contrary this afternoon." He looked at his watch, stood up and laid a fatherly hand on her shoulder. "Let people think what they choose; and send young Delia to me if she gives you any trouble. Your boy won't, you know, nor John Junius either; it must have been a woman who invented that third-and-fourth generation idea . . ."

An elderly maid-servant looked in, and Delia rose; but on the threshold she halted.

"I have an idea it's Charlotte I may have to send to you."

"Charlotte?"

"She'll hate what I'm going to do, you know."

Dr. Lanskell lifted his silver eyebrows. "Yes: poor Charlotte? I suppose she's jealous? That's where the truth of the third-and-fourth generation business comes in, after all. Somebody always has to foot the bill."

"Ah—if only Tina doesn't!"

"Well—that's just what Charlotte will come to recognize in time. So your course is clear."

He guided her out through the dining-room, where some poor people and one or two old patients were already waiting.

Delia's course, in truth, seemed clear enough till, that afternoon, she summoned Charlotte alone to her bedroom. Tina was lying down with a headache: it was in those days the accepted state of young ladies in sentimental dilemmas, and greatly simplified the communion of their elders.

Delia and Charlotte had exchanged only conventional phrases over their midday meal; but Delia still had the sense that her cousin's decision was final. The events of the previous evening had no doubt confirmed Charlotte's view that the time had come for such a decision.

Miss Lovell, closing the bedroom door with her dry deliberateness, advanced toward the chintz lounge between the windows.

"You wanted to see me, Delia?"

"Yes.—Oh, don't sit there," Mrs. Ralston exclaimed uncontrollably.

Charlotte stared: was it possible that she did not remember the sobs of anguish she had once smothered in those very cushions?

"Not—?"

"No; come nearer to me. Sometimes I think I'm a little deaf," Delia nervously explained, pushing a chair up to her own.

"Ah." Charlotte seated herself. "I hadn't remarked it. But if you are, it may have saved you from hearing at what hour of the morning Tina came back from the Vandergraves' last night. She would never forgive herself—inconsiderate as she is—if she thought she'd waked you."

"She didn't wake me," Delia answered. Inwardly she thought: "Charlotte's mind is made up; I shan't be able to move her."

"I suppose Tina enjoyed herself very much at the ball?" she continued.

"Well, she's paying for it with a headache. Such excitements are not meant for her, I've already told you—"

"Yes," Mrs. Ralston interrupted. "It's to continue our talk of last night that I've asked you to come up."

"To continue it?" The brick-red circles appeared on Charlotte's dried cheeks. "Is it worth while? I think I ought to tell you at once that my mind's made up. I suppose you'll admit that I know what's best for Tina."

"Yes; of course. But won't you at least allow me a share in your decision?"

"A share?"

Delia leaned forward, laying a warm hand on her cousin's interlocked fingers. "Charlotte, once in this room, years ago, you asked me to help you—you believed I could. Won't you believe it again?"

Charlotte's lips grew rigid. "I believe the time has come for me to help myself."

"At the cost of Tina's happiness?"

"No; but to spare her greater unhappiness."

"But, Charlotte, Tina's happiness is all I want."

"Oh, I know. You've done all you could do for my child."

"No; not all." Delia rose, and stood before her cousin with a kind of solemnity. "But now I'm going to." It was as if she had pronounced a vow.

Charlotte Lovell looked up at her with a glitter of apprehension in her hunted eyes.

"If you mean that you're going to use your influence with the Halseys— I'm very grateful to you; I shall always be grateful. But I don't want a compulsory marriage for my child."

Delia flushed at the other's incomprehension. It seemed to her that her tremendous purpose must be written on her face. "I'm going to adopt Tina—give her my name," she announced.

Charlotte Lovell stared at her stonily. "Adopt her—adopt her?"

"Don't you see, dear, the difference it will make? There's my mother's money—the Lovell money; it's not much, to be sure; but Jim always wanted it to go back to the Lovells. And my Delia and her brother are so handsomely provided for. There's no reason why my little fortune shouldn't go to Tina. And why she shouldn't be known as Tina Ralston." Delia paused. "I believe—I think I know that Jim would approved of that too."

"Approved?"

"Yes. Can't you see that when he let me take the child he must have foreseen and accepted whatever—whatever might eventually come of it?"

Charlotte stood up also. "Thank you, Delia. But nothing more must come of it, except our leaving you; our leaving you now. I'm sure that's what Jim would have approved."

Mrs. Ralston drew back a step or two. Charlotte's cold resolution benumbed her courage, and she could find no immediate reply.

"Ah, then it's easier for you to sacrifice Tina's happiness than your pride?" she exclaimed.

"My pride? I've no right to any pride, except in my child. And that I'll never sacrifice."

"No one asks you to. You're not reasonable. You're cruel. All I want is to be allowed to help Tina, and you speak as if I were interfering with your rights."

"My rights?" Charlotte echoed the words with a desolate laugh. "What are they? I have no rights, either before the law or in the heart of my own child."

"How can you say such things? You know how Tina loves you."

"Yes; compassionately—as I used to love my old-maid aunts. There were two of them—you remember? Like withered babies! We children used to be warned never to say anything that might shock Aunt Josie or Aunt Nonie; exactly as I heard you telling Tina the other night—"

"Oh—" Delia murmured.

Charlotte Lovell continued to stand before her, haggard, rigid, unrelenting. "No, it's gone on long enough. I mean to tell her everything; and to take her away."

"To tell her about her birth?"

"I was never ashamed of it," Charlotte panted.

"You do sacrifice her, then—sacrifice her to your desire for mastery?"

The two women faced each other, both with weapons spent. Delia, through the tremor of her own indignation, saw her antagonist slowly waver, step backward, sink down with a broken murmur on the lounge. Charlotte hid her face in the cushions, clenching them with violent hands. The same fierce maternal passion that had once flung her down upon those same cushions was now bowing her still lower, in the throes of a bitterer renunciation. Delia seemed to hear the old cry: "But how can I give up my baby?" Her own momentary resentment melted, and she bent over the mother's labouring shoulders.

"Chatty—it won't be like giving her up this time. Can't we just go on loving her together?"

Charlotte did not answer. For a long time she lay silent, immovable, her face hidden: she seemed to fear to turn it to the face bent down to her. But presently Delia was aware of a gradual relaxing of the stretched muscles, and saw that one of her cousin's arms was faintly stirring and grouping. She lowered her hand to the seeking fingers, and it was caught and pressed to Charlotte's lips.

§ 11

Tina Lovell—now Miss Clementina Ralston—was to be married in July to Lanning Halsey. The engagement had been announced only in the previous April; and the female elders of the tribe had begun by crying out against the indelicacy of so brief a betrothal. It was unanimously agreed in the New York of those times that "young people should be given the chance to get to know each other"; though the greater number of the couples constituting New York society had played together as children, and been born of parents as long and as familiarly acquainted, yet some mysterious law of decorum required that the newly affianced should always be regarded as being also newly known to each other. In the southern states things were differently conducted: headlong engagements, even runaway marriages, were not uncommon in their annals; but such rashness was less consonant with the sluggish blood of New York, where the pace of life was still set with a Dutch deliberateness.

In a case as unusual as Tina Ralston's, however, it was no great surprise to any one that tradition should have been disregarded. In the first place, everybody knew that she was no more Tina Ralston than you or I; unless, indeed, one were to credit the rumours about poor Jim's unsuspected "past," and his widow's magnanimity. But the opinion of the majority was against this. People were reluctant to charge a dead man with an offense from which he could not clear himself; and the Ralstons unanimously declared that, thoroughly as they disapproved of Mrs. James Ralston's action, they were convinced that she would not have adopted Tina if her doing so could have been construed as "casting a slur" on her late husband.

No: the girl was perhaps a Lovell—though even that idea was not generally held—but she was certainly not a Ralston. Her brown eyes and flighty ways too obviously excluded her from the clan for any formal excommunication to be needful. In fact, most people believed that—as Dr. Lanksell had always affirmed—her origin was really undiscoverable, that she represented one of the unsolved mysteries which occasionally perplex and irritate well-regulated societies, and that her adoption by Delia Ralston was simply one more proof of the Lovell clannishness, since the child had been taken in by Mrs. Ralston only because her cousin Charlotte was so attached to it. To say that Mrs. Ralston's son and daughter were pleased with the idea of Tina's adoption would be an exaggeration; but they abstained from comment, minimizing the effect of their mother's whim by a dignified silence. It was the old New York way for families thus to screen the eccentricities of an individual member, and where there was "money enough to go round" the heirs would have been thought vulgarly grasping to protest at the alienation of a small sum from the general inheritance.

Nevertheless, Delia Ralston, from the moment of Tina's adoption, was perfectly aware of a different attitude on the part of both her children. They dealt with her patiently, almost parentally, as with a minor in whom one juvenile lapse has been condoned, but who must be subjected, in consequence, to a stricter vigilance; and society treated her in the same indulgent but guarded manner.

She had (it was Sillerton Jackson who first phrased it) an undoubted way of "carrying things off"; since that dauntless woman, Mrs. Manson Mingott, had broken her husband's will, nothing so like her attitude had been seen in New York. But Mrs. Ralston's method was different, and less easy to analyze. What Mrs. Manson Mingott had accomplished by dint of epigram, invective, insistency and runnings to and fro, the other achieved without raising her voice or seeming to take a step from the beaten path. When she had persuaded Jim Ralston to take in the foundling baby, it had been done in the turn of a hand, one didn't know when or how; and the next day he and she were as untroubled and beaming as usual. And now, this adoption—! Well, she had pursued the same method; as Sillerton Jackson said, she behaved as if her adopting Tina had always been an understood thing, as if she wondered that people should wonder. And in face of her wonder theirs seemed foolish, and they gradually desisted.

In reality, behind Delia's assurance there was a tumult of doubts and uncertainties. But she had once learned that one can do almost anything (perhaps even murder) if one does not attempt to explain it; and the lesson had never been forgotten. She had never explained the taking over of the foundling baby; nor was she now going to explain its adoption. She was just going about her business as if nothing had happened that needed to be accounted for; and a long inheritance of moral modesty helped her to keep her questionings to herself.

These questionings were in fact less concerned with public opinion than with Charlotte Lovell's private thoughts. Charlotte, after her first moment of tragic resistance, had shown herself pathetically, almost painfully, grateful. That she had reason to be, Tina's attitude abundantly revealed. Tina, during the first days after her return from the Vandergrave ball, had shown a closed and darkened face that terribly reminded Delia of the ghastliness of Charlotte Lovell's sudden reflection, years before, in Delia's own bedroom mirror. The first chapter of the mother's history was already written in the daughter's eyes; and the Spender blood in Tina might well precipitate the sequence. During those few days of silent observation Delia discovered, with terror and compassion, the justification of Charlotte's fears. The girl had nearly been lost to them both: at all costs such a risk must not be renewed.

The Halseys, on the whole, had behaved admirably. Lanning wished to marry dear Delia Ralston's protégée—who was shortly, it was understood, to take her adopted mother's name, and inherit her fortune. To what better could a Halsey aspire than one more alliance with a Ralston? The families had always intermarried. The Halsey parents gave their blessing with a precipitation which showed that they too had their anxieties, and that the relief of seeing Lanning "settled" would more than compensate for the conceivable drawbacks of the marriage; though, once it was decided on, they would not admit even to themselves that such drawbacks existed. Old New York always thought away whatever interfered with the perfect propriety of its arrangements.

Charlotte Lovell of course perceived and recognized all this. She accepted the situation—in her private hours with Delia—as one more in the long list of mercies bestowed on an undeserving sinner.

And one phrase of hers perhaps gave the clue to her acceptance: "Now at least she'll never suspect the truth." It had come to be the poor creature's ruling purpose that her child should never guess the tie between them . . .

But Delia's chief support was the sight of Tina. The older woman, whose whole life had been shaped and coloured by the faint reflection of a rejected happiness, hung dazzled in the light of bliss accepted. Sometimes, as she watched Tina's changing face, she felt as though her own blood were beating in it, as though she could read every thought and emotion feeding those tumultuous currents. Tina's love was a stormy affair, with continual ups and downs of rapture and depression, arrogance and self-abasement; Delia saw displayed before her, with an artless frankness, all the visions, cravings and imaginings of her own stifled youth.

What the girl really thought of her adoption it was not easy to discover. She had been given, at fourteen, the current version of her origin, and had accepted it as carelessly as a happy child accepts some remote and inconceivable fact which does not alter the familiar order of things. And she accepted her adoption in the same spirit. She knew that the name of Ralston had been given to her to facilitate her marriage with Lanning Halsey; and Delia had the impression that all irrelevant questionings were submerged in an overwhelming gratitude. "I've always thought of you as my Mamma; and now, you dearest, you really are," Tina had whispered, her cheek against Delia's; and Delia had laughed back: "Well, if the lawyers can make me so!" But there the matter dropped, swept away on the current of Tina's bliss. They were all, in those days, Delia, Charlotte, even the gallant Lanning, rather like straws whirling about on a sunlit torrent.

The golden flood bore them onward, nearer and nearer to the enchanted date; and Delia, deep in bridal preparations, wondered at the comparative indifference with which she had ordered and inspected her own daughter's twelve-dozen-of-everything. There had been nothing to quicken the pulse in young Delia's placid bridal; but as Tina's wedding approached imagination burgeoned like the year. The wedding was to be celebrated at Lovell Place, the old house on the Sound where Delia Lovell had herself been married, and where, since her mother's death, she spent her summers. Although the neighbourhood was already overspread with a net-work of mean streets, the old house, with its thin colonnaded verandah, still looked across an uncurtailed lawn and leafy shrubberies to the narrows of Hell Gate; and the drawing-rooms kept their frail slender settees, their Sheraton consoles and cabinets. It had been thought useless to discard them for more fashionable furniture, since the growth of the city made it certain that the place must eventually be sold.

Tina, like Mrs. Ralston, was to have a "house-wedding," though Episcopalian society was beginning to disapprove of such ceremonies, which were regarded as the despised *pis-aller* of Baptists, Methodists, Unitarians and the other altarless sects. In Tina's case, however, both Delia and Charlotte felt that the greater privacy of a marriage in the house made up for its more secular character; and the Halseys favoured their decision. The ladies accordingly settled themselves at Lovell Place before the end of June, and every morning young Lanning Halsey's cat-boat was seen beating across the bay, and furling its sail at the anchorage below the lawn.

There had never been a fairer June in any one's memory. The damask roses and mignonette below the verandah had never sent such a breath of summer through the tall French windows; the gnarled orange-trees brought out from the old arcaded orange-house had never been so thickly blossomed; the very haycocks on the lawn gave out whiffs of Araby.

The evening before the wedding Delia Ralston sat on the verandah watching the moon rise across the Sound. She was tired with the multitude of last preparations, and sad at the thought of Tina's going. On the following evening the house would be empty: till death came, she and Charlotte would sit alone together beside the evening lamp. Such repinings were foolish—they were, she reminded herself, "not like her." But too many memories stirred and murmured in her: her heart was haunted. As she closed the door on the silent drawing-room—already transformed into a chapel, with its lace-hung altar, the tall alabaster vases awaiting their white roses and June lilies, the strip of red carpet dividing the rows of chairs from door to chancel—she felt that it had perhaps been a mistake to come back to Lovell Place for the wedding. She saw herself again, in her high-waisted "India mull" embroidered with daisies, her flat satin sandals, her Brussels veil—saw again her reflection in the shallow pier-glass as she had left that same room on Jim Ralston's triumphant arm, and the one terrified glance she had exchanged with her own image before she took her stand under the bell of white roses in the hall, and smiled upon the congratulating company. Ah, what a different image the pier-glass would reflect tomorrow!

Charlotte Lovell's brisk step sounded indoors, and she came out and joined Mrs. Ralston.

"I've been to the kitchen to tell Melissa Grimes that she'd better count on at least two hundred plates of ice-cream."

"Two hundred? Yes—I suppose she had, with all the Philadelphia connection coming." Delia pondered. "How about the doylies?" she enquired.

"With your aunt Cecilia Vandergrave's we shall manage beautifully."

"Yes.—Thank you, Charlotte, for taking all this trouble."

"Oh—" Charlotte protested, with her flitting sneer; and Delia perceived the irony of thanking a mother for occupying herself with the details of her own daughter's wedding.

"Do sit down, Chatty," she murmured, feeling herself redden at her blunder.

Charlotte, with a sigh of fatigue, sat down on the nearest chair.

"We shall have a beautiful day tomorrow," she said, pensively surveying the placid heaven.

"Yes. Where is Tina?"

"She was very tired. I've sent her upstairs to lie down."

This seemed so eminently suitable that Delia made no immediate answer. After an interval she said: "We shall miss her."

Charlotte's reply was an inarticulate murmur.

The two cousins remained silent, Charlotte as usual bolt upright, her thin hands clutched on the arms of her old-fashioned rush-bottomed seat, Delia somewhat heavily sunk into the depths of a high-backed armchair. The two had exchanged their last remarks on the preparations for the morrow; nothing more remained to be said as to the number of guests, the brewing of the punch, the arrangements for the robing of the clergy, and the disposal of the presents in the best spare-room.

Only one subject had not yet been touched upon, and Delia, as she watched her cousin's profile grimly cut upon the melting twilight, waited for Charlotte to speak. But Charlotte remained silent.

"I have been thinking," Delia at length began, a slight tremor in her voice, "that I ought presently—"

She fancied she saw Charlotte's hands tighten on the knobs of the chair-arms.

"You ought presently—?"

"Well, before Tina goes to bed, perhaps go up for a few minutes—"

Charlotte remained silent, visibly resolved on making no effort to assist her.

"Tomorrow," Delia continued, "we shall be in such a rush from the earliest moment that I don't see how, in the midst of all the interruptions and excitement, I can possibly—"

"Possibly?" Charlotte monotonously echoed.

Delia felt her blush deepening through the dusk. "Well, I suppose you agree with me, don't you, that a word ought to be said to the child as to the new duties and responsibilities that—well—what is usual, in fact, at such a time?" she falteringly ended.

"Yes, I have thought of that," Charlotte answered. She said no more, but Delia divined in her tone the stirring of that obscure opposition which, at the crucial moments of Tina's life, seemed automatically to declare itself. She could not understand why Charlotte should, at such times, grow so enigmatic and inaccessible, and in the present case she saw no reason why this change of mood should interfere with what she deemed to be her own duty. Tina must long for her guiding hand into the new life as much as she herself yearned for the exchange of half-confidences which would be her real farewell to her adopted daughter. Her heart beating a little more quickly than usual, she rose and walked through the open window into the shadowy drawing-room. The moon, between the columns of the verandah, sent a broad band of light across the rows of chairs, irradiated the lace-decked altar with its empty candlesticks and vases, and outlined with silver Delia's heavy reflection in the pier-glass.

She crossed the room toward the hall.

"Delia!" Charlotte's voice sounded behind her. Delia turned, and the two women scrutinized each other in the revealing light. Charlotte's face looked as it had looked on the dreadful day when Delia had suddenly seen it in the looking-glass above her shoulder.

"You were going up now to speak to Tina?" Charlotte asked.

"I—yes. It's nearly nine. I thought . . ."

"Yes; I understand." Miss Lovell made a visible effort at self-control. "Please understand me too, Delia, if I ask you—not to."

Delia looked at her cousin with a vague sense of apprehension. What new mystery did this strange request conceal? But no—such a doubt as flitted across her mind was inadmissible. She was too sure of her Tina!

"I confess I don't understand, Charlotte. You surely feel that, on the night before her wedding, a girl ought to have a mother's counsel, a mother's . . ."

"Yes; I feel that." Charlotte Lovell took a hurried breath. "But the question is: *which of us is her mother?"*

Delia drew back involuntarily. "Which of us—?" she stammered.

"Yes. Oh, don't imagine it's the first time I've asked myself the question! There—I mean to be calm; quite calm. I don't intend to go back to the past. I've accepted—accepted everything—gratefully. Only tonight—just tonight . . ."

Delia felt the rush of pity which always prevailed over every other sensation in her rare interchanges of truth with Charlotte Lovell. Her throat filled with tears, and she remained silent.

"Just tonight," Charlotte concluded, *"I'm* her mother."

"Charlotte! You're not going to tell her so—not now?" broke involuntarily from Delia.

Charlotte gave a faint laugh. "If I did, should you hate it as much as all that?"

"Hate it? What a word, between us!"

"Between us? But it's the word that's been between us since the beginning—the very beginning! Since the day when you discovered that Clement Spender hadn't quite broken his heart because he wasn't good enough for you; since you found your revenge and your triumph in keeping me at your mercy, and in taking his child from me!" Charlotte's words flamed up as if from the depth of the infernal fires; then the blaze dropped, her head sank forward, and she stood before Delia dumb and stricken.

Delia's first movement was one of an indignant recoil. Where she had felt only tenderness, compassion, the impulse to help and befriend, these darknesses had been smouldering in the other's breast! It was as if a poisonous smoke had swept over some pure summer landscape . . .

Usually such feelings were quickly followed by a reaction of sympathy. But now she felt none. An utter weariness possessed her.

"Yes," she said slowly, "I sometimes believe you really have hated me from the very first; hated me for everything I've tried to do for you."

Charlotte raised her head sharply. "To do for me? But everything you've done has been done for Clement Spender!"

Delia stared at her with a kind of terror. "You are horrible, Charlotte. Upon my honour, I haven't thought of Clement Spender for years."

"Ah, but you have—you have! You've always thought of him in thinking of Tina—of him and nobody else! A woman never stops thinking of the man she loves. She thinks of him years afterward, in all sorts of unconscious ways, in thinking of all sorts of things—books, pictures, sunsets, a flower or a ribbon—or a clock on the mantelpiece," Charlotte broke off with her sneering laugh. "That was what I gambled on, you see—that's why I came to you that day. I knew I was giving Tina another mother."

Again the poisonous smoke seemed to envelop Delia: that she and Charlotte, two spent old women, should be standing before Tina's bridal altar and talking to each other of hatred, seemed unimaginably hideous and degrading.

"You wicked woman—you *are* wicked!" she exclaimed.

Then the evil mist cleared away, and through it she saw the baffled pitiful figure of the mother who was not a mother, and who, for every benefit accepted, felt herself robbed of a privilege. She moved nearer to Charlotte and laid a hand on her arm.

"Not here! Don't let us talk like this here."

The other drew away from her. "Wherever you please, then. I'm not particular!"

"But tonight, Charlotte—the night before Tina's wedding? Isn't every place in this house full of her? How could we go on saying cruel things to each other anywhere?" Charlotte was silent, and

Delia continued in a steadier voice: "Nothing you say can really hurt me—for long; and I don't want to hurt you—I never did."

"You tell me that—and you've left nothing undone to divide me from my daughter! Do you suppose it's been easy, all these years, to hear her call you 'mother'? Oh, I know, I know—it was agreed that she must never guess . . . but if you hadn't perpetually come between us she'd have had no one but me, she'd have felt about me as a child feels about its mother, she'd have *had* to love me better than any one else. With all your forbearances and your generosities you've ended by robbing me of my child. And I've put up with it all for her sake—because I knew I had to. But tonight—tonight she belongs to me. Tonight I can't bear that she should call you 'mother'."

Delia Ralston made no immediate reply. It seemed to her that for the first time she had sounded the deepest depths of maternal passion, and she stood awed of the echoes it gave back.

"How you must love her—to say such things to me," she murmured; then, with a final effort: "Yes, you're right. I won't go up to her. It's you who must go."

Charlotte started toward her impulsively; but with a hand lifted as if in defense, Delia moved across the room and out again to the verandah. As she sank down in her chair she heard the drawing-room door open and close, and the sound of Charlotte's feet on the stairs.

Delia sat alone in the night. The last drop of her magnanimity had been spent, and she tried to avert her shuddering mind from Charlotte. What was happening at this moment upstairs? With what dark revelations were Tina's bridal dreams to be defaced? Well, that was not matter for conjecture either. She, Delia Ralston, had played her part, done her utmost: there remained nothing now but to try to lift her spirit above the embittering sense of failure.

There was a strange element of truth in some of the things that Charlotte had said. With what divination her maternal passion had endowed her! Her jealousy seemed to have a million feelers. Yes; it was true that the sweetness and peace of Tina's bridal eve had been filled, for Delia, with visions of her own unrealized past. Softly, imperceptibly, it had reconciled her to the memory of what she had missed. All these last days she had been living the girl's life, she had been Tina, and Tina had been her own girlish self, the far-off Delia Lovell. Now for the first time, without shame, without self-reproach, without a pang or a scruple, Delia could yield to that vision of requited love from which her imagination had always turned away. She had made her choice in youth, and she had accepted it in maturity; and here in this bridal joy, so mysteriously her own, was the compensation for all she had missed and yet never renounced.

Delia understood now that Charlotte had guessed all this, and that the knowledge had filled her with a fierce resentment. Charlotte had said long ago that Clement Spender had never really belonged to her; now she had perceived that it was the same with Clement Spender's child. As the truth stole upon Delia her heart melted with the old compassion for Charlotte. She saw that it was a terrible, a sacrilegious thing to interfere with another's destiny, to lay the tenderest touch upon any human being's right to love and suffer after his own fashion. Delia had twice intervened in Charlotte Lovell's life: it was natural that Charlotte should be her enemy. If only she did not revenge herself by wounding Tina!

The adopted mother's thoughts reverted painfully to the little white room upstairs. She had meant her half-hour with Tina to leave the girl with thoughts as fragrant as the flowers she was to find beside her when she woke. And now—.

Delia started up from her musing. There was a step on the stair —Charlotte coming down through the silent house. Delia rose with a vague impulse of escape: she felt that she could not face her cousin's eyes. She turned the corner of the verandah, hoping to find the shutters of the dining-room unlatched, and to slip away unnoticed to her room; but in a moment Charlotte was beside her.

"Delia!"

"Ah, it's you? I was going up to bed." For the life of her Delia could not keep an edge of hardness from her voice.

"Yes: it's late. You must be very tired." Charlotte paused; her own voice was strained and painful.

"I *am* tired," Delia acknowledged.

In the moonlit hush the other went up to her, laying a timid touch on her arm.

"Not till you've seen Tina."

Delia stiffened. "Tina? But it's late! Isn't she sleeping? I thought you'd stay with her until—"

"I don't know if she's sleeping," Charlotte paused. "I haven't been in—but there's a light under her door."

"You haven't been in?"

"No: I just stood in the passage, and tried—"

"Tried—?"

"To think of something . . . something to say to her without . . . without her guessing . . ." A sob stopped her, but she pressed on with a final effort. "It's no use. You were right: there's nothing I can say. You're her real mother. Go to her. It's not your fault—or mine."

"Oh—" Delia cried.

Charlotte clung to her in inarticulate abasement. "You said I was wicked—I'm not wicked. After all, she was mine when she was little!"

Delia put an arm about her shoulder.

"Hush, dear! We'll go to her together."

The other yielded automatically to her touch, and side by side the two women mounted the stairs, Charlotte timing her impetuous step to Delia's stiffened movements. They walked down the passage to Tina's door; but there Charlotte Lovell paused and shook her head.

"No—you," she whispered, and turned away.

Tina lay in bed, her arms folded under her head, her happy eyes reflecting the silver space of sky which filled the window. She smiled at Delia through her dream.

"I knew you'd come."

Delia sat down beside her, and their clasped hands lay down upon the coverlet. They did not say much, after all; or else their communion had no need of words. Delia never knew how long she sat by the child's side: she abandoned herself to the spell of the moonlit hour.

But suddenly she thought of Charlotte, alone behind the shut door of her own room, watching, struggling, listening. Delia must not, for her own pleasure, prolong that tragic vigil. She bent down to kiss Tina goodnight; then she paused on the threshold and turned back.

"Darling! Just one thing more."

"Yes?" Tina murmured through her dream.

"I want you to promise me—"

"Everything, everything, you darling mother!"

"Well, then, that when you go away tomorrow—at the very last moment, you understand—"

"Yes?"

"After you've said goodbye to me, and to everybody else—just as Lanning helps you into the carriage—"

"Yes?"

"That you'll give your last kiss to Aunt Charlotte. Don't forget—the very last."

PREFATORY NOTE TO "POMEGRANTE SEED" AND "A BOTTLE OF PERRIER"

Edith Wharton wrote ghost stories throughout her life and published two compilations of them, *Tales of Men and Ghosts* and *Ghosts.* Unlike the rest of her fiction this category continued to improve in quality to the end, for being removed from the actual world, it was not weighed down by the doses of clumsy satire that marred the later novels. *Pomegranate Seed,* which appeared in *The World Over* (1930) is the most perfect of her thrillers, for the reader's awareness of who it is that has written the mysterious, illegible letters which so unnerve Kenneth Ashby, comes at just the same moment as his wife's. In this specialized brand of fiction Mrs. Wharton's remarkable craftsmanship can be observed, so to speak, in a vacuum.

A Bottle of Perrier, from *Certain People* (1936) which is not, strictly speaking, a ghost story, but a tale of hatred and murder in the North African desert, is yet quite as eerie and chilling as any of the former category. Mrs. Wharton's style was never richer in setting her background: "The afternoon hung over the place like a great velarium of cloth-of-gold stretched across the battlements and drooping down in ever slacker folds upon the heavy-headed palms." And the final sentence is like a screaming chord from Strauss' *Salome:* "The moon, swinging high above the battlements, sent a searching spear of light down into the guilty darkness of the well."

A Bottle of Perrier

§ 1

A TWO DAYS' struggle over the treacherous trails in a well-intentioned but short-winded "flivver", and a ride of two more on a hired mount of unamiable temper, had disposed young Medford, of the American School of Archæology at Athens, to wonder why his queer English friend, Henry Almodham, had chosen to live in the desert.

Now he understood.

He was leaning against the roof parapet of the old building, half Christian fortress, half Arab palace, which had been Almodham's pretext; or one of them. Below, in an inner court, a little wind, rising as the sun sank, sent through a knot of palms the rain-like rattle so cooling to the pilgrims of the desert. An ancient fig tree, enormous, exuberant, writhed over a whitewashed well-head, sucking life from what appeared to be the only source of moisture within the walls. Beyond these, on every side, stretched away the mystery of the sands, all golden with promise, all livid with menace, as the sun alternately touched or abandoned them.

Young Medford, somewhat weary after his journey from the coast, and awed by his first intimate sense of the omnipresence of the desert, shivered and drew back. Undoubtedly, for a scholar and a misogynist, it was a wonderful refuge; but one would have to be, incurably, both.

"Let's take a look at the house," Medford said to himself, as if speedy contact with man's handiwork were necessary to his reassurance.

The house, he already knew, was empty save for the quick cosmopolitan man-servant, who spoke a sort of palimpsest Cockney lined with Mediterranean tongues and desert dialects—English, Italian or Greek, which was he?—and two or three burnoused underlings who, having carried Medford's bags to his room, had relieved the place of their gliding presences. Mr. Almodham, the servant told him, was away; suddenly summoned by a friendly chief to visit some unexplored ruins to the south, he had ridden off at dawn, too hurriedly to write, but leaving messages of excuse and regret. That evening late he might be back, or next morning. Meanwhile Mr. Medford was to make himself at home.

Almodham, as young Medford knew, was always making these archæological explorations; they had been his ostensible reason for settling in that remote place, and his desultory search had already resulted in the discovery of several early Christian ruins of great interest.

Medford was glad that his host had not stood on ceremony, and rather relieved, on the whole, to have the next few hours to himself. He had had a malarial fever the previous summer, and in spite of his cork helmet he had probably caught a touch of the sun; he felt curiously, helplessly tired, yet deeply content.

And what a place it was to rest in! The silence, the remoteness, the illimitable air! And in the heart of the wilderness green leafage, water, comfort—he had already caught a glimpse of wide wicker chairs under the palms—a humane and welcoming habitation. Yes, he began to understand Almodham. To anyone sick of the Western fret and fever the very walls of this desert fortress exuded peace.

As his foot was on the ladder-like stair leading down from the roof, Medford saw the man-servant's head rising toward him. It rose slowly and Medford had time to remark that it was sallow, bald on the top, diagonally dented with a long white scar, and ringed with thick ash-blond hair. Hitherto Medford had noticed only the man's face—youngish, but sallow also—and been chiefly struck by its wearing an odd expression which could best be defined as surprise.

The servant, moving aside, looked up, and Medford perceived that his air of surprise was produced by the fact that his intensely blue eyes were rather wider open than most eyes, and fringed with thick ash-blond lashes; otherwise there was nothing noticeable about him.

"Just to ask—what wine for dinner, sir? Champagne, or—"

"No wine, thanks."

The man's disciplined lips were played over by a faint flicker of deprecation or irony, or both.

"Not any at all, sir?"

Medford smiled back. "It's not out of respect for Prohibition." He was sure that the man, of whatever nationality, would understand that; and he did.

"Oh, I didn't suppose, sir—"

"Well, no; but I've been rather seedy, and wine's forbidden."

The servant remained incredulous. "Just a little light Moselle, though, to colour the water, sir?"

"No wine at all," said Medford, growing bored. He was still in the stage of convalescence when it is irritating to be argued with about one's dietary.

"Oh—what's your name, by the way?" he added, to soften the curtness of his refusal.

"Gosling," said the other unexpectedly, though Medford didn't in the least know what he had expected him to be called.

"You're English, then?"

"Oh, yes, sir."

"You've been in these parts a good many years, though?"

Yes, he had, Gosling said; rather too long for his own liking; and added that he had been born at Malta. "But I know England well too." His deprecating look returned. "I will confess, sir, I'd like to have 'ad a look at Wembley.* Mr. Almodham 'ad promised me—but there—" As if to minimize the *abandon* of this confidence, he followed it up by a ceremonious request for Medford's keys, and an enquiry as to when he would like to dine. Having received a reply, he still lingered, looking more surprised than ever.

"Just a mineral water, then, sir?"

"Oh, yes—anything."

"Shall we say a bottle of Perrier?"

Perrier in the desert! Medford smiled assentingly, surrendered his keys and strolled away.

* The famous exhibition at Wembley, near London, took place in 1924.

The house turned out to be smaller than he had imagined, or at least the habitable part of it; for above this towered mighty dilapidated walls of yellow stone, and in their crevices clung plaster chambers, one above the other, cedar-beamed, crimson-shuttered but crumbling. Out of this jumble of masonry and stucco, Christian and Moslem, the latest tenant of the fortress had chosen a cluster of rooms tucked into an angle of the ancient keep. These apartments opened on the uppermost court, where the palms chattered and the fig tree coiled above the well. On the broken marble pavement, chairs and a low table were grouped, and a few geraniums and blue morning-glories had been coaxed to grow between the slabs.

A white-skirted boy with watchful eyes was watering the plants; but at Medford's approach he vanished like a wisp of vapour.

There was something vaporous and insubstantial about the whole scene; even the long arcaded room opening on the court, furnished with saddlebag cushions, divans with gazelle skins and rough indigenous rugs; even the table piled with old *Timeses* and ultramodern French and English reviews—all seemed, in that clear mocking air, born of the delusion of some desert wayfarer.

A seat under the fig tree invited Medford to doze, and when he woke the hard blue dome above him was gemmed with stars and the night breeze gossiped with the palms.

Rest—beauty—peace. Wise Almodham!

§ 2

Wise Almodham! Having carried out—with somewhat disappointing results—the excavation with which an archæological society had charged him twenty-five years ago, he had lingered on, taken possession of the Crusaders' stronghold, and turned his attention from ancient to mediæval remains. But even these investigations, Medford suspected, he prosecuted only at intervals, when the enchantment of his leisure did not lie on him too heavily.

The young American had met Henry Almodham at Luxor the previous winter; had dined with him at old Colonel Swordsley's, on that perfumed starlit terrace above the Nile; and, having somehow awakened the archæologist's interest, had been invited to look him up in the desert the following year.

They had spent only that one evening together, with old Swordsley blinking at them under memory-laden lids, and two or three charming women from the Winter Palace chattering and exclaiming; but the two men had ridden back to Luxor together in the moonlight, and during that ride Medford fancied he had puzzled out the essential lines of Henry Almodham's character. A nature saturnine yet sentimental; chronic indolence alternating with spurts of highly intelligent activity; gnawing self-distrust soothed by intimate self-appreciation; a craving for complete solitude coupled with the inability to tolerate it for long.

There was more, too, Medford suspected; a dash of Victorian romance, gratified by the setting, the remoteness, the inaccessibility of his retreat, and by being known as *the* Henry Almodham—"the one who lives in a Crusaders' castle, you know"—the gradual imprisonment in a pose assumed in youth, and into which middle age had slowly stiffened; and something deeper, darker, too, perhaps, though the young man doubted that; probably just the fact that living in that particular way had brought healing to an old wound, an old mortification, something which years ago had touched a vital part and left him writhing. Above all, in Almodham's hesitating movements and the dreaming look of his long well-featured brown face with its shock of gray hair, Medford detected an inertia, mental and moral, which life in this castle of romance must have fostered and excused.

"Once here, how easy not to leave!" he mused, sinking deeper into his deep chair.

"Dinner, sir," Gosling announced.

The table stood in an open arch of the living-room; shaded candles made a rosy pool in the dusk. Each time he emerged into their light the servant, white-jacketed, velvet-footed, looked more competent and more surprised than ever. Such dishes, too—the cook also a Maltese? Ah, they were geniuses, these Maltese! Gosling bridled, smiled his acknowledgment, and started to fill the guest's glass with Chablis.

"No wine," said Medford patiently.

"Sorry, sir. But the fact is—"

"You said there was Perrier?"

"Yes, sir; but I find there's none left. It's been awfully hot, and

Mr. Almodham has been and drank it all up. The new supply isn't due till next week. We 'ave to depend on the caravans going south."

"No matter. Water, then. I really prefer it."

Gosling's surprise widened to amazement. "Not water, sir? Water—in these parts?"

Medford's irritability stirred again. "Something wrong with your water? Boil it then, can't you? I won't—" He pushed away the half-filled wineglass.

"Oh—boiled? Certainly, sir." The man's voice dropped almost to a whisper. He placed on the table a succulent mess of rice and mutton, and vanished.

Medford leaned back, surrendering himself to the night, the coolness, the ripple of wind in the palms.

One agreeable dish succeeded another. As the last appeared, the diner began to feel the pangs of thirst, and at the same moment a beaker of water was placed at his elbow. "Boiled, sir, and I squeezed a lemon into it."

"Right. I suppose at the end of the summer your water gets a bit muddy?"

"That's it, sir. But you'll find this all right, sir."

Medford tasted. "Better than Perrier." He emptied the glass, leaned back and groped in his pocket. A tray was instantly at his hand with cigars and cigarettes.

"You don't—smoke, sir?"

Medford, for answer, held up his cigar to the man's light. "What do you call this?"

"Oh, just so. I meant the other style." Gosling glanced discreetly at the opium pipes of jade and amber laid out on a low table.

Medford shrugged away the invitation—and wondered. Was that perhaps Almodham's other secret—or one of them? For he began to think there might be many; and all, he was sure, safely stored away behind Gosling's vigilant brow.

"No news yet of Mr. Almodham?"

Gosling was gathering up the dishes with dexterous gestures. For a moment he seemed not to hear. Then—from beyond the candle gleam—"News, sir? There couldn't 'ardly be, could there? There's no wireless in the desert, sir; not like London." His respectful tone tempered the slight irony. "But tomorrow evening ought to see him riding in." Gosling paused, drew nearer, swept one of his swift hands across the table in pursuit of the last crumbs, and added tentatively: "You'll surely be able, sir, to stay till then?"

Medford laughed. The night was too rich in healing; it sank on his spirit like wings. Time vanished, fret and trouble were no more. "Stay? I'll stay a year if I have to!"

"Oh—a year?" Gosling echoed it playfully, gathered up the dessert dishes and was gone.

§ 3

Medford had said that he would wait for Almodham a year; but the next morning he found that such arbitrary terms had lost their meaning. There were no time measures in a place like this. The silly face of his watch told its daily tale to emptiness. The wheeling of the constellations over those ruined walls marked only the revolutions of the earth; the spasmodic motions of man meant nothing.

The very fact of being hungry, that stroke of the inward clock, was minimized by the slightness of the sensation—just the ghost of a pang, that might have been quieted by dried fruit and honey. Life had the light monotonous smoothness of eternity.

Toward sunset Medford shook off this queer sense of otherwhereness and climbed to the roof. Across the desert he spied for Almodham. Southward the Mountains of Alabaster hung like a blue veil lined with light. In the west a great column of fire shot up, spraying into plumy cloudlets which turned the sky to a fountain of rose-leaves, the sands beneath to gold.

No riders specked them. Medford watched in vain for his absent host till night fell, and the punctual Gosling invited him once more to table.

In the evening Medford absently fingered the ultra-modern reviews—three months old, and already so stale to the touch—then tossed them aside, flung himself on a divan and dreamed. Almodham must spend a lot of time in dreaming; that was it. Then, just as he felt himself sinking down into torpor, he would be off on one of these dashes across the desert in quest of unknown ruins. Not such a bad life.

Gosling appeared with Turkish coffee in a cup cased in filigree.

"Are there any horses in the stable?" Medford suddenly asked.

"Horses? Only what you might call pack-horses, sir. Mr. Almodham has the two best saddle-horses with him."

"I was thinking I might ride out to meet him."

Gosling considered. "So you might, sir."

"Do you know which way he went?"

"Not rightly, sir. The caid's man was to guide them."

"Them? Who went with him?"

"Just one of our men, sir. They've got the two thoroughbreds. There's a third, but he's lame." Gosling paused. "Do you know the trails, sir? Excuse me, but I don't think I ever saw you here before."

"No," Medford acquiesced, "I've never been here before."

"Oh, then"—Gosling's gesture added: "In that case, even the best thoroughbred wouldn't help you."

"I suppose he may still turn up tonight?"

"Oh, easily, sir. I expect to see you both breakfasting here tomorrow morning," said Gosling cheerfully.

Medford sipped his coffee. "You said you'd never seen me here before. How long have you been here yourself?"

Gosling answered instantly, as though the figures were never long out of his memory: "Eleven years and seven months altogether, sir."

"Nearly twelve years! That's a longish time."

"Yes, it is."

"And I don't suppose you often get away?"

Gosling was moving off with the tray. He halted, turned back, and said with sudden emphasis: "I've never once been away. Not since Mr. Almodham first brought me here."

"Good Lord! Not a single holiday?"

"Not one, sir."

"But Mr. Almodham goes off occasionally. I met him at Luxor last year."

"Just so, sir. But when he's here he needs me for himself; and when he's away he needs me to watch over the others. So you see—"

"Yes, I see. But it must seem to you devilish long."

"It seems long, sir."

"But the others? You mean they're not—wholly trustworthy?"

"Well, sir, they're just Arabs," said Gosling with careless contempt.

"I see. And not a single old reliable among them?"

"The term isn't in their language, sir."

Medford was busy lighting his cigar. When he looked up he found that Gosling still stood a few feet off.

"It wasn't as if it 'adn't been a promise, you know, sir," he said, almost passionately.

"A promise?"

"To let me 'ave my holiday, sir. A promise—agine and agine."

"And the time never came?"

"No, sir. The days just drifted by—"

"Ah. They would, here. Don't sit up for me," Medford added. "I think I shall wait up—wait for Mr. Almodham."

Gosling's stare widened. "Here, sir? Here in the court?"

The young man nodded, and the servant stood still regarding him, turned by the moonlight to a white spectral figure, the unquiet ghost of a patient butler who might have died without his holiday.

"Down here in this court all night, sir? It's a lonely spot. I couldn't 'ear you if you was to call. You're best in bed, sir. The air's bad. You might bring your fever on again."

Medford laughed and stretched himself in his long chair. "Decidedly," he thought, "the fellow needs a change." Aloud he remarked: "Oh, I'm all right. It's you who are nervous, Gosling. When Mr. Almodham comes back I mean to put in a word for you. You shall have your holiday."

Gosling still stood motionless. For a minute he did not speak. "You would, sir, you would?" He gasped it out on a high cracked note, and the last word ran into a laugh—a brief shrill cackle, the laugh of one long unused to such indulgences.

"Thank you, sir. Good night, sir." He was gone.

§ 4

"You do boil my drinking-water, always?" Medford questioned, his hand clasping the glass without lifting it.

The tone was amicable, almost confidential; Medford felt that since his rash promise to secure a holiday for Gosling he and Gosling were on terms of real friendship.

"Boil it? Always, sir. Naturally." Gosling spoke with a slight note of reproach, as though Medford's question implied a slur—unconscious, he hoped—on their newly established relation. He scrutinized Medford with his astonished eyes, in which a genuine concern showed itself through the glaze of professional indifference.

"Because, you know, my bath this morning—"

Gosling was in the act of receiving from the hands of a gliding Arab a fragrant dish of *kuskus*. Under his breath he hissed to the native: "You damned aboriginy, you, can't you even 'old a dish steady? Ugh!" The Arab vanished before the imprecation, and Gosling, with a calm deliberate hand, set the dish before Medford. "All alike, they are." Fastidiously he wiped a trail of grease from his linen sleeve.

"Because, you know, my bath this morning simply stank," said Medford, plunging fork and spoon into the dish.

"Your bath, sir?" Gosling stressed the word. Astonishment, to the exclusion of all other emotion, again filled his eyes as he rested them on Medford. "Now, I wouldn't 'ave 'ad that 'appen for the world," he said self-reproachfully.

"There's only the one well here, eh? The one in the court?"

Gosling aroused himself from absorbed consideration of the visitor's complaint. "Yes, sir; only the one."

"What sort of a well is it? Where does the water come from?"

"Oh, it's just a cistern, sir. Rain-water. There's never been any other here. Not that I ever knew it to fail; but at this season sometimes it does turn queer. Ask any o' them Arabs, sir; they'll tell you. Liars as they are, they won't trouble to lie about that."

Medford was cautiously tasting the water in his glass. "This seems all right," he pronounced.

Sincere satisfaction was depicted on Gosling's countenance. "I seen to its being boiled myself, sir: I always do. I 'ope that Perrier'll turn up tomorrow, sir."

"Oh, tomorrow"—Medford shrugged, taking a second helping. "Tomorrow I may not be here to drink it."

"What—going away, sir?" cried Gosling.

Medford, wheeling round abruptly, caught a new and incomprehensible look in Gosling's eyes. The man had seemed to feel a sort of dog-like affection for him; had wanted, Medford could have sworn, to keep him on, persuade him to patience and delay; yet now, Medford could equally have sworn, there was relief in his look, satisfaction, almost, in his voice.

"So soon, sir?"

"Well, this is the fifth day since my arrival. And as there's no news yet of Mr. Almodham, and you say he may very well have forgotten all about my coming—"

"Oh, I don't say that, sir; not forgotten! Only, when one of those old piles of stones takes 'old of him, he does forget about the time, sir. That's what I meant. The days drift by—'e's in a dream. Very likely he thinks you're just due now, sir." A small thin smile sharpened the lustreless gravity of Gosling's features. It was the first time that Medford had seen him smile.

"Oh, I understand. But still—" Medford paused. Through the spell of inertia laid on him by the drowsy place and its easeful comforts his instinct of alertness was struggling back. "It's odd—"

"What's odd?" Gosling echoed unexpectedly, setting the dried dates and figs on the table.

"Everything," said Medford.

He leaned back in his chair and glanced up through the arch at the lofty sky from which noon was pouring down in cataracts of blue and gold. Almodham was out there somewhere under that canopy of fire, perhaps, as the servant said, absorbed in his dream. The land was full of spells.

"Coffee, sir?" Gosling reminded him. Medford took it.

"It's odd that you say you don't trust any of these fellows—these Arabs—and yet that you don't seem to feel worried at Mr. Almodham's being off God knows where, all alone with them."

Gosling received this attentively, impartially; he saw the point. "Well, sir, no—you wouldn't understand. It's the very thing that can't be taught, when to trust 'em and when not. It's 'ow their interests lie, of course, sir; and their religion, as they call it." His contempt was unlimited. "But even to begin to understand why I'm not worried about Mr. Almodham, you'd 'ave to 'ave lived among them, sir, and you'd 'ave to speak their language."

"But I—" Medford began. He pulled himself up short and bent above his coffee.

"Yes, sir?"

"But I've travelled among them more or less."

"Oh, travelled!" Even Gosling's intonation could hardly conciliate respect with derision in his reception of his boast.

"This makes the fifth day, though," Medford continued argumentatively. The midday heat lay heavy even on the shaded side of the court, and the sinews of his will were weakening.

"I can understand, sir, a gentleman like you 'aving other engagements—being pressed for time, as it were," Gosling reasonably conceded.

He cleared the table, committed its freight to a pair of Arab arms that just showed and vanished, and finally took himself off while Medford sank into the divan. A land of dreams . . .

The afternoon hung over the place like a great velarium of cloth-of-gold stretched across the battlements and drooping down in ever slacker folds upon the heavy-headed palms. When at length the gold turned to violet, and the west to a bow of crystal clasping the dark sands, Medford shook off his sleep and wandered out. But this time, instead of mounting to the roof, he took another direction.

He was surprised to find how little he knew of the place after five days of loitering and waiting. Perhaps this was to be his last evening alone in it. He passed out of the court by a vaulted stone passage which led to another walled enclosure. At his approach two or three Arabs who had been squatting there rose and melted out of sight. It was as if the solid masonry had received them.

Beyond, Medford heard a stamping of hoofs, the stir of a stable at night-fall. He went under another archway and found himself among horses and mules. In the fading light an Arab was rubbing down one of the horses, a powerful young chestnut. He too seemed about to vanish; but Medford caught him by the sleeve.

"Go on with your work," he said in Arabic.

The man, who was young and muscular, with a lean Bedouin face, stopped and looked at him.

"I didn't know your Excellency spoke our language."

"Oh, yes," said Medford.

The man was silent, one hand on the horse's restless neck, the other thrust into his woollen girdle. He and Medford examined each other in the faint light.

"Is that the horse that's lame?" Medford asked.

"Lame?" The Arab's eyes ran down the animal's legs. "Oh, yes; lame," he answered vaguely.

Medford stooped and felt the horse's knees and fetlocks. "He seems pretty fit. Couldn't he carry me for a canter this evening if I felt like it?"

The Arab considered; he was evidently perplexed by the weight of responsibility which the question placed on him.

"Your Excellency would like to go for a ride this evening?"

"Oh, just a fancy. I might or I might not." Medford lit a cigarette and offered one to the groom, whose white teeth flashed his gratification. Over the shared match they drew nearer and the Arab's diffidence seemed to lessen.

"Is this one of Mr. Almodham's own mounts?" Medford asked.

"Yes, sir; it's his favourite," said the groom, his hand passing proudly down the horse's bright shoulder.

"His favourite? Yet he didn't take him on this long expedition?"

The Arab fell silent and stared at the ground.

"Weren't you surprised at that?" Medford queried.

The man's gesture declared that it was not his business to be surprised.

The two remained without speaking while the quick blue night descended.

At length Medford said carelessly: "Where do you suppose your master is at this moment?"

The moon, unperceived in the radiant fall of day, had now suddenly possessed the world, and a broad white beam lay full on the Arab's white smock, his brown face and the turban of camel's hair knotted above it. His agitated eyeballs glistened like jewels.

"If Allah would vouchsafe to let us know!"

"But you suppose he's safe enough, don't you? You don't think it's necessary yet for a party to go out in search of him?"

The Arab appeared to ponder this deeply. The question must have taken him by surprise. He flung a brown arm about the horse's neck and continued to scrutinize the stones of the court.

"When the master is away Mr. Gosling is our master."

"And he doesn't think it necessary?"

The Arab signed: "Not yet."

"But if Mr. Almodham were away much longer—"

The man was again silent, and Medford continued: "You're the head groom, I suppose?"

"Yes, Excellency."

There was another pause. Medford half turned away; then, over his shoulder: "I suppose you know the direction Mr. Almodham took? The place he's gone to?"

"Oh, assuredly, Excellency."

"Then you and I are going to ride after him. Be ready an hour before daylight. Say nothing to any one—Mr. Gosling or anybody else. We two ought to be able to find him without other help."

The Arab's face was all a responsive flash of eyes and teeth. "Oh, sir, I undertake that you and my master shall meet before tomorrow night. And none shall know of it."

"He's as anxious about Almodham as I am," Medford thought; and a faint shiver ran down his back. "All right. Be ready," he repeated.

He strolled back and found the court empty of life, but fantastically peopled by palms of beaten silver and a white marble fig tree.

"After all," he thought irrelevantly, "I'm glad I didn't tell Gosling that I speak Arabic."

He sat down and waited till Gosling, approaching from the living-room, ceremoniously announced for the fifth time that dinner was served.

§ 5

Medford sat up in bed with a jerk which resembles no other. Someone was in his room. The fact reached him not by sight or sound—for the moon had set, and the silence of the night was complete—but by a peculiar faint disturbance of the invisible currents that enclose us.

He was awake in an instant, caught up his electric hand-lamp and flashed it into two astonished eyes. Gosling stood above the bed.

"Mr. Almodham—he's back?" Medford exclaimed.

"No, sir; he's not back." Gosling spoke in low controlled tones. His extreme self-possession gave Medford a sense of danger—he couldn't say why, or of what nature. He sat upright, looking hard at the man.

"Then what's the matter?"

"Well, sir, you might have told me you talk Arabic"—Gosling's tone was now wistfully reproachful—"before you get 'obnobbing with that Selim. Making randy-voos with 'im by night in the desert."

Medford reached for his matches and lit the candle by the bed. He did not know whether to kick Gosling out of the room or to listen to what the man had to say; but a quick movement of curiosity made him determine on the latter course.

"Such folly! First I thought I'd lock you in. I might 'ave." Gosling drew a key from his pocket and held it up. "Or again I might 'ave let you go. Easier than not. But there was Wembley."

"Wembley?" Medford echoed. He began to think the man was going mad. One might, so conceivably, in that place of postponements and enchantments! He wondered whether Almodham himself were not a little mad—if, indeed, Almodham were still in a world where such a fate is possible.

"Wembley. You promised to get Mr. Almodham to give me an 'oliday—to let me go back to England in time for a look at Wembley. Every man 'as 'is fancies, 'asn't 'e, sir? And that's mine. I've told Mr. Almodham so, agine and agine. He'd never listen, or only make believe to; say: 'We'll see, now, Gosling, we'll see'; and no more 'eard of it. But you was different, sir. You said it, and I knew you meant it—about my 'oliday. So I'm going to lock you in."

Gosling spoke composedly, but with an under-thrill of emotion in his queer Mediterranean-Cockney voice.

"Lock me in?"

"Prevent you somehow from going off with that murderer. You don't suppose you'd ever 'ave come back alive from that ride, do you?"

A shiver ran over Medford, as it had the evening before when he had said to himself that the Arab was as anxious as he was about Almodham. He gave a slight laugh.

"I don't know what you're talking about. But you're not going to lock me in."

The effect of this was unexpected. Gosling's face was drawn up into a convulsive grimace and two tears rose to his pale eyelashes and ran down his cheeks.

"You don't trust me, after all," he said plaintively.

Medford leaned on his pillow and considered. Nothing as queer had ever before happened to him. The fellow looked almost ridiculous enough to laugh at; yet his tears were certainly not simulated. Was he weeping for Almodham, already dead, or for Medford, about to be committed to the same grave?

"I should trust you at once," said Medford, "if you'd tell me where your master is."

Gosling's face resumed its usual guarded expression, though the trace of the tears still glittered on it.

"I can't do that, sir."

"Ah, I thought so!"

"Because—'ow do I know?"

Medford thrust a leg out of bed. One hand, under the blanket, lay on his revolver.

"Well, you may go now. Put that key down on the table first. And don't try to do anything to interfere with my plans. If you do I'll shoot you," he added concisely.

"Oh, no, you wouldn't shoot a British subject; it makes such a fuss. Not that I'd care—I've often thought of doing it myself. Sometimes in the sirocco season. That don't scare me. And you shan't go."

Medford was on his feet now, the revolver visible. Gosling eyed it with indifference.

"Then you do know where Mr. Almodham is? And you're determined that I shan't find out?" Medford challenged him.

"Selim's determined," said Gosling, "and all the others are. They all want you out of the way. That's why I've kept 'em to their quarters—done all the waiting on you myself. Now will you stay here? For God's sake, sir! The return caravan is going through to the coast the day after tomorrow. Join it, sir—it's the only safe way! I darsn't let you go with one of our men, not even if you was to swear you'd ride straight for the coast and let this business be."

"This business? What business?"

"This worrying about where Mr. Almodham is, sir. Not that there's anything to worry about. The men all know that. But the plain fact is they've stolen some money from his box, since he's been gone, and if I hadn't winked at it they'd 'ave killed me; and all they want is to get you to ride out after 'im, and put you safe away under a 'eap of sand somewhere off the caravan trails. Easy job. There; that's all, sir. My word it is."

There was a long silence. In the weak candle-light the two men stood considering each other.

Medford's wits began to clear as the sense of peril closed in on him. His mind reached out on all sides into the enfolding mystery, but it was everywhere impenetrable. The odd thing was that, though he did not believe half of what Gosling had told him, the man yet inspired him with a queer sense of confidence as far as their mutual relation was concerned. "He may be lying about Almodham, to hide God knows what; but I don't believe he's lying about Selim."

Medford laid his revolver on the table. "Very well," he said. "I won't ride out to look for Mr. Almodham, since you advise me not to. But I won't leave by the caravan; I'll wait here till he comes back."

He saw Gosling whiten under his sallowness. "Oh, don't do that, sir; I couldn't answer for them if you was to wait. The caravan'll take you to the coast the day after tomorrow as easy as if you was riding in Rotten Row."

"Ah, then you know that Mr. Almodham won't be back by the day after tomorrow?" Medford caught him up.

"I don't know anything, sir."

"Not even where he is now?"

Gosling reflected. "He's been gone too long, sir, for me to know that," he said from the threshold.

The door closed on him.

Medford found sleep unrecoverable. He leaned in his window and watched the stars fade and the dawn break in all its holiness. As the stir of life rose among the ancient walls he marvelled at the contrast between that fountain of purity welling up into the heavens and the evil secrets clinging bat-like to the nest of masonry below.

He no longer knew what to believe or whom. Had some enemy of Almodham's lured him into the desert and bought the connivance of his people? Or had the servants had some reason of their own for spiriting him away, and was Gosling possibly telling the truth when he said that the same fate would befall Medford if he refused to leave?

Medford, as the light brightened, felt his energy return. The very impenetrableness of the mystery stimulated him. He would stay, and he would find out the truth.

§ 6

It was always Gosling himself who brought up the water for Medford's bath; but this morning he failed to appear with it, and when he came it was to bring the breakfast tray. Medford noticed that his face was of a pasty pallor, and that his lids were reddened as if with weeping. The contrast was unpleasant, and a dislike for Gosling began to shape itself in the young man's breast.

"My bath?" he queried.

"Well, sir, you complained yesterday of the water—"

"Can't you boil it?"

"I 'ave, sir."

"Well, then—"

Gosling went out sullenly and presently returned with a brass jug. "It's the time of year—we're dying for rain," he grumbled, pouring a scant measure of water into the tub.

Yes, the well must be pretty low, Medford thought. Even boiled, the water had the disagreeable smell that he had noticed the day before, though of course in a slighter degree. But a bath was a necessity in that climate. He splashed the few cupfuls over himself as best as he could.

He spent the day in rather fruitlessly considering his situation. He had hoped the morning would bring counsel, but it brought only courage and resolution, and these were of small use without enlightenment. Suddenly he remembered that the caravan going south from the coast would pass near the castle that afternoon. Gosling had dwelt on the date often enough, for it was the caravan which was to bring the box of Perrier water.

"Well, I'm not sorry for that," Medford reflected, with a slight shrinking of the flesh. Something sick and viscous, half smell, half substance, seemed to have clung to his skin since his morning bath, and the idea of having to drink that water again was nauseating.

But his chief reason for welcoming the caravan was the hope of finding in it some European, or at any rate some native official from the coast, to whom he might confide his anxiety. He hung about, listening and waiting, and then mounted to the roof to gaze northward along the trail. But in the afternoon glow he saw only three Bedouins guiding laden pack-mules toward the castle.

As they mounted the steep path he recognized some of Almodham's men, and guessed at once that the southward caravan trail did not actually pass under the walls and that the men had been out to meet it, probably at a small oasis behind some fold of the sand-hills. Vexed at his own thoughtlessness in not foreseeing such a possibility, Medford dashed down to the court, hoping the men might have brought back some news of Almodham, though, as the latter had ridden south, he could at best only have crossed the trail by which the caravan had come. Still, even so, some one might know something, some report might have been heard—since everything was always known in the desert.

As Medford reached the court, angry vociferations, and retorts as vehement, rose from the stable-yard. He leaned over the wall and listened. Hitherto nothing had surprised him more than the silence of the place. Gosling must have had a strong arm to subdue the shrill voices of his underlings. Now they had all broken loose, and it was Gosling's own voice—usually so discreet and measured—which dominated them.

Gosling, master of all the desert dialects, was cursing his subordinates in a half-dozen.

"And you didn't bring it—and you tell me it wasn't there, and I tell you it was, and that you know it, and that you either left it on a sand-heap while you were jawing with some of those slimy fellows from the coast, or else fastened it on to the horse so carelessly that it fell off on the way—and all of you too sleepy to notice. Oh, you sons of females I wouldn't soil my lips by naming! Well, back you go to hunt it up, that's all!"

"By Allah and the tomb of his Prophet, you wrong us unpardonably. There was nothing left at the oasis, nor yet dropped off on the way back. It was not there, and that is the truth in its purity."

"Truth! Purity! You miserable lot of shirks and liars, you—and the gentleman here not touching a drop of anything but water—as you profess to do, you liquor-swilling humbugs!"

Medford drew back from the parapet with a smile of relief. It was nothing but a case of Perrier—the missing case—which had raised the passions of these grown men to the pitch of frenzy! The anti-climax lifted a load from his breast. If Gosling, the calm and self-controlled, could waste his wrath on so slight a hitch in the working of the commissariat, he at least must have a free mind. How absurd this homely incident made Medford's speculations seem!

He was at once touched by Gosling's solicitude, and annoyed that he should have been so duped by the hallucinating fancies of the East.

Almodham was off on his own business; very likely the men knew where and what the business was; and even if they had robbed him in his absence, and quarrelled over the spoils, Medford did not see what he could do. It might even be that his eccentric host—with whom, after all, he had had but one evening's acquaintance—repenting of an invitation too rashly given, had ridden away to escape the boredom of entertaining him. As this alternative occurred to Medford it seemed so plausible that he began to wonder if Almodham had not simply withdrawn to some secret suite of that intricate dwelling, and were waiting there for his guest's departure.

So well would this explain Gosling's solicitude to see the visitor off—so completely account for the man's nervous and contradictory behaviour—that Medford, smiling at his own obtuseness, hastily resolved to leave on the morrow. Tranquillized by this decision, he lingered about the court till dusk fell, and then, as usual, went up to the roof. But today his eyes, instead of raking the horizon, fastened on the clustering edifice of which, after six days' residence, he knew so little. Aerial chambers, jutting out at capricious angles, baffled him with closely shuttered windows, or here and there with the enigma of painted panes. Behind which window was his host concealed, spying, it might be, at this very moment on the movements of his lingering guest?

The idea that that strange moody man, with his long brown face and shock of white hair, his half-guessed selfishness and tyranny, and his morbid self-absorption, might be actually within a stone's throw, gave Medford, for the first time, a sharp sense of isolation. He felt himself shut out, unwanted—the place, now that he imagined someone might be living in it unknown to him, became lonely, inhospitable, dangerous.

"Fool that I am—he probably expected me to pack up and go as soon as I found he was away!" the young man reflected. Yes; decidedly, he would leave the next morning.

Gosling had not shown himself all the afternoon. When at length, belatedly, he came to set the table, he wore a look of sullen, almost surly, reserve which Medford had not yet seen on his face. He hardly returned the young man's friendly "Hallo—dinner?" and when Medford was seated handed him the first dish in silence. Medford's glass remained unfilled till he touched its brim.

"Oh, there's nothing to drink, sir. The men lost the case of Perrier—or dropped it and smashed the bottles. They say it never came. 'Ow do I know, when they never open their 'eathen lips but to lie?" Gosling burst out with sudden violence.

He set down the dish he was handing, and Medford saw that he had been obliged to do so because his whole body was shaking as if with fever.

"My dear man, what does it matter? You're going to be ill," Medford exclaimed, laying his hand on the servant's arm. But the latter, muttering: "Oh, God, if I'd only 'a' gone for it myself," jerked away and vanished from the room.

Medford sat pondering; it certainly looked as if poor Gosling were on the edge of a break-down. No wonder, when Medford himself was so oppressed by the uncanniness of the place. Gosling reappeared after an interval, correct, close-lipped, with the dessert and a bottle of white wine. "Sorry, sir."

To pacify him, Medford sipped the wine and then pushed his chair away and returned to the court. He was making for the fig tree by the well when Gosling, slipping ahead, transferred his chair and wicker table to the other end of the court.

"You'll be better here—there'll be a breeze presently," he said. "I'll fetch your coffee."

He disappeared again, and Medford sat gazing up at the pile of masonry and plaster, and wondering whether he had not been moved away from his favourite corner to get him out of—or into?—the angle of vision of the invisible watcher. Gosling, having brought the coffee, went away and Medford sat on.

At length he rose and began to pace up and down as he smoked. The moon was not yet up, and darkness fell solemnly on the ancient walls. Presently the breeze arose and began its secret commerce with the palms.

Medford went back to his seat; but as soon as he had resumed it he fancied that the gaze of his hidden watcher was jealously fixed on the red spark of his cigar. The sensation became increasingly distasteful; he could almost feel Almodham reaching out long ghostly arms from somewhere above him in the darkness. He moved back into the living-room, where a shaded light hung from the ceiling; but the room was airless, and finally he went out again and dragged his seat to its old place under the fig tree. From there the windows which he suspected could not command him, and he felt easier, though the corner was out of the breeze and the heavy air seemed tainted with the exhalation of the adjoining well.

"The water must be very low," Medford mused. The smell, though faint, was unpleasant; it smirched the purity of the night. But he felt safer there, somehow, farther from those unseen eyes which seemed mysteriously to have become his enemies.

"If one of the men had knifed me in the desert, I shouldn't wonder if it would have been at Almodham's orders," Medford thought. He drowsed.

When he woke the moon was pushing up its ponderous orange disk above the walls, and the darkness in the court was less dense. He must have slept for an hour or more. The night was delicious, or would have been anywhere but there. Medford felt a shiver of his old fever and remembered that Gosling had warned him that the court was unhealthy at night.

"On account of the well, I suppose. I've been sitting too close to it," he reflected. His head ached, and he fancied that the sweetish foulish smell clung to his face as it had after his bath. He stood up and approached the well to see how much water was left in it. But the moon was not yet high enough to light those depths, and he peered down into blackness.

Suddenly he felt both shoulders gripped from behind and forcibly pressed forward, as if by someone seeking to push him over the edge. An instant later, almost coinciding with his own swift resistance, the push became a strong tug backward, and he swung round to confront Gosling, whose hands immediately dropped from his shoulders.

"I thought you had the fever, sir—I seemed to see you pitching over," the man stammered.

Medford's wits returned. "We must both have it, for I fancied you were pitching me," he said with a laugh.

"Me, sir?" Gosling gasped. "I pulled you back as 'ard as ever—"

"Of course. I know."

"Whatever are you doing here, anyhow, sir? I warned you it was un'ealthy at night," Gosling continued irritably.

Medford leaned against the well-head and contemplated him. "I believe the whole place is unhealthy."

Gosling was silent. At length he asked: "Aren't you going up to bed, sir?"

"No," said Medford, "I prefer to stay here."

Gosling's face took on an expression of dogged anger. "Well, then, I prefer that you shouldn't."

Medford laughed again. "Why? Because it's the hour when Mr. Almodham comes out to take the air?"

The effect of this question was unexpected. Gosling dropped back a step or two and flung up his hands, pressing them to his lips as if to stifle a low outcry.

"What's the matter?" Medford queried. The man's antics were beginning to get on his nerves.

"Matter?" Gosling still stood away from him, out of the rising slant of moonlight.

"Come! Own up that he's here and have done with it!" cried Medford impatiently.

"Here? What do you mean by 'here'? You 'aven't seen 'im, 'ave you?" Before the words were out of the man's lips he flung up his arms again, stumbled forward and fell in a heap at Medford's feet.

Medford, still leaning against the well-head, smiled down contemptuously at the stricken wretch. His conjecture had been the right one, then; he had not been Gosling's dupe after all.

"Get up, man. Don't be a fool! It's not your fault if I guessed that Mr. Almodham walks here at night—"

"Walks here!" wailed the other, still cowering.

"Well, doesn't he? He won't kill you for owning up, will he?"

"Kill me? Kill me? I wish I'd killed *you!*" Gosling half got to his feet, his head thrown back in ashen terror. "And I might'ave, too, so easy! You felt me pushing of you over, didn't you? Coming 'ere spying and sniffing—" His anguish seemed to choke him.

Medford had not changed his position. The very abjectness of the creature at his feet gave him an easy sense of power. But Gosling's last cry had suddenly deflected the course of his speculations. Almodham was here, then; that was certain; but just where was he, and in what shape? A new fear scuttled down Medford's spine.

"So you did want to push me over?" he said. "Why? As the quickest way of joining your master?"

The effect was more immediate than he had foreseen.

Gosling, getting to his feet, stood there bowed and shrunken in the accusing moonlight.

"Oh, God—and I 'ad you 'arf over! You know I did! And then—it was what you said about Wembley. So help me, sir, I felt you meant it, and it 'eld me back." The man's face was again wet with tears, but this time Medford recoiled from them as if they had been drops splashed up by a falling body from the foul waters below.

Medford was silent. He did not know if Gosling were armed or not, but he was no longer afraid; only aghast, and yet shudderingly lucid.

Gosling continued to ramble on half deliriously:

"And if only that Perrier 'ad of come. I don't believe it'd ever 'ave crossed your mind, if only you'd 'ave 'ad your Perrier regular, now would it? But you say 'e walks—and I knew he would! Only—what was I to do with him, with you turning up like that the very day?"

Still Medford did not move.

"And 'im driving me to madness, sir, sheer madness, that same morning. Will you believe it? The very week before you come, I was to sail for England and 'ave my 'oliday, a 'ole month, sir—and I was entitled to six, if there was any justice—a 'ole month in 'Ammersmith, sir, in a cousin's 'ouse, and the chance to see Wembley thoroughly; and then 'e 'eard you was coming, sir, and 'e was bored and lonely 'ere, you understand—'e 'ad to have new excitements provided for 'im or 'e'd go off 'is bat—and when 'e 'eard you were coming, 'e come out of his black mood in a flash and was 'arf crazy with pleasure, and said: 'I'll keep 'im 'ere all winter—a remarkable young man, Gosling—just my kind.' And when I says to him: 'And 'ow about my 'oliday?' he stares at me with those stony eyes of 'is and says: ' 'Oliday? Oh, to be sure; why, next year—we'll see what can be done about it next year.' Next year, sir, as if 'e was doing me a favour! And that's the way it 'ad been for nigh on twelve years.

"But this time, if you 'adn't 'ave come I do believe I'd 'ave got away, for he was getting used to 'aving Selim about 'im and his 'ealth was never better—and, well, I told 'im as much, and 'ow a man 'ad his rights after all, and my youth was going, and me that 'ad served him so well chained up 'ere like 'is watchdog, and always next year and next year—and, well, sir, 'e just laughed, sneering-like, and lit 'is cigarette. 'Oh, Gosling, cut it out,' 'e says.

"He was standing on the very spot where you are now, sir; and he turned to walk into the 'ouse. And it was then I 'it 'im. He was a heavy man, and he fell against the well kerb. And just when you were expected any minute—oh, my God!"

Gosling's voice died out in a strangled murmur.

Medford, at his last words, had unvoluntarily shrunk back a few feet. The two men stood in the middle of the court and stared at each other without speaking. The moon, swinging high above the battlements, sent a searching spear of light down into the guilty darkness of the well.

Pomegranate Seed

§ 1

CHARLOTTE ASHBY paused on her doorstep. Dark had descended on the brilliancy of the March afternoon, and the grinding rasping street life of the city was at its highest. She turned her back on it, standing for a moment in the old-fashioned, marble-flagged vestibule before she inserted her key in the lock. The sash curtains drawn across the panes of the inner door softened the light within to a warm blur through which no details showed. It was the hour when, in the first months of her marriage to Kenneth Ashby, she had most liked to return to that quiet house in a street long since deserted by business and fashion. The contrast between the soulless roar of New York, its devouring blaze of lights, the oppression of its congested traffic, congested houses, lives, minds and this veiled sanctuary she called home, always stirred her profoundly. In the very heart of the hurricane she had found her tiny islet—or thought she had. And now, in the last months, everything was changed, and she always wavered on the doorstep and had to force herself to enter.

While she stood there she called up the scene within: the hall hung with old prints, the ladderlike stairs, and on the left her husband's long shabby library, full of books and pipes and worn armchairs inviting to meditation. How she had loved that room! Then, upstairs, her own drawing-room, in which, since the death of Kenneth's first wife, neither furniture nor hangings had been changed, because there had never been money enough, but which Charlotte had made her own by moving furniture about and adding more books, another lamp, a table for the new reviews. Even on the occasion of her only visit to the first Mrs. Ashby—a distant, self-centered woman, whom she had known very slightly—she had looked about her with an innocent envy, feeling it to be exactly the drawing-room she would have liked for herself; and now for more than a year it had been hers to deal with as she chose—the room to which she hastened back at dusk on winter days, where she sat reading by the fire, or answering notes at the pleasant roomy desk, or going over her stepchildren's copy books, till she heard her husband's step.

Sometimes friends dropped in; sometimes—oftener—she was alone; and she liked that best, since it was another way of being with Kenneth, thinking over what he had said when they parted in the morning, imagining what he would say when he sprang up the stairs, found her by herself and caught her to him.

Now, instead of this, she thought of one thing only—the letter she might or might not find on the hall table. Until she had made sure whether or not it was there, her mind had no room for anything else. The letter was always the same—a square grayish envelope with "Kenneth Ashby, Esquire.," written on it in bold but faint characters. From the first it had struck Charlotte as peculiar that anyone who wrote such a firm hand should trace the letters so lightly; the address was always written as though there were not enough ink in the pen, or the writer's wrist were too weak to bear upon it. Another curious thing was that, in spite of its masculine curves, the writing was so visibly feminine. Some hands are sexless, some masculine, at first glance; the writing on the gray envelope, for all its strength and assurance, was without doubt a woman's. The envelope never bore anything but the recipient's name; no stamp, no address. The letter was presumably delivered by hand—but by whose? No doubt it was slipped into the letter box, whence the parlour maid, when she closed the shutters and lit the lights, probably extracted it. At any rate, it was always in the evening, after dark, that Charlotte saw it lying there. She thought of the letter in the singular, as "it", because, though there had been several since her marriage—seven, to be exact—they were so alike in appearance that they had become merged in one another in her mind, become one letter, become "it".

The first had come the day after their return from their honeymoon—a journey prolonged to the West Indies, from which they had returned to New York after an absence of more than two months. Re-entering the house with her husband, late on that first evening—they had dined at his mother's—she had seen, alone on the hall table, the gray envelope. Her eye fell on it before Kenneth's, and her first thought was: "Why, I've seen that writing before;" but where she could not recall. The memory was just definite enough for her to identify the script whenever it looked up at her faintly from the same pale envelope; but on that first day she would have thought no more of the letter if, when her husband's glance lit on it, she had not chanced to be looking at him. It all happened in a flash—his seeing the letter, putting out his hand for it, raising it to his short-sighted eyes to decipher the faint writing, and then abruptly withdrawing the arm he had slipped through Charlotte's, and moving away to the hanging light, his back turned to her. She had waited—waited for a sound, an exclamation; waited for him to open the letter; but he had slipped it into his pocket without a word and followed her into the library. And there they sat down by the fire and lit their cigarettes, and he had remained silent, his head thrown back broodingly against the armchair, his eyes fixed on the hearth, and presently had passed his hand over his forehead and said: "Wasn't it unusually hot at my mother's tonight? I've got a splitting head. Mind if I take myself off to bed?"

That was the first time. Since then Charlotte had never been present when he had received the letter. It usually came before he got home from his office, and she had to go upstairs and leave it lying there. But even if she had not seen it, she would have known it had come by the change in his face when he joined her—which, on those evenings, he seldom did before they met for dinner. Evidently, whatever the letter contained, he wanted to be by himself to deal with it; and when he reappeared he looked years older, looked emptied of life and courage, and hardly conscious of her presence. Sometimes he was silent for the rest of the evening; and if he spoke, it was usually to hint some criticism of her household arrangements, suggest some change in the domestic administration, to ask, a little nervously, if she didn't think Joyce's nursery governess was rather young and flighty, or if she herself always saw to it that Peter—whose throat was delicate—was properly wrapped up when he went to school. At such times Charlotte would remember the friendly warnings she had received when she became engaged to Kenneth Ashby: "Marrying a heartbroken widower! Isn't that rather risky? You know Elsie Ashby absolutely dominated him"; and how she had jokingly replied: "He may be glad of a little liberty for a change." And in this respect she had been right. She had needed no one to tell her, during the first months, that her husband was perfectly happy with her. When they came back from their protracted honeymoon the same friends said: "What have you done to Kenneth? He looks twenty years younger"; and this time she answered with careless joy: "I suppose I've got him out of his groove."

But what she noticed after the gray letters began to come was not so much his nervous tentative fault-finding—which always seemed to be uttered against his will—as the look in his eyes when he joined her after receiving one of the letters. The look was not unloving, not even indifferent; it was the look of a man who had been so far away from ordinary events that when he returns to familiar things they seem strange. She minded that more than the fault-finding.

Though she had been sure from the first that the handwriting on the gray envelope was a woman's, it was long before she associated the mysterious letters with any sentimental secret. She was too sure of her husband's love, too confident of filling his life, for such an idea to occur to her. It seemed far more likely that the letters—which certainly did not appear to cause him any sentimental pleasure—were addressed to the busy lawyer than to the private person. Probably they were from some tiresome client—women, he had often told her, were nearly always tiresome as clients—who did not want her letters opened by his secretary and therefore had them carried to his house. Yes; but in that case the unknown female must be unusually troublesome, judging from the effect her letters produced. Then again, though his professional discretion was exemplary, it was odd that he had never uttered an impatient comment, never remarked to Charlotte, in a moment of expansion, that there was a nuisance of a woman who kept badgering him about a case that had gone against her. He had made more than one semi-confidence of the kind—of course without giving names or details; but concerning this mysterious correspondent his lips were sealed.

There was another possibility: what is euphemistically called an "old entanglement". Charlotte Ashby was a sophisticated woman. She had few illusions about the intricacies of the human heart; she knew that there were often old entanglements. But when she had married Kenneth Ashby, her friends, instead of hinting at such a possibility, had said: "You've got your work cut out for you. Marrying a Don Juan is a sinecure to it. Kenneth's never looked at another woman since he first saw Elsie Corder. During all the years of their marriage he was more like an unhappy lover than a comfortably contented husband. He'll never let you move an armchair or change the place of a lamp; and whatever you venture to do, he'll mentally compare with what Elsie would have done in your place."

Except for an occasional nervous mistrust as to her ability to manage the children—a mistrust gradually dispelled by her good humour and the children's obvious fondness for her—none of these forebodings had come true. The desolate widower, of whom his nearest friends said that only his absorbing professional interests had kept him from suicide after his first wife's death, had fallen in love, two years later, with Charlotte Gorse, and after an impetuous wooing had married her and carried her off on a tropical honeymoon. And ever since he had been as tender and loverlike as during those first radiant weeks. Before asking her to marry him he had spoken to her frankly of his great love for his first wife and his despair after her sudden death; but even then he had assumed no stricken attitude, or implied that life offered no possibility of renewal. He had been perfectly simple and natural, and had confessed to Charlotte that from the beginning he had hoped the future held new gifts for him. And when, after their marriage, they returned to the house where his twelve years with his first wife had been spent, he had told Charlotte at once that he was sorry he couldn't afford to do the place over for her, but that he knew every woman had her own views about furniture and all sorts of household arrangements a man would never notice, and had begged her to make any changes she saw fit without bothering to consult him. As a result, she made as few as possible; but his way of beginning their new life in the old setting was so frank and unembarrassed that it put her immediately at her ease, and she was almost sorry to find that the portrait of Elsie Ashby, which used to hang over the desk in his library, had been transferred in their absence to the children's nursery. Knowing herself to be the indirect cause of this banishment, she spoke of it to her husband; but he answered: "Oh, I thought they ought to grow up with her looking down on them." The answer moved Charlotte, and satisfied her; and as time went by she had to confess that she felt more at home in her house, more at ease and in confidence with her husband, since that long coldly beautiful face on the library wall no longer followed her with guarded eyes. It was as if Kenneth's love had penetrated to the secret she hardly acknowledged to her own heart—her passionate need to feel herself the sovereign even of his past.

With all this stored-up happiness to sustain her, it was curious that she had lately found herself yielding to a nervous apprehension. But there the apprehension was; and on this particular afternoon—perhaps because she was more tired than usual, or because of the trouble of finding a new cook or, for some other ridiculously trivial reason, moral or physical—she found herself unable to react against the feeling. Latchkey in hand, she looked back down the silent street to the whirl and illumination of the great thoroughfare beyond, and up at the sky already aflare with the city's nocturnal life. "Outside there," she thought, "sky-scrapers, advertisements, telephones, wireless, aeroplanes, movies, motors, and all the rest of the twentieth century; and on the other side of the door something I can't explain, can't relate to them. Something as old as the world, as mysterious as life . . . Nonsense! What am I worrying about? There hasn't been a letter for three months now—not since the day we came back from the country after Christmas . . . Queer that they always seem to come after our holidays! . . . Why should I imagine there's going to be one tonight!"

No reason why, but that was the worst of it—one of the worsts!—that there were days when she would stand there cold and shivering with the premonition of something inexplicable, intolerable, to be faced on the other side of the curtained panes; and when she opened the door and went in, there would be nothing; and on other days when she felt the same premonitory chill, it was justified by the sight of the gray envelope. So that ever since the last had come she had taken to feeling cold and premonitory every evening, because she never opened the door without thinking the letter might be there.

Well, she'd had enough of it; that was certain. She couldn't go on like that. If her husband turned white and had a headache on the days when the letter came, he seemed to recover afterward; but she couldn't. With her the strain had become chronic, and the reason was not far to seek. Her husband knew from whom the letter came and what was in it; he was prepared beforehand for whatever he had to deal with, and master of the situation, however bad; whereas she was shut out in the dark with her conjectures.

"I can't stand it! I can't stand it another day!" she exclaimed aloud, as she put her key in the lock. She turned the key and went in; and there, on the table, lay the letter.

§ 2

She was almost glad of the sight. It seemed to justify everything, to put a seal of definiteness on the whole blurred business. A letter for her husband; a letter from a woman—no doubt another vulgar case of "old entanglement". What a fool she had been ever to doubt it, to rack her brains for less obvious explanations! She took up the envelope with a steady contemptuous hand, looked closely at the faint letters, held it against the light and just discerned the outline of the folded sheet within. She knew that now she would have no peace till she found out what was written on that sheet.

Her husband had not come in; he seldom got back from his office before half-past six or seven, and it was not yet six. She would have time to take the letter up to the drawing-room, hold it over the tea-kettle which at that hour always simmered by the fire in expectation of her return, solve the mystery and replace the letter where she had found it. No one would be the wiser, and her gnawing uncertainty would be over. The alternative, of course, was to question her husband; but to do that seemed even more difficult. She weighed the letter between thumb and finger, looked at it again under the light, started up the stairs with the envelope—and came down again and laid it on the table.

"No, I evidently can't," she said, disappointed.

What should she do, then? She couldn't go up alone to that warm welcoming room, pour out her tea, look over her correspondence, glance at a book or review—not with that letter lying below and the knowledge that in a little while her husband would come in, open it and turn into the library alone, as he always did on the days when the gray envelope came.

Suddenly she decided. She would wait in the library and see for herself; see what happened between him and the letter when they thought themselves unobserved. She wondered the idea had never occurred to her before. By leaving the door ajar, and sitting in the corner behind it, she could watch him unseen . . . Well, then, she would watch him! She drew a chair into the corner, sat down, her eyes on the crack, and waited.

As far as she could remember, it was the first time she had ever tried to surprise another person's secret, but she was conscious of no compunction. She simply felt as if she were fighting her way through a stifling fog that she must at all costs get out of.

At length she heard Kenneth's latchkey and jumped up. The impulse to rush out and meet him had nearly made her forget why she was there; but she remembered in time and sat down again. From her post she covered the whole range of his movements—saw him enter the hall, draw the key from the door and take off his hat and overcoat. Then he turned to throw his gloves on the hall table, and at that moment he saw the envelope. The light was full on his face, and what Charlotte first noted there was a look of surprise. Evidently he had not expected the letter—had not thought of the possibility of its being there that day. But though he had not expected it, now that he saw it he knew well enough what it contained. He did not open it immediately, but stood motionless, the colour slowly ebbing from his face. Apparently he could not make up his mind to touch it; but at length he put out his hand, opened the envelope, and moved with it to the light. In doing so he turned his back on Charlotte, and she saw only his bent head and slightly stooping shoulders. Apparently all the writing was on one page, for he did not turn the sheet but continued to stare at it for so long that he must have reread it a dozen times—or so it seemed to the woman breathlessly watching him. At length she saw him move; he raised the letter still closer to his eyes, as though he had not fully deciphered it. Then he lowered his head, and she saw his lips touch the sheet.

"Kenneth!" she exclaimed, and went out into the hall.

The letter clutched in his hand, her husband turned and looked at her. "Where were you?" he said, in a low bewildered voice, like a man waked out of his sleep.

"In the library, waiting for you." She tried to steady her voice: "What's the matter! What's in that letter? You look ghastly."

Her agitation seemed to calm him, and he instantly put the envelope into his pocket with a slight laugh. "Ghastly? I'm sorry. I've had a hard day in the office—one or two complicated cases. I look dog-tired, I suppose."

"You didn't look tired when you came in. It was only when you opened that letter—"

He had followed her into the library, and they stood gazing at each other. Charlotte noticed how quickly he had regained his self-control; his profession had trained him to rapid mastery of face and voice. She saw at once that she would be at a disadvantage in any attempt to surprise his secret, but at the same moment she lost all desire to manoeuvre, to trick him into betraying anything he wanted to conceal. Her wish was still to penetrate the mystery, but only that she might help him to bear the burden it implied. "Even if it *is* another woman," she thought.

"Kenneth," she said, her heart beating excitedly, "I waited here on purpose to see you come in. I wanted to watch you while you opened that letter."

His face, which had paled, turned to dark red; then it paled again. "That letter? Why especially that letter?"

"Because I've noticed that whenever one of those letters comes it seems to have such a strange effect on you."

A line of anger she had never seen before came out between his eyes, and she said to herself: "The upper part of his face is too narrow; this is the first time I ever noticed it."

She heard him continue, in the cool and faintly ironic tone of the prosecuting lawyer making a point: "Ah; so you're in the habit of watching people open their letters when they don't know you're there?"

"Not in the habit. I never did such a thing before. But I had to find out what she writes to you, at regular intervals, in those gray envelopes."

He weighed this for a moment; then: "The intervals have not been regular," he said.

"Oh, I daresay you've kept a better account of the dates than I have," she retorted, her magnanimity vanishing at his tone. "All I know is that every time that woman writes to you—"

"Why do you assume it's a woman?"

"It's a woman's writing. Do you deny it?"

He smiled. "No, I don't deny it. I asked only because the writing is generally supposed to look more like a man's."

Charlotte passed this over impatiently. "And this woman—what does she write to you about?"

Again he seemed to consider a moment. "About business."

"Legal business?"

"In a way, yes. Business in general."

"You look after her affairs for her?"

"Yes."

"You've looked after them for a long time?"

"Yes. A very long time."

"Kenneth, dearest, won't you tell me who she is?"

"No. I can't." He paused and brought out, as if with a certain hesitation: "Professional secrecy."

The blood rushed from Charlotte's heart to her temples. "Don't say that—don't!"

"Why not?"

"Because I saw you kiss the letter."

The effect of the words was so disconcerting that she instantly repented having spoken them. Her husband, who had submitted to her cross-questioning with a sort of contemptuous composure, as though he were humouring an unreasonable child, turned on her a face of terror and distress. For a minute he seemed unable to speak; then, collecting himself with an effort, he stammered out: "The writing is very faint; you must have seen me holding the letter close to my eyes to try to decipher it."

"No; I saw you kissing it." He was silent. "Didn't I see you kissing it?"

He sank back into indifference. "Perhaps."

"Kenneth! You stand there and say that—to me?"

"What possible difference can it make to you? The letter is on business, as I told you. Do you suppose I'd lie about it? The writer is a very old friend whom I haven't seen for a long time."

"Men don't kiss business letters, even from women who are very old friends, unless they have been their lovers, and still regret them."

He shrugged his shoulders slightly and turned away, as if he considered the discussion at an end and were faintly disgusted at the turn it had taken.

"Kenneth!" Charlotte moved toward him and caught hold of his arm.

He paused with a look of weariness and laid his hand over hers. "Won't you believe me?" he asked gently.

"How can I? I've watched these letters come to you—for months now they've been coming. Ever since we came back from the West Indies—one of them greeted me the very day we arrived. And after each one of them I see their mysterious effect on you, I see you disturbed, unhappy, as if someone were trying to estrange you from me."

"No, dear; not that. Never!"

She drew back and looked at him with passionate entreaty. "Well, then, prove it to me, darling. It's so easy!"

He forced a smile. "It's not easy to prove anything to a woman who's once taken an idea into her head."

"You've only got to show me the letter."

His hand slipped from hers and he drew back and shook his head.

"You won't?"

"I can't."

"Then the woman who wrote it is your mistress."

"No, dear. No."

"Not now, perhaps. I suppose she's trying to get you back, and you're struggling, out of pity for me. My poor Kenneth!"

"I swear to you she never was my mistress."

Charlotte felt the tears rushing to her eyes. "Ah, that's worse, then—that's hopeless! The prudent ones are the kind that keep their hold on a man. We all know that." She lifted her hands and hid her face in them.

Her husband remained silent; he offered neither consolation nor denial, and at length, wiping away her tears, she raised her eyes almost timidly to his.

"Kenneth, think! We've been married such a short time. Imagine what you're making me suffer. You say you can't show me this letter. You refuse even to explain it."

"I've told you the letter is on business. I will swear to that too."

"A man will swear to anything to screen a woman. If you want me to believe you, at least tell me her name. If you'll do that, I promise you I won't ask to see the letter."

There was a long interval of suspense, during which she felt her heart beating against her ribs in quick admonitory knocks, as if warning her of the danger she was incurring.

"I can't," he said at length.

"Not even her name?"

"No."

"You can't tell me anything more?"

"No."

Again a pause; this time they seemed both to have reached the end of their arguments and to be helplessly facing each other across a baffling waste of incomprehension.

Charlotte stood breathing rapidly, her hands against her breast. She felt as if she had won a hard race and missed the goal. She had meant to move her husband and had succeeded only in irritating him; and this error of reckoning seemed to change him into a stranger, a mysterious incomprehensible being whom no argument or entreaty of hers could reach. The curious thing was that she was aware in him of no hostility or even impatience, but only of a remoteness, an inaccessibility, far more difficult to overcome. She felt herself excluded, ignored, blotted out of his life. But after a moment or two, looking at him more calmly, she saw that he was suffering as much as she was. His distant guarded face was drawn with pain; the coming of the gray envelope, though it always cast a shadow, had never marked him as deeply as this discussion with his wife.

Charlotte took heart; perhaps, after all, she had not spent her last shaft. She drew nearer and once more laid her hand on his arm. "Poor Kenneth! If you knew how sorry I am for you—"

She thought he winced slightly at this expression of sympathy, but he took her hand and pressed it.

"I can think of nothing worse than to be incapable of loving long," she continued; "to feel the beauty of a great love and to be too unstable to bear its burden."

He turned on her a look of wistful reproach. "Oh, don't say that of me. Unstable!"

She felt herself at last on the right tack, and her voice trembled with excitement as she went on: "Then what about me and this other woman? Haven't you already forgotten Elsie twice within a year?"

She seldom pronounced his first wife's name; it did not come naturally to her tongue. She flung it out now as if she were flinging some dangerous explosive into the open space between them, and drew back a step, waiting to hear the mine go off.

Her husband did not move; his expression grew sadder, but showed no resentment. "I have never forgotten Elsie," he said.

Charlotte could not repress a faint laugh. "Then, you poor dear, between the three of us—"

"There are not—" he began; and then broke off and put his hand to his forehead.

"Not what?"

"I'm sorry; I don't believe I know what I'm saying. I've got a blinding headache." He looked wan and furrowed enough for the statement to be true, but she was exasperated by his evasion.

"Ah, yes; the gray-envelope headache!"

She saw the surprise in his eyes. "I'd forgotten how closely I've been watched," he said coldly. "If you'll excuse me, I think I'll go up and try an hour in the dark, to see if I can rid of this neuralgia."

She wavered; then she said, with desperate resolution: "I'm sorry your head aches. But before you go I want to say that sooner or later this question must be settled between us. Someone is trying to separate us, and I don't care what it costs me to find out who it is." She looked him steadily in the eyes. "If it costs me your love, I don't care! If I can't have your confidence I don't want anything from you."

He still looked at her wistfully. "Give me time."

"Time for what? It's only a word to say."

"Time to show you that you haven't lost my love or my confidence."

"Well, I'm waiting."

He turned toward the door, and then glanced back hesitatingly. "Oh, do wait, my love," he said, and went out of the room.

She heard his tired step on the stairs and the closing of his bedroom door above. Then she dropped into a chair and buried her face in her folded arms. Her first movement was one of compunction; she seemed to herself to have been hard, unhuman, unimaginative. "Think of telling him that I didn't care if my insistence cost me his love! The lying rubbish!" She started up to follow him and unsay the meaningless words. But she was checked by a reflection. He had had his way, after all; he had eluded all attacks on his secret, and now he was shut up alone in his room, reading that other woman's letter.

§ 3

She was still reflecting on this when the surprised parlour-maid came in and found her. No, Charlotte said, she wasn't going to dress for dinner; Mr. Ashby didn't want to dine. He was very tired and had gone up to his room to rest; later she would have something brought on a tray to the drawing-room. She mounted the stairs to her bedroom. Her dinner dress was lying on the bed, and at the sight the quiet routine of her daily life took hold of her and she began to feel as if the strange talk she had just had with her husband must have taken place in another world, between two beings who were not Charlotte Gorse and Kenneth Ashby, but phantoms projected by her fevered imagination. She recalled the year since her marriage—her husband's constant devotion; his persistent, almost too insistent tenderness; the feeling he had given her at times of being too eagerly dependent on her, too searchingly close to her, as if there were not air enough between her soul and his. It seemed preposterous, as she recalled all this, that a few moments ago she should have been accusing him of an intrigue with another woman! But, then, what—

Again she was moved by the impulse to go up to him, beg his pardon and try to laugh away the misunderstanding. But she was restrained by the fear of forcing herself upon his privacy. He was troubled and unhappy, oppressed by some grief or fear; and he had shown her that he wanted to fight out his battle alone. It would be wiser, as well as more generous, to respect his wish. Only, how strange, how unbearable, to be there, in the next room to his, and feel herself at the other end of the world! In her nervous agitation she almost regretted not having had the courage to open the letter and put it back on the hall table before he came in. At least she would have known what his secret was, and the bogy might have been laid. For she was beginning now to think of the mystery as something conscious, malevolent: a secret persecution before which he quailed, yet from which he could not free himself. Once or twice in his evasive eyes she thought she had detected a desire for help, an impulse of confession, instantly restrained and suppressed. It was as if he felt she could have helped him if she had known, and yet had been unable to tell her!

There flashed through her mind the idea of going to his mother. She was very fond of old Mrs. Ashby, a firm-fleshed clear-eyed old lady, with an astringent bluntness of speech which responded to the forthright and simple in Charlotte's own nature. There had been a tacit bond between them ever since the day when Mrs. Ashby senior, coming to lunch for the first time with her new daughter-in-law, had been received by Charlotte downstairs in the library, and glancing up at the empty wall above her son's desk, had remarked laconically: "Elsie gone, eh?" adding, at Charlotte's murmured explanation: "Nonsense. Don't have her back. Two's company." Charlotte, at this reading of her thoughts, could hardly refrain from exchanging a smile of complicity with her mother-in-law; and it seemed to her now that Mrs. Ashby's almost uncanny directness might pierce to the core of this new mystery. But here again she hesitated, for the idea almost suggested a betrayal. What right had she to call in any one, even so close a relation, to surprise a secret which her husband was trying to keep from her? "Perhaps, by and by, he'll talk to his mother of his own accord," she thought, and then ended: "But what does it matter? He and I must settle it between us."

She was still brooding over the problem when there was a knock on the door and her husband came in. He was dressed for dinner and seemed surprised to see her sitting there, with her evening dress lying unheeded on the bed.

"Aren't you coming down?"

"I thought you were not well and had gone to bed," she faltered.

He forced a smile. "I'm not particularly well, but we'd better go down." His face, though still drawn, looked calmer than when he had fled upstairs an hour earlier.

"There it is; he knows what's in the letter and has fought his battle out again, whatever it is," she reflected, "while I'm still in darkness." She rang and gave a hurried order that dinner should be served as soon as possible—just a short meal, whatever could be got ready quickly, as both she and Mr. Ashby were rather tired and not very hungry.

Dinner was announced, and they sat down to it. At first neither seemed able to find a word to say; then Ashby began to make conversation with an assumption of ease that was more oppressive than his silence. "How tired he is! How terribly overtired!" Charlotte said to herself, pursuing her own thoughts while he rambled on about municipal politics, aviation, an exhibition of modern French painting, the health of an old aunt and the installing of the automatic telephone. "Good heavens, how tired he is!"

When they dined alone they usually went into the library after dinner, and Charlotte curled herself up on the divan with her knitting while he settled down in his armchair under the lamp and lit a pipe. But this evening, by tacit agreement, they avoided the room in which their strange talk had taken place, and went up to Charlotte's drawing-room.

They sat down near the fire, and Charlotte said: "Your pipe?" after he had put down his hardly tasted coffee.

He shook his head. "No, not tonight."

"You must go to bed early; you look terribly tired. I'm sure they overwork you at the office."

"I suppose we all overwork at times."

She rose and stood before him with sudden resolution. "Well, I'm not going to have you use up your strength slaving in that way. It's absurd. I can see you're ill." She bent over him and laid her hand on his forehead. "My poor old Kenneth. Prepare to be taken away soon on a long holiday."

He looked up at her, startled. "A holdiay?"

"Certainly. Didn't you know I was going to carry you off at Easter? We're going to start in a fortnight on a month's voyage to somewhere or other. On any one of the big cruising steamers." She paused and bent closer, touching his forehead with her lips. "I'm tired, too, Kenneth."

He seemed to pay no heed to her last words, but sat, his hands on his knees, his head drawn back a little from her caress, and looked up at her with a stare of apprehension. "Again? My dear, we can't; I can't possibly go away."

"I don't know why you say 'again', Kenneth; we haven't taken a real holiday this year."

"At Christmas we spent a week with the children in the country."

"Yes, but this time I mean away from the children, from servants, from the house. From everything that's familiar and fatiguing. Your mother will love to have Joyce and Peter with her."

He frowned and slowly shook his head. "No, dear; I can't leave them with my mother."

"Why, Kenneth, how absurd; she adores them. You didn't hesitate to leave them with her for over two months when we went to the West Indies."

He drew a deep breath and stood up uneasily. "That was different."

"Different? Why?"

"I mean, at that time I didn't realize"—He broke off as if to choose his words and then went on: "My mother adores the children, as you say. But she isn't always very judicious. Grandmothers always spoil children. And she sometimes talks before them without thinking." He turned to his wife with an almost pitiful gesture of entreaty. "Don't ask me to, dear."

Charlotte mused. It was true that the elder Mrs. Ashby had a fearless tongue, but she was the last woman in the world to say or hint anything before her grandchildren at which the most scrupulous parent could take offense. Charlotte looked at her husband in perplexity.

"I don't understand."

He continued to turn on her the same troubled and entreating gaze. "Don't try to," he muttered.

"Not try to?"

"Not now—not yet." He put up his hands and pressed them against his temples. "Can't you see that there's no use in insisting? I can't go away, no matter how much I might want to."

Charlotte still scrutinized him gravely. "The question is, *do* you want to?"

He returned her gaze for a moment; then his lips began to tremble, and he said, hardly above his breath: "I want—anything you want."

"And yet—"

"Don't ask me. I can't leave—I can't!"

"You mean that you can't go away out of reach of those letters!"

Her husband had been standing before her in an uneasy half-hesitating attitude; now he turned abruptly away and walked once or twice up and down the length of the room, his head bent, his eyes fixed on the carpet.

Charlotte felt her resentfulness rising with her fears. "It's that," she persisted. "Why not admit it? You can't live without them."

He continued his troubled pacing of the room; then he stopped short, dropped into a chair and covered his face with his hands. From the shaking of his shoulders, Charlotte saw that he was weeping. She had never seen a man cry, except her father after her mother's death, when she was a little girl; and she remembered still how the sight had frightened her. She was frightened now; she felt that her husband was being dragged away from her into some mysterious bondage, and that she must use up her last atom of strength in the struggle for his freedom, and for hers.

"Kenneth—Kenneth!" she pleaded, kneeling down beside him. "Won't you listen to me? Won't you try to see what I'm suffering? I'm not unreasonable, darling; really not. I don't suppose I should ever have noticed the letters if it hadn't been for their effect on you. It's not my way to pry into other people's affairs; and even if the effect had been different—yes, yes; listen to me—if I'd seen that the letters made you happy, that you were watching eagerly for them, counting the days between their coming, that you wanted them, that they gave you something I haven't known how to give—why, Kenneth, I don't say I shouldn't have suffered from that, too; but it would have been in a different way, and I should have had the courage to hide what I felt, and the hope that some day you'd come to feel about me as you did about the writer of the letters. But what I can't bear is to see how you dread them, how they make you suffer, and yet how you can't live without them and won't go away lest you should miss one during your absence. Or perhaps," she added, her voice breaking into a cry of accusation— "perhaps it's because she's actually forbidden you to leave. Kenneth, you must answer me! Is that the reason? Is it because she's forbidden you that you won't go away with me?"

She continued to kneel at his side, and raising her hands, she drew his gently down. She was ashamed of her persistence, ashamed of uncovering that baffled disordered face, yet resolved that no such scruples should arrest her. His eyes were lowered, the muscles of his face quivered; she was making him suffer even more than she suffered herself. Yet this no longer restrained her.

"Kenneth, is it that? She won't let us go away together?"

Still he did not speak or turn his eyes to her; and a sense of defeat swept over her. After all, she thought, the struggle was a losing one. "You needn't answer. I see I'm right," she said.

Suddenly, as she rose, he turned and drew her down again. His hands caught hers and pressed them so tightly that she felt her rings cutting into her flesh. There was something frightened, convulsive in his hold; it was the clutch of a man who felt himself slipping over a precipice. He was staring up at her now as if salvation lay in the face she bent above him. "Of course we'll go away together. We'll go wherever you want," he said in a low confused voice; and putting his arm about her, he drew her close and pressed his lips on hers.

§ 4

Charlotte had said to herself: "I shall sleep tonight," but instead she sat before her fire into the small hours, listening for any sound that came from her husband's room. But he, at any rate, seemed to be resting after the tumult of the evening. Once or twice she stole to the door and in the faint light that came in from the street through his open window she saw him stretched out in heavy sleep—the sleep of weakness and exhaustion. "He's ill," she thought—"he's undoubtedly ill. And it's not overwork; it's this mysterious persecution."

She drew a breath of relief. She had fought through the weary fight and the victory was hers—at least for the moment. If only they could have started at once—started for anywhere! She knew it would be useless to ask him to leave before the holidays; and meanwhile the secret influence—as to which she was still so completely in the dark—would continue to work against her, and she would have to renew the struggle day after day till they started on their journey. But after that everything would be different. If once she could get her husband away under other skies, and all to herself, she never doubted her power to release him from the evil spell he was under. Lulled to quiet by the thought, she too slept at last.

When she woke, it was long past her usual hour, and she sat up in bed surprised and vexed at having overslept herself. She always liked to be down to share her husband's breakfast by the library fire; but a glance at the clock made it clear that he must have started long since for his office. To make sure, she jumped out of bed and went into his room; but it was empty. No doubt he had looked in or on her before leaving, seen that she still slept, and gone downstairs without disturbing her; and their relations were sufficiently loverlike for her to regret having missed their morning hour.

She rang and asked if Mr. Ashby had already gone. Yes, nearly an hour ago, the maid said. He had given orders that Mrs. Ashby should not be waked and that the children should not come to her till she sent for them . . . Yes, he had gone up to the nursery himself to give the order. All this sounded usual enough; and Charlotte hardly knew why she asked: "And did Mr. Ashby leave no other message?"

Yes, the maid said, he did; she was so sorry she'd forgotten. He'd told her, just as he was leaving, to say to Mrs. Ashby that he was going to see about their passages, and would she please be ready to sail tomorrow?

Charlotte echoed the woman's "Tomorrow," and sat staring at her incredulously. "Tomorrow—you're sure he said to sail tomorrow?"

"Oh, ever so sure, ma'am. I don't know how I could have forgotten to mention it."

"Well, it doesn't matter. Draw my bath, please." Charlotte sprang up, dashed through her dressing, and caught herself singing at her image in the glass as she sat brushing her hair. It made her feel young again to have scored such a victory. The other woman vanished to a speck on the horizon, as this one, who ruled the foreground, smiled back at the reflection of her lips and eyes. He loved her, then—he loved her as passionately as ever. He had divined what she had suffered, had understood that their happiness depended on their getting away at once, and finding each other again after yesterday's desperate groping in the fog. The nature of the influence that had come between them did not much matter to Charlotte now; she had faced the phantom and dispelled it. "Courage—that's the secret! If only people who are in love weren't always so afraid of risking their happiness by looking it in the eyes." As she brushed back her light abundant hair it waved electrically above her head, like the palms of victory. Ah, well, some women knew how to manage men, and some didn't—and only the fair—she gaily paraphrased—deserved the brave! Certainly she was looking very pretty.

The morning danced along like a cockleshell on a bright sea—such a sea as they would soon be speeding over. She ordered a particularly good dinner, saw the children off to their classes, had her trunks brought down, consulted with the maid about getting out summer clothes—for of course they would be heading for heat and sunshine—and wondered if she oughtn't to take Kenneth's flannel suits out of camphor. "But how absurd," she reflected, "that I don't yet know where we're going!" She looked at the clock, saw that it was close on noon, and decided to call him up at his office. There was a slight delay; then she heard his secretary's voice saying that Mr. Ashby had looked in for a moment early, and left again almost immediately . . . Oh, very well; Charlotte would ring up later. How soon was he likely to be back? The secretary answered that she couldn't tell; all they knew in the office was that when he left he had said he was in a hurry because he had to go out of town.

Out of town! Charlotte hung up the receiver and sat blankly gazing into new darkness. Why had he gone out of town? And where had he gone? And of all days, why should he have chosen the eve of their suddenly planned departure? She felt a faint shiver of apprehension. Of course he had gone to see that woman—no doubt to get her permission to leave. He was as completely in bondage as that; and Charlotte had been fatuous enough to see the palms of victory on her forehead. She burst into a laugh and, walking across the room, sat down again before her mirror. What a different face she saw! The smile on her pale lips seemed to mock the rosy vision of the other Charlotte. But gradually her colour crept back. After all, she had a right to claim the victory, since her husband was doing what she wanted, not what the other woman exacted of him. It was natural enough, in view of his abrupt decision to leave the next day, that he should have arrangements to make, business matters to wind up; it was not even necessary to suppose that his mysterious trip was a visit to the writer of the letters. He might simply have gone to see a client who lived out of town. Of course they would not tell Charlotte at the office; the secretary had hesitated before imparting even such meagre information as the fact of Mr. Ashby's absence. Meanwhile she would go on with her joyful preparations, content to learn later in the day to what particular island of the blest she was to be carried.

The hours wore on, or rather were swept forward on a rush of eager preparations. At last the entrance of the maid who came to draw the curtains roused Charlotte from her labours, and she saw to her surprise that the clock marked five. And she did not yet know where they were going the next day! She rang up her husband's office and was told that Mr. Ashby had not been there since the early morning. She asked for his partner, but the partner could add nothing to her information, for he himself, his suburban train having been behind time, had reached the office after Ashby had come and gone. Charlotte stood perplexed; then she decided to telephone to her mother-in-law. Of course Kenneth, on the eve of a month's absence, must have gone to see his mother. The mere fact that the children—in spite of his vague objections—would certainly have to be left with old Mrs. Ashby, made it obvious that he would have all sorts of matters to decide with her. At another time Charlotte might have felt a little hurt at being excluded from their conference, but nothing mattered now but that she had won the day, that her husband was still hers and not another woman's. Gaily she called up Mrs. Ashby, heard her friendly voice, and began: "Well, did Kenneth's news surprise you? What do you think of our elopement?"

Almost instantly, before Mrs. Ashby could answer, Charlotte knew what her reply would be. Mrs. Ashby had not seen her son, she had had no word from him and did not know what her daughter-in-law meant. Charlotte stood silent in the intensity of her surprise. "But then, where *has* he been?" she thought. Then, recovering herself, she explained their sudden decision to Mrs. Ashby, and in doing so, gradually regained her own self-confidence, her conviction that nothing could ever again come between Kenneth and herself. Mrs. Ashby took the news calmly and approvingly. She, too, had thought that Kenneth looked worried and overtired, and she agreed with her daughter-in-law that in such cases change was the surest remedy. "I'm always so glad when he gets away. Elsie hated travelling; she was always finding pretexts to prevent his going anywhere. With you, thank goodness, it's different." Nor was Mrs. Ashby surprised at his not having had time to let her know of his departure. He must have been in a rush from the moment the decision was taken; but no doubt he'd drop in before dinner. Five minutes' talk was really all they needed. "I hope you'll gradually cure Kenneth of his mania for going over and over a question that could be settled in a dozen words. He never used to be like that, and if he carried the habit into his professional work he'd soon lose all his clients . . . Yes, do come in for a minute, dear, if you have time; no doubt he'll turn up while you're here." The tonic ring of Mrs. Ashby's voice echoed on reassuringly in the silent room while Charlotte continued her preparations.

Toward seven the telephone rang, and she darted to it. Now she would know! But it was only from the conscientious secretary, to say that Mr. Ashby hadn't been back, or sent any word, and before the office closed she thought she ought to let Mrs. Ashby know. "Oh, that's all right. Thanks a lot!" Charlotte called out cheerfully, and hung up the receiver with a trembling hand. But perhaps by this time, she reflected, he was at his mother's. She shut her drawers and cupboards, put on her hat and coat and called up to the nursery that she was going out for a minute to see the children's grandmother.

Mrs. Ashby lived near by, and during her brief walk through the cold spring dusk Charlotte imagined that every advancing figure was her husband's. But she did not meet him on the way, and when she entered the house she found her mother-in-law alone. Kenneth had neither telephoned nor come. Old Mrs. Ashby sat by her bright fire, her knitting needles flashing steadily through her active old hands, and her mere bodily presence gave reassurance to Charlotte. Yes, it was certainly odd that Kenneth had gone off for the whole day without letting any of them know; but, after all, it was to be expected. A busy lawyer held so many threads in his hands that any sudden change of plan would oblige him to make all sorts of unforeseen arrangements and adjustments. He might have gone to see some client in the suburbs and been detained there; his mother remembered his telling her that he had charge of the legal business of a queer old recluse somewhere in New Jersey, who was immensely rich but too mean to have a telephone. Very likely Kenneth had been stranded there.

But Charlotte felt her nervousness gaining on her. When Mrs. Ashby asked her at what hour they were sailing the next day and she had to say she didn't know—that Kenneth had simply sent her word he was going to take their passages—the uttering of the words again brought home to her the strangeness of the situation. Even Mrs. Ashby conceded that it was odd; but she immediately added that it only showed what a rush he was in.

"But, mother, it's nearly eight o'clock! He must realize that I've got to know when we're starting tomorrow."

"Oh, the boat probably doesn't sail till evening. Sometimes they have to wait till midnight for the tide. Kenneth's probably counting on that. After all, he has a level head."

Charlotte stood up. "It's not that. Something has happened to him."

Mrs. Ashby took off her spectacles and rolled up her knitting. "If you begin to let yourself imagine things—"

"Aren't you in the least anxious?"

"I never am till I have to be. I wish you'd ring for dinner, my dear. You'll stay and dine? He's sure to drop in here on his way home."

Charlotte called up her own house. No, the maid said, Mr. Ashby hadn't come in and hadn't telephoned. She would tell him as soon as he came that Mrs. Ashby was dining at his mother's. Charlotte followed her mother-in-law into the dining-room and sat with parched throat before her empty plate, while Mrs. Ashby dealt calmly and efficiently with a short but carefully prepared repast. "You'd better eat something, child, or you'll be as bad as Kenneth . . . Yes, a little more asparagus, please, Jane."

She insisted on Charlotte's drinking a glass of sherry and nibbling a bit of toast; then they returned to the drawing-room, where the fire had been made up, and the cushions in Mrs. Ashby's armchair shaken out and smoothed. How safe and familiar it all looked; and out there, somewhere in the uncertainty and mystery of the night, lurked the answer to the two women's conjectures, like an indistinguishable figure prowling on the threshold.

At last Charlotte got up and said: "I'd better go back. At this hour Kenneth will certainly go straight home."

Mrs. Ashby smiled indulgently. "It's not very late, my dear. It doesn't take two sparrows long to dine."

"It's after nine." Charlotte bent down to kiss her. "The fact is, I can't keep still."

Mrs. Ashby pushed aside her work and rested her two hands on the arms of her chair. "I'm going with you," she said, helping herself up.

Charlotte protested that it was too late, that it was not necessary, that she would call up as soon as Kenneth came in, but Mrs. Ashby had already rung for her maid. She was slightly lame, and stood resting on her stick while her wraps were brought. "If Mr. Kenneth turns up, tell him he'll find me at his own house," she instructed the maid as the two women got into the taxi which had been summoned. During the short drive Charlotte gave thanks that she was not returning home alone. There was something warm and substantial in the mere fact of Mrs. Ashby's nearness, something that corresponded with the clearness of her eyes and the texture of her fresh firm complexion. As the taxi drew up she laid her hand encouragingly on Charlotte's. "You'll see; there'll be a message."

The door opened at Charlotte's ring and the two entered. Charlotte's heart beat excitedly; the stimulus of her mother-in-law's confidence was beginning to flow through her veins.

"You'll see—you'll see," Mrs. Ashby repeated.

The maid who opened the door said no, Mr. Ashby had not come in, and there had been no message from him.

"You're sure the telephone's not out of order?" his mother suggested; and the maid said, well, it certainly wasn't half an hour ago; but she'd just go and ring up to make sure. She disappeared, and Charlotte turned to take off her hat and cloak. As she did so her eyes lit on the hall table, and there lay a gray envelope, her husband's name faintly traced on it. "Oh!" she cried out, suddenly aware that for the first time in months she had entered her house without wondering if one of the gray letters would be there.

"What is it, my dear?" Mrs. Ashby asked with a glance of surprise.

Charlotte did not answer. She took up the envelope and stood staring at it as if she could force her gaze to penetrate to what was within. Then an idea occurred to her. She turned and held out the envelope to her mother-in-law.

"Do you know that writing?" she asked.

Mrs. Ashby took the letter. She had to feel with her other hand for her eyeglasses, and when she had adjusted them she lifted the envelope to the light. "Why!" she exclaimed; and then stopped. Charlotte noticed that the letter shook in her usually firm hand. "But this is addressed to Kenneth," Mrs. Ashby said at length, in a low voice. Her tone seemed to imply that she felt her daughter-in-law's question to be slightly indiscreet.

"Yes, but no matter," Charlotte spoke with sudden decision. "I want to know—do you know the writing?"

Mrs. Ashby handed back the letter. "No," she said distinctly.

The two women had turned into the library. Charlotte switched on the electric light and shut the door. She still held the envelope in her hand.

"I'm going to open it," she announced.

She caught her mother-in-law's startled glance. "But, dearest—a letter not addressed to you? My dear, you can't!"

"As if I cared about that—now!" She continued to look intently at Mrs. Ashby. "This letter may tell me where Kenneth is."

Mrs. Ashby's glossy bloom was effaced by a quick pallor; her firm cheeks seemed to shrink and wither. "Why should it? What makes you believe— It can't possibly—"

Charlotte held her eyes steadily on that altered face. "Ah, then you *do* know the writing?" she flashed back.

"Know the writing? How should I? With all my son's correspondents . . . What I do know is—" Mrs. Ashby broke off and looked at her daughter-in-law entreatingly, almost timidly.

Charlotte caught her by the wrist. "Mother! What do you know? Tell me! You must!"

"That I don't believe any good ever came of a woman's opening her husband's letters behind his back."

The words sounded to Charlotte's irritated ears as flat as a phrase culled from a book of moral axioms. She laughed impatiently and dropped her mother-in-law's wrist. "Is that all? No good can come of this letter, opened or unopened. I know that well enough. But whatever ill comes, I mean to find out what's in it." Her hands had been trembling as they held the envelope, but now they grew firm, and her voice also. She still gazed intently at Mrs. Ashby. "This is the ninth letter addressed in the same hand that has come for Kenneth since we've been married. Always these same gray envelopes. I've kept count of them because after each one he has been like a man who has had some dreadful shock. It takes him hours to shake off their effect. I've told him so. I've told him I must know from whom they come, because I can see they're killing him. He won't answer my questions; he says he can't tell me anything about the letters; but last night he promised to go away with me—to get away from them."

Mrs. Ashby, with shaking steps, had gone to one of the armchairs and sat down in it, her head drooping forward on her breast. "Ah," she murmured.

"So now you understand—"

"Did he tell you it was to get away from them?"

"He said, to get away—to get away. He was sobbing so that he could hardly speak. But I told him I knew that was why."

"And what did he say?"

"He took me in his arms and said he'd go wherever I wanted."

"Ah, thank God!" said Mrs. Ashby. There was a silence, during which she continued to sit with bowed head, and eyes averted from her daughter-in-law. At last she looked up and spoke. "Are you sure there have been as many as nine?"

"Perfectly. This is the ninth. I've kept count."

"And he has absolutely refused to explain?"

"Absolutely."

Mrs. Ashby spoke through pale contracted lips. "When did they begin to come? Do you remember?"

Charlotte laughed again. "Remember? The first one came the night we got back from our honeymoon."

"All that time?" Mrs. Ashby lifted her head and spoke with sudden energy. "Then— Yes, open it."

The words were so unexpected that Charlotte felt the blood in her temples, and her hands began to tremble again. She tried to slip her finger under the flap of the envelope, but it was so tightly stuck that she had to hunt on her husband's writing table for his ivory letter-opener. As she pushed about the familiar objects his own hands had so lately touched, they sent through her the icy chill emanating from the little personal effects of someone newly dead. In the deep silence of the room the tearing of the paper as she slit the envelope sounded like a human cry. She drew out the sheet and carried it to the lamp.

"Well?" Mrs. Ashby asked below her breath.

Charlotte did not move or answer. She was bending over the page with wrinkled brows, holding it nearer and nearer to the light. Her sight must be blurred, or else dazzled by the reflection of the lamp-light on the smooth surface of the paper, for, strain her eyes as she would, she could discern only a few faint strokes, so faint and faltering as to be nearly undecipherable.

"I can't make it out," she said.

"What do you mean, dear?"

"The writing's too indistinct . . . Wait."

She went back to the table and, sitting down close to Kenneth's reading lamp, slipped the letter under a magnifying glass. All this time she was aware that her mother-in-law was watching her intently.

"Well?" Mrs. Ashby breathed.

"Well, it's no clearer. I can't read it."

"You mean the paper is an absolute blank?"

"No, not quite. There is writing on it. I can make out something like 'mine'—oh, and 'come'. It might be 'come'."

Mrs. Ashby stood up abruptly. Her face was even paler than before. She advanced to the table and, resting her two hands on it, drew a deep breath. "Let me see," she said, as if forcing herself to a hateful effort.

Charlotte felt the contagion of her whiteness. "She knows," she thought. She pushed the letter across the table. Her mother-in-law lowered her head over it in silence, but without touching it with her pale wrinkled hands.

Charlotte stood watching her as she herself, when she had tried to read the letter, had been watched by Mrs. Ashby. The latter fumbled for her glasses, held them to her eyes, and bent still closer to the outspread page, in order, as it seemed, to avoid touching it. The light of the lamp fell directly on her old face, and Charlotte reflected what depths of the unknown may lurk under the clearest and most candid lineaments. She had never seen her mother-in-law's features express any but simple and sound emotions—cordiality, amusement, a kindly sympathy; now and again a flash of wholesome anger. Now they seemed to wear a look of fear and hatred, of incredulous dismay and almost cringing defiance. It was as if the spirits warring within her had distorted her face to their own likeness. At length she raised her head. "I can't—I can't," she said in a voice of childish distress.

"You can't make it out either?"

She shook her head, and Charlotte saw two tears roll down her cheeks.

"Familiar as the writing is to you?" Charlotte insisted with twitching lips.

Mrs. Ashby did not take up the challenge. "I can make out nothing—nothing."

"But you do know the writing?"

Mrs. Ashby lifted her head timidly; her anxious eyes stole with a glance of apprehension around the quiet familiar room. "How can I tell? I was startled at first . . ."

"Startled by the resemblance?"

"Well, I thought—"

"You'd better say it out, mother! You knew at once it was *her* writing?"

"Oh, wait, my dear—wait."

"Wait for what?"

Mrs. Ashby looked up; her eyes, travelling slowly past Charlotte, were lifted to the blank wall behind her son's writing table.

Charlotte, following the glance, burst into a shrill laugh of accusation. "I needn't wait any longer! You've answered me now! You're looking straight at the wall where her picture used to hang!"

Mrs. Ashby lifted her hand with a murmur of warning. "Sh-h."

"Oh, you needn't imagine that anything can ever frighten me again!" Charlotte cried.

Her mother-in-law still leaned against the table. Her lips moved plaintively. "But we're going mad—we're both going mad. We both know such things are impossible."

Her daughter-in-law looked at her with a pitying stare. "I've known for a long time now that everything was possible."

"Even this?"

"Yes, exactly this."

"But this letter—after all, there's nothing in this letter—"

"Perhaps there would be to him. How can I tell? I remember his saying to me once that if you were used to a handwriting the faintest stroke of it became legible. Now I see what he meant. He *was* used to it."

"But the few strokes that I can make out are so pale. No one could possibly read that letter."

Charlotte laughed again. "I suppose everything's pale about a ghost," she said stridently.

"Oh, my child—my child—don't say it!"

"Why shouldn't I say it, when even the bare walls cry it out? What difference does it make if her letters are illegible to you and me? If even you can see her face on that blank wall, why shouldn't he read her writing on this blank paper? Don't you see that she's everywhere in this house, and the closer to him because to everyone else she's become invisible?" Charlotte dropped into a chair and covered her face with her hands. A turmoil of sobbing shook her from head to foot. At length a touch on her shoulder made her look up, and she saw her mother-in-law bending over her. Mrs. Ashby's face seemed to have grown still smaller and more wasted, but it had resumed its usual quiet look. Through all her tossing anguish, Charlotte felt the impact of that resolute spirit.

"Tomorrow—tomorrow. You'll see. There'll be some explanation tomorrow."

Charlotte cut her short. "An explanation? Who's going to give it, I wonder?"

Mrs. Ashby drew back and straightened herself heroically. "Kenneth himself will," she cried out in a strong voice. Charlotte said nothing, and the old woman went on: "But meanwhile we must act; we must notify the police. Now, without a moment's delay. We must do everything—everything."

Charlotte stood up slowly and stiffly; her joints felt as cramped as an old woman's. "Exactly as if we thought it could do any good to do anything?"

Resolutely Mrs. Ashby cried: "Yes!" and Charlotte went up to the telephone and unhooked the receiver.

PREFATORY NOTE TO "HENRY JAMES"

Edith Wharton's name is constantly linked with that of Henry James, as though she were a lesser version of the master in petticoats, yet except for an occasional similarity in subject matter, their novels and tales are widely different. James was super-subtle, speculative and indirect; Edith Wharton was clear and to the point. Her phrases do not have to be read and reread, like his, for richer and deeper disclosures. Nor did either of them ever really appreciate the other's best work. James found Mrs. Wharton at her best when, as in *The Reef,* she was most like himself, and she complained that she could not read his later books because they were too severed from "that thick nourishing human air in which we all live and move." Yet aside from their books they were the best of friends.

If he found her at times too energetic, possibly too bossy, if he called her "the angel of devastation," he still loved to motor with her, to sight-see with her, to gossip with her, to discuss literature (except his own) with her. If she found him fussy, spoiled and stubborn, she still delighted in his wonderful talk and in the largeness of his heart. They make an enchanting contrast as seen in this chapter from her memoirs, she extravagant, he frugal, she always ready to go, he constantly lingering, she summing up, he expanding in further involutions, she masculine when he was feminine, and feminine when he was most masculine. It is as if they saw themselves on a stage of high comedy and enjoyed their own effect.

FROM *A Backward Glance*

CHAPTER 8 HENRY JAMES

§ 1

WHAT is one's personality, detached from that of the friends with whom fate happens to have linked one? I cannot think of myself apart from the influence of the two or three greatest friendships of my life, and any account of my own growth must be that of their stimulating and enlightening influence. From a childhood and youth of complete intellectual isolation—so complete that it accustomed me never to be lonely except in company—I passed, in my early thirties, into an atmosphere of the rarest understanding, the richest and most varied mental comradeship. Some of my friends were men exceptionally distinguished in their own walk of life, without being public figures; others were already celebrated when I first knew them, and of these I shall find it difficult to give an adequate account because of my unhappy lack of verbal memory. Once I had emerged from my long inner solitude my opportunities, though limited in extent (for I have always been fundamentally un-"social"), were of a quality so rare that it ought to illuminate all my pages. I have lived in intimate friendship with two or three great intelligences; but I am not a Boswell myself, and have never had a Boswell of my own, both of which facts I deplore, since in the former case I might have set down the dazzling talk I spent such enchanted hours in absorbing, and in the latter have handed it on to my recording satellite. As it is, having a tendency to pass, when in high company, into a state of exhilaration that precludes anything as precise as taking notes, I enjoy the commerce with great minds as a painter enchanted by the glories of an Alpine meadow rather than as a botanist cataloguing its specimens.

Once, happening to sit next to M. Bergson at a dinner, I confided to him my distress and perplexity over the odd holes in my memory. How was it, I asked, that I could remember, with exasperating accuracy, the most useless and insignificant things, such as the address of every one I knew, and the author of the libretto of every opera I had ever heard since the age of eighteen—while, when it came to poetry, my chiefest passion and my greatest joy, my verbal memory failed me completely, and I heard only the inner cadence, and could hardly ever fill it out with the right words?

I had the impression, before I ended, that my problem did not greatly interest my eminent neighbour; and his reply was distinctly disappointing. *"Mais c'est précisément parce que vous êtes éblouie"* ("It's just because you are dazzled"), he answered quietly, turning to examine the dish which was being handed to him, and making no effort to pursue the subject. It was only afterward that I saw he had really said all there was to say: that the gift of precision in ecstasy (the best definition I can find for the highest poetry) is probably almost as rare in the appreciator as in the creator, and that my years of intellectual solitude had made me so super-sensitive to the joys of great talk that precise recording was impossible to me. Good talk seems, instead, to pass into my mind with a gradual nutritive force sometimes felt only long afterward; it permeates me as a power, an influence, it encloses my universe in a dome of many-coloured glass from which I can detach but few fragments while it builds itself up about me. The reader may here object that I have taken more than a page to say that I have a bad memory; but to say only that would not quite cover the case, since the talk I hear is not forgotten, but stored in some depth from which it still returns in its essential implications, though so seldom in its verbal shape.

Since I have already spoken of Henry James's visits to the Mount, it is perhaps best to put his name first on the list of the friends who composed my closest group during the years I spent there, and those that followed. In fact, however, my first meeting with Henry James happened many years earlier, probably in the late 'eighties; though it is at the Mount that he first comes into the foreground of the picture.

For a long time there seemed small hope of his ever figuring there, for when we first met I was still struck dumb in the presence of greatness, and I had never doubted that Henry James was great, though how great I could not guess till I came to know the man as well as I did his books. The encounter took place at the house of Edward Boit, the brilliant water-colour painter whose talent Sargent so much admired. Boit and his wife, both Bostonians, and old friends of my husband's, had lived for many years in Paris, and it was there that one day they asked us to dine with Henry James. I could hardly believe that such a privilege could befall me, and I could think of only one way of deserving it—to put on my newest Doucet dress, and try to look my prettiest! I was probably not more than twenty-five, those were the principles in which I had been brought up, and it would never have occurred to me that I had anything but my youth, and my pretty frock, to commend me to the man whose shoe-strings I thought myself unworthy to unloose. I can see the dress still—and it *was* pretty; a tea-rose pink, embroidered with iridescent beads. But, alas, it neither gave me the courage to speak, nor attracted the attention of the great man. The evening was a failure, and I went home humbled and discouraged.

A year or two later, in Venice (probably in 1889 or 1890), the same opportunity came my way. Another friend of my husband's, Ralph Curtis of Boston, had the happy thought of inviting us to meet Henry James, who was, I think, staying either with Curtis at the Palazzo Barbaro, or with Robert Browning's old friend, Mrs. Arthur Bronson. Again fortune held out her hand—and again mine slipped out of it. Once more I thought: How can I make myself pretty enough for him to notice me? Well—this time I had a new hat; *a beautiful new hat!* I was almost sure it was becoming, and I felt that if he would only tell me so I might at last pluck up courage to blurt out my admiration for "Daisy Miller" and "The Portrait of a Lady". But he noticed neither the hat nor its wearer—and the second of our meetings fell as flat as the first. When I spoke to him of them years afterward he owned that he could not even remember having seen me on either occasion! And as for the date of the meeting which finally drew us together, without hesitations or preliminaries, we could neither of us ever recall when or where that happened. All we knew was that suddenly it was as if we had always been friends, and were to go on being (as he wrote to me in February 1910) "more and more never apart".

The explanation, of course, was that in the interval I had found myself, and was no longer afraid to talk to Henry James of the things we both cared about; while he, always so helpful and hospitable to younger writers, at once used his magic faculty of drawing out his interlocutor's inmost self. Perhaps it was our common sense of fun that first brought about our understanding. The real marriage of true minds is for any two people to possess a sense of humour or irony pitched in exactly the same key, so that their joint glances at any subject cross like interarching search-lights. I have had good friends between whom and myself that bond was lacking, but they were never really intimate friends; and in that sense Henry James was perhaps the most intimate friend I ever had, though in many ways we were so different.

The Henry James of the early meetings was the bearded Penseroso of Sargent's delicate drawing, soberly fastidious in dress and manner, cut on the approved pattern of the *homme du monde* of the 'eighties; whereas by the time we got to know each other well the compact upright figure had expanded to a rolling and voluminous outline, and the elegance of dress given way to the dictates of comfort, while a clean shave had revealed in all its sculptural beauty the noble Roman mask and the big dramatic mouth. The change typified something deep beneath the surface. In the interval two things had happened: Henry James had taken the measure of the fashionable society which in youth had subjugated his imagination, as it had Balzac's, and was later to subjugate Proust's, and had fled from it to live in the country, carrying with him all the loot his adventure could yield; and in his new solitude he had come to grips with his genius. Exquisite as the early novels are—and in point of perfection probably none can touch "The Portrait of a Lady"—yet measured by what was to come Henry James, when he wrote them, had but skimmed the surface of life and of his art. Even the man who wrote, in "The Portrait of a Lady", the chapter in which Isabel broods over her fate at night by the fire, was far from the man in whom was already ripening that greater night-piece, the picture of Maggie looking in from the terrace at Fawns at the four bridge-players, and renouncing her vengeance as "nothing nearer to experience than a wild eastern caravan, looming into view with crude colours in the sun, fierce pipes in the air, high spears against the sky . . . but turning off short before it reached her and plunging into other defiles".

But though he had found his genius and broken away from the

social routine, he never emancipated himself in small matters from the conformities. Though he now affected to humour the lumbering frame whose physical ease must be considered first, he remained spasmodically fastidious about his dress, and about other trifling social observances, and once when he was motoring with us in France in 1907, and suddenly made up his mind (at Poitiers, of all places!) that he must then and there buy a new hat, almost insuperable difficulties attended its selection. It was not until he had announced his despair of ever making the hatter understand "that what he wanted was a hat like everybody else's", and I had rather impatiently suggested his asking for a head-covering *"pour l'homme moyen sensuel"*, that the joke broke through his indecisions, and to a rich accompaniment of chuckles the hat was bought.

Still more particular about his figure than his dress, he resented any suggestion that his silhouette had lost firmness and acquired volume; and once, when my friend Jacques-Emile Blanche was doing the fine seated profile portrait which is the only one that renders him *as he really was,* he privately implored me to suggest to Blanche "not to lay such stress on the resemblance to Daniel Lambert".

The truth is that he belonged irrevocably to the old America out of which I also came, and of which—almost—it might paradoxically be said that to follow up its last traces one had to come to Europe; as I discovered when my French and English friends told me, on reading "The Age of Innocence", that they had no idea New York life in the 'seventies had been so like that of the English cathedral town, or the French *"ville de province"*, of the same date. As for the nonsense talked by critics of a later generation, who never knew James, much less the world he grew up in, about his having thwarted his genius by living in Europe, and having understood his mistake too late, as a witness of his long sojourns in America in 1904, 1905 and 1910, and of the reactions they produced (expressed in all the letters written at the time), I can affirm that he was never really happy or at home there. He came several times for long visits to the Mount, and during his first visit to America, in 1904-5, he also stayed with us for some time in New York; and responsive as he always was, interested, curious, and heroically hospitable to new ideas, new aspects, new people, the nostalgia of which he speaks so poignantly in one of his letters to Sir Edmund Gosse (written from the Mount) was never for a moment stilled. Henry James was essentially a novelist of manners, and the manners he was qualified by nature and situation to observe were those of the little vanishing group of people among whom he had grown up, or their more picturesque prototypes in older societies. For better or worse he had to seek that food where he could find it, for it was the only food his imagination could fully assimilate. He was acutely conscious of this limitation, and often bewailed to me his total inability to use the "material", financial and industrial, of modern American life. Wall Street, and everything connected with the big business world, remained an impenetrable mystery to him, and knowing this he felt he could never have dealt fully in fiction with the "American scene", and always frankly acknowledged it. The attempt to portray the retired financier in Mr. Verver, and to relate either him or his native "American City" to any sort of concrete reality, is perhaps proof enough of the difficulties James would have found in trying to depict the American money-maker in action.

On his first visit, however, he was still in fairly good health, and in excellent spirits, exhilarated (at first) by the novelty of the adventure, the success of his revolt against his own sedentary habit (he called me "the pendulum-woman" because I crossed the Atlantic every year!), and, above all, captivated by the new experience of motoring. It was the summer when we were experimenting with "Alfred de Musset" and "George"; in spite of many frustrations there were beautiful tours successfully carried out "in the Whartons' commodious new motor, which has fairly converted me to the sense of all the thing may do for one and one may get from it"; and this mode of locomotion seemed to him, as it had to me, an immense enlargement of life.

§ 2

It is particularly regrettable in the case of Henry James that no one among his intimates had a recording mind, or rather that those who had did not apply it to noting down his conversation, for I have never known a case in which an author's talk and his books so enlarged and supplemented each other. Talent is often like an ornamental excrescence; but the quality loosely called genius usually irradiates the whole character. "If he but so much as cut his nails," was Goethe's homely phrase of Schiller, "one saw at once that he was a greater man than any of them." This irradiation, so abundantly basked in by the friends of Henry James, was hidden from those who knew him slightly by a peculiarity due to merely physical causes. His slow way of speech, sometimes mistaken for affectation—or, more quaintly, for an artless form of Anglomania! —was really the partial victory over a stammer which in his boyhood had been thought incurable. The elaborate politeness and the involved phraseology that made off-hand intercourse with him so difficult to casual acquaintances probably sprang from the same defect. To have too much time in which to weigh each word before uttering it could not but lead, in the case of the alertest and most sensitive of minds, to self-consciousness and self-criticism; and this fact explains the hesitating manner that often passed for a mannerism. Once, in New York, when I had arranged a meeting between him and the great Mr. Dooley, whose comments on the world's ways he greatly enjoyed, I perceived, as I watched them after dinner, that Peter Dunne was floundering helplessly in the heavy seas of James's parentheses; and the next time we met, after speaking of his delight in having at last seen James, he added mournfully: "What a pity it takes him so long to say anything! Everything he said was so splendid—but I felt like telling him all the time: 'Just 'pit it right up into Popper's hand'."

To James's intimates, however, these elaborate hesitancies, far from being an obstacle, were like a cobweb bridge flung from his mind to theirs, an invisible passage over which one knew that silver-footed ironies, veiled jokes, tiptoe malices, were stealing to explode a huge laugh at one's feet. This moment of suspense, in which there was time to watch the forces of malice and merriment assembling over the mobile landscape of his face, was perhaps the rarest of all in the unique experience of a talk with Henry James.

His letters, delightful as they are, give but hints and fragments of his talk; the talk that, to his closest friends, when his health and the surrounding conditions were favourable, poured out in a series of images so vivid and appreciations so penetrating, the whole so sunned over by irony, sympathy and wide-flashing fun, that those who heard him at his best will probably agree in saying of him what he once said to me of M. Paul Bourget: "He was the first, easily, of all the talkers I ever encountered."

Of the qualities most impossible to preserve in his letters, because so impossible to explain with whatever fulness of foot-notes, was the quality of fun—often of sheer abstract "fooling"—that was the delicious surprise of his talk. His letter to Walter Berry "on the gift of a dressing-bag" is almost the only instance of this genial play that is intelligible to the general reader. From many of the letters to his most intimate group it was necessary to excise long passages of chaff, and recurring references to old heaped-up pyramidal jokes, huge cairns of hoarded nonsense. Henry James's memory for a joke was prodigious; when he got hold of a good one, he not only preserved it piously, but raised upon it an intricate superstructure of kindred nonsense, into which every addition offered by a friend was skilfully incorporated. Into his nonsense-world, as four-dimensional as that of the Looking Glass, or the Land where the Jumblies live, the reader could hardly have groped his way without a preparatory course in each correspondent's private history and casual experience. The merest hint was usually enough to fire the train; and, as in the writing of his tales a tiny mustard-seed of allusion spread into a many-branched "subject", so his best nonsense flowered out of unremembered trifles.

I recall a bubbling over of this nonsense on one of our happy motor-trips among the hills of Western Massachusetts. We had motored so much together in Europe that allusions to Roman ruins and Gothic cathedrals furnished a great part of the jests with which his mind played over what he has called "the thin empty lonely American beauty"; and one day, when his eye caught the fine peak rising alone in the vale between Deerfield and Springfield, with a wooden barrack of a "summer hotel" on its highest ledge, I told him that the hill was Mount Tom, and the building "the famous Carthusian monastery". "Yes, where the monks make Moxie," he flashed back, referring to a temperance drink that was blighting the landscape that summer from a thousand hoardings.

Sometimes his chaff was not untinged with malice. I remember a painful moment, during one of his visits, when my husband imprudently blurted out an allusion to "Edith's new story—you've seen it in the last 'Scribner'?" My heart sank; I knew it always embarrassed James to be called on, in the author's presence, for an "appreciation". He was himself so engrossed in questions of technique and construction—and so increasingly detached from the short-story form as a medium—that very few "fictions" (as he called them) but his own were of interest to him, except indeed Mr. Wells's, for which he once avowed to me an incurable liking, "because everything he writes is so alive and kicking". At any rate I always tried to keep my own work out of his way, and once accused him of ferreting out and reading it just to annoy me—to which charge his sole response was a guilty chuckle. In the present instance, as usual, he instantly replied: "Oh, yes, my dear Edward, I've read the little work—of course I've read it." A gentle pause, which I knew boded no good; then he softly continued: "Admirable, admirable; a masterly little achievement." He turned to me, full of a terrifying benevolence. "Of course so accomplished a mistress of the art would not, without deliberate intention, have given the tale so curiously conventional a treatment. Though indeed, in the given case, no treatment *but* the conventional was possible; which might conceivably, my dear lady, on further consideration, have led you to reject your subject as—er—in itself a totally unsuitable one."

I will not deny that he may have added a silent twinkle to the shout of laughter with which—on that dear wide sunny terrace of the Mount—his fellow-guests greeted my "dressing-down". Yet it would be a mistake to imagine that he had deliberately started out to destroy my wretched tale. He had begun, I am sure, with the sincere intention of praising it; but no sooner had he opened his lips than he was overmastered by the need to speak the truth, and the whole truth, about anything connected with the art which was sacred to him. Simplicity of heart was combined in him with a brain that Mr. Percy Lubbock has justly called robust, and his tender regard for his friends' feelings was equalled only by the faithfulness with which, on literary questions, he gave them his view of their case when they asked for it—and sometimes when they did not. On all subjects but that of letters his sincerity was tempered by an almost exaggerated tenderness; but when *le métier* was in question no gentler emotion prevailed.

Another day—somewhat later in our friendship, since this time the work under his scalpel was "The Custom of the Country"—after prolonged and really generous praise of my book, he suddenly and irrepressibly burst forth: "But of course you know—as how should you, with your infernal keenness of perception, *not* know?—that in doing your tale you had under your hand a magnificent subject, which ought to have been your main theme, and that you used it as a mere incident and then passed it by?"

He meant by this that for him the chief interest of the book, and its most original theme, was that of a crude young woman such as Undine Spragg entering, all unprepared and unperceiving, into the mysterious labyrinth of family life in the old French aristocracy. I saw his point, and recognized that the contact between the Undine Spraggs and the French families they marry into was, as the French themselves would say, an "actuality" of immense interest to the novelist of manners, and one which as yet had been little dealt with; but I argued that in "The Custom of the Country" I was chronicling the career of a particular young woman, and that to whatever hemisphere her fortunes carried her, my task was to record her ravages and pass on to her next phase. This, however, was no argument to James; he had long since lost all interest in the chronicle-novel, and cared only for the elaborate working out on all sides of a central situation, so that he could merely answer, by implication if not openly: "Then, my dear child, you chose the wrong kind of subject."

Once when he was staying with us in Paris I had a still more amusing experience of this irresistible tendency to speak the truth. He had chanced to nose out the fact that, responding to an S.O.S. from the *Revue des Deux Mondes,* for a given number of which a promised translation of one of my tales had not been ready, I had offered to replace it by writing a story myself—in French! I knew what James would feel about such an experiment, and there was nothing I did not do to conceal the horrid secret from him; but he had found it out before arriving, and when in my presence some idiot challenged him with: "Well, Mr. James, don't you think it's remarkable that Mrs. Wharton should have written a story in French for the *Revue?*" the twinkle which began in the corner of his eyes and trickled slowly down to his twitching lips showed that his answer was ready. "Remarkable—most remarkable! An altogether astonishing feat." He swung around on me slowly. "I do congratulate you, my dear, on the way in which you've picked up every old worn-out literary phrase that's been lying about the streets of Paris for the last twenty years, and managed to pack them all into those few pages." To this withering comment, in talking over the story afterward with one of my friends, he added more seriously, and with singular good sense: "A very creditable episode in her career. *But she must never do it again.*"

He knew I enjoyed our literary rough-and-tumbles, and no doubt for that reason scrupled the less to hit straight from the shoulder; but with others, though he tried to be more merciful, what he really thought was no less manifest. My own experience had taught me that nothing is more difficult than to talk indifferently or insincerely on the subject of one's craft. The writer, without much effort, can reel off polite humbug about pictures, the painter about books; but to fib about the art one practises is incredibly painful, and James's overscrupulous conscience, and passionate reverence for letters, while always inclining him to mercy, made deception doubly impossible.

I think it was James who first made me understand that genius is not an indivisible element, but one variously apportioned, so that the popular system of dividing humanity into geniuses and non-geniuses is a singularly inadequate way of estimating human complexity. In connection with this, I once brought him a phrase culled in a literary review. "Mr.——has *almost a streak* of genius". James, always an eager collector of verbal oddities, fell on the phrase with rapture, and earnest requests to every one to define the exact extent of "almost a streak" caused him amusement for months afterward. I mention this because so few people seem to have known in Henry James the ever-bubbling fountain of fun which was the delight of his intimates.

One of our joys, when the talk touched on any great example of prose or verse, was to get the book from the shelf, and ask one of the company to read the passage aloud. There were some admirable readers in the group, in whose gift I had long delighted; but I had never heard Henry James read aloud—or known that he enjoyed doing so—till one night some one alluded to Emily Bronte's poems, and I said I had never read "Remembrance". Immediately he took the volume from my hand, and, his eyes filling, and some far-away emotion deepening his rich and flexible voice, he began:

> Cold in the earth, and the deep snow piled above thee,
> Far, far removed, cold in the dreary grave,
> Have I forgot, my only Love, to love thee,
> Severed at last by Time's all-severing wave?

I had never before heard poetry read as he read it; and I never have since. He chanted it, and he was not afraid to chant it, as many good readers are, who, though they instinctively feel that the genius of the English poetical idiom requires it to be spoken *as poetry*, are yet afraid of yielding to their instinct because the present-day fashion is to chatter high verse as though it were colloquial prose. James, on the contrary, far from shirking the rhythmic emphasis, gave it full expression. His stammer ceased as by magic as soon as he began to read, and his ear, so sensitive to the convolutions of an intricate prose style, never allowed him to falter over the most complex prosody, but swept him forward on great rollers of sound till the full weight of his voice fell on the last cadence.

James's reading was a thing apart, an emanation of his inmost self, unaffected by fashion or elocutionary artifice. He read from his soul, and no one who never heard him read poetry knows what that soul was. Another day some one spoke of Whitman, and it was a joy to me to discover that James thought him, as I did, the greatest of American poets. "Leaves of Grass" was put into his hands, and all that evening we sat rapt while he wandered from "The Song of Myself" to "When lilacs last in the door-yard bloomed" (when he read "Lovely and soothing Death" his voice filled the hushed room like an organ adagio), and thence let himself be lured on to the mysterious music of "Out of the Cradle", reading, or rather crooning it in a mood of subdued ecstasy till the fivefold invocation to Death tolled out like the knocks in the opening bars of the Fifth Symphony.

James's admiration of Whitman, his immediate response to that mighty appeal, was a new proof of the way in which, above a certain level, the most divergent intelligences walk together like gods. We talked long that night of "Leaves of Grass", tossing back and forth to each other treasure after treasure; but finally James, in one of his sudden humorous drops from the heights, flung up his hands and cried out with the old stammer and twinkle: "Oh, yes, a great genius; undoubtedly a very great genius! Only one cannot help deploring his too-extensive acquaintance with the foreign languages."

§ 3

I believe James enjoyed those days at the Mount as much as he did (or could) anything connected with the American scene; and the proof of it is the length of his visits and their frequency. But on one occasion his stay with us coincided with a protracted heat-wave; a wave of such unusual intensity that even the nights, usually cool and airy at the Mount, were as stifling as the days. My own dislike of heat filled me with sympathy for James, whose sufferings were acute and uncontrollable. Like many men of genius he had a singular inability for dealing with the most ordinary daily incidents, such as giving an order to a servant, deciding what to wear, taking a railway ticket, or getting from one place to another; and I have often smiled to think how far nearer the truth than he could possibly have known was the author of that cataclysmic sketch in the famous "If—" series: "If Henry James had written Bradshaw."

During a heat-wave this curious inadaptability to conditions or situations became positively tragic. His bodily surface, already broad, seemed to expand to meet it, and his imagination to become a part of his body, so that the one dripped words of distress as the other did moisture. Always uneasy about his health, he became visibly anxious in hot weather, and this anxiety added so much to his sufferings that his state was pitiful. Electric fans, iced drinks and cold baths seemed to give no relief; and finally we discovered that the only panacea was incessant motoring. Luckily by that time we had a car which would really go, and go we did, daily, incessantly, over miles and miles of lustrous landscape lying motionless under the still glaze of heat. While we were moving he was refreshed and happy, his spirits rose, the twinkle returned to lips and eyes; and we never halted except for tea on a high hillside, or for a "cooling drink" at a village apothecary's—on one of which occasions he instructed one of us to bring him "something less innocent than Apollinaris", and was enchanted when this was interpreted as meaning an "orange phosphate", a most sophisticated beverage for that day.

On another afternoon we had encamped for tea on a mossy ledge in the shade of great trees, and as he seemed less uneasy than usual somebody pulled out an anthology, and I asked one of the party to read aloud Swinburne's "Triumph of Time", which I knew to be a favourite of James's; but after a stanza or two I saw the twinkle of beatitude fade, and an agonized hand was lifted up. "Perhaps, in view of the abnormal state of the weather, our young friend would have done better to choose a poem of less inordinate length—" and immediately we were all bundled back into the car and started off again on the incessant quest for air.

James was to leave for England in about a fortnight; but his sufferings distressed me so much that, the day after this expedition, feeling sure that there was nothing to detain him in America if he chose to go, I asked a friend who was staying in the house to propose my telephoning for a passage on a Boston steamer which was sailing within two days. My ambassador executed the commission, and hurried back with the report that the mere hint of such a plan had thrown James into a state of helpless perturbation. To change his sailing date at two days' notice—to get from the Mount to Boston (four hours by train) in *two days*—how could I lightly suggest anything so impracticable? And what about his heavy luggage, which was at his brother William's in New Hampshire? And his wash, which had been sent to the laundry only the afternoon before? Between the electric fan clutched in his hand, and the pile of sucked oranges at his elbow, he cowered there, a mountain of misery, repeating in a sort of low despairing chant: "Good God, what a woman—what a woman! Her imagination boggles at nothing! She does not even scruple to project me in a naked flight across the Atlantic . . ." The heat collapse had been as nothing to the depths into which my rash proposal plunged him, and it took several hours to quiet him down and persuade him that, if he preferred enduring the weather to flying from it, we were only too glad to keep him at the Mount.

A similar perturbation could be produced (I later learned, to my cost) by asking him to explain any phrase in his books that did not seem quite clear, or any situation of which the motive was not adequately developed; and still more disastrous was the effect of letting him know that any of his writings had been parodied. I had always regarded the fact of being parodied as one of the surest evidences of fame, and once, when he was staying with us in New York, I brought him with a glee a deliciously droll article on his novels by poor Frank Colby, the author of "Imaginary Obligations". The effect was disastrous. I shall never forget the misery, the mortification even, which tried to conceal itself behind an air of offended dignity. His ever-bubbling sense of fun failed him completely on such occasions; as it did also (I was afterward to find) when one questioned him, in a way that even remotely implied criticism, on any point in the novels. It was in England, I think—when he and I, and a party of intimate friends, were staying together at Howard Sturgis's—that I brought him, in all innocence, a passage from one of his books which, after repeated readings, I still found unintelligible. He took the book from me, read over the passage to himself, and handed it back with a lame attempt at a joke; but I saw—we all saw—that even this slight, and quite involuntary, criticism, had wounded his morbidly delicate sensibility.

Once again—and again unintentionally—I was guilty of a similar blunder. I was naturally much interested in James's technical theories and experiments, though I thought, and still think, that he tended to sacrifice to them that spontaneity which is the life of fiction. Everything, in the lastest novels, had to be fitted into a predestined design, and design, in his strict geometrical sense, is to me one of the least important things in fiction. Therefore, though I greatly admired some of the principles he had formulated, such as that of always letting the tale, as it unfolded, be seen through the mind most capable of reaching to its periphery, I thought it was paying too dear even for such a principle to subordinate to it the irregular and irrelevant movements of life. And one result of the application of his theories puzzled and troubled me. His latest novels, for all their profound moral beauty, seemed to me more and more lacking in atmosphere, more and more severed from that thick nourishing human air in which we all live and move. The characters in "The Wings of the Dove" and "The Golden Bowl" seem isolated in a Crookes tube for our inspection: his stage was cleared like that of the Théâtre Français in the good old days when no chair or table was introduced that was not *relevant to the action* (a good rule for the stage, but an unnecessary embarrassment to fiction). Preoccupied by this, I one day said to him: "What was your idea in suspending the four principal characters in 'The Golden Bowl' in the void? What sort of life did they lead when they were not watching each other, and fencing with each other? Why have you stripped them of all the *human fringes* we necessarily trail after us through life?"

He looked at me in surprise, and I saw at once that the surprise was painful, and wished I had not spoken. I had assumed that his system was a deliberate one, carefully thought out, and had been genuinely anxious to hear his reasons. But after a pause of reflection he answered in a disturbed voice: "My dear—I didn't know I had!" and I saw that my question, instead of starting one of our absorbing literary discussions, had only turned his startled attention on a peculiarity of which he had been completely unconscious.

This sensitiveness to criticism or comment of any sort had nothing to do with vanity; it was caused by the great artist's deep consciousness of his powers, combined with a bitter, a life-long disappointment at his lack of popular recognition. I am not sure that Henry James had not secretly dreamed of being a "best seller" in the days when that odd form of literary fame was at its height; at any rate he certainly suffered all his life—and more and more as time went on—from the lack of recognition among the very readers who had most warmly welcomed his early novels. He could not understand why the success achieved by "Daisy Miller" and "The Portrait of a Lady" should be denied to the great novels of his maturity: and the sense of protracted failure made him miserably alive to the least hint of criticism, even from those who most completely understood, and sympathized with, his later experiments in technique and style.

§ 4

Those long days at the Mount, in the deep summer glow or the crisp glitter of autumn, the walks in the woods, motor-flights over hill and dale, evening talks on the moonlit terrace and readings around the library fire, come back with a mocking radiance as I write—and with them the figures of our other most beloved guests, Walter Berry, Bay Lodge, and three dear friends from England, Gaillard Lapsley, Robert Norton and John Hugh Smith.

Still others, friendly and delightful also, came and went; but these, with Henry James, if not by the actual frequency of their visits, yet from some secret quality of participation, had formed from the first the nucleus of what I have called the inner group. In this group an almost immediate sympathy had established itself between the various members, so that our common stock of allusions, cross-references, pleasantries was always increasing, and new waves of interest in the same book or picture, or any sort of dramatic event in life or letters, would simultaneously flood through our minds.

I think I may safely say that Henry James was never so good as with this little party at the Mount, or when some of its members were reunited, as often happened in after years, under Howard Sturgis's welcoming roof at Windsor. The mere fact that we had in common so many topics, and such innumerable allusions, made James's talk on such occasions easier and wider-ranging than I ever heard it elsewhere; and the free and rapid give-and-take of ideas animated his mind, which so easily drooped in dull company.

In one respect Henry James stood alone among the great talkers I have known, for while he was inexhaustible in repartee, and never had the least tendency to monopolize the talk, yet it was really in monologue that he was most himself. I remember in particular one summer evening, when we sat late on the terrace at the Mount, with the lake shining palely through dark trees, and one of us suddenly said to him (in response to some chance allusion to his Albany relations): "And now tell us about the Emmets—tell us all about them."

The Emmet and Temple families composed, as we knew, the main element of his vast and labyrinthine cousinship—"the Emmetry", as he called it—and for a moment he stood there brooding in the darkness, murmuring over to himself: "Ah, my dear, the Emmets—ah, the Emmets!" Then he began, forgetting us, forgetting the place, forgetting everything but the vision of his lost youth that the question had evoked, the long train of ghosts flung with his enchanter's wand across the wide stage of the summer night. Ghost-like indeed at first, wavering and indistinct, they glimmered at us through a series of disconnected ejaculations, epithets, allusions, parenthetical rectifications and restatements, till not only our brains but the clear night itself seemed filled with a palpable fog; and then, suddenly, by some miracle of shifted lights and accumulated strokes, there they stood before us as they lived, drawn with a million filament-like lines, yet sharp as an Ingres, dense as a Rembrandt; or, to call upon his own art for an analogy, minute and massive as the people of Balzac.

I often saw the trick repeated; saw figures obscure or famous summoned to the white square of his magic-lantern, flickering and wavering there, and slowly solidifying under the turn of his lens; but never perhaps anything so ample, so sustained, as that summoning to life of dead-and-gone Emmets and Temples, old lovelinesses, old follies, old failures, all long laid away and forgotten under old crumbling grave-stones. I wonder if it may not have been that very night, the place and his reawakened associations aiding, that they first came to him and constrained him to make them live for us again in the pages of "A Small Boy" and "A Son and Brother"?

§ 5

In New York James was a different being. He hated the place, as his letters abundantly testify; its aimless ugliness, its noisy irrelevance, wore on his nerves; but he was amused by the social scene, and eager to leave nothing of it unobserved. During his visits, therefore, we invited many people to the house, and he dined out frequently, and went to the play—for he was still intensely interested in the theatre. But this mundane James, his attention scattered, his long and complex periods breaking against a dull wall of incomprehension, and dispersing themselves in nervous politenesses, was a totally different being from our leisurely companion at the Mount. I always enjoyed having him under my roof, wherever that good fortune befell me; but my hurried preoccupied New York guest seemed a mere fragment of the great "Henry" of our country hours.

New York in those days, though more cosmopolitan than in my youth, was still a small place, with so limited a range of intellectual interests and allusions that dinner-table talk was a good deal like the "local items" column in a country newspaper; and I remember depressing evenings when the hosts, contributing orchids and gold plate, remained totally unconscious of the royal gifts their guest had brought them in exchange.

James knew that his treasures were largely unmarketable in Fifth Avenue, but it perplexed and saddened him that they should, as a rule, be equally so in the world of letters, which he was naturally even more eager to explore. I remember one occasion when a dinner was especially arranged to make known to him a brilliant essayist whose books he greatly enjoyed. Unhappily the essayist's opaque countenance revealed nothing of the keenness within, and he on his part, though appreciative of James's genius, was obviously put off by his laborious hesitations. Their comments on the meeting were, on the essayist's side, a joke about James's stammer, and on James's the melancholy exclamation: "What a mug!"

I suspect that he was much happier, and more at his ease, in Boston than in New York. At Cambridge, in the houses of his brother, William James, and of Charles Eliot Norton, and their kindred circles, he had the best of Boston; and in Boston itself, where the sense of the past has always been so much stronger than in New York, he found all sorts of old affinities and relations, and early Beacon Hill traditions, to act as life-belts in the vast ocean of strangeness. He had always clung to his cousinage, and to any one who represented old friendly associations, whether in Albany, New York or Boston, and I remember his once saying: "You see, my dear, they're so much easier to talk to, because I can always ask them questions about uncles and aunts, and other cousins." He had brought this question-asking system to a high state of perfection, and practised it not only on relations and old friends, but on transatlantic pilgrims to Lamb House, whom he would literally silence by a friendly volley of interrogations as to what train they had taken to come down, and whether they had seen all the cathedral towns yet, and what plays they had done; so that they went away aglow with the great man's cordiality, "and, you see, my dear, they hadn't time to talk to me about my books"—the calamity at all costs to be averted.